DuskBourne

SJAQUIWN A. SMALL

DuskBourne
Copyright © 2025 by Sjaquiwn A. Small.

MILTON & HUGO L.L.C.
1001 3rd Avenue West, Suite 430
Bradenton, FL 34205, USA

Website: *www. miltonandhugo.com*
Hotline: *1- 888-778-0033*
Email: *info@miltonandhugo.com*

Ordering Information:
Quantity sales. Special discounts are granted to corporations, associations, and other organizations. For more information on these discounts, please reach out to the publisher using the contact information provided above.

ISBN-13:   979-8-89285-687-4   [Paperback Edition]
              979-8-89285-688-1   [Hardback Edition]
              979-8-89285-686-7   [Digital Edition]

Rev. date: 12/12/2025

This book goes to the countless friends, family, and for those, who couldn't be here now.

Thank you for all your support, and love.

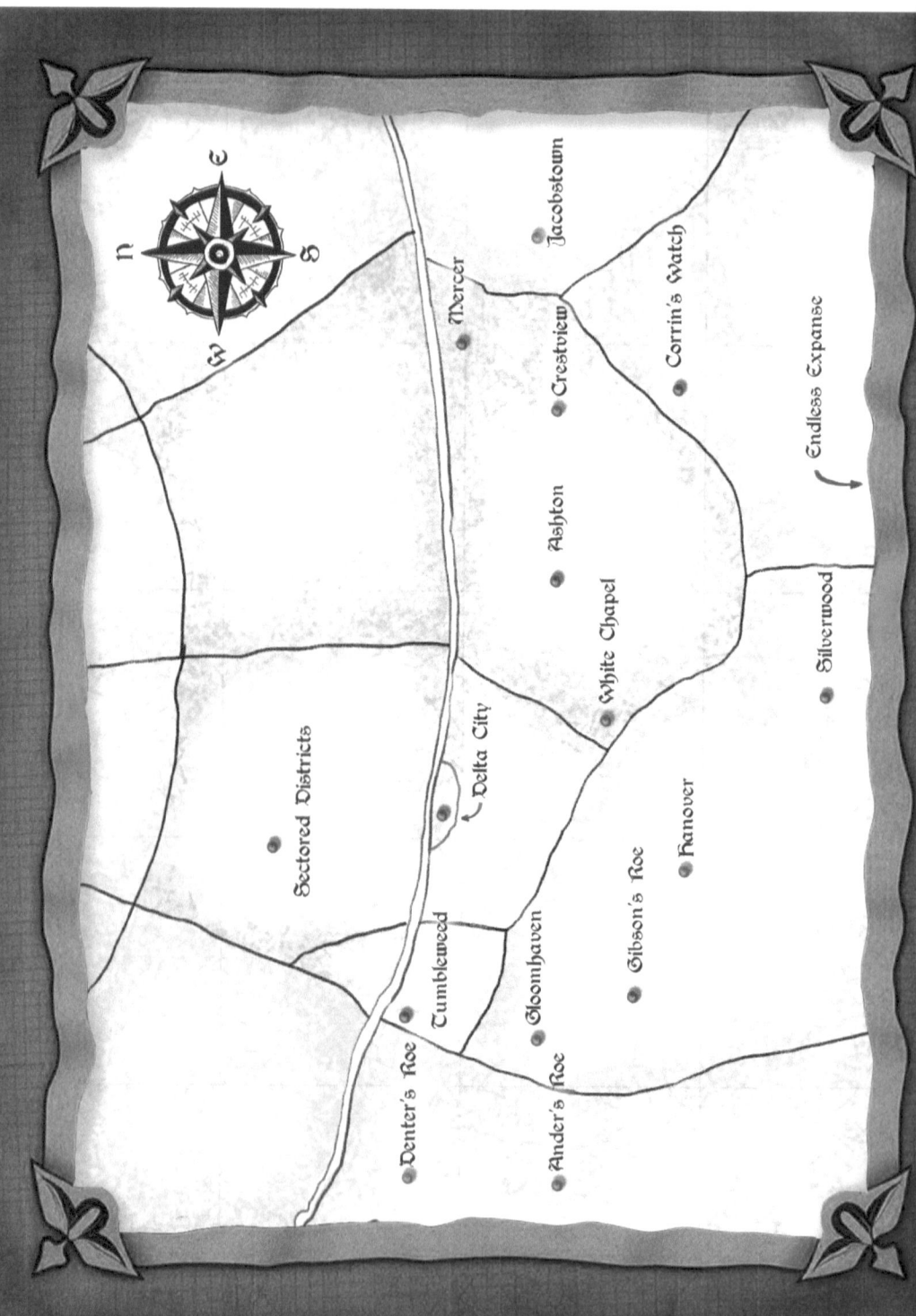

CHAPTER

1

10/18/2055, Tuesday, 6:58 pm

The nomads of the underground bunker: G-XV- 425. Were fast approaching the end of the road. There was an ominous stillness within the rolling plains of the wastelands, a stillness that seemed far to eerie for the groups liking. The closest settlement to their location, *Silverwood*, was the only town for miles around in the middle of nowhere, bordering the endless expanse.

By the suggestion of *The Circle*: A mediating organization that helped to manage the various freelancers that traveled the hazardous, and, dune ridden backdrop of the badlands. Nomads they were called the freelancers (mercenaries) that were under the protection and employment of the independent service outside the conclaves. They were the ones forgotten by the system, and where the most adapted when it came to the harshness of the vast desert. From the bone-dry climate, the voracious and lethally charged wildlife- as sparse as it was, and other dangers that hid just under the surface

Since Silverwood was a fairly new, and a growing settlement in the outskirts of the expanse, there were bound to be jobs for a nomad or two. Afterall, the conclaves would no doubt jump at the chance to send a nomad. Instead of wasting their resources for paid bodyguards from Sector Security. But their journey here, sadly, seemed another waste of their precious time and resources. For like the regions desiccated backdrop- their chance of any good jobs/gigs were equally bone dry. Undeterred if not furious for their bad draw of the dice, they decided after a few weeks of sleuthing the small settlement, that it was high time to pack up and leave. The unexpected lack of jobs caught them all off guard, you'd think being at the crap end of nowhere they'd pony up to the idea of tossing the risk to some nameless nomad. But no... surprisingly, and shockingly, both the two groups were working together on the development of this settlement. S.S in particular, being pretty nasty in there threats for them to leave the small settlement.

So... there only option was to leave and find work elsewhere.

The lead up to their long journey across the wastelands towards the settlement of *Corrin's Watch* was going to be a long one. As far as preparations went, they were nearly set. The routes were triple checked and given the proper time to be scooped out for the possible dangers of raiders, bandits, and other rouge nomads that might complicate the path forward. The seven members of this band each understood the perils of traveling across the badlands. Yet, their plans of a swift retreat from this god forsaken place were equally put on the back burner.

The end of the day was quickly approaching, and the halls of the bunker were quiet, everyone was doing their jobs, and all seemed to be going smoothly... except there was one problem. Two of its members were missing.

Inside one of the rooms of the bunker a lone nomad was holed up inside of the data center: The bleeding heart of the underground hideout, the center of the bunkers systems and subsystems, and a communications center for its inhabitants.

The long rectangular room was filled with servers that were placed against the sides of the walls. Each producing a low hum against the dark steel walls. All lined up half-hazordly, connecting to one another in a sprawling web of cables and wires, some trailing the ground near them. But the true focus of the room was a large terminal at the very back, were every line, cable and wire was connected to.

The sound of typing could be heard under the hum of servers. A girl with long red hair, and tan skin, was typing away at the terminal. Using one hand, as her right arm was wrapped up to her side in a type of black sling. Her freckled round face scrunched up in concentration, the light of the terminal in her brown eyes which lit the semi dark room with a dim glow. She wore a brown leather jacket, over a black shirt- a dirty pair of jeans and black boots- old and scuffed from walking across the sandy outback. Around her neck was a black and yellow bandanna. Which hid the small necklace that hung from her neck.

There was an odd cable that was draped over her right shoulder, a cable that was connected to the small port under her right ear.

"Come on you stupid thing. Where are they? They have to be somewhere around here- can't freaking believe them!" she gritted out in clear frustration.

Her brown eyes began to glow, a small pinprick of green light flowed eerily from her pupils. Her holocalls were still going unanswered, and Susan was increasingly getting worried. Her connection to the network feed was experiencing small communication errors, and her neural link to the others was getting disrupted. Jade, Thomas and Hosea haven't made it back to base yet... and the forecast of the region has already made it clear that a massive storm was on its way.

Not unexpected mind you- being so close to the endless expanse. But it was seriously an inconvenient time for this to happen.

Susan growled in frustration, her nerves at an all-time high, of course those two had to run off with Kingsley's truck. A bid to chase a signal outside the confines of the shelter and further away into the barren wasteland. She thankfully still had a reading of where they were located at, but it was only a small general area, bordering the edge of their neural network.

Hosea their leader and handler was still supposedly at the town of Silverwood. Chasing an unknown call at that small town (Something he barely explained to her as he made his way out) and just disappeared without another word. She couldn't get a signal of his whereabouts. He was, of course, too far away from their shared network to get a reading of his position. She knew Hosea could take care of himself. Yet, she was getting weird readings from the town's direction, unusual... but for now, her true concern lied with the other two.

She flinched- a sharp pain knocking her out of her concentration, a pain that she's been contending with for an entire month. From within her arm sling another jolt of pain made her silently gasp, and with great effort to not set it off again she adjusted the straps of the sling, making sure to further loosen them.

With a grunt, she turned her attention to the screen- there was another odd reading on the map display, of the area surrounding the bunker.

A warning message?

She typed a few commands, before another window popped on screen- it was a weather forecast and by the readings it looked to be a severe one. She cursed, her brown eyes now luminescent in that tall tell color of neon green "Guys! This isn't funny- pick up the damn phone already!" She called out in utter vexation, her patience at wits end. If the weather warning was severe, then it wasn't a by the numbers sandstorm. It was a supercell from the expanse.

If it weren't for this damn arm I could have been out there with them! She thought to herself. Suddenly, she regretted her thoughts as she looked to the sling.

She bit back her anger and bitterness. this wasn't going to get her anywhere, sighing as she reached to her right- grabbing hold of a bag with her left hand- before dropping it onto her lap. Fumbling inside for a brief moment she took out the thing she was looking for. A booster shot with a wicked looking syringe needle on the bottom. Popping the cap off, she grimaced- her brown eyes giving the syringe a hesitant peer. Taking a breath, she placed it on the table just under the keyboard and further undid the strap to her sling.

Revealing the 'arm' which was hidden by the soft black fabric. A prosthetic limb which was surgically attached to the place where her real arm used to be. A dark token from a rival nomad group, which started with an ambush, and likewise ended with her losing a limb.

The prosthetic was an armored prosthesis, full of pneumatic actuators and electrical motors. Linked to her nervous system, fueled by the minuscule pulses that came from her nerves, allowing it to have the same movements as any other limb. She took a nervous breath as she took the syringe into her left, feeling the stinging pain.

Church told her that until the arm has properly adjusted to her nervous system- she will experience lapses of the arm moving on its own accord, and the boosters were a way of helping recovering amputees from accidently causing the prosthetics to spasm. It was like having the sensation of phantom pain all over again, and the best thing she could do was ignore the urge to move her right arm. But for now.... she administered the drug into her shoulder, gulping in pain. She blew a steady breath as the drugs did their work. The neural interface in her vision, glitched for a moment before returning to normal. Eventually she would need to have that checked out by Bella.

Suddenly, she heard footsteps echoing from outside the hall. Becoming tense, instinctively- she reached for the holster on her left hip, the booster falling to the floor with a hollow thud. "Whoa, whoa, relax- it's just me!" A sharp voice called out firmly behind her, a woman's voice to be more precise. Susan froze, her left hand pausing in place, the moment of sudden panic suddenly deflating as she recognized the voice behind her. She's been having those sudden panic episodes for a few days now... it was slightly embarrassing.

She turned around "S-sorry about that... so what brings you here Bell?" The older woman: Bellatrix. A woman, who's messy jet-black hair fell down past her shoulders. Her steel grey eyes- ever calculating, carefully observed Susans abashed expression.

Before lightly shrugging.

Shoving her hands into the pockets of her grey jumpsuit. The red glow of the servers reflecting off the metal buttons that adorned her leather jacket over the jumpsuit.

She walked up to Susan, giving the teenager a small grin "Oh nothing, just going for a little walk is all." She gave the terminal an interested look "So, you managed to find those two punks yet?" Susan snorted "More like idiots! and yes, sorta- I'm just wondering what King is going to do to them once he finds the truck missing."

Bella chuckled "Have any idea what made them take off in the first place?" Susan sighed to herself "Some kinda signal, out there, past the canyon and into the open desert." Bella shook her head, before asking "Which grid did the signal cut off?" Susan typed a few commands into the screen. A map appeared on the screen marking their position, and tagging a marker some clicks to the north past the canyon.

Bella furrowed her brow "Any readings on their biomoniters?"

"So far there still reading ok, but I wouldn't put it pass them to do something reckless." Susan said.

Bella shook her head with a sigh "I'm sure there doing fine... to tell you the truth, I had a feeling they were gonna bail out sooner or later." Bella said, her voice taking on a solemn tone.

Remembering the looks on both their faces: Jade's, and Tom's, during the first moment they saw Susan's severe injury in the aftermath of the ambush. Both of them staying by her side as she went into a short coma.

Bella thinking back on it, remembered the celebration when Sue finally regained consciousness and the improvised surgery to replace the limb with the prosthetic; she definitely wasn't thrilled about the amount of favors she had to call in, in order to get hooked up with the right replacement for the job and the surgery, which was off the books of course.

Scowling to herself, she realized she should have been more observant of those two. She gave the spot where the signal cut off a stern look, the easygoing air she had earlier disappearing in but an instant.

"I'm assuming they weren't following just a random signal?" Susan asked quietly.

"No" Bella answered, still giving the screen a hard look.

"Figures, those two are so stubborn when it comes to these things! Like going on a revenge spree is going to get my freaking arm back!" Susan said, with clear agitation coloring her voice.

It wasn't like she hadn't developed a grudge on the nomads that did this to her. But it wasn't worth it if they ended up dead or worse.

"Relax, those two can handle themselves.... besides, when they do finally get back. If worse comes to worse, King and Hosea will probably tear them a new-"

Suddenly, behind them, a dry chuckle sounded off. Turning around Church walked up, observing the two of them. Wearing a white tee, under a black hooded jacket and well- worn jean pants. He gave the two girls a slightly amused look "I assume those two are at it again." It wasn't even a question.

Bellatrix scoffed "Of course it is, those two can't go a month without causing a ruckus." Church gave a small nod to Susan, pulling back his sand blond hair, he gave the prosthetic a weary look.

"Any problems so far Sue?"

"No, nothing I can't handle... thanks." Susan thought for a moment "Has King woken up yet?"

Church shook his head "Nope, not yet, but... I'll give a quick prayer to those two when he finds out. I mean, the man just got done fixing the framing from the last job."

Bella seemingly forgetting her series mood for a moment, grinned "Oh yeah, that's... hehehe, we probably won't find anything left of them once King finds them."

Susan gulped, Kingsley was their designated mechanic out here in the wastes, with Jade and Tom occasionally lending a hand. She couldn't imagine the old man's wrath if they ended up wreaking it worse than the other job. Though, to be fair, it wouldn't be the first time those two had gotten on his ire. She shook her head in disdain, it couldn't possibly get worse.

Suddenly, the computer flashed red taking her aback, as she watched the monitor begin to flash warning signs.

CODE RED ALERT!!!
CODE RED ALERT!!!

Over and over again, the warning blared loud across the monitor. She froze- the neural link behind her ear was heating up! She only had a moment to brace herself before information concerning the alert overwhelmed her. The OS system in her brain struggling to keep up with the windows of information now popping in her very eyes.

"Susan! Disconnect now!" A voice, whiplike in its command ordered. She forced her eyes closed and ran an instant shutdown of her augmented operating system.

The disconnection was incredibly painful... Opening her eyes she felt someone yank the cable from behind her ear. She stumbled in her chair, the sudden freedom from the net link causing her to become woozy. A hand gently stood her up, and she recognized the person as Bellatrix- who carefully moved her shaking form onto a chair next to another server tower.

"Sorry, it was either the hard disconnect, or a seizure from thermal thralling," Bella said "Just rest here for a bit... I need to see what's going on."

Susan nodded weekly, watching as her vision cleared enough to see Bella take the seat to the monitor, Church moved to Susan putting his hand to her forehead.

"How's your head? Any headaches or burns to your neural port?" he questioned worriedly. She felt her neural port socket with her unbraced hand and shook her head.

"I'll be fine," She focused towards the older woman, who now had the mainframes connector cable inserted to her port. "How's it going Bella?" She wearily asked.

Bellatrix paused, her eyes- twin pieces of grey steel- emitting a greenish hue, widened as the information was processed by her O.S. She shuddered, It was the town that Hosea had supposedly traveled too... the only settlement for miles and the only one to risk being near the expanse.

It was Silverwood... their VM Reactor has gone through a critical meltdown.

The town was doomed.

CHAPTER

2

10/18/2055, Tuesday, 7:49 pm

Jade and Tomas roared in there victory, the bellowing wind of their speed across the desolate desert suffocating their voices for any to hear, as the massive truck zoomed past the many dunes which carpeted the naked landscape. It all went according to plan, they were dead, every last one of them. D. E. A. D. Dead.

The truck had seen better days... but it was all worth it in the end. Their payback was successful.

"Kingsley's going to be pissed when we get back, but to hell with it... completely worth it!" Jade cackled, who's hair was tied into a ponytail, which trailed in the breeze of the speeding monster she was driving. Her thug-like appearance was marred with dirt and grim, with some parts of her clothing drenched in small pockets of blood. Her black kevlar vest under her jacket was dented and scratched with the stray arcs of bullets. "Yeah, let's hope if Hosea is back he won't kick the shit out of us!" Tom remarked back, his hand grasping the cap on his head, covering his wild fro. The wind blowing the collar of his duster around his neck, which was also marred with dirt, sand, blood and the small cuts and dents that covered his kevlar vest over his long sleeve. The setting sun was barely a corona of light over the horizon and the trek back to base was a looming inevitability.

Better to enjoy the drama free ride of freedom while they had it, the moment they got back... King and Hosea both would have their heads.

"You think the loot we got back from that camp will soften the blow?" Tom pondered out loud. Jade shrugged "Probably, probably not...

but, at least we didn't go through all are ammo back there. Those idiots are so incompetent, I'm surprised they made it this far in the badlands." She grumbled, the back seat of the truck was full of cases and cases of loot and weapons, pillaged from the unfortunate bowls of the hidden bunker, from which the ex-nomads had taken over in forced occupation. The previous owners be damned. The circle of life when dealing with nomads that quit the circle.

"Hopefully, this will make the venture here worth it," Tom growled "The circle sending us here in the middle of nowhere, next to that god forsaken town; which- who in their right minds would build near the freaking expanse?!" he repeated not for the first time.

Again Jade shrugged "No clue," she snorted "It's their choice, if they want to build a settlement near no man's land, then it's there deathbeds." Shaking her head "Freaking S.S always so full of themselves." She mumbled ruefully.

Suddenly, a sound, an explosion- something unholy reverberated across the night air. A shockwave which slammed into the pair, Jade struggled- jaw clenched as she tried to hold on for dear life. The truck swerved from the wave of force which slammed into it, their ears popped, and they barely heard their own screams as the truck slid to a stop. A massive bout of sand blew through the air; through the windows, covering them in the course feeling minerals. The ringing was slowly dying down to Toms relief, as Jade angrily brushed sand and gravel from her clothes and hair.

"The hell was that!" She started, only to pause when her eyes, and Tom's, gained that characteristic shimmer signaling a holocall. They both gulped, it was Hosea...

Hesitantly, they looked at the other- both having the same nervous looks on their faces. They understood what was about to happen, and with reluctance, they both silently agreed to get it over with.

"Hosea... let us explain-" Tom began.

Tom! Jade! Do any of you have a stem kit!" Hosea's voice demanded through the holocall. His gruff voice in a state of panic, which completely took them both for a loop. The old hound was not one to lose his cool very often, if ever, and it shocked them to silence.

"TOM!" he shouted.

"Y-yes, yes we got one, where is your position?" Tom stuttered in alarm.

"I'm on route from Silverwood returning to base, both of you meet me halfway, I have a kid bleeding out and he needs one on the double." Tom and Jade paled, a kid, what? The call went dead, they took a second then Jade kicked into high gear. The trucks engine roared, and the beast revved back down the road towards the meeting place.

"What the hell is going on?" Jade stammered "He's never like this... and what the heck does he mean the *kid* is bleeding out, what kid?!" she said outload.

Tom shook his head, silently going over what happened with the earlier shockwave, his mind coming up and crossing out theory after theory. The earlier thrill of their victory now seemingly a distant memory, replaced with a type of uneasiness which dropped a hole into their stomachs. Whatever was going on, it seemed there future punishment would fall to the backseat, until the mysterious circumstances concerning Hosea was behind them.

10/18/2055, Tuesday, 8:19 pm

Kingsley awoke to the sounds of chaos outside, then more pressingly, found the sight of his truck missing. Of course those two idjits had something to do with it, that he already figured.

Inside the garage section of the bunker, the alarm on the walls was blaring, screeching like a banshee even. But... something else caught his attention. Running out of his small room, he came upon Susan. She barely reached up to his chest in height, his long sleeves and cargo pants, dirty and slightly greased from transmission fluid, gave him the look of the typical grease monkey. And her looking utterly panicked from the blaring red of the alarms.

"What happened!" King questioned.

"Silverwood! it's gone... it- it's had a reactor meltdown!" Susan screamed over the alarms, her face horrified. She directed to the open hall, with her good arm.

"Everyone's packing, we gotta leave the bunker- were getting confirmation from the circle that S.S is sending S.P.C.T.R to investigate." The blood drained from King's face.

SPCTR (Special. Commando. Tactical. And Reconnaissance Squad) Where the best of the best. The deadliest squad of solders this side of the conclaves. Physically and cybernetically enhanced to the brink of cyborgification. The Modern Knights as some referred to them; and if they found out there was a bunker this close to Silverwood- after a reactor meltdown of all things.

They both booked it across the garage, towards the Voyager- a massive, eighteen wheeler behemoth of a motorhome- pulled by semitruck. The armored brown hide of the coach was a staple of nomad travel across the perilous wasteland, and right now they had to flee. Susan climbed the stairs into the entrance of the motorhome, as King ran for the truck- ready to start the beast. She rushed inside, fast walking through the dark interior as she passed by a few sofa chairs and the kitchen section of the home. Down the trailer she went until she stopped at the back. The main living room, or the data center was inactive, chairs lined the center in a neat circle, and at the center of the furniture: The holomap projector, a large, round device which jutted up from the floor in a jumble of wires and cables. The top of the saucer was lined with a bunch of consoles which connected to the top. Susan pressed a few buttons, and the interior of the home lit up with activity. The hum of machinery filled the space as the windows of either end lit up with light. A ripple effect could be seen as the looking glass technology reflected outside of the cabin. The armor which covered the windows and sides of the home had the tech to digitally reflect outside. Allowing sights, without, sacrificing protection. Whether from gun fire, or to the elements of the wastes. The projector buzzed and hummed as Susan typed commands into the device. Lights emitted from the solar panel esc top, and gathered in midair forming a broad holographic map of the region.

"Bella where are the others? Do you see them?" Susan demanded into her holocall.

"Don't rush me! There coming, they.... that's Hosea and the others! I'm letting the gate open in the garage now!" Bella breathed "Hold on... who's that with Hosea?" She inquired sounding highly confused.

"Huh!?" Susan started before looking out the window, the massive entrance to the garage slid open with a heavy churning of cogs and cranks: Two vehicles, a car which was heavily armored up, and Kingsley's personal field truck, which slide laboriously into the garage with a screech, battle worn and heavily damaged. Susan grimaced at the blotches of dried blood which covered the passenger's side. Oh! When Kingsley sees this....

Jade and Tom quickly exited out of the truck, both sprinting down the hall and out of the garage. Susan raced out, nearly tripping as she came outside of the voyager. Hosea stepped out, a fairly tall and grizzled looking man, who wore a dark shirt under a desert brown poncho- which was blotched in red (was that blood?)- he lifted himself out of the car, and... Susan's eyes widened, her face becoming drained of color.

Hosea held a boy, maybe six to seven years old in his arms, he was barely moving and there seemed to be bad wound on his forehead. His shirt was utterly ruined with blood stains from his previous injury, with his pants worn and his shoes scoffed with dirt.

From behind the graying hair of Hosea, who's eyes glinted with a sharpness that Susan knew- meant that the old hound was not in a good mood- he turned to her.

"Susan is the map in the voyager operational," He asked "We need to get a route out of here, the circle won't be able to talk S.S down if we're caught here. And the last thing anyone back at base needs is S.S assuming we had anything to do with Silverwood."

She nodded "Yes... I'm on it." She turned around, moving quickly back inside as her mind raced.

What is going on? Silverwood is gone... S.P.C.T.R is on its way... and that kid...

She made it to the console, typing more commands, the map focusing on the region they were in, updating the current news and information of the area, and once again... as if to highlight once and for all, that indeed- Silverwood was gone. Its marker now darkened, a small pit that laid at the edge of civilization. A chill ran through her, not at all comfortable of the implication of being so, so, close to a disaster that's bound to have horrible ramifications for everyone, involved or not.

The map widened, a path was highlighted orange on the holographic image. It would take three and a half days at most to reach *Corrin's Watch*. Her eyes glinted green as a holocall buzzed for her to answer.

"Bella," Susan answered

"Did, the console lock on to Corrins," Bella asked, "I'll be in the voyager in a moment, did you see who was in the car with Hosea?"

"Yes... it was a kid, 6-7 years maybe... what about SPCTR? Are we really going to take the open road to Corrins?" she asked pressingly "With the drones and sensors, I doubt were going to get far."

"We're not taking the road Sue, did you check the map? Give it another look." Bella responded with derision.

Susan looked up and paused... the path to Corrins, it was cutting through the mountains, no... under the mountains. "How...."

"The underground path should take us under the enviro scanners, we just have cut power to the bunker, then we can escape down the auxiliary path... No point staying here any longer, especially with SPCTR on the way," Bella explained, her voice over the coms becoming faintly distorted in static "Last thing we need is S.S finding another old hideout, there really doing their damndest to get rid of our safehouses."

Susan narrowed her eyes, nomads where always going to be a source of strife across the wastes. The Manifest Wars have forever marred them to the general public's eyes.

The Republic's eyes to be precise.

Leave it to them to judge us lowly wasters as less superior than there oh, so, glorious sector districts. Not like they gave a damn when the corporations came down to breath in on our necks! You can barely find a settlement out there that doesn't have corporate sponsorship!

Susan snorted *And they wonder why some settlements go down under...*

She shook her head in agitation, forcing the bitterness from her current mood she looked out the window. Hosea, now joined by Church came rushing towards the voyager- the boy was cradled in Church's arms- as Hosea barged open the door with a crash that made her flinch. In a blur of rapid movement, she saw something that made her freeze in horror, as Church carried the boy his arm dangled limply- all across his semi dark skin- a familiar and horrible sight greeted her.

Dark, vivid, lines of sickly veins covered his arm branching across and under his skin. She breathed an unsteady breath, as the three disappeared down the opposite side towards Hosea's bedroom.

She crossed past the map room into the kitchen area, her disbelief palpable. Suddenly out the entrance she spotted Tom and Jade, both of them came rushing inside the voyager panting heavily, backpacks of clothes and belongings wrapped around them as they tiredly set it on the ground around the kitchen. Susan numbly noticed her pack among the chosen supplies. A moment later Bellatrix came rushing in, not saying a word as she moved towards the bedroom, carrying a similar large sized rucksack of belongings.

"Yo... Sue... What up," Tom breathed out, sliding down against the small fridge. "We got your stuff... we should be good to clear out of this place... hey, you alright?" he said finally noticing the look on her face. "You look like you've seen a ghost."

"Susan?" Jade asked concerned "what's wrong?"

"Cognicrossis," Susan said quietly "That kid... he's got cognicrossis."

CHAPTER

3

10/18/2055, Tuesday, 9:10 pm

The boy was stable....

Yet, the accursed dark veins of cognicrossis forked relentlessly across his body. The sight sent chills across Susan's spine, and it made the skin crawl down her forearm, you knew... that if the dark veins were present. The sufferer of this illness was near the final stages of cognicrossis.

The Voyager was traveling smoothly down the tunnel, by Bella's assessment, they should pop out well away from the general region of XV-425. So long as S.S didn't catch them in the location of the disaster they were safe.

She rubbed the splint holding her prosthetic, absentmindedly thinking- as she sat down near the bed. The boy, laying down asleep with bandages wrapped around his head injury; she thought about Silverwood, the town was for all intense and purposes a no man's land now, the area heavily contaminated with styx matter, which, was currently contaminating the boy as he laid there in bed.

Susan frowned *A death sentence it was... the poor kid. But... how did Hosea come across him- better yet why was the kid even outside Silverwood to begin with? They were both far enough away from the initial explosion of the reactor. And, I think Church said that the contaminating effects of styx matter shouldn't have reached them from that distance...*

She frowned, this sickness was another horrible staple of settlement life, the reactors were needed of course- they shielded settlements from the supercells, which came roaring out of the endless expanse. Yet, styx matter was another beast entirely. The raw and hazardous waste which

16

was a byproduct of burning Ichorcyte: the material which settlements excavated for on the daily.

V.M Reactors and Ichorcyte: the one two combo, which would in theory be able to terraform the wastelands. A dream that seemed to motivate every settler who put up with corporate bullcrap.

She moved over, using her one hand to move his sheets further up, kid was shivering, so at least that meant his nerves weren't too degraded by the illness, he could still feel the temperature of the room, but would his mind be any better? She grimaced, the thought immediately banished from her mind. That.. that was too grim to think about. She moved from her seat, silently heading for the door, taking one last look at the boy as her face became downcast. Someone this young should never have to go through something as hellish as this... and it infuriated her to no end. There insistent need for the reactors were a double-edged sword. One which kept most of the settlements safe from the wastelands horrible storms. So long as the styx matter didn't destroy its populace first.

Her nostrils flared, and of course... the republic loves to brag about how styx matter free their reactors are.

She clicked her tongue, why was it all such a bad joke?

She moved out of the room and through the kitchen area, the movement of the motorhome barely phasing her as she easily walked along, minding the bumps which made the trailer bounce slightly. The scenes from the windows made her stop for a moment, the moving walls of the axes tunnels greeted her... although it wasn't much a view aside from the lights which bounced off the stone walls surface and the brief headlights which spilled across them from the semi's headlamps. King and Hosea where driving up front so there wasn't much answers they could get from their handler at the moment. She shook her head, like she would even ask with the current mood of Hosea. Hosea was hard, very hard to rile up... and whatever he found at Silverwood must have been horrible. Reactors going critical wasn't normal- it was possible, yes. But the problem was there have been only a few that Susan could count with her good hand... it was so rare for it to happen... she remembered one happening when she was the kids age, with previous meltdowns happening way before her time.

She continued on... all this just felt so wrong; the conclaves and S.S working together to establish this settlement away from corporate hands... and it just so happens to go up in smoke. It all stank to high heaven, and Susan was starting to suspect foul play.

What else was new in the wastelands.

"Oh my god! you two are idiots... couldn't you have for once, just for once, waited for the go ahead!" Bella groaned out, covering her face, to the amusement of Church and the aggravation of Jade and Tom. All four where sitting around the holomap, the devices green hue lighting up the semidarkness of the trailer, like a digital variant of a campfire. "Come off it Bell! At the very least we got most of the spent ammo and the credits they were hoarding in their little hideout," Jade snapped "Oh! And don't forget the guns we looted from them!" added Tom with a smug look.

Bella glared at them, her pupils eerily emitting the green pinpricks of light. They both promptly shut up. "We could have contacted the circle about them, if we had done that we could have gotten a bonus pay from the bounty on their heads."

"But all we gotta do is inform them about the location of the hideout and which group we took out," Tom said "I still have the coordinates of the hideout on my O.S, just let me upload the-"

"I doubt that's going to mean anything," Church spoke up "You might wanna delete it, the circle is going to distance itself as much as possible from the disaster. So... they probably won't care that much about the hideout... considering S.P.C.TR is combing the region also."

Tom looked dejected after that. While Susan, in a dour mood, took her seat next to Church. "Hey Church," She whispered to him as Bella continued to admonish the other two.

"Yeah," he answered back quietly, she gestured with the flick of her eye to the other room "Did Bella manage to find out who he is?" He shook his head "No, he doesn't even have a biomonitor." She blinked, that's impossible. Everyone had a biomonitor assigned to them when they were born. A digital codex if you will, which logged and organized credentials, ages, health statuses, identities, and even the family line of each individual in the conclaves, republic both.

It wasn't illegal per say, but it was highly frowned upon. "So, no idea who his family is!" She asked alarmed.

Church shook his head "Not even a name... But I don't need a biomonitor in order to tell how bad the contamination is, but thankfully- cognicrossis isn't transmissible through touch- so we should be good."

"Yeah, but... what do we do when he wakes up!" Susan fretted "How do we handle that? Kids barely older than I was when I first learned about it... and he's stuck with it!" she gave a pained look back to the room "And we both know how badly people are treated with the disease... who's gonna step up for him when we don't even have a biomonitor to identify next of kin?"

Church closed his eyes, his face becoming somber "That's a good question... but... will find out more when we get back to Corrins. If we can get a deep scan maybe will get a match from the S.S database for next of kin." He sounded highly doubtful.

Susan narrowed her eyes "Church... what's that look for?"

Church pulled out a cig "Hosea found him far away from Silverwood, right." she nodded "Two theories: one the kids parents were in Silverwood when the meltdown occurred- still doesn't explain how he got outside the town- but there's the first theory." Susan was about to say something when-

"And the other theory?" asked Bellatrix, with Jade and Tom giving Church their apt attention. He lit the cigar "He might have been abducted." he took a puff from the cigar "wouldn't put it pass raiders or ex nomads to raid and abduct traveling wanderers on the road to Silverwood. Maybe the reactor explosion went off and it proved the best moment for escape." Everyone was silent, Bella pondered while Tom and Jade looked unconvinced, but neither spoke up with any better theories.

"What about Hosea... does he have any ideas? I mean, the boss was the one to find him in the first place." Susan thought outload.

Church shrugged as he puffed a ring of smoke into the hologram which promptly crackled as the smoke passed through, giving the smoke a greenish tinge.

"'Your guess is as good as mine' is what he told me... so no, he doesn't. At least he wasn't heartless enough to leave him outside on the road." Church replied.

"Tch, tell me about it... I know a bunch of people back in corrins who would have done it," Bella scoffed "Doesn't change the fact that the theories are pointless, the kids here and I'm certain that bringing him to S.S is a bad idea... and the circle..." She sighed, covering her face her posture all of a sudden becoming exhausted "This... is unbelievable." She said softly.

"He's alive at the very least, it's not all bad... but church, any medicine for what he's got?" Tom questioned "You're the doctor on hand... so... anything we should watch out for?"

Church looked towards the bedroom "There's nothing much we can do. All we can do for now, until we reach Corrins, is to look out for him. He'll definitely be confused when he wakes up- if he decides to wake up." He sighed before getting up "I'm going to go and take first watch." He said before moving to the back, pressing the bud of his cig into an ashtray by the sink and leaving it there as he disappeared behind the door.

The voyager trudged along through the passage. And after two hours they finally came to the end of the tunnel. Susan watched from the hidden camera on front of the semi as Hosea and Bellatrix accessed the console near the gateway. The entire tunnel underneath the canyon was... honestly the strangest thing she had seen traveling the wastes... who, on earth, had the time to build and plan all this, not to mention the upkeep- building the tunnel in such a way, to last for so long... it was all so crazy to think about. Kingsley was driving his truck behind the voyager, when they stopped, he climbed inside the trailer to have a word with the other two. It was to put it mildly a hilarious moment for Susan, even funnier when Bellatrix spoke up before King could lay into them that he needed to be quiet for their 'guest' in the bedroom. King, confused, went back, then after a minute confronted Jade and Tom promising to have a detailed word with them later on when they reached corrins. They both shivered as he grumbled all the way back to his truck.

The voyager glided out of the tunnel which promptly sealed itself back up again, the massive gate camouflaged by a rocklike surface. It was the middle of the night, and as the headlights revealed the path forwards down the valley, Susan was suddenly hit with an unexpected realization.

The constellations of the night sky... she had forgotten, being inside the bunker they didn't have a good view of the stars...

A weird thought she realized, after all... Her losing an arm, Silverwood and the unfortunate series of events that caused there downfall, to the boy who was in there backroom with a terminal illness... it was a lot, too much to think about.

But.. the night sky- as she laid down on the sofa getting ready to turn in for the night. The night sky tended to stay relatively peaceful, beautiful, serene. Something she could look out in wonder and not think about the horrible things that were happening out there in the wastes.

She grimaced to herself, that wasn't true... the wastelands, even as hostile and desolate as it was- also had moments of tranquility to it- an almost oppressive air of mystery which beckoned you to explore it for all its worth.

She smiled thinking about her favorite constellation, that more than likely, would be seating up there in the night sky at this very moment.

Nocturna Major: a configuration of stars that were drawn together in a wide spiral pattern, like a maelstrom in the dark curtain of space. She clicked her tongue, Nocturna was an odd constellation, it was a pattern that seemed to change constantly, more and more stars seemed to appear and disappear, some have even said that the others were drawn to the center. There light seemingly swimming the infinite abyss in perpetual travel.

A vagabonds north star, an eternal partner for the one partaking in the lonesome road of the wanderer.

She sighed to herself, looking over- Jade, Tom, and Bellatrix- were sleeping around the room taking there sofa of choice to get some rest. Pretty soon Kingsley and Hosea would need a break from the constant driving, though sadly she wouldn't be able to drive this time around. She rolled over, turning her back to the green hologram as the 'windows' brightly began to ripple, the outside view of the rolling dunes and the night sky vanished. She'd have to find Nocturna major on a later night.

Maybe when it was Tom or Jades turn she would join the passenger's side to get a good look.

Yeah... next time, next time I'll find you... She thought, closing her eyes and letting herself fall asleep.

10/18/2055, Wednesday, 3:10 am

She felt a presence behind her... the subtle bump and roll of the voyager across the desert landscape couldn't distract from the feeling of something stalking behind her.

Freezing in alarm, she woke with a jolt- her eyes snapping open- and her thoughts buzzed rapidly.

What the heck was going on now?

She struggled to keep herself still, she saw a small shadow dart in front of her, a silhouette cast by the holomap. She followed the shadow with her eyes, at the same time finally registering the snoring around her, everyone was still asleep, and whatever was circling the holomap had quietly sneaked past them all. The shadow stopped, becoming idle... it was right behind her.

Suddenly she could hear the pressing of a button, the map changed behind her, followed by a low gasp... the voice sounded... young.

Susan blinking her eyes in bewilderment, unknowingly and by the instinct born from living as a nomad she already had her good hand on her gun holster, slowly she moved her hand away, taking a moment to calm herself, she peered behind her back.

It was the boy! His face lit up by the glow of the holomap.

She shivered, his face was still crawling with the dark lines of cognicrossis, all around his eyes and skin. Yet... he was moving... looking at the holomap in muted wounder. Eyes a light with barely contained interest, he pressed another button, the map zoomed out revealing the entire landscape of the wasteland. Their location, the miniscule dot which was crawling laboriously across the region towards Corrins. The boy reached out trying to grasp the image only for his hand to pass through, he paused suddenly, looking at his hand with a curious expression, seemingly for the first time noticing the dark lines all over his palms. Susan slowly turned her body around, the sofa creaked, and she froze, the boy paused and looked up, spotting her looking at him. The two became still, *crap...* she thought, the boy blinked at her- looking confusedly at her splint- and to her surprise the boy approached first. She watched, going from confusion at what he was now doing, to horribly concerned, as he moved towards her. Wasn't he feeling sick, like at all? How was he even still moving in that state? All of that buzzed in her head as he closed the distance. He was finally close enough to be at arm's length, Susan scrambled up, which caused the kid to pause on his approach. The green glow of the map, lit the boy's face, dark brown eyes sizing her up, an oval shaped face, with hawkish-like features, and the bandage covering his forehead- hiding the earlier wound- the disheveled dark hair and the innocent gaze of curiosity unnerved her.

Put her in another firefight with the usual bandits or ex/rogue nomads, but put her with a kid...

"Uh, hi there... what's your name..." Susan began apprehensively, becoming nervous over the kids stare. He blinked his eyes before turning to the map, then to her arm, his expression once again curious.

"Do you wanna know what it is?" she rephrased her question, trying to sound more confident, maybe she could get him to tell who he was and why he was even outside Silverwood to begin with.... well, he was sixish, so maybe she wouldn't get much out of him, but it's worth a try. He gave an excited nod, now smiling- she couldn't help it, she smiled back, though hers was one of relief.

She carefully stood up and made for the map, he followed behind quickly- the kid practically bounced in excitement. And she couldn't stop the small shake of her head at his antics. Excitable scamp wasn't he. Not even feeling the small smile as he reached the map, ready for her as if he were an excitable student waiting on his teacher.

Suddenly, the boy froze, excitement slowly ebbing away as confusion replaced it. Susan stopped, something wasn't right... the boys skin and lips were slowly losing their color, becoming paler and to Susan's horror he began to wobble were he stood near the holomap. Without warning the boy's eyes closed and Susan shouted in surprise as she dived to get him. He fell over at the same time everyone jerked up in alarm and panic, their hands instantly going for their firearms. She moved and without realizing it, instinctively reaching up with her prosthetic arm, it exited the splint in a smooth motion, the gears and actuators guiding it as if it were her previous arm. It dived under and caught him around his chest as she fell with him, guarding him with her body as he went limp. She groaned as her body contacted the floor, but the pain she felt was quickly overridden by the panic of the kids well-being.

"Susan!" "What the hell!" "What going on!?" Susan heard in the background as she sat up carefully and rolled him over, checking his pulse with her other arm. Tom, who was closet, came to her side and immediately looked bewildered at the boy in her arms.

"How'd he sneak by all of us." Tom said absentmindedly, a note of impressed jib in his voice as the two ladies moved towards the two. "Wow what's he doing here!" Jade stuttered trying to figure out what was going on.

"He- he just appeared out of nowhere!" Susan said panicked "Kid was trying to play with the holomap and- I asked him if he wanted to learn how it works- the second we got to it he collapsed!" Susan said rapidly, looking absolutely pale. Suddenly the boy shoot up, causing everyone to jump. He breathed rapidly, suddenly scared, quickly Bellatrix recovered first.

"Hey, hey there," holding her hands up approaching slowly "Are you okay?" the boy took a moment before nodding "Okay, that's good- you can understand me... can you tell me your name." Bella asked sweetly, sitting on the floor, legs crossed, next to Susan who was looking at Bellatrix with surprise. The kid perked up, looking toward her, his face puzzled. Before his hand went to grasp his head, the boy groaned his eyes clenched shut in discomfort. Bella got a bit closer, placing a worried hand to his side.

Suddenly the door past the kitchen flew open with a dull thud as Church rushed out, he paused- shocked at the sight before him- quickly he made a beeline towards the group.

"How long was he up?" he asked hurriedly as he crouched next to Bella.

"Sue!" Jade hissed, getting Susan's attention enough for Church to ask again.

"I- I don't know, he just appeared there looking at the holomap... What's happening with him," she asked frantically "It's normal, suffers of cognicrossis always have mild to severe headaches. That's a stage one occurrence... which is a miracle by the physical symptoms I'm seeing." he answered, carefully grabbing the kids arms "Hey fella, let me get a good look at you... okay."

The boy looked towards church, he slowly let his arms down, and church looked him over. It was only a couple of seconds when Church unexpectedly looked confused "that's odd..." he said softly.

"What is it?" Tom said hoovering over the holomap to get a look.

"The symptoms... they don't seem to be getting worse, it looks to me like there regressing... that's a miracle." Church said, his voice laced with disbelief. Susan didn't look remotely convinced.

"Regressing... the kid just past out on us for a couple of seconds!" Susan exclaimed "He's as cold as ice!" Church put his hand on his forehead, yes... he was cool to the touch, but...

"Look at him carefully, do you see something odd." Church replied patiently.

"His skin, he's losing the paleness by the looks of it." Bella analyzed, Jade, Tom, and Susan looked closer and to their shock, she was right... some of the color was returning to him, not much but it was now becoming more and more obvious, that the dark lines were becoming less intense.

Church looked at the child uneasily, cognicrossis was a death sentence, maybe he was mistaken on how badly the boy was corrupted by it. But... something odd was happening with the boy. Could he be a *deviant?*

"S-Sorin?"

Everyone froze, suddenly taken aback by the kids first words.

The kid looked back to Bellatrix positively beaming "My n-name... is... Sorin." he said happily.

CHAPTER

4

10/18/2055, Wednesday, 6:08 am

The voyager sat idle across the shade of a rocky plateau, everyone had eaten their fill of rations (The kid was reluctant to eat them, to the irritation of Kingsley, but he eventually gave in.) and they were all discussing what to do with him. Hosea, King, Church, and Bellatrix sitting around the campfire outside in the shade, as the other four sat inside the voyager.

Susan was showing him the holomap to his fascination. With Jade and Tom seemingly joking about the 'nickname' he gave her. "Can't believe he asked if you were a knight!" Jade sniggered out, with Susan promptly glaring at her. Tom laughed, the kids parents must have read him a lot of bedtime stories involving them. Those old tales before the great rapture across the endless expanse. At least, that was the theory of how the original nomads came to the wastelands. He shook his head, tall tales and children's stories they were. No... the only knights they had here where the ones that could tear you in halves with shear strength alone. The one to be avoided if you were a nomad. Outside, the other four adults threw theories back and forth.

"Bella, I don't know... I followed the signal, which lead me to a location in Silverwood; an abandoned building on the outskirts of the town, and after that, nothing." Hosea said calmly "The only ghost runners skilled enough to erase memories like that are all the way past the capital of the republic, only the agency that works with S.P.C.T.R are capable of flashing out memory like that."

Bella shook her head "That's... that's just... shit, and you've got some of the best O.S security as far as I know out here.... in this miserable dustbowl of a region," She sighed "But how did you find him?" She flicked towards the voyager.

"When I found out what was wrong, I hunkered down for the moment. You know- checking my systems to see if anything else was tampered with." He shook his head "Everything looked normal, aside from the memory loss, I was perfectly fine... But, I still tried to scan the building for any signs of the runner... couldn't find a trace- and before I could do anything more, that's when the warning reached me on general coms for the region. I booked it- there and then. And by the time I made it back to the road, and contacted Jade and Tom... the meltdown happened."

He looked towards the voyager "I retreated... and there he was... walking slowly down the path out of the city limits. He was a mess... and the bleeding from his forehead was fresh. Someone definitely attacked him, could have been a raider- an animal- but I've got know idea... and none of it feels right."

"I'll say this... will have to travel a lot more carefully for now on. The Conclaves and S.S are going to be out for blood." Kingsley said darkly.

"Hmph, well there's one good thing about this..." Church said dryly.

"And what would that be," Hosea said casually "The raiders and ex-nomads will have to tread more carefully for a while. Cause you know S.P.C.T.R isn't gonna give any chances for a surrender," he scoffed "Same will most likely apply to use sadly..." Church said.

Hosea shrugged "Will just have to go dark for a while, leave this region and regroup at Corrins... can only imagine the settlers reactions to the news feeds. Then again, I wouldn't be surprised if they hadn't yet."

Kingsley gave a hollow chuckle "Yeah... the conclaves and republic both were bragging about their town for months now... and for this to happen." He shook his head sadly "God be with those settlers..."

Bella looked between all three of them as they spoke, her expression ponderous, she gave one lasting look towards the voyager. The cawing of a desert shriek in the distance, the loose trails and grains of sand echoed subtly around them with smaller less noticeable animal life, but unusually Bella couldn't focus on them, no instead she thought about the kid- Sorin- and wondered what they were going to do with him.

"So the kid, are we going to hand him over to the S.S child services?" Everyone became silent at her question.

Hosea closed his eyes and leaned forward on his seat, his appearance seemingly taking a more somber air about him. That was the question wasn't it... and it of course, was a complex and exhausting one at best. S.S and the conclaves ran a program for children.

Who by either accident or by the cruel environment of the wastelands, have tragically lost their families. It wasn't perfect by any means and most children ended up going from shelter to shelter, orphanage to orphanage, and usually sector care tends to let a good few fall into the cracks. Then there was the circle. The Circle could be a lot of things, though primarily and infamously they were the flagship handlers and operators of nomads.

Nomads of course being the trained few who offered a couple of services: Bodyguards, Private security, Cyberspace security, Private investigators, general thug work, and hitmen. But... they also offer programs for children who've also lost family members. Of course, most- see this as them grooming them to become future nomads. But with how crooked and flawed the systems out here in the wastelands where, what other choices could they possibly have? At the end of the day... the circle could be seen as another safety net for those who couldn't be caught by the republic or the conclaves.

But the boy... Sorin. Hosea needed to know first... a deep scan at Corrins, and if needed, the Circle could help fulfil the requirements of a biomonitor serial and id. He grunted, looking towards Bellatrix.

"Will wait till Corrins before making a decision." he turned to Church "Was there something you needed to tell me about him?"

Church nodded slowly "You've heard about deviants, right?" Hosea paused, narrowing his eyes he nodded silently "What of it."

"The kids symptoms are unusual... we both seen it, the dark veins and the pallor of his skin. We all saw what he looked like when we brought him into the voyager." Church stated unnerved.

The door to the voyager opened and Susan walked out, the boy piggybacking on her as she walked outside grumbling to herself. Sorin looked around, his face now devoid of the dark veins and the pallor color, seemingly returning to his light dark skin. He looked around captivated in his surroundings to Hosea's amusement.

"Yeah... I see what you mean, but, we both know what sector security will do if they suspect it." Hosea said.

Kingsley shook his head "I still find it hard to believe. Kids being born with powers... Heh, the type you see in those trashy vids back in the districts."

Bella whistled "Who knows- maybe on are way back to Corrins, the kid will start shooting lasers out of his eyes!" She chuckled "He already looks cognicrossis free, can't really say if I remember any deviant being immune to styx contamination."

Church shook his head "Bell! I'm series... hell, they even got videos of that one kid blowing up a convenience store in Tumbleweed for christ sakes!"

Bella rolled her eyes "Relax church... just teasing, but I agree... if, and I mean if. Will find out with the deep scan. Sides... Richards still owes us for that one job right?"

Hosea nodded, Susan reached them- Soran was still closely observing the surrounding desert- King and Bella got up, both joining in on the conversing and snickering at Susan's state of vexation. Hosea shook his head, the kid was already warming into their hearts by the looks of things... Hosea raised a single brow at Susan's prosthetic, now out of the splint and wrapping around the boys other leg with her other arm.

Seem's she miraculously got used to the prosthetic. Still... will have to watch her carefully, prosthetic arms of that grade tend to be skittish. We'll have to nudge her to get a better one, much later on. And the kid, he's going to be an... interesting problem. Hosea thought calmly.

Hosea pondered to himself by the fire, as Jade and Tom began taking turns playing with the kid. The boy was an odd one, that much Hosea could agree on... and if he was a deviant that would make things a whole lot more complicated.

Deviants are the men and women born in Pangaea with supposed superhuman abilities, abilities that cybernetics are struggling to contend with. At least, that's what some of the general public believed. Hosea grunted, the corporations, the republic and the conclaves seemed very keen on the narrative that it's all baseless rumors. Yet, after seeing Sorin, so suddenly being able to recover from his illness. Cognicrossis wasn't something you could just recover from overnight. It was feared for a reason, and if the neural logical damage didn't kill you, then the mental and physical toll would. It was already a well establish and lethal sickness. Thank god it wasn't something that could normally be passed by contact with the skin, but... with how toxic styx matter was, it only made the illness that much more mysterious and unnerving. Hosea was suddenly taken out of his thoughts as Bella's voice was suddenly barking orders; he looked and his eyes widened, the dark lines have reappeared over the boy's skin, his eyes closing in pain and his skin becoming paler in Jades arms.

"Come on! Let's get em inside," She said frantically.

"I'll get some meds, and see if I can decrease his symptoms!" Church said, as he rushed ahead into the voyager, swiftly followed by the rest.

Hosea made to follow, his poncho flapping from a strong gust of wind, and all to abruptly he paused, the hair on the back of his skin began to raise up. There was something behind him... a familiar presence he felt after the moment he lost his memory. He turned around, his kinetic revolver in hand and pointing forwards faster than the eye can see.

Nothing... there was nothing there... but he could have sworn....

He activated the binocular aug in his eyes, zooming forwards... and there was something there.

A dot, a shape, a figure... finally at approximately 120x magnification, he could make out a dark stranger in the background. He was milliseconds from zooming in, when suddenly a draft of wind picked up the sand behind the figure, it only took a few moments, but the stranger was gone. Disappearing like a mirage.

He stood there silently, his eyes narrowing, what on earth was that? Was that just a product of his overactive imagination? Hosea grunted to himself, this didn't feel right but nothing for it now... He holstered his gun and with one last look back, he moved towards the voyager. After ensuring Sorin was fine (much to Church's astonishment) the voyager crew left behind the camp by the big plateau and set off further down the arduous path towards Corrins Watch. Hosea never told them what he saw, and later on would investigate what he had forgotten before the tragedy of Silverwood. Nothing came of it... for years to come, nobody would ever be able to shed light on the incident.

Silverwood's looming shadow in the following years would slowly mark a dramatic shift to the wastelands. The Republic, The Conclaves, and The Circle. All of them will come to be haunted by the settlements mysterious downfall, near the border of known civilization... The Endless Expanse.

CHAPTER

5

A shadow skittered across the road, the streets of red boulevard drive were barely lit that night, due in part to the weather. The sandstorm from a month ago had surprising wind speeds- strong enough to cause loose debris to fly sporadically in the air. Taking a few streetlights with them. Of course, being in the historic district of Gloomhaven... well... the odds of those lights being replaced were slim at best.

But for the figure hugging the sides of the streets, in a rush to reach his destination without being caught, this was a blessing in disguise.

He only had so much time to get his task done, and they would get suspicious if he didn't make it back before 8pm sharp. He moved silently down the empty streets, walking quickly down an especially long alleyway, the few lights of the windows being his only sources of light. The ten-year-old stopped as he made it to the exit, looking both ways and making sure the cost was clear he stepped out onto Angelo street... a mostly abandoned neighborhood and the location of the nearest junkyard. He turned right and jogged down the street corner, watching his speed as the road dipped down, it was only getting darker and as he held on to the straps of his backpack he prayed he could make it back before the deadline. The junkyard was the only place left were he could get decent parts to fix his bike. Half of Angelo street was a junk yard and deemed too dangerous for most to go in, on account of the Cazador nests and so forth. A lot of junk gets thrown here from the undercity to the central district of gloom. There was a lot of equipment here that was abandoned legally and illegally, from broken down firearms, to ruined augments- not the bodily kind- but most of the general civilian types like attachable inhalers that a few reactor workers decided to throw over the fence, armored skeletal rigs(low end power suits) for heavy lifting, the usual broken down vehicles and dissected scooters and motorbikes. It was a massive junkyard, and hazardous conditions aside, it was the best place to find replacement parts.

He had about an hour and twenty minutes to move in, peruse, and get out before Aunt Dot gets suspicious. He got his delivery run done much earlier than usual in order to make it here. The journey back to the undercity would take him maybe 30 minutes.... so he had to get out in at least 36 minutes total. To make his prepared excuse work. That Chase and his flunkies were giving him a hard time as usual.

Sorin crouched down, removing the black and gold due rag from his head, a memento from Susan and wrapped it around his neck. With that he silently moved towards the spot he scooped out hours ago.

The Junkyard fence was easy to get past, a small hole big enough for him to crawl through, unfortunately, he may have scratched himself as he made it out. The medium sized cut near the lower part of his cargo pants proved this to be a fact, as he groaned to himself in annoyance.

He shook his head and moved forwards, swiping the dirt off his grey long-sleeved shirt. He slid below another fence and low and behold he was at the place he needed to be. Pulling up his black and yellow bandanna over his mouth and nose to block out the smell, he got to searching, the area was filled with mounds of junk and broken husks of vehicles, there had to be some leftover scraps he could use. After a few agonizing minutes of lifting heavy scraps of useless junk and worthless due dads, taking a moment to get his breath back, he held up his watch: **Tuesday, 6/13/ 2061, 7 :25 pm,** he needed to hurry! He tried to get out of the mess he made, when suddenly he tripped on a small pipe.

Catching himself against the side of the ruined car, he spotted his reflection and groaned. His round face and hawklike features were marred with dirt and grim, the only part of his face that wasn't dirtied was his mouth and nose, his black disheveled hair was a mess, and his clothes... also a mess.

He really needed to come up with a *BIG* excuse for the mess... he chuckled, Tom always said he had the face of a scruffy, mischievous imp, now he looked more like a grease monkey... just like Kingsley. Swiping the dirt from his hair, he moved on, this pile was a bust. Moving further down the path he noticed something, there was a faint glint behind the main building of the junkyard. Carefully, he walked over piles of junk in his way, course it wasn't easy- the sun was disappearing over the horizon- and his surroundings were becoming pitch dark, with the only lights being the main building and outside the junkyard. He had a flashlight in his bag, but... he didn't want anybody to suddenly look out there window and spot him waving his light across the yard.

Finally, sidestepping the lights of the building, and finding a good spot to observe what that glint was, he crouched and took off his backpack- carefully he took out the flashlight- a small hand sized puck of a light. Pointing forwards he adjusted the strength and turned it on.

Another massive mound behind the building, with a long fence blocking easy access to it. But looking closer, he noticed a large opening- a hole- in the mound and the yellowish glint was reflecting the light from the building and something blinking from within. At that moment, Sorin forgot about his bike. Was there actually something... valuable in there? He paused for a moment looking around the barge, countless other mounds of junk, could he spare the time to do this...

If its valuable enough, maybe I could trade it with Otto, then I won't have to worry about fixing it... could even buy a new one if its good enough! Sorins eyes were now focusing on the shimmer in the hole, his expression agonizing as he thought about his options. *Church and Aunt Dot... they wouldn't have to worry about wasting credits for my sake either, for once... and Aunt Dot needs the money to keep the bar afloat too...*

Sorin pressed his lips, his mind imagining something super rare inside the junk mound. Maybe some rich central citizen decided to get rid of something valuable, wouldn't be the first time, he witnessed that happen with one of the kids at school, like that one kid... Riley something, something- this one time when he came to school flaunting a new skateboard and one day he apparently threw it away, flaunting another shiny, brand-new bike. Soren was also pretty sure Riley helped Chase break his very own bike the same day...

Sorin's mind was finally made up.

Turning off his flashlight he pocketed it and moved closer to the locked fence, he reached inside his bag and pulled out a small case. Opening it, he pulled out a pick. He inserted it and after 2-3 minutes the lock snapped up, and fell off the door with a thick thud as it landed on the ground. Sorin looked around quickly, like a deer in the headlights, but there wasn't anybody there. No one heard it. He was alone.

Sorin sighed in relief, wiping the sweet off his brow. He walked forwards, it was a massive pile of scrape and garbage. And the opening on the side didn't look super deep; he still felt a bit nervous. He gathered his courage, and taking a moment he looked around one last time and with grimace crawled inside. The garbage and scraps under his hands felt rough and horrible, he would take the longest bath after getting this done. Slowly and methodically he crawled, and eventually the shimmer and glow of the object was getting closer. And then he saw it, the cause of the shimmer, it was some sort of broken headlamp. Its light reflecting on the surface of a smooth dark orange and black oval disc, trash surrounded him all around the inside of this mound, and the disc- which looked to be the size of his forearm- poked out of the wall of scrapes. He put his hands on it and started to pull, the thing was kinda heavy but little by little, it was starting to budge from its spot.

There was a sound, a sound which made him pause... his hands still on the disc, he looked and there was something behind it. An opening of some sort, the color drained from his face, he went to let the disc go, but it slid out before he could stop it.

And what he saw made him want to scream in freight, but he was too scared to say a peep.

There was a fluttering of many wings inside the opening. A Cazador nest... he was inside a hole, next to a Cazador nest... he grabbed the disc slowly, his entire body shacking, terrified, he started to slowly crawl back.

He kept his eyes locked to the nest, to the shadowed silhouettes of the giant wasps. The headlamp inside the tunnel making their shadows jump out of the hole. He felt the bottom of his shoe hit something. There was the sound of something rolling, and suddenly he heard the sound of broken glass, he looked back with a start... he must have kicked a bottle out or something. He turned around and felt a sharp chill travel down his spine and fingers. A Cazador was moving out of the hole, the size of a small dog- crawling creepily over the trash- the blinking lights reflecting from its wings, and its green exoskeleton. Its red compound eyes were looking directly at him. It stood there, flapping its wings aggressively, Sorin immediately obliged its warning. He quickly backed out, keeping his sights to the Cazador which laid idle guarding the nest as more dark silhouettes crawled from within. Suddenly, Sorin fell over and rolled out of the opening. He felt something fall from his backpack as he came to stop outside the mound. Dizzy he felt the heavy disc land at his side. Getting up, he could feel the adrenaline course through his body as he crawled away in fear. No movement, he looked around, it was really dark now, bringing up his watch, he gasped- it was 7 :45pm- he quickly got up, gathered the disc and quickly stuffed it into his backpack still watching the opening of the mound. He moved away from the hole as fast as he could and made for the fence. He picked up the lock and refastened it were it belonged and ran for the exit. Not stopping until he finally reached the hole in the fence a good minute and a half later. He breathed raggedly as he crawled below it to leave the junkyard.

It was all a blur as he kept running and running down the street, and finally he tripped on the ground, laying on all fours as he struggled to get his breath back. He was still shaking as he crawled too and leaned against the wall. Taking his durag cover off so he could breathe in the fresh air unimpeded.

His gaze staring upward toward the sky... he made it out, he actually made it out... There were so many stories out there in the wastelands of settlers getting stung by Cazadores, and none of them pretty. You're body convulsing, the incalculable pain, and finally the moment when your body goes numb, the paralysis and finally... death.

He got up shakily... he was still alive though, still alive and breathing. Taking a moment to calm down he looked down to his watch. It was 8:01 pm. He groaned, cursing to himself. He needed to get home to the nocturne, and he was not looking forward to the confrontation.

6/13/2061, Tuesday, 8 :13 pm

Gloomhaven was a pretty big town. Once a small settlement that was established near a massive canyon, hundreds and hundreds of miles south from the border zone separating the wastelands from republic soil. In the end, that small settlement grew into a massive, two sector town which also had a top layer (The Central and Historic Districts), and a bottom sublayer under the town (The Undercity), sorta like a subterranean tunnel. These tunnels ran all along and inside the ravine walls and from earlier records, the very cliffs of the canyon (or at least... the south side where the town was originally built) were excavated and turned into a type of mining town.

The ichorcyte was the objective, and after years of excavating, the V.M reactor was established. The Historic district was born, and years after that, a bridge was built, linking to the other side of the ravine were the Central district was established north, facing towards the border zone.

Sorin walked through the streets, looking out for settlement officers- at this time of night- he'd be in big trouble if he were to be caught roaming the streets. Especially if they pulled up his biomonitor and found out his connection with the circle. The upper citizens of Gloomhaven don't exactly take kindly to nomads, especially if your biomoniter was issued by the likes of the circle. Not that Sorin had much choice in the matter of who found him that day. Hosea and Bella never said where they found him... and to this day, he wondered who his actual parents were.

He turned left around the street corner and there it was, the undercity elevator- a two-way lift that transported people from the top side of Gloomhaven to one of the sub residential zones under the city.

Sorin grinned, finally! He was going home.

The large concreate structure 10 feet tall and 20 feet wide- standing by itself between two buildings, and housing inside a large metal platform which descended by three layers underground. The first two layers being approximately 60 meters deep in depth and 35 miles wide. With the final layer being 80 meters deep and 50 miles wide(as of right now). Sorin pressed the button near the large vault entrance, the small interface showing the platforms location switched on and a wait message appeared on screen. After a moment the vault door hissed open and the large platform- with a carrying capacity for 12-18 passengers stood silently for him to step on.

Sorin rode the elevator down, grasping the handrails as he sat down on one of the metal benches. It was rare thing having the elevator all to himself, but he didn't pay it any mind- his headspace was occupied with the eventual confrontation he would have back when he got home. Sorin closed his eyes and sighed, he couldn't think of any way out of that. His thoughts turned to the moving elevator as the unseen gears and pulleys gradually brought it down to layer 2, SRZ-10. There were over twenty elevators constructed around the old district. A few of them... six to be exact, no longer functioned due to either maintenance problems or other mechanical system errors. Right now, crazily, Sorin wondered how oh, so, unfortunate it would be if the elevator were to stop working right now... at least he would have had an alibi for him being so late.

The massive cogs and gears of the caged platform groaned out, as the lights of the ceiling flickered. Sorin held on to the safety rails, as he calmly watched the indicator count down the floor levels and with a groan the dial finally reached layer 2. The elevator made another old groan than became idle, the doors opened, and a colorful glow of neon lights filtered onto Sorin. He was almost home, and he was still trying to come up with an excuse for his appearance. He looked out of the entrance door, the long tunnel lead on in a spider web of activity and moving bodies. Of course, at this time there weren't that many people roaming the neon rich passages of the undercity marketplace. Convenience stores, food stops, entertainment shops. All below the historic district, and as Sorin walked with the crowd he felt dejected, wondering if all his troubles were for nothing. The undercity was sprawling, like a labyrinthian maze, the paths forked from passage to passage, and without the many signs pointing the way, Sorin had no doubt that most would end up lost in this underground cavern. But after so many years underneath the historic district, the undercity just kept growing and spreading deeper and deeper into the ravine cliff.

Neighborhoods created from the ever-expanding excavation and with tunnels leading from area to area. The people of the undercity created a thriving subculture, as below the city of Gloomhaven. Sorin shivered, he was about to reach the end of the tunnel marketplace. The chatter of the crowd and the noise of kids his age, and adults walking up and down the tunnel, not able to distract Sorin from the dread building in his chest. There were pockets of neighborhoods in the undercity, they go by many names, but residential zones were the most popular name. The undercity had up to 10 to 20 residential zone for the first and second layers. Although, layer three was a different beast all together: it's the furthest depth below Gloomhaven and was still in the process of excavation to this day.

Thankfully, the nocturne was located in one of the first residential zones of layer two, and Orio- was the name of his residential zone, a large and vast opening where the tunnel branched off- into a huge man-made cavern filled with residential households built from rock, concreate, metal and wood. Forming a quant underground cul-de-sac. Houses medium to small in size, lined back-to-back across the 'street' with the streetlamps casting a soft white illumination across the rocky walls of the cavern, and barely able to reach the very caverns ceiling.

At the end of the street was where his home- The Nocturne- was located. Sorin gulped and left the streaming crowd, climbing down the stone steps and into the empty streets, walking past the neon signs and advertisement boards on the ceilings, a few of which pointed in the direction of the nocturne. He felt his stomach sink with each step he took, and slowly he found himself preparing for the worst.

CHAPTER

6

6/13/ 2061, Tuesday, 8 :29 pm

The Seventh Nocturne...

There were a lot of buildings and residential hotspots within the undercity, from café's, baristas, and diners. The Nocturne could count as all three. but most living in the community of Orio considered the establishment as a bar. Medium sized and a two-story establishment, with a big basement and cellar.

As Sorin climbed the wooden steps, which were illuminated by the neon sign in a velvet purple, proudly proclaiming its name for all to see. He noticed that there was no lights on behind either side of the door from the stained-glass windows. He paused, that was weird, by this time- Aunt Dot or Church would have been home by now. Especially Aunt Dot... She was after all the owner and server of the place.

He walked to the door and crouched down, shifting the welcome mat over and slipped the key from under it. He unlocked the door and stepped inside, flipping a switch to the side he looked around. The main bar area brightened. Florescent lights above the bar, bathed the wooden foundations in calming blues. Along with the other four side booths tucked into the corners of the walls to his left. He walked towards the bar stand to his right taking a seat, and in the middle of the table was a tray of food, covered with a sheet of plastic and a note.

Sorin,

    Have to step out for the moment, a friend needs help with an errand, and It might take a while for me to get back.

    Lock the door, and be sure to eat up.

    P.S Church should be arriving home soon, so you probably won't be alone for long.

    P.S.S Also, don't forget to take your meds!

Sorin couldn't help the sigh of relief as he got done reading the letter, leaning his head on the table he counted his lucky stars. Thinking about it, if the constellations were correct, then that meant tonight would have been the night when Nocturna Major was visible in the night sky this period. He smiled to himself.

I wonder if Susan is looking up at the sky right now. He thought to himself.

"Heh, maybe that's why it didn't sting me back there." Sorin said to himself, thinking back to it. In a way, he always viewed the constellation as his good luck charm in a sense. Ever since the day Susan taught him about the constellations and what they meant. And Bellatrix... who made a fun joke about it one evening before she and Kingsley left for another job. *'You know... Nocturna Major has a lot of old myths surrounding it, wives tales there called. A lot of people... even are dear old Susan believes that the constellation is a guardian of the wanderer, always looking out for the lonesome traveler, and once in a while acting as a guide for those lost. Hehe... there's even an adage to it, believe it or not.*

"Where oh where must we go, those who wonder this path, in search of our better selves." Sorin said to himself, from under his breath.

He began eating his food, a cheeseburger, fries, and a fruit juice. All the while, wondering and thinking about how the others were doing. Tom, Jade, and Susan. Hosea, King and Bellatrix, where they doing fine out there? Sorin drank the rest of his juice, he shook his head, immediately shifting his thoughts to other matters, of course there okay, unlike him...

He unzipped his backpack, and took out the disk. The orangish dark metal, glimmered under the lights of the bar. He gave it a bewildered look, what was it? The thing was like a medium sized frisbee, and to his slight disgust there was a nasty, yellowish, weblike substance on the side of it. He took a napkin and wiped it off, that's when he noticed the odd groves along the sides of it. He raised an eyebrow, and pressed his thumb against the side...

Suddenly, a click was heard!

In his hands the disc began to expand, Sorin yelped in surprise- accidentally knocking his plate and cup on the floor with a thud and thump- and the disc continued to extend. He could hear a grinding like noise from it, and suddenly the dark metal began to separate and detach itself at certain points, becoming almost fin like on the sides, and Sorin dropped it...

The disc now the size of a small platform fell down to the ground. Only for a sharp pulse of energy to ripple from the bottom... there was no sound of a crash, and to Sorin's stone-flabbergasted expression, the platform was now hovering 2-3 feet above the ground. Sorin moved from his seat without thinking, now truly observing it... he slowly looked underneath, the bottom of the platform had a vent like opening under it, which was humming with energy, a blue wave which seemed to push it off the ground.

Sorin's breath hitched, eyes widening in reverence, and excitement coursing through him. He just found something better than a bunch of messily, spare, bicycle parts!

It's a hoverboard... I found a freaking hoverboard! The thought shot through Sorins head like a comet. He approached it, instantly blinded by his excitement and rush to learn how to use it, then suddenly, something felt wrong.

The hoverboard sparked, the thing started to make a low whining sound, then all together the thing started to twitch and jitter madly before-

The board suddenly let out a great wave of energy which made Sorin fly backwards. The air was kicked out of his lungs as the board seemed to fly to the other side of the room. Crashing into the other wall, and snapping back to its previous small disc form, its bottom slightly smoking.

"Ough" Sorin groaned out, using the railing from the bar table to hoist himself up and giving the hoverboard a pained and cautionary look. He slowly approached it, as if he were approaching a cornered animal. Pieces of its metallic shell was lying around it, and the smoke coming off was starting to petter out. His disappointment was severe... and his day took a sudden nosedive, was this it? All that excitement, only for this to happen...

"No..." he breathed out, as he began to ball his fists. *No... This doesn't mean anything. I mean... if I could get to Tom and convince him to help me, maybe we could fix it!* Sorin gazed at the board with a look of hunger, his imagination, suddenly and irrevocably charged with utter jubilation. Visions of him riding it down the streets and tearing through the bottom layers of the undercity at blinding speeds suddenly had him quaking in anticipation. Forget the bike, if he got this hoverboard working... then, that would be freaking amazing! No, awesome!

The carefully put the board back inside his backpack. For now, he needed to find a way to explain how he came across it...

Without going over what happened at the junkyard or for that matter the Cazadors...

Sorin grimaced, that was not going to be an easy thing... then again, Tom or Jade probably wouldn't freak out to much if he told either of them. He grinned, maybe next week he'd get the chance to show em what he found. He realized he would probably have to hide it in his room until then, glancing at the end of the main bar stand further away, across the stairs, leading up was a door, a wooden door that led downstairs into the basement. A large main room which had three paths, the main path which led to the storage room, and the two other paths which forked. Left was Sorin's room, and right was Church's room. While Aunt Dot slept in the room upstairs.

Smiling, he glanced down to the floor, where his plate had fallen. Moving back to the bar stand, he went to reach for the plate. That's when he noticed it, and he froze- dread freezing his insides- His hand outstretched, with the now visible dark- colored veins, developing and forking up across his arm.

A cogni attack, now of all times...

No! no, no, no... My medicine, I need my medicine- Sorin quickly and desperately began to rummage through his backpack... and they weren't there... why weren't they there!

His room, he had to get to his room! Sorin abandoning his backpack and moved quickly towards the end of the main bar.

Sorin slammed the door open with a loud bang, as he moved as fast as possible through the short hallway, but to his growing anxiety he could feel it.... like a dark and terrible shadow looming overhead, the beginning sensations of gnawing pain across his body began to spread as he finally reached the door to his room. He kicked it open and gasped as the gnawing pain evolved into a burning red agony. All across his body, there was only pain. He stumbled, using every bit of his concentration to walk himself inside.

His room for a lack of a better term was a mess, medium sized and shaped like a semicircle, there was junk and parts in a disorganized pile on one side with a workbench in the middle of it all, and on the other side was his bed and nightstand. The straight end was home to three pairs of furniture which included a wardrobe and two trunks on either sides of it. In the middle of the room was a large round table, which had a couple of books, a lamp and a shabby laptop or minicomputer. Sorin supported himself against the table, pulling himself towards his bed. Dimly, through the pain, he felt so much derision for his current situation.

Why? Why did he have to have a flare up *now* of all times...

Was it karma, or just more of his rotten luck. He struggled to balance himself, the room was starting to spin, and he felt his head splitting. Just, just a little bit more...

He collapsed next to the stand, not able to stop the pitiable whimper as he forced himself forward. A green bout of nausea touched his tongue, but he swallowed it down and reached for the drawer, after roughly pulling it open he reached inside and pulled out his spare bottle of meds. His hands shaking from pain, he uncapped the lid and let it fall to the ground as he pulled one white colored tablet from the bottle and quickly dry swallowed it.

His energy finally depleted, he sunk to the floor- the medicine bottle rolling to the side, as tablets spilled out onto the floor. Sorin was on the floor in a ball, hugging himself in whatever attempt he could to endure the pain. It would be a few minutes before the meds kicked in, so he waited and thought about the hoverboard.

And... he couldn't help but laugh, despite the pain he was in. A hoverboard! He found a *hoverboard* of all things in that dump. Of all the lucky draws... maybe for once he was due a good hand.

CHAPTER

7

6/13/ 2061, Tuesday, 9:48 pm

Forty minutes.

Forty minutes of pain, and then after that, ten more minutes of recuperation. All things considered it wasn't that bad compared to past cogni attacks. *A four out of ten... yea me, whoo-hoo...* Sorin thought dryly.

He gripped the rails on the walls, using them to steady himself as he moved out of the basement. He took a moment to think about what he was going to do next, he had to go back and get his meds from the junkyard, that was essential. He had to find a way to sneak back there, and he groaned, it was still there by the Cazador nest. He pinched the bridge of his nose; stupid, stupid- it must have happened when he fell out of the hole- if he had taken the time to just make sure he hadn't...

He shook his head, he screwed up, that's it, get over it, move on. He'll go back and get it the next day. But for now...

He readied himself and walked towards the main bar, picking up his plate and cleaning the mess of broken hoverboard pieces. He really hoped Tom would have a solution to his current problem. He took a seat in one of the booths near the wall, the lights of the main bar being the only illumination that reached his booth. Neon blues and purples reflecting off the clean surface of the table and walls. The lights glinting off his glass cup, he thought about how he should tell Church of his latest cogni attack.

Uhhh... I really hope he doesn't raise the dang dosage again... the stuff is freaking terrible. Sorin thought *Wish there was something I could drink to get rid of the crappy aftertaste.* Though to be fair, the taste of the tablets

45

didn't really click until the attack was said and done. Hince the empty glass cup, after downing two small drinks of fruit juice, the taste still lingered. He rolled his eyes *Whatever... at least its finally over with...*

Suddenly he heard the door open behind him. "Sorin... you here!" a voice called.

"Yeah, I'm right here Aunt Dot." Sorin replied back, waving a hand outside his booth so she could see him.

The tap of heeled footsteps upon the wooden and stone floors reached his ears, and a woman appeared next to him. Crisanta Dottery, the owner of The Seventh Nocturne.

Short-statured, fair-skinned, and she looked positively exhausted. She wore her usual bartender uniform, short sleeved white blouse and black vest over it, with black dress pants. Her teal blue eyes glanced down at his spot on the booth. She froze, mid-step of her taking the rubber band out of her brown hair, which laid over her shoulder in a ponytail. She gaped at his appearance, and Sorin flinched, realizing to late that he forgot to take a well- needed bath, from his escapade at the junkyard.

"Umm... I can explain..." he held his hands up miserably, doing his damndest to look as innocent as possible.

She frowned, folding her arms up and gave him a single raised eyebrow. "I'm listening."

Sorin looked away from her accusing eyes, developing a bad taste in his mouth, not really preferring the obvious excuse, but it was either that or... "I had another attack." He said silently.

She was silent for a moment, her eyes searching, but her expression, not by much mind you- began to soften a little- she unfolded her arms and took a calming breath. "How long ago was it?"

"About fifty minutes ago. Its fine, I took my meds, but... well, it wasn't as bad as last time," Sorin tried to say, only for her to quickly take a seat on the opposite end of the booth. She held out her hand "Let me see." She replied looking at his arm, which still faintly showed the black veins. He sighed before complying, giving her his hand, she looked at it and her brow creased further. "How's the pain." She questioned.

Sorin shrugged "It's not that bad, maybe a four out of ten, maybe," she gave a concerned look "Seriously, it's okay... I can deal with a little pain now and again... how was your day so far?" Sorin asked, now desperate to stop the tirade of usual questions: Is it getting worse? Should we take you to the hospital? Are the meds even working properly? He could think of worst questions... but he'd rather not think about school at the moment. Or the junkyard. She gave him an annoyed look, before frowning, letting him pull his arm back. "You're going to let Church know when he gets back." She said, giving him a look, that said, he didn't have much of a choice but to do so, and that she would ask and check if he did.

Sorin nodded "Yes."

She nodded back, relaxing but not by much. Letting herself fall against the seat "My day was... well, you can see it on me kiddo." Sorin grinned, happy the first confrontation was over.

"Sooo... who's the friend you mentioned?" She snorted, before stretching against her seat. He grimaced at the dubious pops coming from her shoulders. "Nuh-uh... none of your business." Sorin slumped "Why? I just wanna know." She gave him an eye roll "Exactly, and you're already a handful as it is." It was Sorin's turn to raise an eyebrow "You're saying I'm worse than Jade or Tom." She let out a tired laugh.

"Oh no... not that bad... but you're getting there, scamp."

Sorin gave an annoyed grumble. Scamp, why'd she had to call him that of all things! He blamed Susan, ever since she first called him that, the nickname just stuck. He gave a silent glare to Aunt Dot's smug look; thinking about it... Hosea was the only one who didn't use that nickname when referring to him. Though... Jade was also an exception-she just referred to him as 'brat'.

"So is Church ever going to get home soon?" Sorin asked, now desperate again to change the topic away from that cursed word.

She yawned "Maybe, you know how it is... he's got a lot to deal with," She gave him a tired look "Since he just got started up in the historic district, it may take a while for word of mouth to spread about his practice, and he also has to find more people to deliver his packages too." She finished.

Sorin hummed to himself in thought, the courier service that Church started was called Vega Express. A small service that delivered packages of all types around the undercity, and historic districts. The items which included parcels, magazines, books, medications, merchandise, media, and other miscellaneous stuff. And so far against all odds, Church was doing pretty good with it. But...

"So there really gone!" Sorin demanded.

"Yeah, Norman and Andre, Church had to let them go." She answered solemnly, Sorin sat back against the seat shocked "But... why? They loved doing it- I mean- what happened." She grimaced before shaking her head. "Sorry, kid, it's not my place to tell." Sorin clenched his jaw "Was it Orson."

"Alright! Time for bed." She said suddenly

Sorin widened his eyes "But- Aunt Dot!" he stammered out, but his voice died out, Aunt dot gave him a simmering look.

Sorin narrowed his eyes "Fine." He got up to leave, but Dot gently reached out and grabbed his arm, he looked back at her "Listen, Sorin, don't worry about it alright. Right now, things are getting... complicated. Just keep you're cool for now. We can't afford to get in trouble with the settlement badges." Sorin pressed his lips, his anger was bubbling like a hot kettle, but what else was new. No matter what they did, everyone seemed determined to see him and church as nothing but dirty nomads. Or in his case a walking corpse.

He looked to the ground "Yeah, yeah, ok. Good night." She nodded silently before letting him go. He walked over to the bar stand and picked up his bag, the weight of the hoverboard no longer bringing with it happy thoughts of the future. Right now, he just felt so useless, and unsure of where to go or what to do to help. Like a wanderer in the wastes who had nowhere else to go but towards an oncoming storm. With his back to a bottomless ravine.

CHAPTER

8

8/16/ 2061, Friday, 2:48 pm

Sorin ran for his life, behind him a group of boys that were chasing him across the street. Of course Chase, a blonde-haired boy, who wore the standard school uniform of black, and yellows had decided that today was the day to get his revenge, for the apparent slight Sorin did a week ago.

Chase swore up and down, to whoever that was listening, that he-Sorin- had assaulted him outside school. Which wasn't untrue... Sorin had given him a black eye, the part he failed to mention was that Chase had hounded him from school in Vesamer street back to Anderson avenue, the closest elevator back home. A ten minute walk, from elevator to school and back again. Calling him every insult and leer he could think of. Sorin of course greeted his teeth, doing everything he could to ignore the sneering laughter of the other boys behind him. Which was almost a daily occurrence for him, Chase taking pleasure in his misery, with his entourage of idiots. Bill, a large boy who's fancy school outfit barely fit over his round stomach. Frank, his walnut-colored hair and big honker of a nose, laughing stupidly and thick headedly over every word Chase said... and Rhudy, a tall, bald, and equally absentminded follower of Chase.

All four walking behind him and Chase giving him the worst headache he could muster. Silently and stubbornly he ignored every jab, insult, and brainless slander. The worst bits of this, of course, was the ones about his connections to the nomads and the circle.

"Look at the little leaper!" Chase crowed "Those nomads must really be desperate for more pawns in there mudslinger racket!" he chuckled. Sorin simply kept walking, the elevator was right there- all he needed to do was get inside and- "-leaper's parents probably got swindled, when they sold him off to those sharks in the circle. Crap, they must have felt cheated when they realized he was a dead man walking." Chase said, off handedly getting a small chuckle from the other three. Sorin stopped abruptly, causing Chase to bump into his back as he gasped in disgust "Watch it punk! Swear I'll swing if I catch what you've got-" Sorin promptly turned around and swung a left overhead firmly into Chases left eye, the other three stood there shocked as Chase swung with the hit in a half circle, right into the arms of Bill who looked at Sorin's enraged, sneering face and at the now angry black discoloration around Chase's left eye. Frank and Rhudy after getting over there shock, balled there fist, giving Sorin a death glare. Time stopped, Sorin gazed at the two now charging toward him, before feeling a heavy fist connect to his right cheek, the anger froze in place, and Sorin made a quick decision. He also swung with the blow and swallowed the roaring rage in his heart and smoldered it as a new feeling of panic replaced it. He ran for it, towards the elevator, moving as fast as possible as he could feel someone trying to grab the back of his school collar. He immediately turned left into the nearest alley. Running as the shouting behind him grew louder and louder, he made another turn, his lungs complaining to him to stop, but he refused, looking back- Chase had now joined the other three- with Bill quickly falling behind. There were small tears coming from Chase's left eye and Sorin felt a fleeting sense of satisfaction from it.

He ran and finally found the end of the alley, popping out onto Penzel street and booked it to the other elevator entrance. Desperate to get there first with enough time for the doors to close, so he wouldn't be trapped with four punks beating him on the way down to the undercity.

He shot down the street, lungs burning, legs burning, and heart pounding. He slid into the elevator shaft, barely slowing himself down before slamming his fist onto the down button. His back slammed into the far wall as the doors shut themselves as the fingers of the four boys pulled and yanked to open the fenced doors. Shouting dry curses towards Sorin's haggard self. Sorin grinned before holding an obscene hand gesture towards them. Which of course- in hindsight was a terrible idea- as Chase's rat face pulled into a furious sneer, and shouted at him as the elevator groaned and wheezed as it carried him down. Towards the undercity.

Sorin moved quickly down the street, now running uphill, past a few parked cars. He just needed to take another right and he could probably lose them on Norris lane. The current street he was on was sparsely inhabited, Winchester street it was called, and most people avoided this street like the plague. Chase and his cronies were never brave enough to try there machinations in view of passerby's. And Sorin, in a moment of desperation went down here to take advantage of the older elevator at the end of Norris lane. He just needed to take the next right a few meters away. Which had a hidden short cut to Norris. By way of an abandoned building. Looking back, the boys were far, far behind him but Sorin noticed something off. Where did chase disappear to? Suddenly, something barreled into him violently. Knocking the breath out of him, "Knew you'd try to come through here, you punk!" Chase spat at him, as he struggled to lift himself off the ground. Sorin gave him a look of complete hatred, ignoring the pain from his likely scrapped right ankle. "Tch, seriously! You've really got nothing better to do." Sorin grasped the streetlamp, hoisting himself back up to his feet painfully. He groaned, that really freaking hurt. He heard footsteps, the others were quickly gaining ground, and they wouldn't hesitate to jump him. He already went through an earlier, painful beating by their hands two days ago. And he wasn't interested in another.

Church and Aunt Dot, didn't know about this now daily ritual he had to go through. Today was the last day of school for the week and later on today Tom, Jade and Susan were supposed to come visit. And he needed to get home now. There was only one thing to do, he swallowed the pain he felt from his ankle and took off running, ignoring the alley that would loop back around to Norris and moving straight up the street. Looking back, he glimpsed Bill stopping to hoist Chase up only for him to slap his hands away, pointing towards Sorin's direction.

The hill began to even out, to Sorin's relief, he started to do a fast jog downhill. About 10-20 or so meters he would reach the end of the street, Winchester street was mostly uninhabited for a reason. At the end of the street, downhill there was another elevator that could get him to the undercity, but... it was near the abandoned V.M reactor power plant that was decommissioned years ago. A power plant that was shut off, after the new one was constructed in the central district about four years ago.

And it had the reputation of being haunted.

The perfect place to give Chase and the others the slip. The road finally evened out under his feet and with a grunt of pain from his injured ankle he surged forwards. He huffed and huffed, feeling the weight of his backpack and the weight of his school clothes. Now scuffed and dirty from the tackle he received earlier from Chase, and the blood that was staining the area of his injured knee.

Unbeknownst to him, Chase screeched to a halt. On top of that hill, a cold chill traveling down his spine *The leaper is crazy!* He thought suddenly terrified. The other three ahead of him, stood there on the cusps of the high street like they were statues. In the background the skeletal remains of the reactor stood, hauntingly mountainous, just staring back at the four as a powerful gust of wind sighed over them carrying particles of dust along with it, as if the old facility was singing a lonesome dirge of melancholy there way.

And down ahead of them in the foreground, Sorin continued on, his shrinking figure carrying him forward, headless of the apparent danger of the place. *S-screw this! I'm not going in there!* Chase thought shaking his head *Leaper probably planned this all along... screw him.*

Sorin looked up dizzyingly, the sky was a cloudy steel sheet, and the sun completely hidden. Sorin looked back down and felt a dull reassurance that he would finally escape.

The Plant was now in view. An old, ancient, facility that was completely in disrepair. The surrounding buildings facing the plant were also under the same state of disrepair with windows smashed, doors falling off their hinges, various litter across the ground, and vehicles like cars and trucks laid on the sides of the roads rusted and some missing their tires. The old historic district, the original location of the first few settlers of Gloomhaven.

Sorin now fast walking, ducked into one of the side alleys, he walked and walked, then with a final hard gasp, leaned against the wall tuckered out. His stamina finally at its limits.

He listened as he crouched down, nothing, no sounds, no footsteps. Did- did they finally call it quits?

He got control of his breathing and got to his shacking feet, taking a few steps out he looked both ways. Nobody. Looking back down the street and uphill... they were nowhere to be found. He dropped to his knees.

Yes! Yes! he was finally rid of them!

A noise behind- made him jump up back to his feet, turning around quickly- nothing... He scanned the alley he found himself in, finally, processing the place for the first time. Was that just a draft of wind just now?

The alley was a completely torn down location, shabby, filth ridden, and macabre. Sorin scrunched up his nose in disgust, the rotten smell of wet drywall, wood, and trash. An unpleasant combination that he hadn't realized up until know. The pale sky above was the only light source he had, yet the light above barely penetrated the dark expanse of the alley. Sorin pulled himself together, he needed to focus, looking back out- he doubted whether or not Chase and his entourage had decided to give up on their pursuit. They didn't chase him down here so close to the apparent ghost town... Well, guess all he needed to do now was find the other elevator down to the undercity.

Man now that I think about it... the elevator leading down to the undercity in this section of Gloomhaven might be really old... but, I'm pretty sure there's a residential zone below this part of the city... hmmm....

Orio would be a long, long walk from this side of the town. He brought up his watch. It was 3:50 pm, that's it, he has no choice but to continue further. The last thing he needs is to be any latter than he already is.

Sorin continued down the alley, grumbling to himself that if Aunt Dot threw a fit his way he would have to sit through it, with *JADE* of all people likely sniggering at his expense.

Suddenly, his watch began to beep... echoing along the walls of the drab alley. He paused and with an annoyed sigh he took off his backpack.

After swallowing his meds down with a bottle of water, he moved forward through the filthy alleyway, all the while, the invisible clock in his head was ticking. His hope that he could find the nearest elevator down, was the only thing that gave him the confidence to move forward.

CHAPTER

9

8/16/2061, Friday, 4:10 pm

"Dang it, where the heck is it?" Sorin muttered

Walking down the abandoned street he tried to find a sign or any type of indicator of where the nearest elevator was located. He didn't want to admit it, but the empty streets, the silent atmosphere, and this constant feeling of being watch was slowly getting to him.

The streets were also getting worse too. The look and feel of the place was of total decay and degradation.

Rubble and rebar were now littered loosely across the streets and roads, with some buildings looking outright leveled. The entrances to most of them being boarded up and sealed, to busted windows with shards of glass shimmering on the dirty ground. The cool sky and Sorin's lone reflection- reflecting off every piece. The ground he walked on was also terribly uneven, pockmarked with potholes, and cracks snacking all along the far streets.

Sorin shivered, what was going on with this place. He knew this section of the city was abandoned... but, this just didn't feel right. A dull, hot breeze of wind blew through the streets and across Sorin. He paused, by instinct closing his eyes and bringing up an arm to shield himself. All those years traveling in the voyager, and so many moments when he was caught off guard by gusts of sand enriched winds to the face, he could feel the particles of it landing all over his school clothes and groaned.

At least I have my durag on... last thing I need is for it to get all up in my hair. Sorin walked on lightly dusting himself off, he kept walking until he came across something which made him freeze. The reactor plant... he could see it, just a few blocks away, it looked so... old. Sorin looked on in amazement, it was so huge! He never put much thought into what being near a reactor would be like up till now. He read about them in school, heard different people from the bar talk about them casually, heard snippets of information from Susan, Bellatrix, Church, and Hosea. And at most he'd come across a still photo or picture of a reactor from the other settlements out there in the wastes. But... he's never been this close to a reactor before... well, no one likes being near a reactor for that matter. Then again, he was living proof of why nobody tended to make tourists hotspots for them.

Looking at it, as it stood there monolithically in the distance. He couldn't help but feel... he couldn't quite understand it. A familiarity that he had never felt before.

Was it a memory! He paused, searching for whatever triggered the rogue emotion. Was it something that could unlock a stray flash or glimpse of who his parents were, before he lost his memories to this illness.

Nothing, not even a whisp of that feeling remained. Another dead end. He opened his eyes, balling his fists. *Damnit, Damnit, why can't I remember them!? Why is my name the only thing I can remember.* Sorin scrunched his eye close, shaking his head. *No, it-it doesn't matter, just... move on, just move on.*

"I just need to get back... Sides, I don't need to know. Not like it'll do me any good in the long run." Sorin said silently. He unclenched his hands and continued on, he needed to get back home or they would freak.

Moments passed and eventually he found something that put a pep to his step, there was a sign, a semi faded sign on one of the streetlights with the words Undercity Elevator: SRZ 30-20, Layers 1-2, 10m ahead. Sorin breathed a sigh of relief, he broke into a light jog.

He'd be home soon all he needed to do was reach it and pray that the old thing still worked. Eventually he found it, the large subterminal was jutted near one of the collapsed buildings. There was pieces of rubble everywhere, but the subterminal itself still looked to be intact, albeit a little worn down. The entire structure was at least 20 feet tall and 10 feet wide. The front door was metallic and vault-like in appearance. Yet, it didn't really surprise him. Aunt Dot did mention at one point that the elevators near the original foundation of Gloomhaven where pretty archaic in their design. But... was it still working? He moved close to the front gate, pressing a button near the door and waited. He clicked his tongue, did it do anything- Suddenly a noise, a loud, grinding and churning sound began to emanate from the subterminal. Sorins teeth shook from the loud noise, and he couldn't help but step back a little, If it was anything like the other elevators he took underground than it would have been big enough to carry at least ten to fifteen people below ground. He just hoped the old machinery could handle just taking him down at the very least. He sighed, only one way to find out. And since this thing was going to take him to sub residential zone 20, layer 2, that meant he still had a long walk ahead of him.

As he stood there something began to rub him the wrong way, and it wasn't the loud sound of turning cogs from the elevator. No, he felt off... the hairs on the back of his neck began to stand up. He froze, what the heck was going on? The sensation was abrupt, and as he stood there increasingly becoming anxious. He slowly turned his head around towards the open street, nothing, save for a low gust of wind and the tumble of trash floating in the air. He suddenly gasped at the sharp stab of pain in his chest, he grew fearful, was it another attack on its way, but he just took his meds not an hour ago.

A sudden chill crawled under his skin, and wordlessly, like he was being drawn to look up, his eyes scanned the tops of the ruined buildings. His eyes widened, and his heart jumped out of his chest in alarm.

There was somebody cloaked in shadows on top of the building. Sorin backed up, for he had a strong impression that he or she was staring directly at him.

The sound of a crank turning made him jump in fright, looking back as the vault door of the elevator opened up with a loud wheeze, revealing the waiting platform. He turned back around... the figure was gone. He stood there for a moment, the sound of the waiting elevator beckoning him inside, but he looked around frantically. What was that? Was he hallucinating now? Uneasily, and highly unsettled, he backed up onto the platform. His eyes rapidly going to the main controls and outside, he quickly pressed the button for Layer 2, SRZ 20. The metal platform, and rusted fenced gate gave a great shudder, and with one last harrowing look outside the gate, the vault finally sealed shut. The lights in the chamber dimly switched on and with another shudder that forced him to grasp the safety rails, the platform descended. All the while a phantom sensation of familiarity began to haunt him throughout the long descent.

8/16/2061, Friday, 5:18 pm

Sorin moved through the lit chamber, the usual bright advertisements and loud store signs passing by him like a dream. He moved along with the crowd, asking a few passerby's for directions and followed a few signs through the maze of passages and hallways.

He couldn't escape the feeling of dread that was welling up within. Was that a hallucination brought on by his illness? The sudden feeling of being watched just came to him, no warning, not even a sound, just utter instinct.

He kept walking- absentmindedly ignoring the noise and bustle of the crowd around him. The image of the dark figure was completely dominating his mind- like an incessant nagging that wouldn't go away. *Come on, snap out of it.... I was running for up to an hour trying to get away from those idiots. Maybe I'm just exhausted, or it could be the meds... crap, then I'd have to explain were I'd been...* he shook his head, the elevator on the way down was surprisingly still in great shape, which, after walking through old historic was kinda shocking. Maybe when he got home, he could tell Jade and Tom about it. He'd just leave out the fact he was chased there. Looking down at his dirty pants he groaned, guess he'll make an excuse of having to deal with the gusts of winds from the desert. Wouldn't be the first time someone tripped on some loose trash and skinned there ankle on the ground. *Yea.. just keep it simple. Sides, not like Chase is going to admit he lost me at old historic. Heh, I bet the moment he found out where I was going- he ran in the other direction!*

Sorin grinned at the image of Chase's stupid grin falling off his face once he saw the old reactor plant. He continued on down the pathways, eventually, and to his relief, he begun to recognize the passageway he was in. Soon the familiar street advertisements and neon signs began to pass him by. And right now all he needed was a good alibi. Eventually he reached the Orio entrance and... what the heck was with the large crowd!

Sorin looked around alarmed at the various people swarming the open cul-de-sac, stands were everywhere with food, beverages and entertainment of all types. Was it a fair or something?

"YO! Sorin over here!" A familiar voice called out.

It was Tom waving on the steps of the Nocturne, grinning, holding a small cup in hand. His sunglasses reflecting the neon lights of the Nocturne, as his dark jacket and jeans gave him the look of a party goer. Yet, where was Jade? And for that matter Church and Aunt Dot. Who were nowhere to be found in the crowd. Of course, this didn't really matter all that much to Sorin as he excitedly ran up to Tom.

"Tom! When did you get here." Sorin exclaimed as he tackled him with a hug on the steps. Causing the older nomad to cough his drink out. "Oof... damn, you've gotten pretty tall scamp." Tom let out as he nudged Sorin off "And for your information... probably the same time you got to school." Tom looked him up and down "What the heck happened to you by the way?" Sorin shrugged "Fell down and scraped my knee, and had to find another way into the undercity... elevator was out." He lied.

Tom raised an eyebrow then shrugged, taking another sip of his drink "So.... you still got it in your room?"

Sorin grinned "Yep." he turned around "What's with all the people? I mean, what's the occasion."

Tom smiled "The semifinals for F.R.L went off without a hitch, apparently it was the most exciting game they had all year. The Red Seekers won by a country mile and everyone around is celebrating the win."

Sorin's eyes widened, the Formula Racing League was one of the most competitive sports of both the conclaves and the republic. Rift runners taking part in high-speed racing across massive tracks, miles and miles long, while fighting to keep their kinetic shields online to finish their laps. It was exciting, chaotic, and a blast to look at. Sorin would never forget seeing his first race on the television (which sadly broke after a drunk customer threw a bottle at the screen, to the absolute displeasure of Aunt Dot.) Watching the hovercars go nearly 1,000 kilometers an hour after getting sling shotted through rifts never got old. And the players for each region or district was divided into teams of three, who each year, competed for the grand prix prize of a cool million credits.

Sorin laughed "Who lost?"

Tom pressed his lips "The Blue Falcons..."

Sorin gaped "What!" he stammered "But they never lose!" Tom shook his head "They do now, and by the looks of it... there gonna have to work hard if they wanna stay ahead of the competition. There's still one last semifinal match they can sign up for I think. But... that's up to the sponsors." Tom turned to him "But forget that for now... Show me the board."

Sorin nodded "Follow me."

CHAPTER

10

8/16/2061, Friday, 5:56 pm

"Alright, so this thing is modular from what I've researched," Tom began "It's also heavily dependent on augments that binds users to it- kinda like operating systems- like Susan, and Bella to name a few." Tom explained.

The two were sitting around the large table in Sorin's room, with the hoverboard in front of them. Tom's eyes had a subtle green pinprick to them as he scanned the board.

"Susan and Bella? But what about you and Jade, how is it any different?" Sorin asked confused.

Tom shook his head "Here's the thing- yes, both of us, Jade and I, have O.S implants in are heads, so does Hosea and Kingsley, but there made for different purposes... Or, builds if you wanna call it that. Me and Jade for example, have the type of implants best used for... well... for firefights. The operating system is linked to are nervous system and it enhances are speed and strength- not to the point of installed cybernetic hardware like artificial limbs or organs you see on advertisements. But general enhancements,"

Sorin nodded his head- attention set on his every word.

"-and then you have the types of augments like Susan and Bellatrix. Who's are best suited for cyberspace interfication. The system links to their nervous system, and the biomonitor of a user, allowing their brains to figuratively link into different types of machinery." Tom pointed to the hoverboard on the table, giving it a fascinating look.

"This piece of equipment uses a combination of both builds. An O.S that scans the users body and instead of enhancing the user, builds a unique profile to the users poster and preference of flight... as well as the users limits."

"Limits?" Sorin uttered back.

Tom nodded "You remember what happened days ago, right? The energy the board released that knocked you down. Well, when the board scans your body, it's building unique safeguards for users safety."

Tom scooted over to Sorin's laptop, and typed a few words into the search engine. After a moment he turned the laptop over, Sorin looked at the photos on the screen. Which showed a bunch of people riding fancier, slicker looking versions of what he had.

"Wow" Sorin breathed silently, marveling at the grace of what he was seeing, there were even a few videos of some doing insane tricks that looked utterly impossible to pull off.

"Looks insane right? Look closely at the hoverboarders. Do you see anything odd about their bodies?" Tom quipped. Sorin looked closely at the videos and photos... that's when he noticed it. The arms and legs of the borders... they looked off. The lines going through some of the arms and legs looked weird, he thought at first that they must be some trendy tattoos or something but on closer look.

"Cybernetic arms and legs? There all replacement augments!" Sorin said grimacing.

"Um-hmm, the replacement limbs are stronger and can deal with the higher functions of the boards- and don't forget, its modular. So you could theoretically replace parts over and over again and find yourself with a different build each time- for better or worse," Tom said, grinning excitedly at the board "The only thing is, you need a O.S or something similar in order for it to link up with you."

At that moment, Sorins budding grin faded. There was a problem in Tom's summary, he didn't have an O.S augment- worse yet, he wasn't old enough for one. *The age limit for bioaugmentations! Crap, crap, crap! then... that means I won't be able to use it.*

"-But not to worry, I got an idea!" Sorin head shot up, giving Tom a hopeful look. "You do!?" Sorin said "Well... Don't leave me in suspense!"

Tom smirked, giving his own impish grin "Ok, ok, chill out- I got a plan, but it may take a while... so in the meantime I need you to study." He slapped his hand on the pile of books on the table, the titles of said books either being self-help books for beginners programming, to the fundamentals of software help and hardware beginners guides.

"Listen... this stuff is complicated. It takes a lot of know-how, in order to make the most of it, if you're really serious about it, then you're gonna have to learn how to program script, know how to safely scout out the right parts for the board and be able to do most of the heavy lifting yourself." Tom gave him a series look "I already covered for ya, on how you got it with Church and Aunt Dot... You still owe me by the way," Sorin nodded giving an eyeroll "But... I can't guarantee I'll be here to help you fix it. So... it's going to be up to you to get back in working order, can you do it?"

Sorin grinned "Of course! Just you watch, when you and Jade get back I'm gonna be shredding it down in layer 3 at the park." Tom laughed "Ok scamp, sure... come on, lets head out... I'm pretty sure Jade's going to be here any minute. And for the love of god don't press her... she's still pretty upset for losing the bet with the last game."

Sorin cackled "I can't believe she betted against the Red Seekers."

Tom shook his head "I can't believe she thought of betting Hosea on who would win- would ever turn out in her favor, I did warn her..." Tom scowled "Though, I can't say I'm any better... In just one round of poker, he managed to haggle *ME* into betting all my credits.... he's an utter conman." Sorin laughed as the two got back upstairs, ready to enjoy the rest of the festivities.

10/15/2061, Friday, 7:35 pm

Sorin slept silently on his workbench. Arms folded covering his face as the hoverboard stood on its own stand, near the wall. Pieces of its metallic shell were scattered neatly around the table, while various tools-from screwdrivers, wrenches and pliers sat to the sides of the bench.

Two months of research, two months of scavenging and hunting for appropriate parts that where compatible with the board. Which wasn't easy, considering that the undercity wasn't the type of place where one can just peruse for hoverboard parts. That's were Otto's scrape shop came into play. He may not have the rights to sell state-of-the-art hoverboard parts. But Sorin did find out in his research that parts could be made with the right know how- so long as it wasn't the important stuff. Like the kinetic drive, the operating system and the shock absorbers. The board sat in its own stand horizontally, as a long wire connected to the side of the board- linking it to the laptop near Sorin's arm. The boards Status and energy reserves on screen. Sorin grimaced in his sleep, the familiar black lines manifesting themselves across his arms and face. His eyes blearily fluttered open, and he groaned out, with annoyance he sat up and reached for the bag by his feet. After a moment the familiar bottle of meds were in his hands and taking the small thermos in hand, he downed the cool water and pills in one gulp. Completely used to the unpleasant ritual of his breakouts.

Sometimes, the watch and meds were not enough, and he just had to do it ahead of schedule.

He looked towards his computer- the systems looked normal- and the new parts looked compatible and stable to the boards build. Each of the O.S's drivers were in clear communication with the other electronics. He just needed the right tech in order to interface with it...

He sighed, cupping his hands over his eyes, tired, thinking about what Tom said to him before settlement authorities broke up Orio's FRL party later that night. Noise complaints apparently... Sorin figured it had something to do with Orson. Sorin yawned, he should probably come upstairs. Didn't Church have something to say to him?

Rubbing the sleep from his eyes he walked out of the room.

Sorin opened the door to the main bar area, Church, who was taking a seat near the bar stool looked up to the mounted screen tv behind the serving area. Church's blonde hair was slicked back and combed into a neat clinical style. Unlike Sorins wild hair underneath his durag, as Churches outfit was a simple brown collard long-sleeve and buttoned shirt, with black dress pants. Aunt Dot wearing the usual bartender clothes gave the tv screen a dubious look. And Sorins eyes widened at the Tv screen. It was absolute carnage. It looked to be what used to be a highway of a large city- somewhere in the republic maybe? He couldn't tell.

The cameraman zoomed in on the scene before them- a massive interstate with the background of large buildings and skyscrapers on the horizon. The road from what little Sorin could tell was on the side of a large cliff, but enormous sections of the roadway and cliff were utterly destroyed, caved in with rubble and debris still falling from pieces of the road- and into the chasm under it. There were totaled vehicles, squad cars, ambulances everywhere. And a few hover cruisers were taking off into the sky towards the peaking buildings of the city. The camera swung to the crowd who were barricaded from the area of the supposed disaster, from what little he could see, they looked completely besides themselves with shock. A few having injuries on their persons, as others brought up phones and took pictures of something off screen. The cameraman turned around once more, and Aunt Dott gasped.

There were stretchers being carted off to an armored vehicle, the stamp of S.P.C.T.R being on the sides of the massive truck. But that wasn't what got Sorins attention and shock. There was a kid on the stretcher- and what looked like sharp talons or ridged tusks seemed to be breaking through his arms and legs and simultaneously covering him, like armor pieces or something- he couldn't be sure... But Sorin felt a chill go down his spine, it looked like bone... but the way it was sticking out, it didn't look like it was broken bone jutting messily out from his skin. The cameraman panned the camera and more kids, teens, and adults on stretchers came into view. All of them, looking more bizarre than the last.

One guy looked like a fusion of wolf and man, another surrounded by vague vestiges of flame and smoke, and on and on it went. And their eyes... they seemed to glow strikingly, it was to an extinct were Sorin wasn't even sure if they were cybernetic in origin... or something stranger all together.

"Oh my god. There real." Chrisanta whispered "There actually real."

"Yeah, appears so." Church said, his expression troubled "This isn't going to end well."

Sorin looked at Church quizzically "What do you mean by that?"

Church turned around towards him. As Sorin approached the bar with the overhead lights bathing the three of them in smooth purples. Sorin looking back at the screen wide eyed and curious "What's going on? And what's with those people being wheeled into that van?" Church was silent as Chrisanta kept her eyes towards the screen.

"Their deviants." He said looking back to the news feed

"Hey Chris, do you mind bumping up the volume." She nodded taking the remote behind the counter and switching on the volume.

The camera shifted views and Sorin was now looking at the inside of a news broadcasting room. A man in black and a woman in red, dressed in business attire behind a large table that was colored in shades of white and reds, along with the room they were in. The middle-aged man with greying short hair gave a troubled look at the screen with the brown-haired woman looking equally as concerned.

"Thank you Jason for the hands-on view. As you can see folks. S.P.C.T.R has once again done their duty to the good people of Delta city," He tried to give a small, pleasant smile towards the camera, but Sorin wasn't buying it for a moment, his eyes didn't reflect the sense of easygoing air that expression tried to manifest.

"Another string of grizzly scenes that have been plaguing the settlements and cities around the border zone- the 'supposed' deviant outbreak as it were." The lady to his left nodded.

"That's right Tim, the reports have been coming in steadily over the last few months. But authorities in the area have laid... special doubts, of the authenticity of some of the reports," The reporter, Tim, raised an interested eyebrow. "Oh, and what would that be Sharron?"

She gave a level look towards the camera "Well... the authorities have noted- with what little they could share with us over at the bulletin. That most of the crimes reported have been exasperated out of proportion... that the supposed powers of the deviants could in fact be in house, or experimental in nature." She gave an anxious look "That Nomads- I'm sorry, ex-nomads, have been experimenting with illegal bio-augmentation. In effect, a series violation of malpractice."

Tim wavered in his seat, his sunny disposition transforming to concern "That's a pretty series allegation, I assume they have proof backing up this up," he then shrugged "Better yet, are they willing to share their source of information on their supposed 'theory' as to what's going on out there in the conclaves?"

Sharron breathed a disappointed sigh "As of right now, no. No, they are not. What makes this development more complex is the report that S.P.C.T.R has personally came in to work with authorities in the capture, and if possible, detainment of those that are labeled as deviants. And that the new current law, which was passed into effect last month, following another incident in the settlement of Crestview."

The two reporters disappeared as the scene shifted to what looked like an outside view from the lens of a camera. Suspended above a traffic light, looking down to a busy street where vehicles and people streamed back and forth down road and street corner alike. Suddenly, a building shook violently. What looked to be a bookstore- erupted in flames, as the front entrance exploded outwards to the screams and honking of horns from vehicles, who scrambled to steer away from the fireball rushing out of what was left of the store. Sorin gaped at the screen and Aunt Dot's face seemed to drain of color. Church looked on, cool as a cucumber, his eyes narrowing. On the screen, which was now experiencing static, there looked to be a figure limping away, out of the demolished entrance... it was a teenager by the looks of it, he or she came out of the store with fire still trailing behind them as it seemed to swirl around their body. And just as abruptly they fell over... seemingly unconscious.

Sorin leaned on the bar table, just shaking his head in amazement, it looked so real- he could hardly believe it, how was he just now learning about this!

He looked to Church, but was surprised by the look on his face. His expression was pensive, completely deep in thought... but he couldn't spot any traces of surprise or alarm that he and Aunt Dot were currently feeling from the news.

"Church?" Sorin prodded, "Is there something the matter?"

Church looked at him and shook his head "No. Just thinking is all... How was school today." He asked absent-mindedly.

Sorin grimaced, him walking to class alone, no friends, everyone treating him like a pariah, ether because of his illness, or because of his relations to the nomads. Practically the only good thing about today was that he managed to walk all the way home without Chase or his flunkies sitting in wait to ambush him. A small grin broke his lips, and to his excitement that very mourning, he got a message about his package from Tom being on the way to the Nocturne. So all and all, it was a decent day.

"Fine. But what about the deviants? Is it really, real? I mean footage and things can be faked can't they."

Church sighed "Yes... and no."

Sorin looked at him confused "Huh?"

"The deviants are... well, there a complex topic. The general discussion for the average settler is completely mixed. Some believe them to be an absolute hoax designed by the corporations- or the nomads, who have been doing backdoor experiments with new augs. And the others, believe it to be completely real." he gestured to the screen "The ones who believe it to be real fall in two camps- the ones who see them as a danger to the world at large and the rest, who are undecided."

Sorin frowned "A danger to the world? How? I mean, what makes someone having cool powers a bad thing?"

Church rolled his eyes "Simple. The Republic, The Conclaves, and the Corporations all, see it as something that they cannot properly control. They didn't mention it, but the rumors going around aren't really doing them any favors. Kids who have tantrums suddenly manifesting powers and accidently hurting their parents, a person with the ability to go invisible without a camo augment, or a teenager who can bend steel- just by thinking about it."

He pointed to the screen "Imagine, your walking down the street and that happens, as you're walking down the sidewalk to get home. How would you feel if that happened, and you ended up caught in the crossfire?"

Sorin looked at him weekly, rubbing the back of his head "Oh... yeah, I guess that would be pretty terrifying." But then he grinned "But... I wouldn't mind being able to teleport though."

Church looked at him for a moment "Teleporting! Really? That's the power you'd go with?" He looked at him, his expression going from series to amused.

Aunt Dot raised an eyebrow at him, as he took a seat next to Church. Her expression one of pointed suspicion. "Ok... Starting to see where this is going."

Sorin glanced at her with a look of annoyance "What do you mean by that? Teleportation would be an awesome power to have."

Aunt Dot stifled a laugh as she began to wipe out an empty glass cup "More like a way for you to sneak out pass curfew. Or worse, using it as the perfect tool for an alibi. Come on... remember when you tried to sneak into Kings room to steal that bottle of his?" Sorin looked away from Dots direction, suddenly watching the tv as if it was the most interesting thing in the room. Church shifted in his seat "He did what..."

She nodded pressing her lips "Slipped into his room and was caught red handed by the old man. Came into the bar with him wrestling Sorin to the ground. Heh, heh, bottle still in hand." Sorin grumbled "I kept telling him Jade dared me to do it."

She shook her head, as she added the clean cup to the shelf behind her. The lights bouncing off the glass in splashes of green and purple. Sorin looked at the screen, yeah, it was definitely a bad blunder on his part. But... if he could teleport, that would be the coolest thing. He grinned to himself, he would even have the ability to help Church with his business. Well, at least with the hoverboard he could accomplish the same thing. Albeit, when he finally was able to interface with the thing. Suddenly, he felt something tapping his shoulder looking down, his eyes widened.

There was a big package next to him on the wooden table. Wrapped in yellow and orange, there was a sticker on the front of it that made him skip a beat.

Vega Express & Shipping Co.

From: Thomas Reed
1423 Boulevard Ave
Corrins Watch, Lambda District, 44-650-9992

To: Sorin Richter
2077 Orio, Seventh Nocturne
Gloomhaven, Historic District, Undercity, 07-013-2007

Sorin looked up to Church who smiled back at him "Tom sends his regards." He said "-and by the way, Bella and King are going to be visiting later today."

Sorin gaped "What! Seriously! You're kidding!"

Church laughed "Oh no... When Bellatrix learned from Tom what you were up to for the past two months... She apparently decided herself to pay you a visit. King was in the area and decided to tag along- wanted to know how you and Chrisanta where doing also."

Sorin looked down to the yellow package, failing to suppress the rising grin on his face. Bella was coming! How long had it been? A year maybe... with only emails and messages from his computer, with the occasional say so from either Tom, Jade, or Susan. Hosea was also another person he hasn't seen for a while, two years in fact.... and he wondered when he'd see the old nomad again one day.

Church shook his head "Call me curious- but what was supposed to be in here that could help with that board of yours?" Sorin got up from his seat, taking hold of the package and feeling its weight- it was kinda heavy- not super heavy, but he could tell something awesome had to be inside in order for him to interface with the board.

"I don't know," he said shaking his head "But, I- I have to get in my room. I'll be right back!" Sorin was about to sprint to his room, but...

"Whoa! Hold it!" Aunt Dot called out over the counter, Sorin skidded to a halt, looking back and forth in the direction of his room and Aunt Dot frantically.

"Before you mess around with that board, be careful... and I better not hear an explosion, or something blowing up in that room of yours young man."

Sorin nodded eagerly "Yes mam!"

She shook her head lightly and made a shoo gesture as she turned around, and Sorin didn't need to be told twice as he ran quickly down the hall and disappeared behind the door. To the laughter of Church behind him.

CHAPTER

11

10/15/2061, Friday, 9: 06 pm

Sorin crashed onto the seat, in front of him the package laid open- the ripped and scattered shreds of present wrappings laid discarded over the workbench and floor. He sucked in an excited breath as he took out what was inside the box.

It looked like a glove/bracelet hybrid at first- but as he took it out, he noticed the mounted screen on the bracelet portion, with a miniature keyboard underneath it. There was metallic machinery all over the glove, with the main interface of the computer having a waterproof housing around it, with clamps connecting to the bottom of it. There looked to be a large USB housing on it to the side, which had a plug like cable connected to it. Sorin instantly realized it was an interface cable. The glove portion of the gadget had an almost fingerless-esc design to it, with another piece of machinery connected to the underside of the hand part. Was that a biometric reader? The entire device was in a black and red finish. There was also a logo on the bottom of the screen and on top of the mini keyboard in bold silver text: EBON-DYNE FUTUREISTICS

Sorin looked at the dubious piece of hardware in silent astonishment. He's skimmed over this exact description over and over again in the many books that sat on his table. The ones Bellatrix had sent him, concerning early programming hardware and technology.

He couldn't believe it... he had a *Cyberdeck* on his workbench, an actual cyberdeck! He slipped his hand into and through the compartment, his fingers slipping comfortably through the wrist mounted gauntlet. The glove was a complete fit, and he took a second to admire the cyberdeck on his arm. Suddenly, he felt something click into place. He felt the magnetic locks binding the mechanism to his arm, and what felt like many needle-like incisions puncture themselves along his arm, and the underside of his right hand. Was that the biometrics locking on? He tested the gauntlet, moving and flexing his wrist, there was hardly any resistance. Surprising, after what felt like four to five needles piercing his arm. Though, it felt a little snug now. But, it looked pretty cool, and he was perfectly willing to let it slide.

With an electric whirr of machinery, he could feel a dull heat run down his entire right hand and arm. There was sharp beep, and the monochrome screen was suddenly lit up in activity. The logo of an eclipsed sun appeared on the monitor, on the bottom, pieces of letters began to appear on the screen until the earlier company name appears once again under the logo. Sorin watched as lines of code replaced the logo and company name.

```
08294738924098239843938439439880934892483834938493349834877998

09349283948894458437584758787480949w49w4899w84995u4989348789434

09893321398293892833828839298390939102938108923929032320934093

00949894999854953045094838289490994843939828930903324005450094

04938234983493844802390890302090959894893499389223938409034944

08598995368356959875989475895950459438 95839848995949934939
```

---{Attention}---

<BIOMONITOR>....57%

{Cognitive Stability: Fine}

{Physical Stability: Questionable}

{Neural Stability: Questionable}

```
<ID Chain code>....50%

{Alias: Sorin Richter (K/a: SCAMP)}

{Birthday: October 27, 2050}

{Gender: Male}

{Chain code: 06261997-11261990-031963(CI)}
```

Sorin gave the monitor a double take, it was really monitoring his biomoniter info. He sighed, way to remind him that he was still lucky to be alive- the constant fear of an 8 out of 10 pain scale, non withstanding anyway. His chain code and the alias tags made him raise an eyebrow, especially at the 'scamp' tag. *Tom must have put it in... but how did he do it without connecting himself to the cyberdeck? I thought the only way to activate it, was to wear it first.*

Sorin remembered the needle like punctures from the deck, as of right now, it was currently leaching his body to power itself. Very, very, creepy to think about. But it works, that's what truly mattered to him. He looked at the board, taking it from its pedestal, he placed it on the table. He unlatched the USB cable from the deck and carefully moved the board so he could have an easier time manipulating it. Months and months of tinkering, and months of collecting parts and repairing the board. He slid the top plate from the front of the board revealing the USB port hidden behind it. He inserted the cord, and the monitor of the deck exploded with data, too much for him to keep up with.

Oh crap! What's going on... did I mess it up somehow! He thought, close to panicking. When suddenly the mad scroll of code stopped. He watched, wide eyed as folders, upon folders, upon more folders began to pop up on screen.

He silently looked between the oval disc on his table and the deck, and was slightly unsure of where to go from there. Picking up the board carefully, he moved to the large table in his room and looked through a few of the dusty volumes sitting near his laptop, till he found what he was looking for. *The beginners guide to programming/software care and setup.* Sorin flipped through a few pages trying to find something that could help him with his current problem. Finally after a few minutes of sifting through pages he found it. A page detailing data migration, using premade packages of configured O.S builds.

So... basically a USB drive that holds all of the user data. But I don't got one on me, so how do I...

Suddenly, Sorin looked back to the empty parcel on the floor next to his workbench and disconnected his the USB drive from the board. He quickly gathered the box and held it upside down above the table. Two small black flash drives tumbled out onto the table to his delight. "Yes" Sorin exclaimed as he gathered them up. He inserted it inside the port of his Cyberdeck and watched the screen light up with more activity. An app appeared on his monitor window *Partition Manager.* He took the drive off and placed it on the table.

All right, the book says that in order to move data from one hard drive to another. There needs to be a file to safety transport the data from both devices. Sorin carefully read aloud the book instructions.

"Okay... Okay, so... does that mean I can transfer my biomoniter data to the board? I mean, Tom did mention, that, this was how these things worked. Can that also work as a user setup?" He paused for moment... was he really just talking to himself out loud just now? He shrugged, eh, whatever.

Thinking about it, he was really skirting the line right now. When it came to underage cybernetics. Heck, a Cyberdeck was not even close to a modern operating system. Yet, would the settlement officers even approve of him having this? He grimaced, for now... he'd keep this to himself, below the undercity.

He typed a few commands to his cyberdeck, copying and pasting the information to a new folder and used the app now installed to his deck. A moment later a message appeared on screen. The partition was ready! And it only took a couple of minutes too! Sorin grinned, unhooking his USB cable again he hooked it into the board. After typing a few more commands and finding the right folder, he activated the partition data.

A massive loading screen appeared on the monitor and Sorin found himself waiting almost an hour before finally the cyberdeck made a loud beep.

Sorin jumped back as the board- on its own, sprang to life. Expanding out, and blowing papers and books off the table as a pulse of blue light emanated from the hovering platform. Sorin gave the board a wide berth at first, not forgetting what happened the last time he got launched across the room. After a few minutes he carefully approached. His cyberdeck was still connected to it, after hesitantly grabbing the board and feeling a spurt of relief that it didn't go haywire he disconnected with it. The purr of pulsing energies seemed to dim the moment he took a hold of it. Holding it with both hands he marveled at the board. It was like a miniature surfboard, oval shaped, like the kinds he heard about in the republic. The board was nearly as tall as him, from neck to his knees, a far cry of what it once was in its idle state as a medium sized disc, about the size of his forearm. Yet, he could feel the power of its jet like propulsion from the bottom of the vents- which he held outward away from him. The top of the board had a black like finish to it, with the dark orange fins on the side subtly moving with the pulsing streams of energy below it. Sorin knew by know that those metal fins were steer assists. Also customizable. The thing almost felt like it had a life of its own, and it was his to do with as he pleased...

He could feel the broad smile on his face. It was time to test it, he moved further from the table and moved his chair out of the way. With a calming breath he let it drop to the ground. And the board immediately pulsed up, catching itself on the ground, as if reading his intentions. He gave an excited holler, it was just hovering there, three feet off the ground. A steady rhythmic pulse as it hovered freely, seemingly inviting him to step on. He obliged, and with shaky knees he stepped onto the platform.

The board didn't give. His right leg left the ground and like that he was hoovering off the floor three feet in the air. This... was satisfying in a way he had never know before. He felt as light as a feather, utterly content with the accomplishment. And like that, his mind was suddenly hit with possibilities over possibilities. The many ways he could customize and possibly make the board truly his own. But he needed to get to layer three if he wanted to understand what he had to work with. Then his eyes widened, how does he even make it go? Does he lean on it or...

Suddenly, there was a knock on his door which startled him. Causing him to fall painfully on his rump. The board sliding out of the way towards his bed, and Sorin sucking in a pained gasp. The door swung open, and a familiar face appeared from the doorway.

Bellatrix's head peaked into the room, her expression going from excited to alarmed as she looked around his room. Till her gaze fell on Sorin, who hoisted himself off the ground using the table. The door swung further revealing Kingsley, his dirty duster and moth-eaten hat casting a shadow over his face and body from the dark hallway. Bella carefully walked in with her usual black leather jacket and jumpsuit on. Sorin looked up and paused, like a deer In the headlights he stared at the two in his room.

"Heya kiddo! That's a nice Cyberdeck you got there... Oh, I see you got the board work-" She didn't get to finish as Sorin tackled her with a bear hug "Bella!" he exclaimed out.

She laughed as she held him. Ruffling his head, and shacking the durag off his scalp. Her grey eyes scanned the room. Her expression amused at the mess of books on the table and taking in the piles of discarded scrap and tools on his workbench. She looked to King who was looking around with a silent double take.

"Hmph, kids starting to pick up on your habits now. Bell." Kingsley quipped "Boys going to end up a bleeding ghost runner in no time."

Sorin turned to King excitedly unhanding Bellatrix "Really, a ghost runner!" he asked looking between them both.

Bella shook her head "Whoa, hold on their King- the cyberdeck and hoverboard is impressive, I'll admit that," she picked up Sorin's durag and handed it back to him "But... the scamp's got a long way to go before he gets to that point." She held up his arm with the cyberdeck "How's it feel... anything odd?"

Sorin shook his head excited, still supercharged after the confirmation of his board working. "Nuh-uh, nothing unusual so far.

By the way, is it supposed to have scamp in the alias tag?" he asked the question with a note of suspicion in his voice, narrowing his eyes at her.

She smiled back innocently "No. not normally, and what's with the look?" she answered back now looking somewhat faux-naïf in her supposed act of ignorance. Or at least, that's what Sorin thought. "You now I'm not the only hacker in this little family we got going here, right." Sorin crossed his arms, rolling his eyes, she was of course referring to Susan- but he wasn't fooled, of all people, Susan would be least likely to use his annoying nickname. At least, if he didn't purposefully get on her nerves.

Before turning to Kingsley, he grinned before rubbing the back of his head sheepishly. "Hi King, um... you're not still mad about..."

King raised an eyebrow before making a low grunt "Oh no, I'm still not forgiving ya for that. But... don't worry, I took my displeasure out on Jade."

Sorin gave a nervous chuckle, not at all curious about what he did. "So what's the deal with the hoverboard, hmm... I assume you're getting into sports now?" King asked, his baritone voice curious as he watched it float near the bed.

Sorin shook his head "Nah, I wanted to see if I could help Church with his business thing. You know, running the packages for him in the undercity."

"Oh really, that's... huh, never mind." King nodded

Sorin gave him an annoyed look "What? What you think I was gonna do?"

Sorin watched with irritation, as the lips behind Kings beard arched in a subtle grin "Heh, oh you know what I meant by that. You, Tom, Jade and," He glanced to Bella's direction who gave him a mock glare "Troublemakers, the lot of ya."

Sorin shook his head "Hey, Aunt Dot said I wasn't nearly as bad as Tom and especially Jade, and what about Sue- she's done some crazy stuff too!" King shook his head, as he passed Sorin patting him on the head to his dismay "Consequences for being in the wrong crowd." As he walked out of his room.

"More like being biased to her side." Sorin grumbled.

Bella rolled her eyes, as she tapped him on the shoulder "Come on, Chrisanta had us come in so we could tell you that dinner was ready. I wouldn't wanna keep her waiting." She said, "And by the way, proud of what you did- knew you could do it." she said patting him on the back as she walked out.

Sorin couldn't help the proud grin as he followed behind.

CHAPTER

12

10/6/2061, Wednesday, 10: 06 am

A week ago, near the large settlement of Halcyon 5, a curious event was taking place. A man and one holo-call.

While Sorin at the time, was researching, and gathering the tools to fix his hoverboard, something strange was happening near a city maybe thousands of miles away from Gloomhaven. Nothing noteworthy at the time, and nothing so grand, as to involve the town within the soil of the republic. But for one individual inside a manor looking out the window, something of terrible note was happening, something of vast and personal conflict of interest.

His name was Nathaniel Raynor, in his office overlooking the expansive overview of the district town in the distance of his old manor. The verdant fields of grass and sparse expanse of treetops didn't take away from the background even further from the settlement, who's foreground of nature between him and Halcyon-5 couldn't distract from the ever- present feeling of a gouged hole being dug further, and further into his stomach. His face still a stoic mask of tough resilience, he stared at the object of his hidden torment.

The border wall, a small pinprick in the distance. Back, and further beyond the reaches of Halcyon. He blinked his eyes, the weather outside was somber- heavily melancholic with the winds blowing through the trees and forcing the grass in a simple frolic of motion. The weather, a dark and overbearing cloud of steel sleet. A perfect symbol of his current and dwindling head space.

He backed away, staring at his reflection upon the window, his dark pinstriped suit and graying hair, the crow's feet in his eyes and the barely concealed scowl on his face. Days, upon days of silence, they were back there. Behind that infernal wall, they had it- the thing most precious to him, the only thing in the world that mattered more to him then his duty as a sector official.

He turned around, his hand pulling the silver chain from his pocket. A locket, which he turned over in his open palm. He gave the accessory a pensive look, a pain beyond description falling over his pale face. The locket popped open, and the picture of a woman appeared- at the top of the open lid. She was beautiful, eyes of twin blue ponds and long flowing hair of blonde platinum. Her smile soft, welcoming, something he desperately wished he could behold in person once more.

And the other- another person- this one younger, and bearing the same likeness as the one above. The same beauty, and the same eyes.

He turned back to the window, locket now closed and squeezed tight in his bald fist. The silver chain swinging limply.

He had to do it. There was no other way, the republics secrets be damned. He. Would. Not. Lose. Her!

His dark eyes showed the familiar pinpricks of enabling a holocall, he switched channels- no one needed to know who he was contacting. And the embedded channels of his work or house lines would not do.

The circle had to be contacted immediately... From there, he would contact an old friend. And as this call was made, he was more than aware of the dark deeds being committed as he waited for the phone to be answered.

He just prayed that he could weather the oncoming storm to come... and hoped that the incoming disaster could be mitigated from a critical catastrophe.

10/16/2061, Saturday, 11: 06 am

Sorin screamed as he once again fell off the board, the grainy mixture of sand and brim doing little to cushion his fall. He rolled to a stop a moment latter groaning to himself.

"Seriously." He huffed, as he got himself up once more.

It was nearly afternoon, and since waking up at 9 sharp. He came down here to practice as much as he could with the board. It was fun trying to learn, but boy was it frustrating! He picked up his board, looking around the expansive underground park of the foundry. Massive sand dunes the color of grey ash, surrounded him as he stood in the shoulder of the wide trail looping and zigzagging across the enclosed park. The cavern's ceiling was full of openings that streamed down pools of sunlight reflected by fiber crystals and the natural limestone from above.

The vast cavern of layer 3 was the best place to learn how to use his board. The location of the park itself was found right after the first two layers of the undercity was established, and from what Sorin heard from Aunt Dot- the foundry was naturally formed from the sand blown through the canyon separating central and historic from one another. Supercells, so strong, that the resulting sandblasting created the enormous cavern that he stood in. Which was located in the very walls underneath the historic districts, maybe near the very bottom, where some caves still undiscovered to this day stretched and twisted around one another like the roots beneath a vast tree.

Sorin walked up a large sand dune, standing on top- he looked towards the furthest point away from the main plaza of the foundry, where all the play equipment that kids younger than him would be found, securely within viewing distance of their parents or relatives. He looked back towards the section of the park, with the most people gathered around the main area. Baulders lodge being the main plaza center and monument of the park. Named after the original expedition leader of the maze-like paths further past the security and gated sections of the park.

Sorin sighed, he was currently in the backtrails of the park. With the paths leading in and out of the main plaza no longer paved with concrete, instead, being lightly covered with dark gravel. He was at least... a mile or two from the lodge, and barely scrapping the security fences which gated unauthorized civilians away from the perilous caves leading to god knows where.

Sorin straightened himself, before carefully moving back down the dune. He already let Church, and the others know where he was going. And informed the officers of the park of what he was doing. By the suggestion of Aunt Dot (a few of the officers knew Dot personally).

Sorin rolled his eyes, he didn't know why she was so worried. If he didn't know any better he was almost sure she'd believe him crazy enough to go past the gate. He shuddered, he braved going into the junkyard and towards the abandoned streets leading to the decommissioned reactor. But the unplotted and unexplored caves further past the security gate. Nu-uh, no thanks, he'd stay away from that one.

He let the board drop to the ground. The platform let out a puff of energy, with sand and loose gravel being pushed away from the center, as the board pushed itself off the ground. Sorin put one foot in the middle of the board, readying himself before using his other foot on the ground to push forward. The dunes swept past him, as he struggled to balance himself on the fast-moving platform. His cyberdeck, which was connected to the board. Monitored his speed and gave him a diegetic map of the park. He looked at the wrist mounted computer, uneasily, as he pushed past 15 miles per hour. Crazy how fast this thing was going, but from what Tom said- it cheeked out. The board was still in the training wheels phase. So... until he learned how to navigate and properly balance himself on it, it would keep him at the current speed.

Sorin huffed, as he focused on the path ahead. All the while, awkwardly moving his body parts to adjust to the demands of his new center of gravity. The winds lightly blew past him and through his hair. His durag was still in his room at the nocturne, as he was too excited to put it on that mourning. He regretted that decision so badly. Cause since coming here he has been falling and falling constantly- only now was he able to get a grasp of balance on the board itself. The clothes on his back, his hair and face were covered in trail dust and sand in some very uncomfortable places. He was lucky enough that the board seemed to always shift and throw him away from the loose gravel. And instead, on the dunes close to the trail. He leaned in, his path creating a small dust cloud in his wake. And even after all the falls and failures, he couldn't stop marveling over the board. Even as the board glided over the gravel trail, he could almost feel every bump and shift of the small rocks beneath him. As if the board were simulating the ground under him. He sucked in a breath as he unexpectedly gained a little height from a small mound of gravel, before landing- causing him to almost spasm off the board- in a panicked wave of his arms.

He cursed, snarling at his near fall, the fear of falling made him nearly manic there. He just needed to be patient, get his balance right, and then he'd be one step closer to getting use to riding this thing.

Yes, all he had to do was get used to it. Then the hard part would be over.

The trail bent to the right, and Sorin uncomfortably moved his body to make the board move in the right direction. He felt the board roll over a smidge, the bottom vents to the left pulsing with energy as the board responded to his movement to shift right. The metallic fins on the side began to stretch out as the one on the right pulled in. Sorin adjusted his stance, feeling gravity push him down as he continued to accelerate forwards.

Come on, come on, come on... you got this, you can do this, just a little bit more!

Suddenly, he felt a dangerous lurch on his right foot. And suddenly panic... his ankle bent on the board, and he cried out in pain. A few things happened, the board automatically decelerated and before he could fall over headfirst, to the instinctual drive to grasp his ankle the board centered and somehow catapulted him from the hard gravel to the nearby dune.

He felt the air get knocked out of him as he rolled against the mound of sand. As his ankle screamed in pain.

Sorin hissed, as he grasped the injured ankle. Cursing himself in frustration for that stupid mistake. The cyberdeck flashed yellow as a diagram of his body showed his ankle, he sat up watching the board move towards him, before quickly compacting itself into its small disc state. Before plopping onto the ground. Sorin groaned as his head slammed back down onto the sandy mound. Realizing, that he would need to wait for his ankle to heal for the moment. Rolling up his pant sleeve, it didn't look bad, probably put too much weight on it during that particular turn.

He looked towards the dark ceiling of the cavern and blew out an annoyed sigh. This was gonna take a while. And all he had left was to think, and think he did.

Time passed... and it was now 12:24 pm. Sorin was utterly laid out on the dune. Now completely covered in white sand. All the while thinking and just going over everything he'd learned from the first two hours of his practice sessions. And... he was still confident he'd get the hang of it. Sooner or later. He just needed to work on his balance. He gave the board a look.

Or... maybe he was a little brash trying to ride it in the beginning. He stood up and tested his ankle, still a little sore, but he was finally able to stand on it.

He picked it up, and began to walk down the path. Taking care not to put too much weight in his right ankle. He remembered a small bench somewhere near the concreate path- he could just sit there and think. And he wasn't feeling so confident standing on the board with a sore ankle. He'll get to a point where he can ride it with no trouble, but for now he was admitting temporary defeat.

After a couple of minutes walking he made it, a small metal bench sitting on the shoulder of a dark path near a small lake just south of the lodge. An underground lake, but still a lake. Sorin sat down, breathing a sigh of relief. But his reprieve didn't last long as footsteps, not his own, began to approach. Further down the path to his surprise was Bellatrix, who was casually walking down the paved trail towards him. She stood before him, taking in his dirty, sandy, and otherwise exhausted form. As he finally noticed the duffle bag over her shoulders.

She gave him an understandably amused look "Hmph, looks like the board is giving ya some trouble. You look like crap kid." Sorin shrugged "I'm making progress... just taking a break is all."

She nodded casually as she took a seat next to him, looking around the park. "I see the foundry has gotten bigger since I've last been here." She said absentmindedly, her steel-colored eyes scanning the environment, before settling on the board. Sorin looked at the duffle bag she placed near him on the ground.

"What's with the bag?" She smiled, crossing her arms as she leaned into the bench seat.

"Open it and see." She replied. Sorin giving the bag an odd look, sat up and reached for the zipper. He gasped, it was a full set of protective gear: Wrist guards, elbow pads, shoulder guards, a helmet and knee pads. All colored a brownish orange.

Sorin lost his voice for a moment, thinking to himself, how much? How much was all of this? He turned to ask her but was cut off, as a hand firmly landed over his mouth.

"Bellmmrph!" Sorin's voice came out muffled, to Bella's annoyed eye roll. "Don't worry about it scamp! Just look at it like this... its free and on the house."

She said grinning.

"Besides, seeing as you're really putting everything you have into riding that thing. I thought best to go ahead and buy you some new gear for it..." She grew silent as her small grin began to slip into a frown "And will be leaving tomorrow morning. So, I thought it would make a good going away present."

Sorin eyes widened, whatever budding excitement he had was completely blown out like a candle from those words.

Already... he thought.

Her hand came off and he gave her a disappointed look, which was crazy considering the gift she just gave him, but... "Is it a new gig?" Sorin asked quietly.

She nodded "Hosea called, said it was big... can't say anything more... but, that's what's up."

Sorin looked towards the gear, looking unsure with what he wanted to say next. Suddenly a beep from his cyberdeck alerted him, he gave a tired sigh before fumbling into the deep pockets of his cargo pants. He fished out his meds (all the while emptying the loose sand which had gotten there.) and took two capsules, swallowing hard in order to get them down. Bella gave him a weird look "You sure you don't need a bottle of water or-"

"Nah I'm good..." She gave him a concerned look "Do the new meds help, I mean I haven't seen any flare ups since..." She bit her tongue, not liking where that particular memory was taking her. Sorin shook his head "Yeah, kinda... it still happens, but it's not as bad as that one time... still hurts like hell though."

Bella narrowed her eyes before softly raking his head. Causing Sorin to give her an annoyed look "Hey!"

"Nu-uh, language." She said giving him a bewildered look "Looks like someone's been spending much time with Tom and Jade."

He turned away grumbling softly, rolling her eyes she pulled him into a hug. Sorin groaned "Bella! Not here!"

"Oh pipe it, you little rascal you! I'm still proud of you for getting the hang of that Cyberdeck." She held him, shacking him to his annoyance "And, you'll be eleven years old soon! Next week I believe."

Sorin paused, he totally forgot about that. Though it technically wasn't his birthday, more like a place holder of his original biomoniter serial code, issued by the circle. He frowned, as Bella continued to hold him, he wondered if he really was going to be eleven next week... he closed his eyes banishing the train of thought, better not to over think it.

"But Sorin, one more thing about the cyberdeck and board. I want you to be responsible with them Sorin. Don't bring it with you to school, and better yet, avoid taking it up to central or historic. Last thing we need is for Orson to find out."

Sorin growled, a venomous scowl forming on his face. That jerk of a corpo stooge had it out for Church and Aunt Dot, if he had the chance he'd give him something to cry about. Ever since he and Church began their lives here in Gloomhaven, Orson was at their door day one, with city officers at his beck and call. Something to do with Church's business impeding his own business contracts or so forth. From that fancy company of his.

Sorin couldn't quite understand all the stuff that went into all this legal nonsense- but it was bullcrap, nothing short and nothing less.

"Yeah, I know... But... Orson shouldn't be able to get in the way of Church's job like this! It's not fair Bell!" Sorin exclaimed "And he somehow got to Norman and Andre!"

She narrowed her eyes "Yeah, I heard. But don't worry about them, there fine from what Church told me. And Orson... don't let him get to you kid. Sooner or later, he won't be a problem anymore. Not with the way he's been muscling in on the other small business. Heck, wouldn't be surprised if he ends up eventually biting on more than he can chew with the other corpos." She spoke with a cold tone in her voice, that never failed to send shivers down Sorin's spine.

"And I meant what I said Sorin, do not take those things outside the undercity. Promise me." Her voice was full of cold authority.

He nodded silently, and at the same time he paused, blinking under her calculated gaze, he felt like he was being dissected for any looks that might betray false compliance. It looked pretty intimidating from where he sat on the bench, like the cool, bubbly persona she had had suddenly evaporated into mist at the mention of Orson.

"Okay." Sorin agreed and Bella nodded back "Good." She said calmly.

Suddenly they both turned their heads to the sound of more approaching footsteps, Sorin assumed it might have been just a runner or jogger going down the path, but no... what looked like a settlement officer was making their way towards them. He was dark skinned, wearing the usual dark blue officers uniform with the Gloomhaven/Conclave patch sewn on to his left breast pocket, and a S.S badge on his right breast pocket. A few other pins were on his leather jacket over the uniform, with the usual sidearm attached to the hip of his dark khakis. And he was fast approaching their location.

CHAPTER

13

10/16/2061, Saturday, 12: 01 pm

Sorin became nervous at the sight of the approaching guard. Were they somehow in trouble? He looked to Bellatrix but... She was smiling again, suddenly back to her carefree persona. Never mind that, she was now waving towards the officer who waved back in turn.

Sorin now felt lost, his befuddlement growing as he could now clearly see the approaching officers face. Who was beaming back towards Bella with obvious familiarity.

"Marshal? Is that you!" Bella exclaimed happily as she stood up.

"The one and only!" The officer laughed back, a drawling lisp in his voice which caught Sorin off guard. Looking at him, he looked... different. Nothing like the other settlers. No, more like, he wasn't really native to these parts. Which honestly raised Sorin's curiosity of who this man was.

Sorin watched the two embrace, and at the same time marveling at how odd it looked. Most of the officers who worked for the city and by extension the conclaves, weren't really fans of Nomads. Although some were nicer than others, and paradoxically a few could be pretty abusive with their authority. Sorin learned pretty quickly to avoid and give them a wide birth. Though, it didn't stop him from sometimes getting near one just to ward of Chase and his cronies. Turns out, even they abided by that rule, perhaps a little bit more so than him. Looking down at his cyberdeck, the clock on the screen read twelve past ten. Soon he'd need to get back to practicing on the board.

"So they finally accepted your transfer to Gloomhaven, eh, that's great. Bet your breathing easier being out of Cynthogene's crosshairs." Bella said, leading him to the other side of the bench. "Um-hmm... Though, it pains me to leave the force over at Delta, but..." He shook his head, face grimacing in contempt "I just couldn't deal with the rampant corruption of Cynthogene, the day they signed that contract was the day everything became much worse over in the Batista district."

Sorin looked over at the officer in shock. *Wait! Did he just say Delta? As in Delta city near the border wall? That Delta City!*

"Wait you're from Delta?" Sorin got out, suddenly reminded of the news feed from last night. The bridge, the deviants, and more importantly the large city he saw in the background of the channel.

"Hm." the man said. Turning his attention to Sorin, with a casual air to him. As if this was the first time he noticed that he was there. "Oh, who might this be Bells?" he asked giving a friendly look of interest.

"Oh him?" before Sorin could stop her, or even get away. Her hand came and softly landed on his head. Causing the boy to groan in annoyance as she once again ruffled his wild and sand enriched hair "This little scamp right here is Soran." She said grinning at him.

"So this is the one you've been telling me about... so, what about Tom, Jade, and Susan? How are those three doing? If you don't mind me asking."

Bella sighed "The usual. Tom and Jade being the reckless, rabblerousers of the two and Susan, well, she's pretty much the 'responsible' one if you get my meaning."

He raised an eyebrow "Still the only sane man of the group ya. Hmm, surprised she hadn't choked them out by now." Bella shrugged "I'm just as amazed as you are."

He turned to Sorin "Nice to meet you by the way," he held out his open hand to him across Bella who leaned back "My name is Marshal, Marshal Owens" Sorin looked at the open hand and firmly grabbed his, before shaking it like Hosea taught him.

"Hello" he said smiling, deciding he must be alright if he knew Susan and the others.

"I take it you must be curious about Delta from what I gather." he all but stated as their handshake ended.

Sorin nodded "Yeah, I saw the news last night. Is it true, do deviants really exist? And they're not just showing us fake footage."

Marshal pressed his lips, his expression becoming thoughtful "Well... to be honest I've never come across a deviant myself before I was transferred to gloom. But, I have heard from friends in the force that have, or... in there reports they have."

Sorins eyes widened excitedly "That's really cool! So... do they know why people are getting powers?"

Marshal shook his head, but the amused smile on his face grew wider "No, as far as it goes, I know just as much as everyone else- which of course isn't a lot. Alas, sadly no... there not really revealing much to the public about it and even if I knew, I doubt I'd be allowed to tell you." he gave him a curious look "You seemed terribly interested in the topic by the way, why is that, if I may ask."

Sorin looked at him in disbelief "Why not, I mean... if I could wake up with powers one day that would be so awesome." He looked down at his sand covered body "Beats what I already have, that's for certain."

Marshal raised an eyebrow at the answer, but when he looked up, he was surprised by the look that fell on Bellatrix's face. A clear look of pain crossed her expression, but in a moment it was gone before Sorin could notice it.

What was that? Marshal thought to himself, he checked it under something he would ask Bells later if they had the time. If, she was willing to talk to him about it. He looked to the gear by his feet and the small orangish disc besides the boy.

"Hold on... is that a hoverboard!?" Marshal asked surprised to see that near him *I would never have thought a kid in these parts would be able to afford one... let alone ride it without the proper augs, I guess that's what the fancy wrist gadget is for, I guess.*

Sorin looked at the board, then with growing excitement, picked it up in hand.

"Yep, Tom found it and gave it to me for fixing." He lied

"Managed to mostly repair it and get it in working order again... I'm just trying to figure out how to ride it is all, it's why I'm here in the first place." He said, especially sounding pleased with himself to the eyeroll of Bellatrix.

"Uh oh, better watch out Marsh. Kid is going to talk you death about it if you don't watch out." she said chuckling, to the annoyed glare of Sorin.

Marshal laughed "Oh I'm fine with it, he must be pretty tech savvy to pull that off. I remember back in Delta when I had to take a few dispatch calls concerning a few, less... than savvy individuals trying to repair their boards," he looked up towards the lodge, face reminiscent of the past "A bunch of parents and would be pro boarders, ended up either: blowing up their roofs and needing EMS assistance due to burns. Or, and my favorite, riding them in an enclosed space- with no room to ride them..." he shook his head.

Sorin did a double take, before laughing "Seriously, I mean- I had moments when the board shocked me or did a little jump in my room. But nothing that bad." Marshal grimaced "Apparently, the cause for most incidents happened because- either they didn't know what they were doing and assumed it was as simple as removing and putting on a new part. Or they decided to simply sell it to someone else, while they go and by a new one, of course." Sorin stopped laughing, just like that, a new, more disturbing thought came to him. Afterall, wasn't that the same conclusion he came to when he first found it. And like Marshal said, the moment he activated it, it erupted in a pulse of energy. He winced, oh yeah... definitely a good hand of luck.

The three talked for another hour, but eventually it was time for Marshal to head back to his post. Sorin and Bella waved as he made his way down to the large, fenced guard post out of sight and past the outer paths of the trails. A moment later saw Sorin putting on the protective gear for his board as Bella watched from the shoulder of the road.

"Alright kiddo, I'm going to head back to the Nocturne. And remember, when it gets to five o'clock it's time to wrap it up and head home."

Sorin nodded "Okay, oh... and will Church be home by seven? I heard from Aunt Dot that he went on some kind of business trip."

Bella frowned "Yeah, I think so... why?"

Sorin went into his pocket, bringing out the orange pill bottle "I'm almost out of meds." The bottle, which had the word: Ambroxicavalol on it with 120mg to the right of the prescription name. "Do you have enough for right now?" Bella stepped up, quickly asking as she got a look inside the bottle.

Sorin nodded "I got enough for today and tomorrow. But I couldn't catch him this morning, before I left for the park."

Bella sucked in a small breath "Okay," she said quietly "I'll let him know if I see him, and I'll give Chrisanta a call too, so she can also reach him. But Sorin remember–"

Sorin nodded "Yeah, I'll be back before five." He said giving her an annoyed look, which earned him a customary hair ruffle. "Alright, okay, I'll leave you to your board.

Catch you back at the nocturne scamp." before turning and moving back down the path, Sorin sighed as he put on the helmet, ready to start another couple of hours of him wiping out across the park.

10/16/2061, Saturday, 3: 58 pm

Sorin gasped, the wind whistling past him as he flew back across the graveled straight path. After two hours of riding and enumerable wipe outs, he was finally achieving some progress. The board was going a steady 20 mph, and the protective gear made it easier to recover from especially hard falls.

He shifted his weight, the board began to list to the right as another short turn to the right drew near. Carefully and with learned precision, he shifted his weight to accommodate the weight of his turn, the board responding in kind, as its fins retracted and expanded to let out puffs of energy, all the while the ground under him was kicked up by the maneuver. And like that... he cleared his fifth turn, without having to slow down nearly as much. The winds buffeting his face as he squinted his eyes. Crouching and bracing as the board accelerated forward.

He breathed an exhilarated howl, his small form darting across the trail.

Finally! he thought. *finally, some progress... actual progress!*

He looked down to his cyberdeck, the speedometer was in the 30's now- a far cry from the speed he started with. The measly 10mph couldn't hold a candle to this current velocity. He couldn't stop the mad smirk curving his lips, as he bent forward on the platform. His computer at home, his cyberdeck, all said the same things about his current build of the board.

If he kept up with his practice, he could reach the top speed of a whooping 75mph. Granted... he still needed to find a place that was long enough for him to go that fast. As excited as he was to reach that lofty goal, he was also adamant to avoid becoming another statistic like the people in Marshal's story.

Susan, Bellatrix, Aunt Dot and especially Church wouldn't let him hear the end of it. And he shuddered what Hosea would probably say if this were to occur.

The lights of the foundry began to dim, the pools of sunlight shifting in tone, as the sunset outside made the vapid lights go from a cool luminescence to a stark canvas of orange and reds. The overhead lights around the foundry activated one by one with loud cranks which snapped Sorin out of his thoughts, he looked to the clock and gave a disappointed sigh it was nearing four till thirty, it was time to call it. With hesitation he slowed down, clearing another turn as he began to make for the bench with the duffle bag near the paved path. From where he was, he could see the lodge off in the distance. He considered riding his way there but shook his head, he more than likely wouldn't be able to balance the bag on his shoulder while on the board, loath as he was to admit it to himself, and he didn't want to risk other people on the paved paths who were still walking along them. Thinking about it, as he slowed down further, he was lucky that no one was taking the gravel paths outside the paved ones.

He slowed to a stop right before he got to the bench, and jumped off, kicking the board up to catch it. The pulse of energy from the vents abruptly cut off with a sharp sigh as if breathing a relief of rest. A moment later, the board folded in on itself, collapsing back into its idle oval disc form.

A few minutes later, Sorin took off the last of his protective gear and placing them inside the bag along with his board. He didn't want to admit it, but, he felt beat. It hit him just as he zipped the bag up and lifted it to his shoulder. He smiled though, he was finally at the point where he could reliably stay on it. He walked down the path, and as the overhead lights gleamed on like search lights. Highlighting most of the foundry as the waning sunlight above continued to dim and ebb.

He was nearly halfway to the lodge when he heard someone calling his name, looking over his shoulder it was Mr. Owens.

"Glad I could catch up to you," he said panting "I found this near the gravel path and saw your name on it."

It was his medications, eyes widening he checked his pockets. He gasped, when did it drop out? He could have been heading home and if an attack had happened...

"Oh man... Thanks Mr. Owens! I didn't even..." "Don't mention it." Owen said with a relieved laugh.

Sorin took the bottle, and put inside the side pouch of his bag, still in disbelief that he hadn't even felt the bottle slip out when he was riding on the board.

"That must have been very important by the look on your face. Come on, I'll walk to the nearest elevator up top."

"Thanks."

Sorin and Mr. Owens walked clear of the paved path, the lodge to their left. A medium-sized concrete and steel building with a small pavilion on each side. To their right was the kids play area. The usual swings, slides, see saws, and sand box. Currently there wasn't anybody around the park or lodge. Right now it was just Sorin and Owens walking down the paved path as they exited the park, once again nearing the main street towards the elevator. Lafander road, it was called; and calling it a street was sorta laughable, there weren't that many houses down here, and what little you could find down in layer three where mostly shacks, and or warehouses.

While Baldurs lodge attracted settlers around historic or the undercity, it was mostly the only safe attraction down here. The places beyond the park and past the security gates were home to the incalculable underground tunnels outside the undercity limits or the bottomless pits that the excavation teams dimmed too dangerous to venture through. The idea that Ichorcyte could still be discoverable this side of the cliff was also abandoned- the tunnels down there where seen as too unstable, and rife with nests of Cazadors.

Or at least, that's what Owens was told by the other officers of the guard.

"So... no one is willing to test the waters outside of the safe zone," Owens continued on "Honestly, I can't blame um. Just imagine... walking down those catacombs, the lights of your flashlights barely covering 5 feet ahead of you, and all the while having to watch out for the occasional sign, smell, or sound of a Cazador nest." Owens shook his head "Not ashamed to admit, I'd have trouble stepping a foot in there."

Sorin eyes were wide as he told him what he knew about the tunnels "But what about augmentation? Shouldn't there be, I don't know, like those implants that allow you to see in the dark? You'd think the conclaves could afford something like that for the workers."

Owens chuckled "You give em to much credit Sor. I'd think after excavating and clearing the park, that they must have done enough to say they given it there all. After all, if someone where to get into an accident while trying to clear a passage, or worst, find themselves stepping onto a lose ledge and falling to their doom. Why... I'd hate to see the manpower, time and effort that would be needed to check and see if they were still with us in the land of the living. And don't forget about the Cazadors. One sting, and you're going to experience the worst pain imaginable, if that doesn't finish you- the neuro toxin will."

Sorin grimaced "Uh..."

Owens nodded "And the implants. That would mean ether getting a sponsor from a corporation, or going to the republic for help. And I doubt the city wants to go for either options. Heck, the conclaves themselves don't want to involve the republic. So, long story short the city is simply strapped."

Sorin nodded, the two finally reached the elevator. Before Sorin could press the button, Owens touched his shoulder, he had a troubled look to him.

"Before you leave... I have to ask you a question, if you're comfortable of course, I'm not forcing you to say one or the other."

Sorin gave him a confused look "What is it?"

He nodded to the bag "That medicine you have... that's not... it's not a medication for cognicrossis is it?"

Sorin paused then frowned, then with a heavy sigh he nodded.

"Oh... is it serious? If you don't mind me asking." he gave an apologetic look "I'm not asking to be nosy for nosy's sake by the way, just wanted to make sure a friend is alright." Sorin smiled and nodded "It's not too bad... painful, but, manageable I guess."

Owens pressed his lips in thought "I see, is that what you meant earlier? When you said you'd rather be a deviant?"

Sorin nodded "Church said that people were scared of them, said that... the republic and the conclaves didn't really like the idea of them. But... I can't help but think how cool they are." He said beaming

"It's weird to say it, but, if I were a deviant- think of the things I could do with powers like that! If I were lucky enough to get an ability like that I could help out with Church or Aunt dot." He held up his bag.

"I wanted to learn how to ride this so I could help with Church's courier business, not up in the historic district but maybe down in the undercity- to get the load off him for once." Sorin said.

Owens eyes widened at what he was saying "That's... an interesting goal you got there, but, I don't think you need to be deviant to do that." He patted the bag "You seem to be pretty gifted when it comes to working on hoverboards. Maybe when you get older you can look up a job in fixing them, or, better yet- creating hoverboard parts or even engines!" Sorins eyes widened at what he heard.

"What!"

Owens nodded "Yeah... if you were dedicated enough to get that thing working, what stops you from getting good enough to do that? Now, does it sound like you need superpowers, or an aug, to accomplish that?"

Sorin blinked, never once did a thought like that cross his mind as he fixed the board. Why had he never thought of that?

"I... could I do that?" Sorin whispered to himself, as another thought came to him, a bleaker one. Would his body even hold out long enough to accomplish that?

A hand landed on his shoulder, knocking him out of his thoughts "Sorin?" Owen said his name concerned "You alright there?"

"Y-yeah, just thinking... you seriously think I could do that? Do they even have jobs like that in the conclaves?" Sorin asked meekly.

"I don't know, maybe when you get home you should ask Bella if such a thing is possible out here in Gloomhaven." Owens replied.

Sorin was quite for a moment, then with a heavy heart, he nodded.

Sorin activated the elevator back to layer two, soon after he and Owens bid farewell to each other. Leaving Sorin to stand there with plenty on his mind; ideas upon ideas shaping themselves in his head as the elevator made a ragged thump on the ground. The elevator doors opened, and he found himself in the very back of the large platform. All the while, the question of whether or not he would live to see that happen was totally up for debate. The doors closed shut, and alone he made himself comfortable, as the platform made its ascent upwards to the next layer.

CHAPTER

14

10/16/2061, Saturday, 9: 28 pm

Kingsley felt a sinking suspicion as he went over what he found earlier that day. Currently, he and Bellatrix were inside a small hotel. One they frequented when on the usual visit to see Sorin. It was called the Eight Flaggs motel. But this, wasn't really important, what was important was the feeling both of them experienced the moment they made it back to the hotel.

Bellatrix wasn't sure, but she felt something was off. A familiar and less than savory sensation of being watched outside her immediate field of view. If it weren't for her being a ghost runner, she would have called it the usual bout of temporary paranoia one gets every so often. But she wasn't so ordinary to begin with. It happened as they were just rounding the corner from exiting Orio, she was reminiscing about what Sorin asked her earlier, a career in hoverboard building... Something she was genially curious about looking up herself. When all of a sudden King tapped her on the shoulder just as they made it to the residential zone for their hotel. That's when she felt it, a sensation of her skin crawling behind her neck, on the side of the passage leading to the entrance of the residential zone of Monroe. She spotted the nearest camera above one of the stores, a ramen shop maybe? Anyway, she interfaced with it, she moved to the side as Kingsley blocked her from view.

Her eyes glared from the breached camera lens of the security camera. A figure was tailing them, and watching from a distance were she couldn't get a good bead on him.

Nothing more than a silhouette hidden by the throng of moving bodies, she immediately tried to get a better view, switching to another camera she could see above a gaming store.

The pursuer was one step ahead though, she jumped to the other camera, and a small glimpse of a digitized silhouette greeted her. In the next instance, however, the camera experienced a fatal surge of energy, somehow shorting out, before exploding into a shower of sparks and fiber optics- which I gotta tell ya, really scared the crap out of the other passerby's.

The connection ended there, and Kingsley couldn't see hide nor tell of the one following them. Bella made a fowl sneer, palming the gun hidden in her jacket. But with a glance from King, they both silently moved on, ignoring the small crowd looking at the now busted camera- now quietly fuming smoke. And as King and her discussed it in their room, they received a holocall from Susan.

"Slow down Sue, what do you mean things didn't go as planned?" Bella breathed, her eyes widening.

"Bell... it wasn't just some random ex-nomads hitting the facility... it was him, Carver was there, and he took something. We don't know what- and the circle is being very suspicious about what there not telling us. Not only that, but... they seem nervous." Bella paused.

Carver! He was still alive!? And what could possibly have the circle spooked? "What about the contractor- any word from him?"

Sue was silent on the other end for moment, then too Bella's surprise the line switched "Bella, this is Hosea... the entire contract has become far more complicated than we could have ever imagined... and the circle isn't playing ball with us." She narrowed her eyes, judging by his tone, he sounded royally pissed off, which could only mean one thing.

"Are they withholding information on us?" Kingsley spoke up "We both know the circle can be fickle sometimes when it comes to the details, but, by the sounds of it- are we walking headlong into a fubar'd situation with this gig."

"Yes, indeed we are. And this job comes from the top. The heads of the circle need us specifically for this upcoming gig," He said. "Moreover... as Susan explained, Carver is active, and he's stolen from a top-secret facility in the wastes... which is property of an agency from the republic."

"The republic you say- and the conclaves are cool with that?!" Bella remarked

"They haven't a choice on the matter. What is held within is classified as highly dangerous. What little info they gave me- that the circle gave me. Is honestly lacking in every corner of detail about what they stole. But... from the gest of it- it's a catastrophic loss." Hosea finished.

Bella was silent for a moment, thinking critically about every detail of his explanation of the job. Then a dark thought came to her, the figure following them...

"Hosea, we just got back to our motel, and I swear... someone was tailing us." Bella narrowed her eyes at the window outside. "I tried to get an id, but are little friend seemed very camera shy. He managed to hide his identity from the camera feed, not only that- managed to counter hack and blow up the blasted thing." She sighed, pinching her brow.

"It was a professional, no doubt about it." Hosea was quite over the line for the moment.

"Do you feel he was on your trail since the nocturne?" he asked calmly, placidly. "No clue, it was only after nearly entering Monroe- that I felt something wrong," King took over "I can't be sure, but, should one of us stay and... keep the nocturne accompanied for the time being?"

Hosea gave a tired sigh, the concern coming from the old handler was subtle, but spoke volumes of the situation they were in. The uneasiness was stifling, and Bellatrix felt an all too familiar cold and venomous surge of hatred, pooling just beneath the surface- bringing with it unpleasant memories of dealing with Carver, and his rogue faction of nomads.

Afterall, he was to blame for stealing Susan's arm in the first place. And whatever remnants of his old vanguards that remained, were swiftly delt with by either the circle or Hosea himself.

"There's just not enough to go off of," Bella said, mostly to herself "We simply can't be sure for how long we've been tailed... but what if we don't have to. The security feed from one of the cameras outside Orio, should have a good angle of when it started."

"If that's the case, then go ahead and get on it, and keep me posted... I need to have a talk with are client." Hosea replied, before cutting the feed.

King scowled "I swear, just when you think things couldn't get worse. Bleeding Carver had to reappear from the woodwork."

Bella sighed "Think you can get a cup of coffee from reception, Its going to be a long night. Oh, we should make sure Church is in the know."

King grunted "Do you got a working back door then, for the two residential zones security systems?"

Bella nodded as she got comfortable in bed, King snorted "Alright, coffee coming up- and I'll contact church on the private channel."

He exited the room, closing her eyes she activated her auto-sync function. The nearest camera in the room, which she hacked and placed dummy footage on a loop. Suddenly lifted up, a green glow pierced through the lens as Bella stared at her body from the camera's perspective. Without her operating chair she would be limited in what she could do, but her current O.S should be more than enough to scan and peruse through the grid with no one the wiser. Living up to her title as a ghost runner, always, gave her a momentary thrill. Too bad this wasn't one of those times. As she shuffled through the grid, her digital avatar zipping through the available access points and nodes, she couldn't help but feel an uncomfortable pit forming in her stomach back at the hotel. With the threat of Carver in the horizon, there was no telling where this current gig could go.

??????????????

Caspien Barabbas Orson had his back against the wall in maddening terror, his worst nightmare was standing there, in front of his desk, cloaked in shadow.

He was in his windowless office, a large room with luxurious furnishing. The monotone grand mural wallpapers of his office, would have made anyone entering his room believe that they were stepping into a beautiful forest. Or at least that's what Orson thought, in his highly valued opinion. The usual riffraff of wasters outside this god forsaken settlement, could do with a reminder of what the republic could offer this quant town. Should they give their support to him and his employers at Yggdrasil Enterprise.

After all, anything beats casting ones lot with the sniveling beggars of the conclaves. Or the barbaric independence of the nomad circles. Murderers. Thugs and thieves, the lot of them! And the worst of the worst was standing in front of his desk, gun out, smoking barrel still pointed at the spot where the bullet left a hole by Orson's fat and round face. His overweight, and sharply dressed form cowering at the opposite wall. With the silhouettes of his dead bodyguards on either side of him. Still bleeding, with the dark liquid pooling on his fancy wooden floors.

He was utterly tongue twisted, unable to even whimper out the simplest of words, knowing that any form of persuasion wouldn't work with the butcher that stared silently. The hood covering his face in shadows.

"Is this where you've been hiding after all these years?" the hooded figure scanned the room "My... you've made an impressive living while I was gone... recovering from the treachery of your betrayal." He said casually, the bodies of his fallen guards and his trembling form a mere token of amusement for the ex-nomad. Going by his deep voice.

"C-Carver, Carver... look, it, it's not a bother- I'll give you anything, anything you want- my treat!" Orson finally spoke up, barely audible and pathetic "Look! Look! I didn't have a choice! If I didn't give up the information- the circle would have killed me!"

He fell to his knees head bowed as Carver's dark shape moved up, a shrouded hand came and ripped the desk off the floor. Orson didn't see the heavy desk impact with the wall, only the resulting crash and splintering of wood on wood.

"I don't need excuses Orson what I need is information," Swiftly his hand came forward wrapping around his neck as the fat man was lifted off his feet and into the air. Orson couldn't even scream, his fingers digging into the fabric of Carver's cloak. Legs kicking and flailing in the air, he made an audible gurgle as he once again couldn't get a good look of his face. But something he could see, made him howl in silent horror, behind Carver- wrapped firmly in the fingers of darkness, pale white eyes shining through like a flashlight in the deep sea. Staring at his helpless form, waiting, motionless. Something within the hood glowed an eerie red "And you don't need to be alive for me to get it."

The stranger turned and threw the man behind him, his body slamming onto the floor with bone crushing force. The sound of agony brutally forced its way out of his lips, and there it was, through the miasma of pain, he sensed movement. He didn't get a chance to scream, nor was he given the decency of a quick death. Through the darkness, a frenzy of moving bodies and the movement of many limbs beat, stabbed, clawed, and gouged. All the while, those pale deathless eyes continued to stare, until he was mercifully cut off from consciousness.

Miles away, out of central, towards the historic district and below the two layers of the undercity. Sorin wakes up with a start. Sitting bolt upright on his bed, his t-shirt drenched in sweet, and his sheets sprawled onto the floor.

Sorin looked around the darkness of his room, breathing heavily, fumbling around in the dark for the light switch. The lamp on his stand lit up the room, casting his books and laptop of the roundtable in eerie shadows. He struggled to calm down, grasping his head as a vicious headache tore his skull asunder. He groaned horribly, his back against the wall. He couldn't understand it, couldn't comprehend it, what kind of freaky nightmare was that!? Flashes of scenes coming and going, running rampant past his eyes, phantom images scrawled into the dark shadows cast by the objects of his room. The bloody scenes of a murder- unforgiving in its imagery, and yet, too vapid for him to make since of at all.

He shook, the agonizing pain in his head now reduced to a hard throb. He sat there just breathing, trying to control himself but having a hard time. He looked towards his end table- a new pill bottle, near the side of his lamp. Could it have been the new meds that Church gave him? He shook his head, the pain continued to settle, but his heartbeat, it was in his ears, jackhammering madly. He couldn't get the images out.

He sat there for a while, forcing his mind shut, closing his eyes and focusing on his breathing. Eventually, and to his relief the shaking began to get better, and his heart rate began to slow down. It was currently two-fifty in the morning, and the sounds of his heart finally faded from his ears.

But the fragments from that nightmare stayed with him. Harrowingly so.

Orson. That had to be Orson, he could recognize that sniveling attitude and his pudgy overweight form from anywhere... but, that was; he closed his eyes. Too horrified to go over the details, there was no sounds in the dream, no way of discerning what was being said, or at least, Sorin assumed the two were talking with one another. Until the moment the figure tossed the heavy desk like it were a mere softball across the room. Then the act itself... the fractured and fragmented scenes of it made the hairs on his neck stand on in.

He greatly despised Orson... that wasn't something he hid, nor did he even attempt to ever mask it. Ever since that day, when he came on their doorstep the first time to threaten Church. He'd never forgotten the sheer rage he felt when it occurred. Or forgiven his arrogant attitude towards them, acting like he was better than them.

But this... this was sick...

What the heck could have brought about a horrible dream like this, and why had it felt so eerily vivid up until that horrible moment?

Sorin would go over this in his head throughout the night, up until nearly four in the morning when at last he was too tired to keep himself awake. He laid back down, no longer able to fight off the weight of his closing eye lids, and the last thought to go through his mind were the pale eyes in the dark.

He didn't bother to turn the lamp back off.

10/17/2061, Sunday, 5: 58 am

Bellatrix massaged her temples, back against the head of the bed.

She couldn't find anything. Not a scrape of evidence of their apparent stalker. At least, nowhere near the Nocturne or Orio.

The only signs of his or her presence was as far back as the entrance to the Monroe RZ. From there they don't appear much, only subtle glimpses here and there. The skill level here was off the charts! And to make matters worse, every camera that had a scrape of their appearance was heavily distorted. Whatever trace they left behind, once they were spotted, quickly turned up empty, and any leads or whereabouts from then on, became less, and less frequent. The trail was officially cold, and she was exhausted.

She bit her bottom lip in frustration, wondering if any of their phone lines were tapped. If they were still in the area, what other means- aside the camera in their room or the window- could they use to spy on them? She took a calming breath, she would need to contact Hosea and Church soon... but not over the holonetwork. The door opened, and King moved to his opposite bed, taking a moment to sit down and make a weary sigh.

She turned to him giving him a hopeful look.

"Any better on your end?" she asked.

"No, nothing. Couldn't find anything that could lead us back to whomever was following us." He answered shaking his head. "Did you come across anything meaningful?"

She shook her head, giving a humorless smile "Nope, whoever it was... their pretty skilled, like, republic agent skilled- I couldn't find anything on the surrounding video feeds, and are tail in question has already scrubbed every identifying frame, and piece of data about his appearance. It's so subtle in fact, I doubt local police could find anything wrong with the footage."

King sighed "Bloody hell, I'm guess were at the final countdown when it comes to it, eh," He turned to the outside window, glaring at the now empty streets below. "We using the emergency communicators then."

She nodded back. "Yeah... better safe than sorry."

The two pulled out a small phone-like device with an antenna on it, black in color and square in shape. An analog communicator from the Manifest war days. Old enough to be considered primitive tech, but simpler to use, albeit, more manual than their holocalls and harder to hack or bug.

Bella nodded to King "You get Hosea, and I'll contact Church. Best to keep him in the loop."

King nodded back

Bella about to switch on the communicator, was suddenly hit with an alarm from her O.S. She froze, eyes widening as the message passed over her eyes. She dropped the com unit in shock. The little bug that she had placed in a particular node over in the central district had been triggered. A dispatch call, that had been recorded and sent over to her by the little critters over the grid.

"Bell!" King said, suddenly on guard. Hearing the dull bump of the device upon the carpeted floor. Bellatrix's now confused expression began to read the report.

"These reports... something bad just happened over at the central district, a report of homicide- no, manslaughter!" she stood up, suddenly very, very disturbed by the data packet which reached her. She recognized this address, but an identification of the remains, by the report, read inconclusive- until further evidence could be gathered.

"King, something wicked just happened over at Kingston avenue, near Orson's office in central." She said, her voice becoming mildly unnerved.

"What was it?" King said, not liking the look Bella was giving him. For as long as he known her, there have been only a few cases where she has given that disturbed expression, and she had seen plenty brutal, repugnant stuff over the years as a runner. This... must rank high if it's got her this riled up.

"From what authorities are gathering, a massacre happened in his office... and their having trouble identifying the remains." She answered. Face grimacing as more and more data came through. Information that was updated on real time by investigators on scene of the crime, but... only readable data no videos or feeds- too risky for that. But the descriptions where more than enough to make her do a double take.

In the worst way possible, the exhaustion that had been creeping up on her was immediately dashed to the side. As an ominous feeling replaced it. Bella could only guess at what was now starting to rear its ugly head in Gloomhaven.

CHAPTER

15

10/17/2061, Sunday, 10:17 am

Church watched Sorin ride around the gravel paths of the park. Sitting under the pavilion watching as Sorin speedily passed dune mounds and trails alike. Church had to hand it to em, he really got the hang of riding that thing in such a short time. Though... there were moments.

Moments when he overturned on a step curve on one of the paths, wiping out from turning to hard to his own alarm, witnessing him pull himself from one of the sand mounds- only to march to his board and ride off again. Determined to do better. Church couldn't help the small curve that formed on his lips, he was on his feet ready to move towards him when that first happened. But... that kid was simply just tenacious to learn. Whatever the setback he encountered.

It was times like this, when he forgot that he was sick. That, at the moment he looked like any other kid- absorbed in whatever sport or game they found interest in. And for that to be hoverboarding of all things... Such an interesting choice of pursuit.

He looked further away into the background, the gate wall, which was much farther away from their current position and was the limit of the foundry park. Officer Owens was there on duty at the moment, and if he had the time he would like to visit himself and thank the man for his kind words to Sorin. Church glanced back to the foreground, where Sorin sped past- the dirt and smoke being kicked up into a long dust trail, as he continued to move, not breaking his speed as he made another sharp turn. Church's hands retreated into the pockets of his pants, a small breeze blowing through the pavilion and his hair, from the direction of the wall. He wished he could relax more- it was certainly a fine day for it, but something troubled him greatly- and he wasn't necessarily excluding the early morning in the nocturne either.

Two things: First was Sorin, he was not his usual self that mourning-something happened, that much he was sure of. But what was the question. He tried to nudge the truth out of him, but stubbornly as ever he refused. Maybe it was a cogni attack late at night, or maybe he found something unsavory about his new goal of becoming a part builder for hoverboards. Church just couldn't find out what it was, but to his relief, Sorin still asked if he could come down to the foundry to practice, and happy to see some normalcy- he agreed, with him joining in turn. Second, and the cause of his... shall we say- mild uncomfortable disposition. Kingsley's emergency call that mourning, just as they made for the foundry... They were apparently tailed, and thankfully they weren't spotted in Orio. But the last piece of news had him feel like his whole day had taken a nosedive.

Carver was still alive... still loose somewhere in the wastelands.

His skin tingled, a sudden automatic urge to grab a non-existent cigarette from his pockets settled over him. It's been what, two to three years since he quit smoking. And just the mention of Carver's name, made him want to reconsider his tobacco cessation. He chuckled, by god he believed the nightmare of him, and his gang was over and behind them.

He grimaced, after what happened with Susan... It was a relief.

Only for that monster to somehow survive, after all this years... Knowing Hosea he's probably throwing a fit right about now. But my question is how... how on earth did Carver survive... after what happened to him?

Church gave a worried sigh, it was a lot of bad news lately, with a bit of good spliced in here and there. He just hoped that things would somehow work its way out. For all their sakes.

10/17/2061, Sunday, 10: 45 am

Sorin zoomed across the dark road of gravel, and pondered. Not truly focused on where he was going, though he knew he should be- he's wiped out a couple of times by now, and normally he'd admonish himself for such a careless mistake. But... the nightmare from last night just wouldn't leave him.

The whistle of the wind didn't do much to clear his thoughts, although he was thankful that at least a small part of him managed to convince himself to come and practice. Which he felt was coming along pretty well. His balance was manageable when he was properly focused, and he could actually take the turns without losing too much momentum or losing his balance. He was steadily improving... yet, his focus was absolutely bogged down by momentary flashes that his mind, periodically, recalled against his better wishes. The fragments of the nightmare would intrusively interrupt his train of thoughts, which more than once got him to accidentally wonder off the shoulder of the road, or worse yet drive him into a sand mound. Frustrating as it was. He'd pick himself up and moved on from the embarrassing occurrence. At the back of his head, he realized that he'd forgotten that Church was here with him. And at some point he started to realize how odd he himself, had been acting. He had a hoverboard dang it! Where'd his zeal for the future go?

He wondered to himself as the dunes slid past him, the wheeze of wind blowing around his ears, and the sound of the dirt trailing up behind him, which could only do so much to distract him from what he was feeling. As the excitement and wonder of yesterday was barely noticeable to his discomfort. He sighed to himself, shaking his head, at the very least he could admire how good he was doing on the board. He completed another turn around a sharp bend, surprisingly for the first time that day- he felt uplifted.

Yes... that's more like it... I'm getting better, I can do this, just gotta keep going. A small smile formed on his face *Yeah! Forget about the dream... it's Sunday, and I got all day to practice with this beauty!* Sorin now grinning from ear to ear. Began to gun the engine of the board, revving his speed all the way to 40mph. He felt a sudden and amazing gratification towards Bella for giving him the protective gear he wore currently. As the straps of his durag, from under his helmet, fluttered around from the breeze he kicked up. And he remembered to tie the dark cloth over his hair this time around. Anything to avoid the pain of having his head absolutely covered in sand again. Even after taking that bath the other night his head still itched from the amount of sand that used to be in it.

The trails were empty on the outer rings further away from the center of the park, more than enough space to go all out on what he was capable of on the board. The first three hours of him coming out of his dour mood, was meet with complete bliss, as he sonic'd across the trails, eventually, he even got to a point where he could make sharp turns- without having to sacrifice all of his speed to keep on the flying platform. Something he researched online before he went to bed. Videos of other boarders using power slide maneuver's around hard turns, like he was doing now, angling the board sideways and letting the jets of the bottom vents slow him down so that he could achieve a drifting maneuver across turns. Though it wasn't always a perfect drift, the times he slid from the road and into another sand mound was numerous to say the least. But... like always, he was making progress. It helped massively that it was extremely fun and exhilarating to pull off.

The day rolled over smoothly, Sorin rode the board and eventually the nightmare finally stopped haunting his thoughts. It was almost a quarter after one, and Sorin was on his way to take another break to chat with Church. He was near the road that would take him closer to the pavilion when something odd happened.

He suddenly closed his eyes for a moment, slowing down as something felt off. He looked around, a tingling at the back of his head, no, more like... a pull, maybe? He felt a sudden stab of pain enter his head, causing him to stop completely in the middle of the road. He stepped off the board the pain was starting to get worse. He dropped down to his knee, another cogni attack? He groaned out gnashing his teeth in agitation. No, this... this wasn't a cogni-attack. By now, the nerves of his entire body would have erupted in agonizing pain. It was all centered in his head, like something was groping around inside of his skull.

Suddenly he felt his eyes open, seemingly on their own as the tugging of an invisible string seemed to force him to look to his immediate right. Unbeknownst to him, his cyberdeck suddenly started to flash red as a warning message played across the screen.

WARNING! WARNING! WARNING!
ABNORMAL COGNISANT LEVELS DETECTED
\\\\\\\\\\\\\\\\\\\\\\\|/////////////////
WARNING! WARNING! WARNING!
ABNORMAL PHYSICAL LEVELS DETECTED
\\\\\\\\\\\\\\\\\\\\\\\|/////////////////
WARNING! WARNING! WARNING!
ABNORMAL NEURAL LEVELS DETECTED

Sorin froze, someone was standing there. Far, far into the +distance. He couldn't quite make them out- but, it looked familiar. On top of a distant sand mound the figure seemed to be looking in his direction.

Sorin rubbed his eyes, feeling another mild wave of an aching pain around his head. He stood up opening his eyes and the figure was gone, the distant dot disappearing like a mirage. *Crap, am I hallucinating now?*

"Man, what's wrong with me?" he muttered to himself.

Sorin suddenly had a thought, random in the way it just popped into his head, but, that didn't make it any less true. Was it suddenly darker? Like looking around he became startled- the lights above the massive cavern seemed to slowly ebb and lessen. Was there something wrong with the mirrors reflecting the lights outside? He looked around becoming antsy, he moved back onto his board, as the sudden urge to find Church was increasingly looking like a good idea. His head was still experiencing a dull ache, but he could worry about that later. He was about to kick off when he spotted someone approaching dead ahead. It was Officer Owens.

Sorin was immediately alarmed by the look on Owen's face, something was definitely wrong. Stepping back off he carried the board surfer style as the bottom vents turned off automatically.

"Sorin! Come on, let's get out of here!" he said pointing towards the lodge.

"What...What's going on?" Sorin asked, looking around the park as he moved with Owens. Messaging his head, still not noticing the warning message from his cyberdeck.

"Supercells coming, that's what." He replied, walking quickly down the paved path as what looked like sand particles began to lightly snow from the ceiling of the cavern.

"This far north! That's crazy... but what about the foundry? Don't they have anyway to seal off outside!?" Sorin exclaimed, now anxious, remembering the moments during his time in the voyager when a supercell occurred.

"The ceiling hatches will direct lose debris from pouring down into the park," Owens said, as he gave a momentary glance upwards as they fast walked down the path towards the pavilion "But... it's not a guaranteed safeguard, and the tunnels past the outside gate could have severe winds blowing sand through the passages. Definitely something you don't wanna be caught in the middle of kid. Last thing we need is for your skin to get peeled off from a bad case of sandblasting." Sorin shivered, not at all a fan of the gruesome image that popped into his head.

Owens put two fingers to his temple as his eyes glowed with the usual green pricks signaling a holocall "Why is no one responding?" Sorin heard him mutter under his breath "Is something wrong?" Sorin asked, glancing worriedly at Owens, but he gave no indication that he heard him, trying once again to get an answer from his call. Sorin walked faster, trying to stay next to him, still trying to ignore the headache that wouldn't leave- when a sudden splash of red got his attention making him to glance downwards. His eyes widened at the status message from his cyberdeck.

"What the..." Sorin whispered, reading the three warning alerts. *No, no, no what the heck is going on!*

"Hey sir! I'd advise you to come with us towards the lodge, for your safety!" He heard Mr. Owens call out.

Sorin glanced up and froze, ahead of them, a stranger who was wearing a familiar cloak in the distance. Looking closer it was actually a large, hooded cardigan, but the wearer was far less bulky than the figure he seen in his nightmare- but the similarity was still striking. He hissed as the headache seemed to spike the moment he looked towards the figure. Owens stopped and gave Sorin a startled look "Sorin? Whoa, what's wrong!" Sorin shook his head, not being able to voice the problem at the moment. Owens then noticed the cyberdeck, eyes widening at the warning message displayed by the monitor. *Oh hell... is he going through a cogni attack?* He was about to pick him back up to his feet, when the sound of footsteps alerted him, looking back up the stranger was on approach.

Suddenly, Owens was on guard, something wasn't right here... That's when he saw it, from the hood of the person walking towards them- a green hue was emanating from out of the hood, and as the dwindling light of the cavern continued to dissipate, a sudden realization came to Owens, why were the emergency floodlights not activating?

That's when it hit him- a maddening degree of white-hot pain pierced his forehead and behind his very eyes. Followed by a warning from his onboard interface menu, he immediately grasped that the O.S in his head was alerting him of an enemy breach, and he needn't guess who was currently attempting such an assault on his faculties. He blocked out the noise and pain of his aching head, a few seconds, that's all he had to interrupt either a paralyzing daemon hack: to brutally knock him out of consciousness, or worse, a lethal O.S short circuit, which would fry the cybernetics behind his eyes and inside his brain- killing him.

He wasn't interested in finding out whether which would occur...

He slipped the handgun out of his holster in a smooth motion, a learned reflex from his time at Delta. Sorin wasn't prepared or ready for the loud barks of kinetic handgun rounds which echoed out of the barrel, and towards the stranger who jerked back from the hits to his torso and chest. The stranger collapsed to his knees and Sorins exclamation of 'What the heck are you doing!' rang on deaf ears to the officer who glared ahead.

"Sorin move, and get down on the ground, and stay down!" Owens barked and Sorin, startled, was frozen in fear, what was going on?

Another loud shot rang into the air, but it wasn't Owens' gun. Sorin jumped in fright as Owens was taken off his feet and flung forwards down onto the ground. Sorin held his mouth open in a voiceless scream, his brain shutting down, trying to figure out what was happening around him, and when he finally snapped out of it he realized he was moving towards Owens downed form... he was motionless, not moving an inch no matter how much Sorin called his name or tried to shake him awake. The hoverboard laying were he dropped it behind him.

Sorin gasped at the bullet wound lodged into Owens' back near the left shoulder blade. It was now starting to bleed, he found himself holding his hands to the wound, applying pressure.

"Moris, you fool! The hell were you thinking- standing there and assuming he would just let you hack him!" A gravelly voice called out behind Sorin, he turned around and grew deathly cold. It was him, the same figure he saw in his nightmare last night!

He wore a large trench coat, which looked well-worn and full of holes. The hood over his head was up enough for Sorin to make out a dark mask covering most of his face. His clothing under the duster, was hidden by the ballistic vest which was covered by nicks, scrapes, bullet holes and other assortment of battle worn scars. His pants had signs of ballistic pads weaved onto the knees and legs, with the army boots also looking scuffed and worn. The gun in his right hand still outstretched and lightly smoking.

It was a nomad... that much Sorin knew. But he was too preoccupied with Owens- who still wasn't moving. "So this is the brat, right." Suddenly Sorin felt himself get lifted by the scruff of his neck. His feet leaving the ground, he couldn't do anything as the man pulled him to his feet faster than he could keep up. He gritted his teeth, a sudden surge of anger overriding any common sense he otherwise would have had. He struck out, his fist flying and landing painfully against the man's torso. The man barely budged from the hit, and Sorin found the large hand holding his collar retreat. He would have run for it, if it weren't for the brutal back hand that got him full in the face. Causing him to see stars, as he rolled painfully on the ground.

"Huh, savage little thing ain't ya! Hmph, Hosea... Always the softie when it comes to desert urchins," the voice chuckled darkly "Although thinking about it, they do make the most loyal solders, the younger the better they say." His voice had such a clear note oily contempt in it. The sound of it made Sorin, if possible, even more enraged. He struggled to get up, sending him the ugliest glare he could manage from the horrible pain of his jaw, which of course felt shattered from the small backhand of the larger man.

The man chuckled "My, what a particularly nasty look. Give a few years you'd make an interesting nomad..." He turned from Sorin, giving the other guy his attention with Sorin finally doubling over, not being able to ignore the flaring pain of his jaw anymore as he grasped it. "Moris, what's the holdup- we gotta go!" the man called "I'm coming, it's just this stupid thing... it's not doing what its told!"

The other cowled figure: Moris, answered back, clutching his chest in pain as he struggled to stay upright. Suddenly the pull from earlier returned and Sorin howled in excruciating pain, clutching his head.

Moris also doubled over howling at the same time "Gah! What the hell is going on with this piece of crap?"

Startled the large man took a step back before suddenly clutching his head "No, what is-" he turned back to Sorin, narrowing his eyes as the pain finally reached him. "Even after all this time, and all the precautions we made- it's still trying to resist the conditions set on it. Damnit!"

Sorin glanced back up, his head was still throbbing- but even in his excruciating state of pain, he could make out something which shocked him into open mouthed terror. Everything became still for a moment, as the stranger held up a device, hand shaking and his deep voice struggling to hold in his labored breathing. But that's not what earned Sorin's silent horror.

There was something covering the top part of the brute's masked face. It looked metallic and was moving around like liquid silver, and suddenly it formed the same pale-like eyes from his nightmare. Milky white, cloudy and appearing completely blind from under his hood which glared back onto his own.

The futuristic gun in his hands seemed to arc with electricity. Suddenly, a loud crackle of electricity echoed into the air, with a blinding light Sorin felt a surge of electricity smack him against the chest causing him to fly a short distance from the impact. He landed against a nearby sand dune and the last thought that registered in the fading vestiges of his consciousness was the forking pain which traveled all along his chest, before mercifully, all went dark.

CHAPTER

16

10/17/2061, Sunday, 7: 47 pm

Church, Bellatrix, and Kingsley sat in the main bar room of the nocturne. The air was wrought with tension, the initial shock and rage had finally wore off, and the news was already given to the others outside the city. Sorin was gone... and they had no new leads to where he could be at the moment.

Officer Owens was in the hospital, still alive to everyone's relief- as strained as it was. Church was seating in the front bar table, a lit smoke in his shaking hands. As he struggled to keep calm. Bellatrix and King sitting on either side of Church as they both looked pale under the lights of the bar, with Aunt Dot still in her room, with the lights still on as the sound of muffled sobs could be heard from the other side.

"Is this really all we can do?" Kingsley asked, his voice low, a dangerous edge to it "How the hell did we not see this coming?" he whispered.

Bellatrix narrowed her eyes to her reflection, a clear look of subdued rage brewing underneath. "Don't start King... Right now, losing are collective shits isn't going to help Sorin." She turned to Church lightly grasping his shoulder "We'll find him Church... I swear it to you we will find him, and we'll make them pay for this." She spat out lowly.

Church slowly, painfully, nodded. Hours after the abduction... and yet no news to speak of. He knew this would be the case, but the idea of going a night without him being found... it... did something to him.

"Let me go and check up on Chrisanta... she doesn't need to be alone right now." They both nodded as Church moved upstairs. King sighed "How much did the camera's capture?"

"Not much, the supercell messed up some of the footage. Most of it came from the security cameras from the pavilions," she rolled her sleeves revealing a small device attached to her wrists "You mind," King shook his head "Go ahead." Her eyes flashed green, and a wire shot out of the small opening from the device, she grabbed it and connected it to Kings neural port. The footage displayed in front of Kings hud, and he watched as the camera panned forwards, zooming in on the two figures moving towards the outer wall of the park limits. Sorin was being carried by the larger one, on his shoulder, as the other carried what looked like the hoverboard under his arm.

"Where are they going? Towards the outer gate- but the guards-" Bella shook her head "Dead." King narrowed his eyes. "So... where did they disappear to? Do you have any more footage outside the park?" She frowned "Yes... but the footage has been tampered with, and those were the hidden ones near the tunnel entrances- the other camera's where also destroyed." She scowled "I don't get how they were able to plan something like this... the timing alone would have been insane to pull off, and don't get me started on the supercell."

King gave humorless laugh "I think they would have made do- even if the supercell wasn't part of the equation. What I want to know is why, why Sorin of all people!" he banged his fist on the bar table.

Bella bit her lips "They finally called it in by the way, the slaughter at central. They finally identified the remains as Orson, and it can't be a coincidence that this happens only hours apart from one another."

She unhooked the cable and cupped both her hands to her face "It was Carver, the one who was carrying Sorin... It had to be him, no doubt about it."

King leaned in on the table "They must have used the tunnels past the gate as an escape route... I don't see any other way they could have gotten out of the undercity, especially with Sorin in tow."

"How confident are you in that hypothesis?" Bella asked.

"I'm not... but it's the only theory that makes sense." Kings eyes narrowed "Think this has anything to do with Hosea's team, I mean...

not long after Carver gets away with highly dangerous and classified republic artifact does he reappear again, here, in Gloomhaven. And judging by the video... that has to be the same guy that was tailing us last night." Bella nodded "Would explain the corrupt footage- but something tells me that that wasn't just some by-the-numbers runner. The way he was able to brute force and corrupt the footage, I've never seen anything like it." She said shaking her head mystified.

"Probably seeing those classified weapons in action." King said, "But what about Owens, not that I'm saying I ain't grateful that the fella is still alive... but, how is he still kicking after what happened with the other guards?"

Bella gave a bewildered look "That's the thing, in the footage- I went back in time, and it looks like he was having trouble halfway through his protocol hacks. Guy was simultaneously breeching up to eleven cameras at once, and he just suddenly started to lose control of it. I thought he was running daemons into the system, but looks like he was using raw processing power to do it." She shook her head "It's unbelievable- I've never seen an O.S. with that kind of ram space for something like that."

King shook his head "Must have been some experimental augments, Susan did say they stole something from that facility. Maybe this was their first test run."

She snorted "And Orson? Pretty intense system breech to rip him apart like that. Overkill that was, even that slimeball didn't deserve to go out like that. We still got time before Hosea contacts us, will need to be ready when that happens." King nodded "Yeah, for Sorin's sake. I hope he can hold out until we can find em."

Bella turned to the mirror, the bags under her eyes weren't pretty. But she didn't care, if she had to scour every inch of cyberspace for even the smallest bread crumb to his location, she would do it, and god help Carver if she finds him first. She'd make damn sure he stayed dead this time around.

?????????/?????????/?????????

Sorin was swimming in a rolling molasses of pain and fatigue. His sore jaw from that quick backhand was still aching, and the left-over pain from whatever that jerk shot him with was still in effect. As well as the burning sensation from his chest.

He felt drained and barely in control of his limbs, like a fuse somewhere between his nervous system and brain was short-circuited. Depriving his muscles of the proper instructions to get out of this nightmare. It had to be another nightmare, right? The scene of Mr. Owens getting shot kept replaying in his head. Was he still alive? That one question seemed to create a hollow fissure within his chest. And why on earth would someone wanna kidnap him? Just the sentence alone felt unreal to him, a cruel joke maybe. But no, the jostling of his subdued body around the back seat of a vehicle felt painfully real enough. The vehicle stopped, he could feel that at the very least. Sadly, he couldn't see, one of them tied something over his eyes and mouth. It tasted like crap. He heard the click of a door opening, and with an uncomfortable lurch, he was lifted from the seat and was seemingly being carried over the shoulder. He growled, wishing he had the strength to punch or kick whoever was carrying him. Instead, he was being hauled like a dirty sack of potatoes to god's knows where.

"What's with the fancy bracelet on his arm? Think we could sell it, like his board?" a voice pressed.

"It's a cyberdeck, an old toy from before the age of the manifest wars. And no, those things are considered obsolete for a reason, still..." the deep voice of the one who shot and smacked him chuckled "It's mighty impressive for someone this young to be in possession of it; too bad we can't remove it without getting rid of his arm... but we needn't bother. Even your O.S. could fry that thing if you were series enough."

The other man clicked his tongue "We throwing him in with the freak," there was a tone of amusement in his voice "If it's still pissed off, I hazard a guess it'll do worser to him than it did to Brick!"

Sorin narrowed his eyes. What where they planning to do with him now? This thought made his insides constrict, and he desperately wished he could see what was going on. They were walking, that much he knew. Then suddenly, he heard something, a lock maybe? But it sounded bigger than a petty lock, more like a large crank, it actually reminded him of the elevators of the undercity. But this sounded massive in scale-like a large gate of some sort. The walking continued and something hit his nose that made him do a double take. The air had a dusty quality to it, there was a massive thud of something closing behind them- they had to be somewhere hidden. But where? They just got out of a vehicle- but where they still near Gloomhaven?

He struggled to keep himself calm, but he was failing miserably. Between the aching jaw and the shotty control of his limbs... he felt so.... helpless. Something destroyed his train of thought, abruptly, the familiar feeling of something probing his head started a new. He clenched his teeth, scrunching his eyes shut in complete disorientation. So strong was the feeing he felt like he was spinning. On they walked and from what little Sorin could piece together, they were walking down pretty long hallways, turning, descending.... yet still not a clue of where they could be. Till finally- they stopped. There was the familiar sound of closed doors the type of which belonged to an elevator. His observation was proven correct when he felt the descent downwards. After half a minute, they continued walking and eventually after moving down yet another long hallway he heard a new voice, another guy by the sound of it.

"Looks like the brat is starting to feel it too- wait till he sees his new roommate!" the new voice cackled, he turned his head towards the direction of the voice. He tried to talk, tried to curse them out as it were- but all that came out was gibberish, indignant filled gibberish, but gibberish all the same.

"Here we are, you two play nice now." Someone else crowed. A woman by the sound of it.

He gave a muffled yelp as he was swung quickly off the guys shoulder. Sorin didn't have time to orient himself at all- as the blindfold and gag were removed. The room in front of him was obviously a holding cell, with one small florescent light bulb hanging in the center of the ceiling. A few mattress beds under it and blankets, a large square room of concrete walls and floors. There was a massive crater in the wall ahead of him, like something small and heavy was smashed into it leaving spider web cracks all over and a clear depression. That was all he could make out before he was pushed in, collapsing painfully inside the room with barely any time to catch himself. The door- a massive slab of iron, steel and concrete swung closed with a bang. He could only watch with downing horror as the sound of heavy cranks sealed him shut inside the semi dark room.

Sorin groaned, his body failing him as he slowly collapsed to the floor. Under the light of the ceiling he started to crawl away, dragging himself to the opposite wall. The big indent above his head. He could feel the creeping fatigue, his eyes where refusing to stay open and he could barely feel his limbs. Arms and legs, all four, feeling absolutely numb. He looked down to his cyberdeck, the monitor was off. A monochrome screen with nothing displayed other than his dark reflection from the light of the ceiling.

His hoverboard protective gear was gone. The only thing on him seemed to be the clothes on his back, and the black durag still covering his hair. His brown long sleeve shirt was filthy and mildly scorched from that stun gun (That's what Sorin was currently classifying it as) and his cargo pants and shoes- also dirty and sand covered. He closed his eyes- he had to do something, there had to be something he could do... Sorin made an unsteady breath and scrunched his face in concentration. Pulling himself up, using the hard wall as leverage- it took a minute, but he got back on his shacky feet. Trembling, he made his way back to the door.

That's when he finally noticed the dent and scratch marks over the surface of it. Which made him even more terrified. How many more prisoners were thrown in here before him? There was a small opening on top, maybe he could see outside and get a feel of where he was at. He reached the door and peered outside- a long hallway stared back at him. A line of florescent lights reveled the way forward into what looked like a t-shaped hallway going left to right.

But to where? Sorin thought Wait a moment... is this a bunker? Oh no, I'm in a bunker!

This one thought, had a very scary implication, and Sorin was forced to take a steady breath. This was definitely a worst-case scenario. It meant one thing, that he was definitely far, far away from Gloomhaven. He took a step back, wishing desperately that he was just going through another vivid nightmare. That he was back at the Nocturne about to wake up for another crappy day at school. But his better judgement kept forcing him back to this bleak reality. He had been successfully kidnapped, and he had no clue of where he was and how far he could be from home. The numbness persisted but he was able to hold himself up. At least there was that, but... what should he do next? What was there to do next?

He shook his head slowly "This can't get any worse... there's no way after getting the coolest thing imaginable, that I end up... *here* of all places!" he mumbled to himself, completely at a loss.

Suddenly, a sound knocked him out of his growing panic. His miniature breakdown, halted by a sound which sent shivers up his spine, and caused him to face the source of the noise. A shape, there was a dark shape further in the darkness of the far wall. To his immediate right. Just out of reach from the light he stood over. In the corner of the room, and the shape was making a low, warning growl in his direction. He swallowed, the noise made his stomach drop, and caused his legs to tremble. What was it that they said earlier? That the nameless nomad had mentioned about this room. *'We throwing him in with the freak? If it's still pissed off, I hazard a guess it'll do worser to him than it did to Brick!'* Sorin focused on the figure, but the lack of illumination away from the dim light made it tough to pick out any more details. So far, all he could make out was that whatever was with him seemed to be wearing a hoodie. Maybe... sorta? The soft growling echoed around the room, giving Sorin a horrible sense of negative dissonance.

He gulped, why where they growling at him? *It sounds too much like an animal to belong to a man, but it's got to be a person, it has to be. Can they understand me?*

"H-hello." his voice echoed back, barely audible over the growls.

"Hey... Um, can you understand me... Do you know where we are?" he asked, not liking the lack of communication. Suddenly the growling stopped, Sorin nervously peered into the darkness, trying to make out any movement or even a nod. Nothing.

Sorin felt utter unnervement, every cell in his body telling him to just leave them alone. To just back away and stick close to the other side of the wall.

Anything, but, getting closer to the strange individual in the cover of darkness. But he needed answers, and was he terrified, yes. But what good would it be if he couldn't find out the motive. And maybe this person could shed some light on his situation (outside of getting abducted and stuffed into a dank prison cell).

With a quaking step, he moved closer, his footsteps echoing around the cell as the soft illumination from the bulb slowly slid over him, to finally resting on his back as he stepped into the darkness. The figure remained idle. He made another step closer, still idle... he was now standing as close as he dared. And... was that a dress! He could finally make out some of the clothing. *She...* was wearing what looked like a jacket slash hoodie, over a dress with tennis shoes. He couldn't exactly tell the color of the dress or the jacket from the lack of light but... that's all he could really make out, her face was hidden by the large hoodie, speaking of which, the jacket she wore was pretty big on her. Was it someone else's jacket? She sat in the corner in the position of a ball. Her hands hidden in her jacket pockets. So many questions, not enough answers. But... she looked to be his age. Hard to believe those growls originated from her.

He bit his lip, was she okay? He was too afraid to get closer, but, could he at least check to see if she was alright. Taking a shaky breath- he already knew what his answer was going to be.

"Hey... are you... alright?" he said nervously. The girl started to move. Sorin froze, like a deer caught in the headlights, he watched as her hoodie moved upwards. As if she just realized that someone was standing before her, Sorin gulped, now or never.

"Listen do you know where we are? I just got thrown here and I have no idea-"

Sorin jumped back. The girl, in a staggeringly fast motion- took her hands out of the jacket pockets, and in a blur of motion, faster than Sorin could keep up with- her hand slammed into the wall next to her.

He screamed, her hand sunk into the concrete wall like it was sinking through fragile glass. Causing an echoing crunch of hard rock as small shards of debris flew around her wrist. She hoisted herself up, growling so loud that it rumbled Sorin's insides; something, that by all rights, shouldn't be able to come out of a girls throat. He back peddled wildly, trying to get back, but she was already upon him. Her hand flashed forwards and he couldn't breath as he was hoisted up in the air. Before being thrown back bodily across the room- and landing back in the center- the light of the bulb shining over him like a poor spotlight. His head swam and whatever energy he had left, simply vanished. His surroundings began to get darker, his jaw began to flare up once again in pain, and he could only watch weekly as she stepped out of the darkness.

Her large jacket was red, in opposition of her dress which was dirty white, the hood was up enough to get a glimpse of bared fangs, while still hiding the top part of her face, her hands had claws at the end of her fingers. She continued to stalk closer, her growls rabid in intensity, and the last thing he saw before all went pitch black was of her crouching down, fist drawn, ready to punch a hole through his face. Before succumbing to darkness.

CHAPTER

17

Carver stood in a large chamber. a vault chamber to be more precise. Boxes of heavy looking equipment filled the room, with other strange and assorted items sitting around gathering dust. He sat down, a locket clasped in his hands and in front of him, the prototype. A smooth sphere like anomaly which floated inside of a chamber-esc containment unit. A vessel which contained, monitored, and controlled the metallic orb. Keeping it 'docile' as his contractor informed him.

The sphere - it had a will of its own. A fact that Carver has learned firsthand. In his later assignment of capturing the boy, he realized quickly that if it weren't for the contingencies in place, this thing would have taken him over. The powers of this artifact were substantial, yet, so steep in secrets that it gave him genuine excitement to peel back its layers, and sooner, would indeed be better than letting things take their current course. The orb had a peculiar reach, a reach that everyone- but the deviant in the cell- could feel. Almost like a dark spell.

Sometimes a pounding at the back of your head or even a tight probing which shuffled around and seemed to hang around like another tenant, forcibly taking living space where it didn't belong. His hands twitched, ever since their acquisition of it, from the hands of the circle and sector security, Carver had the strangest sense that it has been watching them since the very beginning. For now, until his contact arrives they would have no choice but to bear with it... he turned his head over his shoulders, footsteps were soundly shuffling from outside the vault.

He sneered to himself, he could only guess at what the sniveling excuse would be this time. He turned back to the Orb, its metallic sheen eerily reflecting the light of the vault. It's spherical shell, subtly moving and twisting on itself. Like a ball of liquid metal floating in the air, suspended by the strange powers that be. He glanced at it in reverence. Once he mastered this artefact, and its strange powers- the circle and specifically Hosea, would regret the day they crossed him, and his vengeance would be oh so sweet indeed.

Taking a moment he wrapped the chain of the locket around the safety railing of the orbs containment unit. Letting it hang there he moved towards the vaults sealed hatch, Its bulky frame, weighing over 42 metric tons of raw steel, and being 16 feet in height, was a formidable security measure guarding the orb. Yet for how thick it was... it couldn't do the job of shielding the nomads outside it from its invisible fingers.

The vault opened, the heavy cogs and pressurized hydraulics of the doors interiors- laboriously pulled the vault door open, and Carver moved out of the vault. Meeting the nomad in front of him with a level stare, he would need to prepare himself soon, their future operation would depend on it. Afterall, a supposed suicide mission required heavy contingencies.

??????????? / ?????????? / ??????????

Sorin was lost. His legs continued to take him further and further into the vast desert. A storm was raging around him, painting the sky and land around him in a dense bog of brown. The only thing he knew for certain was that he was lost and had no memory of even why he was there to begin with.

Was he dreaming? Or was this a form of limbo? The funnel of wind and sand continued to howl around him, yet, he marched on. Not particularly concerned, tired, or even all that hungry or needing his thirst quenched. No, he seemed to be searching for something, something important, but also not having the first or slightest clue of what he was searching for. He looked up, and the sky was in a blink perfectly clear, the storm halted, the winds died abruptly, and the sun suddenly and all to unnaturally began to fast forward down- below the horizon.

The stars were out, and the constellations now dotted the night sky. He looked down, and something moved in the corner of his eye. He looked around, still unnervingly calm, and spotted something in the distance. The glow of the moon in the night sky and the constellations gave him the illumination to spot a distant figure standing on top of a large sand dune.

His mouth moved, but no sound came from his lips. The figure pointed, he didn't know how he could tell, but he could. He was gesturing behind him, he turned around and a sign followed by what looked like a distant town or small settlement appeared further behind him.

The sign read *Silverwood*, a name that sounded strangely familiar. He looked up, and he knew that somehow, this was the right place to be. His feet crunched down on the sandy floor, and once again he found himself moving across the desert towards the town. A town with a familiar constellation hanging above it like a stellar beacon. A swirl pattern of stars, the usual guide of the lonesome wanderers of the wastelands.

??????????? / ??????????? / ???????????

His eyes slowly opened, and he winced. The effort of trying to move, instantly bringing with it a world of hurt.

Sorin's head was in a vice. His body a throbbing patch of work that pulsed with pain. A cogni-attack... his mind instantly recognized. His head was against the wall, now seemingly in a new position with a makeshift pillow of rags and cloth under his head.

Someone placed him on the matt near the wall, the sheets covering him where moth eaten, but better than nothing. He slipped the blanket off, and caught a glimpse of his hand. A mess of black veins. If he were back home right now, a quick view of his mirror would show the awful discoloration of his skin. A forking, branching line of black veins creepily spreading around from head to toe. He then groaned, realizing that he didn't have his meds on him. The pain was horrible, but thankfully it felt like a 3 out of 10. More than manageable enough. He tried to sit up, but the pain radiating off his body quickly forced him back down with a frustrated grunt. That's when it hit him, a probing like sensation that pierced his head and made him clench his teeth. The same feeling he had when entering this stupid bunker. He forced his nausea down and had a strange thought that he had forgotten something.

Suddenly, a noise caught his attention. A gasp, somewhere in the darkness. He could barely look up to see, but something was peering at him from the dark. He could feel it. He heard a shuffling of movement and the sound of slow footsteps approaching. Sorin suddenly grew tense, the last memory before he lost consciousness snapping back in full force. He tried to get up, tried to move, but it was hopeless. The pain, still a weight which held him in place and the throbbing ache of his head made things difficult to orient himself. The first thing he could see were her shoes, which were barely in the lights reach. A dark greyish color- and their owner was standing pensively in the dark, half out and half in, enough to see the red and dirty white, respectively of her jacket and dress which came down past her knees, while the jacket stopped at her hips. The red hood of the leather jacket hid the top part of her face, but that didn't matter much to Sorin who looked on anxiously. Wondering how he was still alive, his last memory of her drawing back a fist, ready to take him out. The scattered pieces and chunks of the wall where still littered around the floor on her side.

Sorin felt another flare of pain, a wave which momentarily made him forget the girl. As his limbs seized from the electric jolt of agony rippling through them. The girl made a sudden movement and Sorin in a moment of panic and vulnerability held up his arms in a defensive stance. Not to dissimilar to the one he would do when being ganged up upon by Chase's cronies.

"Wait!" the girls voice spoke up, "Please, I-I'm sorry... I thought you were one of them. I-I didn't mean to do that..." her voice, a shacky nervous ramble that Sorin could barely follow for how fast she spat it out. Her tone was different, a type of accent maybe? Not something the other kids at the school or undercity had.

"Are you okay? You don't look okay- I mean... obviously, um..." She shifted nervously and Sorin was immediately thrown off by the awkwardness. Now having a hard time comparing the growling noise and terrifying aggressiveness to the same person before him. He hesitantly let his arms down, glancing back towards her direction. She was now standing at the precipice of the lights reach, her once intimidating posture, now replaced with a timid reproach. Sorin looked at her, his headache still present and body still going through the painful episode. "I-I'm fine... who... who are you?" Sorin responded weakly. Struggling to pull himself up from the matt.

She slowly stepped out of the darkness. "Zorah... er, just, call me Zoe. Zoe Raynor.... what's your name?"

"Sorin... Sorin Richter." He answered. His back now positioned against the wall.

Finally in the light of the room, Sorin could feel her eyes looking him over. "Are you... sick?" She walked over and crouched next to him. Sorin looked at her confused, most kids his age tended to avoid him-when they spotted the dark veins appear during a flare up. "Yeah... have you never seen cognicrossis before?" Sorin asked, looking at her quizzically. She froze "Cognicrossis?.... you mean... that illness from the wastelands? That cognicrossis!"

Sorin frowned, not liking where this was going. He nodded in answer, before shuffling the blanket off himself. He pulled up his cyberdeck and pressed the switch on the monitor. The screen flashed on and to Sorin's annoyance the device was still highlighting his status in deep reds.

Zoe froze at the device on his arm "What's that?"

"My cyberdeck... I just wanna check something is all." Sorin mumbled as he checked his status page. The probing sensation in his head... was it just a headache from his current cogni attack? Or was it something more? He wondered if the deck could read it. It was after all linked to his biomoniter. Heck, maybe it could trace the cause of it too.

"Hey, can I ask you a question?" Sorin said glancing towards Zoe "This might sound weird... but, do you feel something... I don't know, groping around in your head by any chance?"

Zoe looked at him for a moment; silently, Sorin wondered if he may have weirded her out with the question. "Depends... what does it feel like?" Sorin after mentally breathing a sigh of relief, tried to describe the feeling as best he could. When he was done her lips formed a frown from under the hood. Sorin was about to ask when he noticed something, the end of her lips... what were those subtle lines tracing away from the ends of them?

"I don't think you're the only one who's going through that. It looks like everyone's complaining about that around here," She said "They use to have guards around the opening of the cell, and they wouldn't stop complaining about it. Something to do with a.... prototype... I think."

Sorin blinked, a prototype? "What happened to the guards?"

Her poster became rigid, as she averted her gaze for the moment. "Um..." she began sheepishly. Sorin gave her a quizzical look "Zoe?" he started. She gave a tired sigh "I... happened..." Sorin blinked "Wha-what did you do?" She groaned "Its... well, I sorta attacked them. I kinda flew off the handle when one of them, a nomad, threw one of those crappy ration bars at me." She glanced at the door "The jerk kept poking and prodding me...calling me things, terrible things, and I snapped after he came in and threw it at me." Sorin glanced at the door, eyes widening "Was that you? The claw marks and dents on the door, that was actually you!?" She crossed her arms, growling softly "How would you feel being called a freak of nature. Every. Single. Time, that jerk opened the door." Sorin blinked "Not to good myself... I guess." He said sheepishly.

"I ended up breaking his arm, I think... though, all I did was grab it." she added almost matter of factly. As she rubbed the back of her neck.

Sorin looked at her pointedly "You broke his arm... by just grabbing it? How strong are you?" he asked unnerved, remembering when she slammed her fist on the wall and left a small depression in it. She looked back at him, and shrugged, her lips pressed "I don't know... strong enough to almost make it out, I guess."

Sorin leaned in suddenly, causing her to jump back in surprise "You almost escaped!" he exclaimed "What stopped you from making it?"

She gave him a weird look "One of the nomads... he looked like a cyborg or something. I don't know what he was, but... he managed to overpower me and then he threw me back in here." She gestured to the wall above Sorin.

Sorin turned around, and he had to stop his jaw from limply hanging in shook. The massive depression on the wall behind him... Zoe created that! "H-he threw you that hard... how are you still..." He looked at her completely amazed.

She looked away from his stare. "Hey! It still hurt you know. Besides, it wasn't that long since it happened. Like... maybe a day or two ago." She clicked her tongue in annoyance "You saw the aftermath of it anyway... me, in that corner. Just trying to recuperate from that throw he did, and that's when you showed up." She turned back to him "Sorry... by the way." She said her voice becoming somewhat timid.

Sorin shook his head "No problem... you know, you're kinda cool! I wish I could do that type of stuff."

She froze "What?" she got out, as if she didn't hear him right.

Sorin nodded, bringing up his arm- which still had the black marks across it. "So, are you one of those deviants I saw on the television?" She gave a small growl at the question. Which, Sorin immediately held his hands up in alarm.

"Hey! Hey! I didn't mean anything by it... I'm just curious is all. I mean you hear about this things on tv, but hardly anyone wants to talk about it outside." He looked at her beaming.

"Like, how does it work? Being that strong and all- and without any augments too." Sorin was slowly becoming more excited, even though Mr. Owen's had given him a new perspective on being born with powers or not. It didn't mean the topic no longer interested him.

She was silent for a moment "Your... you're not joking. You really think I'm... cool?" Sorin nodded "Yeah, that is what I just said."

She shook her head "Believe me, it's anything but cool. Heck, look what I almost did to you... h-how are you not even scared."

Sorin paused, his expression becoming ponderous. "Well yeah, I was definitely, positively, scared at first- I mean, when you threw me like that. It was definitely scary. But..." he held up the blanket and glanced at the makeshift pillow "I mean... this didn't just spring on me while I was knocked out. If you wanted me dead, I simply would have been dead. No too ways about it." he shrugged "That... and you don't really come across as a bad person. So, yeah."

Zoe stood stalk still as he listened to his reasoning. Glancing at him mysteriously under her hood. Sorin looked at her and wondered if she was okay. Suddenly, she shook her head in what looked like mild disbelief. "You're really, really, weird... you know that."

Sorin shrugged once again "Eh, I had worse."

The two were silent for a moment before they both started laughing. After which, Zoe could be found sitting against the wall. Next to Sorin.

"But seriously, why a deviant? I mean, you've seen how it is on the news. Where just freaks, at least, that's what everyone else sees us as." Zoe asked sounding frustrated.

Sorin brought up his arm, which still had the black marks upon it. A constant, painful, reminder of his terminal illness. He did research on it during those months when he was fixing the hoverboard and found something amazing. Apparently Deviants were incapable of getting cognicrossis. Although it was mostly rumors and hear say. He couldn't stop himself thinking how lucky it would have been if he were born as a deviant.

He shrugged letting his arm down "Just beats what I currently have you know. But, I gotta ask... where are you from?" she looked at him "What do you mean?"

"You don't sound like you're from here," Sorin said "Your accent... yeah, it sounds different."

"Ok, what do you mean by here? Do you know where I even am? The guards don't exactly care to tell me anything. No matter how much I yell at them... or beat em." Zoe said, growling the last part.

"Well since where inside a bunker, I kinda figured where somewhere in the wastelands. You know the conclave regions?" He said, trying to find any type of familiarity in her posture. That's when Sorin realized he must have said something wrong, Zoe seemed to freeze when he mentioned the wastelands.

She looked down after a moment, slowly shaking her head in what looked like disbelief "No way... there's no way I'm that far from... I mean, how would they even manage to..."

Sorin carefully observed her, growing very concerned for how she was acting. She was now leaning against the wall, trembling as she held herself in a ball. He leaned in, touching her shoulder "Zoe?" Sorin said.

"Sorin, I'm from Rosaria," She turned to him "From Sector 9, district 4." Sorin's eyes widened "You're from the Republic." He said silently. She nodded slowly. Sorin grimaced, he may have been potentially hundreds of miles from his home. But Zoe... judging by wherever this Rosaria was, she was likely thousands and thousands of leagues from hers.

CHAPTER

18

??????????? / ??????????? / ???????????

Sorin looked up at the craggily ceiling, from his position on the matt. It was presumably night and Zoe was asleep, retreating to her corner of the room with Sorin also moving somewhat into the darkness of the large cell. He couldn't find the means to sleep, and strangely he was fine with it. Looking at his cyberdeck, the time and date where still not showing on the top right of the monitor. And the scan of his biomoniter was inconclusive.

He shook his head in disappointment, a part of him- actually wished there was something the deck could do to point out what was wrong with him. Even before the mention of this so-called prototype, and the effects it was having on him and the guards. It didn't explain his dreams or nightmares he was having before the abduction. He was more than willing to believe that it was just his new prescription of medicine, but now, he had other ideas. The dream he experienced, came to mind at that moment. It was an odd one to say the least. He could remember it now in vivid detail. Like a faded memory reappearing from nowhere, only it wasn't a memory... as far as Sorin could tell. The faraway town in the distance for instance, felt eerily familiar, but he couldn't put his finger on it. He shivered, the lone figure in the distance. That was the third instance of seeing him. At first he was sure it was just the nomad who knocked him out with that weird stun gun. But no, he was strangely unsure. Not just unsure- he felt it wasn't the same person at all. Once on top of a building standing on the edge, peering at him mysteriously. The second time on top of a sand dune as he was riding his hoverboard. And the third time... In his dream, pointing mysteriously at a town he was, maybe, sure he's never been too. He folded his arms, shivering under the covers, and all the times he's seen him he developed a headache soon after. Strange, considering the sensation was too similar to the subtle probing in his head.

But the same nomad appeared in my nightmare, at the nocturne, the same one who murdered Orson... how do I even explain that? Crap, what the heck was going on?

Sorin closed his eyes, things were getting stranger and stranger, and that's before his kidnapping ever took place. A memory drifted to the surface, and with that he felt as if a bucket of cold water had been dumped on him. The kidnapping, and worst of all *Mr. Owens! oh my god, he can't be dead, he just can't!* Try as he might, the moment of the gunshot, and Owens getting taken off his feet- like a marionette who's wires had been severed- was now making its brutal rounds inside his head. On top of everything that was happening to him, this one single nightmarish scene kept playing on repeat. He sneered, whoever that guy was that shot him... he'd get his. Sorin was counting on it.

The probing sensation was now a dull flutter at the back of his head. As he fell asleep, anger shifted to unease. He wondered if Hosea, Bella, and the rest would be able to locate him. Did Zoe have someone searching for her whereabouts too? He sighed, something to ask her when they both woke up.

?????????? / ?????????? / ??????????

The level of contempt that resided within Carver was slowly rising in its potency. This damnable orb continued to float there in its chamber. Its metallic sheen reflecting his snarl back at him, as if, it were silently mocking the ex-nomad. It has been nearly half a month since the operation to spirit away the girl, and now this boy- His relation to Hosea notwithstanding- was important to the operation.

Apparently, his employer deemed him a top priority. Not only in relation of forcing Hosea and his company to back off (The team sent to retrieve the other artifact from site-20, made off without a hitch, with nary a casualty.) But... for another purpose, that involved the artifact.

For what purpose- he couldn't understand. Yet, the moment this child entered his line of sight at the park. His half of the artifact and the half currently bounded with Moris- began to act up, far more than usual. Even the mode of transport back to base was beyond what he had expected. Their employer was hiding more than what he was letting on, and the boy was also a factor in his suspicions.

There was more to this child than meets the eye. But for now, he had to wait... if he were to rush it now, he could lose everything. And this growing corruption within his body- which was steadily marching on, slowly and methodically. Time was of the essence, and later today he would have his answers. Carver in alarm suddenly moved from his seat- something in the corner of his eyes moved. He looked around, as the chair fell over from his quick movement with a low thud on the hard floor. An unease began to settle on the veteran nomad, a shape was standing in the corner of the room- he was sure of it. Was it his imagination? He narrowed his eyes at the orb. This thing was slowly getting to him.

He shook his head, moving to stand the chair back up. It was time to leave, he needed to talk with Trace- his resident runner for the bunker. Moris had suddenly come down with a sickness, and the fool has of yet to return his half of the original artifact. He shook his head, as he made for the exit for the vault.

Yes, soon he would have his answers.

??????????? / ??????????? / ???????????

Sorin trembled in bed, his heartbeat was currently drumming inside his ears. Something was wrong, and it wasn't the probing sensation at the back of his head, he sat up and looked around. The cell was quite, and Zoe was still crouched in the dark, a soft snoring sound gently wafting from the shaded corner.

His eyes adjusted to the dark, squinting, scanning around the cell- movement in the corner of his eye- to his immediate left. Sorin made a sudden involuntary intake of breath, there was something behind the cell door- looking straight at him, in his position just out of the illumination of the overhead ceiling light. The back of his cranium was a sudden jolt of activity- he felt a pressure behind his head that he couldn't begin to put into words, his eyes closed, and a feeling of un-equilibrium fell over him. Like he was sinking into a pit of quicksand. He looked towards the cell door, and the pressure was gone, and the figure was gone, its dark faceless silhouette no longer blocking the now empty hallway.

That couldn't have been the nomad that kidnapped him. This thought was like a stranger in and of itself to him. As spontaneous as the figures rapid appearances. Sorin was now wide awake, and breathing fast, his eyes wide. That was probably the closest he's seen the figure. It was getting closer to him...

The rising, trickling, pool of dread was slowly streaming past the mental barrier of control he had enacted for himself. Whatever was happening, he felt to his growing disturbance that there wouldn't be anywhere to hide from this inevitable encounter.

??????????? / ??????????? / ???????????

Moris was dead.

When Carver reached the med bay, he was suddenly overcome with a massive wave of nausea, and Morris, on that bunk bed- began to convulse and scream like a mad man.

His body contorting upon itself, all the while, as the other men struggled to latch him back to the bed. The green gem attached to the silver mask on his face, pulsed with an emerald glow. The ugly dark marks on his open chest was festering all across his body. Most of the marks seemed to coalesce around his earlier bullet wounds from the guard who shot him. Carver forced himself forward, as Moris screamed and choked on his words in a crazed ramble. Carver wouldn't at all be surprised if he accidentally bit off his tongue.

"LEAVE ME ALONE!" he would bellow in a frenzy "CAN'T YOU SEE IT! IT'S REACHING FOR ME! GET IT AWAY! GET IT AWAY!" Carver grabbed the crazed man, bringing him up to his face by the robe of his neck "Look at me you fool! Focus- there's nothing there!" he commanded, no- insisted.

Moris's eyes slowly began to roll back into their sockets. The dark veins under his skin grew more opaque, rapidly spreading before their eyes, trailing down below his stomach as Carver released his robe in disgust. The man fell down on the bed, still squirming in silent panic, his body suddenly seized, his once flailing limbs now stiffening in place, as his skin became paler and paler. Then abruptly... his body relaxed, his arms falling to the bed limply as one final breath was exhaled from his now dead body.

The vault entrance slid back close. Carver exhaled a disturbed breath, shaken, but not keen on admitting his unease to any of the men and women under his command. The orb was in the center of the vault- its metallic sheen reflecting his stubborn glare. He walked towards the chamber, his discomfort- screaming at him to back away from this accursed machine. No... After everything he's seen, he couldn't just see it as a new piece of shiny hardware any longer. There was something, deeply, unnatural about this thing. But what choice did he have. It was ether the artifact... or... eventual death at the hands of cognicrossis. He stepped to the containment unit, and after typing the pass codes into the console, the id socket unfurled. He pulled down the sleeve of his desert robe and activated his neural link. The screen lit up with activity, as it scanned his credentials and with a loud series of beeps, the console accepted his code.

The containment unit hissed as the cylinder chamber opened. For a moment, a piercing chill seemed to settle over him. Like an invisible gale of the coldest wind he had ever had the displeasure of experiencing.

This... is worser than the first time I've opened it. Almost like its laughing at me. Carver thought with a scowl.

He took a moment to breath, then with every scrape of willpower he could muster- he forced his arm forward. Holding a curious object in his hand. A metallic mask, the one that Moris once had, towards the floating ball of liquid metal. And with a sudden jerk of movement, Carver was ready. The ball seemed to move, stretching towards the mask. A long silvery tendril of god knows what came forward. Carver's skin prickled, the mask began to move and stretch- Carver unhanded it before his piece of the artifact felt inclined to abandon him. The green gem on the mask glowed a brilliant emerald as something within the orb pulsed with deep, deep indigo. Before the mask disappeared, melting back into the main body of the artifact. Carver hurriedly accessed the console, and reactivated the containment unit. The lid closed, and the unearthly cold disappeared along with it. Carver backed up, teeth clenched, the probing has started again- worse than the last time and far more viciously.

He moved to his chair, and after closing his eyes, allowed the sensation to tick away at the back of his head, as he slowly got accustomed to it again.

??????????? / ??????????? / ???????????

Sorin gnashed his teeth, just when he thought he had gotten accustomed to the pain- It decided to get worse!

He stood against the wall, checking his status on the cyberdecks monitor. The device still couldn't pinpoint the cause of the pain. But... his cogni attack had finally ceased and he could reliably stand on his two feet again. There was a small yawn further in the darkness and footsteps as Zoe's form walked to the light of the room.

Sorin paused, her hood... it was drawn up- Zoe had unknowingly let her hood slip up. His eyes widened at her appearance: She had long blonde hair ending bellow her collar bone and back, enough to make him wonder how she managed to keep it all behind her. The hair in front didn't hide her actual face- and from Sorin's position in the light, she looked almost... like any other girl his age. Her eyes and mouth were the things that made her seem... almost alien. Her two eyes where compound in appearance- the type of compound that eerily reminded him of the Cazadors back at the dump in Gloomhaven. But her's where strangely beautiful, forest green's that where traced in a hexagonal pattern- made visible by the lights refracting from her eye's. Her mouth had subtle black lines tracing from the ends of them. Making him wonder if it was some sort of strange makeup or something more. Her fair skin had an almost 'hardened' quality to it, like a partial exoskeleton. But from far away, it was easy to miss. Unlike now, where she was arm's length away from him.

"Sorin... wha- what is it?" She asked confused, still seemingly disoriented from coming out of sleep.

"Um," Sorin began, forgetting the drumming in his head for the moment "Nothing to be worried about." He said trying to be as casual as possible.

She yawned, scratching her head, only to freeze. Her eyes widening, her clawed hands reaching up to her uncovered head as she searched for her missing hood. Sorin lips were in the motion of forming a sentence, maybe something reassuring, when he froze. Suddenly caught off guard by the look of sheer mortification on the deviants face. He winced, when a sharp, and horrified squeal resonated from her as she turned around and sunk rapidly into the veiling reach of her dark corner. He stood there, not able to ignore the dawning shroud of awkwardness that fell over him. He heard the hasty flip of her jacket hood and knew it was back over her face.

"Zoe?" Sorin began "Uh... you good?"

He heard a gibberish collection of words as her response. Sorin blinked, open mouthed in confusion.

"Zoe... It- It's okay, why are you freaking out!" Sorin asked, flabbergasted by the girls sudden distress. "What's the matter?" he said about to walk in the dark to maybe attempt some sort of reassurance... when.

"What's the matter? What's the matter!" Zoe's voice called out from the dark "You saw what I look like... I'm a freak!" she cried out mortified, absolute self-loathing coloring the edges of her voice.

Sorin paused, looking confused, but he shook his head, before shrugging- he proceeded to move out of the light from the center of the room and moved forward into the darkness. It was getting easier to see her anyway. He carefully made his way to her- using the wall to his left to feel where he was going. Spotting her position at the corner, crouched down against the wall, head down- her hands seemingly covering her face. Sorin sat down next to her. He poked her shoulder, making her jump.

"Zoe," Sorin said "Listen, I don't think it looks that bad." Zoe was now looking at him. That much he could tell "Yeah, it's different but...

I don't really think you're a freak." Sorin said shrugging, even though she probably couldn't see him.

"What." Zoe uttered back silently.

"I'm just saying... Look, you go to school right? I mean before the whole kidnapping thing right?" Sorin asked. He could see her silhouette nod back.

"Okay listen, a lot of the other kids at my school- use to talk about people getting surgical augments- augments that alter appearances and what not. And Church, my uh... my uncle... used to have a medical practice before switching to a courier service. And he would tell me stories of people who had jaws removed, eyes switched out for fancy eye prosthetics that... kinda looked like animal eyes and so forth." Sorin shook his head chuckling "He told me that a lot of them needed them to be removed or switched out. Either because, they weren't put in right. Or because they were not compatible. Sometimes, I would walk into his office while he was with a customer, and they would look so messed up and off..." he carefully grabbed her shoulder "Believe me, you don't look that bad. Heck it kinda looks cool."

"You... you really mean that?" she said, still sounding somewhat doubtful.

"Yeah, sides you get the awesome super strength to go along with it." Sorin replied back with a grin. "And two... well, it can't be all bad. I mean if you were normal I'm pretty sure we wouldn't be talking now," he gestured to the depression of the wall behind him "If you know what I mean."

She snorted "I guess." She turned to him "You're uncle... he's not a doctor anymore... why not?"

Sorin grimaced, the main reason for Church having to close his budding medical practice was because of a larger firm by the name of Zeta-Dynamics. They used their influence too sabotage Church, which after a few months, Church decided to abandon the practice- in favor of a courier service. Sorin looked down.

"Gloomhaven and their stupid regulations." He replied "You can't go a couple of feet without stepping on red tape. Worse, it's harder if you're not with a company or with a family that has good enough standing with the settlement heads. But... it's okay, he's got the courier job going... and Aunt Dot, she's got the bar.

So, it's good enough." He sighed.

"Wait, a bar. You're aunt works at a bar?" Zoe said curiously "She owns it." Sorin corrected "Though it's not the biggest... but, it's still home." At that she completely turned around. "You live in a bar!" she exclaimed. Sorin raised his eyebrow "Yes," he said dubiously "There something wrong with that?"

"No, it's just... I mean, when you said you lived out there in the wastelands. I kinda, well... never mind." She said lamely.

"What? That we lived in the desert? No way, not in the open desert at least. I live in a settlement." Sorin said

"Gloomhaven, right?" Zoe asked, Sorin nodded "Yeah, has a population of 10,000... I think."

"Oh... wow. And how do you know that?" Sorin smiled "It's a settlement, they always boast about their numbers down here... makes it easier to attract sponsors and corp shareholders. At least, that's what Aunt Dot tells me." He shrugged. "Oh, and the undercity."

"Undercity? What's an undercity?" Zoe spoke, completely lost again.

Sorin sighed before explaining what the undercity was. And from there, the two started to talk, informing and describing what their two hometowns were like. Sorin about Gloomhaven, and Zoe about Rosaria, back and forth. For most of the day they talked about home and what life was like in their respective locations. From the deserts of the wastelands, to the forests and rivers surrounding Rosaria. For the time being this was the only thing they could do, in their present situation talking was the only way for either of them to forget... a way to make time go by, or even a way to keep the fear of what may happen to ether of them at bay.

Neither of them doubted the fact that a rescue... would be their only way out of this place...

CHAPTER

19

??????????? / ??????????? / ???????????

Carver could barely keep his eyes open. The artifact was still acting up, he realized that the infernal thing was up to something, what that something was he couldn't begin to understand, let alone comprehend.

Whatever systems were linked up to the vault and the containment unit inside was disconnected. After Moris's death, he refused to give this thing any more leeway. He assigned Trace too monitor it from the bunkers data center, now that the second piece of the artifact was back in place, he dared not chance this thing getting into the bunkers mainframe- after the wonders that Moris pulled off with Gloomhaven's maintenance and security systems. He realized this thing was not to be underestimated. He still had his piece of the artifact, but he kept it away from the vault. He know sat in his room, pouring over the report that was given from Moris's autopsy.

The two kids were given their daily rations for the day, and he was slightly surprised to see the boy had managed to get on the girls good side. But for how long? He shook his head, their contact should have been here by now. But the constant supercells close to their location was mucking up their schedule. He chuckled to himself again as he thought about an old saying his father once told him when he was the brats age. *Something's going down beyond the expanse tike, better pray the dark wanderer doesn't come a knocking!* He snorted once again, oh how gullible he was at that age. The supercells originated from the expanse, and being caught outside a settlement during one is considered a death sentence, plain and simple death. Which- is where the void mass reactors came in. The reactors generated a field which nulled the storms effects, but outside the range of a null wave- you either get to cover, or you hide out in a bunker.

Carver snorted, even with the protection of the reactors shield, it still wasn't a full proof solution. Yes, settlements had the benefit of the barrier. Yet it didn't stop the dangerous wind speeds or the threat of being pelted by the debris- kicked up by the storm. Carver couldn't count the amount of times his crew had stumbled on a poor fool caught during one. The remains either being charred from the intense lightning strikes or reduced to pulp from the force of the winds and pieces of debris swept up from the sand charged gales.

Were there other ways to travel during a storm. Yes... Were they horribly expensive and rare to come by. Also yes, there was of course the option of armored looking glass shards, which could be attached to vehicles in place of windows and the usual customed armored tire jobs. But, the expense alone would be ludicrous. Factor in the wind speeds and the unpredictability of the supercells. Bunkers and Settlement shelters were the best options every time.

Unless you were a bandit, then you used other unsavory methods. *Methods that the circle no longer allowed us to use.* Carver thought ruefully.

The bunker they were in was made to be a shelter, with the tools and room needed for a small band of nomads to rest and recuperate. His gang was only 19-23 strong, with one down due to Moris's untimely death. It was moments like these, that made the mortuary rooms a god send for them. Rooms that were supplied with coffins and sealed containment chambers.

Moris's cadaver was in one such containment chamber. He tucked the info inside of his robe- the body was practically bone dry of any styx contamination when the piece was pried from his face. Yet, the brain was still showing a little bit of activity after the mask was off, which was eerie, considering the heart was no longer beating. *At least the body didn't have a bad reaction to the artifact. With what happened with Orson, it probably would have been a disaster, the artifacts have been acting far too strange as of late.* The throbbing from the vault had finally quieted down, it was still there- just not as severe as it once was. But Carver was still unsure of how long that would last.

??????????? / ??????????? / ???????????

Trace stirred in his reverie, the runner carefully adjusted himself within the confines of his operators chair. A large dentist chair looking contraption that was connected to the data centers main console and surrounded by server towers, his room was stuffed to the brim with tables and tables of old hardware and busted scrape. The brats hoverboard and backpack was sitting patiently on one of his tables. Spare parts and hardware he could put to better use than a piece of crap board.

The small hallway leading into the semi-dark room was awash with the glow of the servers and the chairs led lights. The monitors surrounding the chair glowing a soft white light. But looking around the room, you'd be remised if you considered his small slice of heaven as anything but a comfort to him. A runner surrounded by his tech and electronics was considered a perfectly normal and everyday occurrence. And yet... something wasn't right.

Trace breathed a calming breath- attempting to get the disorientation to settle. After all, he disconnected from the interface in a hurry. For he felt a creepy sense that he was not alone in the room. He sat up, gun in hand, as his cybernetic eyes scanned the room- the security cameras fixed outside and inside scanning along with him- by his mental command.

Nothing... Nothing, and still nothing.

He called the video recording of the rooms security footage in his main interface. Separate from the operating chairs, and still nothing, not a shadow, not a peep. He checked the main entrance leading inside this very room, the magnetic locks were still operational, and hydraulic motor still sealed. Nothing in the log of the door opening for the past two hours.

He winced, the cable connected to him painfully pulled at the back of his head, he had leaned a little too hard there. *By the expanse, get a grip. Last thing we need is this getting uncoupled.* He relaxed, carefully adjusting the other cables connecting to various ports throughout his body. The plug suit he wore was doing its best to cool him down, yet the cybernetics running across his body- connected to the chair- were heating up. Each nod around his arms and legs allowed him to better integrate with the bunkers systems. But the effects of limited cyberspace was already wearing on him.

And that wasn't normal.

He's had sessions of being under for hours and hours at a time. Yet, ever since they brought that damn artifact to base something has been nagging at the back of his head. He shook his head, he needed to prepare himself to lay back down. The large massage like chair, was specifically made for the allowance of emergency disconnects- but the process was still horribly disorienting and nausea inducing.

The bunkers systems have been spliced off from the vault room... But, the left-over nodes I installed are still picking up activity from that creepy ass ball of metallic sludge.

The nodes he left behind were harmless, none of them connecting to any other system of the bunker, and the hidden cameras inside of the vault still weren't picking up anything. So why the hell was he so worried. *Oh please... you know why.* Trace thought to himself sleeking back his greasy hair *That artifact... that thing is wrong. Hell, it's even got the boss unnerved... though, I'd never admit it to his face.* It seemed the only thing that wasn't affected by that thing, was the freak down in level 3.

The fact that it was the officials daughter had him and the others laughing.

No wonder they kept her in that mansion. Little freak of nature is liable to rip your face off, than to allow you give it any orders. Small wounders Carver and his crew were able to knock her out while she was unaware.

It was time to go back under. He put the gun back down in his holster and laid back down, the leather-bound upholstery depressed back as the cable connected to his head sunk back into the chair. Closing his eyes- the room felt like it was sinking, before long he opened his eyes and cyberspace greeted him back. Well... calling it cyberspace was a bit much. His digital avatar looked around, networks of digital trails running in series of complex paths from branch to branch.

And each branch a cluster of systems and subsystems, with the leaves being the end points of those systems. Be it a camera, a door, a security system, lights, etc.

It wasn't cyberspace in its entirety. But, it was the main nexus center of the entire bunker. Which he carefully toggled off and separated the main line trailing back to the other bunkers on the grid. It was fairly difficult, but not impossible. No one needed to know where they were currently located at.

He brought up the holographic menu, and commanded the other 'branches' to form up around him. The trunks formed up, each branch and twig of the complex nexus- furled around him like a massive sphere with him in its center. Bringing up a hand he silently ordered one of the branches to unfurl towards him. Its tip dropped down, and with a snap of his finger, the twig stretched- its form reshaping itself digitally into a projection- a camera feed which showed the inside of a cell in level three.

Trace watched lazily, as the screen showed the two kids who seemed to be talking. Sliding it back in place, and letting the digital screen dissolve in a cluster of light, he glanced around the grid- nothing out of the ordinary. He unfurled the other branches, each one showing a status page and video of the room or system that was connected to it. Still nothing. Sept for the activity alert from the vault. He grimaced, before lazily scanning around the other systems. The biomoniter status page was also good to go- with one less reading (Moris) on the list. As far as he could tell, everyone's readings were in the green. Well... all except for the boss and the boy that he threw in the cell. Both of them were all over the place. And the other one- the deviant- well, her kind weren't compatible with cybernetics. As far as he heard at least. For now he wasn't worried all that much about her. If she was resilient enough to get punted all the way, and halfway- through a wall, by Bastien no less- than she was probably fine.

But he still couldn't shake the feeling that something wasn't right. Like an incessant tick at the back of his head that wouldn't go away. And the constant, but subtle, prodding at the back of his skull wouldn't let up.

Everyone could feel it- even Bastien - the guy had gone through partial cyborgification, and he still wasn't spared the constant mental probing. God knows, if they didn't need this job, this one last job, they would all have said to hell with it. But the circle, and the conclaves. Would sooner see them dead than free of their sphere of influence. Trace sneered, as Carver would say 'It's not are faults that the circle have become soft over the years, with that joke of an old nomad in charge- people like Hosea have slowly risen in the ranks, and screwed everything up.' Trace narrowed his eyes, peering through the 'branches' and 'leaves' observing every connection in and out of the bunker.

The foundations of the bunker were as far as he could see secure. And for now all he could do was keep the watch ongoing. It wouldn't be for another two and a half hours until something broke his concentration yet again.

Suddenly an alert, Trace's avatar froze, and his physical body twitched. The vault was showing a massive disturbance, a hidden camera... it was picking up something in the vault- he couldn't read the signature- was that an intruder! He pulled the branch towards him as a digital screen made of light manifested around it. The light transformed into a hologram of the cameras feed. His physical body's heart skipped a beat, and his digital avatar observed, transfixed.

There was a dark figure, who stood before the now open containment unit. His large robes were tattered, shredded, and well worn. Yet even though the strangers back was turned to the camera, he could tell that the mysterious intruder was rather lithe in build. How the hell had he gotten in there? There was no possible way he could have gotten inside- the vault door was keyed to Carver's signature, and the alarms would have alerted him way before he even managed to open the damned thing!

He pulled up Carver on the holocall, as he pulled the other source of the alarm. The mortuary room?

He pulled up the feed.

Nothing but static. All the cameras near and around the entrance and main hallway were down.

"What is it." Carvers gravelly voice called.

"Got two wings on alert," Trace answered back quickly "The vault room and the mortuary room. Carver- there's an intruder in the vault room! And all cameras in and near the mortuary are not responding!"

Carver was silent for a moment "I'll gather the men for the vault, I need you to send another team for the morgue, on the double!"

"Already on it!" Trace answered.

He paged the nearest nomads close to the mortuary chamber. A holographic map digitized itself in front of his face; the maze-like diagram of the 2nd level floor of the bunker, projected the mortuary in a bright light as the closest nomads near the room answered his hails. Three men, and two women- there biomoniter tags appearing before him. All five where now in route to the chamber in the south wing of the bunker, while Carvers marker within the map was heading towards the west end of the bunker, towards the vault room.

Just what the hell have we gotten ourselves into now?

??????????? / ??????????? / ???????????

Carver felt years of combat experience settle over him like a well-worn glove. The deep rage and inky throes of malevolence was barely tempered by the razors edge of adrenaline.

The footsteps of his fellow nomads and his very own, stomped down the halls leading towards the vault. His heavy rifle poised in front of him, he wondered to himself, as he made that final turn, leading towards the heavy vault door. The client, their plans, the boy, and this sudden knowledge that all wasn't what it seemed. It was all building to this... he could feel it. Whatever was happening now the artifact was at the center of it all and his life would be absolutely forfeit without the artifact, and the boon it gave for his symptoms. This was a move of desperation on his part, the only move he had left- and the only path in his plan to maybe recapture his glory as the best of the best. So what choice did he have to follow this path. The artifacts he was gathering would lead him to a prize greater than what the circle sought in cooperation with the various corporations infesting their once glorious wastelands. Those under him chose this freely along with him, and death was always mutually assured. But he would be damned if he would let this chance of retribution fall through his fingers, like the sands which blew freely in the winds of the wastelands. The blood of his clan would be paid in full.

The others formed up behind him, a few meters back- with guns trained on the vault door. Carver moved to the console, and stuck his arm into the id scanner. A medium sized compartment with a scanner at the end for his open palm, the vault hissed, and the cranks unfurled themselves from their magnetic locks.

Carver backed up, cocking his gun, and readied himself. The vault swung from its sealed position. Its cogs roaring laboriously as the hydraulics opened the massive gear-shaped door from its sealed hatch and Carver's eyes widened, a heavy mist fell out of the cracks, the hatch continued to turn, and more and more heavy fog poured out, Carver held his gun with a harder grip as a thick cloud of dark grey mist seeped from the unsealed chamber vault. Everyone behind him began to move with unease. Guns trained and slightly shacking from anxiousness. The obscured chamber in front of them was silent, not even a sign of movement wafting inside the room.

"Trace! What's going on in there! Do you have any visual past the fog?" Carver demanded over the holonet. Suddenly he gave a pained grunt, as his coms began to experience major signal interference. His onboard interface immediately alerted him of something hijacking communications.

Carver immediately growled, something in the vault- maybe the intruder, or the artifact itself- was the source of the interference. He cocked his gun and gave the signal for a recon scanner. If there operator was being cut off, then they would need to use caution. A moment later, a nomad- Varrik- aimed, and tossed a small round looking metal device through the dense fog. A second later, there was a metallic thud and the scanner went live. Carver put his fingers to his temple, as a soft electronic noise filtered out of the chamber. He switched on his interface, the scanner inside the chamber was rendering a 3d model of the room. But from the scan, no biological readings were currently inside, no sign of traps, or any other weird signs of an ambush. He narrowed his eyes, either the intruder was somehow shielding his signature or something far more bizarre was at foot.

He held up a hand, and closed it into a fist. *Fine... hide, scurry in the fog like a coward. Let's see how far that gets you.* The four nomads at his side filed into the fog on either side, hugging each side of the wall and not moving through the center and Carver followed suit- his robes bellowing behind him- as he was enveloped by the thick shroud of fog.

Trace's avatar froze in horror, the men and women that disappeared down in west wing... their biomoniters... most have gone dark. With Bastien- their resident heavy wreaker- being the only one who's biomoniter was still partially active. But it was wild and heavily sporadic. He was doing everything in his power to get communications up again with Carver, but the moment he opened that vault everything on the west end went dark. He looked around frantically, all feeds for both ends of the bunker where down. And any nomad around the two sides were cut off, someone had done the impossible and snaked their way into his subsystems without his knowing. And the main systems before his eyes were being hijacked as he rushed to cut the enemy hacker off.

Suddenly, Trace paused, his thoughts which were running ragged in an attempt to fix this was suddenly and abruptly halted.

The once golden branches of his nexus were turning the shade of diluted tar, as the physical representation of his view of the nexus was being thoroughly and ruthlessly corrupted out of his control.

Yet, this wasn't the thing that got his notice. For he was once again under the horrible impression, that... someone... or something, was inside the data center, near his body. Trace's eyes widened, as the central nexus of his cyberspace was suddenly plunged into a veil of darkness.

He felt his world suddenly shift and contract. His consciousness crashing back into the land of the real, and with a horrible bout of nausea and the feeling of his head being split open, he was greeted by a familiar figure in tattered robes. Who's face- shielded by the semi-darkness of the room- was barely distinguishable.

The only thing that Trace could see in his growing terror, as he laid their bound by the numerous cables of his operating chair, was that of the dark strangers glowing red eyes. Which peered down at him, no more similar to the hallucination of a paralysis demon. That one would be unfortunate enough to encounter during the aftermath of a vivid nightmare.

CHAPTER

20

??????????? / ??????????? / ???????????

Zoe was walking around in circles, her every instinct was on red alert, maybe for the first time in weeks she could fathom the past guards irritation. She paced around the cell. Wondering what on earth was happening outside.

Sorin was asleep again, his face grimacing under the moth-eaten covers, as the black veins creeped under his eyes and face. The sight of which never failed to disturb her, how could somebody bare such pain? It once again made her think how unfair it all was... Of all the powers she could have gotten in the lottery, she instead got this freak form... instead of something more useful, the ability to heal maybe. She shook her head, looking upon Sorin in the light against the wall. A deep remorse bubbled within the surface.

The boy wasn't at all what she had considered people from the wastelands to be like. Then again, after her capture from her home. She was dead set in the belief- like the other kids at her school, before she started home schooling- that most of them were probably thuggish. Of course, Sorin did look kinda impish... But more dorkish than anything else.... in a good way of course. Yet, in light of all this... he looked at her and didn't once think of her a freak. If that wasn't just the oddest thing to encounter, and right after having to put up with the horrible way she had been treated for the past week. Barely any food or water, the constant jeers and looks from the nomads passing her daily rations. Only for them to throw someone else in a cell with her. Knowing she might lose it on sight, just as she did with the other nomad days ago.

She paused in her pacing. Another sharp sensation of anxiousness hitting her. Her lips curled inward, an instinctual growl slowly escaping her lips. The room subtly shook under her feet, upstairs- the vibrations as far as she could tell were coming upstairs. Something bad was happening outside, that much she could sense. She clenched her fist and closed her eyes, forcing the primal buzzing back where it belonged, she couldn't afford to lose control now.

Not with Sorin close by like this.

Her compound eyes glaring towards the door, as a small snarl of frustration came from her. She'd find a way out of this... sooner or later, and she'd make them pay for this. Her hands twitched at the idea of beating the crap out of them, and maybe she would be able to take back what they stole from her as well.

??????????? / ??????????? / ???????????

There where shouts and sounds of gunfire rolling from the dark hallways of the morgue. An explosion or two from inside the chamber, the glimpse of a dark figure getting thrown bodily outside through the hall and impacting against the concreate wall on the opposite end, leaving a sizable depression on the surface.

Outside... further away from the morgue, jumbled scenes of carnage, gunfire, explosions, and images of random bodies getting dropped to the floor. Blood and chaos seemed to rule other parts of the bunker.

The scene shifted, he was witnessing something from inside a heavily fogged chamber. The mist obscured all, and the four figures standing within weren't moving an inch, weapons laying uselessly upon the ground, and all looked still.

Their leader stood close by, looking to be in an equal deep trance- the dark lines now vividly scrawling across his face. Eyes rolled back, and eerily still and before him... stood a dark stranger.

It turned its gaze towards the other small containment unit. The sphere floating inside the containment unit, its metallic sheen rolled and churned, and it was whispering... unintelligible ramblings... and an odd, out of place chirping noise began to echo out.

The dark strangers hood turned once again, past the leader, and past the other nomads, and stared pointedly towards the exit of the chamber. The dark figure moved, past everyone and out the chamber silently, the thick fog parting away from him like an invisible hand was drawing them aside like that of a drawn curtain.

Sorin's eyes shot open, as he stood himself up from his laying position on the wall, his face drenched in sweat. Suddenly he doubled over, a sharp pain stabbing him inside the chest. His heart! What was this pain coming from his heart! He gagged, getting the attention of Zoe.

"Sorin?" She said moving closer to him "What's wrong?"

"I don't know!" Sorin said, shaking his head, and making a pained face. He grabbed his head, he could feel his head pulsing with pressure, that dull probing hours ago was currently transforming into something constricting.

"Hey, hey, whoa... hold on!" Zoe said alarmed, crouching down and righting Sorin back to the wall and holding him steady. Sorin nodded gratefully "Help- Help me up for a minute." He asked.

Zoe looked unsure "Are you sure! You said your heart was-"

Sorin shook his head "That's not the problem, something's very wrong, and it's got nothing to do with me." He nodded upward "Something is going on up there, right? I can feel that at the very least."

Zoe gave him an uneasy look "Yeah... h- how do you know?" Sorin shook his head silently, not wanting to give credit to the odd hallucination he just saw. "Just a gut feeling, I- I don't really know... ever since Carver arrived at Gloomhaven... I've been having really weird hunches as of late."

Zoe blinked "Okay, well... I'm also getting a bad feeling."

Sorin nodded, then closed his eyes as another throbbing headache hit him. Zoe carefully braced Sorin and lifted him up to his feet, she barely had to try in order to accomplish it. But, looking at his current state, she was slowly becoming unsure of the decision of picking him up.

"Listen, maybe somebody finally sent help... Maybe, my dad found us." Zoe said her voice becoming hopeful. Sorin looked at her, his eyes narrowed from the headache "You think?" Suddenly he paused "Wait, when you mean by help, do you mean your dad, as in your dad could be here to help?"

Zoe nodded beaming, Sorin's eyes widened "Who is your dad?"

"My dad? Well, he's the chief security officer of-" suddenly Zoe froze in mid-sentence, her poster becoming stiff, as her eyes widened behind her hood.

"Zoe? Zoe what's wron-" Sorin began, only for Zoe to let go of him. He quickly put a hand against the wall, steadying himself, as Zoe moved in front of him, her back to him as she growled towards the door. Sorin growing further alarmed, as he watched Zoe scan the room. Her poster was completely alert- terrified even.

"What is it?" he breathed.

"There's something coming, I can feel it... but, I- I can't see anyone through the doors window!" Zoe growled out fearful.

Sorin looked where she was looking and yelped, there was a dark figure standing in front of the doorway. It's red eyes through the dark shroud peering directly at him.

Zoe jumped "What! What is it!" she exclaimed startled.

Sorin pointed at the door "You don't see it! It's right there!" She turned looking directly at the stranger, but she looked back at him with equal parts frustration and confusion "You really don't see him?" Sorin said at a loss for words.

She looked back and shook her head, her mouth set in a frown from under her hood, Sorin now completely uneasy, watched as the figure moved away from the window. Suddenly there was the sound of a bolt being moved, Zoe jumped back claws out, and Sorin watched silently as the echoes of a crank being turned emanated from the reinforced door.

Sorin and Zoe watched as the door swung open, as if by some invisible force, which slammed against the wall. Revealing the now accessible long and dimly lit hallway to the elevator. Sorin was completely disturbed by what he had just seen; at first, he was under the impression that he was having a hallucination. But after witnessing the door seemingly unlatch itself, he couldn't fall back on the theory of him simply losing his mind any longer.

Zoe was simply speechless, her mind picking apart what she had just seen and coming up blank.

"Did... did that just happen." Sorin got out silently.

"Y-yeah... I think it just did." Zoe answered, looking at the hall with disturbed perplexation.

The dim hallway was open to them, stretching to a very old looking elevator, similar to the ones in Gloomhaven- but far more compact- he glanced around, but he couldn't find any traces of where that mysterious figure disappeared too.

"I don't see him... do you see anything fishy?" Sorin said.

"What do you mean him! I'm telling you there was no one on the other side of the door Sorin!" Zoe exclaimed.

Sorin narrowed his eyes at the hall "Oh, and I assume the sound of the bolt getting moved was also me hearing things, no?" he retorted.

She looked back and forth, between him and the hallway, lips pressed in an uneasy scowl. "A-anyway, the doors open... shouldn't we clear out?"

Sorin grimaced, any other time he would have jumped at the chance to get out of this stupid cell. But his gut was telling him that something was amiss. And... why did he feel like they were about to encounter something bad up there.

"Sorin?" Zoe said looking at him.

Sorin closed his eyes and nodded "Yeah... we should get out of here. Maybe, I could call for help using this." He brought up his cyberdeck "And... I gotta tell you something." Zoe glanced back down the hall. "What?"

"My family, if I'm able to contact them. You should know... their nomads."

Zoe turned to him quickly giving him a double take "What!" she exclaimed backing away.

Sorin held his hands up "Whoa, whoa... chill, there nothing like the people here who kidnapped us. Honest... But, if your dad is an official of whatever-"

"Sector Security," She growled, Sorin could feel her glaring at him "Well, I'd doubt this thing would be able to reach all the way to the republic. And they more than likely are already out their looking for me... if I can get a signal, then I could call in for a rescue." He gave her a serious look "If where in the middle of the wastelands, then where better off contacting Hosea, it's not safe wandering the deserts without transportation anyway."

She gave him a frustrated look "Wait… are you suggesting we stay close to the bunker!" she said shaking her head.

Sorin groaned "I'm telling you, as someone who traveled with nomads for a year or two. That the open desert is not a good place to be without shelter or even a ride. The wildlife and supercells alone would be the end of us." He said.

The Direwolves, Cazadors, Outback scorpions, Duneraptors, and no telling what else, was waiting out there for them. And he refused to lie about their odds if they chose to make a run for it in the open deserts. He's heard enough horror stories and tales of missing, lost, or dead wanderers who meet a terrible end out there. He really hoped that if they did find a way out of the bunker, that there will at least be something nearby that they could use for temporary shelter. Till helped arrived… if, they could contact someone that is.

Zoe cupped her hands to her face, and from what Sorin could tell, was probably attempting to calm herself down "Fine." She said silently her voice muffled. "Fine, I'll trust you, just… let's just get out of here." She said morosely.

Sorin gave her an apologetic look "Listen, we can try and leave the bunker. But, I'm just saying. We can't go out there and expect things to just work out. But… thanks for trusting me. I promise, I'm not pulling your leg."

Zoe was silent before nodding. The two reluctantly left the cell behind, and as they passed through the hallway towards the elevator, both felt a heightened sense of unease, what would be awaiting them on the next floor?

CHAPTER

21

??????????? / ??????????? / ???????????

The elevator whined as the two rode it upwards. Its flickering lights and raggedy condition not helping the slow apprehension of confronting what awaited them up top.

Sorin focused on what needed to be done. If he could find a way to contact help, maybe both of them would be able to go back home in one piece. Zoe tensed her muscles, her body ready to pounce on the first nomad she could see. Her anger and need to release it on someone deserving was becoming a very, very appealing prospect. Needless to say, the both of them were tense. The pressure was building and the past events leading up to them leaving their cell, has caused them to subconsciously prepare for the worst.

Neither of them were prepared for what happened next, as the elevator halted its ascent, the doors slide open as the stark color of red bleached the inside of the elevator causing Sorin and Zoe to shield their eyes, as the alarm systems echoed across the halls. Unshielding their eyes, they both paused at what greeted them ten feet away lying in the middle of the floor.

It was a body... someone was lying face down on the floor... gun right next to him. The alarm system blaring, and casting shadows of red and yellows as the person laid there, splayed out, in the middle of the floor.

Sorin froze, and Zoe made a harsh intake of breath. The hallway further beyond led to a t-section. With one room each on either side further away. But that didn't matter much to the two kids walking slowly out of the elevator, nerves freezing at the sight before them. Zoe's fury and longing for payback was thoroughly evaporating at the sight of the body....

Was it a body?

Sorin gulped as they finally stopped close enough to get a better look. The man was shaggy haired, and had a dirty full beard around his mouth. His desert fatigues and sash were well worn and old. The silver pendant on his shirt was dirty and crumpled, but the symbol of a bird perched on a twig with what looked like a sun behind it stood out; It was an odd detail on him, but that wasn't the point of interest.

"Sorin... is that-" Zoe began, till she spotted his expression and the question fell to the wayside. Sorin nodded, not trusting his voice at the moment.

The man's face was pale, lips purple, and the familiar dark veins spreading vividly from under his skin. The question was no longer if the man on the floor was dead. The answer was obvious. But the how- that is what currently disturbed Sorin. Looking at the palled face, he shivered to himself, a brittle chill running deeper than he had ever know possible- down to his very soul even. How many times had he... in those vulnerable moments of dubious introspection... had he envisioned his own face, his own body in such a state.

He tore his eyes off the corpse, moving them down the hall and avoiding Zoe's gaze. "Let's get out of here." He said, quieter than he had meant to say.

Zoe was silent for a moment, Sorin's haunted expression tore through her in a way she hadn't expected. The body in front of them may have rattled the both of them. But... she wasn't stupid enough to think that it bothered her the most. She kept quiet, looking away from the expression on his face, an expression he was obviously having trouble in concealing. A horrible feeling of numbness settled over Sorin as he walked past the body. Zoe increasingly became unnerved at the bodies appearance- before looking at Sorin's retreating back in concern, as she slowly followed him. Their eyes set dead ahead, determined not to look at the cadaver a few feet behind them, pretending as it were, that it didn't exist. They both moved down the hall, past both empty rooms on either side and made a right turn into another hallway. Sorin forced himself to think of other things, things that would kill the incessant thoughts back to the nameless body behind them, of which, he was having a horrible time of it...

The call for help... That's right... Focus on that, just keep moving, don't think about it.

Sorin thought back, remembering the times before Gloomhaven. The times when the voyager crew would temporarily hide out in a bunker. There should be a place that could help him make a SOS broadcast, or something to get the word out...

They kept moving forward. The alarm now becoming a silent one as the lights kept painting the hall in red. Sorin moved past a room and stopped, causing Zoe to glance back in interest. Sorin paced back and looked into the other room, a storage closet, and there was a sign on the wall to his right, a map by the looks of it. The layout of the 2nd floor showed the room names, directions, and their current location. He scanned the sign and found what he was looking for.

"You found something?" Zoe questioned following his gaze.

"The data center... that's where we need to go next. And... I think... yeah, if we can reach it, I could probably get an SOS out." Sorin answered.

He followed the directions, and eureka! The data center was all the way towards the center of the 2nd floor and...

"Geez, this place is pretty big for a bunker," Sorin uttered, scratching the back of his head. "I've been in bunkers a lot smaller than this!"

Zoe turned to look at him "Huh? But didn't you say you lived in a settlement?" Sorin nodded "Yeah, after a year or two, when they first found me." He shrugged "I don't really remember much... they told me they found me near the expanse when I was just six, and they brought me with them. Two years later they made arrangements for me to live with Aunt dot and Church, and I've been living with them since."

Zoe was silent for a moment, a frown on her lips. "Ok, but... What about your mom and dad? Didn't they find them. I mean... you said your family, but the way you're saying it. They could only find your aunt?"

Sorin shook his head "Nope," he turned to her raising an eyebrow "Aunt Dot, isn't really my Aunt... I just, refer to her as that you know..." Sorin gave her an odd look "Is there something wrong with that?"

Zoe blinked under her hood, before shaking her head vehemently. "No, I was just wondering how that works is all." She frowned "I'm not exactly a tourist here, ya know... Heck, I was outside my house drawing- when I was shot in the back by that guy," Her voice became quite, her tone hard and growly "Jerk shot me three times I think before I passed out... And when I woke up..." She shook her head, hands clenching and unclenching.

"You mean that stun gun looking gadget he had? Well, that's what he used on me also... though, it took only one shot to knock me out though." Sorin muttered the last part, also rubbing his jaw, remembering the brutal back hand he got before the shot. Zoe glanced at him "Is that why you were so out of it- when they first threw you in the cell with me? I mean... the dark lines all over you."

Sorin shook his head, he reached out and ripped the map from the wall. "No, that's normal for me. I don't have my meds to suppress the symptoms, so... me getting out of here is kinda a must right now."

Zoe paused, eyes going wide behind her hood, before nodding "Okay... The data center, right?" Sorin nodded.

They both moved down the corridor, past rooms that had been sealed by security shutters. Sorin glanced at the map, the layouts put them in the east wing of the bunkers 2nd level, and it looked like they would be going through the storage and generator rooms.

They both slipped through a few more hallways and rooms, before finding themselves ascending a short staircase and arriving in one such room. On either side of the corridor- were generators, large industrial machines that surprisingly didn't make much noise. The coiled rods on top of each one gave a low hum of electricity running through the various wires and cables connecting to each device. Sorin and Zoe looked around, amazed, taking a moment to just gawk at the technology on display. The various consoles, gauges, and other gizmos attached to them gave an almost retro feel to them. Definitely not like the modern equivalents you would see in a settlement. They exited the corridor and took another turn back downstairs, which brought them into a wider hall. Sorin checking the map finally gave a relieved breath. Just another corner... and... Sorin paused, with Zoe looking down at the map, they both turned their heads to the right and saw it- directly ahead of them.

The only entrance inside the data center. They both jogged down the hall, only to slow down nearly halfway, they stopped, both gagging as a horrible smell reached their nostrils.

Something smelling of copper and, mixed with the aroma of burnt charcoal. They looked at each other uneasily before moving closer to the door.

When they got close enough, Sorin couldn't help the scowl which formed on his face, his mood immediately becoming prickly, the door was mag locked and sealed.

"Crap! You've got to be kidding me!" Sorin growled. "Maybe I could lift it." Zoe said, grimacing at the door.

Sorin shook his head "The door is held in place by interlocking seals, and each seal in the mag lock is supported by a hydraulic motor. Those motors affect 3300 lbs. of pressure. So... crap!" Sorin said kicking the lock door.

Zoe growled "But... there has to be another way to get this piece of junk too open..." Zoe suddenly paused, her hands clenching and unclenching, she turned to Sorin.

"Wait a minute, how do you even know about that... the door I mean..." Zoe uttered giving him a searching look.

Sorin now pacing glanced back "Bella... she told me about it, during my first year... I was sick and bored... and..." Suddenly he stopped "We were joking... something about Jade and Tom propping the doors, pranking Susan about something or another..." Sorin moved towards the door, whispering something to himself, before his eyes widened.

"Hey, Zoe, how strong are you... exactly?" She gave him a quizzical look "Don't really know, why, you got a plan?"

Sorin pressed his lips, before putting a hand on the door, narrowing his eyes he nodded. He looked up to the fluorescent lamp above the door, which was still green. So... there was still technically power running through it. So that meant it had to be automatic right?

"It's a long shot... but, maybe I could force a manual override." He answered.

Looking around, he scanned the wall near the door- hoping to find the thing he was looking for. After a moment he found it, a marking on the wall, subtle, and just under the green florescent light above the door, he followed it- head craned upward as the line lead further down the hallway. Zoe followed behind giving Sorin a mystified look, and on he walked, making a right turn and following the marking which lead into another room on their right. Sorin went in as Zoe- eyes widening, and wondering where he was leading her- continued to follow. Sorin looked around, it looked to be a storage closet, medium in size and filled with cleaning supplies and the like, shelves lined with various miscellaneous items and what not. And a few storage boxes...

Sorin paused for a moment. The line near the ceiling disappeared behind one of the cupboards. Sorin, with some effort, managed to move the cupboard a little to the side (The thing was full of industrial cleaning equipment).

Using his cyberdecks screen as a small light source, he gave a relieved laugh. The light cast by the deck illuminated a large grate in the wall where the line disappeared into. Solid black, with a vent like opening around the metal latches holding it in place. He narrowed his eyes, there looked to be a small locks in place holding the latches closed. And there was no set of keys in sight for the three latches sealing the vent in place.

Sorin smiled, and this, was were Zoe came in.

Suddenly he felt a hand on his shoulder, turning around Zoe was looking at the vent cover with intrigued interest. "Is that what we're looking for then?" She asked. Sorin nodded "I don't have any keys to open it... So, think you can rip it open for me?" he asked, giving her a sheepish look.

Being this close to her, he could spot the eye roll from under her hood.

She gestured for him to get back, Sorin obliged- moving out of her way, and standing next to the doors entrance. She moved in front of the grate, giving the vent cover a look over. She made a small exhale of breath, before swiftly striking the vent, causing Sorin to flinch. The grate gave a shrill wine, as her punch crumpled the metallic lock. Zoe released a relieved breath, before doing the same to the other two locks. The vent rattled in place as the locks- now crushed into slag, laid uselessly on the floor. The vent wheezed and retracted outwards, allowing access inside the maintenance space.

"Will that work." Zoe asked, now sounding thoroughly pleased with herself.

"Yup," Sorin said, giving a thumbs up "Let's see if what I'm looking for is inside."

After a moment Sorin was crawling through the grate, taking a moment to right himself, he got to his feet within the cramped space. Wiring, pipes, and valves of all sizes spanned across the entire concrete walls of the maintenance hatch. He looked around using the illumination from his deck to get a better look of his surroundings- until he spotted what he was looking for. The small circuit box was close to his right, Sorin grunted struggling to shuffle himself around to reach the box. Turning around so that he would be facing it, he slid the protective lid off partway and groaned.

"How did those two... manage this? I can barely fit in here. Let alone get this stupid cover off." Sorin muttered to himself. But with a final push the lid fell to the floor.

Sorin groaned at the mess in front of him.

The circuit box had up to 10 switches all blinking red and green- with the other ends being a mess of circuits and wires jumbled together half hazordly- some cut and others... Sorin gaped at the jerry-rigged mess of duct tape and hastily put together circuits. Where on earth was the pressure release? Sorin closed his eyes and breathed out slowly. He carefully scanned the mess of wires, carefully moving some around to get a better picture of what he was dealing with. That's when he came across something that gave him hope. There was a USB port near the very bottom, a recent edition once again jerry rigged into place and shining more light he saw the little thin line he used to find the maintenance grate was leading right into it.

Sorin gave a relieved laugh, this had to be the manual override, it had to be!

Leaning against the wall he uncoupled the USB cable from his cyberdeck and carefully slid it into the port interface. "Sorin, you okay in there?" Zoe's voice echoed from the other side of the wall.

"Yeah! I'm good- I think I found the pressure release... gotta interface with it first... might take a bit!" Sorin spoke back, his voice echoing in the enclosed space "Just sit tight, I'll be out soon."

Zoe was silent for the moment "Okay! I'll just... sit here then."

Sorin nodded "At least you get to sit." He muttered quietly.

"What was that?" Zoe's voice bounced back. Sorin could have sworn he heard a warning growl in her voice.

"Nothing, Nothing." Sorin spoke quickly "Okay." Zoe's voice now back to its casual tone repeated back.

Note to self... watch out for her hearing... Sorin thought to himself as the cyberdecks menu popped on screen. *Alright, let's get started.*

CHAPTER

22

??????????? / ??????????? / ???????????

Zoe gave a bored yawn, as she sat on a small crate.

Legs dangling from the box in a lazy swing. It's been what? Maybe half an hour since he got started on the thing. And she was already fighting the urge to just crawl in, just to see what he was doing in there. But from what little he was able to explain, he was using his cyber... deck? Yeah! His cyberdeck thingy to hack into the system for the door.

She cringed, that was her basic understanding for it anyway.

She sighed, wondering to herself where her locket must be. The jerk that knocked her out might still have it, failing that- she was prepared to search the entire bunker for it. She grimaced, would they even have the time for that? Before shaking her head, she had to tell him at some point, maybe when they got the SOS out.

But part of her was still curious about Sorin's life outside this place... even though he was related to his own group of nomads, he still didn't strike her as a thug or seemed any more bad than the usual word of mouth of what everyone at home thought of wastelanders. Back at home she would just stay at her house, a small mansion bordering the outskirts of Rosaria, facing the wooded outback and rolling rosary fields.

And yet here she was in a bunker at the back ends of the conclaves. She hugged herself, if what he was saying was true... then she would be surrounded by deserts. Nothing but arid wastelands, empty, dry, and she was in the middle of it all. She shook her head and jumped off the crate, she really hoped they could get help.

Well... at least I can depend on Sorin to get me through this. He hasn't let me down, yet...

Suddenly, she heard a sharp crack of electricity behind her. Causing her to make a surprised yelp. But hers didn't come close to the one Sorin made, which had her eyes widen by the painful note of it.

"Sorin! You okay!" She exclaimed.

There was silence for a full minute, and Zoe was about to charge her way inside to see if he was okay. But paused when she spotted the gloved hand of his cyberdeck, followed by his black durag covered head appearing out of the vent hole. He staggered to his feet, and Zoe hurried to his side, carefully gauging her strength as she helped him up.

"Thanks," Sorin mumbled, as he rubbed his forehead "The dang thing shocked the crap out of me!" he said. Left eye twitching.

Zoe gave a sigh of relief "Well you scared the crap out of me!" she remarked back. He gave her surprised look "Oh... sorry. By the way I got the door unlocked." He said now grinning "I can't believe I was able to pull it off!" he said happily "Though, I could have gone without getting shocked." He grumbled.

Zoe gave a small smile "Cool, so that means we can finally get someone to help us out of this place."

Sorin nodded "Yeah, lets head to the data center."

??????????? / ??????????? / ???????????

The two approached the data centers entrance, the light of Sorin's cyberdeck cutting through the darkness of the room. Yet, even as the two made their way through the now open door. Something was definitely wrong. Sorin covered his nose- the burnt smell was getting worse- and Zoe had to gag for a moment, pausing in her step inside the cusp of the rooms entrance.

"Zoe?" Sorin said.

Backing up out of the room, she shook her head, both hands clasped around her nose.

"I-I'm sorry... the smell... it's so bad..." her muffled voice came out apologetically.

Sorin paused, looking from Zoe to the dark room "Yeah, its bad, but-"

"No, Sorin- I can't! I can barely stand it!" She shook her head frantically, Sorin glanced and saw something that immediately got him worried. Something wet was falling from between her fingers.

"Zoe! What's wrong!" Sorin exclaimed approaching her.

She backed up "No, don't worry about it- just do what you gotta do... I need to get out of here, the smell is making my eyes water." She turned around and hurried out of the hall, gagging on her way out.

Sorin still worried, turned around, the hum of the servers now his only companion. He gulped, the sooner he finished here, the sooner he could leave. Moving further through hallway, the dim glow of the server towers on either side, painting the short hallway in greens and reds. He squinted, the lights of the servers weren't enough to properly count as a permeable light source. But the glow of his cyberdeck managed to suffice. He walked further, the smell grew worse, and an acrid taste of copper appeared in his tongue, as he approached what looked like another room. Sorin stopped, his footsteps echoing around the round room, tables full of junk and scrape lined the sides of the walls and in front of him- what looked like a dentist chair facing away from him. He immediately recognized the operators chair in front of him. Various consoles, small screens and neural cables were poking out of the sophisticated contraption- a custom modified chair- at least, that's what he assumed it was. Definitely different than the one Bellatrix would use in her sessions inside cyberspace. Suddenly, his stomach lurched- there was something in the chair... something still interfaced with it...

Sorin felt a familiar cold numbness envelope him, no sooner as the thought of what laid in front of him in the darkness crossed his mind, an electronic hum filled the air. He could only widen his eyes as the monitors and consoles around the operating chamber suddenly lit up. The dim lights slowly and gradually increasing in strength. Sorin grimaced, a shaky breath coming from his open mouth. The lights now painting the room in red, as the thin trail of smoke, now visible under the red lights, wafted around the room... as the body within the chair became uncomfortably visible. Charred and black, the plug suit burned and singed as the nameless runner in the chair held his head up- jaw open in a voiceless scream. The light smoke wafting from him, reflected the red light from the screens in an ominous halo.

Sorin redirected his gaze away, having an even worser time holding his nausea back. He could feel the bile trying to escape his mouth, but he somehow managed to hold it in. Continuing to look away, he looked towards the tables around the room. Anything to preoccupy his focus. Scrape, scrape, scrape and more scrape.... then to his shock and muted delight... he spotted a few familiar objects.

His backpack, and right next to it, his hoverboard!

Sorin rushed toward the table, taking a moment to look over his board, which still looked to be intact- but his backpack was empty and void of any of the tools he carried with him to the foundry, before his kidnapping. His riding gear was also nowhere to be seen, and... he scrunched his eyes... as happy as he was that his board was still intact... he felt a nob develop in his throat.

The operating chair and the body.

He still needed to establish a connection to the outside world. He slipped the backpack on and put his board over his left armpit. Trying to find any sense of comfort from the familiar device.

Just don't look at it... just ignore the smell... you have to do this... if you don't, how will they ever find you...

His legs felt like jello, and the nausea was slowly coming back up. He shook his head, grimacing to himself. "Come on you idiot, move, you have to move!" he scowled at himself. Turning back around, he took a few shaking steps towards the chair in the center of the room. He kept his eyes locked on the chair, pretending the body didn't exist- similar to the first one they encountered- he got to his knees and put his board on the floor.

Thinking back... Before his inevitable departure to Gloomhaven, and long after his 9th birthday... He was definitely in a similar room like this, in another one of the smaller bunkers. It was during a supercell... and the voyager crew were just waiting for it to pass.

At the time, Bellatrix was instructing Susan on the fundamentals of cyberspace. Susan- after getting the proper cyber modifications, was finally able to interface herself into an operatives chair. Something she had been training for under the watchful eye of Bellatrix. But Bella, being ever vigilant and cautious on the dangers of the net, decided to create a simulation. Specifically tailored to Susan and the skills she needed to have in order to be an effective runner. Sorin frowned as he tied his durag around his nose and mouth, making sure to filter out the horrible smell so that he could focus. He closed his eyes, the details of the day coming little by little. He remembered, when he was really bored he would find himself in the data center. Bella and Susan, usually near the operating chair- would be discussing and talking about what made it all tick. Susan would sometimes let Sorin sit with her- during one of Bella's long and passionate lectures on how cyberspace functioned. Sorin with a strange fondness remembered his enthralled expressions of wonder as he listened to her (Heck, half the time he didn't even understand what she was talking about. But her raw passion was so compelling!) But thinking about it now, there was a chilling main theme to all her lessons, to Susan- and by proxy to Sorin. The main idea, of which, was how cyberspace could both enlighten... and ruin you....

Sorin unplugged the USB cable from his cyberdeck, there had to be a manual interface jack somewhere on this thing. The multitude of interface nodes connecting from the charred bodies plug suit and the chair was a mess. Burned and slagged just like the body... yet, the main node- connected to the neck- looked suspiciously less burnt. Sorin refused to touch it, but following the cable he noticed another jumble of switches and nodes on the bottom of the chair.

Crouching down, he thought about the sessions where Susan dived into cyberspace. Via- the guided simulations cooked up by Bella. How even when she was exploring a safer, more approachable slice of the net, it was still overwhelming in all its vastness. Cyberspace was made up of hard lines, radio links, cell networks, and any other piece of technology or signal that could be used to share information from one computer to another.

It was data at its purest form. A mass communication network that could be accessed by the brain computers of ghost runners or operatives. And as Bella once described it- the cyberdeck allowed a runner to create a personal network. Which could give someone access- by mental command- over a piece of machinery added to their domain. It's how runners could, with the help of their cyberdecks, hack into things: like cameras, security gates, vehicles... anything that could receive a signal or transmission, in theory, could be vulnerable to a hacker. It's the same for cyberspace... the only difference was that you were shooting your consciousness into a digitized sprawl of data and binary systems.

An endless digital frontier, where the ghost runner prowling the net could be likened to an electronic wraith.

The mind being their offense and defense inside the net. With the software available to their mental figure tips acting as their figurative sword and shield.

Overwhelming, vast, hectic, exhilarating, but most importantly dangerous.

Susan... during one notary session was overwhelmed by the net. And Soran- observing Bella- watched as she hooked her neural link into the chair. Using her expertise to guide Susan back to her body, letting her own personal network act as a guiding light to bring her consciousness back to the real world.

Sorin carefully guided his USB cable into the interface jack, below the headrest. He didn't have a personal network. Nor did he have the implants to dive into cyberspace... But... he could still link the operating chair to the greater net. The bunkers sub matrix wouldn't be of any use to him cut off from the grid. So... for his plan to work, he needed the bunker connected to the open net. From there, he would have to count on Bella searching high and low for his whereabouts. He groaned behind his makeshift mask, this was going to be infuriatingly difficult-ignoring the body and the horrible odor of burnt flesh- he began typing commands onto the screen. Time flew by, and with every menu, system and subsystem accessed, the more he began to realize that something truly horrible happened to the bunker. Making him actually thankful he didn't have the capability to go into cyberspace. The bunkers systems were completely in disarray. Even someone as green as him could tell how corrupt the data was. Heck, being able to interact with the system as is, was nothing short of a miracle.

But what could have caused this?

Suddenly a soft muffled gasp came from behind him, turning around, it was Zoe. Sorin paused in his typing, she seemed to have wrapped a cloth mask over her nose and mouth. Her hood was pulled up enough to spot the look of horror in her compound eyes.

"Oh my... gosh..." she turned around, the retching noise causing him to jump up in alarm "Zoe!" Sorin started.

She turned back around shaking her head, her eyes fell on Sorin's cyberdeck, hands still covering her mouth, she walked over. Sorin could only silently move aside as she gave him a questioning look.

"I'm trying link the bunker to the greater net," Sorin explained slowly "If I can reestablish a link... then I can probably send out a call for help. I know someone who is probably at this very minute searching for me. So... I figure if I send a big enough signal out there she'll find it and it will lead her back to this bunker... wherever were at." Sorin summarized.

Zoe blinked, before nodding.

"There's something I gotta tell you..." she said, her voice even.

"What is it?" Sorin said, not liking the troubled look she was giving him.

"I decided to explore around," Zoe said "I followed the other map directions... and the main exit leading to the 1st floor is collapsed. Just a complete pile of rubble, and the main elevator is also broken... there... there were bodies-" she shivered, shaking like a leaf.

"Zoe.. are you okay." Sorin asked, bringing a hand to her shoulder. She shook her head, her eyes getting a wet quality to them "No... no, I'm not alright. I mean... I was ready to beat the crap out of them... but this... what the heck is going on here?" She said, her voice shaking.

Sorin moved and grabbed her other shoulder "Hey, hey, it's okay... I'm with you... I can barely stand being so close to... well..." he gestured to the body behind him "Will escape, just you watch." He said, trying his hardest to give a confident grin "But first, let me get this thing done so we can get out of this room." Zoe gave him a small smile, before nodding.

Almost an hour later, it was done- the grid was switched on and Sorin had sent out a tag with his nickname on it. After scouring high and low he figured out how to switch the main nexus switch on. Forcing the grid to reconnect with the bunker. After doing so, he used the dead nomads still interfaced biomoniter as the flare to attract attention to the bunker. Just like how Bella used her own private network as a flare for Susan.

SOS_SCAMP_ExE was officially online and ready to go.

Sorin grimaced at what he had to do- compared to using his cursed nickname to make the owner of the signal obvious to Bellatrix or Susan. He felt... nasty... using the dead nomad like this. But... what other choice did he have?

He typed the command to run the program, and disconnected from the chair, finally free of this horrible mess. He moved away... to find Zoe searching through the scarp of one of the tables lining the circular room. She looked agitated, shoving the discarded pieces off the table and onto the floor in a frustrated bid. Sorin unsure of what was going on, moved closer.

"Zoe?" he asked, giving her questioning look.

She twitched at the sound of his voice, but sighed in answer "yeah," she turned to him "Are you done with that thing?"

Sorin nodded "What's up?"

She looked at the mess she made, before giving him a nervous look "I... there's something else I need to tell you."

"Okay..." Sorin said "What is it?"

"When they kidnapped me... I had a necklace on me... and after I woke up it was gone." She balled her fists "That necklace was the only thing I had left of my mom... and they stole it from me... I- I don't know where they could have taken it... if it's not too much trouble, could we-"

Sorin blinked then nodded "Sure... I don't mind looking for it," he moved back to the operating chair and picked up his hoverboard "They stole this from me also... I honestly forgot about it, until a saw it on the table behind you." He gave her a determined look "Will find it, and will get the heck out of this place."

Zoe beamed at him "T-thanks!" she then glanced at the board "So... what even is that?" Sorin gave her flabbergasted look "It's a hoverboard... you don't know what a hoverboard is!" she gave him a surprised look "A hoverboard? Oh..."

Sorin gave her a weak look "Oh?... I mean... it's awesome- why are you looking at me like that?" Zoe shook her head "Eh... nothing, a lot of the other boys at my old school wouldn't stop talking about those things. Tch, they didn't even keep them for very long... apparently they were too hard to ride."

Sorin scoffed "Please... it's not that hard. You just gotta stick with it is all..."

Zoe rolled her eyes, a small monotone giggle emanating out of her mask as she turned to walk out of the room "Yeah, okay..."

Sorin hurried to catch her and was about to call her back, demanding what was so funny, he made it almost to the entrance...

When a sound caused him turn back to the operating chair. The head of the body was staring at him, seemingly peering around to look at him... Sorin froze in silent fear... the mouth was still open in that silent scream, and those eyes stared sightlessly back at him...

Did that... did it just move... is he still alive...

Sorin was about to flee, when suddenly, something popped out of the device still attached to the side of its head. A long, black, chip piece... of some sort, flew out of the neural port and slide towards the entrance. Towards him.

Zoe turned back, not hearing the footsteps of Sorin walking behind her. She looked confused for a moment, that's when she noticed it... the new position of the corpse, and gave an alarmed, terrified yelp. She jump back when the chip shot out of the things neck hole. Sliding towards the exit and suspiciously next to Sorin's shoe.

Sorin's eyes widened, the chip just stopped in front of him, he looked back... only to yelp when the runners face crashed into the ground, its body following suit, crumpling into a mess as the neural cables detached from the various spots of the plug suit. But the main cable stayed put... apparently burned into the main interface port at the nap of his neck.

Zoe was shaking... what on earth was going on?

Sorin looked down, hesitatingly he picked up the chip. His eyes widened as he flipped it over, realizing what he held in his gloved hand. He set the hoverboard down and took the chip in his other hand.

"Hey... wha- what are you doing!" Zoe exclaimed in a small voice.

Sorin looked back to her "Zoe... this- this is a datacypher... Susan told me about these things... there like portable hack indexes... I could probably hack my way into any of the systems here with it."

Zoe gave him a fretful look "Whatever! Let's get out of this place... unless, you wanna stay with him!"

Sorin grimaced "Good point!"

Sorin gathered his hoverboard and rushed out of the room with Zoe, the datacypher in hand. The body of Trace silently laid there in a heap, as the lights of the room and the operatives chair began to slowly dim. As the gruesome contents of the data center where once again hidden in shadow.

CHAPTER

23

??????????? / ??????????? / ???????????

After inserting the Datacypher into his cyberdeck, Sorin was amazed to learn that he was right, and so much more.

The datacypher supplied his Cyberdeck with not only a map of the entire bunker. But gave him the means to access any of the other locked rooms and hidden maintenance hatches of the bunker. Sorin and Zoe used this to explore the east wing of the bunker... Sadly, they yielded no results from their search. The necklace was still in the wind, and they were eventually forced to make their way down to the south wing. An hour had nearly passed since their flight from the data center. All that time exploring the east side with nothing to show for it... Zoe was crushed, and Sorin couldn't find any shortcut pass the blockage of debris barring them from entering the atrium in the north and into freedom.

So the south wing was there current goal...

"There's a maintenance shaft that will take us to the west wing... and another that's connected to north wing... the west wing is also blocked off by that crap in the way- so this is the only way I can see us getting out of here." Sorin said, showing Zoe the layout on the cyberdecks screen.

Zoe narrowed her eyes at the monitor "Wait a moment... what does that word mean? What's a mortuary?" Sorin looked to where she was pointing and groaned "You've gotta be kidding me..."

They made their way out of the east wing, and passed the path to the data center. Both feeling a chill run down their spine as they passed the now dark hallway into the server room. Neither of them spoke, their only goal at the moment reaching the entrance to the south wing and directly towards the mortuary. There was a maintenance shaft, that could take them into the west wing of the mortuary... But, as they walked through the south wing- they began to realize to their horror- that seemingly... a small war must have taken place down here.

They both walked down the damaged hallway. A few bodies littered the hallway towards the morgue, the florescent lights flickered over the grizzly scene, with bullet shells mixed with the debris of the damaged walls and ceilings, littering the floor. They were both silent, not able to voice the horror of what they were encountering. But most of all... they were both confused... bewildered even...

What could have possibly caused this madness?

They entered the morgue. There was a massive, behemoth of a man inside... Zoe had her hands clasped over her mouth in shock, and Sorin immediately recognized him for what he was. The man was heavily augmented, that much was obvious- tall, buff, and brute-like in build and weight- his desert scrubs of custom military armor and cloak didn't cover either of his cybernetic limbs. Both looked to be prosthetic in design... if they were made from industrial parts. Massive and bulky, the guy looked like he could crush stone and probably bulldoze a building if he wanted to.

And he was in horrible shape... Slumped against the wall, head down and with more nomads across the floor, unmoving.

His body was covered in injuries, his armor and scrubs were torn and battle worn, blood covered his body, and his right cybernetic limb was separated from his body... the dark oil splattering the wall and floor to his side.

Sorin looked to his cyberdeck... the maintenance shaft leading to the west wing was directly ahead of them. Seemingly behind the giant. Sorin showed Zoe and she looked at him like he was crazy. Not that he could blame her. A moment later, after a lot of convincing they both got to work. Sorin knew he wouldn't be much help, compared to Zoe's monstrous strength, he knew he wasn't much of a match. But, the moral support of him feebly pushing with her- seemed to help in its own way. The giant cyborg began to list to the side, as they both pushed as hard as they could. Sorin pushed from the side, forcing himself to ignore the sticky, oily fluid covering the still attached-but damaged- cybernetic limb. And Zoe pulled, pulling his right leg by the calf... tugging the limb like you would a rope in a tug of war. She growled, the body slowly moving across the floor- and Sorin heaved, using everything he had to move the behemoth (Even though he knew he wasn't doing much to move it.) Both his arms were screaming in protest- trying to shove the guys torso, with his legs also burning in fatigue... and his lungs... Sorin by that point imagined them to be two blown out balloons.

"Hey! Hey, Sorin. Let's take a break." Zoe called, letting his leg down on the ground.

Sorin silently agreed, taking his shoulder off the brute and felt his face grimace at the nasty feeling of something sticky coated his long sleeve. Zoe moved away from the cyborg, the look of sheer remorse on her face was palpable.

"This.. this feels so wrong... oh gosh, he could be alive... couldn't he?" She said looking at the cyborg, her face mixed with both fear and guilt.

Sorin, his feelings similarly mixed, shrugged. Although he'd rather not think about it- more than likely he wasn't. "If he was- he'd probably let us know real quick..." he sighed "This sucks... there's gotta be a better way to move em." suddenly, Sorin paused. He looked over to his hoverboard and got an idea. Gathering the metallic disk in hand he extended it, causing Zoe to glance at it curiously *What's he doing now?*

The board pulsed with energy, Zoe twitched from the effect and was suddenly apprehensive "Sorin? What are planning now?" Sorin gave her a tired look "Let's work smarter, not harder." He let the board fall to the ground next to the cyborg, catching itself in the air. "Help me push him on it... and I'll move him out the way with the board. I think it should be able to support him."

The two grunted in exertion, and finally, the body fell over. Landing heavily on the board which pulsed with energy as it powered up to stay afloat. Sorin gave it a moment... and it was still supporting the giants weight. Giving Zoe a tired thumbs up, he typed a few commands to his cyberdeck... the board powered up and Sorin remotely commanded it to move him out of the way from the maintenance hatch. His legs and one arm dragging across the ground. Sorin commanded the board to tilt itself- causing the dead nomad's body to slide off against the wall- Sorin winced, feeling a little guilty on how the body looked in that position.

Crap, Zoe's right... this sucks...

Even when these nomads had done the crappiest things to them, for who knows how long. He still couldn't help the... what was it? Sympathy, pity, condolences... they were rogue nomads, had to be. Tom, Susan, and Jade would always speak negatively about them. Those who abandoned the circle, and committed terrible acts around the wastelands. The worst of the worst. Bandits in all but name.

So why did he feel so bad about the slumped body near the wall? He glanced to Zoe, and she looked just about as reproachable as he felt... with a bitter sigh, and a hesitant nod from Zoe... they carefully righted the cyborgs body. Giving the fallen behemoth *some* dignity.

After a moment, the two moved on. Sorin used his cyberdeck to open the maintenance hatch and they both crawled inside. The hatch was just as narrow as the one he used earlier. Pipes and wiring across the walls as they crossed the grated floor. The passage was submerged in darkness, and if not for Sorin's cyberdeck, it would have been a far more miserable trek. Sorin and Zoe brushed the cobwebs out of their way (Zoe especially didn't care for the abundance of cobwebs.) and carefully navigated some of the broken pipes and faulty wiring (Sorin was especially appalled at the state of the crawlspace, how on earth did they manage to keep this place running up till know?) they managed to reach a bend in the crawlspace, which lid them to a ladder. After making their way up, they noticed that the grated floor showed another hallway on the bottom; effectively they were now on an elevated catwalk. Sorin and Zoe moved forwards- their footsteps clacking against the steel grating- with the lights of the switches and wiring to the side revealing the way to the next ladder down.

Sorin walked, ready to get out of this maintenance shaft... Suddenly, something horribly cold settled on Sorin, a frigid air so ruthless and abrupt, it caused him to double over. Behind him, Zoe was immediately on edge... a cold sheet of ice seemed to envelope the young deviant- and it left her instincts screaming in alarm- so bad was it that her hands around the safety rails on either side of her where immediately crumpled from her grip.

Come....

    Come, child....

        Come....

A raspy voice... something, otherworldly... seemed to whisper directly into his ears as if it were standing next to him. Sorin could only widen his eyes in terror.

His breath hitched, a sudden and familiar pain began to radiate from his body. As the familiar dark lines began to appear under his eyes and over his skin. He groaned, his hand grasping for the nearest thing to keep him steady. The safety rail seemed to vibrate under his hand or was that just him? He fell to a knee on the hard girded surface, he could barely register the pain in his knee, as his entire body was enveloped in a cover of pain. Zoe closed her eyes, counting from one to five, her grip on the twisted steel rail faltered and an uneasy breath escaped from her mouth, She opened her eyes back up- and finally noticed the state of Sorin.

The boy leaned on the rail weakly, his face pulled in a snarl, he needed to get up. He didn't have time for this. Shakily he began to get back on his feet, when suddenly something grabbed hold, putting his arm over her shoulder, Zoe lifted him up back to his feet.

"T-thanks Zoe." Zoe nodded silently, still trying to shake the horrible assault on her faculties.

Whatever happened, it caused every fraction of her to seize up. If she hadn't have grabbed hold of the rail... she probably would have bolted. She bit her lip, as they moved forward- she began to silently become concerned for Sorin's sake. The black marks under his skin scared her, as it painfully reminded her of the first body they encountered during their escape. Sorin was silently shaken, the pain of his cogni attack somehow paled in comparison of the voice that spoke within his head. He had to fight the impulse to look from side to side. Whatever was going on in this bunker... he desperately wanted out, to escape this nightmare, and to flee from whatever plagued this horrible place.

They reached another ladder leading back down, and after making sure Sorin could make the descent down safely- they both found themselves in front of the exit hatch.

The hallways of the west wing somehow was more damaged and ruined than the wing before it. After exiting the hatch and stepping into a seemingly empty locker room, they peeked outside and gasped. The hall was not just ruined... but obliterated. The walls, floors, ceilings were scarred by slash marks, pock-a-dotted by the left-over remnants of bullet holes, soot like residue and debris left behind by explosions. Their eyes were as wide as saucers, and mouths agape in silent horror. The bodies prone on the ground or slumped across the walls were bloodied and black. You name it- bullet wounds, gauge marks, crushed by debris, and the ones that they could make out... had the same dark like veins covering their skin, which was as palled and white as the first body they came across. A few of them still had their cybernetic weapons still activated. Hidden cyberware that was installed inside the body- killing tools- such as: hidden blades in arms, mini grenade launchers, razor filament links, flamethrowers, concealed guns that pop out of the arm (or knee, to Sorin's bewilderment), mini chainsaws, and a few that the pair just couldn't make out or recognize.

On a few of the bodies, sat the same silver pendant; looking at it now, some of the bodies had the pendants shape as tattoos on their arms, faces, or any place that showed some skin. But looking at the symbol: the bird perched on the twig, there were shapes hanging below the branch it stood on. Sorin, in a moment of unease decided to look away from the detail.

But the strangest thing about the terrible scene... was the weird, dark, ash- like substance on the floors or on some of the deceased nomads. A dark tarlike substance was also in some of the halls leading towards the next maintenance shaft they needed to reach. They were puzzled by its origin, but there was something ominous about its presence... something that made the skin on Sorin's arm break out in goosebumps.

Sorin paused, the dark veins visible across his skin continued to pain him. Not nearly as bad as the maintenance shaft, but enough to slow his movements.

"Sorry about this... wish I could move faster." Sorin unexpectedly apologized to Zoe, who gave him a surprised look.

Sorin forced his gaze forward, ignoring the burning shame in his heart. *Useless...* this illness, made him feel so useless at times...

"Sorin... there's nothing to apologize for," Zoe scoffed, her compound green's seemingly boring holes into his own eyes "Were would we be if you weren't here? I mean... you're the whole reason we've gotten this far!" She reasoned "All the things you've done and said... I never would have thought about or even known what to do to get out of here. It's alright... if you're feeling bad, will work through it. You've had my back, let me have yours." She said.

Sorin paused, before nodding, smiling gratefully "Yeah... thanks, and I'll have yours." Zoe smiled "That's a promise." The two were about to move on... when a loud sound caused them both to freeze.

The hallway ahead of them lead to a wide corridor. Bending from left to right, and on the right bend... a sound... a distorted moan... something that made the hairs of Sorin's neck stand on end, echoed down the hall and over the pair. The flickering lights of the hallway on the right began to trace a slow-moving silhouette. Projecting the black shape across the wall ahead of them. Zoe went stock still, and Sorin began to feel something dangerous rise from the girl holding him. A soft snarl emanated from under her hood. Sorin became tense, feeling a level of anxiety that surpassed the experience of first being thrown into that cell. Suddenly, a sharp, stabbing pain began to slowly drum within his head. A skull cracking headache, too similar to the one he had after the Orson nightmare.

Zoe slowly began to unhand Sorin, who moved towards the wall on his right to center himself. The figure finally stepped out from behind the wall... The flickering lights and slow dancing shadows made it hard to make out the figure, but through the migraine he could make out the nomad desert garb, the silver pendant over ballistic armor and fatigues... but then the light suddenly hit the figures face... and he was suddenly speechless...

The man before them was not normal in the slightest, his face was utterly ruined with the black marks of cognicrossis- but to a level that Sorin had never seen or heard of. His eyes... they were both black pits, sclera dipped into the blackest of inks, and irises the color of spoiled milk. He breathed rapidly, enough to make Sorin believe he wasn't getting air properly into his lungs. All the while a thin, vapor of dark mist was seeping from his breath like smoke or ash.

Sorin was suddenly hit with a terrible feeling of deja-vu. Those eyes weren't too dissimilar to the pair wrapped in the claws of darkness... which had not so long ago, tore into the Orson of his nightmare.

Suddenly the thing leveled a disturbing glare across the hall, directly landing upon them both. Sorin flinched back and Zoe gave a warning growl, her claws drawn and ready. Then... quicker than Sorin could track... the thing was sprinting down the hall, a blood curdling scream of frenzy reverberating down the corridor. Zoe roared and charged forward. Meeting the crazed nomad head on. The sound of impact rattled Sorin to his core, as Zoe- just in the nick of time- ducked under a thrown fist, which collided into the wall where her head had been a mere second ago. Taking a chunk out of it. Zoe swiftly moved around and under to the left of the nomad, before turning and slashing at the man's back.

Sorin's eyes widened (as did Zoe's) when instead of blood, a miasma of black vapor and the same dark liquid across the halls spluttered out.

Zoe was unprepared as the nomad swiftly backhanded her across the side, causing her to fly down the ruined corridor, before crashing into the far wall, leaving a sizable depression in her shape. Zoe's world exploded in pain, the breath knocked out of her as she landed on the ground in a heap. "ZOE! LOOK OUT!" her head shot up, the nomad was already on her, fist drawn and chambered, before shooting downward.

She flipped to her side, rolling out of the way as a horrible CRUNCH of impact rattled the hallway. She got back to her feet in time to dodge another wild one aimed at her face, she moved, dodged, rolled, before finally using the momentum of his wild barrage against him. In an enraged roar, she grabbed his arm and flipped him... throwing him back against the wall, before coming in and slashing heavily across his temple.

Sorin could only tremble at the impact from the open palm slam she did to him, causing his head to buckle and draw back from the force. The nomad flew face first into the other wall. Cracking it, before falling over like a broken marionette to his side.

Zoe was breathing heavily, her body shaking. As she looked over the unmoving nomad. Suddenly, she stumbled, becoming unsteady on her own two feet before catching herself against the wall.

Sorin was already moving, desperate to help, when suddenly... there was movement from the nomad. He skidded to a stop, as Zoe looked on in fear. The nomad was getting back up.

Unnaturally, inhumanly... he pulled himself back up from the ground. His neck cracking as more black smoke poured from his mouth and eyes. Zoe didn't get the chance to put up a guard, before a closed fist landed against her chest, causing the girl to cry out in pain as she was sent flying across the ground in a heap.

Sorin felt a bucket of cold water splash over him, as the nomad began to follow up on his attack. He stalked to her unmoving position on the ground, as she squirmed in pain. Sorin desperate to do something... anything... pressed the switch on his cyberdeck. Forcing the hoverboard in his hand to extend as he launched it forward in a blaze of energy. Just as the nomad was about to reach her with an extended hand out. The hoverboard in a pulse of energy, slammed into the things torso-plucking it off its feet and ramming him against the wall with a brutal CRUNCH. The board rebounded and shot into the other hallway, as the thing... slid back down twitching, and growling at Sorin who rushed to Zoe's aid.

Sorin frantically gathered Zoe up, and tried to get her arm over his shoulder, they had to get away from this thing... it wasn't human... it couldn't be human... He couldn't even be sure if he was another deviant....

Sorin was dragging Zoe away around the right bend, when a noise forced him to turn around. There was a blur of movement, and suddenly Zoe crumpled to the ground in a moaning heap. As Sorin struggled to breath, he barely registered that his feet had left the ground before his head exploded in pain. The monster had, in the swiftest of movements, gotten back up, rushed and choked slammed him into the nearest wall above the flickering light of the ceiling. His vision swam and his back radiated pain. He could only stare at the things piercing glare, as his fingers dug into the things wrists, desperate to get air back in his lungs.

Suddenly, the air was charged with a strange electricity. Everything started to lag and falter, as if Sorins reality was experiencing a major time dilatation effect. The pounding and groping at the back of his head started to lengthen and intensify, his vision- once barely incoherent- suddenly sharpened...

We are here....

closer... you must come closer...

The last survivor... must.. not... be... lost...

Something drummed within his ears. A booming crescendo that pulsed throughout his body. Sorin felt as if he were falling backwards... the darkness reached out and everything around him started lose focus. The iron grip around his neck, the pain and throbbing of his back and head...

There was an animalistic roar of somebody far, far, away... before the grip enclosed around his throat abruptly loosened... and Zoe.... in a deep fury... lashed out.

Sorin slide down the wall entranced. Watching... numbly... as the girl slashed in a crazed frenzy. The nomad howled in fury and struck true. Causing Zoe to fly backwards down the hall, she dug her claws into the floor- and coming to a sliding halt, he went for another crushing strike, only for the thing to quickly back off in alarm.

Something shot out of Zoe's back... with the SHHRRIP! of fabric, as two long, chitinous pincers each, erupted through the left and right sides of her back, puncturing out of her jacket, and hung in the air around her. The sharp, razored- edges- pointing menacingly towards the nomad. Her compound eyes glaring sightlessly ahead in a trance of berserker rage. Before roaring in a mad dash towards her target. Her four pincers carrying her at high speeds, skittering down the hall past Sorin in a mad fury.

CHAPTER

24

??????????? / ??????????? / ???????????

Sorin was far away, further than he had ever felt before mentally or physically. The world seemed to have lost its color, like a tub of muted greyscale had bleached the world in monochrome, the sounds of chaos and conflict were strangely unimportant...

Sorin dispassionately observed the spectacle before him- Zoe slashing like a mad berserker, her razor-sharp pincers gouging the concrete walls and floors as sparks SCREECHED from the rapid flurry motions against concrete. Each razor blade tracing a series of jagged slashes towards its target. The creature- formerly a nomad- could only retreat back defensively, dodging and rolling away from the wild slashes barely giving him the opening to fight back, as wound after wound, and laceration after laceration accumulated rapidly. Zoe roared aggressively giving chase down the hall and through the ruined, debris strewn corridor.

Sorin weather by his own will or something more... slowly got back to his feet. He stood there inert, still looking- premeditatedly blank- as the two disappeared behind the right bend. Something pushed him forward... a distorted thumping of a heartbeat sounded in his ears... he moved, robotically, sluggishly down the corridor. He reached the end and turned his head to the left- a dead end- rubble strewn everywhere blocking the exit out of the west wing.

Turning right, there they were.... still at it, still fighting, still moving down the hall... The creature roared in frustration, the multiple cuts and slashes across the now ruined and battle worn nomad garb began to 'bleed' the same dark mist that seeped from the things open mouth. Sorin mutely followed, The creature bellowed, not out of pain, but of deep frustration- before throwing a reckless fist forwards-

Zoe moved under it, her clawed hand slashing the underside of his thigh, before her pincers surged forwards slashing into his arms and legs, the thing jumped away, but Zoe pressed the assault onwards past another hall to the left and onwards still. The two were a blur of motion. And Sorin still in a trance paused when he arrived at the left turn.

He glanced down the empty hallway, and the distorted heartbeat drummed again in his ears. The hallway lead towards what looked like a massive crank in the wall... the monochrome invading his world suddenly seemed to recolor around the crank... his vision cleared, the heartbeat intensified, and an invisible string seemed to pull him towards it.

He's near...

The last survivor is near....

You're survival... and its own... depends on unity...

An alarm began to blare in the background, the sounds- muffled- bounced across the corridor as the crank in the wall began to hiss heavily. A thick, dark fog began to churn out of the widening gap of the vault door. The churning miasma crawled from the massive door, traveling across the ground as if it were beckoning Sorin forward.

The string started to pull again, his feet picked up without his conscious thought, shoes disappearing inside the heavy fog- and a feeling of familiarity, as strange as everything that has been transpiring since the opening of his cell, abruptly stung through the veil shrouding his mind. He stepped through the vault door. The obscured vault chamber was quite. Unlike the monotone voices swirling around in his head. The heavy fog slowly parted around him, moving as if by a will of its own. Figures... four of them... began to appear in front of him, all their heads bowed down, in a similar trance to him. Stock still inside the fog, like lost specters. He moved past them and paused, there it was. His vison cleared, the monochrome effect was drawing away from the center of his vision. A large capsule-like device in the center of the room, surrounded by safety rails and attached to numerous consoles and gadgets that Sorin in the best of times wouldn't have had a clue of their functions. A body was crumpled over the safety rail, someone strangely familiar, but the contents of the capsule was what pulled Sorins focus by that invisible string. The capsule opened with a hiss, the voices whispering from the fog suddenly silenced.

A metallic orb was hoovering within. A silvery, metallic substance that Sorin neither understood nor cared to know in his current state; it was moving... rippling around as if gravity itself was rendered moot. The orb and whatever the substance was, twitched at his approach. The standing figures all began to collapse behind Sorin, and something seemed to touch his mind- something alien. He moved closer, the drumming beat now a crescendo in his ears. Sorin finally at the rail- extended a hand towards the now open capsule- towards the orb which began to slowly move towards him. The orb began to surge with movement, before coming apart, like a complex origami sculpture or a budding flower... Sorin focused on the center, fixed in the middle of the shifting anomaly were three gems... Red, green and indigo respectively. Of varying sizes with the Red piece being the biggest and the green one being the smallest.

Sorin felt his body getting pulled as if he were being magnetized, but he didn't pay no mind, docile to the artifacts hold. A tendril of liquid silver began to reach for his outstretched hand.

Suddenly a glint of something bright caught his eye. Further down, dangling from the safety rail near the body draped across it...

It was a locket. The lid was open, revealing the picture of a woman with blonde hair and the bluest eyes. Her dress was regal, like something he'd never seen anyone wear in the wastelands, something you'd probably find out in the republic sectors. But that's not what really caught his attention. There was something under the picture, a black gem of some sort, something glinting back a white glare into his eye.

The alien hold on his mind began to faulter... the string holding him in place and the gravitational pull began to null and cease. The heartbeat began to skip out of rhythm and its rapid pounding in his ear also stopped. Suddenly, as if coming from a deep slumber, Sorin's eyes shot open wide- looking around in confusion and fear... until his eyes settled onto his outstretched hand... and the thing reaching towards it.

Sorin howled in fright, quickly drawing back his arm so hard he fell back down onto the floor. His other hand reached out in alarm of his fall and grabbed the only thing close by, the locket- which fell with him as it became untangled from the rail.

The orb went berserk- the thing expanded and began to sprout out multiple tendrils from the opening of the capsule. Causing Sorin to crawl back in horror.

The substance surged out of the containment unit, over the body draped over the rail- that he now recognized as Carver. He bumped into one of the bodies on the floor and this caused him to scramble up to his feet, his arms out ahead of him, he ran for it, through the dark fog- in his hands the locket, dangling from his closed fist.

Sorin didn't look back the adrenaline surging through his legs. Not caring where they took him, so long as they got him away, anything to get away from the thing inside the capsule.

The fog suddenly started to weaken... and like a thin curtain being brushed away he was suddenly back outside the vault- a sound forced him to turn around, something unholy- echoing from the dark miasma, he sprinted down the hall disappearing down the left turn into another hallway.

That's when he was forced to remember everything that had happened... What? Just barely 6-9 minutes ago. Zoe, the creature, his neck getting crushed in its grip... then nothing... until he woke up in that foggy place... Zoe! Where was Zoe!

His eyes widened, as he began to panic, the walls and floors of the hall were demolished- and the slash marks leading further towards the corridor. He ran through it, tripping on some of the fallen rubble in his way as he hurriedly tried to catch up, desperate, hoping there was anything he could do to help. He ran past his hoverboard which was still extended- gently floating on the ground- as he made another turn following the signs of carnage. Before abruptly skidding to a stop.

Why was it so quiet? No sounds of conflict anywhere. Sorin looked around, his focus primarily in locating Zoe. All he could do was follow the collateral damage of the brawl between the two. The slash and claw mark trail in the floor and walls lead to another room. Sorin didn't waste any time, he moved swiftly- arriving through the entrance and looked around.

It was another locker room. Bigger than he would have figured for such a bunker, but then again, with how big this place was... He shook his head he needed to focus. The lights were dimmed, and the place was also thoroughly trashed. With a few large locker cabinets seemingly bisected from a crazy sharp object, with claw marks, fist sized dent marks around the walls and indents on a few surfaces with cracks webbing around the depressions left behind from a body or two colliding with it. This was... how was he to locate her now? Could the security footage give him any clues...

Suddenly a sound caught his ear. A small sound, maybe of something tapping against a hard surface? He suddenly felt tense- the sudden urge to call for her name was instantly cut off. Feeling a cold tingle travel from head to his toes. He felt like he was being watched from somewhere.

He gulped, what in the world was going on, where was she... Suddenly, there was movement... below him... a shadow? He looked up and two pairs of compound eyes were glaring sightlessly from the wall above.

Sorin mouth agape in silent astonishment- watched as Zoe. In an eerily similar vein of a spider, perched herself to the surface of the wall above him. And... what the heck were those coming out of her back! There was a spine-chilling hiss coming from beneath her hood, something utterly removed from anything resembling how she normally was, and he couldn't stop himself from backing away in fright towards the locker. Away from the entrance and away from Zoe. The shadow of her hood obscured her mouth, but her eyes were hauntingly visible from the dim light of the room.

She suddenly dropped down on all fours... No, all eights. THUMP! SCREECH! onto the ground. Her sharp pincers stabbing into the floor, as her dirty ripped dress and large red jacket covered her. She glared at him, her pincers ripping from the tile flooring and now, pointed menacingly towards him. He began to tremble... a sudden memory of her berserk rampage on the creature- who was nowhere to be found- popped into his head.

He was completely outclassed here... there was no way he could hope to fight her off.

He held his arms up shakily, as non-threatingly as he could, giving her a pleading look... he had to convince her it was safe... he had to get through to her... it was the only way...

"Zoe... it's me... please, you gotta snap out of it." he said slowly, cautiously, making every syllable as clear as he could. Zoe meanwhile began to growl, a harsh feral sound that didn't belong to her whatsoever.

Sorin froze as she stood up. Her pincers still pointing- and her posture, something he didn't think was possible, became more aggressive. He stood stock still, back against the locker, the faintest feeling of sweat going down his brow, there had to be something he could do to reach her. Suddenly, another sound of something falling in the background. She twitched, head whipping around as her pincers moved in conjunction. Sorin immediately ran for it. Moving to the side as he jumped a pair of collapsed lockers, he heard a howl of rage behind him, followed by a collection of sounds of something rapidly stabbing into the concrete floor. Sorin sprinted, rushed through the short maze of lockers as the puncture sounds got closer. He made another random turn- and suddenly felt his stomach drop to his feet. Time slowed down, his eyes widened, as a horrified inhalation of air escaped him. The rabid nomad that had nearly choked the life out of him... he was inside, imbedded into the back wall of the far wall- creating a miniature crater around him.

He... he was also melting. His body evaporating into the same dark mist from earlier as his black pits stared sightlessly into his. With more than half of his body already gone. The remains of his cloths being the only thing left...

You're making a mistake...

You need it...

Your survival depends on it...

Sorin feeling overwhelming fear, backed away from the thing. Almost too scared to process what he heard echoing inside his head. Suddenly, he felt the back of his collar pulled roughly back, as his feet left the ground. An animalistic growl to his ear as he was twirled in mid-air, before his back crashed into the wall above the melting body. The pain radiating from his back didn't distract from what was now in front of him.

Now... similar to the thing below, choking him with one hand as the other pressed painfully onto his chest. The claws digging through his shirt, Zoe's pincers where stabbed into the wall latching her and him to it as she bared her sharp teeth, her long blonde hair now dangling from behind her red hood. Sorin was gasping, eyes widening in panic, he had a full view under her hood, and it was terrifying. The subtle lines trailing from the corners of her mouth had seemingly parted, revealing another row of sharp teeth. He reflexively grabbed her wrist, and something jingled from around his right hand, something sliver- a locket? Suddenly, Zoe stopped all movement. Her growling died in her throat as her compound eyes widened. The lockets lid opened and closed as it dangled from Sorin's fist, and each time it opened a light seemed to draw Zoe's eyes towards it.

Sorin focused on her, eyes moving between her and the locket... and quickly, driven by a gut feeling of survival he used whatever strength remaining in him to move the locket closer to Zoe. Keeping it level enough for her to see the opened accessory. Her predator-like posture began to slowly ebb away as she looked at the contents of the necklace.

Suddenly, almost like she were coming back from a deep sleep, her eyes, void of the death stare locked onto his own... a small whimper came from her mouth- now back to normal as the black lines joined back together, hiding the extra row of teeth.

Her breathing quickened as her grip instantly relented, allowing Sorin to breath. His vision swam, and he wasn't aware of his feet touching the floor again until he slid down to the ground, struggling to get air back into his lungs. Opening his eyes he was further away from the body of the nomad... now seemingly a pile of ashes.

And Zoe... who was further away at the opposite side of him, her pincers gone- her head down and huddled in a fetal position against the back of one of the broken lockers. Her muffled sobs breaking the silence of the locker room.

Sorin had to recuperate for nearly a minute before he could move. His throat was absolutely sore, with his chest feeling like it was recently pressed by a road roller. He struggled to pick himself up, but after a moment he was able to collect himself. He swayed on his feet, using the metal bench next to him to keep himself steady. He gingerly moved towards Zoe, who was no longer sobbing, but still looked to be in a horrible state of morale. No different than him really... the voices echoing around his head, wouldn't leave him be.

No matter how hard he tried to bury it.

He reached out a hand towards her, his concern palpable, she suddenly and timidly glanced up... what little of her expression he could see under her hood looked utterly guilt ridden. He paused, before slowly kneeling towards her and gingerly pulling the hoody off.

Ashamed, reproachful, mortified. Her eyes were looking away from his and she seemed half ready to bolt...

"Zoe," Sorin said making her freeze "I-it's okay... I understand, I was scared too..." She shook her head, lip trembling "I-I almost..." Sorin frowned looking towards the pile of dark ash.

"You saved me. End of story... if you hadn't jumped in, I would have died. then and there," he shook his head "You did more than I ever could. And I was knocked out for the duration of the fight..." he paused, the rest of the words dying in his throat. Yes, he was out cold. But not in a way that could be considered normal in the least. "It's nothing to be ashamed of, you don't need to be ashamed of what you can do-"

Zoe finally looked at him, her compound eyes glaring into his own "Sorin! I almost killed you!" she exclaimed "I practically didn't recognize you... your my friend- and I almost..." She shook her head, squeezing her knees tighter to her chest. Her face wet with tears, she was lightly shaking, very close to crying again.

"But you didn't." Sorin gave her a firm look "You. Saved. My. Life." he held the silver locket in front of her. "You may have lost control for the moment, but, you still pulled through in the end. You had my back, so, let me have yours." She suddenly gave him a double take, her eyes locking onto the necklace. She reached a trembling hand to the locket, her eyes widening "W-where did you get this?" she asked softly.

"I came across it looking for you." Sorin said, suddenly remembering the moment his eyes laid upon it. The phantom sensation of waking up from a deep sleep still fresh in his mind. "The lady in the picture reminded me of you... so, I kinda assumed-" Sorin couldn't finish his sentence. Zoe had, faster than he could comprehend, pulled him into a deep hug. She was now freely crying over his shoulder, and Sorin was kinda besides himself. Wondering whether or not he had said the right thing.

CHAPTER

25

??????????? / ??????????? / ???????????

Almost an hour had passed, before the two were once again heading for the maintenance hatch for the north wing. Sorin was helping Zoe forward down the hall, after pulling herself together, she quickly realized her body felt like it had been put through the meat grinder.

Sorin had went back to gather his hoverboard first, with Zoe giving the large platform a seemingly small look of respect "That thing sure packs a punch." She replied with a nod. Sorin collapsed it back into its small disk form with a small grin, before stuffing it back into his backpack. Zoe was limping down the hall as Sorin helped carry her. Sorin didn't mention the vault chamber- he was still shaken by the words which reverberated around his skull- the fog, inhabited by the tranced induced nomads, and the man he finally realized was the same who kidnapped him... all seemingly dead....

And at the center of it all was that... thing... inside the capsule like device.

Sorin developed a cold sweet just thinking about it. Whatever it was... whatever it wanted him for... **Survival...** he wanted no part of it. He just wanted to get Zoe and himself out of this cursed bunker. They reached the other maintenance hatch inside another room. A living quarters to be exact. Sorin stopped, causing Zoe to glance at him, before following his line of sight- towards a large desk. That seemed to be brimming with loads of papers and documents. Her eyes feel on one large document that had a photograph on it... It was Sorin. Sorin moved towards the desk, with Zoe moving alongside. The picture looked to be taken on the day he was riding his hoverboard for the first time. Maybe from a camera hanging on one of the lamps dotting the foundry. During the moment he was sitting at the bench with Bellatrix and Mr. Owens...

Sorin paused as Owens' face, as a flash and bang of a gun, suddenly rattled through him. His breathing quickened, but he looked away.

"Sorin? What's the matter?" Zoe asked, not liking the look on his face.

Sorin looked at her, not really knowing what to say, he had to be still alive... right? "That's Mr. Owens and Bellatrix in the photo with me." he said, his voice barely a whisper "Oh." Zoe said, regarding the woman sitting next to Sorin. She looked just as wild and impish as the boy next to her. And the dark-skinned man sitting across them... was that an officer of some sort? "And the guy, Mr. Owens right? who is he supposed to be?" she asked.

She glanced back at him, she was startled by his expression. Sorin looked transfixed... almost sick even. Not the black vein type sick, but something more... something possibly worse, and she couldn't begin to fathom what it was.

"Sorin, what's wrong with you? Are you okay?" She asked, turning around and putting a hand to his forehead. He lightly shook his head, turning to her in surprise. "I- I'm fine. I just... I hope my signal managed to reach one of them." he turned back to the document before flipping the first page- moving the photograph, and Mr. Owens, from view. The inside of the document was filled to the brim with notes, reports, and detailed descriptions of some sort of facility. And in the middle of it all... was the orb. Codename G.K.R. Sorin looked at the diagram of the capsule and the orb, all of it flying over his head. Equations, theorems, and theories that he had no way of comprehending or understanding.

"Meta-mor-pho-sis... what the heck does that even mean?" Sorin whispered to himself, reading the word as slowly as possible.

Zoe looked through the photos, each one, ether of a building in the distance of a large desert canyon, or of the orb thing in the capsule. "Creepy." she responded, looking at the diagram with a mixture of discomfort and uncertainty. Sorin agreed, taking a look at the orb and feeling once again the voice whisper in his ears *You need it...* he shook his head, closing the file and gathered the rest of the notes and diagrams inside it. Before stuffing it alongside his hoverboard. When help came, he'd pass this over to Hosea and Bella, maybe they would know what to do with it.

After that, they both found the hatch behind another closed door in the room.

At this point, Sorin understood this must have been the large guys room, the one who incapacitated him and Zoe; the place barely shed any more light on how he managed to come across this thing. With no answers in sight of the reason for his capture either. Sorin simply shrugged, so long as they could escape with their lives- the answer could stay buried.

The two walked through the maintenance tunnel, Zoe told him she was fine to move on her own now, though once in a while they did need to stop for a moment before continuing on.

They exited the hatch. The hallways of the north wing were less damaged than the previous wings. But signs of battle were still present. A few bodies here and there, a lot of which the two tried carefully to navigate past without touching. The were both moving slowly- ears and eyes open- after whatever that thing was that attacked them, they both decided to be more cautious. But before they could go for the exit, there was one thing they needed to do.

They had to stop by the mess hall.

Using his cyberdeck Sorin was able to locate it. Thankfully there were no bodies to be found here, and with Zoe using her strength, they were able to break into the supply closets. Rations, water, camping supplies and the utensils to use them. The deserts outside the bunker would be brutal, and there was no telling how long help would arrive. They needed to make this count. They exited the cafeteria when they were done foraging around, and made their way to the main atrium on the map.

The atrium was huge, a lot larger than the cafeteria, and seemed to be divided into two individual floors: The bottom floor(which they currently inhabited) and the 2nd floor above. A brief flight of stairs led upwards to what seemed to be more rooms. The current floor was full of various furniture and appliances, some of which Sorin would probably have imagined being inside a small hotel lobby or something similar.

With the general vibe of the atrium feeling strangely welcoming- a polar opposite tone to what the two experienced downstairs.

Not a body in sight either.

Uneasily, they both moved forwards. Zoe, even though she felt relief at the upcoming thought of freedom. She was feeling a lingering hesitation at the prospect of confronting the wastelands in its entirety. A surreal nail in the coffin that she was hundreds, thousands, of miles from all she knew. Sorin was glad to be rid of this stupid bunker, ready to get as far away as he could from that vault. Similarly, he wasn't looking forwards to the silent dissonance of the wastelands. This time, without the safety of the voyager or Gloomhaven to shield him from its dangers. The two ascended the staircase to the second floor; Zoe had to move a little bit slower than Sorin, her whole body was still sore from the fight with the nomad. But the worst feeling came from her back, it was almost like an ache, like a kind of pressure. She stopped and groaned. Sorin turned back, looking at her worried "Zoe, are you alright?" She grimaced in response.

"My back... It feels weird." She said.

Sorin blinked "Is it those things you got? The things that came for your back?" he asked

She looked at him strangely for a moment, then images flashed in front of her, like from a blurry reel- scenes of her chasing someone, something, down the hall with... four other bladed limbs... spider limbs... she shivered.

Suddenly, if possible... she became far more aware of the pressure building within her back. Four points in particular between the shoulder blades and lower back. Two sharp pins from left to right. "Zoe?" Sorin said, wondering what was going on with her.

She shook her head "Wait a minute... I think... I remember..." suddenly a new realization came to her, this pressure, it felt self-inflicted, like she herself was unconsciously gripping something closed, in the same vain as someone who unconsciously clenches their fist- only its focused on the four points. She widened her eyes, what if she stopped clenching? Stopped holding it back? And without meaning too, an instinctual, animal part of her let go of the pressure...

Suddenly Sorin and Zoe heard the SHERIPPP! of fabric being torn. Zoe yelped, and Sorin watched transfixed...

The four long and sharp pincers shot out of her back, before curving forwards sporadically. Zoe trembled, the sudden sensation of four new limbs shocking and catching her off guard. They moved, twitched and jabbed at the floor around her. With one slicing clean through one of the guardrails- which caused sparks to fly everywhere.

"Whoa! Zoe! How are you-" Sorin began walking back a bit, minding the sharpness of the pincers "I-I don't-" she began, looking close to freaking out. Sorin suddenly stopped "Wait... calm down, just chill... just take a moment too get a handle on it..." Sorin insisted, hands out, gesturing her to freeze- which she did. She paused, her new limbs jerked and slowly froze with her.

Her eyes widened "O-okay" she breathed "This... oh god, this is... it feels sooooo weird..." she mumbled out weakly.

Sorin cautiously approached one dug into the floor. He carefully reached out, poking it, the thing felt both brittle and strong all at once- he dared not touch the sharpened edges of it.

"Well," Sorin observed "These outta come in handy out there." He offered "So... how does it feel? Is it just like moving your arms? Or legs?" he asked giving her a curious look.

She looked at him flustered "What... what does it matter?" she demanded. Sorin looked at her confused "I'm just asking-" She stomped her foot "That's the least of my worries! Who sprouts extra pairs of bladed limbs out of their backs?" she groaned "This can't get any worse..." Sorin blinked "You know... if you were able to pull them out maybe you can... I don't know... retract them. Maybe?"

He gave them another curious look, before poking it again. She shot him a weathering glare. He stopped.

"Okay... lets... let's see if I can pull it back... my jacket... oh no, my jacket..." she looked down, turning herself to observe the torn shreds of her jacket on the ground behind her.

She turned back to him looking utterly miserable. Sorin feeling some pity at the sight, he approached and carefully patted her on the shoulder, minding the sharp blades on either side of her. "Don't worry about it... will be out of this place in no time... just think about that."

Suddenly he felt movement. Looking up, he watched as Zoe brought her pincers upwards. Sorin couldn't help feeling a little nervous seeing those razor- sharp limbs curl up, before watching in amazement as they seemed to retract back into Zoe's back. She was surprised to find that the pressure building up in her back was gone. Almost like extending the pincers may have relieved the muscles extending them outward. She would have been relieved, if it didn't cost her prized jacket. Both her dress and jacket needed to be fixed.

She stood up and gave Sorin a dejected look "My jacket is ruined. This sucks..." Sorin could only nod silently in agreement "It's okay, now let's head out of this dump." He replied. Zoe sighed and nodded, before following him towards the atriums exit.

The stairs leading up from the atrium lead to the front entrance and garage. Sorin whistled to himself, the place was packed with vehicles. Armored with the same tech as the voyager- looking glass armor rigs- and other modifications that would have had even Kingsley impressed. Let alone Jade or Tom...

Zoe couldn't help but stare at the various vehicles dotting the garage. Sorin told her about looking glass rigs, described how they looked and functioned, and even told her about the rig he rode in with his nomad family, but she never imagined this... They looked like something you would see in one of the fantasy vids at home, decked out in heavy metallic shells- over the windows and windshields- with funny little do-dads in various places, from antennas, small radar looking dishes, even what looked like gun placements. What world was she about to step into out there? Sorin moved past the vehicles with Zoe close behind, the entrance to the vault was huge, big enough to fit two cars at once even. The massive crank vault was similar to the one downstairs, just much bigger. The console was further to the right, inside of what looked like a small security checkpoint. Sorin looked up and noticed something at the top of the entrance. Two medium-sized compartments above the ceiling. Making a note of it, he moved for the checkpoint.

Entering it, Sorin had to do a double take- the console was *huge*. With three screens over it. The camera footage, presumably displaying outside the bunker was sadly not working- the digital snow of static was buzzing on all three of the screens.

Why couldn't there be a manual? Or better yet a guide for this stuff? Sorin thought ruefully.

The keyboard didn't have any obvious buttons which would open the gate. Number keys, arrow keys, switches, dials, levers, and other blinking buttons. Nothing was ever simple. He did see a few USB ports under and to the sides of the console- Sorin wasn't surprised, who knew how long ago this bunker was built. Hosea certainly didn't know; the origin of who built the underground bunkers dotting the wastelands were surrounded in mystery, and Sorin remembered asking him at one point... before his move to Gloomhaven.

'No one knows any more kid. The original architects of the underground bunkers have long since been lost, with the locations and layouts of the other hidden bunkers. The circle has a few charts and other scattered maps detailing whereabouts of a few others. But it's nowhere near the estimated total, barely even a 10th of the remaining lot. The wastelands are vast Sorin... and god knows how many more are still hidden to this day.'

Hosea chuckled 'We only know of this bunker, because an old friend found it by accident, so... who knows. Maybe you'll discover one if you're lucky.'

Sorin snorted, like that will ever be the day. After this, he would happily go without ever wondering into another bunker again... He connected his USB port and got to work. One of these codes from the dead runner should open the massive gate. Zoe meanwhile walked along the cars and trucks, observing the gizmos and gadgets of each in morbid fascination. She gripped the locket around her neck, the familiar cool locket was a small source of comfort. One of the only things she had left of her mother. She closed her eyes, taking the locket in her palm she opened the lid, there she was... beautiful, normal... she stiffened, the black gem on the bottom began to glimmer its mysterious light- she hastily closed it- grimacing to herself, the luxury of the gems power was something she couldn't afford at the moment. She'd be willing to use it, once her and Sorins safety was guaranteed.

She shoved the pendant down her dress, and zipped her ruined jacket up. She'd soon be out of this horrible place.

There was a loud CRASH from outside the garage. Sorin all the way at the security checkpoint popped his head up startled, Zoe turned around with a start. That came from the atrium...

Zoe immediately ran for the security checkpoint, her speed a small blur of motion to Sorin, as she skidded to a stop outside the door. Sorin let her in and engaged the locks. They both crouched, below the glass window- peering out to see what was going on.

"What if it's another one of those monsters?" Zoe breathed silently.

"I don't know," Sorin whispered back "Let me-" he didn't get a chance to finish.

The lights suddenly shut off, plunging them both in darkness, then they flickered back on unstably. Sorin glanced at his cyberdeck, it wasn't him... he looked at his progress- the breach commands he sent into the system was still in progress of unlocking the gate controls for him. He looked back out and suddenly he shivered. His body felt like it was breaking out in goosebumps, the air seemed to become charged in static and the whole atmosphere in the room felt like it got dipped inside of an ice-cold freezer. The lights started to flicker again, and the screens near the console started to sparkle and emit smoke. Causing Zoe to yelp in fright.

"What's going on now!" She whispered frantically, her focus had been outside when the screens started fizzing.

She paused, suddenly aware Sorin wasn't making a sound, nor reacting to the room... She looked to her right and froze. Sorin had the black veins traveling all over his body, and he looked to be in complete agony, he was grasping his chest and was doubled over stunned.

Before she could even do something to help, another series of CRASHES racketed across the schizophrenically flickering garage.

She looked back up and nearly screamed in horror, something was standing at the far end of the garage entrance... and it radiated a wrongness that chilled her to the bone, cloaked in darkness with the flickering lights barely illuminating the idle shape. Something was moving, slithering around it hypnotically, she crouched down further... scooting over to Sorin who was struggling to type in commands to his deck. Her instincts were going berserk, the small animal inside was in a frenzy, desperate to escape whatever was coming. But she refused, she'd never again let it consume her...

Sorin growled in defiance of the pain. A horrible presence invading the back of his head. The pain of his sudden cogni attack caught him off guard, but he wouldn't let it stop him, he began to commit another hack- something separate from the console breech. He was glad that he could engage more than one hack at a time. Although the invisible probing was making things unnecessarily difficult. Sorin midway into his hack froze... the probing was getting worse... and he could hear the voices clearer and clearer. He seized up, fingers frozen and his body increasingly getting colder.

Sorin...

Zoe's hands gathered him up before he could dip further down to the ground. She carefully moved him under the window, both sitting below it against the wall. She had to keep her breathing under control, she no longer had any sight on the thing... suddenly there was a noise, a cold menacing HISSSS that was uncomfortably near their location.

She peeked out the window... She immediately regretted it...

The thing in the middle of the garage was monstrous. Its metallic, chitinous, armor-esc hide reflected the ceiling lights shining across its body. With what little she could see from the flashing lights- rippled with muscular potential. The briefest vestiges of torn rags hung from its body, with the coiling, snake-like metallic tendrils swishing from behind its back and shoulders. The thing didn't have eyes- but its mouth was a row of sharp razors, with its hateful lips pulled into a sneer. It stood there, holding its head upwards, as if it were tasting the air. Its head was covered in a hard shell- how it was able to see- Zoe couldn't begin to fathom.

She hastily stopped looking, shaking in fear despite her best attempts. Sorin was able to pull himself up. Zoe shook her head, but it was too late. Before she could hoist him back down, he got a good look... and dropped right back down. A silent slew of curses came from the boy's mouth, before he could stop himself- thank god Bella wasn't there to hear him say those things. The monster was huge! It had to be 8ft tall at the least!

"Sorin... I hope you got a plan... because, I'm definitely not going out there." She whispered.

Sorin gave her a nervous look "I might have one... don't know if it'll do much good with that thing." Suddenly a loud ding, sounded from the console startling the both of them.

Zoe peaked back up, and the thing suddenly stiffened... before looking in their direction. The garage was suddenly bathed in a revolving yellow light- the massive front entrance began to HISSS loudly as the pneumatic actuators and gears within the entrance began to grind over themselves.

The first breech was complete, and the gate was opening.

CHAPTER

26

??????????? / ??????????? / ???????????

The creature growled, its eyeless stare homing in on the opening entrance.

Zoe came back down, her expression fearful and anxious, Sorin glanced at his cyberdeck the 2nd hack was almost done. And he wondered to himself if this was a good idea, there was no telling if this could work.

There was a deafening CRASH above them as shattered glass rained down around them. Sorin yelled, startled by the sudden sensation of constriction around his waist, arms, and legs. Zoe yelled as her eyes widened in horror, multiple silvery ropes busted through the glass, and some shearing through the metal walls, only to wrap around Sorin who was quickly hoisted up into the air. Sorin roared in anger, feeling himself being lifted up- he struggled to move, turning his head behind him and froze in place. The thing was standing idle a few feet behind the checkpoint.

Sorin could feel its eyeless gaze peering into his own eyes. He quivered, as a horrible presence suddenly intruded his mind. The invisible hand seemed to grasp his entire head, forcing him to look upon the abomination in front of him.

Sorin... Survival... Need... Unity...

The words pierced his brain like jagged ice picks, his vision got redder, and time seemed to lag and slow down. A gradual pain started to build; a small corner of his mind believed it to be his cogni attack building in severity- but he quickly realized this was nothing like that, his chest... his chest felt like it was on fire. Like something was building and building ready to burst. Beyond his peripherals, something flashed in front of him, he fell down as two arms wrapping around his waist, and four long bladed pincers sheered through the other tendrils wrapped around him.

"Let go of him!" Zoe roared as she pulled back, yanking him out of the tendrils grasp. Sorin grimaced in pain, his vision hazy, Zoe jumped back with Sorin in tow- with Sorin recalling the USB cord, the cable snapping back in place with a SNAP! The creature made a distorted roar of frustration, a horrible fusion of guttural, primal fury.

Zoe used her other pincers to jab the rest of the window out of frame. The creature lunged and Zoe suddenly tightened her hold, Sorin could only widen his eyes as she launched them both out of the window- using her pincers to spider crawl out of the way. The monster crashed heavily into the station, reducing the small checkpoint into rubble and warped metal. Sorin forced himself to move, ignoring the splitting headache he typed furiously into his cyberdeck.

Zoe skittered over a fortified vehicle with Sorin in tow, she looked over her shoulder and did a double take. The entrance was almost open- but that wasn't what got her attention. Above the vault door, the two compartments on the ceiling suddenly opened. The creature roared in rage, bursting out of the collapsed ruin that used to be the checkpoint. Glass and debris flew in each direction, as the monster bounded for them. Sorin pressed enter, and Zoe could only gasp as she moved around another vehicle.

Descending from the two compartments, two large metallic pillars came down, with two long barrels on either sides of them, as they began to spin at insane speeds. Sorin and Zoe felt their teeth chatter as the loudest most recussive noise began to deafen them and reverb around the entire garage. BRBRBRBRRBR the barrels went- as round after round shot out of the gun turret. The pulse rounds crashed into the creature, causing the most uncomfortable shriek the pair had ever heard. Bullet cases began to thump on the floor below the turrets, creating an expanding pile on the floor. Zoe and Sorin watched with wide eyes as the rounds decimated the area around the creature, which had immediately retreated to cover at the other end of the garage behind another large vehicle: a van, which was getting disintegrated by the concentrated fire. Suddenly they had to avert their eyes, the van exploded- along with the other vehicles near it causing them to similarly explode into pieces. They both ducked down, BOOM, BOOM, as shards of warped armor pieces and debris rained everywhere. With the sudden heat washing over the two, Sorin turned to Zoe who was gawking at the two turrets.

"THAT WAS YOUR PLAN!" she screamed over the roar of turret fire, and the creatures enraged howls.

"YES! WE NEED TO MOVE! I DON'T KNOW HOW LONG ITS GOING TO LAST!" Sorin screamed, she turned from him and the turrets, then the creatures location at the other side of the garage. Now presumably being burned alive by the flames. She growled, her grip on him tightened- "HANG ON!" she yelled before stretching her pincers and pulling them into a furious charge to the now nearly opened gate. Sorin tried to keep himself steady as possible, but as his feet glided above the ground, the pincers around him scurrying forward in surprising speeds. He felt like he was riding a roller coaster. Not as fast as his hoverboard, but still really fast.

Suddenly another enraged roar boomed from the growing flames behind them. They turned their heads around and Zoe nearly faltered in her mad dash towards the exit. The creature was charging after them, as the rounds of the turrets followed closely behind the creature, the thing was using the other vehicles as cover- suddenly there was a loud SSSHHRRIPPPP of metal getting ripped from something. The creature suddenly jumped high in the air in an arc- over an armored truck and suddenly threw something huge over their heads.

It was a large piece of serrated metal torn from one of the vehicles, thrown like a frisbee as the metal sheet cleaved through the right-hand turret. Causing it to fall to the ground with a harsh thud and a series of pounding beats as the still spinning drums hit the hard concrete. Sorin and Zoe could only yelp in fright as the thing THUDED! near them, before surging ahead of them, Zoe having no choice but to alter her course- as the live rounds followed the creature, forced her pincers to spring her and by proxy Sorin, behind another car as cover, as bullets washed over it, causing the vehicle to creek and moan heavily from the impacts of the rounds. They both peered over the vehicle, and watched in a terrible spectacle- as the creature recklessly charged through the solo rounds of the remaining turret.

Its body being pierced and run through by the kinetic rounds. As eerie dark mist poured from the wounds, its dark metallic form whipped its arm out- and a massive tendril lashed out- SHEEKT! The metallic whip cleaved through the other turret. To the horror of the two kids behind cover. The creature skidded to a halt and turned in on the spot- the turret crashed onto the ground and the monster swiftly charged for their position.

Sorin and Zoe didn't get the chance to react before it was already upon them.

The monster pounced, landing on the roof of the car- crumpling it and the armor underneath. Sorin heard a faint "Run!" before he was suddenly flying through the air- for Zoe had thrown him out of harm's way, faster than he could have processed. She immediately went on the offensive, desperate to buy time so that he could at least escape. She launched herself up, pincers ready to slash the abomination above her, only for a massive open hand to smash into her side.

Causing the deviant to fly a good ten feet away before crashing into the far wall- leaving a large indenture where she landed. Then limply falling down into a heap. Her pincers sliding back into her back.

Sorin landed on the ground, before rolling to a painful stop, his world was spinning- but he quickly picked himself up, the pain of his cogni attack hardly registered as complete fear for Zoe snapped him back up to his feet.

His eyes landed on her unmoving form at the far wall, further from the gate- she threw him in its general direction... past the monster, but it didn't matter. The creature, faster than he could react, was already barreling down on him. He couldn't even scream as tendrils snaked through the air towards him, they wrapped around him once more, so tight that his struggles where rendered mute- as it pulled him into the air in front of it. The presence invaded his mind, far more relentless than last time as his body seized from the sharp intrusion. But still, Sorin struggled, desperate to do something... anything...

Zoe's unmoving body- suddenly forced flashbacks of Mr. Owen's similar fate. His body limp and unmoving with him being unable to do anything...

Something inside him started to build.

The presence continued its assault- its influence pouring its will against his own, vying to turn him passive. But something dark and venomous started to rage within the boy- a black flash of malevolence roared deep within him, and only got worse the more of he could see of Zoe's unmoving body. His chest began to throb, and a sharp pressure started to cook just beneath the point in which his heart resided. Sorin felt his eyes drawing away from Zoe. Past the eyeless face of the creature and moved further down to its chest. Its armored hide and torso suddenly rippled like water... and three familiar gems suddenly surfaced from the metallic substance. The three gems: Red, green, and indigo shined brightly. But the maelstrom of dark pressure was still, steadily building... and suddenly, that same presence that was vying to pacify him, started to grow nervous, until a tick of panic suddenly shot across the invisible link binding it and Sorin.

Stop...

You don't understand...

The dark oath will claim you...

If you draw from its source unfiltered...

The voice in his ears was muffled, nearly drowned out by the tempest growing inside his chest. His heartbeat drummed in his ears, and the dark veins growing and branching across his skin- began to emit an eerie glow.

The beast reached forwards. Its desperation plain to see, as more tendrils quickly wrapped around the boy. Pulling him towards the three gems, Sorin began to shake within the confines of his bindings. A power began to radiate out of his chest, casting visible light from within his bounds. He was finally at the tipping point: the rage of his capture, the hatred of his condition, and the fear of losing someone else he had only just met- released an explosion of utter cataclysm that pulsed from his bindings. The raw unstable force surged through his veins and out of the pours of his skin, ripped through his bounds, and crashed into the creature picking it off its feet.

Sorin roared, a guttural howl distorted by a monochrome flare which consumed the two and muffled the roaring fire behind them.

BOOOOMMMMMM!

Sorin flew backwards, landing hard against the floor. The creature was flung back like a ragdoll, invisible force throwing it howling back towards the flames with a harsh crash of impact. The shredded tendrils that once bound him fell to the floor in heaps, before disintegrating into the air.

The mental line connecting them both suddenly, and abruptly snapped. All was quiet, save the roaring inferno and the periodic electric zaps of the ruined checkpoint and severed gun turrets. Smoke started to gather in the garage and Sorin coughed. He slowly got back to his feet, his vision going in and out.

He felt detached from his body, a distorted sense of dissociation which separated him from mind, body and emotion. The unimaginable pain radiating across his body, felt distant, like the still burning embers of a since past bonfire. But despite it all he picked himself up, the only thing that seemed to register was his quickened pace towards Zoe's unmoving body. He reached her just across from the raging fire as his arms extended to move her, he spotted the dark veins of his cognicrossis as it was running down his arm, and they were glowing in front of his very eyes. He paused, the marks were starting to disappear- losing their translucency, before quickly becoming transparent.

The pain was gone, but the uncanny drumbeat of his heart began to take an almost worrying quality to it. Why did he feel like he was hearing two heartbeats instead of one? Was it shell shock? No... he needed to focus. He had to get Zoe out of here. He touched her neck, scared, but to his infinite relief there was a pulse!

He pulled out his hoverboard and gathered her up piggy-back style. He slipped his backpack to his torso and got on the board. He wasn't sure he had the balance for this, but he didn't care. With Zoe's weight on his back, he commanded the board to move forward, and with a blast of energy he sped with Zoe away from the gout of flames, the ruined checkpoint and finally out of the now open bunker entrance. The bullet casings of the spent turret jingling as he sped onwards. His path curved upward, forcing him to lean on the board to keep his balance. Zoe's weight and the backpack attached to his torso made everything so much worse to get his bearings. All the while- the potential threat of death behind him created a level of concentration so unheard of, that it made his practice at the foundry look absolutely simple by comparison. Never before had he felt so aware of his state of being, the constant thump of his heart and the exhale and inhalation of his lungs. Sorin blinked as a bright light started to filter down the path ahead... and then, his ascent came to an end.

He didn't have time to slow down as he flew upward, and suddenly his face was slapped by the bright sunlight of a setting sun. He slammed back down with a rough pulse of energy as his surroundings came into focus. The hoverboard hummed, as the large platform carried him down the ruined streets ahead of him, the half decayed and falling apart buildings on either side of him... this was definitely not Gloomhaven. For even the historic district wasn't *this* rundown and abandoned.

Glancing back behind him, the entrance to the bunker was located around a wide dead-end street. In the middle of four ruined buildings. Smoke was slowly rising from out of the entrance. Sorin really hoped the fire wouldn't reach outside.

He turned back and quickly had to swerve to avoid colliding with an abandoned vehicle. What used to be a truck, now a rusted shell parked on its side in the middle of the road. Sorin grunted, teeth clenched as he fought to regain his balance. Zoe by herself wasn't super heavy, but her and the backpack filled with supplies was throwing off his balance. He concentrated, dodging and moving between broken chunks of building and disabled abandoned wrecks on the road. The general roads themselves not being of any help. Massive cracks and potholes, with signs, streetlamps and other hazards dotting the path in his way.

Sorin growled in irritation, where the heck was he? What the heck kind of settlement was this... the state of the buildings, the horrible condition of the streets, and the lack of people. All of it was wrong.

Yet, after driving around with Zoe on his back. He was quickly flabbergasted by the size of the settlement... he wasn't big on history like Tom- but, this felt much, much older than the historic district back home. Even the abandoned carcasses of rusted vehicles in the middle, and sides of the roads where all older models of vehicles he'd seen back at Gloomhaven. There was barely any legible street signs, advertisements, and graffiti which could identify where he was or what the name of the settlement was.

I'm in an actual ghost town... are we the only ones alive here, for miles around?... Sorin thought.

He focused ahead, slowing down his acceleration. For now all he could do was keep going; he sent the SoS signal, maybe heading back closer to the bunker was the best choice... he shook his head, the sudden flash of the monster giving him a fresh wave of goosebumps. He needed shelter and time to think, at the same time- he needed to take care of Zoe until she either woke up or help arrived.

He sighed, yeah... he needed to make a stop and figure out his next move.

Sorin kicked the underside of the boarded door. After searching for a stable enough building to hideout, he found this small corner store- tucked away between two four story buildings on a curve. The front of the store was heavily barricaded, but the back of the store was thankfully rotted. Zoe was currently laying on the hoverboard, which hovered behind Sorin who had his backpack in hand. The underside portion of the entrance gave way to his shoe- crawling inside he used the light from his cyberdeck to scan the small store.

The place was completely empty, the small store and its seven to eight aisles- barely had a lick of products inside. The ones that Sorin did come across were old and moldy. With the aisle shelves similarly filled with dust and spider webs. *At least there are no signs of Cazador nests* Sorin thought as he spotted the checkout area, which was also covered in layers of dust. The cash register was blanketed by the same filth which covered the store, with its cash drawer extended and void of money. Replaced instead with a bed of grime. Shaking his head in disgust he moved back to the back door, typing commands into the deck he carefully kicked the hole he made into the door. After making sure the entrance was big enough he ordered the board to slide itself and Zoe under the opening.

After a moment Sorin had Zoe against the wall, Her hood off as he checked her for injuries. Under the light of his cyberdeck she only had a few scratches and cuts around her right shoulder and forehead, with a few more cuts going down her right arm. Taking some supplies out he carefully covered the wounds. Using what he learned from watching Church dress wounds back at Gloomhaven. Sorin couldn't help but feel amazed at the state of her wounds. She was barely bleeding from the cuts dotting her arm and head, with there being no signs of bruising from the moments she was thrown into a wall. With the small indentures she left on the hard surfaces you'd think she'd have a sign of such intense damage. Wrapping the last cut, he sat her up against the wall, covering her with one of the blankets they packed from the other rooms inside the bunker.

He sat down on his hoverboard, breathing a calming sigh. They were finally out of the bunker. But what else were they going to do in the meantime? The supplies they raided from the cafeteria probably wouldn't hold them for another two- three days.

He stood up. Bella or Susan would probably come across the SOS. But if they didn't... what else could he do to get help?

Sorin moved in circles, his mind going over everything that happened in the last hours since escaping the cell. Until finally he moved back to his hoverboard and sat down. Rummaging through his bag he pulled out the document, he narrowed his eyes at the photo in front of it- the orb, the voices, and that monster that appeared inside the garage. All of it was connected to him somehow.

But how? He wasn't anything special... just another kid who was unlucky enough to get contaminated by styx matter. So why was it so gun-ho about getting to him?

He once again opened the document. The notes and files inside of it referred the orb as some kind of artifact, but it didn't go into much detail about it. The other stuff drew theories and different speculations about how it worked. With another diagram of the orb and its capsule having a word written in red above it.

"Metamorphosis," Sorin read silently "Tch, this stupid word."

He placed the document down on the floor and closed his eyes in thought. It was probably a bad idea for him to take this thing. But... after everything he experienced inside that bunker, he just had to know what was going on.

Suddenly an itch started to develop behind the nape of his neck. The air once again began to tingle. And he shoot upwards to his feet, suddenly shaking in fright.

"No... no, no, no." Sorin repeated to himself. A second later, what felt like a sharp pin suddenly pierced his head. His head throbbed as he closed his eyes, dropping to one knee, clutching his head in pain.

It was back, the fire inside the garage hadn't killed it, and it was coming for him.

CHAPTER

27

??????????? / ??????????? / ???????????

Sorin could feel it through the connection. And through the link he could sense its approach, and if it found him here... Zoe.

He forced himself up, he had to get out of here. Just being here placed Zoe in complete harm's way. But where could he go? He wracked his brains for an answer, but nothing was coming up. He looked outside past the boarded window, and like that he realized the true gravity of the situation. The link... there was truly nowhere else to turn. The link would simply lead it right to him, no matter the distance. Sorin greeted his teeth, there had to be a way to break it... He suddenly went to Zoe, the locket- could it work like it did last time? He pulled the silver chain up carefully and held the locket in his hand, opening it- the black gem shined from the light of his cyberdeck. But nothing was happening. He waited a few more moments but still nothing. He cursed, gently letting the locket go. He felt an incredible shroud of fear take hold of him. Every iota of his brain was filled with the prospect of the future encounter with the beast, and he could hardly bear it.

The bodies within the bunker flashed into his mind, the nomad who was barely human came to the forefront- his black eyes peering at him with total malice. The creature... it was racing through the city at this very moment. He could feel it homing in on his location with the guidance of the invisible tether binding them both

And he didn't know what to do...

His thoughts went back to the moment when it held him, the moment his heart drummed within his chest, an explosion of power that was just as mysterious to him, as was the mystery of the things relentless pursuit of him.

Yet, no matter the reasons he refused to be turned into whatever that nomad had become.

He gulped, feeling a knot sliding down his throat. His nerves were fraught with anxiety. And he was once again highly aware of his state of being, and how alive he was at that very moment. This was it... for now, until he could think of something, he would have to lead it away from her. That's the only course of action he could commit. His limbs shaking, he put his backpack filled with rations next to Zoe, after making sure she was situated he moved towards the back door of the store. Hoverboard in hand, with the sun still over the horizon, he moved towards the entrance of the alley to the side of the store. The streets outside were quiet, the ruin and decay of his surroundings was as depressing a sight as usual. He tried to keep his breathing even but for the life of him it was almost impossible; the buzzing at the back of his head was getting louder, and the strand connecting the both of them was slowly becoming stronger. Like a lost signal that was slowly regaining its reception. His heart thumped in his chest, so abrupt was it, that his hand went right over it.

It was close, he extended his board and let it drop before him. He needed to get ready. He jumped on, the platform pulsed with energy- as if the machine itself was amp with anticipation.

Sorin looked both ways, wondering what the best direction would be to go. CRASH! The sound ripped through the air to his left, the opposite of where he was looking- and his choice was made for him; he kicked off frantically, the wind buffeted his face as he blasted off forwards towards the opposite direction.

The sounds of carnage boomed behind him. He glanced back and there it was, crashing through the rusted shell of a car, the ruptured pieces flying everywhere as it bounded for him on all fours- moving impossibly fast for its massive bulk. Its eyeless face trained on his retreating form, and its horrible mouth pulled into a spiteful sneer. Sorin turned around and gunned it, his speedometer on the deck rising from 20mph- to 40mph- and finally 50mph. He focused, his stance on the board instantly set as the added weight of his bag and Zoe were no longer a factor in weighing him down; It took every shred of concentration to swerve, dodge, and jump over every obstacle in his way. All the while, it was in a relentless pursuit, its distance staying just behind him- no longer gaining any ground, but not losing it either.

That's when Sorin noticed something... the dead streetlamps that should have been off and without power, began to blink. Each piece of machinery that he was now hastily speeding past began to emit light in some form or fashion, like a mysterious breath of life was being blown into the abandoned street he was being chased through. He suddenly swerved hard, nearly colliding with a barrier that extended up from the ground with a CRUNCH of debris and dust flying upwards. He held on to his board as the vents underneath hummed from the sudden sharp turn. Sparks began to jump from the metal fins being scrapped across the ground. And Sorin clenched his teeth from the effort, his legs and arms screaming in protests as he angled the drifts momentum into the nearby alleyway. With a SWOOSH he plunged into the narrow path. Sorin looked behind him In fright and watched with alarm as the creature turned and crashed into the narrow passage, with the two buildings seemingly shaking from the impact. To Sorin's shock he could see one of the gems; the green one by the suns glare upon it, was poking from out of its forehead.

Suddenly, he was reminded of the garage. How the lights and some of the machinery was reacting at the time... it wasn't him doing that by mistake... it was this things doing...

The thing roared as it struggled to enter the alleyway, like a giant cat trying to reach for a pesky mouse. Then suddenly, its massive face moved- its hulking frame dashing away from the alleyway entrance. And Sorin was out of the alley, shooting out and moving clear across the next street, he only had a moment to spare before his velocity once again took him into another alley ahead. There was a noise above him, he looked up and a fast-moving shadow rushed down from above. He cried in pain as something sharp flashed through the air next to him, cutting his face, and slashing at his back. He ducked on the board as fresh blood flew from his cut cheek, with the steady trickle of it oozing from his back. The new wounds stung horribly, but they didn't feel major.

Sorin growled in anger, he continued to crouch down on the board as the two tendrils lashed about in the air above him. How had it climbed up that fast? He looked ahead- the alley was nearly at an end, he needed to think of something fast!

He smashed on the breaks, propping the board up and using the thrust of the boards vents to counter thrust his current velocity. The massive shadow zoomed further up ahead and with great effort he swiveled around, using the fins to further twist the board into the opposite direction. With a blast of energy he was moving, flying back from wince he came; he bent down, keeping his eyes forward as he held up his cyberdeck and began to activate the breech program. There had to be something around he could quick hack. Anything he could use to slow this thing down.

He swerved to his right as he exited the alley flying down the sidewalk, which wasn't as thronged with loose debris and fragments of ruin. Sorin's eye caught movement below to his left, that's when he caught sight of a shadow, a massive running figure that was blocking the sunlight on top of the building.

So fast... how can I shake it if it's able to catch up so quickly! Sorin looked around frantically, there had to be a way, there just had to be...

CRUNCH! There was a shower of rubble from above. Sorin veered away, back into the street as the creature landed where he had just been with a loud thud of impact. The creature was further behind after making that failed jump. But this didn't relieve Sorin, not one bit. He knew it would be back on him soon enough, Sorin twisted forward desperate for something to use. Suddenly, another series of barricades sprang up from the ground in front of him and Sorin quickly aimed his quick hack at the barricade- if the barricades were able to pick up a signal than surely he could reach it with his new breach program from the dead runner.

He locked on the barricades and gave the command. They shut with a loud BANG and Sorin grinned. Maybe the best relief alongside finding out that Zoe still had a pulse. He zoomed past the barricade and after a few seconds reengaged them... he heard an enraged howl behind him followed by the ear-splitting sound of metal getting torn up. Looking back with a frown, the wind buffeting his back, the metal barrier was completely torn and thrown off its hinges. Thrown to the wayside as the freak of nature charged through them. Its lips were curled in absolute loathing, those glossy teeth bared. Sorin turned back around, shaking his head in frustration, there had to be something in this dump of a settlement that could help him. He couldn't do this forever...

Sorin zoomed down the road, his speed staying at a constant 55mph, and all the while, he was forced to make counter hack after counter hack. He couldn't afford to go faster on his board, not if he wanted the reaction time to survive whatever ridiculous breech this thing behind him was attempting; Its digital fingers were absolutely fumbling with its quick hacks to stop him by any means necessary. From bringing up barriers, blowing out streetlamps as he passed them by (Forcing him to shield his eyes when they exploded from a surge of power), forcing down old crossing signs in his path. Blowing up pipelines in front of him (one of which singed his left arm), uncoupling streetlights and dropping them on him (one of which cut into his left leg from the shards of plastic). The ones he couldn't counter hack in time, he simply tried his hardest to swerve or dodge out of the way.

He was moving down another rubble strewn street, his cyberdeck alerting him to multiple enemy breeches. Most, he was able to cancel and throw back as a temporary distraction. But he had a problem. He was running out of road.

The road ahead was a dead end, with two ruined buildings on either side- and one huge building dead ahead. The sunset reflecting off the massive arch window at the front of the building; this had to be near the city's center. The massive turned-over statue at the front- which was laying on its side pointing towards the massive window, certainly looked super important enough. The gold statue depicted a man who was holding a sword above his head. But that's not what concerned Sorin, who was quickly and stressingly running out of ideas.

He looked around, hoping, begging for somewhere else he could turn, but there was nowhere else. He was approaching the last few buildings, and he glanced behind himself. The creature was gaining... its jaw open, roaring in definite frustration at its prey.

He looked forward, he zoomed past the other few buildings and suddenly- Sorin had a thought, a crazy thought, and honestly it was the only idea he had. It would ether work... or it would fail miserably.

The statue... it was leaning down at a fifty-degree angle and was low enough to be pointed at the large window on the 3rd floor. Sorin with absolute exhaustion realized this would probably be his only way out of this situation. The building looked to be on its last legs, with the ruined structure looking barely held together under the weight of gravity.

Sorin narrowed his eyes and concentrated. The path forwards wasn't nearly as broken as the numerous stretches of broken and cracked road he had been racing over for the past half hour. He needed to get his speed up, and his velocity on point. He leaned in on the board, changing his stance to get a better degree of balance, and with a silent prayer that this would work, he engaged the board to go as fast as possible.

He really hoped the window wasn't as sturdy as it looked.

The vents below the hoverboard crackled with energy as Sorin shoot down the path like a bullet. The fins on either side of the board closed up, compressing the energy from the boards engine- out the back- shooting the board faster than ever. Sorin braced himself- using what he learned from the foundry to keep his stance steady, he lowered and readied himself as the winds buffeted his face and body.

The speedometer reading jumped from 50mph to 75mph. He gritted his teeth, as he finally reached the tilted statue, the board bumped against the stand, his posture was nearly broken from the rough vibration traveling from the board and up his legs; but to his relief and exhilaration the long platform hoisted itself up, and shot across the length of the massive statue, and Sorin was finally airborne- his speed carrying him closer and closer to the window. The sunlight glared from the clear frame and Sorin quickly and without much thought, going completely on reflex, brought his hoverboard up. Scared that he would collide face first with the window, he brought the bottom of the board facing upwards towards the bright window. He willed the board to blow out a massive pulse of energy- hoping the exhaust would at least shield him. The board blasted energy out the bottom, the vents pulsing with the effort, and Sorin let out a loud curse, as the bright glare of the window and the bottom of his board became too bright for him to look anymore. He closed his eyes.

Sorin heard the shatter, felt the force of the board going through the windows frame, and felt shards of glass being splintered across the area around him. the only thing protecting him from getting ripped to shreds by the millions of glass pieces- was the energy radiating from the vents below the board. It didn't stop a few small splinters from piercing his upper torso and his arms which had gone to instinctly cover his face. His board suddenly landed on something wobbly, his eyes shot open, and he was zooming through the decayed insides of the buildings third floor. Speeding out of the large room and moving through the peeling halls of the top floor.

The speedometer rapidly dropped down towards the low thirties, he was desperately trying to slow himself down, but as he rode through the uneven terrain of the dilapidated hallway, he heard something.

There was a massive shockwave that seemed to travel through the floor. The hall around him splintered, and Sorin did not like the horrible moan and groaning sounds coming from inside the walls. There was another heavy vibration, followed by another and another. He looked behind him and sneered in utter contempt. Of course it jumped up with him...

The beasts hulking frame bulldozed into the building, causing even more debris and chunks of rotted wall to rain down around him. His speed was now at the low twenties and as he looked back forwards... he was approaching the staircase!

Sorin had enough time to realize that it was, in fact, a massive stairwell he was about to fly into. The problem, was that it was just as deteriorated as the surrounding hall... and behind him- the beasts was surging through the hall, claws digging onto the wooden floor- quickly moving to tackle the boy as the room behind it began to collapse in on itself with broken chunks of ceiling. The creature was utterly demolishing the surrounding hallway to get to its target, as the many flailing tendrils behind it whipped around, shredding through the already fragile state of the building's interior.

Sorin, with the added adrenaline, realized something as he was about to approach the moment of no return... The stairwell was deteriorated, but it should have enough room for him to do a very, very, hard drift around the spiral staircase. Maybe enough to reach the bottom floor even. But would it hold? Sorin widened his eyes, the staircase was getting closer, and his mind was going haywire trying to figure it out. But all to suddenly, a calm began to settle in his head. Either his practice at the foundry would pay off... or he would wipe out... inside of a likely collapsing building- with this stupid thing still on his tail.

Screw it!

Sorin put on a burst of speed- he didn't know how fast, just enough to at least get the speed he needed to keep going. Once he committed, there would be no retries.

He finally passed the last room, and he twisted himself around to his left, switching his poster, and letting the board close its side fins to the right. Sorin greeted his teeth and tilted just like he did back at the foundry all those days ago, the left fins on the board suddenly opened wide, as a large gout of energy pulsed from the left side of the board. The acceleration forced the board and Sorin to drift to the side as Sorin finally descended the steps. He was immediately thankful for the propulsion of the bottom vents... without it, he would have felt every sharp edge of the stairs as he descended down. It was almost a blur, his speed seemed to increase as he descended, and with all the concentration he had, he kept the nose of the board pointed away from the rusted balusters... and with timing he couldn't have dreamed of pulling off... he shot forward down the hall. The energy blowing from the left finally abating as the right fins gasped open. The board exhaled and the rest of that energy was quickly ejected backwards. Just behind him the stairwell finally collapsed, the echoing crash following him down the hallway with a heavy series of THUDS.

He quickly looked to his speedometer, 37mph and dropping, Sorin felt another rumble above, and the ceiling began to crumble, he held his arms up to shield from the debris, there was another quake, and something massive shoot down from the ceiling with a loud CRASH!

Sorin cursed, and just like that, the monster was once again behind him. leaving a gaping collection of holes from the rooms above. Sorin quickly began to speed up as the thing gave chase. The ceiling rained down, now huge chunks were falling around him as he moved left to right trying to dodge whatever thudded in front of him. A door stood leagues away, the word exit was blinking rapidly above it.

Sorin gasped as something heavy landed on his shoulder, and with a cry he was knocked off his board. He rolled on to the broken floor for a moment before coming to a painful stop, he heard a roar of victory close behind him, which was quickly and abruptly replaced with a shrill of pain. Looking behind himself from the floor, he was frozen by what he saw- the creature was impaled... a massive metal beam or support looked to have fallen right on top of the things back- running it through, the bottom end impaling into the broken floor. A gout of black smoke was ejecting from the wound.

Sorin scooted back frantically as a massive, clawed hand landed exactly where his leg once was. Causing the hard stone of the floor to be gouged.

Sorin struggled to pull himself up as the falling debris got worse, and he shouted in pain as more heavy pieces landed on him, the building began to shake and Sorin was thrown into the opposite wall, desperately he moved, crawling away on the ground as the creature howled pulling itself forward- and dragging the lodged beam across the floor. He collected the board which was waiting patiently a few leagues from the door and ran full pelt. Holding the platform above him, and using it as a shield for the falling pieces of ceiling. With every ounce of strength and the adrenaline flooding his veins, he barged into the door in front of him using the board as a ram. There was a pulse of energy, and the old door was reduced to splinters. Sorin charged outside as the building gave a thunderous roar, and he was blown down as debris shot above him, he didn't get the chance to get back up as layers of smoke went everywhere.

The sunlight barely penetrated the smokescreen over the dead-end street. And Sorin laid there, on his stomach completely worn out, his entire body aching from what he was put through. Both his arms felt like pincushions, the tiny glass shards from earlier did a number on him; his right shoulder still felt raw from that piece of debris which landed on it. He coughed from the smoke still in the air, the haze of the setting sun being the only thing to illuminate his surroundings; he flipped over to his back and regretted it- the vertical slash on his back screamed in response causing him to gasp out. Carefully, slowly, he got up back to his feet. Not really looking where his hands landed on to gain purchase. And leaning on whatever was close, he began to feel the cut upon his cheek- the wound was hot, and the pain was irritating, but he forced himself to ignore it...

"Is it finally dead?" Sorin muttered to himself.

Moving away from the thing he was leaning on, he took a step forward; the hoverboard was right there, face down on the ground, he went to pick it up. Suddenly, his hand moved back over his chest, the sensation was unmistakable, and he snarled in utter contempt.

"Oh you can't be series!" he roared toward the direction of the now demolished building. "What do you want from me? Could you freaking take the hint already!" he said kicking a small rock towards the debris, a low rumble could be heard shacking inside the ruble. "SCREW YOU! YOU HEAR ME! YOU WON'T HAVE ME, AND YOU"LL NEVER CATCH ME!" He raised his voice, his rage pouring into his words as it echoed across the dead-end street, before dissipating out into the dead settlement. Sorin glared at the demolished building; his hands balling and closing, as his hatred for this thing was now reaching astronomical levels. He grumbled to himself silently, before collecting himself, he reached down and got his board; looking around, he realized he was back in front of the building and behind him was the very statue he had used as a ramp. Closing his eyes, he could feel the collective pain of his injuries, which panged across his entire body.

He needed to do something about that... Church would have immediately gone to treat and bandage his wounds... if he was here, that is. He grumbled to himself shaking his head. *Focus, I have to focus... there has to be a place I can go to... somewhere far away, where I can have enough time to do something about these cuts...*

He gave the razed collection of debris in front of him another withering stare; before tossing down his board and jumping on, he kicked off- zooming past the golden statue and flying down the streets. He carefully readjusted the black and gold durag on top of his head; the thing was filthy, he could feel the dirt and grim covering it. Just another thing he needed to fix when he was finally rescued from this horrible place.

CHAPTER

28

??????????? / ??????????? / ???????????

Sorin cursed in frustration. He was far, far away from the dead-end valley.

But he had no idea where he was; the abandoned convenience store he had left Zoe to recuperate was nowhere to be found, and the sun was steadily creeping from the sky. After having to contend with and fend off the monster, the way back to the store ended up being the last thing on his mind.

Not like he could go back if he wanted to... but with the eventual return of the creature on the dwindling horizon, going back and placing Zoe in harms way was not an option. So what could Sorin do but find a place where he could get these wounds taken care of.

That was his plan, but he was having a difficult time of it; Sorin cursed again, most of the buildings in this part of the settlement were to unstable to go inside, and the other ones had the unfortunate infestation of the deserts wildlife...

Cazadors were aplenty in this area. And trying to find shelter outside the streets was slowly getting more and more challenging. At one point he tried to enter a building that looked somewhat more stable than the rest- only to look up and catch the movement of a green exoskeleton illuminated by the light of his cyberdeck; those massive compound eyes were wholly more malevolent than the ones from Zoe. The sudden movement above and in front of him, followed by the aggressive buzzing noise got his heart to lodge up his throat in panic. He backed out of the building in a hurry and quickly jumped back on the board- flying further down the street, just behind him the large dog-sized insect came skittering out the door, watching his retreat. Sorin breathed a massive sigh of relief as the dirt kicked up behind him; he traveled further down the path looking for something that could be of use. Suddenly, his eyes widened, and he immediately came skidding to a halt on the board. In the middle of the street, the boy stood idle, caught off guard by the sight before him.

The city limit... he was finally near the city limit.

The wastelands sprawled before him, past the city entrance gate, the flat expanse of the desert stretching unendingly into the horizon. The dark cement of the broken road he was on lead seemingly forever into the distant background. He felt a chill go down his spine, the setting sun in the background casting the unknowing expanse before him in vibrant oranges and deep reds, the sands blowing in the winds lazily.

The sight almost made Sorin forget where he was at, and what was eventually coming for him. He shook his head and made to turn around when he spotted something, to his right, a big gas station seated maybe couple of meters near the entrance gate- an island on a foundation of concreate housing a bunch of fuel stations in between two collapsed buildings. The station itself, surprisingly, looked to be in great condition if one didn't mind the dust, sand and cobwebs that seemed to litter and cake the place. Sorin stared at the station; it was old, like- he'd been transported back in time old...

He floated over to the building looking it over, "What is this?" he murmured to himself as he began to make out small signs over the barricaded doors and windows. But only one was mostly legible.

Welcome! Welcome! ...

.... Whitechapel! .... Next great jewel of the conclaves! Sponsored by .... and StarCore international ...

Sorin looked at the only legible sign above the door to the station. Whitechapel? StarCore International? he'd never heard of those names up till now.

But, he assumed Whitechapel must have been the name of this abandoned settlement. While StarCore international must have been the corporation that sponsored the place. After all, he'd walked past loads of ads at Gloomhaven with the exact same advertising.

But... this place is in ruins. What the heck happened here?

Shaking his head at the ironic words of the ad, he moved on; there had to be a way inside this place...

He didn't have to search long; Sorin realized the windows weren't that covered up, he picked up a brick on the side of the road and with a grunt- threw it at the boarded window. There was a loud crash of the window shattering, and the soft thump of the brick sailing through the rotted 2x4 and landing inside somewhere within the station.

Sorin jumped off the board and proceeded to hop over the ledge, taking care not to cut himself, slipping through the jagged edges of the window he was relieved that the inside of the station was mostly clear. No signs of any cazadors, no obvious signs of structural weaknesses, and for once, the smell of rotted wood and peeling plaster hadn't assaulted his nostrils. Stepping into the room hoverboard in hand, the place was lightly furnished, almost like the front entrance used to be a waiting room or something similar. It was a large room with white (Now dirty brown) colored walls and a few advertisement flyers on some of them. Aisles of empty shelves and the aforementioned furniture gathered at the back of the room in front of an old, analog Tv (Which also sported a huge crack in the middle of the screen). Thinking about it... the pumps outside the station did look big enough to fill up a rig as big as the voyager or something similar. This was probably the first stop for a lot of travelers journeying across the wastes.

"This must have been a really popular place to visit." Sorin thought out loud "It's so big... did Gloomhaven have any fuel stations like this? No, I don't think so." he frowned "Geez, what happened here?" Sorin asked no one in particular, this was the first time he had ever stepped foot in an abandoned settlement. But to be in such a massive city out in the middle of nowhere... with no sign or any given tells of how it ended up like this.

It was creepy. To him at the very least... But now that he was here. Was there anything salvageable in this dump?

Sorin looked behind the large checkout area, the place also seemed to have served as a convenient store, the cash register was busted, and the bottom shelves were also empty... Sorin paused for a moment, he spotted something behind one of the desks, moving it a little bit to the side.

There was a medium sized box, which was as old looking as the other stuff in the room- but the medical symbol on the front of the case got his attention. Opening the box, there was a bunch of supplies inside... medical gauze, ointment, emergency lights, and a flare gun! Sorin looked through the boxes contents- everything looked sanitary (Church's constant habits of throwing away things that didn't meet his view of being sanitarily safe, had unfortunately, rubbed off on Sorin... Seeing how he would always volunteer his help for him.) he took out the ointment and medical gauze, and sighed, this was going to hurt...

???????????????????????

The sun was almost gone and the streets outside were slowly getting blanketed by the creeping darkness; the wounds under his gauze bandages stung from the medical ointment. Sorin looked out the broken window, and he uneasily swallowed the lump in his throat.

He still couldn't feel nothing... The wait for this things eventual pursuit was wreaking havoc on his state of mind; he saw things in the shadows that weren't there, he flinched at the random sounds of the old station and settlement outside, and his mind went to Zoe... wondering if she was pulling through. The SoS he sent out, even that was becoming a source of anxiety for him. Could he be sure that it would reach them? Did he somehow mess up when making it? Did it even send out into the digital landscape of cyberspace? So many things buzzing around in his head... and he was just as flummoxed about where he was to go from here.

What else could he do? The thing just wouldn't stay down, and he was increasingly becoming nervous at the idea of having to flee once more- especially if it meant going out there in the setting sun.

He sat down on the hoverboard (he refused to sit on the furniture, which looked absolutely finicky) and he tried to brainstorm. There had to be a reliable way to keep it down... A way to finally stop this thing from taking him. He shivered, it was slowly getting colder; He looked back outside, his eyes scanning the horizon, before landing on the fuel stations outside. Not the small ones, but the massive oil cannisters tucked to the sides, where big rigs could use far away from the other small stations.

As he sat there, an idea suddenly surfaced into his mind. The idea was fleeting, a small iceberg which surfaced unannounced, and just as suddenly, sunk back into the deep. But then he paused, his mind suddenly yanking the idea back as he hugged himself. The idea was an absolutely desperate one... and if Hosea, Bella, King, Church or Aunt Dot had access to his thoughts at the moment- they would have called it reckless and foolish. But, Sorin was scared, he was tired, and he was cold. The idea was dangerously looking more and more tempting.

He shook his head, no, no... there had to be something else he could do, anything else...

He heard a noise and jumped up, this didn't sound like a random noise from the station. It was coming from outside, Sorin looked out the window; the dimming rays of the sun was painting the dead settlement in elongated shadows, the streets were looking darker, with the sunlight barely able to reach past the surrounding buildings. And Sorin saw it- just stalking from the shadows further down the street. Four massive wolfhounds slinking out from the dark; their short coats of yellowish dark fur seemed to blend in with the shadows. *Direwolves! You've got to be kidding me!!!* Sorin thought to himself, both his hands grabbing his head in panic.

The board! Sorin tapped his cyberdeck and the board immediately moved next him. He needed to be ready to move just in case.

Suddenly he felt it- the invisible string in his head immediately started to pull itself taught. It was coming, and Sorin scowled to himself... The direwolves weren't so intimidating anymore. Something worse would be coming for him soon.

Wait a minute... that thing makes all the electronics around it go haywire. Could I use that to my advantage... The gas pumps... are they manual or are they automated?

Right now he couldn't be sure... the stations power was not working, he already checked earlier. He didn't have the technical know-how of manipulating the fuel stations; but, if he could hack the subsystems for the fuel pumps and canisters maybe he wouldn't need to. If the systems linked to all the pumps here, he could force the pumps to leak oil. And maybe cause those big rig oil tanks at the side of the store to explode.

With the monster caught in the middle of it...

Sorin found himself getting increasingly anxious, he was actually considering this... Actually going through with it; his hands trembled, and a cold sensation traveled down his body- the image of the station he was in suddenly being enveloped in a massive fireball popped in front of his eyes.

Yet, the mental thread in his head was not lying. It was getting closer, and he was once again coming up blank on any other ideas. He took a moment to calm himself down, counting from one to ten; the direwolves outside were quiet, and he couldn't hear any sounds of them moving all that much. Getting nervous he looked up, they were all together in a tight nit group, hair bristling and teeth bared- they could probably sense it too. One by one, they all began to clear out. And Sorin found himself hoping they wouldn't go.

Stading up, he swallowed another lump. This was probably going to be it. One last plan- he could only hope for the best at this point; The sun was now barely over the horizon, and that sunset was quickly being reduced to embers, the abandoned streets where barely illuminated, and the evening sky was getting darker. The beast hasn't even arrived yet. No sign, no sounds, all was quite- and Sorin was becoming antsy. He was checking the fuel stations in front of the store, with the light of his cyberdeck he found what he was looking for, a symbol- a small logo of the cities ACCT(Administrators Of Cyberspace Communication Transmissions). He wondered how the bunker below the city had cut into the ACCTS domain over there corner of cyberspace, but those questions could wait later when he reunited with Bella; he had the proof he needed that this thing could be linked by his cyberdeck- more like breeched; Sorin scowled to himself, his fist clenching- for his plan to work, he needed the thing to keep close to the station. He wasn't sure of how far the thing needed to be in order to cause machinery to turn on by itself- but he would soon find out. Keep it chasing him, and keep it close to the station while the breech works on the station, and above all, don't let it catch up...

His hand moved down to the flare gun in his pocket, once again checking to see if it was still there. He checked the other pockets of his cargo pants; he only had two rounds for the gun, and he hoped against hoped that his aim wouldn't be lousy. All he needed now was the creature to show its ugly face.

He clenched his board tightly, but where was it? The link binding them both was barely receptive, almost weaker than it had started out; Sorin hated the link, but it was his only way of tracking how close it was... Suddenly, nothing, not even the dull throb remained. He froze, became deathly still, something was wrong he could feel it, he moved away from the station and looked around his eyes barely able to discern any detail lurking outside his field of view. The darkness being cut by the light of his cyberdeck, and streets leading towards into the settlement looked as far as he could tell, looked empty. He narrowed his eyes, paranoia causing him to quicken his steps; he couldn't believe it, there was no way it was just giving up.

What's it playing at?... is it really, finally calling it quits? No, somethings up, maybe I should...

Sorin heard a noise behind him, he turned around throwing his board up like a shield... nothing.

He began to breath quicker, he was struggling to keep it under control, he threw the board down and hopped on it, he was ready to move at a moment's notice. Another sound behind him, he turned; the hoverboard pulsing with energy and was primed to bolt with him on it. But he paused, there was something in front of him a few meters in the distance, barely illuminated by the light of his cyberdeck

A figure was standing there, observing him; the hood of its long cloak was shrouded in darkness, not giving any details of its face. But what he could see had him frozen in fear. The shapes eyes seemed to glow white, two glints of glowing silver that shined from within the depths of its hood- he could sense its stare, and it was somehow more frightening than the eyeless ones of the beast.

Sorin's mouth open and closed, but nothing came out, to spooked by what he was seeing; the same stranger he kept encountering in Gloomhaven, the bunker, and now once again in front of him. Was he about to die? Like the nomads before him...

"*Sorin*," A voice, a hollow unearthly voice echoed into his head "*The time is near, and the gatekeeper is your only salvation.*"

CHAPTER

29

???????????? / ???????????? / ????????????

Sorin was silent; the shapes words echoing inside his head. Who was he... and why did he feel strangely familiar?

"H-how do you know my name and who the heck are you!?" Sorin demanded louder than he had intended to ask; there was something wrong here, something that revolved around him, and he had no idea what...

But everyone seemed to think he was key to something- that was the only thing he could reach after seeing the documents in the file.

"Wait a minute... Gatekeeper? What the heck is a gatekeeper?" Sorin inquired.

"Could you just tell me what the heck is going on already!" Sorin roared towards the figure. But he remained silent and Sorin swore out loud "Screw this! I'm outta here!" he turned around and the figure was suddenly facing him, he yelped, switching the hoverboard in reverse- but in a swift motion, the hand of the stranger (an appendage wrapped in black cloth) came to rest upon his chest, exactly where his heart was...

Sorin froze, something jumped within his chest; a sensation so alien, it caused him to gasp. There was something freezing where the strangers hand laid, a surge of cold so all-consuming that it caused him to double over. His knees landed on the board as he grasped his chest, struggling to draw breath as it filled his entire chest; Sorin's face was pulled into a expression of complete rage.

"WHAT DID YOU-" he looked back up, his vision swimming; and the stranger began to turn transparent- his form disappearing back into the shadows like a phantasm. Sorin with his eyes widening could only yell "WAIT!" as the figure finally disappeared into the dark veil of the buildings shadow. Sorin's hand immediately went to his cyberdeck increasing the brightness of the lights, but it didn't change anything... the reach of the light only extended for a few feet; but the stranger was gone...

Once again alone in the parking lot, between fuel pumps and gas station; Sorin cursed to himself, his body freezing from whatever that... thing, did to him. He tried to stand up, but it was a struggle- the cold persisted and his vision was still blurry. He gasped, something in his chest lurched; grasping where his heart was over his chest he began to panic.

"What did he do to me?" Sorin breathed in a hushed tone "What the heck did he-"

Sorin was abruptly distracted; in the corner of his eyes he noticed something, a bright, rapid interval of lights down the street leading further into the settlement. Streetlamps. They were rapidly switching on and spreading towards his location. Sorin's eyes widened in alarm, it was coming, he could feel it now... it was close. The mental thread between it and him began to tighten. But the direction of the source was completely sporadic.

No, it was moving fast. Very, very, fast.

The gas station suddenly exploded in light. Sorin gasped in fright, and he looked down at his cyberdeck. Multiple electronic sources began to connect to his index; and the fuel stations were one of them. He immediately sent a breech on them, and connected to the other electronics around the area. He had to lock them down, he needed to stay close to the station, and he couldn't afford to multitask with counter hacking and fleeing at the same time... Not with this horrible pain spreading from his chest.

His vision was still wonky, but he persisted- looking up occasionally to see what was going on around him... But, to his unnervement there wasn't a sound, not a peep out of place. The thing was close, yet for the life of him, he couldn't understand why it wasn't taking the bait.

No, Sorin shook his head. *It did take the bait, but why hasn't it shown itself yet?* He hovered in the parking lot, looking desperately for this thing. His right foot was on the hard pavement ready to kick off in the direction he needed to go. Sorin began to wonder to himself could it be possible that it's guessed what he's planning on doing? He couldn't be sure if this thing knew that it was hacking its environment- but what if it figured out what was going on with the fuel pumps?

Suddenly, the gas station went dark plunging him in near total darkness. Sorin yelled in alarm, his cyberdeck once again his only light source, looking down at the screen, the breech connection paused- showing an error message over its progress. He looked around, pointing the screen forward trying to make something out of the only illumination he had, and that's when he heard it. Facing the ground next to him; something silver shot out from between the floor grates, a thick metallic thread which quickly latched onto his arm.

It was like a jolt of electricity shot out of the metallic thread, he was suddenly seized by a hoarfrost temperature going up his leg- his knee hit the platform, and his arm felt completely frozen. He groaned in pain, as the floor grate next to him began to crack as sounds started to emanate from between the bars.

Suddenly with a harsh CRASH! And CRUNCH! a humongous fist crashed through the ground; Sorin could only bring his right arm to shield from some of the pieces of asphalt which flew everywhere. Now his left arm was going numb, and he could barely lift it. More tendrils began to wrap themselves around the board, causing it to whine in protest. As tendrils went into the vents. Then another quickly wrapped around his left arm.

The creature ripped itself from the rubble; Sorin growled in rage, giving the freak a defiant glare. He then noticed how different it looked; it was still massive, but thinner, its muscles seemed to have shrunk on themselves, giving it a malnourished look. This of course didn't help in making it any less terrifying, not one bit.

The creature turned its eyeless gaze towards him, its big granite colored face giving him a sightless glare, its mouth pulled into an ugly sneer. Sorin's eyes widened, there was a gaping hole where the metal beam had skewered it, from the front of its chest, all the way to the back, he blanched being able to see through to the other side like a macabre hole in the wall. How on earth was it still alive?

The tendril from its back was firmly wrapped around his left arm; he quickly went into his other pocket, while kicking back on the ground, hoping the board could get him some distance. Instead... the creature growled and quickly reached out with an arm grabbing Sorin around the torso in a crushing grip. Sorin felt the oxygen in his lungs getting squeezed out as he gasped involuntarily from the things strength. His entire hand was completely wrapped around his torso, and he couldn't do a thing as he was lifted up off the board. His legs dangling from the ground; he was forced to watch as the three gems in its forehead began to push themselves forward. The monster started to howl in the night sky, in a seeming roar of victory; the three gems glowed brightly: the red, green, and indigo pulsing from its head.

The gas station erupted in lights; so bright where they that Sorin had to close his eye for a moment as the pain radiated across his torso and arm, which was excruciating. Opening them again, he could only watch as more tendrils began to wrap around his legs and arms. The lights from the streetlamps and the other surrounding electronics began to flicker unstably, as a few seemed to spark and shortly explode from whatever power was being forced through them. Sorin looked to his cyberdeck, the connection looked to be reestablished, and the breech was starting back up, all he needed was twenty seconds... Sorin fighting through the pain dropped his right arm down to reach for his left pocket. The creature faced him, and to his disturbance, made a horrible grin, formed from its glossy teeth.

SCREW YOU! Sorin thought with all his being as his fingers finally wrapped around the flare gun.

Summoning every bit of contempt he had for this thing, he brought it out and pointed it forward, just in time- as it roared in his face, in what was probably in its mind a roar of jeering mockery. CRACK! The gun fired out the round which crashed into the things open mouth. The thing froze... then with a loud BANG! The night sky was filled with the sudden agonized roars escaping from its wide jaws. Sorin was unhanded, as the tendrils snaked off his limbs.

He fell back down landing on his board, back first before his head bumped onto the platform causing stars exploded in his head. The board sprang from the impact as the monster roared in fury as it backed off, trying to claw the burning flare from its throat; the red illumination from the flare and smoke was completely filling the area around it and

Sorin, who struggled to sit himself up, the cold was now spreading further. There was a beep from his wrist.

The breech was complete. Using his other hand which was still numb, he gave the command. The fuel stations made a horrible noise, the pumps started move as pressure began to build within the hoses connected to the pump handles. The hoses started to expand, while the fuel nozzles began to spray oil inside of their holsters on the pumps. The stations started to groan as more and more pressure continued to build within the silos. The massive fuel canisters on the side of the building began to open. The hoses finally exploded, the thick plastic ripping itself free as fuel sprayed everywhere, some of it nearly spraying on him. The monster gave enraged howl as the flare continued to burn within its mouth; its scaly hide was then drenched in the dark liquid by the fuel station that it had backed into by mistake. The large silos behind to the sides started to overflow; Sorin commanded the hoverboard to back up. The platform with a pulse of energy, proceeded to backpaddle away. The tendrils binding it- were quickly snapped by the torque of the hoverboards engine.

He grimaced, the overpowering stench of fuel wafted through the air. His breech command forced the subsystem to purge the left-over fuel inside of the stations underground storage tanks. He didn't have time to set the exact pressure for the fuels dispenser system, and he switched off the safety measures for the dispensers- causing the automated system to pump it out with full pressure. The same was happening with the giant fuel silos at the opposite end of the building.

The fuel sloshed forward, splashing across the monsters metallic hide; the flare gun slipped from Sorins hands, clacking onto the concrete below; the frigid chill from his chest spread down to his hands and other limbs. His vision was getting worse... and everything was starting to spin.

That's when it happened, more fuel exploded everywhere from another hose that could no longer contain the pressure. A sheet of petroleum landed on the beast, in its face and into its wide jaws... and the flare was still burning...

Sorin averted his eyes, the gas on the creature suddenly ignited and he was engulfed in flames. Sorin couldn't hear the beasts roar over the intense inferno. The flames stretched their fingers out to the other pools of petroleum on the ground and like a lit match, the flame roared forwards, slurping the fuel up before finally reaching the other fuel stations.

BOOM! BOOM! BOOM!

The stations detonated with horrible force, one after another in quick succession. A wave of pure heat surging forward, as the obliterated remains of the fuel stations erupted into a pillar fire. Sorin, who was rapidly gaining distance from the explosions was bombarded by the sudden heat wave, and like a blanket the temperature surrounded him at all sides. He peeked ahead and was barely able to swerve the board out of the way from colliding with a streetlamp. While behind him the explosions increased in size, and the shockwaves they produced rattled him to his core. Another shockwave, this one from the eruption of the massive oil silos to the side of the gas station, and Sorin was sent careening out of control, fragments of station and pieces of asphalt and smoldered metal rained across the streets. And Sorin screamed as something sharp embedded into the back his right leg. While the board zipped away. Sorin, who was occupied by the horrible pain cutting into his leg, was not prepared as the board shoulder checked into a fire hydrant in the way, causing him to shake and tumble off the fleeing platform.

He was barely able to tuck and roll from the impact of him hitting the concrete floor at such a speed; at the back of his mind, he must have been going maybe 15-25 mph as he was thrown off the board, he rolled roughly on the ground, and with a horrible thud, his uncontrolled roll was cut short when he slammed into the nearby side of a building.

The station, with one final roar, imploded in a catastrophic explosion; the glass behind the other nearby building shattered from the shockwave as Sorin slipped into a ball upon the floor, another wave of heat and condensed air rolled over him. As glass fell onto the ground shattering around him. The night sky was lit by a large mushroom cloud of smoke and fire, as the street around him was cast in a orange glow of dancing lights and shadows.

Sorin couldn't help the groan which escaped his mouth. His world was nothing but pain, his body a collection of bump and bruises with the fragment of ripped metal lodged into his leg. He squirmed, he couldn't even find the strength to get up at this point. Looking down, and painfully moving his right leg- he could just make out the small piece of metal sticking out of his lower calf. Feeling nauseous at the sight, he looked away and turning over to his stomach on the side of the sidewalk, he looked back towards what used to be the gas station. Now a burning ruin.

Sorin gasped in shock, he couldn't believe it... he was still alive... but, was it finally dead?

He closed his eyes, breathing a ragged moan of pain as a sudden wave of agony surged from his injured leg, and when he opened them- he noticed his cyberdeck. The screen was cracked, and fragments of metal were sticking out of it. The screen was glitched and barely readable. Sorin felt his heart sink into his frozen chest, a deep pain flashing within at the sight of his beloved cyberdeck.

He reached a shaking hand to the command prompt, and typed a few commands. The screen made a few glitched noises, but... it looked like it was still functioning, if barely. He made to call the board to him, but something caught his eye; a shadow was moving away from the intense flames leading out of the settlement. Its form a silhouette in front of the blazing fire. Sorin's relief was deflated like a ballon, and with a desperate, frantic motion pressed the keys of his cyberdeck. His board! he needed his board, he had to escape...

The shadow flickered and seemed to phase right in front of him. The effect of which seemed to distort the space around it in its wake, as the sound of the burning inferno became warped; Sorin flinched back, his fear filling his heart with lead, as he struggled to look up at the things face. But there was nothing, nothing but those silver points for eyes, as the shadows cast by its long hood covered whatever its face may have looked like. The stranger crouched to one knee, its bandaged arm pulling something from its ragged robes, a smoking orb in its hands...

Sorin tried to pull away, tried to get up, flee, anything... but his injuries weighed him down. The frigid cold, which this thing was culpable of- was now completely filling his entire body.

The orb was stark silver in the strangers bandaged wrapped hand; Sorin felt a powerful surge of electricity travel across his body, the origin of which seemed to radiate from within his chest.

He could feel it... the thin and ethereal thread connecting him and it seemed to rise in its potency... the resonance of its pull, veiling a foggy shroud as thick as the mist from that chamber inside of the bunker. The orb in his mist addled eyes seemed to shiver along with him- the orb began to peel itself back, exactly as it had back in its capsule. Only... there was just two gems this time, poking from within its center: the red and green gems and their respective hues. Sorin felt trapped, his head was not his own anymore, and it was getting harder and harder to think...

Suddenly, the pseudo- metallic flower extended out two vines of silver.

With barely any conscious will on his part, and by instinctual reflex of his animal brain- his right arm shot out to block the dual tendrils coming for his face. The creepy vines latched to his cyberdeck covered wrist instead, with the gloved gauntlet beeping an alarm that Sorin could hardly hear as his mind seemed to go blank. The orb suddenly yanked itself forward towards his arm, the metallic substance covering his gloved hand and the cyberdeck under it. Sorin shivered uncontrollably, as the small shadow within his consciousness understood the degree of pain he was in. Sorin shook, his arm feeling like it was covered in a blazing inferno of pain, as a scream of agony came unbidden from his lips.

> "May the gatekeeper serve you well. The unity you form with it, shall protect you from the inevitable corruption to come," the figure stood up, its body rippling from the heat of the distant fire "You have grown child, you're survival of Silverwood was a fortunate outcome... Your mother, she would have been proud..."

The figure vanished, its body fading from view; Sorin fell over unconscious, his face falling across the pavement floor as his right arm eerily reflected the blazing fire in the distance. The silver substance, continued to spread over his arm- before slowly halting in its movement, then gathered itself back, collecting itself across the boys right forearm as the two gems appeared over the back of his hand.

CHAPTER

30

??????????? / ??????????? / ???????????

When Zoe finally opened her eyes, her first thoughts were one of total confusion; the dark and dreary surroundings of the old, and small convenience store caught her completely for a loop. The sunsets light was breeching through the cracks of the old wooden barricades of the window, giving her a horrible view of the store's scenery.

Where was she? and how had she?

Her eyes widened, the flashes of memory which caught up to her, had her springing back to her feet. The blanket fell across the floor as her left shoe bumped into the backpack to the side...

Sorin's backpack...

She looked around, her eyes now truly drinking the environment in, but there was no sign of the boy that had seemingly saved her life. The creature... how on earth had he managed to escape and bring her here? That's when she realized she was out of the bunker, but what did that information mean at all to her if she was the only one to get out. Her compound eyes began to well up, tears threatening to fall, what was going on... she moved her arm a little too hard and cried out in pain, her hand went to her right arm and felt the bandages covering the affected wound. Her head and arm both bandaged up... So, he must have had plenty of time to apply them... so why wasn't he here?

Did he go out to gather more supplies... No, she shook her head. Her concern was palpable, and the only thing that made sense- was that maybe the monster was still alive. She had to find him now, he needed help!

She grabbed the backpack and blanket, stuffing it inside she slipped the bag on. The door ahead was still barricaded but she couldn't have cared less. She smashed open the barricaded door using all her strength, as the door and particle wood holding it in place was reduced to splinters from her kick.

She had to find him... he had to be somewhere... she couldn't be the only one alive... after everything they went through! She sped outside and her jaw almost hit the floor. A hand went to her mouth as the sheer ruin of the surrounding environment finally processed into her mind.

"Oh my gosh... this is..." she said in a hushed tone of voice "What happened here!?"

She moved across the ruined street and immediately became nervous at the signs of a fight, the way the ruined vehicle in front of her looked... like something had cannonballed through it. She needed to find a better view, anything to discover where she was at in this massive city.

"Settlement... he called it a settlement." Zoe corrected herself silently.

She moved towards a ruined building; applying tension to her back, She could feel the pincers extend from behind- as her instincts pointed her above the building. A vantage point... that's what she needed. She crouched down, the pincers skewering into the pavement. she bounded upwards, using the sharpened extra limbs to spring herself further up in the air- 5 meters- before sending all her pincers skewering into the walls of the building before her, all four pulling her upwards like a spider, she used her arms and legs to climb faster. In the back of her mind, she was eerily surprised at how fast she was climbing up, but she filed it away for now, the only thing she was focused on was locating her friend.

She pulled herself up and made her way across the rooftop, before coming to a stop at the edge. Her eyes widened, the expanse of the settlement completely floored her. It was huge... most of the buildings were like the one she stood on, maybe 3-5 stories tall, but the sight of it was beyond what she imagined back home.

Especially, with how some of the people from her hometown described settlements. That they were hodgepodges of communities out there in the conclaves, vying for the settlement of a barren wasteland. But what she saw made her shake her head in horror. The city was dead, it looked so old and abandoned; by the light of the setting sun she was completely flabbergasted, where was she going to start looking?

She unconsciously pecked the ground bellow her with her pincers; the slight breeze from the wind blowing across her tattered dress, which gave her chills. The temperature was dropping- how cold did it get in the wastelands at night? She frowned to herself... she would have to hurry... the last thing she needed was for the little bit of sunlight she had to disappear, and it was progressively getting darker as she stood over the edge thinking.

But as she was about to vault off the building, she heard a noise... She paused; closing her eyes and focusing, she began to realize to her astonishment, that those were voices she was hearing in the distance.

She gasped, the SOS he sent out... Did his nomad family finally arrive to help? She began to focus, using her acute hearing to pinpoint the direction of the voices talking. It was faint and barely audible, but it was there, she just had to figure out the direction...

"There... I got it." Zoe mumbled to herself as she made her way in the direction of the noises.

The light of the sun continued to dip, till finally the light of the sun hid over the horizon, causing small vestiges of orange and reds to streak across the waning sunset; and Zoe was having a rough time making her way across the rooftops of the city, with most of the buildings being in horrible conditions.

Her agility gave her a small edge in navigating the dangerous surroundings; she was especially amazed that the buildings were still standing regardless of the horrible state of disrepair that they were in. She jumped another hazardous gap between seemingly collapsed spaces of one rooftop, using her pincers to skewer and pull herself over massive stretches of collapsed roofing. She scaled and descended whenever necessary over the stretches of the rooftops to make her way over to her destination. Which, she began to realize wasn't just voices per say. She paused on top of one roof, now that she was closer, she could definitely recognize the low rumbles of a vehicle... a working vehicle. She continued to move. Her excitement causing her movements to become quicker. She flipped through a broken window and scaled up the ruined façade inside of the building and wall- crawled upwards.

She pulled herself upwards onto the roof and she slowed down; pulling her pincers behind her as she got closer to the edge of a building, and below her...

She blinked in confusion, where those kids... and they looked to be of her own age!

There was two of them, one girl and one boy; the girl was dressed in what looked like punk clothes and the boy seemed to be dressed like a young rocker or something similar. Scratch that, after looking harder the girl looked a little bit older and the boy younger. They seemed to be arguing with one another; of course, that wasn't what interested Zoe. The green van they were standing next to was pretty big, and judging from the muffled sounds from it- more people were inside.

She bit her lip; Zoe was confused, she didn't remember Sorin ever mentioning any other kids like them... Did she make a mistake? She gave a nervous groan to herself. What should she do? She couldn't afford to waste more time, not when she had no idea where he even was in this dead city...

"There's gotta be something I can do... something!" She whispered to herself; her pincers began to once again tap around her in her anxiety, creating small *tick, tick* noises against the asphalt of the roof. She squeezed the rails in front of her, which began to groan and compress under the girls strength. But then, something felt wrong; Zoe paused, the noises below and the sounds of the argument between the two kids was suddenly silent. She looked back down and felt her heart go into her throat. The boy, he was pointing directly at her and the girl she was also pointing an outstretched hand towards her position... Zoe, looked on confused. What was that trailing around her arm... was that electricity!

Zoe gave a massive yelp, as the girl suddenly shot out a bolt of pure lighting from her hand. The heavy CRAKLE ripping through the air faster than she could blink- which speared past, nearly hitting where her head had been.

She flipped backwards, her instincts once again saving her life... She came to skidding stop away from the edge, her heart pounding. Suddenly a massive force ripped through the section of roof under her feet; the floor below her began to crack and rumble, and using all her reflexes she jumped... just in time as a section of the roof she stood on collapsed; she wall jumped off the opposite wall and used her pincers to yank herself away from the collapsed section. Zoe screamed a bit, her momentum carrying her off the building and dropping her off the side; she stretched her pincers, all four skewering either side of the other building, which slowed her fall. She landed on the ground gracefully, and a voice "It went this way!" called from out of the open street.

Fearing for her life, she growled and tried to slip further into the alley; the walls of the building gave a horrible CRUCH and loosened a pair of large debris which fell directly in front of her, she gave a hiss of frustration before darting back out of the alley- right into the open street, and right in front of the two kids.

They both jumped back in alarm; their faces pulled into an expression of fear. Zoe, even in her near feral state, grimaced at the looks- the image of Sorin's exact reaction when they first meet passing her by in a flash.

The teen in front of her crackled with energy, ice blue electricity traveling along her body and clothes; her blue eyes, under her dark bangs had miniature sparks pulsing from them. She had medium long hair, which fell past her shoulders as she wore a dark blue long sleeve shirt and collar with the words *CombiDrone* blazoned in the middle in red font, with dark colored pants and shoes. The boy was her own age, she could tell that much at least; he wore an orange and black weathered jacket which looked a few sizes too big on him, with a plain white shirt under it. His skin was tanner than the girls, who's skin was fairer in shade; the boy had wild brown hair, fuzzed up in way to look rock star esc (Zoe had seen plenty of boys at her old school with the same look, before she started home schooling) he wore black jeans and white shoes.

The girl and boy tensed, and Zoe nervously backed away, ready to make a run for it. Her pincers behind her raised, ready to carry her away.

"ROXANNE! JACK! WHATS HAPPENING!" A voice, a woman's voice cut through the air. Zoe flinched, her eyes widening as two adult from out of the van came up from behind the two kids.

She froze, were these the parents? An older man skidded in front of the two, between them and her, he definitely looked to be the boy's father; a man of dark skin, with brown hair and beard, his dark brown eyes looked between the two groups- he wore a dark shirt and faded jeans and brown leather boots.

"Dad! Look out, you're in the way!" the older girl cried, raising her open hand as a ball of electricity gathered around it.

"Both of you! Cut it off now!" the man barked back "Did she attack? Or done anything at all aggressive to you yet? Or, did you jump the gun like usual?" The girl froze, as the boy looked tensely at Zoe. Who froze, trying to look as non- combative as possible.

"Hey, both of you calm down!" a woman said, pulling herself in front of the two kids. Zoe watched, the woman looked to be the girl's mother, sharing the same light skin tone, with dark hair tied into a long-braided ponytail. She wore a dark jacket and light jeans, with dark brown shoes. The two kids looked at their parents; with clear hesitation, a moment later they began to relax. The two parents walked forwards towards Zoe, who looked on with clear nervousness, what had she gotten herself into?

"Hey there," the woman greeted "My name is Meryl, and this is my husband Robert... what's your name?" she asked kindly.

Zoe looked them both over; they looked nice enough, and maybe they could help her. "Z-Zoe..." she said nervously "C-could you help me... I'm looking for my friend, but I don't know where he is."

They both gave a double take "You're friend?" the man said, his voice a low rumble, but she couldn't mistake the kindness coming from it "So you're not alone then?"

Zoe shook her head "We were both taken by Nomads, and we were held prisoner inside of a nearby bunker... t-there all dead. Something killed them and we escaped- but something huge attacked us." She shivered "It knocked me out, and Sorin... I-I don't know what happened after- but, I woke up in one of the abandoned stores and he wasn't there." She shook her head "I don't know where he's at." she trembled.

"Hey, hey, it's okay." Meryl lightly laid a hand on both her shoulders, her pincers inched back, no longer primed to carry her away, "It's okay, will see what we can do... do you have any idea of where he could have gone?" she questioned. Zoe shook her head rapidly, she wiped her eyes, tears threating to spill.

"Mom... Dad..." the boys voice interjected, he walked up, his face pulled into an expression of concentration. Zoe's eyes widened, the air seemed to ripple around him, as his eyes glowed a goldish tinge. "I hear something... no, I hear somebody shouting in the distance," he turned to Zoe "Is this Sorin person a boy my age?" Zoe was suddenly at attention "Yes! Y-you can hear him- where is he?" she demanded frantically, but then she paused, something was wrong, the boy seemed to get paler in color...

"Jack?" the man asked, "What's wrong?"

The girl- Roxanne- Zoe, believed her name was, walked up to the boy. "Hey, what gives? Something happening?" she asked. He gave her a confused look "It sounds like... is that fire?"

KABOOM!

Before Zoe could say anything else, a rumble ripped through the ground, rolling over them. They all cried out in alarm as a massive explosion lit the now sunless night sky, followed by a shockwave that knocked them off their feet. Zoe struggled to keep herself level, using her pincers to dig into the ground as she found herself holding on too Meryle. She kept the woman from falling over as her husband dropped to one knee, he looked up frantically, and was horrified at the massive plume of smoke in the distance. "What in god's name." he whispered as he checked on his two kids who were both getting up from the ground. "Is everybody alright?" he called, followed by a chorus of yesses. Zoe looked up at the mushroom cloud in terror "W-what was that?" she uttered out.

"Guys! I can hear him! It's coming from that direction, towards the smoke!" Jack cried out.

Zoe felt herself freeze, her eyes widening in horror and shock. *Sorin... wha... what happened!*

She unhanded Meryl, and with a surprised yelp from the older woman, who could only watch as the girl in the red jacket ran off, far faster than any of her age could have moved. Jack looked on, his mouth becoming slack jawed as the girl covered the length of the street... before scaling the building in front of them- like a spider- before disappearing above and moving out from view... directly towards the column of smoke...

"Wholly crap, she's fast..." Roxanne replied, to the numb agreement of Jack, who could only nod in response.

"Everybody in the van," Robert called "Will meet her there."

??????????? / ??????????? / ???????????

246

Zoe coughed and gagged as she got closer and closer to the source of the explosion. The air was becoming wavy as the heat began to climb. This was so much worse than the fire of the garage, with the acrid smell of lit fuel everywhere. She vaulted over another rooftop close by, her pincers giving her plenty of leverage to get across from building to building. She squinted, coughing as a miasma of dark smoke began to roll over her.

She paused, overlooking the carnage below. She covered her mouth, what happened? Was Sorin truly in the middle of all this? She searched the streets below, desperate to find him. She suddenly froze, her compound eyes spotting movement below; something floating near the sidewalk at the other side of the street. Nearly covered by the dense smoke in the air.

She sucked in a breath, that was his hoverboard! She dived below, using her pincers and claws to slow her decent on the brick walls. With a heavy landing on the ground she sprinted forward- reaching the board in nearly two seconds as she skidded to a halt. *The boards here... but where is he...* She scanned the street, frantically blowing the smoke out of her eyes and face. The heat was starting to get worse.

"Help..." She froze, that was him, he sounded weak... really weak. "SORIN! WERE ARE YOU!" She shouted out.

"R...Right here... I...I'm right here." His voice gagged and coughed, struggling to get out.

She ran through the dense smoke, coughing as she went deeper and deeper, as the heat continued to rise- the flames were dancing in the shadows ahead and she was terrified of what his possible wounds could be. His voice continued to call, and with a cry of relief she could finally spot his hunched form against the wall, the smoke in the air made things hard to pick out, but as she got closer she had to do a double take at his horrible appearance.

His black and gold durag was shredded and torn, some of his dark hair poking out of the holes. His left cheek was cut across, as blood lightly spiled down from the wound, as similar injuries dotted the bandages on his arms and right shoulder just under his long sleeve shirt, which sported more cut marks and bloody gauze. Turning him over, there was deep claw like scratches on his back. She felt the breath leave her throat when she spotted the worse one, embedded into his lower right leg, a jagged piece of metal.

He was currently going in and out, struggling to stay awake- and she moved, carefully picking him up with her strength, before moving him to a piggy-back position. She moved the backpack to her front and sprinted back out; taking care not to jerk him to much, as she got away from the spreading fire, which seemed to jump to the other structures behind her. Anything that was covered in wood became a host to the growing flames.

She finally cleared the worst of the smoke, her vision improving as she reached the other end where she started; before moving past the hoverboard; she heard a noise and looked back, eyes widening as the board began to follow her from behind. Two large pools of light began to approach the street; she made another relieved breath as the families van pulled into the street. The green van came to a screeching halt as she finally approached the vans headlights, she slowed down as she reached the side door which slide open revealing Jack, Roxanne and Meryl. The three didn't waste time in helping Zoe get Sorins battered form into the van; only to cry out in surprise as the hoverboard jumped into the van behind Zoe.

The inside of the van was spacious enough to put Sorin on the floor; the place had two cabin seats each, front to back, with another bench seat in the back, further behind the bench seat was the trunk section, where Zoe spotted a few bags of luggage. The inside of the van was old and fairly lived in- albeit with a few items- probably the twins stuff, scattered around the back bench. Which mostly blended with the background to Zoe, who, was completely panicking at Sorin's current state. Under the ceiling lights his injuries looked far worse, as the signs of his cognicrossis was appearing around his eyes and skin.

Suddenly Roxanne cried in fright, jumping back from Sorin, her eyes widening. "What the heck is THAT!" Zoe looked to where she was looking at in alarm, what could have possibly...

There was something on Sorins arm...

A life-like looking gauntlet, of a dark silver and reddish design; complex looking as its sharpened plates looked scale like. There were two gems sticking out at the back middle of the hand: one large red gem in the middle, and a small green one in the lower right. It covered his right hand and forearm; and to Zoe- It looked so creepy- like his arm was removed and replaced with something wholly alien in appearance.

"Dude! What is that!?" Jack blurted out "Is that his actual hand? Wait, is he a deviant?" he glanced at Zoe "Like us?"

Zoe looked at the clawed gauntlet with unease; shaking her head mutely back and forth, "No," she bleated out "That- that wasn't there the last time I saw him... the monster!" Zoe blurted out without thinking "It did something to him, it must have... even his cyberdeck is gone." She looked towards them and paused, the family had a strange look about them; Zoe cringed, she must sound crazy to them. They looked at Zoe, and she wasn't prepared for the somber atmosphere of the room. Robert put the van in reverse, as Meryl got closer to Zoe.

"How long have you know you were a deviant?" Meryl asked, as she stepped closer to Zoe and Sorin, sitting next to her as she brought up his arm and checking for his pulse.

Zoe looked at her confused "What?" she breathed, "Have you had your powers long?" Roxanne continued, leaning out of her seat to look Zoe in her eyes "You said the monster... so, does that mean you encountered one? You know- the dark eyed ones?" Zoe suddenly froze, the image of the feral nomad coming to view.

"W-what are they?" she whispered.

"We don't know." Jack answered, "They tried to kill us both... if it weren't for mum and dad- we'd be goners." Zoe turned around, and watched as Robert parked the van further away from the street and moved next to Meryl. Who was still in the process of checking Sorin's wounds.

"Hey, it's okay. Mom is a nurse and Dad... well, he used to work in the mines. The ones were they excavated for ichorcyte; he's really good at patching up injuries," Jack said as he moved closer to put a hand on Zoe's shoulder "Are you good by the way?" he asked.

Zoe looked to Sorin and shook her head "I don't know. Are there more of us? Deviants I mean, have any of you come across any more out there?"

Roxanne shook her head "Nope. Wastelands aren't exactly a good place for meeting any random kids like us with powers... we'll... except you, of course..." She scratched her head "Sorry... about blasting you by the way. Thought you were one of those freaks trying to jump us again." Zoe paused, she actually forgot that happened a while back. "I-its fine. Just happy Sorin is alive... can't believe were actually out of that bunker..." she sighed, suddenly something bumped into her, and she turned around looking behind her; the hoverboard was still floating, as if it were waiting for something.

"Yo... I've been wanting to ask- is that his?" Jack asked, wide eyed as his voice took on a tone of admiration. She gave him a dead pan look, before rolling her eyes.

Boys...

"Yeah, it's his... he must have used it to escape that thing." She said.

Jack whistled "So... when I heard that building collapsing earlier, and the sounds I was hearing further in the settlement. That was all him? This guy is crazy!" he cried, as a zap of electricity made him and Zoe jump, with Jack cradling his rump, while glaring at his sister.

"What was that for!" He said, through clenched teeth.

"Dude, really, I mean... come on! The guy is literally laying right there- and is in bad shape no less... and you call him crazy..." She retorted, giving him a look that screamed moron.

"Well, if you had let me finish! I was gonna say he was super cool for doing it! Like... five star awesome cool!" She rolled her eyes as she brought up what looked like a cellphone. Jack grumbled as he sat down in the back. Zoe, to her surprise, was trying not to chuckle at the twins antics. She glanced back to Sorin. She could only watch as Meryl redid his bandages and treat his new wounds on the spot. Much later, the hoverboard collapsed on itself. Becoming a medium sized oval disk once again (To the amazement of Jack.) Zoe placed it below the bench seat. While putting his backpack with the others in the very back.

Outside, the fire raged on, and after nearly thirty minutes, the green van made its way past the city limits. Sorin and Zoe, now two more passengers on a ride outside the abandoned ghost town, and into the awaiting stretches of the wastelands.

CHAPTER

31

10/24/2061, Sunday, 7:28 pm

The wastelands outside the van was vast and serenely quite; every grain of sand that was shifted from the hot breeze wafted across the side and back windows.

Sorin remained unresponsive on the bench chair, the heavy wind blowing across the window above his head. His short wild tangle of black hair was a mess. As his bandanna was missing, taken off to make sure there wasn't any more fragments of glass or splinters lodged into its fabric. Mrs. Murdock said she would see if there was anything to be salvaged from it, as she took out a her sewing kit.

The gauntlet upon his right arm twitched under the covers on top of Sorin. And Zoe's ear twitched at the spastic and sudden movement; it does it periodically, a weird and creepy characteristic of the odd gauntlet. The thing also refused to come off. Robert already tried to remove it, without too much success, and after driving down the trail leading further into the desert... Well, the twins gave it a go... to another bout of resounding failure. *'Thing might as well be superglued to his arm'* Zoe said, after failing to take it off as well.

Jack huffed as he sat back on the captain's chair. "So... any ideas on how were going to remove it?" Roxy shrugged "I'm certainly out of ideas." Zoe groaned "If I pull anymore I might end up pulling his arm off. This is ridiculous!" She growled crashing against the chair to the side.

The sound of creaking could be heard as the gauntlet made its involuntary movement. Zoe grimaced, it was like the thing was mocking them. Jack sighed, his ears twitching from the things movement. "That thing just sounds wrong... and I mean... wrong." He said.

Zoe gave him a curious look "Hey, you never told me what you could do. I mean, I can understand Roxy and her electric powers... but, what can you do?" Jack eyed her before grinning "Sound." he answered, "I can control it, and even send out small shockwaves... though, it kinda varies on how much frequency I use." Zoe raised an eyebrow "Frequencies?"

"Yeah." Zoe jumped, his voice somehow whispered into her ear, from the opposite side of the chair, where the window was at. "How did you-"

"Like I said, frequencies." He smiled "Well, more like sound waves... but you get my meaning." She gave him a weird look "And I thought I had the weird powers."

Roxy sorted "So how do you do it? I mean before you were kidnapped and all... did you always have on the hood and jacket when you were outside?" Zoe blinked at her question "I... well, hold on." She fished under her shirt before bringing up her locket. "Zoe?" Roxy questioned, looking at the small locket in her hand with confusion. "This is how." She opened the locket and stared at the black rock inside of it. Jack and Roxy looked to one another about to voice aloud what she was doing. Only to be interrupted when the rock suddenly glowed a bright purple; so bright was it that the two parents looked back in alarm. The van coming to a quick halt.

"What in the world is going on back there!" Meryle started, only for the light to quickly dim. The two siblings stopped shielding their eyes and focused back on Zoe. They both felt their jaws go slack.

Zoe let down her hood, and parted her long blonde hair back. Her compound eyes and her insect-like appearance was suddenly gone. replaced with the normal appearance of any other girl her age. The green eyes staring back at the twins looked remarkably like the ones seen in the picture of the older blonde woman- except they were blue. With Zoe sharing in the woman's good looks, only in a younger form. Even the dark lines spreading from the ends of her lips were gone.

She scratched the back of her head looking embarrassed, "S-sorry! I forgot how bright the thing can get when I use it." Jack looked at her as if she had suddenly did a magic trick "Whoa... How did you do that!?" Roxy just looked at the necklace with clear shock on her features.

Zoe gave a sad look, before holding the necklace up for them to see. "I don't really know. My dad gave it to me when I had my first transformation, he told me my mom had it.... and when I put it on, well," she shrugged "It turned me back to normal, though... it doesn't do anything about my strength, and it only works when I have it on and look at periodically." She explained "If I don't, I revert back to that." Before slipping the locket on and pushing it down her dress.

Roxy blinked "Wait... you said your mother had it first. So the lady in the picture... that's your mum?" Zoe nodded "Yeah, it's... the only thing I have of her."

Roxy slowly sat back in her chair, "Oh... sorry, didn't mean to pry-" Zoe shook her head "Its fine," She smiled "Heck, when I got kidnapped-those nomads took it from me..." she nodded to Sorin "If it wasn't for him, I probably be stuck looking like that."

Meryl smiled from her spot on the seat "Hmm, sounds like that young man down there must be a real gentleman, from the way your saying it."

Zoe paused, before shaking her head "Actually, he's kinda a dork. And he's a little strange- smart too, but really strange."

Roxy doubled over laughing, as Jack, similarly held his stomach in laughter. Robert, who had gotten back on the road, couldn't help the small chuckle. "Ah, gotta love kids their age, huh dear." Meryl shook her head, a small smile on her face.

Three days later, his condition was still the same. Sorin was still in a comatose state, and Zoe was getting increasingly worried about him. Even the random twitching of the gauntlet had finally ceased; Sorin sometimes mumbled in his sleep deliriously, and other times, the gauntlet would subtly glow under the sheets... something, Zoe and the others caught on random occurrences. By the location of the light, it seemed to come from the gauntlets two inlaid gems.

That night, the traveling unit made camp around 9'after; Sorin was situated, and his wounds were mostly healed. Though, to the Murdocks horror, he did have periods were he would break out into one of his cognicrossis episodes, although he was nonconscious for them. Zoe hastily told them that this was normal. To the Murdock's shock.

"What... how long has he had it? Did he ever mention it, or..." Robert stopped, his features becoming gut wrenched by the discovery. Meryl looked at Sorin's pale constitution under the light, the black veins spreading all across his body. "This... this is severe, does he have any meds for this?" she asked her, Zoe shook her head "Said he dropped them when he got taken." She looked back to Sorin and sighed "See... it's going away now." They both looked back, and to their bafflement- and the twins disbelief- the veins slowly receded away, his pale skin going back to its original light brownish color. "He's been like that since I meet him, something about an incident when he was 6 years old I think."

Roberts shook his head slowly "That's incredible, positively a miracle that he's still alive!"

Zoe suddenly grew still "What!"

Meryl gave her a heartbroken look "Dear... its cognicrossis. The meds that settlers are given for it amount to painkillers at most, and at worst..." She shook her head "Its deadly, it doesn't matter the age or how fit one is during the initial contamination. The body never gets better during a cogni attack; for some it varies... but most people tend to only get worse. With a few, here and there- that are on direct care, twenty-four seven."

Zoe paled, mouth hanging open, desperate to form words that wouldn't come to mind. The images played inside her head like a slide show, and there were so many of them that showed him going down to one knee or being unable to move in their cell. That's how frequent they were- and she's saying that it only gets worse!

"B-But it's like I said! He's only sick for a moment- then he's back to normal." She bleated.

The group was silent for a moment in the van. Everyone processing what was discussed- shocking as the information was.

"Um... hey Zoe. Where are you from? If you don't mind me asking." Jack asked, now looking at her ponderously.

"I'm from Rosaria. Sector 9, district 4." She sighed, *Here it comes...*

Jack sucked in a breath, as the others glanced at her, horrified. "Yeah... they kidnapped me and... brought me here." She said weakly

"Sorry, I'm not really familiar with everything down in the conclaves." She mumbled out.

Robert sat down and gave a tired breath. Looking at Zoe with clear sympathy "God... you're really far from home aren't you. Listen, I don't mean to pry... but, could you explain what happened. I just wanna understand what's been going on in that forgotten settlement."

Zoe blinked, before nodding "Um, sure... but, it's a long story though."

Jack grinned "Well, if that's the case. Hey mom! Could we make some soup while Zoe tells us what happened."

Roxy rolled her eyes, smacking her brother in the back of the head. To his annoyance. Zoe couldn't help the nervous laugh as the two exited the van, followed by their parents- who were shouting warnings for the other two to slow down. *Dang... if Sorin was awake, I could have gotten him to explain everything. There is no way I'm going to be able to explain that gadget on his arm... or even what a cyberspace is supposed to be.* She sighed, before moving out of the van and hastily bringing her hood up from the cold breeze that caught her unawares.

Meryle took one good look at her and shook her head, "Why don't we get you out of those torn clothes... I'm pretty sure Roxy's got a few spares for you in the trunk."

Zoe looked at Mrs. Murdock aghast "Wait a minute! Are you sure? I don't wanna be a bother-" she was interrupted; from further ahead, Roxy looked back and waved a lazy hand in the air, as she zapped a few twigs to make a small fire "Yeah, sure! Go ahead... should be in the big one next to Jacks!" Zoe wasn't able to say anything else as Mrs. Murdock gently pulled her to the back of the van (She didn't have the heart to remain stalk still, even though she was more than capable of doing so).

The two went behind the van, and once again as her shoes sunk into the desert floor, she couldn't help but feel a little nervous at the pitch blackness surrounding the campsite. There were large rocky plateaus surrounding them, poking high into the pitch sky, most of them blending in with the background; it was a bone dry section of the desert and there was barely any fauna or animals to be seen. But, she could at least admit to one thing that was beautiful out here. The night sky, which was full of stars, to many to count even by her best efforts.

Likewise, the mourning and setting sun, both to her astonishment and sometimes unease. Were also breath taking- so long as you weren't overwhelmed by the sheer vastness of it; the stories Sorin told her of the fathomless wastelands looked to all be true.

Mrs. Murdock loaned her Roxy's clothes, and she hesitantly thanked her.

All the while, back inside the van. Sorin laid there on the bench seat. His head gently moving around, as the gauntlet under the covers began to pulse with red and green hues.

??????????? / ??????????? / ???????????

A colorless void surrounded him. Probably the closest he's ever come to experiencing the idea of what an ocean was like. It was endless, an ethereal wave or force that moved through and around him. It called to him, guiding him in its impartial flow.

Whether he was currently alive or dead he couldn't be sure. But the voices whispering around him wouldn't let up. They weren't necessarily aggressive to him, but they did sound incredibly confused, lost in a perpetual echo chamber, bodyless vagabonds cut off from his side of reality. He couldn't see anything, but something was closing in on him- whether or not it was a threat- he couldn't be sure.

There was a sound, a sound of somebody chocking- that strangely filled him with dread and claustrophobia. His eyes opened and he was no longer on the burning street.

He was trapped! Inside an enclosed space, his hands were pressed upon something sealing him in. A door? Or maybe a hatch? There was weird symbols and diagrams upon it, glowing a golden hue. There meaning unimportant as his little hands slammed upon the sealed cover; his breathing quickened, there was movement from beyond this enclosed space- he didn't know how he knew, but he knew- sounds of a scuffle outside and loud voices shouting.

Suddenly, the golden hue of the symbols disappeared. The hatch hissed loudly, steam blowing around him as light began to slip through the cracks of the opening seal. His eyes hurt; the light now pouring inside of his prison, looking away and down to his body- he could spot various wires, maybe IVs or neural interface plugs trailing under his shirt. He froze, had he gotten smaller? No, younger? Suddenly, there was a shadow standing over him. Blocking the intense light and standing as a silhouette above him.

He shivered, the cold air rushing into the pod freezing him in place.

"*Sorin.*" A voice, a gentle voice... a woman's voice, whispered into his head.

"*I'm so sorry, but... I'm afraid are time is up, and... and I need you to be brave. Can you do that for me.*" Sorin struggled to look up, to focus on her face, but his vison began to warp- like a damaged holovid or a fading dream- and yet, the only thought that came to mind was a strange one.

Why does she sound so sad?

Suddenly, the light, the enclosed space, the nail biting cold... and her. All of it, began to darken and lose focus... collapsing upon itself and draining away like liquid through a faucet. His vision was all to suddenly plunged into another veil of ceaseless shapes and dark whispers; the sudden inhalation of air into his throat burned him, and caused him to hack and sputter. His body felt weak, and something heavy laid upon him. He opened his eyes and quickly closed them, the light above the ceiling, it caused his head to throb horribly...

That's when something unexpectantly strange happened. His right arm, feeing like it was being weighed down by a ton of bricks, suddenly got lighter. A feeling in his chest that he didn't know was there, until now, immediately began to make its presence known.

It was like a small ember was inside of his chest. A cold star, that seemed to prickle with subdued heat. A small pygmy that barely registered to Sorin, up till now. The star slowly began to heat up, a pulse of movement that caused Sorin to gasp as something surged from his chest down to his right arm. There was a red shimmer- further below to his right- under the covers... exactly where his hand was...

His eyes widened, and suddenly there was a pulse of green... and the van was lit up with activity.

CHAPTER

32

10/24/2061, Sunday, 9:28 pm

Zoe and Jack froze... the sounds of heavy, spastic inhalation of breaths catching them both unawares. Just as Zoe had slipped on her new grey shirt and pants from behind the van, something caused her instincts to flare up in alarm.

Then, abruptly, there was chaos. The van went crazy. Both her and Mrs. Murdock screamed in alarm as the van made spastic, electronic sounds. The lights from inside and outside going on and off. She lifted and moved Mrs. Murdock away (much to her surprise!) as the van cranked up, and began to reverse and drive forwards. Nearly running into the pair, as they watched from the other side of the van now covered in a little bit of trail dust. Zoe went slack jawed as the van seemingly drove by itself a few meters down the road before coming to a dead stop- the lights flickering on and off.

"Yo! What the-" "Meryl- Zoe, you two alright!" "What the heck is happening with the van!"

Zoe and Myrel got up from the ground, both to absorbed to answer back as the van continued to flicker- before suddenly switching back in reverse. The van wheeled itself backwards again, before sliding back to halt once more, Zoe snapped out of it and moved towards the possessed vehicle.

"What in the world is going on in there!" She breathed as she made for the hijacked van.

??????????? / ??????????? / ???????????

Sorin was freaking out!

What the heck was on his arm! He tried to get his breathing under control, tried to sit up and look around but his body was weak and sluggish, and he just couldn't get his thoughts together.

The thing that was on his right arm was pulsing with green light and the lights above the ceiling kept flickering on and off. He raised his right arm above his head- it was literally the only thing he had strength to move, yet he was completely in disbelief of its current appearance.

Where was he? how did he get from the street to here? Where was Zoe? Nothing made sense! Suddenly, he became aware of the things movement; the gauntlet was stretching down, manifesting more armor down his bicep and shoulder, covering his long sleeve- which looked otherworldly in its design. Frightened he tried to get up, only to yelp as the room suddenly lurched, nearly causing him to fall off the bed... No, bench chair? He looked around, the flickering lights giving him enough faculty of sight to make out the inside of a van. But, the van was mobile- driving itself by the crazed turning of the wheel.

How in the world...

Suddenly, something cool began to crawl up his neck; involuntarily, he let out an uncomfortable intake of breath as it quickly swarmed over his cheek and covered his right eye. A horrible ache began to pound against his upper cranium, a pressure that wouldn't relent as the van suddenly came to a stop, causing him to slide from the seat. To his confusion, he landed on something metallic which pulsed with energy, catching him before he could hit the floor. His hoverboard! Thank goodness, something familiar...

The van came to sudden stop, and he was grasping at the sides of the board, trying to get himself situated, or at best stable. The room was spinning now and the flickering lights all around him made everything that much more disorienting. He looked around, his gaze meeting the window and consequently outside- it was dark. The outside view of the van showed him that he was indeed out of the dead settlement. Instead, he had somehow found himself back in the open desert, without the comfort of the voyager, or its crew... He tried to stand up, but his legs were still unresponsive and sluggish, he grunted to himself in exhaustion, clear visible frustration at his body for not responding to his input. At this point he just wanted to get back on the seat, at the very least! There was another surge from his chest, and the most alien sensation he had ever felt began to sprout from his back.

He didn't know how... but, he could *feel* the armor on his shoulder suddenly extend outwards... He gasped, something was pulling him back onto the seat... he looked behind him and felt his stomach twist into a rough knot, followed by a strangled cry, for there was something metallic wrapping around the van's bench seat- like dead vines crawling around a tree. Three long tendrils pulling him backwards and somehow doing it with impossible skill. He was completely frozen in fear, the blanket over him was now on the floor- and the blinking lights only made things so much worse than it already was. Was this a nightmare? He brought up the clawed gauntlet, it's dark silver finish glistening under the blinking lights- the two gems are what really got his attention- he shook his head, the two gems glowed with their respective colors: the large one in the middle glowing beat red, and the one on the bottom right of it, enshrouded in an emerald green.

There was suddenly the sound of footsteps, and Sorin jumped in fright as the side door slide open. Sorin's eyes widened, as a familiar long shade of blonde hair surged into the van. There was something glowing purple which dangled around her neck as she turned around.

"Zoe?" Sorin got out weakly, she blinked, her now compound eyes staring unbelievably towards him. Before backing up in alarm at what was on him... and around him.

"Sorin!? What in the..." she began, her face paling at the sight before her. The tendrils trailing from spots of the armor behind his right shoulder was completely unexpected, like the last thing she would ever think of seeing when entering the family van.

Suddenly, Sorin doubled over, closing his eyes as his right arm moved to cover his head; a splitting headache coming to him without warning. Sorin opened his eyes; the pain was a complete low blow, he was getting absolutely tired of this...

Something was appearing on the thing over his right eye. The 'lens' or whatever it was began to display text over the now, small, transparent screen.

<-----*{Neural Metamorphosis Executive}* ----->

Nervous Mapping... 100%	Muscle mapping 100%
Neural Mapping... 100%	Tendon mapping. 100%
Skeletal matrix mapping... 100%	Biomoniter mapping...100%
Interface Matrix Mapping... 100%	Cognition mapping... 100%

{}

{}

{}

{}

< ----------------*{Results}*--------------->

USER SYMBYOSIS GRADE... PERFECT
Styx Matter Synthesis... Perfect
Warning Missing Component Core

<-->

Zoe approached cautiously, as Sorin looked at the text over his right eye in silent apprehension; the text was corrupt and broken, like something was having a horrible time translating the bizarre systems report... and that's when he realized... his cyberdeck... where was his cyberdeck... and then the last memory of what happened slammed into him like a truck.

The stranger, the orb in his hand, the way it latched to him and... it swallowed his cyberdeck... he looked at the gauntlet in growing horror. Just what had he done to him!?

He felt something on both his shoulders, looking up, it was Zoe, who was grabbing both his shoulders in an attempt to get his attention, her face was completely terrified.

"Sorin! The van... a- are you doing this!?" she asked loudly.

"What," Sorin questioned, his voice absolutely dry and weak "Where am I?"

Sorin grunted, a sharp pang of something pounding within his chest alerted him of something wrong. He grasped her arm with his right hand, the dark silver gauntlet seemingly obeying his will as the tendrils moved to grasp at Zoe who yelped out of the way. Her wrist slide quickly from his hand as Sorin felt his strength rapidly failing, his right arm growing heavier; The armor around his shoulder began to smoke, the dark silver pauldrons and armor around his upper arm began to slowly disintegrate. He vision began to darken, and the gauntlets light started to dim, both gems seemingly losing their luster as the boys eyes became heavier. The van lurched to a stop, the lights finally ceasing in their rapid blinking.

Zoe gaped in shock, the weird armor around his arm and shoulder where disintegrating into a silvery mist before her very eyes. Along with the tendrils hovering protectively around him; taking her hands off the two side chairs for support, she took a cautious step forward, watching silently as the last of it disappeared leaving no trace. Sorin was looking at her weakly, his confusion and fear causing her to move to his side. The gauntlet was seemingly back to its idle state. The two gems now lightless, as Sorin struggled to remain awake.

"I-Is it dead?" he got out "The thing that was chasing me, is it finally gone?" his exhaustion causing his head to lay back against the pillow. Zoe's ears twitched as she could hear shouts outside. A voice, probably Mr. Murdocks telling the others that it was finally safe to approach.

Zoe looking at his state in total worry, and nodded numbly, the sudden events that had transpired finally registering for her. "Y-yes, it didn't come back... after I found you near the gas station. It must have died in the fire... you're safe Sorin- the Murdocks found us, and they got us out of that place."

Sorin was silent for a moment, before nodding slowly; his eyes closed, finally unable to keep them open. "G-good."

Zoe blinked, and just like that he was out again. His breaths coming out softly. She frowned, the armor, the tendrils... it unnerved her.

She hesitated, before carefully moving the gauntlet covered hand back to the seat. The Murdocks barged in soon after, just as she was placing the blanket back on Sorin.

"Zoe! What happened- are you alright!?" Mr. Murdock exclaimed out of breath. Leaning against the chair, as the other three appeared looking completely bewildered.

Zoe looked down to Sorin's still form, her mind abuzz with thoughts, none of which helped alleviate what she was currently feeling. The gauntlet was doing something to him, and she had no idea how to explain what she had just seen. She grasped the locket in her hand, the small silver necklace barely soothing the shear worry she was feeling. Just what had she missed, when Sorin was fighting for his life, alone out there?

CHAPTER

33

10/25/2061, Monday, 4:23 am

His eyes opened to a partially illuminated ceiling. The van, that's right, he was currently inside of a van. Pushing the covers off himself for a moment, Sorin felt his body ache as he stood up from the bench chair.

The fact that he was even aware of the fact was a miracle in and of itself. His hand came to message his aching head, and he ended up nearly screaming at what he saw in front of him. Crazy, considering he had already experienced the new look of his arm. The lights from outside the draped window poured into the van, giving him enough visibility to see. And what he saw on his arm made him completely uncomfortable.

Just... what in the world was this thing? He remembered the moment it jumped on his cyberdeck and the pain, the horrible pain that he felt as if his arm was being immolated away. Every nerve a web of searing hot wires of flames, it was something he would never forget. Suddenly, a noise caused him to look to his left, breaking him out of his recollections. Three shapes- three bodies- laying inside of a mattress behind his seat. With a swelling of his heart he recognized Zoe. To the right, with one boy his age and an older girl to the left. Neither of which he was too familiar with. Looking to his right, towards the drivers and passengers side, he spotted another pair, two adults laying on a mattress near the front of the van.

A ghostly voice suddenly whispered 'The Murdocks got us out of there' in his ear.

He looked down, taking in his appearance- his dirty and ripped clothes still over him. He could feel the bandages around his various wounds. Had they really helped him with those? They felt far better than the ones he applied at the gas station. But all together he was able to move, albeit, with a bit of effort on his part. Was this due to the gas explosion? Or was it due to the gauntlet?

Positioning his back against the chair he grimaced, the back of his right leg- in the calf section- felt somewhat painful to move; that shard of debris that had pierced the back of his leg, he couldn't see any signs of it under the bandages around the spot. He moved his right arm, narrowing his eyes at how the gauntlets fingers brushed the spot on his leg. It was so eerie... it didn't feel like he was wearing a gauntlet at all... like a literal extension of his arm... completely fit to form... he clicked his tongue silently, it didn't help his unease at all, like his arm was replaced by something wholly unnatural.

But that was the weird part. The gauntlet, as alien as it looked-concurrently seemed beautiful. Maybe it was the filtered starlight from the drapes, which seemed to bounce off the metallic finish. Giving it this subdued sheen, like a partial diffuse of light on its cool metallic cast. With the red edges between the plates of the gauntlet looking almost alive in a sense. He suddenly grabbed the gauntlet with his other arm and began to pull, a few seconds passed, and he wasn't getting any closer to getting it off. He breathed in silent frustration. The thing was latched on to him- like some kind of screwed up prosthetic limb.

He shivered, how would he be able to explain this to Hosea and the others, let alone what happened back at the settlement. Suddenly, his face pulled into an expression of pain. The gauntlet began to subtly gleam from its central gem. A red light which glowed hazily in the partial darkness.

He held the groan to himself silently, not really keen to waking everyone else up. It felt like a cogni attack- thankfully a less severe one-but still plenty painful. He sighed, what were the odds that he were to have one now. Just as he was waking up. Taking a moment to test his right leg, he discovered it was possible to stand on it, just... not too fast. After a few minutes, he realized his black and gold bandanna was not wrapped around his head. He looked around before shortly giving up, his shoulders slumped as he made it to the door carefully... it must have been burned by the explosion, he himself caused. With a careful push he moved the side door back as quietly as he could, taking care to slip by the two parents who seemed deep in sleep.

Sorin gazed up at the night sky, the stars were stretched all around, as the vast wastelands surrounded him on all sides. It was rocky where they were at, but, the lack of vegetation and the rolling sand dunes around them meant they must be deep in the conclavian deserts. The sand crunched under his shoes, and a subtle wind danced around him- picking up the sand and throwing it carefully a ways in front of him. None of it- aside from the starry sky- really mattered to him. His only thought at the moment was to reach the remains of the campfire a few meters away from the van. The pain was growing, but it wasn't anything worse than what he's had to deal with before. He reached a big rock by the fires remains, the twigs under a bit of solid ground kinda threw him off, but, he reasoned that the Murdocks must have took some firewood before coming this far south. Suddenly, he felt the need to smack himself. Of course they were this far south! In all his panicking, he failed to realize one simple thing. If there was an abandoned settlement, that meant you were in a local near the border of the endless expanse, which was south of known civilization.

Not directly near the border mind you, but, it's been well known that the weirdest, most outlandish rumors come from the various locations near no man's land. Heck, Sorin's heard plenty tales of the endless expanse from Tom, Jade, King... Hosea.

'The place was practically famous, as well as the most avoided place in Pangaea's history.' He remembered that phrase from the school's history textbook, at the very least.

Sitting down on the rock near the pile of ashen remains, he looked up at the night sky. The pain was finally at its zenith, and as he hugged himself he chuckled, the past events coming back to him... He'd been kidnapped, nearly killed, been mind-controlled by some orb in a jar, and he was currently wearing, said orb, on his right hand and arm (With the remains of his cyberdeck, most likely fused into it) and somehow... he was still breathing- in pain, but still breathing. He wondered how everyone else was doing back at home, how was Aunt Dot doing, Church, Bella, King... Mr. Owens...

He felt the clawed talons of the gauntlet bite into his other arm. Mr. Owens kept popping up abruptly in his thoughts, and every time it happened he felt himself cringe up, like his very being was wounded from the memory- not just the memory... the gun shot, and the moment he goes limp after crashing to the ground.

All because that psycho of a nomad wanted him, Sorin, as a way to access the very thing on his arm... He scoffed to himself, feeling the insides of his guts grow hot from the sudden revelation. All this... just for the thing on his arm...

And it wouldn't come off.

He closed his eyes as a surge of pain traveled throughout his body. Looking back up to the sky, he suppressed his anger, the maddening unease of the past events where slowly being overtaken by the need to star gaze. He opened his eyes and looked around. The night was practically a carpet for the interstellar points dotting the black expanse. "Where are you?" Sorin muttered "You've got to be here somewhere. Crap, it's been ages since I've done this." He sighed, this wasn't really the same without Susan or Hosea. But... anything to distract himself from the pain. Besides, stargazing fascinated him. Without the lights from the city, and the ceiling of a entire underground tunnel blocking his view, he had full reign to search and identify the constellations above him.

Sorin scanned the stars, tracing the lines and remembering the locations of the paths. The night sky was ever changing, ever revolving. Every location of the constellations changed, the position of the planet around the suns orbit could do that, and like Susan once told him *'Sometimes, you really have to hunt them down in order to find them.'* and this would be no different; it would be better if he had a telescope... but, all well...

"Two Sisters, Castellanos, Remus and Salvator, Minor Costilla, Ursa Horrox," Sorin whispered the names, each one popping into his head as he spotted them; finding that one star that looked familiar and tracing it to figure out where it belonged in the pattern. A generally difficult task, if you didn't know where to look, but enough to keep his mind distracted. A simple routine that he had strangely missed. "Minor Astraea, Minor Sythea, Altus Dipper...."

He saw it and he paused, eyes focusing on the familiar and his favorite constellation. "Nocturna Major." He whispered, the spiral arrangement of stars finally revealing itself. His guardian angel and interstellar good luck charm, so to speak.

The little winds blowing around him seemed to agree with him. Blowing directly from where the constellation was from the sky, and trialing behind him towards the van. So, did that mean he was supposed to stay with the Murdocks? He shrugged, *Probably looking too deep into it... I swear, after everything that's happened, it's like I'm questioning everything that comes my way now. Hope this means I'm not going crazy...* he thought grimly.

The van was at his back, and the pain was still in motion. The worst companion to have while star gazing, but he made do; after identifying a few more, the pain slowly began to peter out. But he felt something odd as the pain finally lessoned. There was a subtle sensation in his chest, that seemed wholly different than the red-hot pain going through his every nerve. He touched the spot with his right hand- and something was beginning to feel strange. Just under the red affliction of his cognicrossis, laid another sensation that felt... cold... he froze, the feeling in his chest suddenly taking on scary familiarity. His vision abruptly filled with what happened earlier, the growth of the gauntlet over his arm, the eerie glow of both gems, and the metallic tendrils-extensions of an even weirder armor- produced by something trying to pull him back to the bench seat.

He gasped, how long had this been inside of him!? His mind went back, and dug up the image of the hooded stranger- the one who had rested his palm onto his chest (exactly where his heart had been).

Suddenly, he stood up. But this wasn't the only time he had that feeling; that vault chamber that was suffused with the heavy mist, the garage, and even at the gas station when he was priming it to explode. All of it came right after his encounter with the man in the dark robes. The wind began to blow all around him, the burnt ashes where shuffled around the ground as Sorin stood stock still, his mind folding in on itself.

He blinked, like a fractured, incomplete recording- voices began to repeat themselves inside his head.

'Your survival of Silverwood was a fortunate outcome... your mother, she would have been proud' 'Sorin, I'm so sorry, but... I'm afraid are time is up, and... and I need you to be brave. Can you do that for me.'

He slowly fell back to the rock, his brain felt unclogged, like a heavy veil had lifted from his head. The words that came to him... one from the stranger as he was going through horrible torment, and the other... her voice... could that had been...

Sorin felt a pregnant pause fall over him. His mind going blank; was that really who he thought it was, could that really have been his... mom... talking to him? He grabbed his head, desperate for more, anything that could confirm what he was thinking... but nothing came, nothing at all but the silent wind blowing around him. He looked back up, the night sky was slowly beginning to show the first vestiges of sunlight. His precious constellations were all but gone. Leaving him with so many questions, enough so to drive him mad.

He unhanded himself and looked down to the gauntlet covering his hand and arm. How many times now had these sudden revelations of his past come to the forefront due to this thing on his arm. He couldn't feel the cogni flare up anymore, but this didn't matter to him, the only thing that mattered was the cold sensation still smoldering deep within his chest.

And... if he released it... could he remember more?

Sorin sucked in a breath; it would only be a moment, just enough to see if anything could be jostled from his styx infested head. His expression turned pained, a longing which seemed to unexpectantly gnaw at his insides until they were raw. Completely reminded of how he felt months ago and the times before that. How hopeless it felt, not being able to remember a thing about where he came from. How easier it was too turn back, and simply not think about it. There was no answers to be found, nothing concrete, nothing to latch on to. But know he had something, and he couldn't look away, no matter how much he wanted too.

The sun was creeping out of the background, orange and red light was now spilling above and covering the grey sky in dappled patches and spots. And below Sorin began to tremble with effort.

He looked back, thinking about the memories in which it started. How it felt back in that burning garage, how it felt ripping through his chest and surging throughout his body. He focused on that tight ball, like a seemingly infinite point of mass density that refused to yield. His eyes narrowed, his fist balling themselves up; tensing whatever muscles that were in his small body, looking for any tells, and signs of how he could get it to work. He cycled through memories, pouring through every emotion he felt in the bunker and the city, desperate for anything that could give him a trigger for this surge, this raw unfiltered energy that seemed to be hiding within him.

His body began to grow hot, was it another cogni attack- he didn't care- his focus was pointed only in one direction.

His emotions were now becoming wild, his pupils dilating from the effort, growing bigger, and suddenly he felt something trail from that load- a thread, a small needle of sensation that caused him to gasp. Focusing on that thread, now visibly shaking from the effort. All the while, the boys skin began to show visible signs of a typical cogni attack. But, so focused was he- on this mental and physical tug of war, that the pain was barely a fly on the wall to the boys desperation for answers.

There was a moment of stillness, a moment where Sorins eyes widened, it was like the solar discharge of a sun. flare ribbons of something cold and warm at the same time began to radiate from somewhere within his heart. He gasped, he could feel it moving through his very nerves. A sensation: as burning hot, as it was cold as ice, running without direction. He quickly focused, looking to the gauntlet on his arm. Mentally shouting at it do something, anything, so he may have his answers.

The gauntlet responded to his call.

The gems on the back of the gauntlet burst into action, the red and green glare nearly blinding Sorin as the energy ribbons seemed to travel from his chest and plunge into his arm like a raging river.

The gauntlet began to lengthen down his arm, metallic armor manifesting along, and up, over his shoulder. He gasped but closed his eyes, instead focusing on his task. Praying, hoping for something to pop into his brain. The feeling of it traveling across and around his neck, before surging around and encasing his other arm, hand, and fingers. Which moved up his throat and across his cheeks, before covering the bridge of his nose and both his eyes. More of it spreading down, covering half his back before stopping. Surging to cover his upper chest before finally ceasing.

He opened his eyes, his vision now incased in something like a mask lens. As he caught sight of his other hand and both arms. Sharpened, alien-like armor, as sleek as it was barely heavy. His left hand, now covered in a similar looking glove like the original. The green gem seems to have migrated behind his left hand. Sorin scanned the suit, it had an almost organic like aesthetic to it; a mix of mechanical plating and a 'muscle-tendon' like texture running between the sharpened plates of the armor. The texture had a subtle white glow to it, a seemingly ethereal-like power running between the armors inner layer; more than likely the same thing inside of him this very moment.

Sorin sat there encased in his one third suit. Not able to help the growing disappointment welling within. All this, only to find out that nothing was shaken out from the cobwebs at the back of his head. No recollections of who he even was, not even the truth of his parents. He leaned over, his arms falling slowly down as another wave of depression settled over him, with nothing once again to cling to. He sat there for a moment wondering what else was there to do. He looked up, through the lens of the mask on his face, he could see the sun now climbing slowly above the horizon. The light bouncing softly off the armor on his arms, he widened his eyes at the effect, and was slightly surprised, creeped out as the mask seemed to animate with the subtle movement of his eyes. He flexed the fingers of his other hand, it was exactly like the original gauntlet, no restrictions on his movement with the armor around his shoulders and arms barely even feelable. Strange. He really hoped there was a way to turn it off-

"Holy Shit!" a voice- a boys voice, screamed behind him- causing Sorin to jump in alarm.

He turned around. Zoe and the two other kids where looking in his direction slack jawed. There was a pregnant pause, where they all stared at one another. *Oh... this isn't good...* Sorin thought to himself, completely sheepish by the looks of shock and mingled unease from the other three.

"Uhm... hi.." he greeted lamely, waving a clawed hand (still glowing with a red glare) reflecting some of the mourning sunlight from its dark silver finish.

CHAPTER

34

10/25/2061, Monday, 6:03 am

Sorin blinked, the mask lens around his eyes widening with him as he noticed something even stranger than his weird armor.

Zoe looked normal! Her compound eyes were normal greens, her claws gone, and the subtle lines tracing the edge of her lips- all gone, she looked like a mini version of the woman from that picture in her locket.

"Whoa," he stood up carefully, his leg still sore "Zoe what happened to you?

You look... different." Sorin said, wondering how this had occurred. What had he missed while he was out?

Zoe was silent; her eyes scanning the armor around Sorin, her demeaner becoming a little uneasy. Roxy and Jack were still looking positively dumbfounded by his appearance. Roxy being mostly nonplussed and Jack...

"Yo... never mind that, how did you... aren't you sick?" Jack asked, his expression amazed. "Like... how are you even standing, and that stuff over you..."

Sorin turned his head to Jack, his eyes focusing on him... to Jack's mild unease... the red lens of the mask, honestly looked kinda creepy. Sorin frowned "Well yeah, I've always been sick... Sorry about that- once it started I decided to walk out," he rubbed the back of his head "Didn't wanna wake anybody while I was having a flare up in the van." Zoe grimaced, as Roxy stiffened "You were having a cognicrossis attack, and you're still alive?" she looked very pale at the revelation.

Sorin nodded "Nothing to bad this time. Maybe a 3 out of 10 on the pain scale," he brought up both his hands, looking at the metallic gloves which covered them "Though, I'm kinda wondering how I'm gonna turn this off." He grimaced, thinking about it- he could still feel the steady flow of energy still moving from his chest to the glove.

"Sorin, how do you feel?" Zoe finally asked, "Are you feeling okay, or..." she gestured weakly to the armor "What's that thing doing to you?"

Sorin blinked "I don't really know. Been thinking about for most of the early morning and..." he shook his head, the idea of explaining himself suddenly becoming too personal for his own liking. Honestly... what was he thinking? Like he was gonna suddenly get answers just like that... he needed to grow up.

"Was trying to find something out about this thing, and well," he gestured to his arms and face "This happened, it feels weird, but... I don't really feel like I'm in anymore pain. So, I guess I'm fine for now." He shrugged.

Zoe was silent, a small frown on her face, but she seemed to accept his answer before moving closer to him. The others looked to one another, unsure of what to make of him so far, but Jack shrugged before moving to catch up to Zoe, with Roxy moving last.

Zoe was now giving him a glare, as she stopped just in front of him, which had Sorin nervously back up a bit "Okay, what the heck happened back at the city Sorin?" she asked with a small growl "-and how on earth did that gas station explode in the first place!" she exclaimed, throwing her hands up.

Sorin who was trying not to sweat bullets, looked away from her bewildered expression "Yeah... about that, it wasn't... completely my fault." He said carefully.

Zoe's eyes widened "No.... you couldn't have-"

"Look." Sorin cut her off "I'm telling you, I was completely out of ideas. I tried everything. I tried to outrun it- and it didn't work, tried to lose it in the alleyways- also didn't work." Sorin counted off from his fingers "Even a whole building collapsing on it didn't work-"

Zoe went pale, shaking her head in disbelief "You dropped a building on it... how..."

"No!" Sorin whined "It brought the building down on me! While, I was riding through it with the hoverboard." he said with a shudder.

"You rode the hoverboard through a building! Seriously!?" Jack said in complete awe. Sorin nodded his head rapidly "Yeah! I literally launched myself from a downed statue and entered through a window... it followed me inside and just, brought the whole thing down on my head, I barely survived." Sorin said shaking his head, cringing at the memory "And it still came after me later on at night."

A hand came to rest on his shoulder, and he flinched from the serious look the older girl was giving him "Okay... why don't you sit down and just explain to us what happened," she held up her hand and made electricity shoot out from her fingertips... to Sorin's alarm.

"Trust me, we've seen some stuff too." She finished.

Sorin thinking about everything that happened, slowly nodded his head, before sitting down and explaining what happened after Zoe got knocked out.

Sorin later on learned both their names: Jack Murdock and Roxanne 'Roxy' Murdock; they both listened as he explained all the encounters he had with the creature. Zoe shaking her head in horror, finally began to understand the numerous injuries she spotted while the older Murdocks were patching him up in the van.

What surprised her most... was when he described the moments when he could feel it coming for him. Like a mini radar (in Jacks own words). He could tell when it was on the hunt for him, and reasoned that taking Zoe would have simply just put her in more danger.

"So... you didn't have a plan, nothing- you were just outrunning it this entire time?" Roxy said in disbelief.

Sorin shook his head "No. No plan, other than surviving as long as I could. Until it chased me too the gas station..." he explained more, finally getting to the gas station as he detailed what happened. He paused, thinking about the stranger, who brought the dang thing to him in the first place. He jumped past that for now. Still not sure what to make of it.

"Then I woke up, heard you calling me, and you know the rest." Sorin finished.

Zoe looked at him, her face troubled "Do you remember anything else, like anything else at all?" Sorin thought for a moment "I think I remember waking up- I guess, the other day... maybe?" he grabbed the side of his head. A sudden throb making him narrow his eyes.

Zoe sighed "So you remember waking up last night. So, I guess that means you hijacked the van by accident then." Roxy and Jack suddenly looked at Zoe with mingled surprise.

Sorin blinked, "What?"

Zoe gave him a level look "Yeah... when you woke up. The van went haywire- nearly ran Mrs. Murdock and me over last night." Sorin suddenly went rigged on his seat, the memories of him first discovering the gauntlet on his hand, and how panicked he was when he woke up... to the flashing lights and the wheel turning itself.

I did that!

Cringing he gave her an apologetic look. "S-sorry- I didn't know." Zoe shook her head "I'm fine."

Roxy gave him an odd look "Wait a minute. We really stumbled on a hacker of all things." She shook her head, baffled by the two new kids in their midst.

"Cool." Jack quipped "And here I thought this trip couldn't get any more awesome! We got a freaking ghost runner in our group."

Looking at his left and right hand, he was reminded of the beasts eyeless face; there were three gems, two of which were encrusted on the back of his hands. The memories of the beasts attempts at hacking him off his board coming back to his unease. But... where was the third one? The purple one?

He gave an unsure look "Can't really say I'm in the same league as a ghost runner. But yeah, I know a few things- here and there. But..." he held up his right hand "I really don't know about this."

Zoe looked to his left hand, her expression ponderous "Well, when I reached the van. That gem right there was glowing like it is now." She gestured to the van "Could you... I don't know- call your board?" she suggested. Sorin blinked for a moment, before nodding, bringing up the left hand he wondered how he was supposed to do that. There wasn't any keyboard or screen he could use to-

Suddenly, text began to appear on the lenses of his mask; there was a soft chirping noise that caused the others to look around in alarm, that didn't sound like any bird local to the surrounding desert. Sorin,

Roxy and Jack especially knew that for a fact. The text flickered; Sorin blinked, was this an interface? Numbers and various lines of code began to scroll down the screen; the gem on his left hand began glow brighter. The interface flickered again, and a digital diagram of his hoverboard traced itself in front of his eyes. It looked like it was drawn in its idle mode: the disc form. He watched as lines of text appeared around the sides of it; to his bafflement, it looked as if the interface... No, the gauntlet. Was connecting and downloading the boards specs.

Wide eyed, he watched as the traced diagram of the board began to animate itself on screen- expanding itself into its active mode before suddenly-

There was a startled couple of shouts from the van. Jack and Roxy froze, as Sorin, followed by Zoe paled in response. The van's side door; which was still cracked halfway open, had something wide zoom out of the open crack. The hoverboard, flying vertically out the opening- flipped itself in midair and landed back on the ground- kicking sand everywhere as it missiled directly for Sorin.

"Whoa! Whoa! Whoa!" Sorin exclaimed as Zoe immediately moved to tackle him down to the ground, who screamed as the board zoomed above her head like a disc shaped projectile moving at ridiculous speeds. The board immediately course corrected, kicking up sand as it arched around and darted directly for him once again. Jack ran forwards before his sister could stop him, quickly moving in front of the two on the ground and held out his hands.

Sorin watched as the air rippled around him, before the board was suddenly repelled away by a massive wave of force. The board flew back, not looking any worse for wear as Sorin wide-eyed and alarmed, got back up as he held a hand towards the board now careening back towards him.

"STOP!" he raised his voice, and just as the board reached him- with Jack ready to blow it back and Roxy getting ready to blast it, electricity dancing around her arms- the board suddenly halted. The repulsers on its sides and the vents under it suddenly humming in response. Sorin breathing heavily, looked back and immediately began to help Zoe up- who was giving the board a freaked out stare.

That thing nearly took my head off!' she would complain to Sorin in the near future.

"Okay... are you good?" Sorin asked the board hesitantly, now moving towards the now levitating platform. Which seemed to be patiently waiting for his input.

"You rode *that* around the settlement!" demanded Zoe, sounding absolutely aghast, "How are you even still alive!?"

Sorin looked back at her "Practice," he answered simply "A lot of practice." He brought a hand to the board, which, abruptly cut off its propulsion forcing him to grab on with the other hand before it could drop to the ground. Sorin was baffled to say the least when more lines of code began to appear on his interface. The board flashed a blue pulse of light, which startled everyone, before more lines of code began to appear over his screen.

9893892090896789890909090909099900

0293090281883493094040490393049309

2939232932067903490430490349459

79230293834530594398453686504950

34839494934954059049500039832092

49940490909430490590495042830292

794834983439483840804348598302

598860495049039403580489498028

----{Attention}----

>[New Operating System on file]<

{User Id Scan} ... 100%   {User Cyberware Compatibility} ... 100%
{User Biomonitor Scan} ... 100%   {User Board Compatibility} ... 100%

Hoverboard model: SR2_FF68196_SR21206

{HBD_Safety_Lock}... Lax
{HBD_Master_Key}... Unlocked
HBD Recognizes Sorin Richter as sole owner...

----{System Report Finished}----

Sorin looked at the notification, having to reread it through a second time, not believing what was being said in the report. The board recognized him as its sole owner? Suddenly, like a ghost from his past, Tom's words came back to him, *'You remember what happened days ago, right? The energy the board released that knocked you down. Well, when the board scans your body, it's building unique safeguards for the users safety.'* Sorin let the board go; Zoe walked up, cautiously looking at the boards idle levitation; Sorin couldn't believe it- the report from his interface is essentially saying that he, has the compatible cyberware for the boards full capabilities.

Does that mean I can go faster! Seventy-five miles was the limit with my old cyberdeck... So, how fast can I go now?

"Dude, you okay?" Jack asked, pulling himself in front of Sorin. Who nodded, not being able to stop the small grin forming on his face in turn. "Yeah, I think I'm good- though," he glanced down at the board "I gotta check this thing out later, and see if it's good to ride on."

He looking at the green gem, and he started to concentrate on it, wondering if he could collapse the board through the gauntlets connection. Sorin looked on with silent amazement as the board flashed blue, the green gem lightly glowing.

The board gave off a small pulse of energy before collapsing on itself, much to Jacks shock "Ok... how did you do that?" he said looking between him and the collapsed metal disk on the sandy ground.

Sorin rubbed the back of his head "I don't really know, I just... concentrated on the gem thing, on the back of my hand- and it just worked." He shrugged "Kinda feels like a got a more advanced cyberdeck on me."

Jack blinked at him "A cyberdeck? Uh... What's that?"

"It's like an operating system. like the kind those people from the republic have- you know- the computer augments that get installed inside the brain. Which allows you to interface with stuff."

Roxy raised an eyebrow towards Sorin, crossing her arms "Ok... and you learned this, where, exactly?"

"Well... my family-" Sorin froze mid-sentence; the sudden pain that was emanating from his heart caused him to double over, knee landing on the sandy ground, he could feel his body go rigged.

"Whoa! Dude! You just said you were-" Jack who was already by his side, could only widen his eyes as the armor covering him began to... smoke? No, it was evaporating- mist like- before his very eyes.

Sorin gasped, the pain was sudden, and to his irritation wasn't any different than a small flare up of his cognicrossis. Sorin carefully got back to his feet with Jack's help. His upper body now armor less, the rest of it falling to the ground in pieces as slithering vestiges of metallic silver retreated back across to his right shoulder. Sorin watched as the green gem took its original spot below the bigger red one at the center. The gauntlet's gems dimmed in brilliance before finally dissipating.

Sorin flinched, as the mask covering half his face began to smoke as well, before finally detaching. Joining the rest in silver smoke.

The interface was gone, leaving his face completely bare for all to see... Zoe gasped, and Roxy grimaced... Jack sucked in a breath at Sorin's face, who's skin was covered in dark veins branching down from his eyes and cheeks. Sorin looked at everyone with a questionable look "What is it?" he mumbled, suddenly feeling tired; whatever force that was pumping that energy into his arm, it felt faint, like it was no longer able to sustain the steady flow powering the gauntlet on his arm. He just wished he didn't feel so groggy. Like he had just come out of sleep.

Well... at least I know how to turn it off, I think...

The door to the van slid open; Mr. and Mrs. Murdock scrambled out looking distressed, their faces searching the campsite before falling on Zoe and Roxy "Hey girls! have you seen the boy- he's not on the chair- and the board below the seat it..." Mrs. Murdocks voice caught in her throat, her eyes now landing on Jack, and then Sorin, who was giving them both looks of interest.

"Oh, hi." Sorin greeted weakly, waving at them both "Thanks for the new bandages. The ones I put on myself didn't feel nearly as good as the ones you put on me." He said smiling gratefully, while at the same time feeling the minor pain which was now starting to pass through his body in waves.

Mr. and Mrs. Murdock looked at him with mingled alarm and confusion, and as Mr. Murdock was the first to make it to him, his expression was quickly replaced with clear concern "My god, are you okay- how bad is it so far? Do you need anything or..."

Sorin shrugged, much to everyone's (except Zoe's) shock. "It's not that bad."

Mrs. Murdock scrutinized him, looking at his sickly appearance in complete dubiousness; she moved closer to him, taking a moment to crouch down and looked directly at him (much to Sorin's embarrassment). After nearly a minute, she relented. Giving her husband an astonished look "It looks like the first to second stages of the illness. But- I don't see any signs of escalation." She turned back to him "Your really not in any worse pain!?"

Sorin nodded, "It's actually coming to a stop right now," he said bringing up his left hand; the black veins on his skin was already starting to go transparent. Jack watched his expression mixed "What about the glove? As cool as it looked, it was kinda creepy dude- not gonna lie."

Sorin nodded, holding his right hand in front of him. "Yeah, it kinda is."

Meryl and Robert blinked at the two's conversation. "The gauntlet? Did something happen, while we were getting up?"

Sorin and Jack shared a look "Mom, Dad, you two might wanna sit down. Sorin's got one heck of a story to tell you guys." Jack quipped.

Sorin sighed "Ah, man. And I just got done telling you guys what happened. and now I gotta do it again..." Jack laughed as Mr. and Mrs. Murdock looked at one another, unsure of how to respond.

Roxy chuckled "Hey Zoe," she whispered, "You're description of him- super accurate." Zoe smiled "Yeah, and he's still a dork."

CHAPTER

35

10/25/2061, Monday, 8:17 am

Sorin scarfed down his oatmeal, toast, and bacon. The moment Mrs. Murdock passed him his plate, was when he finally realized how hungry he was.

Everyone was around the fire eating their share; the pot and pan was set over a metal trey, which was positioned over the small fire. All the while Sorin was telling the elder Murdocks of what happened. Going over his side of the story, since Zoe told him that she summarized her side; or more accurately, the parts she was conscious for.

Sorin went over everything again, the moment of the kidnapping, waking up and being carried over to his cell, meeting Zoe (Who looked away embarrassed, still feeling guilty how that played out), their eventual escape, all the way to the moment when Sorin- reluctantly and with hesitation- told them about the moment when they encountered the monster in the garage. Sorin taking Zoe and the eventual chase between it and him. then the gas explosion.

"I'm telling you after the building fell down on top of it... I-I didn't know what else to do," Sorin explained, "The metal girder ripped a hole right through it... and it was still trying to get me."

He detailed how the monster snuck up on him, and how he ended up using the cyberdeck to force the gas out of the pumps, before shooting the thing in the mouth with the flare gun.

'Huh... that explains the flare rounds in your pocket.' Mr. Murdock would mutter to himself.

He ended the story with him going in and out of conscious. To the moment when the thing belonging to the monster latched onto his cyberdeck. Before being discovered by Zoe. He then went and retrieved his backpack before explaining the pains he was feeling in his chest and how the gauntlet reacted to it. Sorin rummaged through his backpack, before pulling out the document file with his photo on it- before handing it to them.

"It was the same thing in document, the orb thing- I think it came from that thing chasing me." Sorin said.

The family looked at the pictures and diagrams; the files didn't give much in the way of answers as to what the orb was, but the uncanny nature of the document file still seemed to give the Murdocks an uneasy feeling.

"Er... Sorin," Roxy said, "This isn't what I meant- when I said we've dealt with the same things." Jack looked at his sister unsure "But it has to! I mean, both of them described the same thing. It's another one of those black-eyed freaks trying to do us in."

Zoe bit her lip "Jack, I think you're forgetting something." Jack looked towards Zoe "Huh?"

She sighed "Sorin isn't a deviant."

Roxy and Jack gave a discomforting look towards one another.

Zoe turned to Sorin "So you could feel it coming after you? So, it was just like the other nomads in the bunker. They were all complaining about the headaches and what not- so it has to be linked to this orb thing. Um... that's currently... on your arm."

Sorin held up his right arm, which was still firmly covered by the complex gauntlet. The light of the sun dancing somewhat on the dark silverish surface, yet, no faint glow or pulse of light emanated from the gems adorned on the back of the hand. He could still feel the lukewarm sphere of uncertainty, as it contracted itself inside his chest; a muscle, it was almost like the contraction of another muscle inside of him- something now barely hidden by the subtle beat of his heart.

"Yeah, and it felt like something was poking my head with a screwdriver." (Zoe grimaced) "At least its finally over. Those 'headaches' were annoying, especially when I was trying to get my wounds taken care of." Sorin replied, scratching his head with his right arm.

"Hmm, Sorin if you don't mind. Let me try something." Mrs. Murdock said.

She moved to seat next to him; in her hand, she carried a bag and after setting it down she rummaged through it. To Sorin's puzzlement, she brought up a stethoscope. "You mind? I'll be quick." She offered. Sorin shrugged before nodding. She slipped the earpieces on and moved the chest piece over where his heart was at. Sorin waited, as everyone else looked with interest. She slowly narrowed her eyes; shaking her head she removed the chest piece and the stethoscope, before placing the tool back in the bag.

"Anything wrong, Hun?" Mr. Murdock asked as he got more helpings of bacon from the trey. "No. I don't hear anything from his chest. Lungs and heart both sound normal, well... considering."

Sorin frowned "Hey Jack, Roxy," they both turned to him "What is it like- when you use your powers I mean?" he asked.

They both looked at him, before Jack shrugged "Honestly, I guess it kinda feels like using another muscle I suppose. You know, when controlling sound- it sorta feels like I'm splashing waves around, like water. It's like a switch, and I'm suddenly seeing the waves everyone makes when they shift the sand around or when it bounces off walls or other surfaces." He looked to Roxy who rolled her eyes at him.

"It's like the dummy said- but it's more like warm water to me. I can ether produce the electricity myself, or..." she brought up her phone; Sorin watched wide eyed as electricity began to flow out of the device and into her hand, traveling around her finger like a tangle of glowing worms "-I can just take it from other places. I can also feel it around other stuff: like lights, tv's, phones or the van..."

She paused before giving his gauntlet an unsure look "Can't feel anything from that thing though. Or you, at least... not in the way your describing what's inside ya." She sighed before focusing on her phone again, a small surge of electricity slipped into the cell phone causing it to light up. Before slipping it back into her pocket.

"Oh," Sorin said "Well... you said you guys went through something similar right? Do you guys know what those things are?" he said remembering the nomad from the bunker, his eyes nothing more than a black abyss. "The guy that attacked Zoe and me... the way he disappeared when he-" Robert sighed as he set his plate down, before giving Sorin a tired look.

"To tell you the truth Sorin, we don't know." He leaned on his seat, giving Sorin an uneasy look "Listen, are home settlement: Ashton. It isn't a sprawling town like Corrin's Watch or as multilayered as your hometown Gloomhaven. But it's still a big place. We have three districts: The Highland District, where most of the settlement heads can be found. The Industrial District, where the locals work at the factory and prospect ichorcyte in the nearby mines, and The Quarter District: Where most of the workers, and most of the families of Ashton lived- where we lived." Robert explained "A few weeks ago something broke into are home. We lived near the back of the Quarter District, where it's pretty much a dead end- lived there for about 10 years or so. Are home isn't exactly in the middle of the neighborhood, so when this thing came and reduced are door to splinters... help wasn't likely to arrive on time."

Sorin's eyes widened "What happened?"

"Me and Jack, that's what happened." Roxy growled "When dad came with the gun- it barely did *anything* to it! I thought it must have been one of those crazy raiders or something- until I saw what was coming out of it. The thing had smoke coming out of its chest- where dad shoot it."

"Yeah, that's what happened with us! Well, I missed most of the fight. But, I was there when Zoe took it out... what is that stuff coming out of it?" Sorin inquired. *Finally, some answers!*

Jack shrugged "No idea man, all I know is that me and Rox threw are powers at it and it eventually stopped moving. And... well, it melted." He looked sheepish "Honestly, thought I was having a nightmare or something." Roxy rolled her eyes "Course you did, wouldn't be surprised- since you saw that movie the other night before it happened." Zoe suddenly grumbled, much to Sorin's confusion.

"Anyway, we waited- for maybe an hour or two before the guards arrived. They didn't even come out of their car, they looked at the damages and simply left.

Not a single word or platitude given." Mrs. Murdock said, her face for the first time looking extremely angry. "I had half the mind to call the security head... but... something was wrong, very wrong."

"Nobody came to check up on us, and we were all to shaken to go to sleep," Robert sighed "That's when he called, and old friend, Garret; somehow he knew what had just happened hours ago, and he called to warn us about another attack on the way." Sorin looked uneasily at the family; of all the things he was hearing, he was not expecting the conversation to go in this direction. "Long story short; Garret is an ex-nomad, and he came to our settlement a wonderer, he was treated very poorly by the settlers, and he came to our door for a place to stay for the night. We accepted and gave him a bed and some food. Next mourning the settlers where a knocking on our door, demanding him to leave."

Robert clicked his tongue "He left that afternoon. That was like, maybe a year ago, I believe. So, after everything that happened I was skeptical about trusting anyone after that. But then he told me about what was going on. That deviants were apparently targets of these things, and that it has been going on for a while now; not just in the wastelands, but everywhere, from the conclaves to the Sector Districts."

Sorin's eyes widened, something began to feel off to him, something he couldn't quite place. "Everywhere? but, how- I mean, wouldn't someone have said something about it, done something about it even?"

Robert glanced at the van "That's the thing, apparently some have already been doing that; not helping the situation mind you, I mean suppressing it, and that news forecast a week ago was probably the first time in a long time, where settlers and citizens of the republic alike had no choice but to see it for themselves."

It was like a bulb clicked in his head; Sorin remembered, the news broadcast a week ago, before he was kidnapped in the foundry, before getting his cyberdeck and forgetting the news feed entirely. Was that what happened? The same things that attacked Sorin, Zoe and the Murdocks- chased after, and caused that chaotic incident near Delta.

"You mean the news feed from Delta City." Sorin said silently.

"Yeah, the very same one." Robert nodded "It's what got me to believe what Garret was talking about, as crazy as it was, and there was nothin else for it; I called in a favor that morning and a day later we were hitting the road." He crossed his arms "He explained that for the past year, he had been escorting deviants to safety across the border- to a place where deviants could be safe. Now as far as safe goes, he told me it wasn't full proof, but, it was better than being out in the open where more could come a knocking."

Sorin blinked "So, how far have you been traveling the wastes? Couldn't have been easy with the wildlife and storms."

Robert smiled and shrugged "We've been lucky so far, the occasional sandstorms and bad road conditions have made a few things difficult but... we're getting by just fine all things considered. Haven't even gone astray with the Duneraptors or the direwolves."

Sorin looked down thinking; his SOS had to have been a dud, not only that, he had no way of contacting them even if he wanted to. So what other options did he have of getting back to Gloomhaven? "Hey guys, how long have I been out?"

Mrs. Murdock gave him a sympathetic look "About six and a half days. If it helps, we found you both on the 19th of October, and right now it's the 25th." She sighed "I had a feeling you would have wanted to know what the date was also." Sorin blinked at this information, he'd been out of it for that long... his shoulders sagged, that meant... his birthday... it was two days from now. How long had he been from home? Had it really been weeks now at this point! He was barely able to keep his calm as he asked his next question "The person who's taking you across the border, he's ex-nomad right?" Robbert nodded silently.

Sorin gave a nervous look "Is it possible for me to stick with you all for a while? I um... well, I'm kinda related to nomads too." He felt nervous admitting this; since when has admitting that your related to nomads ever been a good idea in the wastelands. But, if they trusted this Garret, and he was a former nomad, surely they wouldn't just up and abandon him, right? "I'm sorta adopted, and my foster family are nomads too. So, is it possible that Garret could contact someone for me."

Mrs. and Mr. Murdock looked at him as if he had grown another head, with the other two giving him similar looks. "And... why on earth would we ever consider *not* taking you with us," Mrs. Murdock said, sounding mighty offended by the idea. Sorin held his hands up "Just saying, most people don't like me is all, especially when they find out I'm related to the circle... in any way shape or form." Zoe looked at him confused *The circle?*

Robert smiled "Look kid, your good to come with us. We're not just going to throw you out just because your related to nomads or the circle. Frankly, it's stupid. While understandable, given the nature of some nomads, not all are the same." Robert rummaged from under his shirt; the necklace that dangled from his hand caught Sorin's attention; the necklace was old and creased, like a military dog tag in a sense. "My great-grandfather was only a kid when a nomad saved his life, and it was during a major conflict. Yet, even though he was on the enemies side he still went out of his way to save his life." Sorin looked at the necklace shocked "Why he do it?" Robert shrugged, before putting the necklace back under his shirt "Unfortunately, Granddad never found out. He tried to find out a couple of years later, but no one could give him a clear answer. The man who saved him, well, he died in a fire after he pulled him out. The necklace was the only thing he had left of em."

Sorin blinked "Oh..."

Robert sighed "What I'm trying to say Sorin, is that sometimes the world isn't as black and white as it seems- sometimes it is, but, most people are far more than just a label." Sorin thought about what he said for a moment then nodded. Satisfied he turned to Jack and Roxy "You two mind helping cleaning this up, where going to have to pack up and leave soon, hopefully we can get closer to Hanover before the day is over."

Jack looked at the food "Can I get second helpings before we go first." Mrs. Murdock chuckled "Sure, just be sure to clean the trey set before we go- and not forget it *this* time." She gave Jack a small glare, who was looking at the food with renewed interest; Sorin with a disturbed familiarity, recognized that type of look from none other than Bellatrix. A look that promised dire consequences if the instructions we're not met. Roxy grinning at Jack proceeded to move back to the van, as Zoe poked him in the shoulder "Later on," she whispered, "Can I have a word... it's about that gauntlet on your arm." Sorin glanced at her, confused, but he nodded back silently.

An hour later, the camping set was packed up in the van, and his hoverboard, safely back inside of his bag along with the documents. The van moved, down the path towards the abandoned town of Hanover. Sorin, as he sat down on the bench chair; couldn't help but wonder what was in store for the upcoming days ahead. Maybe, by then, he would be reunited with Hosea and the others.

CHAPTER

36

10/25/2061, Monday, 6: 54 pm

Sorin stepped out of the van; the many plateaus dotting the region have suddenly reduced in number, creating a far more open desert than the last stop they made. Hours upon hours of driving and taking small breaks in between have made his legs and back slightly stiff... though, he didn't have it as bad as the others.

"Finally! My legs feel like they're about to pop off." Jack moaned, stretching himself out happily.

Zoe came out with a slump of her shoulders, after being woken up, she couldn't shake the grogginess from her four hour long rest. Roxanne hopped out, giving her brother an annoyed look as she brought up her phone and scrolled through it. Sorin looked at the three with curious appraisal, the memories of traveling the deserts in the voyager coming to mind. The beast of a mobile home was spacious and had plenty breathing room to stretch and not be in the situation they were in. But, oddly enough, Sorin didn't much mind; if anything, a part of him missed this. Somehow traveling with the Murdocks and Zoe... inside of a medium sized van brought with it an unexpected nostalgia of something long past.

Sorin's musings was sadly interrupted as something was tapping him on the shoulder. Turning around he was meet with Mrs. Murdock, who was holding a bundle of clothes to him.

Sorin blinked "Hey Sorin... I already gave Zoe some new clothes because of how torn they were. It looks like it's your turn." She said giving him a small smile "Jack said he didn't mind lending these to you."

Sorin stared at the clothes before turning towards Jack who was walking towards the two. "What up." he said "Don't know if you're a fan of The Nuromancers, but I've already got a few to spare. So help yourself."

Sorin blinked, wordlessly he took the bundle from Mrs. Murdock and nodded his thanks to them, before moving inside the van to change. Moments later, his torn and ripped brown long sleeve was replaced by a light grey one, which was adorned with a green microchip pattern that traced along the sleeves and creeped up the bottom of the shirt, before joining together in the middle. Tracing a brain like logo in the center of the shirt. His cargo pants were likewise replaced by a pair of charcoal grey jeans with the same digital, microchip brain logo on the sides of the pockets. His shoes were the same; if by some miracle he was able to find his way back to Gloomhaven, then finding and buying a new pair would be the top of his list.

Sorin checked himself out, to his surprise he kinda liked the cool designs of the new threads... Most of the gauntlet was covered by the long sleeve.

Thankfully the sun wasn't too hot this evening, and the van's ac was working good. He paused, thinking back to a moment when the voyagers ac unit broke. He shuddered, reminiscing on that one- painfully hot day. Shaking his head he headed back towards the others, ready to help with the campfire for the night.

The campfire was set up half an hour later, and Sorin was sitting inside the van; his hoverboard on the bench seat in pieces as Jack, Roxy, and Zoe watched in silent curiosity. The older Murdocks were preparing dinner, leaving Sorin with plenty of time to see how his board was doing.

"Man, I still can't believe you found it in a Cazador nest of all places." Jack whistled "Like, are you some sort of thrill seeker or..." Sorin gave him an alarmed look.

"What? No! I mean- I stumbled into it. Like I said, I was just trying to find some cheap parts for my bike. And I thought maybe I could trade it at Otto's and get something better for my troubles." He turned back "I just didn't expect it to be lodged in a Cazador nest is all. Though to be fair, if I'd known, I *definitely* wouldn't have tried it." he shrugged "But I got an awesome board out of it... so, worth it."

Zoe looked at the board; her estimates on it had been dead wrong, it was one thing to see it support the weight of a massive cyborg on it, it was another to finally see the inside of it and realize why it felt so... Powerful? Dangerous? Stupidly complicated?

"So you really took months fixing this thing. Where did you learn how to do it?" she asked.

Sorin shrugged "Looked it up on the net- from my laptop, and Tom sent me books and programming guides for it. It was really hard, but, I got the hang of it somewhat. The most difficult stuff, I simply called him for help."

He reattached some the main casing of the metallic shell, screwing on the bolts with a screwdriver he borrowed from Mr. Murdock. The kinetic drive, shock absorbers and exhaust vents looked fine- albeit, lightly covered in sand which he blew off; but the board was fine, he just needed to figure out how to use it with the gauntlet, now that the strange artifact (as the document described it) was filling in for his late cyberdeck.

He screwed in the last piece; after making sure the extended platform was properly fixed in place, he allowed it to contract to its idle mode. Satisfied he picked it up, and placed it inside his bag.

Maybe after I get done eating I can see how it rides. I really wanna see what It can do, since it's given me full access to its systems... Just gotta make sure I don't break a leg while doing it.

"Still wondering about that gauntlet of yours, it seems kinda weird doesn't it." Roxy said, "It's like something out of a sci-fi movie... You know what, nah. More like a horror movie." She smiled at Zoe who growled in annoyance "Oh, would you knock it off. I'm not watching it!" She exclaimed.

Sorin stared, while Jack chuckled to himself. "Come on, Zoe, I swear the movie's good. It's got a little bit of horror in it. But I'm telling you you'll love it." Roxy replied, lifting up her phone. Zoe's simply gave an annoyed huff, getting up, she quickly left the van. Roxy sighed as she called out to her, before steeping out herself.

Sorin raised an eyebrow to Jack who laughed. "Rox has a few movies downloaded on her phone. She offered Zoe one, but, she seems to really hate horror movies in particular." He shook his head "Sis is a movie buff, so she probably ain't giving up anytime soon." He explained.

Sorin laughed, with Jack joining in "So what? Are you into movies as much as her or something?" he asked. Jack shook his head "Nah, I mean, I enjoy a good flick or two. But, music is more my thing."

Sorin with his interest peaked grinned "Hmm, makes sense I guess... I mean, you are the guy with the sound powers after all." Jack snorted at this "Actually, it was my dad. Back home, he had a lot of old Cd's and music tapes that he would collect. Told me Grandma Arlene got him into it... and, I guess the sound powers did have some involvement I suppose." Jack shrugged "Well, anyway you can't blame me. I mean, bro, if you could see and feel what I feel, you'd probably like it just as much as I do."

Sorin looked at him questionably "Okay, I can probably understand the feel part. But, what do you mean by see?"

Jack squeezed past Sorin; he leaned over the back seat and brought out a big duffle bag from the trunk section. He took a seat and handed Sorin the bag, who took it, giving it an inquisitive look.

"Open it up," Jack said, "Trust me, it's awesome."

Sorin shrugged, before opening the zipper, his eyes widened; Cd's and video cassettes, all of them contained inside large Cd folder cases, and music cassette boxes- all organized and numbered. He sifted through them, amazed at the massive collection on his lap. He liked music, maybe not as much as Tom or Susan. But he didn't mind it now and again. This however, put the both of them to shame. By just looking at the playlist on the sides and covers of the portfolios, he was flabbergasted, there must have been thousands of tracks in here!

"H-Have you listened to all of these!?" Sorin asked, amazed by the massive collection. Jack shook his head "I've listened to a lot of them, but... I'm barely halfway there." He rubbed the back of his head sheepishly "Dads been collecting these for a while now, and the ones I prefer, are the more modern ones. Mostly rock." He grinned "Whenever I'm using my powers, I can feel each and every beat of the music, it's like... well, it's like I explained earlier. It's like waves brushing around and through you. It's... that's the best way I can explain it." he said, sounding somewhat frustrated.

Sorin blinked, looking back at the collection in his hands. The explanation, as brief as it was... sounded incredible- it felt like something along the lines of Bella and Susan; the way they talked about cyberspace, and the similar frustration in describing it. Jack's explanation had similar vibes too it.

"BOYS!" Sorin and Jack glanced outside, Mrs. Murdocks voice called from the campsite "The foods ready, come get it while its hot!"

Jack turned to him, a sudden excitement alighting his eyes. "Once we get done eating, your gonna ride the board?" Sorin nodded "Yep, I gotta see how fast I can go on it, now that I got this on my arm." They both grinned at one another "Lets hurry up, I gotta see how it works!" Sorin zipped the bag up and placed it back in the trunk section of the van. The boys quickly moved out, ready to eat and test the hoverboard.

The food was good. The rations that Sorin and Zoe had raided from the kitchens of the bunker were used in the diner prepared by Mrs. Murdock. Colored rice and beef stew. Once the two kids were done with their bowls, Sorin and Jack ran for the van before coming out with the hoverboard, to the amusement of Zoe and Roxy, and mild concern of Mrs. Murdock- who looked at the hoverboard with clear skepticism, Mr. Murdock simply raised an eyebrow at the board clutched by Sorin, as he continued to eat. Sorin sat the board down on the ground a few meters from the campsite. He didn't want to go too far, Mrs. Murdock told him to keep close to the camp, after all.

"Okay, here goes nothing." Sorin said, flexing his gloved hand. The sun was already dipping partly down the horizon, and he needed to do this before the last traces of sunlight disappeared.

Roxy and Zoe soon joined the two, watching the board with interest as it laid on the ground. "Hmph, this outta be good." Roxy quipped, "Don't mind me guys, I'm just gonna stand here, out of collision distance." Said Zoe, eyeing the board with caution, as she stood further behind Roxy and Jack.

Sorin gave them an annoyed look, the girls were further behind Jack, looking over his shoulder as if he was about to blow himself up or something. Rolling his eyes, he returned his attention to the task at hand, he focused- prodding that tight ball in the center of his heart.

He thought about his right arm. *The green one... it was the green one right? Pretty sure Zoe said the green gem was glowing when the van went crazy...*

Sorin focused, grimacing as the core within his chest began to tighten. Suddenly, there was a discharge- a sudden pulse of energy which felt paradoxically cold and warm- and it was flowing freely from chest- to right arm.

The gauntlet still moved much to his annoyance, as the metallic material began to stretch. The laps of his long sleeve was consumed, the material creating armor along his arm and running past his shoulder. But... to his relief, the stretching armor seemed to stop halfway around his chest and back, while the rest stretched up, over the top of his ear and covered his right eye.

The metallic eye patch was cool to the touch, and for a moment he couldn't see out of the lens, before it abruptly turned transparent; the interface soon followed, as the heads-up display appeared (to his surprise) like his late cyberdeck. Showing the company logo in a distorted and glitched animation. The others watched; Zoe looked at the growing substance as it formed the armor around him, there was something so eerie about how it moved, as enchanting as it was creepy; the twins were awed as it finally stopped moving, the organic-like tendons inlaying in-between the sharpened mechanical plates had a subtle glow, which bounced softly onto the darkish silver of the armors metal. Sorin breathed in, trying to halt the energy, it seemed the armor was listening to him (as strange as it sounded) The armor pulsed with a subtle hew, and Sorin watched to his amazement as a speedometer displayed itself on his hud. His red lens focused onto the board, and blue windows appeared- each a separate spec of the board. Sorin glanced at the window which had the command: Ignition, in blue. he focused on the word, and watched as it seemed to highlight itself.

With a cry of surprise from him and the others watching. The hoverboard immediately pulsed, extending itself to its active state and blowing sand everywhere from its propulsion upwards. Floating in front of Sorin patiently waiting for him to step on.

"Whoa!" Jack gasped in awe, while the others watched the hoverboard, and Sorins half covered arm warily; Roxy and Zoe in the current situation could only become more apprehensive as Sorin stepped on the board, which dipped slightly as he put his weight on it.

Meanwhile, Sorin felt relief. The separate windows disappeared, and he was finally able to focus on the board itself. The boards propulsion and kinetic drives looked and felt good; energy pulsed from the boards vents, escaping in spurts from the fins on either side; leaning on the board he checked the interface from his 'eyepatch'.

If it responded to his thoughts, then didn't this technically mean he had, well, in essence- something conventionally close to the type of cyberdeck that Bellatrix currently had installed in her head? Sorin's focus was suddenly pulled away from the board. The speedometer moved to the right, a targeting reticle appeared center vision; he looked around watching as the reticle focused on rocks, objects in the camp, and finally landed on the van- which became highlighted.

"What the..." Sorin whispered, a menu appeared on the side of the hud, as options appeared, not many, just two: Breach and System Control. He paused, looking in disbelief- suddenly reminded of what Zoe said earlier.

"Sorin?" Zoe questioned, looking where he was looking "What's up? Something wrong?"

Sorin shook his head "It's nothing, I'm good." he said quietly.

He couldn't believe it.... he looked back to his board and pulled his other foot up. Now standing on the platform, he had to control his breathing. For now, he just needed to concentrate on the task at hand. As awesome as it was... he wondered what he was getting himself into?

The board's bottom vents hummed, the fins on the sides opened, and Sorin focused- drowning out the surprised cries from the others as sand fanned from beneath the boards exhaust. Sorin shoot forwards; Zoe, Roxy and Jack covered their faces as sand blasted up in his wake. Bringing their arms down, they watched, stunned, as a blue blazing shimmer left a trail of kicked up dust, which was the only way they could identify Sorin's location- he moved, curving around the campground in a massive circle- his speed making him a brief blur moving almost out of their field of view.

Sorin was buffeted by the turbulence of his path... The breeze ruffling his hair... His left eye watering and a massive grin (despite his surprise and shock) split his lips... The right eyepatch on his face began to stretch, moving across the bridge of his nose and covering his other eye... the last vestiges of silver moved above his other ear; he could only imagine what it looked like, an improvised pair of silver red goggles was his best guess. But the grin stayed, the sheer exhilaration drowning whatever unease that was forming at the gauntlets abilities. Almost like the thing was reading his mind... The board must have been reading him too, his stance was barely affected by the rolling sands under him, and as he surged past 95mph... he realized that his earlier hunch was correct... and he absolutely loved it! His velocity was constant, and little by little, he began to increase his distance from the camp, slowly getting further and further away- as an almost addicting level of freedom filled him. The constant hardship and struggle of the last six days slowly becoming shrouded by a veil of carefree experimentation.

He turned, moving in the direction of a smaller dune directly ahead. Sorin crouched down before the jump and blasting off nearly at the zenith. His balance on the board was hardly affected as his experience from the dead settlement came to him as muscle memory. He grabbed the middle side of the board, using his backhand, between his feet and turned. Doing a full rotation in air, the fins opening and assisting with the movement, before landing vertical along a bigger dune, the vents below the board humming in response. As dust was kicked up in a cone behind him as he surfed back down to stable ground. Looking up at the sky, he realized that the sun was nearly over the horizon; *the camp!* Sorin's eyes widened below the mask. *Shoot! I almost forgot about staying near the camp...*

He shifted his direction, moving back, and heading directly for the lights which was slowly becoming a small beacon, in leu of the darkening sky; bringing his right arm up and glancing at the gauntlet, he gave the strange artefact another once over. Feelings of guilt began to bubble up as his recent zeal slowly began to wear off. Pushing his exhilaration down... he realized it was impossible to forget everything he went through just six days ago... No, more than six days ago... Mr. Owens, the bunker, the orb, and the stranger. All of it, because he was somehow tied into something he couldn't possibly understand.

It was also linked to his past. By the logic of that stranger, he needed this thing on him. But what he really wanted to know, was the answers concerning the mysterious source hidden within his chest. *I have to reach Hosea... maybe then I can find out what is wrong with me.*

He traveled back across the desert landscape, his exhilaration had made him go further than his planned test. But now that it was out of his system (Partly out of his system) he recognized that it was time to head back. He moved around some of the taller dunes, and carefully began to back pedal on the throttle. Last thing he wanted to do was come in to fast and get sand every-

His right hand twitched; a sound suddenly caught his attention, a sharp chirp which caused him to look around, no birds anywhere... he looked down and froze, something was happening with the gauntlet, something strange... He slowed the board down, almost coming to a full stop and to his astonishment... the chirping noises... it was coming from gauntlet!

His mouth slightly agape, he brought up his arm and to his growing uneasiness the gauntlet let out another chirp. Now that it was closer, and he was fully paying attention. The sound was nearly identical to the chirping or twittering of a small bird, but it still felt too natural to be a digital recording or even a sound effect for that matter... like an actual bird was inside of the thing. The armor covering his whole arm and shoulder began to subtly tighten, each small twitter and chirp followed by a small contraction, maybe, by the life-like muscular texture between the armor plating.

This was almost to surreal for him, the gauntlet on his arm at this very moment felt alive in the truest sense of the word. He shivered, a chill running down his spine. Just what had that guy attached to him? His earlier excitement and exhilaration where now gone, and replaced by a creeping unease.

CHAPTER

37

10/25/2061, Monday, 8: 46 pm

The sun was nearly down over the horizon, shooting a waning disk of oranges and blues in the distance; Zoe stood on top of the van, her compound eyes scrutinizing the foreground for the blueish glow of the hoverboards light.

"You see em?" Jack called below.

"No, not yet." She replied back, "My visions good, but it's not good enough to see in the dark. Jack." She sighed. "Can you hear him?"

Jack shrugged, "Barely, the sound is coming back muffled. Must be the surrounding dunes."

Below the van, leaning against the hood. Roxy concentrated, the ambient electricity in the air from the van was like a small lighthouse surrounded by the vast emptiness of the desert. It was the opposite of being at the settlement with all that electric power surrounding her at all sides. Yet it made her appreciate one thing. In all the dull nothing, she at the very least had an easier time identifying one lone signature of energy, coming rapidly in their direction.

"Wait a minute, I think that's him- or at least, I can feel the board coming back directly ahead of us." Roxy called up.

Zoe looked back and she breathed a small sigh of relief. Near maybe 150 meters away (By Zoe's estimates... more or less) she could see a hue of clear blue riding back between a few small dunes. Only to widen her eyes at the speed he was going; she found herself wondering how he was keeping himself on that thing.

Without much thought, she jumped, doing a front flip off the van and landing beside jack, who jumped up in surprise. She stopped, looked at him and gave a embarrassed look "Sorry."

Jack shook his head "You kidding? That was awesome. Like, did you learn how to do that or-" Zoe frowned, shaking her head "No... it's quite simple for me, ever since I first changed I've been able to do it." she looked towards the desert, where the blue hue in the distance was getting brighter. The distant sounds of the board getting closer. "I could run faster, lift really heavy stuff more easily, and it made climbing the trees at my home easier too-" Jack looked at her quizzically "Climbing tree's... Oh, that's right. You're from the republic. What kind of trees? The only tree's we got down here in the conclaves are these dried up twigs. The things would sooner break under ya, then remain sturdy enough to climb." Jack chuckled "Roxy could tell ya more, she climbed one once and fell on her ass-" suddenly a fork of electricity shot between his feet, causing him to curse in alarm; Zoe simply moved to the side, already knowing that it would be the wise choice to stay out of Roxy's way (Who looked thoroughly displeased at her brother).

Roxy glared at her brother, electricity traveling down her arm and fingers. "Not. Another. Word." She hissed.

Jack frantically nodded, and Zoe shook her head at their antics.

Roxy grumbled, as she forced the electricity down; glancing back to Zoe "Anyway, like the punk was saying. What do you mean by climbing?" she suddenly grinned a small chuckle coming from her lips "Any cool hobbies a rich girl like you would be in too?"

Zoe rolled her eyes, while folding her arms; She smiled, "Well, I don't know about cool... but, I do like drawing." Roxy looked at her quizzically "Oh, and this ties into climbing tree's how-"

"Landscapes." Zoe said, "Rosaria is surrounded by large trees: Eastern Hemlock is what they're called, and some can reach about 250 feet high... You wouldn't believe the view from up there." She said.

Roxy looked at Zoe with mild interest, "Okay... you have to give me details. Like, what's it like? Being surrounded by tree's and the like?" she questioned before gesturing around her "Don't know if you noticed, but it's really hard to find a good tree out here to climb, and even more rare to find an actual river around these parts."

Jack laughed "Yeah, it's really weird to say this but... my mom had to convince me that there was other places besides the wastelands. Heck, seeing the vids at home of how big the forests are in the republic is crazy to me. Though, I don't think Roxy could take living in the republic... the rainfall could probably take her out."

Roxy gave him a small glare, before jabbing him in the arm "Oh, whatever. So you climb a super high tree, and you draw pictures of the landscape. Er, not bad I guess, but how high do you even go? Do you just prop yourself on one of the branches or something?"

Zoe nodded "Yeah, most of the time I sit on one of the branches near the top of the tree. From there I would just sit against the trunk and start sketching away." she blinked "It's surprising really, I mean... the enhanced vision I get from my powers really helps with spotting things around the trees, and the animals below: mostly birds, black tailed deer, rabbits and other critters. Eventually I got really good at moving from tree to tree," she scratched the back of her head in embarrassment "and scared plenty of squirrels while I was at it."

Roxy giggled "I'm really trying not to picture it- Your head popping out of the canopy and giving a squirrel a heart attack!"

Zoe rubbed the back of her head sheepishly "I wouldn't say that, more like they gave me a heart attack. You'd be amazed how vicious those things can be when they feel like there being backed into a corner."

She shivered at the memory; her swinging on a particular branch in the forests around her home... and landing near a group of the furry critters. It was on that day she became thankful for her hardened skin; the little monsters became buzzsaws at that exact moment, ripping up her clothes and forcing her to abandon that particular branch. Using her agility to pounce off the branch in a frantic bid of escape and latching onto the trunk of the tree and sliding all the way to the ground. She came home that day, having to explain to her dad and Mrs. Gloria (the house maid) how she ended up in such a disheveled state, her dress and backpack sporting holes and bitemarks everywhere. To her complete shock. They may not have done any lasting damage to her, but she learned to never cross there territory again.

"Anyway... that's what I mostly did when I wasn't doing home schooling. I'd grab my bag, climb up the nearest tree and draw for hours... it was really fun."

"Huh, that's interesting." A voice said behind her, she yelped, jumping forward and turning around... only to be meet by Sorin. The hoverboard grasped in hand; as the top part of his face was behind what looked like a domino-esc mask, which made her shiver at how creepy it was. The red lens over his eyes focused on her as the mask seemed to animate around his face. Showing more expression than any mask had any right to make. Almost like an organic extension of his body.

Sorin, of course, was a little worried by Zoe's reaction- who was staring at him like he was a stranger. "Is the mask that bad?" he said, raising an eyebrow.

Jack gave him a sympathetic look "I mean, the way it moves around your face is kinda..." Sorin blinked "You know what... how does this look on my face? Is it like a pair of goggles or..."

Zoe shook her head "It kinda looks like a messed-up version of a domino mask. Only its moving... like, hold on-" Zoe moved past him, before disappearing inside the van. A moment later she jumped out, followed by Mr. and Mrs. Murdock. Who of course paused in their tracks when they spotted Sorin, and his lengthened armor covering his arm and shoulder, ending at the mask covering the bridge of his nose and eyes.

"Oh, dear..." Mrs. Murdock muttered, giving Sorin a double take. Along with Mr. Murdock.

Sorin gave them an exhausted look "Not you guys too."

"Here," Zoe held a small mirror to him "Take a look for yourself."

Sorin held the mirror to his face and grimaced "Oh... I guess it is that bad."

She was right about it being a mask (though, he had no idea what a domino mask was) but it didn't look like a pair of goggles. Instead, the mask seemed to be designed around the contours of his face; molded around him, with the same armor-like pieces around the bridge of his nose, the cheeks and brow above his eyes. The red lens looked fairly intimidating. Though, he wondered why it looked so... glossy. It reminded him of something Hosea once told him, that some species of birds or lizards in the wastelands had a third eyelid to protect their eyes from wind, debris and dust. A nicti-something membrane, or something along those lines; but the part that he found kinda creepy was how it gave his eyes this almost sunken-like appearance; the mask moved along with his expression. Emoting, and he could see his eyes (vaguely) through the lens. As the metal moved, the organic- like texture between the plates pulling them subtly together, almost mimicking his expression of unease.

"Yeah, never mind... that is kinda weird." Sorin agreed, handing her back the mirror. Sorin felt something poking his right shoulder, turning around he gave Roxy a questioning look; she was poking the metallic armor with an inquisitive expression, he gave her an annoyed look "Enjoying yourself." He asked.

"How does it feel to wear this thing? Kinda feels warm to the touch, It does." She observed.

"Roxy... stop doing that." Mr. Murdock sighed, as Mrs. Murdock walked to Sorin. "Have you had anymore cogni attacks recently Sorin?" She asked. He shook his head "None so far. Sorry for hacking your van by the way."

She shook her head "It's alright, though you gave us quite the scare..." She smiled "Actually, it reminds me of the times when Jack and Roxy had trouble controlling their gifts." She gave the gauntlet a slightly dubious look "But... I'm assuming that device on your arm is a different beast all together."

Sorin shrugged, "Feels just like my old cyberdeck. I just wish I knew how to take it off."

"Why would you wanna take it off?" Jack questioned, looking confused "I mean, it's kinda awesome- a little creepy at times, but awesome!" Sorin gave the gauntlet a suspicious look "But I never asked for it. The thing forced itself on me- I mean, if something grew to the size of a tank and decided to chase you around an abandoned settlement, then latch itself on to your arm, wouldn't you be a little suspicious?"

"Okay... why did it latch on to you, in particular?" Mr. Murdock asked, before Jack could give his answer.

Sorin froze, the words of the stranger echoing in his ear; the gauntlets status reports coming back to him. "It had something to do with the thing in my chest." He said slowly, his expression concentrating on the report and what it said specifically "It came up when I woke up that night- the night I accidentally hacked the van. It was like a status page." he looked to Mr. Murdock who was drinking in his words, as the others listened.

"There was one stat in the log that was strange... styx matter... synthesis... I think that's what it said." He said uncertainly, giving him a questioning look "What does that even mean?"

Mr. Murdock rubbed his neck, looking just as unsure; Mrs. Murdock had a strange look to her. She seemed to be thinking hard on what he just said; her expression changed slowly, to one of silent bafflement "Synthesis?" she muttered to herself. The ex-nurse gave the gauntlet a strange look.

"Well, whatever it means," Jack said "It's somehow able to create that wicked armor on you. So... what else can it do?"

Zoe clicked her tongue "You sure that's a good idea? It's not like us, Jack. like he said... you should have seen what happened to the other nomads in the bunker. It was a horror show in there- bodies everywhere and the way that nomad looked when he attacked us..." she grimaced.

Roxy was quiet, leaning against the van, her expression ponderous. Sorin sighed heavily to himself, the whole business with this thing on his arm was ominous no matter which way he looked at it. As cool as it all was, he needed to be thoroughly convinced before he could rest easy on the idea of this thing being attached to him. Taking a moment to look around as Jack and Zoe talked about the gauntlet. He spotted his backpack; and he moved to collect it. He laid his hoverboard on the rock and sat down beside it and as he reached over to grab his bag, Sorin abruptly realized something was wrong... He felt movement along his arm. There was a swift flick of motion, something silvery stretched, reflecting the embers of the campfire as it moved like a coiled rope or snake.

There was a sudden cry of alarm. The closest person to catch what happened: Roxy, glanced down where he was at, and caught the sudden burst of movement, to her shock, and Mr. and Mrs. Murdock- who jumped when it happened.

Zoe and Jack whipped their heads around... only for Jack to utter a sudden "Whoa!"

The gauntlets main gem blazed red; the sudden sharp tendril unfurled itself around his arm, as it shot out from below the wrist. CRACK! The whip sounded out. Wrapping itself around the bag like a serpent, with a sudden cry from Sorin; not of pain, but of sheer alarm! The bag was hoisted into the air. Before crashing into his stomach. Causing Sorin's eyes to bulge underneath his mask from the force- like getting hit with a medium sized ball. *That freaking hurt!* The whip immediately moved back and recoiled around his arm.

Everyone stared with wide eyes. Sorin glanced wide eyed at the gauntlet, mouth agape, the tendril was wrapped around his arm like a chain; he could feel the things tension along his arm, poised to uncoil and strike out.

"Sorin, what in the world..." Mrs. Murdock breathed. He quickly looked up and saw everyone's expressions. "I swear, I didn't mean to do that!"

Needless to say, he was too scared to move, afraid it would strike out on its own volition. Until a hand grasped his armor-clad shoulder. "Jack!" Roxy screeched, hands grasping the sides of her head in panic, completely horrified at what her brother was doing.

"Whoa, that's a neat trick!" Jack said in awe "Like, is it like one of those thingy ma-jigs you told us about... um... neuro what's it's?" he questioned unsure.

Sorin stared at him wide eyed "Y-you mean a neuro link? Is that what you meant?" Jack nodded, "Yeah! That's the one!"

Zoe shuddered at the cracking noise it made, the sound seemed to echo in the air. It sounded like it would hurt something terrible if it hit someone. "That thing looks so painful," she breathed "What does that even feel like!?"

Sorin looked at her unsure of what to say, with a hesitant start he moved his arm. The thread of silver looked embedded into the gauntlet, making it look like a natural part of its sharpened exterior; he held his arm straight, the sharpened tendril was coiled around the arm like a spiral, like a tattoo, but with a deadly edge to it. To his unease, it made the gauntlet look even more alien than it had looked earlier. Something he would have thought impossible.

Please, don't cut me... He thought as he moved his left hand towards the whip. Jack watched, taking his hand off his shoulder and for some reason getting tensed up. Sorin felt the metal of his tendril-whip, which he assumed would be cool to the touch. Instead, it was slightly warm to the touch. And it felt strangely like a part of him. He grimaced, the bladed edge felt almost like dull barb to him. With a flex of his arm, he tried to will the tendril to move and far too easily it obliged. He gasped, the feeling of the tendrils movement around his arm was so strange and with seamless fluidity, the tendril snaked out from around his arm in a motion as smooth as water. Deploying out from under his wrist- exactly like Bellatrix's neurolink. Only the tendril was hovering in front of him, moving like an underwater serpent, he looked to Zoe... and of course, she looked ready to freak out. Along with everyone else, who were watching in silent unease; feeling like he was a part of a circus, he wondered what else this thing was hiding from him.

He willed it to stop it's movement, and it dropped down to the ground. Sorin made a face, he could feel the sand as the whip laid upon it; his eyes widened- like an extension of his arm- he could feel the long appendages subtle movements along the soft yet gritty surface. Sorin sighed, he didn't even need to look behind him, he could totally feel the bewildered stares behind him. Moving his other hand he grabbed the whip (Taking great care not to cut himself with it, but to his relief, the bladed edges of the whip still felt dull to him.) he examined it, the thing still felt warm to the touch, strong and highly flexible. Yet, it still felt metallic at its core.

"Dude... like, what can that thing not do?" Jack uttered, moving closer to inspect the whip like appendage. Sorin gave him a bewildered look "How should I know, It didn't exactly come with a manual." He let go of the tendril, which proceeded to quickly shoot back around his right arm. Much to the fascination of Jack, and the apprehension of the girls.

"Hey Sorin," Mr. Murdock said as he took a seat next to him "When you mentioned styx matter, that got me thinking... what were there other status reports in that log you told us about." Sorin paused, regarding him with an unsure expression "Let me think."

Mr. Murdock was slowly becoming troubled, the phrase 'Styx Matter synthesis' sounding ominous the more he thought about it. Everyone took their seats around Sorin- with a few (Zoe and Roxy) giving his right arm a wide berth. Instead moving a bit further from the camp and taking a seat on some rocks.

"Hey!" Roxy whispered to Zoe "Huh?" she blinked, moving over to better hear what she was saying.

"I don't like it, there's something fishy about that thing on his arm... just wish I knew what it was, or who would ever wanna make something so... creepy."

Zoe gave an uncertain look towards Sorin "I'm worried. It reminds me to much of the monster that knocked me out. The monster that broke into your home, it's almost exactly like the nomad we encountered in the bunker... but that thing from the garage, it just... it felt nothing like the nomad with black eyes. If you'd seen it, then you'd understand what I was talking about." She whispered, "I'm just... I still don't understand what they could have gained from kidnapping the both of us. I mean, were they just after more weapons, like the thing on Sorins arm? Or... was it something even worse?"

Roxy shook her head "No idea... Me and my family are just trying to get someplace safe. Away from this whole business. I swear, it's like were all involved into some crazy conspiracy or something... It's freaking stupid. I don't understand why everyone has to make such a big deal about me or Jack having powers." She folded her arms "Ashton practically disowned us from the settlement when the heads got word of us being deviants, jerks were referring to us like we weren't even human." She growled "Even my friends at school didn't want anything to do with me, or Jack too."

Zoe paused, grimacing at the horrible things she was saying and reminded of why she was pulled out of school too. "I didn't have many friends at school either; I... kinda got into a fight at school. I pushed a girl, and she flew into the far wall." Zoe looked pained, "Things happened, and I started home schooling soon after.

That's when my face changed," she shivered "It was a pretty bad day." She ended lamely.

Roxy sighed "Sorry to hear that, that sounds pretty rough."

Zoe nodded "But, I haven't come across any of those monsters back at home. So, is it something that only happens in the conclaves?" Roxy shrugged "No, idea. Your guess is as good as mine."

Zoe nodded, before glancing back across the campsite. Sorin, Jack, Mrs. and Mr. Murdock were talking... and something seemed wrong. Both the parents looked stressed, and Sorin and Jack seemed unnerved. Zoe and Roxy looked to one another, before quickly rejoining the camp- wondering what insane feat the metal glove could be doing now.

CHAPTER

38

"It's just an idea, nothing will probably happen." Mr. Murdock said "It's like you said Meryl, if its styx matter- we can't just wait and see what happens. Let's see if a reading pops up from the scanner."

Sorin sat on the rock near the remains of the campfire; the two adults were talking about him doing some kind of test, or something similar in that effect. But he had a bad feeling. "Are you guys sure about this? Not saying I don't trust you- I'm just a little-" he started. "Oh no, its fine kid." Mr. Murdock reassured "The scanner won't hurt at all. I just want to test a theory; The log mentioned Styx matter right." Sorin nodded hesitantly, "Well, the scanner I have is good at picking up styx matter within ichorsyte mines." Mr. Murdock explained.

"Styx Matter in the mines? What do you mean?" Sorin asked.

Mr. Murdock sighed "Styx matter isn't just a biproduct of V.M reactors. It's all a result of ichorsyte, most people inside of the conclaves don't know this, and even less outside of the conclaves. Ichorsyte can sometimes be unstable, something to do with the minerals makeup or something along those lines, but, when it happens- styx matter is formed." He looked towards the gauntlet "I can tell you one thing, that styx counter inside the van has saved my life countless times. Styx Matter on contact is deadly Sorin, the stuff that comes out of the reactors is mostly inactive, or inert, if you want to call it that. But the stuff you find below, near ichorsyte- it's extremely dangerous."

Sorin paled, inactive? What in the world was active styx matter like? "What does it mean if its active?"

Mr. Murdock grew troubled "Colorless. It's like a pitch-black fire that eats at anything around it. Usually when the counter detects it- that's when we deploy drones to drill and collect whatever minerals are safe enough to gather. Then we book it. Seal up the tunnel and leave behind markers to warn others not to drill in that location or risk potential styx contamination... But, moving on," He gave Sorin a reassuring look "I just wanna see if the counter can detect anything with the gauntlet." Sorin nodded silently; Mr. Murdock left for the van with Mrs. Murdock following close behind, and Sorin, while sitting on that rock felt a slow building tension in his gut. An unnerving jolt, which seemed to cause him a moment of terrible introspection.

Colorless... pitch-black... fire...

The monochrome flash as the monster from the garage first took hold of him. The rage, the desperation, and the fear for Zoe's life.

Jack observed Sorin, he'd been thinking about what his father had said and as he turned to Sorin, he immediately noticed his troubled expression. "Dude, you good?" Jack asked, concern coloring his voice.

Sorin silently nodded; at that moment Zoe and Roxy arrived. Jack looked up "Yo, what up." He greeted.

Roxy simply rolled her eyes "Bored, that's what," she glanced at Sorin's arm "Anything else weird happen yet." Jack shrugged "Dad wants to try and scan Sorin with the counter." Roxy raised an eyebrow at that. While Zoe looked confused "A counter?" she said.

Roxy explained what it was to Zoe. Meanwhile, Jack fished inside of his pants pocket. He tapped Sorin on the shoulder, the metallic armor around his shoulder still feeling slightly warm. Sorin glanced up at him, and the reticle from his interface immediately focused on the small water bottle in his hand.

"Hey, wanna try something," Jack asked, his expression becoming somewhat excited. Sorin gave him a weird look "What is it?"

He presented the water bottle to him "Think you can catch the bottle if I throw it over there?" Sorin stared at him "Well, sure, I guess-" Jack shook his head "Not with your hand... I mean, the tentacle thing around your arm."

Sorin gave an unsure look at it "Er... maybe."

Jack nodded his head rapidly "Well if that's the case let's try it! I mean, you're stuck with it for the time being. So... Let's see what it can do," Jack grinned "Besides, I think it would be for the best. Can't have too much practice with it, especially if we come across more of those black-eyed things trying to do us in."

Sorin thought about it for a moment, before nodding, he got up from his seat and focused on his gauntlet. The tendril seemed to respond and proceeded to untether itself from his arm. "Alright, you ready to throw." He asked him. Jack nodded, before winding his arm back for a throw.

Roxy had just got done explaining what her dad's scanner was, when she caught sight of the tendrils movement, she immediately jumped back in alarm, which got Zoe's attention, who turned around and froze at the sight that greeted her. The metallic whip was unfurled, flashing through the air in a swift movement, before wrapping tightly around a small water bottle in mid-air, the bottle seemed to burst from the impact, as a dulled CRACK echoed in the night air. Her eyes widened as the bottle was zipped out of the air, yanked backwards like a fish getting caught by a hook, as water trailed back downward. Her eyes followed the bottles path; Sorins outstretched hand was suddenly struck by the crushed bottle like a softball. As the rest of the water ran down his hand. He winced, lightly shaking his hand from the impact. The whip draping around him near the ground, tense and ready to be deployed again.

"Holy crap! That hurt!" Sorin winced.

Jack gaped at what happened "I threw that as hard as I could... and it plucked it out of the air like it was a piece of meat."

Zoe and Roxy looked at the scene with disbelief.

Sorin looked at the crumpled bottle; just like the sand, he could feel the bottle give around the tendrils strength. He set the bottle down and looked at the whip, still moving on the ground near him. *Was that what the log meant? All those notifications on the neurological mappings... was it for this reason?*.

"Okay, seriously... could you cut it out. Thing reminds me too much of a snake." Roxy said, cringing at the tendrils movement. Sorin looked to her direction "Right, sorry about that." He thought for a moment, before willing the tendril to move; everyone watched as the tendril gathered itself up; Sorin held his hand open and watched as the metallic whip rolled itself in his hand, now looking like a silverish lasso.

"I hope I never get hit with that." Jack said "The cracking noise makes my hairs stand up."

Sorin nodded "Yeah... I'm probably going to have to practice with this thing.

I'd rather not hurt anyone by mistake." He sighed "Bella and Susan are going to freak if they see this."

Zoe moved closer, giving the tendril a cautious look "So.. are you in control of that? Or... is it the gauntlet doing all the movement?" Sorin looked at her and gave a troubled look "A little bit of both if I'm being honest. I can actually feel it moving around in the sand, and I could even feel it when it wrapped around the bottle earlier; It's kinda awesome- just wish it didn't feel so weird." He grew ponderous.

"Hey Zoe." She regarded him "Yeah?"

"Does your pincers work the same way? Like you can feel them move and all, but is it kinda like another limb?" he held up the tendril in front of her, she blinked at it, her expression becoming quizzical "That thing... really?" before nodding hesitantly "Yeah, that's what mine feels like, well, when I have them out that is." Zoe paused "Wait a sec," Sorin watched the necklace within her black shirt glow a purplish hue, suddenly her appearance shifted; green eyes shifting to compound ones and her skin hardened, with the claws and lines once again appearing at the edges of her mouth. Zoe turned to Roxy "You mind if I use them?" Roxy regarded her appearance, before sighing "Go ahead, it's not my favorite shirt." Zoe nodded before the soft rip of fabric reached his ears. All four pincers extended from her back and folded around her, their sharp tips piercing the sandy ground.

"Doesn't feel too strange now... though, I hate the fact I gotta sacrifice a shirt or two, in order to bring them out." Zoe said, rubbing her arms as she glanced at her pincers with annoyance.

"Hey Sorin." Sorin turned around and was greeted by Mr. Murdock; looking up, he spotted the device in his hand. It looked like a large handheld gadget with a cylinder tube and a carrying handle on the top. On the side of the device there looked to be a carrying compartment which reminded Sorin of his late cyberdeck. On top there was a display with numbers on it and a needle, alongside a digital screen above it. Mr. Murdock now crouching down, took the handle with his other hand, before taking out a small metal rode from the devices side compartment. The rode was attached to a wire connected to the device; Mr. Murdock then regarded Sorin, "Alright, if you don't mind... can I use this on your arm."

Sorin stared at the metal rod "Is that supposed to detect styx matter? The rod thing in your hand?"

Mr. Murdock nodded "It's the sensor, allows you to detect traces of styx matter; the substance gives off an energy signature that the device can detect and gives a warning on its general direction." He tapped the dial "This, monitors the radiation levels."

Sorin gulped "Okay... should I sit down?"

Mr. Murdock shook his head "That won't be necessary, just hold still for me." Mrs. Murdock appeared later, moving across the two and taking a seat next to Jack. She looked closely towards Sorin's direction, brow furrowed, her expression concerned "Hey mom, something wrong?" Jack asked, she shook her head "Just thinking, don't worry about it hon." She replied.

Sorin watched as the metal rode got closer to his arm. Zoe and the rest watched with bated breath; Sorin felt himself get tense as a soft beep could be heard emanating from the counter. But to his relief, it seemed to be barely moving past the first level of styx contamination, the needle was waving rapidly across the 1st number, of which, the counter went up to a total of 10SyR (Styx Absorption Rating); Mr. Murdock hummed to himself "What is it?" Sorin asked.

"It's bizarre... the gauntlet itself has a similar reading to ichorsyte... Actually, it's the exact same level as ichorsyte." He breathed "But... something is off-" suddenly there was a sharp series of beeps from the counter, just as the rode finally got to the end of Sorins forearm; the counters digital screen on top of the display suddenly flashed a red warning sign. To Sorin's frozen terror, an arrow appeared on the screen...

Pointing directly towards Sorins chest... exactly where his heart is.

Sorin felt a lurch in his chest, the constricted ball of energy where the mysterious flow of power originated from, suddenly, began to pulse with activity. He grasped his chest, and the gauntlet began to glow a brilliant red. Mr. Murdock paled, the readings from the gauntlet jumped up with alarming speed. The rod still pointing to the gauntlet was now reading at a level of 5SyR.

They both stared at the counter, horrified, Mr. Murdock stood up shaking "That's impossible... that reading pushes the survivability limit..." he whispered, completely transfixed.

Mrs. Murdock rushed to his side looking at the counters reading; she put a hand to her mouth, "What on earth," she whispered "Sorin hold still."

Sorin gave them a conflicted look; everyone was getting nervous, and that surge of power from his chest was still there, still ever presently radiating that power towards his gauntlet arm. "Sorin, could you remove your hand for a second." Mr. Murdock asked him. Sorin looked at the rod, and hesitated, before removing his right arm. The rod moved up the gauntlet, and finally rested on his chest- directly over his heart and It was like clockwork. The arrow on display shot up faster than the three could comprehend, moving all the way to 10SyR; the counters series of beeps were now frantically chittering, the display screen lit up and the arrow pointing to his chest disappeared. Replaced with a red exclamation sign and another symbol, one that Sorin didn't recognize, a circular sign featuring a central circle within, surrounded by what looked like five propeller symbols around the circle like a spiral.

Mr. Murdock eyes looked at the second symbol with clear disbelief, eyes bulging, he looked at Sorin as if he were a ghost.

"Mr. Murdock," Sorin asked quietly "What is it... what does that symbol mean?" he demanded, as Mrs. Murdock crouched down on her knee, looking absolutely besides herself with shock.

"That can't be right... there has to be something wrong with it... Robert, is it malfunctioning?" Mrs. Murdock asked, turning towards Mr. Murdock.

He shook his head "No, this is a brand new one I got from the mines- before we left... it's completely functional." He said rubbing his chin.

"Would you guys tell me what's wrong already! What's got you both so spooked!?" Sorin raised his voice, looking back at the counter, clearly uncomfortable with how they both were acting.

Mr. Murdock hesitated, his jaw tightened at the symbol on the counter. Before sighing heavily, he sat down and gave Sorin a remorseful look. "Sorin... this is serious. Are you *sure* your cogni attacks aren't any worse than a mild aching across your body?" he asked.

Sorin taking note of how serous he was acting, and still growing more uneasy by the second, nodded his head "Well, recently none of my cogni attacks have been that bad. Honestly, the worst one I had was during the bunker. When I first got thrown into the cell." He held up his gauntlet "But the strange thing about it... At first, I thought it was because I wasn't taking my medications. But, ever since I encountered the monster, I think the orb was the real reason for that flare up I was having at that settlement."

Mr. Murdock shook his head "I... I don't think it's that simple Sorin... I don't know how else to tell you about this. But... that medicine your taking, what's it called?"

Sorin gave them a confused look "Ambro-something 120mgs" he answered.

Mrs. Murdock gave him a skeptical look, mouthing the 'Ambro' part of what he said. "You don't mean Ambroxicavalol right?" Sorin nodded quickly "Yes, that's the one!"

She shook her head slowly, brow furrowing as she recalled the medication. "120 milligrams.... of Ambroxicavalol... that can't be right, that... that wouldn't do a thing. Especially not with the reading on that counter." She shook her head "Sorin... it's a miracle that your still standing."

Sorin gave them both an impatient look "Seriously, could you two stop being so cryptic and tell me what's going on." He demanded.

They both turned to one another before giving him a dire look. "Sorin, that sign on the counter... that's the symbol for *active* styx matter." Mr. Murdock said grimly "If it was just the 10SyR alone- that would have been bad, but... you have actual live styx matter radiating from your *chest* kid. Frankly, you're a living miracle if I've ever seen one."

Sorin looked at him, the words sounding foreign to himself; that couldn't be, he'd been sick for so long- ever since the first day he'd been discovered by the voyager crew. But to hear it from both their mouths. This was the furthest thing he expected from this little test with the counter. His eyes widened, the black flash in the garage days ago... was that active styx matter he saw... how was that even possible?

"But... How.... I've never- I've never been that worse off. Unless I was having an 8 or a 10 level attack... it's never gotten worse for me... so how-" he trailed off, the mental slide show of all the small to large cogni attacks playing back-to-back.

Nothing was making sense!

"Sorin!" Mrs. Murdock grabbed his shoulders, the metallic shoulder pads dulling the sharpened edges of their interlocked plates. Sorin looked up startled. "Listen... we're not trying to scare you... we're just concerned, this is something that's never happened before, in any case of styx poisoning. Especially for someone harboring active styx matter inside them. It's simply not possible."

Sorin flinched "Why?" he asked, "How is it worse than usual?"

The outside wind of the desert blew over the pair. Sorin looked around, and everyone was standing up around him; Roxy, Jack, and Zoe had moved closer to him and Mrs. Murdock obviously trying to hear what was going on. All three, giving him varying degrees of anxious alarm and worry- none more so than Zoe. The lights from the van and campfire being the only source of illumination in the dark space of the surrounding wastelands. Yet, Sorin felt a creeping dread seize his heart. The looks of worry from everyone, should have... in some way touched him. He was a stranger in their mists, but they've chosen to care about him. Regardless of his connections to the nomads, his status as a cognicrossis sufferer, or.. the thing currently attached to his arm. He should have felt relieved; but instead, he felt isolated, scared and confused for why this was happening to him.

"I'm not going to waste time explaining the usual symptoms of styx matter." Mrs. Murdock explained "But active styx-matter is different, normal cognicrossis takes time to run its course, with other stages getting worse, and worse as time goes on.... until the final stages. But when someone is under contamination from active styx matter, their nervous system isn't just attacked, their immolated." Sorin paled "What."

She sighed, shaking her head "What's a better way to explain this... it's like an invisible fire Sorin, it's radiation that has no visible light, and when it comes in contact with anything organic- it disintegrates it. It's the same comparison of someone standing in front of the sun. You die well before you get close enough to it." She said quietly.

Mr. Murdock put a hand on his wife's shoulder "I heard stories back in Ashton, of minors in other settlements coming across catches of active styx matter deep in the earth. There rare, very, very rare. But when there unearthed, its always reported as devastating." He grimaced "It's like a horror story for miners of ichorsyte; something the workers would always tell a green horn on the first few weeks of the job." He said, "And I'm telling you, the people who live to tell about it, there not the same soon after." He finished.

Sorin looked down, clutching the spot over his heart, the place where he could still feel the energy traveling down into his gauntlet arm. The mental image of something otherworldly and abstract living within his veins now taking on a more horrible shape. How something so ruinous could be coming from his heart, but the memory of that moment in the garage was not a hoax. That was active styx matter... there was no doubt in his mind now... and the words of the stranger came to him. Every cryptic line and ominous message now once more seared into his brain.

"But this thing on my arm. That has to be what's powering it, so... what does it all mean?" he asked uneasily.

Mr. Murdock shook his head "I'm sorry but I can't answer that for you. But... when we reach Hanover- maybe then you can contact your family. Perhaps they can make sense of that document you have in your bag."

Mrs. Murdock gave a reassuring smile "Look, as dour as this is... your still alive Sorin... let's look at it in that perspective right now. If you were like any other boy your age... well, I'd rather not think about that."

Sorin looked to his gauntlet unsure if he could look at everything that happened in a more positive light. But she was right... right now he was alive, even if everything he'd learned so far was paradoxical to what should have happened by now. That still didn't make him feel any better about his situation. Or, reduce the feeling of uncomfortableness around the mysteries surrounding him... The gauntlet over his arm, or the signature of active styx matter radiating from his heart.

"Mom." Roxy said "What if Sorin is like us? With everything he and Zoe has told us so far why can't that be the case?" Jack walked up next to Sorin's side "Yeah! And that also explains why the giant monster thing could have been after him. You know, aside from the big metal ball thing attaching to his... uh..." he looked to Sorin, who sighed "Cyberdeck." Jack nodded "Right, the cyberdeck."

Mrs. Murdock sighed "That's the problem. It's all speculation. We don't really know how much of this is something related to deviants... or, whatever it is those nomads were doing. I swear kidnapping *children*... the nerve of them!" she hissed. Which caused Jack and Roxy to stare at their mother in surprise. "If there was ever a bunch of cowards that deserved to be hunted out of their holes by S.P.C.T.R, they would have it coming."

Sorin felt a stab of unease, touched by Mrs. Murdocks concern as he was, the nomads in the bunker would no longer be able to answer for whatever crimes they have meted out in the wastelands. Suddenly, Sorin felt himself becoming dizzy. He grasped his head before crouching down, his right knee landing on the dirt as he groaned. Everyone turned to him in alarm.

He winced, *Oh that's just perfect... another flare up, now of all times.*

Mrs. Murdock was already crouched down with him, her hand moving to his armor-clad shoulder, only to swipe her hand away in shock as the sharpened pauldron suddenly began to smoke. The effect was immediate as Sorins interface began to smoke too, the silverish mist disappearing as the armor around his arm and shoulder slowly began to disintegrate. The night wind of the wasteland began to pick up, and with another gasp from Sorin, the rest of the armor suddenly gave way, the mask interface, the armor running up his arm and shoulder became a large cloud of silver mist. The wind died down, carrying whatever was left of his armor. Leaving Sorin with a now deactivated gauntlet; the red light dimming, and the energy from his chest; now identified as active styx matter, simply cut off. The tightened core of his chest was suddenly and irritatingly hidden by a wall of pain; courtesy of his cogni flare up. Sorin looked up and Mrs. Murdock grimaced, his face was a branch of small dark veins around the underside of his eyes and cheeks. Going down his neck and disappearing past his grey shirt.

"Crap." Sorin muttered, he forced himself to stand up; much to Mrs. Murdocks worry, as she frantically held on to him. Mr. Murdock was also at his side, who held a large arm behind him- to Sorin's gratitude, as he could feel himself list a bit from the effort.

"That came outta nowhere," Sorin said, taking note of how suddenly exhausted he was "Where the heck did my energy go?" he said to himself out loud as the two adults set him on one of the rocks by the campfire "Feels like a ran a marathon."

Zoe was moving forward, her eyes worried... but at the same time perplexed. The way in which the armor evaporated into the air was just so odd to her. Roxy and Jack of course were watching as the rest of the mist disappeared; Jack specifically, was remembering how the armor felt under his hand. How solid and sharp it was... yet he was baffled by the quick dispersal of the metallic substance that covered him... it was all so strange. Sorin glanced at his left hand, spotting the visible black lines covering them; even though the glove was supposedly using the styx matter in his body as a power source, he was still subjected to the harsh effects of his illness. Although, he has yet to experience a cogni attack past a 5 out of 10 yet... He sighed, looking at his gauntlet covered arm; the thing unnerved him and the constant things he's been finding out about his condition have made him question everything he's been told by Church, Hosea and Bella.

He had to find out why. They had to have known about the active styx matter... by what the Murdocks have been telling him, he should have been died.... a thought which scared him totally.

"Sorin how bad is it." Mr. Murdock asked, observing the boy leaning on the rock. Mr. Murdock held onto Sorin, making sure he wouldn't fall over. "It's not that bad," Sorin replied back after a moment "Just feel really tired."

Roxy stepped closer as she looked him over; feeling uneasy, to her the guy in front of her looked like death, and that's right after learning what's coursing through him. "Are you sure, you look like your about to fall over on us."

"Yeah, what she said," Jack said on his side "I guess using the gauntlet for so long has its draw backs... kinda like me and Rox actually."

Zoe carefully walked up to Sorin. Not liking the marks just under his skin. "Ditto, maybe you should stop using it for the moment, yeah."

Sorin sighed, "Sure, sure.... but can someone get my hoverboard real quick. I'm not sure I put it back in my bag..." Sorin suddenly listed, much to everyone's alarm.

Zoe was already next to him as he leaned forward. His eyes rolling into the back of his head; Mr. Murdock already had him before he could lean further. For a moment everyone was panicking; Sorin's eyes had closed, and he had gone completely limp in Mr. Murdocks arms.

"Oh Crap! Is he okay!" Roxy hollered over the commotion, only for Jack to suddenly say "Wait! I think he's just asleep..." Mrs. Murdock held a finger to his neck and gasped with relief as snores began to emanate from him.

Zoe leaned over in a crouch, her sudden terror of the worst happening abruptly replaced with utter vexation. "Oh my gosh, is he serious... he nearly gave me a freaking heart attack!"

Mr. Murdock sighed "Zoe... It's okay, just calm down... let's... let's get him back in the van." Mrs. Murdock nodded and carefully scooped him up in her arms, before moving towards the van.

Mr. Murdock glanced at the gauntlet which was over Meryl's shoulder. He looked up to the now bright stars of the night sky; everything he's seen and learned today, it was impossible, he knew that... yet what the boy had in his body, it defied explanation... As he watched his two kids and Zoe follow behind his wife, he felt a growing sense of unease in his gut- a strong note of concern, over what possible explanation for the boys... unique circumstance. That gauntlet was the center of his unease, and the energy signature from his styx counter was still buzzing the horrible noise of warning in his ear, as a phantom echo.

He prayed for his sake that nothing more sinister was at work. He followed behind, the desert nights pitch black curtain, howling an unseen wind which tousled the distant sand dunes.

CHAPTER

39

10/26/2061, Tuesday, 4:57 am

Sorin opened his eyes, the ceiling of the van's interior greeting him in turn.

He laid there, his head over a pillow, propped on the bench seats arm rest. The light from the window wasn't as luminous as the other nights. Looking past the curtain covering the window from his position on the armrest, he couldn't see much of the skyline outside.

He gave a silent exhalation of breath, a sad sigh as it were... the stars weren't out tonight. Everyone was fast asleep, and once again he found himself to be the only one awake.

He groaned silently, his memory catching him up. The fragments of him falling asleep floated to the surface. The sudden dreariness and loss of balance, culminating in him losing consciousness. The embarrassment soon came a moment after. The abruptness of it wounding his pride. He bit his tongue, choosing instead to direct his frustration elsewhere, for there was nothing else for it now. The revelations of hours past followed by the onset of cognicrossis... was that what he had to look forward to if he overused the gauntlet? He could feel the clawed talons of the gauntlet brush his thigh, bringing it up out of the covers, its dark silverish metal barely reflecting the light outside. Resting his right arm on his stomach he felt torn. On one hand he loved the idea of having his own operating system. On the other, the thing was still this big, massive mystery, which grew more and more complicated by the minute.

Sorin snorted quietly, shaking his head at everything that's happened, never in a million years would he have expect something like *this* to happen.

So not fair... I finally get a working cyberdeck and Hoverboard. Only for me to end up kidnapped, then, a freaking loon under a hood forces a stupid experiment on me, which, I don't know if its alive or not. Oh! Don't forget the mysterious thing in my chest- which, is generating live styx matter...

Why can't I have anything for free, just this once!

Suddenly he felt movement, just behind the couch, he made to get up and peak. But a hand came and clamped around his mouth. His gauntlet arm shot up, grabbing the wrist of whoever... he looked up and the dark outline of something he recognized made him pause.

His eyes widened, by the dim light of the window- he recognized the clawed hand as Zoe's.

"Shhhhhh!" she whispered, her other hand making the silence gesture over her lips. Something he could barely make out in the semi darkness of the van. Sorin didn't know what was going on, but he squeezed her wrist, hopefully she could see his look of bewilderment in the dark better than he could.

She suddenly pointed away, following where she was pointing he landed on the sliding door leading outside. He looked back to her, and she nodded toward its direction. "Let's get outside... away from Jack's range... I gotta ask you something." She whispered.

Sorin looked at her before nodding slowly, unhanding her wrist she let go of his mouth; he carefully moved the blanket off him and reached down for his shoes. Zoe moved over the couch, silently swinging a leg over the head of the large seat and maneuvering herself over it like a cat.

The two made for the door, silently minding the two adults on the small mattress, as they slept on. Sorin cringed to himself as he tiptoed to the door, his sneakers making small scuff noises on the vans floor, while Zoe, of course, was quitter than a mouse- hardly making any noise whatsoever. The door creaked and slid back, Sorin and Zoe slipped by the cracked door into the semi-dark outside.

The sky was still a dark blue sheet covering the skyline, a pale light just creeping on the horizons edge, the rolling dunes of sand on the bottom looking like shaded shadows on the wastelands horizon. Sorin carefully closed the door, making sure a rogue wind didn't blow a truffe of sand inside and onto the sleeping husband and wife. Sorin and Zoe moved, away from the van, further past the campground and stopping a few odd meters away from the site. On top a large sand dune and looking down back towards the van and campsite. The early morning winds whistled around them, ruffling over his short unkempt hair, and tossing Zoe's long blonde hair over and around her shoulders.

Zoe was in her transformed state, her green compound eyes looking unsure of themselves. Sorin kept a steady eye on the van, something in him finding the van a more interesting sight than looking directly into Zoe's eyes. He had a small feeling in his gut about what she wanted to talk about.

He sighed "You know, with how far he was able to hear inside the settlement. I doubt this will be far enough away from Jacks powers," he turned to her looking somewhat wary "But I guess it'll have to do. What did you wanna talk about?"

She looked at him, her eyes moving down to the sandy floor "There's more to your story than just the orb jumping onto your cyberdeck... isn't there?" Her tone wasn't accusing, but her words were nervous, like she was dreading whatever else he could have potentially left out. "When... when I went berserk back in the bunker, something else happened... Didn't it." she stated, looking back at him "The way you were looking at the document back at the desk. What really happened in that vault room?"

Sorin looked at her, feeling nervous; this was it... he'd seen it coming ever since she gave him that look. When he first told his side of the story to the Murdocks. He was honestly afraid and confused about the whole thing; but... the weight of everything he experienced from the stranger and the mystery surrounding the orbs abilities... it scared him.

He talked, explaining the out-of-control compulsion that came over him when the nomad had held him against the wall, his puppet like march to the vault door, the voices in his head, his first encounter with the orb, the moment after she was knocked out with the black flash of active styx matter, and last but not least... the stranger. And how he seemed to know more than, even what he knew about himself... including his throwaway mention of his (maybe) mother. It was like a part of the heavy load had been taken off his shoulders, the more he talked about it.

"I don't have anything to remember them Zoe, nothing. No photo, no video, not even a necklace or anything... And this guy somehow knows me, and everything about it just stinks." Sorin said "You couldn't even see him, and somehow he was able to open the cell door. He was there before the gas station explosion... and he did something to me. Held his hand where my heart was and it felt like I was dying." he said becoming immeasurably uncomfortable. "And he just kept saying I needed it- that my survival depended on it- and I still can't make any since out of it!" he rambled, becoming more and more anxious with each passing second.

"Sorin wait!" Zoe said, wide eyed and worried, both hands now over his shoulders.

"Slow down, breath. Just... look," she said trying to look as reassuring as she could "Will get answers... I don't know how- but, maybe my dad will know more about this." she reassured. "And your nomad family will probably know even more. I mean they have to have known." She reasoned "Maybe... there was a good reason for it, maybe..." She said, almost lamely at the end, her tone unsure.

Sorin cringed, what other reason could there be to hide this from him? For the longest time, he simply saw himself as firmly in-between the mildest stages of cognicrossis. It sucked. But, he never would have imagined himself in such a horrible position. Knowing what's inside of him... it, it stung. If Hosea and the rest knew about this, then what else could they have been hiding from him? Did he even want to know? Sorin was silent, not able to say anything in reply. Zoe cringed, becoming more concerned. His explanation striking a cord with her; this was beyond what she could have guessed, and worser than whatever she could have thought possible. Sorin seemed dragged down, an invisible weight which settled onto his shoulders. His eyes unseeing, looking deep in thought and simultaneously dispirited.

She paused, she had to do something, anything to get his mind somewhere else. "Sorin." she lightly shook him, causing him to glance back at her "Look, I'm pretty sure will find out what's really going on after we reach Hanover. So for now, let's not overthink it... Besides, the view out here is awesome."

She glanced to the side while pulling him to look along with her, over to the rising sun in the background. Just halfway out of the horizon, filtering a red and copper hue across the now visible clouds in the sky. "Beautiful." she breathed, watching the sunlight run across the dune filled desert. A golden carpet below the mourning dawn, stretching across an ocean of dunes. It was so surreal to her, as an empty void in the middle of the desert- it was strangely peaceful.

Maybe when I get home, I can see about drawing this. She thought.

Sorin glanced in the direction of the rising sun, his thoughts still on the stranger, but as he looked towards the horizon something caught his eye. Lazily he looked towards the small figure moving in a straight line towards the suns direction. Zoe gasped, her green eyes focusing on the shape in the distance.

Compound eyes reflecting some of the light from her retinas like mirrors. Focusing her vision, she could make out some details. The thing had a small body with a brownish hide, membrane bat-like wings from what little sunlight she could catch washing over its scaled hide; the things head was shaped like an arrow, a beak like mouth from what she could make out from the growing distance.

"What is that?" she whispered, not recognizing it from any species of bird back home.

Sorin looked at her confused, and then did a mental face palm. *Duh! Of course she wouldn't know what a biodactyl is. Probably doesn't have them in the republic...*

"That's a biodactyl." Sorin said, Zoe turned giving him a bewildered look "A bio... dactyl?" she stammered, looking perplexedly back to the now retreating dot over the horizon.

Sorin nodded "Their mostly sand burrowers; they eat small animals like... uh- snakes, rodents, insects, and other small lizards... I forgot what else they eat... but, their mostly harmless."

Zoe stared at him "How do you even know this..."

Sorin shrugged "Hosea, Kingsley, and Susan- but mostly Hosea. He pretty much told me a lot about the animals down here. Though...

there aren't a whole lot of em." He explained, thinking back to those times when he was still traveling around in the voyager.

"The way he said it- living in the middle of the desert is rough, its eat or be eaten out here, and water is incredibly scarce too. So most of the wildlife is kinda vicious. Its why we have Duneraptors, Direwolves, and Cazadors... Which are the worst things you can encounter out here. Though cazadors are more likely to nest in dark, wet, and dirty places. Like abandoned buildings or trash barges. Direwolves are mostly everywhere, but their mostly nocturnal, and only travel at night or late evenings."

Zoe expression became apprehensive "And here I thought the squirrels at home were bad." She mumbled to herself "And what exactly are duneraptors? Are they supposed to be giant dinosaurs or something?"

"No," Sorin said "A bird."

Zoe raised an eyebrow "Oh... so, it's like the biodactyl then, harmless right?"

Sorin shook his head, before chuckling to himself, oh this was going to be good. "Uhm... No. Definitely no... more like a giant predatory bird that makes a nest inside one of the plateaus, or inside the walls of a large canyons. They also have a large hunting ground- I actually forgot how big of an area they hunt, but they're really territorial. Dangerously so." He suddenly had a ponderous look "You know what... I'm pretty sure I almost got attacked by one when I was still traveling in the voyager."

Zoe stared at him looking very horrified "What!"

Sorin laughed "Yeah, I was eight when it happened. Completely unaware of it too; I was with Hosea outside of the voyager, and we came across a bunch of odd stuff around camp. Food going missing, and stuff started breaking around camp, and odd noises at night. Well... as he put it, I was wondering around when he noticed a shadow over me. Turns out the reason why all are stuff was going missing or likewise getting destroyed, was because we were in a duneraptors nesting ground. Hosea had no choice but to shoot it down; I didn't know what was going on and he literally carried me away before I could see that anything was wrong. Didn't want me seeing the dead animal." He explained.

Zoe looked ill "Your telling me that thing almost... that's horrible!"

"Oh... Yeah, it was. Glad Hosea was there when it did happen." He grinned looking sheepish.

She shook her head "Gosh this place is scary. How do you people deal with it? I mean, the Murdocks already told me about the raiders and other ex-nomads. How can the conclaves even hope to bring order to this place... it feels lawless out here."

Sorin shrugged "No idea. But corps sure love to boast about their continued progress. Like it really means anything." He snorted "More like bleeding the settlements dry."

Zoe raised an eyebrow, but shook her head; taking note of his dislike for the corporations in the conclaves... Just like the Murdocks. "So... how's the arm doing? Is it feeling weird, and can you still hear voices?"

Sorin paused, before shaking his head "Nope, haven't heard any voices for a while now actually. They kinda stopped once we got out of that settlement, not that I'm not happy about it." He brought up his right hand, "Just wish this thing had a manual to go with it. And it's amazing that I can still hack stuff with it... Heck, it's even better than my old cyberdeck."

Zoe gave the gauntlet a wary look "Don't forget about the creepy bladed tentacle thing that came out of it... I swear when you were whipping that thing around it looked soooo weird." She thought about it for a moment, before giggling.

Sorin gave her an odd look "What?"

Zoe smiled "You kinda remind me of one of those stage performers back home. There was this circus that came around town this one time, and one of the performers had duel whips- kinda like your gauntlet, only it was less creepy and made of fabric I think- anyway, he did a bunch of neat tricks on stage. Like striking targets thrown at him or pulling stuff out of the air using the whip." She giggled again, thinking about yesterday when Jack tossed the water bottle.

Sorin sighed "Why geez, thanks. Maybe I'll think about joining one in the future."

Zoe laughed "Oh... I'd pay to see that!"

Sorin rolled his eyes at her; the sun was just about over the horizon, casting bright red ribbons across the sky. The sand dunes of the gold carpet stretched before them, the endless desert now visible over the dawn. In the distance to Sorin's surprise he could hear the low-pitched cries of something in the distance. A cawing noise, to be precise. More than likely a Merwink. A small to medium sized bird that caws in the early mornings. They had yellowish sandy feathers and were mostly scavengers that dined on bugs, or again, smaller animals. It was flock communication. They mostly hunted by themselves, but would fan out and sometimes hunt in small groups. Kingsley simply called them the wastelands version of crows. Only difference was they were venomous.

Another sound joined in... but this one was much closer than the nearby flock of merwinks.

Sorin paused, there it was again... A soft chirping sound that was emanating from below... immediately guessing its source he brought up his right arm. The soft light of the mourning dawn bounced upon the iridescent dark silver, its red texture between the plates were softly hewed in a dim glow. The chirping was resonating from between the plates; a faintly musical tone within its notes, an altogether different vibe than the one he got the first or second time he heard it.

It was more... emotive. Not just twittering or chirping, but a mixture that shocked him by how complex it sounded, as soft and meticulous as it was.

"W-What is that?" Zoe spoke looking around, her eyes wide and expression awed "That sounds so beautiful... Sorin, do you-" she stopped, her eyes falling to him then suddenly looking confused. Her eyes darted down and landed on the gauntlet. She paused; absolutely dumbfounded, she took a small step forward and balked at what was happening before her. The gauntlet continued its small symphony. Sorin held his right hand up, the gems underside of the gauntlet faintly shimmering; he couldn't believe it, so this wasn't in his own head after all...

"H-how is it doing that?" Zoe stammered, her eyes staring mystified towards the silver glove.

Sorin shook his head, her guess was as good as his at the moment. "Sorin... Zoe..." a voice called out.

Sorin turned around and Ms. Murdock was standing there behind them, arms folded, she looked sternly at the two of them. Sorin glanced down; the gauntlets song had abruptly ended, much to his confusion.

Zoe was paralyzed, suddenly looking very nervous at Mrs. Murdocks unexpected arrival.

Sorin, maybe out of his current bewilderment of the gauntlets surprise bout of bird song, wasn't feeling as worried as he should have been. He looked to her stern expression and gave her a sheepish smile.

"Oh, mourning Mrs. Murdock." He greeted.

She looked between the two of them her expression unreadable. "What are you two doing so far from the campsite this early in the morning? Especially when there could be direwolves still roaming around?" she said sounding less than amused.

Sorin looked to Zoe who was shifting her foot uneasily, very likely scared to admit it was her idea to come out here in the first place. Sorin turned to her "Um... it was me. I asked her to come outside. Thought I could explain the constellations in the sky but weren't any stars out." He said.

Mrs. Murdock raised an eyebrow. Sorin scratched the back of his head, "But I was able to tell her about the biodactyls though."

Mrs. Murdock sighed heavily "Okay, Sorin. I understand you're trying to be helpful. But this isn't a playground. There's no telling what could be out there." Sorin was silent; her tone was series, and he was getting scary Bellatrix vibes at the moment.

He nodded "Yes mam, sorry..."

She turned to Zoe who flinched "Zoe, do you understand." She nodded her head rapidly "Yes, sorry"

She sighed, before glancing back over her shoulder. "Looks like were the only ones awake right now..." she turned to Sorin, her expression relaxing just a smidge, as a questioning look taking its place "What was that tune I was hearing earlier? Didn't sound like anything from this parts." She asked.

Sorin and Zoe shared a look. Sorin was about to ask her how much she heard, until the gauntlet beat him too it; he groaned, the musical melody which had been interrupted by Mrs. Murdocks sudden arrival had reemerged, and ramped up in volume.

As if the gauntlet itself was more than happy enough to oblige the apparent need of its music.

Mrs. Murdock paused, the melody coming from Sorin, who looked completely annoyed by something. "Sorin? What's the matter?" Sorin looked up and gave her an exasperated look "Nothing, just the gauntlet doing something random, as usual." he said.

She creased her brow at his words. Then looked at the gauntlet on his arm; she sucked in a small breath- there was no mistaking it, the sounds were coming from it. But how...

"Sorin, how on earth?" she said moving closer "Since when has it started doing that?"

"Might have been doing it since the first time I woke up with it... I mean, I thought I was hearing things or something... no one seemed to hear it, except for me... Well, until now." He explained.

Zoe nodded quickly "It started happening when he told me about the biodactyls," she gave an expression that Sorin couldn't read "Its sounds so weird, it's like the birds back home in Rosaria." she looked at the gauntlet with a torn expression; the gauntlets ominous vibes had her feeling a distinct lack of trust with it, but the sudden sounds it was making had her conflicted... how could something so out of this world strange, produce something so... beautiful?

Mrs. Murdock was quite, taking in what Zoe and Sorin had to say about it. She stared at the gauntlet, looking at the strange device over the young man's arm. Her eyes widened, suddenly a look of familiarity came over her. "That couldn't be... but, it sounds exactly like it." she mumbled to herself.

Sorin and Zoe looked to one another. *Sounded like what?* They both thought in unison. "Um... Mrs. Murdock? what are you-" Sorin began, only to stare as Mrs. Murdock turned around and fast walked back to the van.

"I'll be right back! Just hold on for a moment!" she called back as she quickly moved past the campsite and into the van. Much to Sorin and Zoe's complete shock and alarm. The moment Mrs. Murdock left, the music from the gauntlet began to dimmer and stop. Much to both of their surprise.

After a moment Zoe regarded Sorin- her expression looking guilty "Why did you tell her it was your idea?" she agonized, "You didn't have to get in trouble for my sake."

Sorin shrugged, "Why not, I'm used to it- getting in trouble I mean. Besides, I owe you for saving me from that burning street." He shook his head "Still can't believe that happened- if not for that hooded guy I probably could've gotten away."

She grimaced, shaking her head she sighed. "Thanks... but, next time let me do the talking. Mrs. M looked like she was going blow a gasket."

Sorin cringed "Yeah, she kinda did."

CHAPTER

40

10/26/2061, Tuesday, 6:04 am

A moment later Mrs. Murdock returned carrying something in her hands. Zoe and Sorin observed the device.

It was a small wooden box the size of a matchbox, with carvings along the sides, top, and bottom: depicting ornate sketches of flowers and birds perched on top of them. There was a small piece of metal, like a hook, holding a notch screwed into the lid of the box.

"Have a listen to this real quick and let me know if this doesn't sound the same to you." She said before pulling the hook off; the lid opened immediately and inside of the box was a small metal contraption that had small gears and wires attached to a comb and cylinder like peace in the middle of it.

Sorin's eyes widened, the cylinder began to revolve around the metal comb over it. The small pins attached to the cylinder plucked the metallic teeth of the comb- producing a nearly identical note of bird song.

Zoe silently regarded the little music box; the music it was producing was beautiful, exactly like the gauntlet's melody.

"My grandmother made this for me when I was your age," Mrs. Murdock said "She used to live in the sectored regions when she was younger, and made this for me on my birthday. She told me that the birdsong was from a species of bird called a nightingale." She sighed "There mostly an endangered species now... A lot of the capitals in the sectored regions have cut off a lot of their habitats." She closed the box, cutting off the music as Zoe looked at her wide-eyed

"That's sad. It sounds really beautiful Mrs. M." Zoe said, looking at the gauntlet, which was now quiet.

"It is. To be honest, I kinda like it," Mrs. Murdock admitted "It's probably the closest thing to a nightingales song I'll ever hear. The only reason it reminded me of the music box is because its well known how varied and complex a nightingales singing can be."

Mrs. Murdock was about to say more- but the gauntlet beat her to it. All three silently listened as the gauntlet began to sing another varied mix of chirping, twittering swells. It wasn't long before they recognized the musical notes. Which were the very same from the music box.

Sorin held up his right arm, observing the gauntlet with renewed curiosity Seems to learn quickly, it didn't feel like a recording... he could literally feel something clicking from within the thing. As odd as it was, it really felt like it was physically creating the chirping noises. How it was able to do so was once again a matter of debate for Sorin.

His cyberdeck was gone and in its place the gauntlet; to bad there wasn't another name he could call it...

Sorin furrowed his brow, as Zoe glanced at the gauntlets gems. There was nary a shimmer from either gems on the back of thing, so this had to be some kind of idle thing it does when it's not active... at least, that's what she assumed. The mourning sun was now clear past the horizon; the cloudless cerulean sky and the gentle ribbons of the mourning sunlight cast the dune rich desert in its brilliance. But as Mrs. Murdock looked onwards towards the horizon, the moment of peacefulness which was accompanied by the birdsong of the gauntlet had finally reached its zenith for her. Pretty soon Robert, Jack and Roxanne would be waking up... its time she got ready to prepare breakfast.

"Well... it's time to head back the campsite," she sighed, getting both Sorin and Zoes attention "Lets head back, breakfast isn't going to make itself." She said.

Sorin paused, the sudden mention of food suddenly making his stomach growl in response. Zoe feeling a similar disturbance could only nod vigorously.

"You're right Mrs. M! I'm starving... I'll go fetch the camp supplies. Hey Sorin mind giving me a hand."

Sorin grinned, his stomach now taking charge of his list of priorities. Placing whatever thoughts concerning the gauntlet into the back foot. "Yeah. I'm pretty sure we got some instant grits with the supplies we took from the bunker. Hey Mrs. M can we see if it's any good."

Mrs. Murdock laughed "Go ahead, be my guest. I'll also check and see if we got enough to go around... Jack will probably want seconds." She said matter of factly.

Sorin and Zoe laughed as they made for the van, the image of Jack stuffing himself with food from the last meal they shared yesterday still fresh in there minds. Along with Roxy's disgust over her little brother's... lack, of mealtime manners. Of course, too Sorin- with Roxy's general personality reminding him too much of Jade and likewise of Susan. It felt even more hilarious to him.

10/26/2061, Tuesday, 7: 27 am

"Oh my god," Roxy groaned "Would you freaking chew your food!"

"I am!" growled Jack.

Or at least, that's what Sorin believed he heard him say. Who's mouth was stuffed with cheese grits and bacon. Zoe simply giggled at the twins antics.

Entertainment without the tv was her thoughts as she watched on.

"Would the both of you behave!" Mr. Murdock admonished with a tired sigh, his expression exasperated. "It's way too early for this..."

The early morning went by in a flash for Sorin, as Zoe and him took out the cooking set. Mrs. Murdock saw to the rest of the supplies they took from the old bunker. And after half an hour later the food was ready. Jack, Roxy and Mr. Murdock were up soon after; Sorin and Zoe both decided to put there earlier conversation on hold as the two enjoyed their food, while Jack and Roxy simply did what they did best. Staying on each other's throats. The aftermath of mourning supper heralded a weird moment for Sorin; while the two Murdock siblings bickered with one another like usual, with Zoe joining in with the two siblings now playing mediator, and learning more about their powers and experiences with them- Sorin was left alone to pounder, Mrs. and Mr. Murdock excused themselves from the campfire and went inside the van for a private discussion. Sorin, meanwhile thought about the gauntlet.

Not of its origin or of the lingering mysterious surrounding it. Whatever secrets it held hidden inside of its gem encrusted exterior... it all felt strangely unimportant at the moment.

The Gauntlet...

The Artifact...

The Orb...

Doesn't this thing have an actual name? Something more... convenient to call it, other than the gauntlet all the time?

The two Murdocks were looking away from one another, both having their respective powers activated: the air around Jack rippled subtly, and cerulean electricity jumped around Roxy; and Zoe who was looking at the both of them in muted interest. Whatever they were talking about, Sorin was seized by the urge to pick his bag up and jumble through it.

Jack sighed "It's kinda painful actually, sometimes when I'm not focused enough- I can totally get the crap scared out of me. It's like... imagine going to bed. Its late at night, a dog barks- and it's like a megaphone going off in your ear. Crap hurts!" he said annoyed.

Roxy rolled her eyes "Please... you think that's bad. Imagine wanting to jump into a swimming pool, only to accidently forget you got lightning powers- aaanndd oops... you accidently electrocuted the people inside the pool. Well, that almost happened at least. Dad grabbed me before I could jump in." She glared at Jack "Or, if your punk of a brother decides to splash cold water on you when your asleep in bed!"

Jack looked away "Yeah... not my finest prank. But you deserved it for zapping me- when I was in the freaking bathtub!"

Zoe simply shook her head at the two, laughing nervously, and wondering if she was lucky to be the only child.

All the while. Sorin fished out the document. The medium sized file containing barely enough information about the artifact now stuck to his right arm.

Flipping a page past the photo of him. To the diagram of the orb and its containment cell. The large acronym at the top of the page: G.K.R, it isn't exactly explained what those three letters mean.

He sighed, there had to be something better he could refer it too. Even Susan had a pet name for her first cyberdeck. Jerry 0.0.7.

Sorin grinned, the memory cracking an involuntary smile. The word was short for jerry-rigged...

She and Bella decided to craft their own cyberdeck from cheaper ones they bought on the market. Something about backwards compatibility... and wanting something flexible for her first interface system. Something she could experiment with and later find something more to her needs... Jerry after all, wasn't exactly the most cutting edge- and was reliable enough to help her figure out her preferences in a deck.

Sorin thought back to all the moments when the gauntlet used its bizarre abilities. Something that really, really stood out. Something that was unique to the gauntlet.

I'm not going to name it something creepy that's for sure... Come on... Silver was too on the nose... Maybe something involving the colorful gems on it? Or maybe I could just call it the prototype... Er, no... something more unique maybe...

Sorin hummed to himself in deep thought; meanwhile, the other three were finally picking up on how silent Sorin was being.

"Yo Sor, you okay over there?" Jack called, looking at Sorins idle form on the other side of the campfire. Sitting on a chair, with the document open over his lap. "Dang... he looks out of it again." He said getting up and moving towards him.

Sorin began to grumble to himself- his brain going blank with ideas. Why was it so hard to come up with a good name for it! With everything this thing could do, it was getting harder and harder to nail down a good, reasonable nickname for it. It could hack machinery, create weird and complex armor over him, and it's able to sprout out tendrils of liquid metal from its silverish makeup.

Yeah... that doesn't help him in the least bit. Suddenly he was shaken from his stupor.

"Yo, feeling sick again?" Jack asked casually, looking him over, trying to spot any black veins appearing under his skin. Sorin with annoyance shook his head "No," he sighed "Trying to come up with a better name for this thing."

Jack blinked "A name?"

Sorin nodded "Just something I've been thinking about. Thought I'd give it a nickname- something better than calling it the glove or gauntlet. You know, something more... cooler, I guess."

Jack gave him an odd look, before grinning "Wow... So, any luck so far? I mean, with everything it can do- wait a moment, why not name it after a song or something!" he said, his eyes lighting up.

Sorin stared at him "A song? You mean after one of the cd's in your portfolio collection?"

"Exactly!" Jack grinned "There's nearly hundreds of band names and rock songs that could fit the gauntlet like a tee. I'm thinking heavy metal, or synth electronic- like the shirt your wearing." He said pointing excitedly at the shirt he lent Sorin a day or two ago.

Sorin looked down at the microchip pattern which formed the cybernetic skull in the middle of the shirt...

"What's the name of the band again?" he asked Jack

"The Nuromancers," Jack answered "Heavy rock with emphasis on electronic vocals and synthetic synthesizers. There a really good band, with a small storyline in most of their songs."

Sorin raised an eyebrow "And what would that be?"

Jack smiled "How A.I will one day rise up and terminate all humans on the face of the earth. With the A.I creating powerful cyborgs in the guise of normal humans... called Nuromancers. Who could actively shape shift themselves into anything and anyone- because there outer shells are maintained by nano machines. Giving them total control of their bodies appearance."

Sorin stared at him "You got all that... from a song?"

Jack shrugged "I looked some of it up, still cool by the way."

Sorin frowned, the name nuromancer sounded cool. But it still felt wrong, that, and he didn't want his gauntlet sharing the name of something that was made to exterminate humans. He shivered, which didn't go unnoticed by Jack who gave him an odd look. He was suddenly reminded of the bodies which littered the halls of the bunker, and the standing, unmoving figures shrouded within the fog of the vault chamber.

No... Nuromancer just wouldn't work. It felt like he was almost jinxing himself by even considering that nickname for the gauntlet. It needed to be something else.

Sorin shook his head "Er, sorry... but no. It's gotta be something else." He said.

Jack scratched his head, wondering what got into him just a second ago. "Okay... well, I don't know. Let me see if I can find something in my collection. There's gotta be something there we could use for name." Turning around only to be met with Roxy and Zoe who were both looking at the two of them with a sneaking suspicion.

"What are you two up too now." Roxy grumbled, her arms folded, and a frown aimed directly at her brother. Jack glared back "What! We're just trying to come up with a name for the glove on his arm."

Sorin rolled his eyes at the two; organizing the pages of the documents before closing the file and slipping it into the bag. He stood up, a slight feeling of ambiguity coming over him as he stared back at the two girls dubious looks. His head still churning with ideas to name it. What a headache this was turning into.

Zoe gave him a questioning look "You're seriously trying to come up with a name for it? Isn't that a bit weird, Sorin?" she said, staring at the gauntlet with a wary expression "Seems kinda possessive, ya know."

Sorin shrugged silently "Nothing possessive at all about it. Just wanna call it something other than the glove all the time. Besides... the thing is stuck to me. So, I might as well come up with a good name for it in the meantime." He gave the gauntlet an agitated look "But I'm having trouble with actually finding a good name for it!"

Roxy snorted, before sniggering "You know with that attitude, I'm surprised you haven't come up with a pet name for that hoverboard of yours yet." Zoe smiled "Probably hasn't gotten around to it yet."

Sorin rolled his eyes, before giving a dry laugh "Very funny. You two outta be comedians; heck, you might even find a way to make getting nearly eaten by squirrels an even funnier segway." Zoe gave a silent snort at that. "Or getting a cold water wake up- courtesy of Jack." He said, smiling.

Jack looked between his sister and Sorin. Looking like he was considering ducking for cover.

Roxy gave Sorin a thin smile "Oh, didn't think you were taking notes back there." There was a slight look of respect from the older teen. "Where'd you learn how to be so bold- if you don't mind me asking."

Sorin closed his eyes, his mind flashing back to a year ago, when Jade woke him up the same way... with a large bucket of cold water, in the middle of the night, without the slightest pip of her visiting beforehand.

"Jade." He said simply

She raised an eyebrow "So, is she like a younger sister?"

Sorin was silent for a moment "More like an older sister, and she didn't even give me towel after that." He sighed.

Jack cringed "Oh god, she sounds worse than Roxy." Sorin groaned in agreement.

Zoe laughed as Roxy rolled her eyes "Whatever," she glanced at the gauntlet "Anyway, why don't you just name it something simple- I mean, come on, what's the most accurate thing about it?"

Sorin held up his right arm "It can hack things, can create a weird armor like shell around me, and it sprouts out whip like tentacles." He said, giving Roxy a tired look. "Is there even a word that can sum that all up."

"The worlds craziest multitool." Zoe quipped. Sorin gave her an exasperated look "You've gotta be kidding me."

"Oh wait! I got one!" Roxy interjected, an evil grin on her face "Let's call it the Shogoth!" Sorin gave her a double look "What!" She pulled out her phone, chuckling madly as she scrolled through it; Sorin, suddenly and uncomfortably, was reminded heavily of Jade by that look on her face. She turned her phone around and Sorin felt his jaw drop in horror.

The screen of her phone showed a tentacled monstrosity, a gelatinous surface of a stark black tar like constitution. Its form was covered in hundreds of eye like tumors; its massive body looked to be steamrolling towards a camera being held by a stranger in the middle of the street. As vehicles and people were trampled and flung to the sides like ragdolls. There were other people and cars harrowingly wrapped around bus sized tendrils, with the bottom of the picture having the stylized font of:

At The Shadows of Madness.

"Like it," she smiled evilly "It's called Homora Shogoth. A space alien that crashed down in the center of a small town. In the movie it was discovered inside of a spaceship, and it has the ability to break into the minds of people who look at it. And.... it even has the ability to hack into the net inside of the movie." Sorin looked at her wide eyed.

"See... it's perfect." Roxy beamed at him.

Sorin shook his head, pinching the bridge of his nose with his right arm, completely speechless. Roxy turned to Zoe and Jack "I think he likes it."

"A-are you two trying to jinx me or something?" Sorin asked, looking at Jack and Roxy with a look of total bewilderment. "Do you want this thing to grow and take over my body or something!?"

Jack raised an eyebrow "Oh relax... I actually agree with Roxy for once. That sounds like an awesome name for it." Roxy looked at him with a look of astonishment "Hold up, is there something wrong with you? Are you actually agreeing with me for once... you gotta be sick or something."

Jack gave her rude gesture with his finger, only to receive a small electric jolt in the rear, much to his cursing vexation. Zoe and Sorin meanwhile were still discussing the matter of the name. Ignoring the two Murdock twins small scuffle in the background.

"Alrighty... barring Roxy's name. What else do think could work?" Zoe asked, "I mean, there isn't much else for it, isn't it." she paused "Wait a minute... why don't you name it after your old cyberdeck." Sorin thought about it "Nah, I didn't really have a nick name for it... But... I really wanna name it something unique you know. Something maybe Susan or Bellatrix would-"

Suddenly, alarmingly, the nearby merwinks began to caw. Zoe gasped, as the two Murdock siblings paused. A flock of them: Sorin counted maybe 10-15 of them. Flew in a tight arrow formation. Hawk and raptor like in appearance, but much smaller and frailer, than there off shot cousins the duneraptors. And right on cue, the gauntlet began to sing back in response, copying the cries of the merwinks; but to Sorins surprise, the gauntlet seemed to be remixing the sounds of the merwinks. Creating flourishes and subtle variations of the small desert birds song. He was reminded of Mrs. Murdocks words: the uniqueness of the gauntlets bird song. Sorin blinked, abruptly realizing what he could call the gauntlet, and it was staring him in the face! How couldn't he see it until now? It was a simple name. And it was probably the only thing that *didn't* disturb, or likewise, make him feel uneasy about its attachment to his right arm.

"Songbird." Sorin said, getting everyone's attention "That's what I'll call it for now on. Songbird."

Zoe blinked "Songbird? Oh! you mean after what Mrs. M told us about the nightingales!" Sorin nodded.

"Songbird... Songbird..." Jack said, feeling the name as it rolled off his tongue. He shrugged "Eh, it's not bad I suppose." Roxy however slumped "Man... Shogoth would have been an awesome name."

Sorin laughed "Too bad, I hereby dub thee Songbird." He said dramatically as he held the gauntlet up, which continued to sing out a series of slow, soft musical twitters. The merwinks however disappeared over the horizon. The desert wind blowing over the four kids as they continued to talk and enjoy the rest of the mourning. Hours later, they were off. The green van once again traveling further into the desert.

The distant settlement of Hanover the ultimate goal of the traveling band.

CHAPTER

41

10/26/2061, Tuesday, 12:04 pm

The cerulean sky was now a steel plate of grey. Sorin leaned against the window, the rolling sandy hills moving past like a slideshow; the sand dunes were getting shorter, and in their place, a desert canyon full of rocky plateaus with the underbrush of weeds poking out of the ground in small tuffs.

Hanover was apparently a big settlement that got abandoned after the manifest wars. Stuck in a region of the wastelands were it was more rock than desert sand; judging by the shortening sand dunes and the subtle changes in scenery, they were getting close. Still a day's travel ahead, but close. Sorin observed the rocky columns as they passed by, his mind's eye picturing himself using some of the other rocks as ramps for his hoverboard. There curved structure looking perfect for it. Some of the sharp edges of the rocks jutting out of the environment got him thinking. There was a video he remembered watching of a few hoverboarders using the environment to do some neat tricks. The one he was itching to learn were the ones involving grinding on rails. Though, he would be kinda hesitant on grinding the sharp ridges of the distant rock formations further away in the background. Picturing himself falling and likewise getting ran through by the sharp points. The hoverboards bottom was also pretty sturdy, but he was unsure if the bottom vents would be able to handle it.

He looked to his gauntlet- now christened with its new name: Songbird. The path ahead was still unknown, but at least he gave the gauntlet something to make it less... alien. A name that was in stark contrast with what he now knew it was capable of, or at least, what he knew currently it was capable of.

Sorin looked back and narrowed his eyes. There were more animals outside than he thought, pretty unusual. Small flickering blurs of movement going in and out of the weed brushes, probably more merwinks and biodactyls. Even direwolves! He gasped, eyes widening as the large desert canines ran in a tight pack of six to seven. Disappearing past the brush and behind the larger plateaus. And none of them were even paying mind to the other small critters around them. Something was wrong, that was obvious, but what? Sorin stared, the wind was picking up. The sky was darkening. There was a gasp behind him, Zoe was bending over in her seat next to him; her appearance had shifted to her deviant form. Compound eyes were closed, and her face was contorted in pain. Jack and Roxy were no different. Roxy was hugging herself in her seat, as electricity sparked and snaked around her. Jack was grasping his head, the air reverberating around him- his eyes were wide and glowing a copper like hue.

"Dad- Mom- somethings wrong!" he grunted out.

Mr. Murdock turned his head for a moment and did a double take. Before frantically pulling over to the side of the road. Mrs. M was already moving before he could pull the van over, the look of absolute worry on her face as she looked all three deviants over. Sorin moved to look at Zoe, who was also grabbing the sides of her head, growling lowly, he went to grab her shoulder and she snarled- causing him to slide back cautiously.

"Zoe?" he got out nervously "What's wrong!?"

She suddenly seemed to realize what she did and looked guiltily. "S-sorry, head... feels like its being split open." She got out.

Sorin turned to the window, looking around as the sky continued to darken, the draft outside getting stronger and stronger. As large tuffs of sand and grass were being blown across the road and surrounding plateaus. Mr. M was now looking over his two kids, the concern on his face was palpable, he turned his head and saw Sorin looking out the window; Sorin gasped, his expression becoming panicked as he realized what was going on. Mr. M cleared the blinds from the door, and what he saw outside made him pale in dawning horror.

Over the horizon, maybe northwest of their position. An ominous dark haze was gathering, getting closer and closer. The wind roared outside, and clumps of debris were getting flown across the air. The dark clouds cracked with lighting and thunder. Sorin gulped as he witnessed the color of it. A bright shade of molten red.

It was a supercell... and it was approaching fast!

Suddenly, making everyone jump from their seats, a rock smacked into the window, causing a small crack to form on its surface as a combination of sand and reeds where blown across the van, causing a rapid dull sound of small impacts across the van. Mr. Murdock cursed and moved back to the driver's seat. The van roared to life and with a cry Sorin was forced to hold on to the edge of the seat. Zoe, Roxy, Jack, and Mrs. Murdock held on for dear life as the vehicle tore down the path.

"We need to get to cover!" Mrs. Murdock hollard to Mr. Murdock "Yeah, I know!" he answered back "The canyon ridge we passed earlier... that should be enough to wither the storm." He pressed, grappling the wheel as the van exited the main road and darted across the uneven path to the high canyon outcropping's. Sorin could feel the armor slowly begin to creep up his arm; Zoe's eyes were darting all over the place her expression now becoming anxious; Sorin cringed, debating on moving a hand to her shoulder, this would technically be her first supercell event...

And the first time was always the roughest.

"Zoe," he said, she quickly faced him- her poster slowly becoming more, and more feral, and tense. Still holding the bench arm he gestured to her with his free hand to calm down. "You gotta calm down, it's just a supercell- so long as we get into cover will be fine."

"How do you know that!?" she exclaimed frantically "My head is throbbing, and it's like every part of me wants to run... I-I'm scared..." she whispered, her breathing turning more rapid. "Zoe, it's okay, just... chill out," Jack interjected "Look, if it makes you feel better use your pincers to anchor yourself... dang, that storm over there is loud!" he groaned, pressing his hands over his ears.

Zoe growled, then closing her eyes she extended her pincers- all 4 prehensible limbs skewering the floor and ceiling, with a metallic *SCREEK!!!* Sorin flinched as the spear like pincer moved around him- stabbing into the side of the van's wall near the window; the bladed limb was positioned across his stomach, making him suddenly picture the handlebars of roller-coaster "Sorry, hope this helps." Zoe said apologetically, her teeth gritted in an effort to keep herself under control.

"Yeah, thanks." Sorin answered, as the metallic armor of Songbird moved to cover the back of his neck, before enshrouding his other arm; on either side, the silver substance moved up the side of his neck and proceeded to cover the bridge of his nose and finally his eyes. The interface activated and an alarm symbol was displayed in the center of his vision. *I didn't even use the thing in my chest to activate it... is this some kind of emergency protocol or something?* Either way, the armor and mask were now covering half his face and both arms, with more armor going halfway down his back. *I guess Songbird is preparing for the worst.* The display highlighted everything that was in the center of his vision, but when he turned his attention to the window and moved towards the now... uncomfortably fast approaching supercell; he saw something that gave him pause...

The interface highlighted the storm in a bright blueish tint, and the readings from the storm made his eyes widen in alarm.

{---*Warning*---}

Wind speeds: 167–184mph   *Storm pressure: 850mm*
Direction of Travel: Northwest   *CG:BFTB: Severe Lightning*

ATIVE S TYX MATTER CONTAINMENATION ALERT!!!

Sorin blinked at the approaching supercell speechless; Songbird was reading active styx contamination... from where... the supercell?

Wait a minute... that's actually possible? Styx matter can be absorbed into the weather? But... supercells come from the endless expanse... so how...

Sorin was knocked out of his musings as the entire van suddenly had a massive jump, which caused him to yelp in alarm. He felt himself launch from the seat only to crash into the unsharpened side of Zoe's pincer- knocking the breath out of him. He gagged as he held his stomach in pain, Zoe suddenly turned her head looking shocked "Oh crap! Are you okay!?" she exclaimed.

Sorin groaned, before giving the thumbs up. Not able to speak from the sudden loss of air. Looking towards the front of the van, he watched as Mr. Murdock seemed to drive the van further inside a tightly enclosed rock valley. The outcropping towering into the sky as the view of the oncoming storm was now suddenly and completely blocked by the rock walls. Sorin was forced to hold on to Zoe's pincer as he watched Mr. M flip on the vans headlights. Cutting through the dark enclosed space. He slid into a nearby crevice, a large cave which had everyone cry in alarm; he jerked the wheel, and the van slid again before crashing into the side of the rock wall- coming to another abrupt stop. Sorin could feel the teeth in his gums tremble over the vans impact on the side of the wall. The windows rattled and he was pretty sure the side of the van bent a little from crash. The front of the van was facing the outside of cave entrance. The sky above got darker, and the flashes of red made everyone in the van flinch, the ongoing roar of debris and wind began to rush outside past the entrance. Sorin could feel goosebumps form on his arms below the protective armor. This was easily the one thing in the wastelands that scared him more than the threat of wildlife, raiders/ex- nomads, or even the sudden sandstorms.

Supercells are one of the great enigmas of the wastelands. An anomaly which carried with it a horrible wake of destruction under its path. If you weren't in a settlement that had a V.M reactor to shield you from the worst of the storm. Either that, or you find the nearest big rock or best piece of cover you could find. If not, you were guaranteed to be ether pelted to death by the debris it kicked up, blown away and dashed into whatever was in your path, or getting incinerated by the deadly spears of lightening.

All this was a byproduct of the endless expanse... And to this day no one could quite understand the origin of such a collection of lethal storms...

The small valley they found themselves in would hopefully shield them from the worst of the storm. Sorin was certainly praying for that outcome at the very least. Suddenly there was a blinding flash which forced all of them to shield their eyes. A fork of lighting came and crashed in front of their cave entrance maybe a good 10 meters away. The effect was chilling. A massive hole was blown into the dry ground in front of them- the sand around the blackened crater was superheated into a slick surface. On and on it went, the band were forced to shield their eyes as lighting the shade of vermillion crashed onto the ground, or the walls of the canyon, a few very nearly got within a few meters of their cave entrance.

Roxy was the only one not averting her eyes. Her focus completely locked onto the caves entrance. Her electricity surging around her.

The boomings of thunder was rocking the van, crashes of lightening and the ever-present striking red flashes were slowly becoming less and less numerous, and as the howl of the wind began to die down, Sorin began to feel a slow bubble of relief, it was almost over.

Sorin paused, his bubble of relief bursting- as something at the back of his head began to throb. A familiar feeling which had him suddenly freeze in cold fear.

SORIN...

A voice scrapped over his ear, and the sound seemed to echo horribly from within his brain. A cold feeling of dread sipped down his spine and made him feel ill. The armor around him similarly tensed up.

It couldn't be... why now... what could he possibly want from him now...

They are coming...

You need to be ready...

They are in pursuit...

Roxy was suddenly on her feet. Her eyes were wide with fright, something was coming, she could feel it...

Sorin looked up and suddenly the doorway to the side of the van was opened, he heard the horrified cry of Mrs. Murdock too late, followed by the sudden alarm and angry yell of Mr. Murdock as his daughter charged out of the van. Before he could even scream at her to come back and follow to give chase, something terrible happened. An explosion of force which caused everyone to crane their necks in horror, up to the flashing red light show in the sky. As brilliant red webs of forked lighting crawled over the howling clouds above them. Sorin watched open mouthed as time seemed to slow down. Not a moment later, or was it an eternity? A massive column of pure plasma- a great red spear in the sky shot down- its trajectory speeding directly towards them.

Suddenly, just as it was about to strike the van. The massive spear of energy seemed to curve inwards, its path altered before his eyes, until it was moving below like a constricted tide of water disappearing around the arms of Roxy.

She stood there in front of the van, acting as a lightning rod and absorbing the rogue discharge; suddenly there was a surge of power, and with a cry of pain from Roxy the raging funnel of electricity around her arms suddenly jumped- towards the van, and with unnatural movement began to surge around and inside the front of the van's grille, the red stream of rogue plasma moved with sinister purpose. The inside of the van was chaos, sparks jumping from the dashboard and Mr. Murdock could only shield and avert his eyes. Without warning, Mr. Murdock cried in alarm as he crashed to the floor frantically, animal instinct forcing him to move, as a surge of red electricity forked from the wheel, the radio, and even the speedometer. Everyone cried out as the rogue discharge- surged out of the dash board- and into the air towards the back, past Mrs. M and Jack before curving in midair.

Sorin wasn't prepared for what happened next. To the horrified cries of Zoe and the others- the rogue bolt of electricity smashed directly into his chest. Right where his heart was.

He seized up, his mouth open in a silent scream.

But instead of searing pain, an indescribable sensation was surging throughout his body, the electric red of the rogue bolt scrambled around his paralyzed body, over his clothes and around the armor. Songbirds two gems blazed with power, and Sorin could feel himself being pulled away from his seat, away from the van, and out of his body. The world around him became still, and an image seemed to burn itself in front of his mask covered face. A familiar eyeless monstrosity roaring in rage, its glare of implied hatred aimed directly at Sorin who could only grit his teeth in a struggle to break free.

The monsters face suddenly grew still, and something began to poke out of its forehead, the gem glowed a brilliant indigo. The image rippled in front of him before disappearing, melting away as if it were the byproduct of a vivid dream, and just as suddenly time resumed.

The electric charge ceased, and he found himself crumpling over Zoe's pincer. Zoe moved, gathering Sorin back up onto the seat and with a sudden heavy gasp of breath he grasped his chest, the place over his heart was know burning, and as the sensation prickled around his upper torso, a feeling of deep dread settled over his heart and shrouded the pain he was feeling.

It was still alive... and it was still coming for him.

The door to the van opened and Roxy rushed inside- her steps were labored and exhausted, Mrs. Murdock and Jack were already at her side as Mr. Murdock was next to Sorin his eyes going from Sorin to Roxy unsure of what to do or say.

"Is everyone alright?" Roxy started "I could feel it coming for us... had to do something." She said drowsily, her long shirt sleeves were in tatters as her skin looked to be slightly burned from the effort. Mrs. Murdock and Jack were wide eyed at the state of her arms. The damage wasn't minor, it was almost a second- degree burn, something that has never happened when she absorbed electricity.

"It's... how is that possible?" Jack whispered to himself.

Sorin in a similar state of exhaustion, as the armor around him began to fade away, remembered Songbirds readings of the supercell.

"Mr. Murdock," he said, getting his attention "The supercell... S-songbird scanned the supercell, it was full of active styx matter. Just like me." He said.

Mr. Murdocks paled "What," He said slowly

"When it hit me, I could feel it... it was definitely styx matter," he turned to Roxy "It's probably why it hurt her arms... it's not normal lightning."

Roxy shivered, her hands shaking from the constant burning sensation going through them. But that didn't worry the teen as much as it should have. As her mother came in with the bandages and Sorin moved behind the couch, so they could sit her down on the seat. She felt a horrible shadow envelope her, a feeling that was almost indescribable; the usual sensation of cool water that ran throughout her body when she absorbed electricity was not there. Instead, she found herself agreeing with Sorin. This rogue lighting strike, she hoped she'd never have to feel its sting ever again.

Electricity was supposed to be neutral, like water to her, but this felt so wrong, and on a fundamental level too. It felt like rage, like a burning contempt of concentrated malice. The feeling alone felt as if she were being marked in its shadow, and she couldn't bear to think about it, what disturbed her most was how it somehow managed to get past her- which unexpectantly jumped onto Sorin, like a lingering presence within the raging bolt had jumped from her grasp and escaped to hit its actual target...

But, this was lighting we were talking about. Lightning wasn't alive, right?

The storm was finally over. After bandaging and checking Roxy's hands and arms, Sorin was next. But, to Mrs. Murdocks surprise the discharge didn't seem to leave any lasting burns or any signs of damage on him. Sorin barely able to respond in his current headspace of panic, said he was fine, that songbird must have shielded him from the electric shock. But Mrs. Murdock wasn't having it, and decided to give him another once over.

After a while, and when Mrs. Murdock was satisfied he was okay, the van was finally pulling out of the large cave.

Zoe, Jack and Roxy were silent; all of them shocked by the storm's path of destruction. But Zoe, even in her shaken state, was giving Sorin a nervous glance. Not at all liking the faraway look on his face.

The ground underneath the van crunched, the lightning strikes from the styx enriched supercell heated the sand and caused it to turn into glass like fragments. Mr. Murdock cursed, having to pull the van carefully to avoid an accidental puncture of the vans tires. The entire valley was an absolute warzone; torn asunder by the volleys of rogue discharges with scattered fragments of rock, grass and other pieces of debris strewn across the environment. But after a few minutes of navigating from the outcroppings of plateaus and rigged rock formations, they were finally approaching the road in which they had fled from the storm. Once again, the group were continuing their journey to Hanover. Roxy was currently laying down on the bench seat, with Zoe sitting in the seat next to Jack and Sorin.

Sorin was quiet- scratch that, everyone was quiet; the storm had shaken them all to their core, even Mr. Murdock didn't have the heart to berate his daughter for scaring the life out of him, even if her intentions were pure; her injuries sustained from that horrible discharge of lighting had shocked the entire family. Whatever the styx enriched lightning did... it caused the lighting to actually *injure* Roxy. Something they had never seen before; but for Sorin, it only made the mystery surrounding the endless expanse more ominous... more unnatural in a sense... like nature itself was being horribly and irreparably changed for the worst.

This wasn't his first time being inside of a supercell, but the recent scan from songbird created far more questions than he was comfortable with.

The discharge didn't hurt him, but the way it jumped from Roxy and traveled inside of the van... that however, had the blood in his veins freeze over. It felt horribly intentional, and he understood why, and he found himself becoming afraid again. Not just for himself, but everyone in the vicinity of him.

The target was once again on his back, and he was completely unsure of what he could even do about it.

CHAPTER

42

10/26/2061, Tuesday, 8:13 pm

Sorin could barely eat his dinner; the chicken and rice were barely touched, and everyone was looking at him strangely. Of course, the whole group was silent for the first few hours, after escaping with their lives from the storm; hours later they were mostly back to their old selves.

Jack and Roxy were fretting with renewed vigor, albeit this was after Jack made sure his sister was alright (to her minor annoyance) which lead them slowly falling back to their old habits. Zoe was chuckling somewhat at their antics, With Mr. and Mrs. Murdock discussing the journey and what needed to be done after making it to Hanover; but at the back of everyone's minds, Sorin was unusually quiet; not deathly so mind you, he still responded somewhat, but the fact remained.

Sorin was completely lost. No matter how he looked at it, the thing that chased him throughout the dead settlement was once again on his heels. The status report from the gauntlet- Songbird- immediately popped into his memory: A missing core... how had he not put two and two together sooner... and now- what else could he possibly do? It survived a gas explosion! What hope did he have of killing it? At this rate, all he was doing was leading it back towards Zoe and the others...

The dark blue gem in its forehead... it looks just like the ones on Songbird... it has to be a connection; but how can I stop it if it comes for me?

"Sorin?" a voice, Mrs. M's voice called his name.

He looked up, Mrs. M was crouching down in front of him. She looked very worried; looking around, everyone was giving him looks. Glancing at his food, he had barely eaten anything on his plate.

"Sorin, what's up? You've been acting strange since the storm. Did that discharge do anything to you?" she asked looking him over.

Sorin looked at her, his mouth dry and the stares from the others not helping him in the slightest. Interestingly, Roxy seemed strangely different, there was an expression on her face, a look that seemed slightly pained. Then, abruptly, the expression changed. To his surprise, Roxy stood up, moving with purpose towards him. Before coming to a stop next to him.

"Hey, I'm sorry if you got shocked back there." She said looking away from him. She held up her hands, which were still lightly bandaged from the rogue strike. "It felt nothing like the usual surge of electricity... it was- I don't even know how to describe it... I mean- it was freaking lighting! I was redirecting! But, it was wrong and out of control..." She breathed.

Crossing her arms she looked at him guiltily "It's my fault, you getting caught up in it. I wasn't prepared for something that... strong... Sorry Sorin." she said, now nervously messaging her shoulders. Sorin blinked, for the first time since the storm. Being able to properly put himself back in the present. Her words jumbled him from the intense panic he was going through.

"N-no, that's not- you didn't do anything wrong." Sorin said, completely taken aback "Its... I... I have to tell you all something." He began, looking very worried now.

Roxy uncrossed her arms and quickly became alarmed over his expression. Heck, even becoming slightly baffled by his response. Zoe hearing what he said immediately got up, followed by Jack who was looking at everything with a sense of wariness- wondering what could make Sorin so... scared. Mr. Murdock joined in a moment later, brow furrowed, having a bad feeling.

"It's alive." Sorin said, "The thing that was chasing me around the settlement- its alive, and its tracking me down."

Sorin told them about the creature; telling them about the invisible link he had with it during its pursuit of him, explaining how it could use it to track him wherever he went. And somehow, it had managed to reestablish that link with him- however faint it was- and it was pursuing him at this very moment. He hesitated, for a moment, everyone was giving him strange looks. Looks that he didn't like.

But he had to convince them somehow... He looked to Zoe, whom at the moment seemed to be sharing in his fear. Jack looked utterly bewildered, trying and failing to wrap his head around what he just heard. Mr. and Mrs. Murdock were looking at him uneasily- no, not at him... but Songbird.

"Is that what I felt in that lightning bolt!" Roxy started, her expression becoming sick. "I could feel it when I was redirecting the bolt away from the van... it was horrible. It felt like I was trying to take hold of a rabid animal, kinda like Mrs. Martin's dog back at home." She said, an unpleasant look on her face. Something Jack seemed to be familiar with.

"But it was lightning from a storm Roxy, are you sure it wasn't just something you haven't had experience with until know?" Mr. Murdock asked, his expression calm and inquisitive.

"No, this felt... wrong. Really, really, wrong." She implored, shaking her head, as a deep frown curved her lips, eyes glancing at the bandages covering her arms. "Look, everything he's saying is freaking weird. But... after feeling whatever it was inside that lighting strike... I can't rule it out, dad. It just... his explanation makes the most sense." She sighed.

Sorin stared at her arms; the miniscule thread that seemed to flutter in the wind was still there. A mental link that he has despised since the day it had latched on to him. It may have been the faintest it had ever felt, like a barely perceptible pinprick in his brain, but it was there, waiting to flare up when the creature inevitably got in range.

"It feels like burning needles doesn't it." Sorin said quietly, getting Roxy's attention "The moment the lighting strike hit you, it felt like a piercing needle was going through your hands. Like something was sending every signal or whatever means to communicate how much it wanted to hurt you. Like it was personally painting a target on your back."

Roxy paled, her posture stiffing, the experience of the red lance of energy making her shiver. He just described the moment exactly as she had felt it.

"I-is it like that all the time?" she demanded, looking at him with mingled horror. Sorin nodded, his eyes sparking with desperation.

"Yes. It feels fainter than it's ever been- but it's there, it's coming, and I don't know what to do." He said clenching his fists, Songbirds main core glowing a faint red.

"Well, maybe Garret will have someone that can help us," Jack suggested "You did say that he was going to introduce us to someone who's dealt with those things chasing us, right dad. I mean, that thing chasing after Sorin is practically the same ain't it!?"

Mr. Murdock straitened, rubbing the back of his head "That's... I don't know Jack. Everything I've seen involving Sorin has gone well and beyond my own understanding of the situation," he turned to Sorin "no offense by the way."

He shrugged "None taken." He replied, glancing down at songbird.

"Whatever's on the heels of Sorin. Well, where just going to have to push it towards Hanover, we only got a day left before we reach it."

Zoe rubbed her arm, looking very anxious "Sorin... that thing from the bunker, is there anything that can really hurt it? Aside from the gas explosion, I mean."

Sorin frowned, thinking back to the chase before shaking his head. "Nu-uh, I was too busy running away from it. That gas explosion was the only thing I could think of, and look where we are."

Mrs. Murdock couldn't help arch an eyebrow at Sorin, feeling very torn with what the boy in front of her just said. On one hand she'd normally be appalled by such a suggestion, on the other, she understood the reasoning for it... as disturbing as it was for a boy his age to think of such things.

"Come on, let's get ready for the night. We better leave early in the mourning just in case." Mrs. Murdock said.

Sorin looked as she got up, as Jack and Roxy followed suit, neither saying a word or even the usual barb between the other. Mr. Murdock put a hand to his shoulder "Sorin, look will get through this. Let's keep are chins up for now, alright, we can't afford to let this bring us down."

He said, the reassurance somewhat helping his mood, but only just. Sorin nodded before standing up; Mr. Murdock walked ahead as Zoe walked side by side with Sorin to the van.

"He's right Sorin. As scary as it is, we just gotta reach that guy at Hanover. Maybe dad, or your family will be able to kill it." she suggested. "I beat they have loads of stuff they could use on it." She continued "Not only that, but it has to be weaker after that whole mess... It has to be."

"Yeah," he agreed, "that fire was enormous! There's no way it got out of that unscathed, and Garret will probably have more than enough firepower to kill it." Sorin reasoned.

Zoe nodded "Yep, all we gotta do is get to Hanover and will be home free. I just hope we don't have to go through another supercell... I don't think I could deal with another one." She shuddered.

The two climbed into the van, and after a few moments they were all laying down. Sorin in the back with Zoe and Jack this time around, as Roxy slept on the bench chair. Sorin's right arm grasped his blankets upon the sleep mattress in worry. Laying stock still, as not to disturb the other two. He absentmindedly couldn't stop his mind from going back to the eyeless visage pulled into that hateful snarl; the indigo gem or core poking out of its forehead as the only illumination of the harrowing picture. He clenched his fists over his covers, and closed his eyes. No matter what, he had to reach Hanover, whatever Garret was going to do to help the Murdocks and Zoe. He hoped he could find a way for him to reach Hosea and the rest of the voyager crew. Time was of the essence. And he wasn't really sure if the thing *could* be stopped.

10/27/2061, Wednesday, 8: 26 am

The dusty air sighed through the open window as Sorin leaned on the side of the seat. His right arm locked into position as he held his head up, staring outside as the rolling sand dunes have finally disappeared. Giving way to a dry expanse of sandy flatlands, reedy brushes, and thorny plants.

The very road the van traveled upon was cracked and beaten, stretching themselves seemingly for miles and miles; for Sorin it made him seriously question how some desert wanderers were able to make it from settlement to settlement on foot. The things he's seen and the overlong stretches of road between civilization and nowhere was utterly mystifying.

He took his gaze from the moving background outside; glancing behind himself, Zoe, Jack, and Roxy were having a small debate.

"Okay, okay, here me out Zoe," Roxy reasoned "the places around the endless expanse are not even proper settlements yet... more like... there kinda like outposts if were being real, real, about it." she said.

Zoe gave her a dubious look "Outposts? Seriously, you're joking right. You make it sound like there on the lookout for something."

Jack and Roxy looked at each other for a moment, before nodding back to her "Exactly." They both said in unison.

She groaned "Ok... what's the deal with the endless expanse anyway? Everyone back at home always gossips about the expanse like it's some kind of haunted house attraction or something." She grumbled, folding her arms in agitation. "And it's not like the other countries outside the republic or the conclaves either. In all of Pangaea, the endless expanse is the most avoided... Why?" She questioned.

Roxy twisted a strand of her dark hair, fixing Zoe with a baffled expression. "What's with all the interest in the expanse anyway? I mean, there are loads more places more interesting than that stretch of the wastelands. Look at Andoria- that country further north of the republic. I heard they got a bunch of crazy ruins hidden in the snowy mountains around there." She said.

Zoe shook her head "Look where I am. Before the home schooling, and even before I got my powers... all the teachers, refused to even brush the subject of that place. Heck, this one time in class, when one of the other kids asked about it- and this was like- the smartest kid in class no less. The teacher just wouldn't budge. Until the entire class began to ask about it, then eventually- maybe to shut us all up- she finally gave in. She told us, that the endless expanse was much like outer space... That it's mostly a waste of time to even go over the subject, because there hasn't been anything of note discovered from exploring it."

Zoe's eyes were now gleaming with curiosity "Even my dad refuses to talk about it; the way he looks when I do ask him... it's strange. The teachers at school usually give me annoyed looks when I ask them. But dad, well, he looks odd..." she said, with a scowl.

Sorin looked at her "What do you mean by odd?"

Zoe shook her head "I don't know... nervous, I guess."

Jack gave a small chuckle "Ok, I can believe that. That place is just bad news. I mean, bad juju type vibes."

Roxy snorted "More like cursed. I heard a lot of rumors from school about it... people disappearing when they go near the border of that place. Like horror movie type stuff." She said with a small smile.

Zoe stiffened "What?"

Jack nodded, smiling "Yeah, didn't they make movies about that place. Crap... I think most of them are scary too. Maybe more than half of them I think; but I gotta admit, the whole outer space comparison is actually new to me."

Sorin smiled at Zoe "Zoe? You didn't happen to think that the expanse was like space, did you?"

Zoe gave him an agitated look "What! No! I'm just saying... It's the only shred of info I can find about that place. Like... how can one place be so... I don't know... Mysterious... Yeah, mysterious for so long and no one has decided to explore it in full yet? I mean, wouldn't you be curious too?"

Sorin shrugged "I mean, you're not wrong. But, after everything Jade and Tom told me about it... I think I'm good where I'm at."

Zoe gave him a look, which made Sorin immediately regret what he just said as Zoe beamed at him. "Oh, and what was that?" she said curiously.

Sorin sighed "Well, Jade and Tom are nomads right. So, let's say they've been around and have come across other nomads. Well... they just happened to meet one of their old friends. They talk, they catch up, and there friend mentions that another nomad they knew took a very odd job from a client."

At this point, Jack, Roxy, and even Mrs. and Mr. Murdock were listening in on the conversation.

"The job... was too escort them close to the endless expanses borders. Apparently something to do with untapped ichorsyte deposits I think- anyway, they get there, and the guy vanishes. No trace, no trail, nothing." Sorin explained, scrunching his brow, trying to remember everything Tom told him. "The weirdest part was that all his clothes, possessions, and even his weapons, where still in his tent, untouched. So this wasn't raiders, or bandits. Whatever happened, happened fast. Like this was in the middle of the day, and the nomad guy's friend said that he was only in his tent for a moment. He gets up and his client was nowhere to be found."

The excitement in Zoe's face drained, the light of curiosity vanished from her green eyes. "So... wait, that's it? But what happened? did he just decide to up and leave without going to look for em- or-" she stammered puzzled, her expression now becoming uneasy.

Sorin shrugged "No clue, and there are a lot of stories like that too. Around the wastelands I mean... people wanting to discover what's past the border and suddenly disappearing."

Zoe grimaced "Seriously. Well, hasn't the conclaves ever thought about exploring past it? I mean, if there story is true, wouldn't that mean people thought they could get more ichorsyte from the other side."

"They did Zoe," Mr. Murdock said unexpectedly from the front "Actually, both Sector Security and the conclaves have tried to do just that. Which resulted in the town of Silverwood."

Sorin paused, the name sounding strangely familiar. "Silverwood? Where is that?" Zoe said.

"A town that was once situated near the border of the endless expanse. Not much is known about it, but, the town and all its inhabitants were unfortunately wiped out by a reactor meltdown." Robert explained from up front, his eyes still locked firmly on the road. Zoe could only widen her eyes, reminded of what Sorin told her about them, in the bunker.

"Reactors? You mean the V.M reactors that Sorin told me about?" she asked sitting up from her seat. Mr. Murdock nodded from behind the wheel. "Those are the ones." He glanced up the mirror to see her confused expression "What's the matter?" he said.

"What do you mean by a meltdown?" Zoe asked, her brow furrowing.

Sorin felt something in him grow tense. He couldn't explain what it was, but the mention of that name jogged something from his mind. Something he couldn't place. Songbird unbeknownst to him was emitting a dim hue of red from its main gem.

"There was something wrong with the reactor." Mrs. Murdock said sadly "Apparently, there was a critical failure, or some sort of system malfunction. No one really knows which, but, the reactor went critical and took the whole town and settlers out."

"Everything?" Jack said "Seriously... that can happen!" he exclaimed horrified. Mr. Murdock nodded grimly.

"To be fair Jack, it is rare... and I mean extremely rare for that to happen. I'm no expert, but the conclaves had help from sector security when they commissioned the reactor for the town, and from what they released to the public, everything seemed to be going smoothly in its construction." Mr. Murdock said, his eyes glancing from the rear-view mirror and the road in front of him. "It was a terrible tragedy. Something no one saw coming." He looked to the rear-view mirror; His eyes landing on Sorin in the back, who looked odd, his expression confused.

"What's on your mind Sorin?" he asked, getting his attention.

"Oh, uh, nothing... just thinking is all." He said, shaking his head. The fleeting sense of familiarity disappearing like mist on a windshield.

That was weird...

Sorin leaned on his seat; he could just picture it- the reactor going critical and wiping the town off the map... it was genially scary stuff.

Come to think of it, wasn't that the reason for why they decommissioned that reactor back in the historic district of Gloomhaven. And yet wasn't the last settlement he left behind just the same... then again, he didn't get the chance to see the reactor in that place...

"It's actually crazy now that I think about it," Sorin replied, "Silverwood, and the settlement were going to... There really are a lot of abandoned settlements out here." He said, his expression becoming pensive.

Mrs. Murdock nodded "It's just how it is. Sometimes a settlement just can't get the proper funding, or even the right conditions to sustain itself in the elements. Reactor or not, there's more to the survival of a town than just the potential ichorsyte that can be mined. As stupid as it is... sometimes the partnership of a corporation can go a long way in keeping a settlement afloat."

Mr. Murdock grimaced "Dear... of all places. I don't think we can say the same for Whitechapel."

Mrs. Murdock suddenly made a face "Oh, yeah... that's..." She sighed "Your right... never mind what I just said." She replied, her voice full of reproach.

"What are you two talking about?" Roxy asked, "Whitechapel? What's a Whitechapel?"

Sorin blinked, his memory of the gas stations front door adorned with the many old signs and banners. "Wait, are you guys talking about the settlement where you found us!" Zoe blinked, the ruined buildings and demolished roads of the massive settlement threaded a deep uneasiness within her. The state of such a massive city, abandoned in the middle of nowhere conjured so many questions of how it became the ghost town it is today.

"What happened to that place?" She asked.

Mr. Murdock hummed lowly in response "The town was abandoned I think maybe fifty or sixty years ago; you all saw how big it was, originally the whole settlement was supposed to be a trading hub for this side of the region. It was also the stomping grounds for a couple of corporations that moved here during the manifest era."

"Um, manifest era? What does that mean again?" Jack asked, looking a little sheepish from not understanding the term.

Mr. Murdock raised an eyebrow to the mirror "Not paying attention in class again I see." He sighed "To keep it short, the period in the late 20st century when the corporations moved out of the republic sectors and came down to the Conclavien province. Essentially for more work and to get away from the restrictive laws of the republic. Now, getting back to Whitechapel- there are two corporations we gotta mention. First: *Z&R* or *Zoldycks and Rythenfall*, and the second: *StarCore International*. These two corporations ended up waging war with one another inside the settlement and beyond. Causing it all to go to ruin."

Sorin blinked, "Wait a minute, just those two corporations, caused all that? How is that even possible?"

Mr. Murdock gave him an odd look "Why not? You gotta understand one thing about the corpos back then. They were greedy, and I'm not just talking about credits. No... they wanted it all. Territory, partnerships, economic influence, and all the icorsyte they could ever have. V.M Reactors were still fairly new, and they were pushing the technology into new heights. All of it, to fulfil their original promise to the conclavien government. The terraformation of the wastelands."

Everyone looked confused for a moment aside from Mrs. Murdock, the kids didn't know what that meant.

Mr. Murdock smiled "Basically, they wanted to use the reactors as a form of terraforming. Altering the atmosphere, the temperature and surface of the wasteland. Essentially they wanted to make survival outside the wastelands more manageable, I'd even guess to say more habitable for human life."

"T-that's possible?" Zoe gasped.

Mr. Murdock nodded "Of course, that's why corporations like Z&R and StarCore were so open arms about gathering ichorsyte. They probably didn't share the dream of creating a more habitable wasteland. But they loved the amount of credits they were raking in- for the mining and refinement of the mineral. They also had smaller corporations on beck and call, small subsidiaries, here and there, spreading their influence left and right. Till it got to the point where there were actual territories of the two spheres of influence."

Mr. Murdocks expression grew grim "Whitechapel continued to grow and expand. But StarCore and Z&R were also growing further in influence. Most of the heads of the settlement, and even a few other business within the town became wholly loyal to one or the other. It was corruption of the highest order. Coercion, blackmail, embezzlement, bribery, it got worse and worse. Eventually, the two companies began to get hostile with one another, fighting and waging war in the shadows until a fight broke out in the middle of the day,"

The kids listened, baffled by what they were hearing. Sorin wouldn't even pretend to understand what some of those crimes meant. But it sounded really bad.

"-the gunfight lasted for an hour and a half, it was chaos... The settlement guards were struggling to contain the shootout, and from what little accounts there were of the incident. The shootout took place inside of a restaurant owned by StarCore, and a few settlement guards- with Z&R- came to lean on one of the people eating at the place. One thing lead to another, and a firefight broke out. Incidents like this kept repeating all throughout the settlement. Eventually, another very bad firefight happened, this one a failed assassination attempt, and the aftermath claimed many lives... and the conclaves have had enough by that point."

Roxy was listening to everything he said, her expression unreadable, but her eyes showed a steady uneasiness. But that paled in comparison to Zoe; who was completely horrified by what she was hearing, her disgust palpable; Sorin and Jack were of the same wavelength, both grimacing at what was being said and picturing in there minds of the harrowing firefights.

"Let's see... that's right, the other settlements that were closest to Whitechapel also fell into pandemonium. I think it was around this time when cyberware and the like were becoming more widespread. So this made things even more grisly. But, to be fair, I don't really recall all the other stuff that happened. So... let me fast forward a bit, and gloss over some details." He said, his expression becoming sheepish.

"Now for the main reason why Whitechapel is in ruins. You see much later on, I say around... maybe, somewhere, between 2008 or 9'ish is when things ramped up for the worst. A major incident took place in Whitechapel, something about a corporate experiment going wrong during the refinement of ichorsyte. Well half a block was destroyed, taking the lives of about 20 people and injuring 50 more. Apparently, the incident wasn't an incident at all, but sabotage orchestrated by Z&R. This lead to civil war within the settlement, with similar fights breaking out in other settlements near or around Whitechapel."

"That's when the conclaves contacted the republic for aid." Mrs. Murdock said, her expression now unreadable.

"After much preparation and deals behind the scenes, both the republic and the conclaves joined forces to get a hold of the rampant violence across the wastelands. This lead to the formation of Sector Security and after its creation, a campaign of war was started against the company controlled settlements. And after a lot of conflict- which lasted for a few years- Whitechapel was the last one standing, with both Z&R and StarCore being forced to join sides against sector security. The conclaves and republic won the war, but this ended up with the whole town of Whitechapel in ruins." Mr. Murdock finished.

CHAPTER

43

10/27/2061, Wednesday, 10: 06 am

Zoe balked at the horrible truth. Her eyes scrutinizing everything she just heard, with clear disgust pulling at her expression. "Oh my gosh," she mumbled to herself "That's horrible... But what happened to Z&R and StarCore?" she demanded.

Mr. Murdock shrugged "Don't know. But, they were dissolved via dissolution. They both were the cause of a regional civil war: The Manifest War as it's known. Which, went on for eight years I think, so... 2016 to 17ish is when it officially ended. That means Z&R and Starcore's leadership were tried and executed- with the subsidiaries under them either becoming liquidated or seized. So both companies were closed, and sector security was officially deemed a success."

"Oh... so that's how my dad's job started." Zoe said, looking surprised, and a bit torn at the revelation.

Mr. Murdock nodded "Yes, and one thing I forgot to mention. That's how the circle was formed too." Sorin did a double take. "Wait, what- really... how?"

Mr. Murdock smiled "The corporations didn't do all the fighting now. They hired bandits, thugs, and nomads. Basically, it was them fighting on the Corpo's behalf. A proxy war, if you wanna be more technical. The credits and prestige rewarded to the people who were contracted by the two corporations, was leagues better than desert life in the fringes. But like all things, the relationship soured, and the circle was formed- which distanced themselves from the losing war- and offered their support with S.S."

Sorin widened his eyes at this "But why, why did the circle become... Well, what they are now?"

Mr. Murdock sighed "Who knows Sorin, maybe they just didn't want to be included into the life of a settler. You gotta think, before the conclaves were even formed; you know- civilized life as it was after the formation of the republic, the nomads were apparently native here- of the wastelands. They traveled, they hunted, they lived off the land as it was."

Sorin blinked, that was a lot to take in. All this talk about Whitechapel, and he somehow learns that nomads were once natives of the wastelands. He had so many questions to ask Hosea when he finally meet him again.

"Dad, where did you learn all this stuff?" Roxy asked, completely amazed at everything he just explained; it was like she was in history class, only the teacher (her dad) was going over all the cool stuff, instead of all the boring subjects.

Mr. Murdock shrugged "I got hobbies too you know; aside from music, I really enjoyed learning about the history of how things happened. Certain things tend to repeat- history I mean- like a cycle. It's interesting to talk about these old subjects. Your mom would certainly agree with me, after all, it's how I meet her in the first place."

Mrs. Murdock nodded with an eyeroll, smiling all the same "And that... is why I don't bring up anything to do with history; your old man will talk your ear off, in a heartbeat, if given the chance. I learned that the hard way when we first met at Corrin's watch."

10/27/2061, Wednesday, 12:18 pm

Sorin was mulling over the things he had learned over the course of the past hour. The backstory of Whitechapel sticking with him well after Mr. Murdocks explanation. Funnily enough, Roxy, in her morbid fascination with the surrounding settlements, asked for more stories surrounding the other settlements that met an unfortunate end.

Salvation's Square, Shady Sands, Primsworth, and finally Hanover... their locations not even featured on any modern maps- as explained by Mr. Murdock.

All connected to the doomed settlement of Whitechapel, and all, likewise abandoned. Sorin was left disturbed by Hanover's story: The town was the furthest of the four settlements from Whitechapel, and had the misfortune of being overrun by raider attacks. Sector Security did what they could, but by the horrible hand of fate- the towns reactor- was irrevocably destroyed in the struggle. Causing the entire settlement to be suffused in live styx matter radiation; sections of the old settlement are also host of hotspots for live styx matter, and as rumor had it, the center of the town is reportedly the most intense of these hotspots.

But, to everyone's relief. They wouldn't be going into the town itself, instead, they would be venturing near the outskirts of the settlement. An old Steel mill, which used to be one of the towns landmark attractions.

But in light of the grizzly tale of Hanover, everyone seemed to be in good spirits. The journey was almost over. This thought seemed to give everyone a moral boost; considering there supplies for camp were dwindling, it was a welcome prospect. Sorin of course was still mildly worried, as interesting as the backstory of all this settlements were, he still felt a little on edge. Whatever happened, if he finally got in contact with Hosea he would inevitably have to ask about the thing in his chest.

That... and the other horrible issue of the creature still alive and kicking. Whether or not he wanted it, Songbird was now a part of him, and until he could get his answers he was stuck with it.

On a minor note... Sorin, in a moment of sheer amazement. Realized that today was his birthday. October 27th. So much has happened since the day he was kidnapped, and now, unexpectantly, it was here, and he'd forgotten all about it.

Sorin looked up, his thoughts interrupted as Zoe put something on his lap. It was a medium sized tablet of some sort, the electronic monitor showing what looked like a map on its screen. Sorin with mild confused scanned the screen; was that some sort of town? What was all the green markings around it? He turned to Zoe who was beaming at him.

"What is it?" he questioned.

"It's the map Mr. Murdock is using to get to Hanover. He said we could use it for a moment; I wanted to see if I could find my home with it. See," she gestured to the digital topography, and the vegetation surrounding a huge landmass "-its right there." She said pointing to the screen.

Sure enough, he began to recognize Rosaria. Surprisingly, it wasn't that massive of a sector city. But, to his fascination, he noticed all the blue lines around the left section of the forest surrounding the town. Where those supposed to be rivers? He moved the map a little, looking around the large expanse of trees and waterbodies "Where is your house at? Can this even show it?" he wondered aloud. Zoe smiled, before taking the tablet. After a moment of scrolling she handed it back to him. Sorin felt his eyes widen a bit when he noticed how large the house was. From the top-down view of the satellite image, the house was pretty big; situated outside town and further from the main road leading to it. Just about as isolated as it gets, and miles from town. With long stretches of forests and lakes separating the household from view. Being a kid from Gloomhaven, it was hard to imagine a land dominated by stretches and stretches of shrubbery, while the sky itself was nearly hidden by the surrounding tree line. To his credit he was having a fun time imagining what her house must have looked like in person.

"Seriously, your house is huge! And the forests surrounding it. Like, doesn't it get... I don't know, overwhelming being outside town like that?" Sorin's expression was intrigued, his eyes alite with glowing imagination, as he asked in a voice tinged with awe.

Zoe shrugged "I don't know about it being overwhelming. But It was quiet, that's for sure. Nothing really interesting ever happens back at home, aside from being able to climb trees and watching the wildlife pass by, it was pretty calm... I kinda miss it though..." she had a faraway look in her eyes. Zoe was no longer in her deviant form; her expression was obviously homesick, as a small tinge of longing showed in her features.

"It's all so stupid, I was just... I was just walking back home, thinking about showing Gloria what I managed to draw that day. And before you know it- I'm waking up in a dark cell." She whispered.

Sorin grimaced, that's exactly how it was for him. A bad dream here and there, and suddenly in a short span of time he was ripped away from his normal everyday life in the most brutal way imaginable... and yet, strangely, what would he be doing if it never happened? He'd be safe at home obviously, but...

Zoe, the Murdock twins and Mr. and Mrs. Murdock...

Sorin sighed "Man, this kinda sucks," Zoe looked at him questionably "I mean, if you were never kidnapped in the first place, if we were never taken from home, we never would have met. Me, you, the Murdocks..." Sorin sat back in his chair, holding up songbird, expression unreadable "Crazy, isn't it."

Zoe was silent, looking at him in surprise; her expression now torn, she could only give a weak nod. "Yeah..." She said after a moment. In front of them on either side of the two captain seats, Jack and Roxy sat in their respective seats, fast asleep.

The desert had finally given way to an expanse of craggy flatlands; the massive canyons and plateaus have disappeared, leaving the ever expanding and nearly deteriorated main road in their wake. Pretty soon they would be at their destination. Sorin sighed to himself, the journey was almost over; but still, there hasn't even been a whiff of danger from the connection, binding him and that abomination together.

"You know... I wonder if this thing could show use Gloomhaven." Zoe said, her face beaming once more. Sorin turned to her "Gloomhaven?... I don't know, let's see.."

He tapped the screen and brought up the field of view, the topography shrunk and the familiar visual of Zoe's house and the town of Rosaria disappeared from the increasing height of the digital screen. Sorin was amazed at how big the supercontinent of Pangaea actually was. The massive landmass was in the shape of a C, with the bulk of its mass near the bottom middle; the conclavien continent, and the other six countries above it: The Republic or Neo America in the middle of the c, Andoria at the very top of the C, Ranslvania to the left beyond the republic, Cyslodian islands off to the right of the republic and into the ocean, The Bolitarian islands below the Cyslodians; Sorin glanced at the final 'continent'. The Endless Expanse, which, was seemingly dominated by a black stretchmark- no one knew the actual length of the expanse. So, why bother making up topography for it.

Sorin spotted there position on the map; he tapped the dot, and watched as it zoomed in. There they were, slowly moving northwest towards Hanover now only hours away. He switched the view back up and moved the curser around, until finally he spotted Gloomhaven.

He sucked in a breath, his expression pulling back in shock; the town was thousands of miles away from Hanover, much further north. How on earth had they been able to get him from such a long distance away? It's impossible...

Zoe went slack jawed at the size of the settlement. She could only imagine what the place must look like in person. The left and right side, which she assumed was the central and historic districts were huge. She looked to Sorin amazed "What about the undercity?" she asked, looking towards the map, trying to find its location.

"I guess the map doesn't show it. It's right under the right side here- the historic district. The line in the middle of the canyon is the main bridge, I've never been on it, I mostly stayed in the historic or in the undercity. The school I went too was near the bridge though. " He described to her.

"That's Gloomhaven?" Sorin looked up, Jack was looking over the chair rubbing the sleep from his eyes "Whoa... the place is even bigger than Ashton!" he gaped. He took his orange jacket off himself, and pushed it to the side.

Roxy stirred in her sleep, puffing a breath that brushed her short bangs to the side. Parting her hair she looked back, curious, but also annoyed at the loud voice of her younger brother. Sorin scooted over as Jack joined them on the bench seat.

Jack was completely dumbfounded by the settlements size. Ashton was by no means small, but this was something else entirely- the place was nearly as big as the other settlement they stopped at: Whitechapel.

He glanced up to the grumpy stare of his big sister, "Yo Rox, check this out! Look how big Sorin's settlement is!"

She glanced down at the pad. "Ok... Where's the undercity he's been telling us about?" she said, voice still drowsy from sleep.

"The map doesn't show it." Zoe said.

"That- and the map doesn't even show the elevators you can use to get there. Really messed up they didn't include it... it's kinda like the undercity doesn't exists." Sorin complained, who was low-key excited about showing Zoe Orio, and by extension, the nocturne. Then again, to Sorin's best guest to whomever programed this- probably wouldn't go to the trouble of detailing the three lower floors of the undercity.

"Oh well," Zoe shrugged "It still looks cool. Maybe one day dad can take me here for a visit... and maybe you can show me the undercity yourself." She smiled.

Sorin nodded "Sure."

Jack grinned "That would be awesome. Though... I wonder if will ever get the chance to visit. I mean... what do you think Garrot will do once we reach him?"

"Who knows," Roxy shrugged "All I know, is that I hope he's got a plan for the freaks chasing us." she replied, now flipping through her phone.

Sorin handed Zoe back the tablet while moving closer to the window, he glanced down to his right arm; Songbird has been quite for a while now, the taloned gauntlet wasn't making a chirp, or even an instance of the armor choosing to move up his sleeve by its own lonesome. Whether or not the gauntlet had a mind of its own- it, like him, seemed to be just along for the ride.

"Zoe? How old are you?" Jack asked.

"Um, eleven... why?" Zoe said, looking at him strangely.

"Dang, I'm still ten." Jack grumbled "I wanna get a cellphone like Roxy," (Roxy proceeded to shoot her tongue at him) "Mom and dad says I gotta wait till I'm thirteen!"

Zoe sighed, shaking her head. Sorin, of course, couldn't help but suppress a chuckle. Jack turned to him, causing him to freeze as he leveled a curious look his way.

"Ok... Sorin, how old are you?" Jack inquired.

Sorin stared at him "Ten." he answered, causing Jack to have a relieved exhale of breath "Yesterday." Jack paused, giving him a double take. With Zoe and Roxy blinking at what he just said. "C-come again?" Jack stammered.

Sorin looked at them all sheepishly "I sorta forgot today is my birthday... crazy right."

All three gapped at him for a moment. Sorin observed their reactions "Guys?"

"T-today, today is your birthday," Zoe got out slowly "What! Why didn't you tell us!" She exclaimed.

Sorin shrugged "Like I said, I forgot. I mean a lots happened..."

"So your freaking eleven now!" Jack groaned "Man, I'm the only one that's still ten... this sucks!"

Roxy chuckled "Yes, baby brother, you are." Jack glared back at her ready to throw another obscene gesture her way.

"What's going on back here!?" Mrs. Murdocks voice reprimanded, as she carefully moved across the moving van. She looked over everyone, her expression tight with irritation.

"It's Sorin mom, today's his birthday and he hasn't even said a word of it till now!" Jack exclaimed to her, causing the older Murdock to pause, her expression untensing, as complete surprise replaced it.

"S-Sorin... is this true?" she asked, a twinge of reproach coloring her voice. "Yes." Sorin answered with a bit of irritation.

Mrs. Murdock gasped at him "So how old are you now?" Sorin shrugged "Eleven, I think." She gave him a confused look "You think?" Sorin scratched the back of his head before nodding. "Well, at least... it's what they decided my birthday was." He replied with another shrug.

Mrs. Murdock paused, as well as everyone present; Zoe gave him a confused look, what did he mean by that? Mr. Murdock glanced up at the rearview mirror, brow furrowing at what the boy just said...

"What do you mean- are you saying you don't remember..." Mr. Murdock suddenly bit his tongue, his eyes glancing back down to the road; he could feel his face pulling into a grimace.

Sorin glanced at Mr. Murdock, before nodding "It's like I said. I don't remember anything after Hosea found me. I don't remember my settlement, my birthday, or my mom and dad." He said simply "Bellatrix was the one who came up with the birthday. She needed something to put on the biomonitor for me- for the circle."

Roxy and Jack stared at him. He said it so casually, like nothing was wrong with that at all. The moment went from being almost celebratory, to veering towards melancholic in an instant.

Zoe found herself unable to speak for a second; her stomach twisting on the spot, a sudden realization almost making her cringe. Sorin had already told her how he was feeling that night- when he explained the parts that were missing in his side of the story; the parts of which, that stood out the most to her, was the pain etched on his face, as he told her what the stranger had said. It was a moment of bleak comprehension. Finally causing her to understand, truly, what he meant by those words, and why they had such a horrible effect on him.

"Well... your eleven know Sorin. That at least has to be a cause for celebration." Mrs. Murdock said, meanwhile in the back of her mind she was crying for the boy. He doesn't even remember his parents... Somehow, she had hoped that he had been lucky to escape the worsts effects of cognicrossis; she had been dead wrong.

"Look, I'll be right back. I think I got something for the occasion." She said, before turning around and moving back to the front passenger seat. Sorin was about to say that it was fine, that he didn't need anything. But she had moved on before he could get a word out.

Nonetheless, Zoe tapped Sorin on the shoulder getting his attention. She had quickly recovered from the realization, as Roxy and Jack seemed to file away the moment for later. "So, I was thinking... maybe much later, when this is all over you could show me that foundry place. At the bottom of the undercity. Do you think I could draw it?" Zoe asked, eyes becoming bright "The way you describe it- it sounds beautiful."

Sorin shrugged "I guess, you think the nomad at Hanover will be able to help us out?" he directed the question towards Jack, who nodded fervently "Absolutely! Garret wasn't with us long, but he seemed kinda cool; that and he told us a lot of cool stories when he was staying with us." He replied earnestly.

Sorin was about to say something when Mrs. Murdock moved back; In her arms was a familiar red jacket that she pushed towards Zoe- who gasped when she saw what it was. Sorin's eyes widened when she held something to him. It was his bandanna! The black and gold cloth looked almost brand new (As long as one didn't pay any mind to the various stitch marks across the accessories fabric) Sorin looked at Mrs. Murdocks smiling face, lost for words.

"W-Wow! Thanks Mrs. M! How can I ever repay you." He stammered.

"Don't. it's your birthday Sorin. It's the least I can do-" She was suddenly interrupted as Zoe- now wearing her mended red jacket- was hugging Mrs. Murdock tightly, much to her expense. "Oh, dear-" she gasped, surprised by the blonde's strength. "Thank you! thank you-" Zoe repeated in a complete frenzy, as everyone immediately tried to get her off.

"Whoa, Zoe! Calm down for a moment!" Roxy exclaimed, heaving with all her might against the girls arm.

"Zoe! Don't break my mom's back!" Jack screamed, as he struggled to remove her.

Sorin simply found himself laughing, as he struggled with the siblings to get Zoe off Mrs. Murdock. Who was simply amazed at the position she found herself in. All of this, was of course to Mr. Murdocks amusement, who shook his head at the rear-view mirror.

What a weird bunch we are... Mr. Murdock thought to himself. As a grin pulled at his lips from the show behind him. The van continued down the road, with Hanover now closer than ever before.

CHAPTER

44

10/27/2061, Wednesday, 1: 37 pm

The large building overlooked the ruined sprawl before it.

An enormous collection of steel warehouses and ironwork scaffolding running across some of the infrastructures that stretched as far as the eye could see. The industrial plant. Or, as it was called back during its operation: Hanover Steel & Iron.

Once a cornerstone of Hanover life, which tied almost to the processing of the settlements mining and refinement of ichorsyte. Now, a shadow of its former self. The steel works seemed to periodically drone with the hollow warping and flexing of its steel infostructure. The winds of the desert howling around and traveling across the barren expanse. Brick and mortar, iron and steel, a rusting skeleton dotting the map near the faded town of Hanover. Another ghost town, like the once great Whitechapel.

But unlike a faded jewel, Hanover was a styx matter death trap. A place where no one would be foolish enough to venture...

Well, the figure standing watch near the side of the window, could only laugh at the irony of that statement.

The figure was adorned with a dark hooded poncho which stretched all the way down to his knees, the only thing that could be spotted from the dark room were both his arms- which, were currently crossed. The rest of his lower body was hidden in the darkness of the room, whatever light that spilled in from the cracked and likewise dust covered window was fleeting at best. The sun that afternoon was barely able to send any traces of its shine past the now encompassing clouds. The wastelands looked to be restless. An ill omen for the nomad inside of the abandoned six-story building. Now situated inside of an old office overlooking what was left of the front entrance. The shadow of his hood was pointing out the window, observing from his vantage point, as the limpid illumination from outside could barely trace the figures face. A storm was close. The drone he had sent out was already transmitting the forecast for the area. The only good news was that the constant hotspots from within the city- barely- had the strength to reach this old steel mill. He could only pray that the Murdocks would make it in time.

Something big was on the horizon. And he wasn't sure if his contacts would make it to the field on time...

A sound alerted the figure, he glanced to his right, a green flash from his laptop caused him to tense; the communicator near the computer was flashing, that only meant one thing.

Twin pearls of green light appeared from within the hood. Illuminating the figures face. A fair complexion, with a full beard and long dark hair; the figure's cyberlink connected with the computer. The electronics within his brain linking the computers audio to his.

"Garrot? You there?" a familiar voice said through the static filled line.

"Rob, I hear you... how far are you from the mill?" Garrot's calm voice echoed across the dark room.

"According to the GPS we're about an hour away. Listen... there's something you should know. We found two more kids, one girl, and one boy- where not sure if he's a deviant or not, but, he has something on his arm. And from what he tells us... those *things* are on their way." Rob answered back, his tone delicate.

Garrot narrowed his eye, but silently held whatever he was going to say at bay. "Okay, give me details."

"Listen, have you ever heard of a boy reported missing or kidnapped? Near the settlement of Gloomhaven? And a girl that was likewise kidnapped from the sectored districts." Robert asked.

Garrot paused again, for a moment he was stunned; that sounded eerily similar to something that his last contact had mentioned over the holo. She was abnormally serious... deathly so at the time; something wholly surreal to how she usually was. All of it centered around a boy she considered one of her own. The girl he knew next to nothing about. But the boy...

"Give me a name." he said.

"Which one?" Robert replied.

"The boy you picked up, what his name?"

"Sorin Richter."

10/27/2061, Wednesday, 2: 54 pm

Litter flew across the desolate roads between the old buildings on either side of the road. The sky above was thickened by the heavy mixture of dark clouds, casting the abandoned mill in an atmosphere of gloom.

As the buildings moved past the windows of the van, Sorin once again felt nervous. While not as utterly deteriorated as Whitechapel, the windows from each building gave nothing away, but eerie blackness; the whole state of the steel mill was totally deserted. Sorin felt his right arm itch; the gauntlet covering his hand felt clammy, that was a first...

His durag was now firmly covering his unruly hair, with the ribbon trailing down his neck; he felt some measure of comfort feeling his keepsake from Susan on him once again. But only just.

There are so many ghost towns in this region... and so many of them are just... collateral... could this happen to Gloomhaven one day?

Zoe watched the buildings from her position on the seat; the emptiness of the mill giving her an uncomfortable feeling of déjà vu; she pulled the hood down from her red jacket, as her taloned hands dove into the jackets pockets. She was in her deviant form. Compound eyes scanned the buildings, and the empty roads, wondering where Garrot was, and pining for the hope of getting in contact with dad. Jack and Roxy where simply vibing. Jack looking around the buildings with carefree zeal, and Roxy... on her cellphone, making brief glances out the window, then, going back to her small screen. Sorin could only envy the two's casual air.

Mr. and Mrs. Murdock were observing their surroundings, looking for the sign that would lead them to Garrots position in this god forsaken place.

"He said he would give us a sign, right?" Mrs. Murdock asked, "Did he tell you what it was going to be?" Mr. Murdock nodded "Don't worry, he was pretty confident we wouldn't miss it."

Mrs. Murdock narrowed her eyes, something about that didn't sit right with her, but, she brushed it off. They were here now... best not to question whether or not this was the right choice now... especially with those things after her kids. Mr. Murdock felt his nerves heighten ever more; this was it, this was the place where Jack, Roxy and hopefully Sorin and Zoe could be safe for the moment. Ever since that day, when that abomination broke into their house. He'd had more than one unpleasant dream of those things finding them in the desert. Thankfully this never happened, or at least, they never got the chance to catch up with them... the last supercell could have slowed them down, but, he was still unsure of that. But for now, beggars couldn't be choosers. They've arrived, all that needed to be done was to meet up with Garrot.

Suddenly there was movement ahead. Mr. Murdock put his foot on the breaks; Sorin and co were forced to hold on as the van came to an abrupt halt, tires skidding below them on the ruined concrete; Sorin leaned in, looking over Roxy's shoulder. There was something ten meters ahead of their position, an object which was suspended in the air; Sorin felt the armor spread to his right eye- only to cringe for a second; as the small eyepatch brought up the interface, his vision quickly zoomed in, giving him the ability to finally make it out. It definitely looked like a drone, or, something similar to one at the very least.

The flying aircraft was definitely not one of the best money could buy, but, the drone looked well cared for, not slick- but it was similar in appearance to his hoverboards collapsed mode, but more bulkier- with wings on either side of the device. Sorin watched the dark yellow drone, wondering what it was doing. Until a light began to blink at the end of its wings, and in front of the drones head piece. Sorin, and by extension the others, jumped when the GPS tablet on the dashboard began to emit a sharp noise; the sound of static ripped through the air, with Sorin wincing from the sudden racket out of the tablet. Only for the noise too come to an abrupt halt.

"Robert... are you there... current situation..." the voice, garbled by sparse static called from the tablet.

Jack's mood suddenly brightened, and Roxy slipped her cellphone away- eyes centered on the tablet. Sorin at the moment realized who the voice probably belonged too.

"Is that supposed to be the Garrot guy?" Zoe asked Jack, who nodded fervently, with a huge grin on his face. "Yes! Garrot, this is Robert speaking... is that supposed to be yours, a few meters away?" Mr. Murdock inquired, staring at the nearby drone with clear caution.

"Ah, so that's you in the van then. I see, so Cole came through with the favor." The voice spoke back, and from what Sorin could make out, he seemed relieved to hear back from Mr. Murdock.

"Yeah, but mind showing us where we need to go. It's not too far, is it?" Mr. Murdock asked, just happy to know that Garrot was here, and that the journey was almost over.

"Oh no, I got you covered. Just follow the drone- it shouldn't take but a few minutes to get where I set up shop." He replied.

The blinking lights of the drone cut off as it turned around ready to move, followed by the tablet; Sorin with growing interest realized something, did he hack the tablet through the drone in order to talk with them? Suddenly, as if reading his mind, Songbird began to scan the drone...

The lights turned back on, and Sorin felt himself shiver, like static electricity was running from his eye to the gauntlet. The drone suddenly swiveled, the lights on again as the tablet switched back on.

"You... with the gauntlet... Did you just scan my drone?" his voice was calm, but there was a mysterious note in his voice that he couldn't place. Oh crap, was he in trouble? Mixed stares of confusion or shock where pointed at him, and Sorin sheepishly looked at the drone "Y-yeah, sorry about that. I'm still getting used to this thing. Songbird, I mean. That's what I call it anyway." The tablet was quite for a moment "Huh, that's interesting." Sorin sighed, happy he didn't make him angry "Bellatrix is going to be interested to hear this." Sorin paused for a moment, thinking he must have misheard "Wait, W-what did you just say? You know Bella!?" he asked completely shocked.

Everyone was looking between the tablet and Sorin, somewhat at a loss for what was going on. "Yes, but listen. When you get here, will have a talk once everything is settled. That a deal?" Sorin looked at the drone numbly "Uh, yeah... sure."

The tablet cut off and the drone turned back around. Jack turned around, as Zoe, Roxy, and the elder Murdocks looked to Sorin. Sorin felt the silver eyepatch dissolve, as he forced himself out of his surprised stupor.

"Well, Sor... what do you think of Garrot?" Jack asked grinning. "He seems kinda cool, I guess." Was his answer after a moment.

CHAPTER

45

Sorin exited the van, which was parked near the entrance of a large building; a pregnant wind brushed over him, the twin tails of his durag blew along with it as Zoe came out of van from behind, her hood down and looking around the abandoned the mill with a dubious expression. Sorin carefully adjusted the straps of his backpack, which carried his hoverboard and the folder of documents.

The Murdocks were already outside, following the drone through the entrance. Mr. Murdock, Roxy, and Jack disappeared within the buildings old and raggedy entrance. Mrs. Murdock however, stood at the entrance waiting for them.

"Hey, you two, don't fall behind." She called, gesturing them inside.

The place was completely barren of any furniture. Save for the reception area, which was instead full of cobwebs, dirt, and some chairs (half-eaten or broken down). Sorin following behind the other two, quickly caught up with the other three. Who were waiting next to an elevator.

"Are we really going to step into that?" Zoe asked, raising an eyebrow at the old elevator.

Abruptly the elevator made a loud dinging noise which caused everyone to jump. They watched as the doors slid open, welcoming them inside its dirt encrusted abode; the lighting of the elevator flickering with the hum of electricity; causing Zoe to become nervous of stepping into its... less than savory appearance. Sorin observed the inside of the elevator; how was this thing still running? Did he redirect power from an old generator or something? He shrugged, before moving inside-much to everyone's hesitation. "Hey guys, you coming?" he asked, as the drone joined him inside. Much to everyone's dismay. Well, except maybe for...

"Yeah, I don't hear anything wrong with it." Jack responded, as he walked inside, joining the drone and Sorin.

Roxy grumbled to herself, as Mr. and Mrs. Murdock joined in, both looking absolutely besides themselves at the haggard interior of the box. Leaving her and Zoe outside the elevator. "I swear, if this thing breaks- I'm gonna kill the both of you, and Garrot!" she growled, pulling Zoe forward into the elevator.

10/27/2061, Wednesday, 3: 40 pm

The nomad opened his eyes with a start, the syringe of memetic coolant in hand. The skin under his clothes feeling the same consistency as a frozen tv dinner; but that was the far better alternative than letting his subdermal network fry him like pork.

Garrot sat up in his seat, the room felt like it was spinning as he collected himself. He grasped the contraption over his head and pulled the visor up; the moment he did this, he was immediately able to recover. He stood up slowly from his chair in front of his personal laptop- the connection to his other drones temporarily cut as they went to autopilot. He sat the cyberdeck down to the floor; his personal head jack- a portable network device he used to connect with cyberspace, or the remnants of cyberspace. The small tethers of net space that remained after the disconnection of the local net. Something they never tell you in class, even when a settlement is in ruin or abandoned, there are still traces left behind of the old net. The ghostly vestiges of a past abandoned telecommunications network, which will probably remain well after this generation or the next. Cyberspace was old, and there where many ways to access its dusty servers. His eyes flashed green, the notifications on his hud giving him an approximate reading of the steel mill. They would be here in a moment. He looked to his watch, Bellatrix and Hosea's group would be arriving today, along with his own party, maybe four to five hours at the most...

If Robert was right, then that was how long it would take for backup to arrive... and that last supercell... a day ago it crashed into Bella's side hard. Garrot cursed, he was really hoping the info Robert gave him was false... This would be a rough day if true.

The ding of the elevator signaled their arrival.

He sighed, it was time to see how everyone faired on their journey here. He stepped out of the dark room and made for the waiting room.

Sorin stepped inside. It must have been something when the mill was still operational. The waiting room was pretty large, windowless with loose traces of chairs and small tables near the sides of the room. The walls were peeling, and some holes could be seen staring back at him, with the pipes gleaming from the fluorescent lights of the ceiling, as faint as they were. The drone flew past each of the Murdocks and floated to the doorway behind the desk on the left, which must have been the receptions desk, and as the drone disappeared into the dark room, a man stepped out; Sorin paused when he spotted him, while the other two: Roxy and Jack, immediately rushed to him, followed by their parents.

"Garrot! Where did you get the awesome drone!" Jack exclaimed, a massive grin plastered on his face.

Garrot pulled his hood down, giving Jack a tired nod "Just something I found near Hanover; had to repair it with scrape, the other ones were loaned, and I see your as loud as ever."

He glanced at Roxy "How you been Rox? Keeping Jack in line?"

Roxy rolled her eyes "I'm good- and keep him in line... please... I'd be better off pretending he didn't exist." Jack simply blew his tongue at her, which she ignored for once.

Mr. Murdock held out his hand, face lit up with relief "I see your still breathing along with the rest of us." Garrot shook his hand "Barely," he replied "The supercells are getting worse, and the sandstorms are also becoming more frequent. It looks like the expanse further south is becoming more agitated as of late." The two finished there shake, and Mrs. Murdock stepped up hugging Garrot despite his slightly dirty, and gruff appearance. "It was a rough ride getting here, but we made it... and we came across two more additions in are strange little family."

She said, turning towards Sorin and Zoe, with the former of which looked nervous.

"Oh, yeah." He turned to Zoe, much to her unease "They told me you're a long way from home. Sorry to hear about what happened in Whitechapel; the gang that abducted you- they had a silver pendent or emblem on their clothes, right?"

Zoe thought for a moment then nodded "Y-yeah, it was a bird perched on a twig I think. And it had what looked like a setting sun behind it." she said, sounding somewhat unsure.

Sorin nodded "There were also shapes hanging from below it- I think they were attached to a branch. But, I'm not really sure what it means."

Garrot's eyes narrowed as Zoe told him about the pendant, and he grimaced when Sorin gave him the added details, an unpleasant look settled on his features. "The Shrikes then... So, that means there still a bunch of them running around out there..."

Sorin looked to his gauntlet, a dark memory of the hallway filled with dead nomads surfaced in an unpleasant flash.

"Um... I don't think you'll have to worry about them anymore." Sorin said quietly "There all dead now... the thing they kidnapped us for, it did them in." he said, feeling an uncomfortable twitch from Songbird.

Garrot was quite for a moment. "Your name is Sorin right? I got in contact with Bellatrix," Sorin looked up "I gave her your description and told her you hitched a ride with the Murdocks to meet me here." He turned to Zoe "Your father, is Nathanial Raynor- correct?" Zoe nodded, hope settling on her features "He's with Bellatrix right now, and are on their way here as we speak. But there's something you should all know." Garrot said, getting everyone's attention

"They also passed a warning to me. That they've been on the trail of something dangerous, and extremely fast. Moving northwest from Whitechapel, for a few days now- and whatever it is... It's headed exactly for Hanover, and they couldn't do much to slow them down."

The temperature in the room plummeted; the Murdocks, Sorin and Zoe, immediately glanced askew from one to another, the implications of what he was saying brought a feeling of dread to all in the room. Sorin in particular felt his stomach twist into a not; that confirmed exactly what he'd been saying, and feeling since the other day.

Sorin paused...did he say them? What did he mean by *them*!?

"D-did you just say them? That thing from Whitechapel was alone the last time it tried to kill me..." Sorin stammered, starring at Garrot and hoping desperately that he had misheard him. "Sorry kid, Bella informed me that four in total where making their way across the desert on foot; no vehicles or any form of transportation in sight."

Garrot sighed, his expression troubled "Quasimorphs... that's the only explanation." Sorin knitted his brow "Quasi... morph?" he repeated, unsure if he said it right.

"Yes, you pronounced it right," Garrot nodded, folding his arms "That's what there referred to."

"Those things that attacked us at our home, and these two?" Mrs. Murdock questioned. Garrot nodded again "What... what are they? And where do they come from?" Garrot shook his head "Thats... it's complicated. What I can tell you is that they use to be people. People. like you, or me... but they were mutated, turned into killing machines that seem... almost hyper fixated in hunting down deviants."

Everyone stared at Garrot, shocked at the information he was just giving them for free. Days of not knowing what they were, and now to finally be given answers...

"W-why," Roxy stammered, her eyes settled firmly on Garrot, her skin becoming paler under the light of the room. "Why us... what did we ever do to deserve that!"

Garrot looked at her, his face unreadable and his eyes casting a somber gaze back at her. "I don't know... and frankly, I'm not supposed to be telling you any of this. But you, your brother, and..." he turned to Zoe "All of you should know and understand this fact. As far as the source of the transformation," his expression going from stoic sympathy to genuine unease "it's been linked to styx matter." Sorin felt a prickling in his upper cranium. Everyone was silent. A collective moment of shared horror- something as spontaneous as it was earth shattering... but it made sense. In its own morbid twisted way. The dark mist which seeped out of the mutated nomad, the monster from Whitechapel- which had the same substance pour from its grizzly wound. If styx matter was the cause of that. Then how on earth did the artifact attached to his arm, and the thing within his chest have a factor in all of this?

"That can't be possible." Mr. Murdock uttered "If that were true everyone would know... someone would have known..."

Garret nodded grimly "Your right, they do know. The conclaves, the republic... there all aware of it and the darndest thing about it, nobody can pinpoint the trigger for the initial change." He frowned "Excuse me for saying this Sorin, but, you're more likely to contract cognicrossis then trigger a quasimorph transformation. But recently, the number of cases of quasimorphs have also been slightly on the rise, as of late."

While everyone in the room listened or asked him questions, Zoe could only glance around at Sorin... who was now against the wall, his face unreadable. He put a hand on Songbird for a moment; the subject of the room being discussed was slowly but surely making him think hard about everything that had happened. Since first having that nightmare. His dream of Orson back at home, and the nomad leader who kidnapped him... so those things in his dream... those were quasimorphs? And the thing which chased him through Whitechapel... could he wind up turning into that?

"Hey Garrot," Sorin said, pulling off his backpack "Can you take a look at this. It's about the gauntlet on my arm- I found this on the nomad guys desk." Garrot, glancing at the youth could only widen his eyes as Sorin pulled out the document. "What is this?" he asked as Sorin handed it to him.

Sorin held up Songbird for Garrot to see "The thing inside of the case jumped on my cyberdeck. And it turned into this. Does Zoe's dad happen to know anything at all about it?" Sorin asked, trying really hard to hide how desperate he was for answers.

Garrot looked the gauntlet over; this was actually the first time he had the chance to really look at it in detail, and what he saw intrigued him. If not for Bella's summary of the bunker located at Whitechapel, then he honestly would have assumed that he was like Zoe... But by Bella's admission, he knew that Sorin wasn't a deviant. The fact that he even had cognicrossis to begin with was a dead giveaway, and the second reason: He didn't have the genetic key that all deviants shared: The Anakim Strand. The gene which gave deviants their powers, or superhuman characteristics. He flipped through the pages, eyes narrowing at the photo of Sorin, Bellatrix, and the person whose name he wasn't familiar with on the bench. Every detail of this dossier was painstakingly gathered to the last detail. But the thing that really got his attention was that one phrase... Metamorphosis... that's the same thing *he* mentioned... Mr. Raynor's colleague... He paused, thinking about what his old acquaintance use to say about the nature of Deviants and how Quasimorphs factored into them... as well as the normal population of humans...

"Garrot?" Sorin asked, wondering what was on his mind along with the others.

"Let's move to the next room. I'll see if I can reach Bella and Mr. Raynor on the net." He said closing the file. Sorin slowly nodded, feeling the metallic fingers of songbird twitch as everyone followed him into the dark room.

CHAPTER

46

10/27/2061, Wednesday, 4: 05 pm

"Sorin, hey man, can we talk for a moment?" Jack asked. "Huh?" Sorin mumbled, coming out of his daydream.

He was sitting near the window; Garrot was currently in cyberspace, well, from what he said, an old portion of it and that he was going to see if he could reach Bella from the other end. He understood some of what he said at the very least... unlike the others, which strangely made him feel a bit embarrassed. Weird. But before that, he had to talk with Zoe, Jack, and Roxy. Something about a certain someone coming to meet with them about their powers.

So, Sorin found himself near the window- looking outside and thinking about the things on route to the steel mill. Quasimorphs, that word had such a bizarre ring to it. Did the others know about their existence? Hosea and the rest.

They were nomads, and no matter how many times he'd ask them about their gigs they'd never go into much detail- aside from doing a few questionable things, here and there.

Before Jack had interrupted his train of thoughts. He wondered, how many contracts did they get for quasimorphs? If any at all for that matter...

"What up?" he asked. Looking over his grinning face.

"Man, you'll never believe the stuff Garrot told us." he said pulling another seat to sit down next to him "About the other kids like us!" he exclaimed in marvel.

Sorin raised an eyebrow "Oh, well... like what? Can't imagine anything stranger than what I've seen in the past few days." Jack chuckled at that.

"Don't believe me. Okay, get this, there have been a few deviants like Zoe that he's come across; you know- can transform and are crazy strong or fast- but most importantly are animal like: Wolves, snakes, bears, birds, you name it! But that's not the coolest part... apparently those types of deviants go by a category." Jack paused, for dramatic effect- which Sorin simply rolled his eyes, but he humored him.

"A chimera!" he exclaimed.

"Chimera?" Sorin said slowly before sniggering "Can't imagine Zoe liking that very much." Jack laughed nervously "By the look on her face when Garrot explained it to her... No, no she did not. But you gotta admit it sounds so cool."

Sorin sat back laughing "Okay... so she's a chimera. What does that make you and Roxy?"

Jack smirked "Espers... I think that's how he said it."

Sorin shook his head, a small humorless smile on his face; he brought up songbird "I wonder what type of category I'd be if I were a deviant."

Jack snorted "Probably something super complicated... I mean, you can hack stuff, you can make that super cool armor, and that whip thing from songbird is gnarly- but in a good way." He added last second.

Sorin scratched the back of his head nervously, with his right hand "Yeah, when you say it like that. But I don't know... sounds too good to be true almost. I nearly get killed by, what, a monster that I've never heard of until now, and I get this weird gauntlet, cyberdeck combo from it. I mean, doesn't that sound crazy to you?" Sorin inquired.

Jack shrugged "Crazy doesn't seem the right word. How about... karma, yeah karma!" Sorin looked at him questionably, baffled by his answer "Karma?" he repeated.

"Yeah, look at this way. You saved Zoe, from getting killed by that thing from the garage. You, freaking, out raced it, across the entire settlement. You brought a building down on it," 'More like it brought the building down on us.' Sorin muttered "And!" Jack continued on "You blew the thing up with a gas station! Like- who can say that, and not sound really, really, cool!?" he looked utterly astonished saying it.

"Heck, you didn't even have any powers!" Jack exclaimed, now waving his arms around.

Sorin opened his mouth trying to say something, but the only thing that could come to mind "I don't think Hosea or Bellatrix are going to see it as cool." He gulped.

Jack groaned "Come on man! Work with me here..."

Sorin looked at Jack sheepishly "My bad, I mean putting it like that... It does sound kinda awesome... Just wish it didn't involve me getting kidnapped."

Jack sighed before nodding "Yeah, the part about getting nabbed from your home is still kinda messed up... don't think anything can un-screw something like that up."

"Hey, Sorin, you got a minute." Roxy called, joining the two along with Zoe.

Sorin looked up and nodded to her direction only to pause at the look Zoe was giving him "Uh, you okay Zoe?" She beamed "Yeah, I'm good. Listen... Garrot wants to see you in the other room. Just you by the way." She added quickly. Sorin wasn't sure, but, Zoe looked really, really pleased, practically beaming from how happy she was.

Sorin with a small feeling of bafflement, made for the other room.

The conference room was a lot larger than the main office behind the waiting room, and tucked to the side of the office. The room was spacious, able to accommodate maybe 8 to 10 people- but the place was also in similar dishevelment: rusted metal chairs, broken furniture, peeling wall plaster, you name it. The place had a few large windows to the side, but they were boarded up. So, the only lights in the room, came from a few more smaller computer terminals around another chair, which had a few monitors attached to it. Sitting in it was none other than Garrot... Who also had a weird contraption on the conference table- helmet like, but with a few notable features he didn't recognize; it sorta reminded him of one of those VR headsets. Garrot sat there near the long table seemingly tinkering with the front sensor part of the helmets visor, Sorin watched silently, the tools strewn over the table, and wires stretched from the back portion of the helmet. A few of them, draped over the document that he had given him earlier- the many papers of the file, spread across the other side of his tools. Sorin shook his head; kicking himself for getting so easily distracted.

"Garrot? You have somethin to tell me?" Sorin asked.

Garrot nodded silently, placing the screwdriver on the table and glancing up at him. "Just wanted to ask you a few questions about the gauntlet on your arm." giving the gauntlet a curious look "By the way... you named it Songbird?" he asked, raising an amused eyebrow.

Sorin sighed "Yeah. but look, if you knew the sound it makes someti-"

Maybe it was coincidence, or just serendipity, but Songbird at that exact moment began to twitter; the green light of the gauntlet piercing the semidarkness. And the helmet turning on in front of Garrot. Much to his surprise.

"Hey!" Sorin started annoyed "Not now, quit it!" the green light faded, and the gauntlet made another small twit before cutting off.

"Sorry about that." Sorin sighed. "It turns itself on sometimes... and does things..."

Garrot narrowed his eyes, now truly observing the gauntlet on the boys right arm. The moment he felt the breach from his drone, and traced it back to Sorin, he was shocked to say the least. Now that he knew the boy was related to Bellatrix, it cleared some things up, but also made things stranger. The document that Sorin handed him- made things worse- and he'd even go as far as unnerving. The gauntlet seemed to have a strange sentience, and calling it just a strange new form of cyberware didn't give it any justice. Whatever the shrikes were doing with the artifact on the boys arm... it can't have been any good. This would prove far more challenging than just another deviant relocation.

"That's interesting... pretty powerful breach that thing casted on the visor. And here I was thinking the I.C.E I had installed was pretty good." Garrot said, his voice sounding strangely impressed.

"Huh?" Sorin muttered, glancing at Garrot in bewilderment. "Ice?"

"Intrusion countermeasure electronics... I.C.E for short." Garrot explained casually. "Your gauntlet- Songbird was it? The breach it threw against my drone and now my cyberdeck. It was surprisingly effective." He said.

Sorin cringed "Sorry."

"Nah, don't worry about it. If you don't mind... I wanna test something." Emerald light gleamed in Garrots eyes; the helmets front lights switched on, as the light of the monitor from his laptop illuminated the room. He slipped the helmet on and pulled up the visor; he motioned for Sorin to get closer, much to the youths apprehensive interest. Wondering where this was possibly going.

"Songbird is able to breach into different forms of electronics, right? Not just drones or the main systems of a van, correct?" he asked.

Sorin nodded "Yeah, it's how I'm able to use my hoverboard."

Garret wore a ponderous expression "So... does that mean its capable of interfacing with my cyberware."

Sorin paused for a moment; could Songbird do that? Hacking electronics was one thing, but hacking into a person's cyberware or neuralware was a whole other matter entirely. He felt nervous of that logical leap. How many horror stories had Jade or Tom for that matter shared with him on the subject. Even Bellatrix- who gave him, in her own words the PG explanation- still managed to creep him out on how dangerous a cyberware hack could be. He shuddered, that's almost what happened with Mr. Owens...

"M-maybe, I not really sure I wanna find out." He admitted.

Garrot noted the boys sudden unnervement. To the surprise of Sorin, the experienced nomad gave him a knowing look. He smiled, not a big one, and not necessarily one that had genuine cheer within it, but the type of which were he was silently telling him, he knew what he was thinking- that he understood why it was bothering him.

"It's alright kid, I assume you must have seen certain things during and after your abduction. I'm also guessing Bellatrix explained the 'PG' version of getting hacked by another runner."

Sorin stood their silently, then after a moment, gave a slow nod.

Garrot nodded back "Thought so... well, don't worry about *that*. I'm asking if you wanna try another method of talking with Bellatrix," he tapped the helmet "By using my connection across cyberspace that I set up earlier. You could follow me- partly- through cyberspace for the meet."

Sorin stood there for a moment, his face scrunched up in confusion, before gawking at Garrot; follow him through cyberspace... that was possible? Without an operatives chair! Garrot observed him; apparently she hadn't told him everything there was to know about cyberspace. Good, the less he knew the better. But unfortunately they needed to take advantage of this. Well, he assumed the gauntlet could partway connect with his interface.

"But how is that possible? I thought you needed an operators chair in order to do that." He said, regarding Garrot with clear perplexation.

"Remember kid. Cyberspace when it comes down to it, is just a digital plane where computer systems communicate with each other. Doesn't matter how old, or how obsolete it is. If it can send and interpret a signal, than it can act as a medium that ghost runners can travel." Sorin blinked, taking in what he was saying "and since there are old subsystems still functioning this far out of Hanover... there's bound to be a pathway we can use for that very purpose of connection. You just need to find the right one." Sorin watched as Garrot slipped a small cable from his laptop to his cyberdeck visor. He moved his hair back, and showed Sorin the neurolink socket near the nap of his neck. Sorin gave it an uneasy look; he'd witnessed Church plug in neural interface cables at the same spot, when he needed to scan the biomonitor of his patients. Checking neuralware compatibility and health; he looked at Songbird wondering if he could do the same thing. Garrot smiled before pulling up a chair for him to sit, which, Sorin took. "You wanna see if it works kid?" he asked calmly.

Sorin, despite himself, couldn't help but nod in agreement; how many times had he been there when Susan described a cyberspace dive with Tom and Jade. The captivating tone of her voice always struck him, and now, he had the chance to see if he could experience the same... By Sorins will, Songbird stretched across his arm and eyes, feeling a powerful surge of energy pulse from inside his chest. He could only tense up as the pain slowly blossomed from the effort of giving Songbird what it needed to manifest the armor. Even Garrot was forced to do a small double-take as the gauntlet stretched like water across the boys upper body. Sorin opened his eyes, the interface coming to life as the reticle focused around Garrot. The two red lens falling on the veteran runner. He breathed easy, the pain slowly dimming in sharpness as he held up Songbird.

"Is it okay for me to connect to your headjack?" Sorin asked, trying hard to quell his growing anxiousness.

Garrot raised an eyebrow "Does your gauntlet have a neurolink? I don't see one."

Sorin balled his fist, and Garrot observed as the gauntlet once again shifted. Small, curved spikes rippled around the gauntlets forearm like a serpent, its sharp fin sliding around like a shark cutting the surface of a body of water, before slowly extending out of the wrist, from the underside of his palm. The cable of silver levitated before his eyes. Garrot blinked, then shrugged to himself. That would have to do. The thread of silver in front of him looked vaguely like a neurolink, so it might work. Sorin gave him an odd look; usually everyone would look at Songbird with clear unease or shock, but the nomad before him seemed almost completely unfazed by the gauntlets abilities.

"You seem pretty unbothered by this... I guess, you've seen weirder?" Sorin all but questioned, completely baffled by the nomads continued composure.

Garrot frowned "Oh, no, that gauntlet of yours is definitely unusual. But... I've meet other deviants that have powers similar to what Songbird is doing now. Kids that can create a protective shell around them out of bone, or other chimera like Zoe- only they have a much more pronounced exoskeleton," Sorin widened his eyes at that "But, none of them have been able to hack into any machinery, or electronics like you have. Alright, bring the cable here, I wanna see if it's possible to form an interface share."

Sorin not really knowing what to expect, allowed the tendril to move around Garrots head. Garrot grabbed the silver cord and moved it close to his headjack. Suddenly, the interface in front of Sorin began to change. Focusing on the headjack; Sorin watched the reticule target the back of his neck, and found himself gawking at what the tendril was doing. Songbird seemed to understand what Garrot needed it to do, as the end of the tendril looked very similar to the plug he saw back in that bunkers data center; the very same one that was plugged to the dead runner in his operating chair. The tendril slid into the headjack, and Sorin felt a cold chill run through the cord and up his right arm; the room seemed to darken, the lights of the laptops began to lose their illumination, and he was slowly starting to feel weightless; it reminded him of the time he jumped that statue like a ramp back in Whitechapel, only far more dragged out than his adrenaline stewed brain could process in his bid for survival. His body felt like it was being pulled in, like a gravity well had opened in front of him, its dark jaws, inhaling all light around him and causing his equilibrium to further deteriorate under the strain of gravity.

"Hey, Sorin, don't fight it. You're alright, your partially connecting with cyberspace right now as we speak- just stay calm and follow my lead."

Sorin could only nod, not trusting himself to form words, his stomach felt like it was twisting from the weightlessness he felt.

"Alright, close your eyes and focus on my voice. We're diving in... one... two... three..."

CHAPTER

47

??

The world shifted around him, a horrible constriction that pressed his head from all sides.

Like he was being pulled into a narrow passage; Sorin felt overwhelmed, his body... or was it his consciousness? Was currently free falling into what looked to be a wormhole of data. like gravity had finally abandoned him, and left the fabric of reality untethered while doing so.

To call it a rush was far too generous.

He felt severed, like he was in two places at once. The feeling was comparable to that of a lucid dream. Sorin understood that he was still sitting in the conference room on the top floor of a building, understood that he was currently interfaced with Garrot's body, and he understood that... for the first time ever... he was in cyberspace. The stories, the lectures, and general explanations from Bellatrix echoed and replayed themselves. Well, to his surprise, cyberspace looked strikingly a lot like outer space. As far as the eye could see, from every direction, star bodies hung suspended and gleaming, a multitude of shades of color, all varying in size and distance; they surrounded him, like he had his very own local galaxy. And for some reason, he felt a weak pull towards the stars closest to him.

Sorin was completely forgetting the apprehension he held in interfacing with Garrot. It was like he was back on his hoverboard, a type of freedom he longed for was slowly poising him to investigate.

His building interest was only hampered by the fact that he didn't have any way of getting closer.

He couldn't feel his body within cyberspace, no, he felt more like a disembodied presence floating within a static void. The sensation was strange, a surreal state of existence he couldn't fully understand or articulate. He paused, something appeared, another presence? Sorin turned on the spot, and behind him a familiar sight. Garrot. The nomad was a transparent blue hologram, which digitally looked to be fading in and out. Floating like an eponymous ghost. And made up seemingly of a thousand bytes of data; his expression was uncannily a spitting image of his real one outside.

And to Sorin's surprise, he was observing him; the experienced ghost runner looked at Sorin with amused curiosity, looking him up and down. He seemed impressed.

He then spoke, his voice, sounding like it was under an electronic synthesizer "Interesting... your completely synced in. You hardly have any neuralware for a full cyberspace dive and yet, you already have a underdeveloped icon."

"What?" Sorin's voice, disembodied, and spoken without the aid of a mouth or tongue. Carried through the vacuum of space.

"Your icon." Garrot said "A three-dimensional rendering that's created by a cybermodem. More specifically Songbird."

"Songbird?" Sorin's voice cut through the void again. "Counts as a cybermodem? What can't it do?" he froze, that came out of nowhere, why did he say that out loud!?

"Kid, a word of advice. Be careful with your thoughts. At your age, being able to send out a holocall is almost unheard of. Last thing we need is you sharing something... embarrassing." Garrot spoke again, Sorin watched as a small smirk played across his lips, barely conceivable due to the rendering of his icon.

Sorin immediately froze, a holocall, that's what's been happening! His eyeless gaze focused on Garrot's image, to shocked to say/think anything.

"Wait, before you blow a gasket trying to figure everything else out yourself. Just calm down. Take it one step at a time, and above all else, just follow my lead." Garrot instructed.

Outside of cyberspace, the boy's body tensed, his eyeballs behind the mask began to rapidly dart around in random movement. Even during the REM phase of his cyberspace dive- Sorin replayed the instructions given to him; one step at a time, that's all he needed to do... take it one step at a time... and moments later, Sorin could feel his body outside of the digital landscape slowly release the tension built up; the absolute excitement of his surprise plunge into the frontiers of the net, was slowly becoming manageable. His rapid eye movement slowly dimmed.

Finally, now he felt strangely displaced; the outer reaches of net space stretched before him, yet the dual feelings of a bodiless existence within that space unnerved him.

This didn't fit with every detail of Susan's tale of cyberspace...

"Alright, looks like your calming down. I need to ask you something. How do you feel right now?" Garrot questioned "Take it slow... just tell me at your own pace."

Sorin heard him, and for the moment he was having trouble thinking of the words to say; but eventually, after almost ten seconds of silence "I feel... lost... why do I... feel so... strange here?" his voice garbled and glitched.

"It's your first time. Your mind is currently separated from your physical body, but your body in the real world is still linked to your consciousness. It's an out of body experience or a feedback loop. You'll catch up eventually."

"Why does cyberspace... look like... outer space?" Sorin said, his words coming out better that time.

"It's how your mind interprets cyberspace, with the help of your cyberdeck. Right now, your brain is interpreting the connections, electronics, and data branches that are being shared by other forms of signals." Garrot looked around "And one of them is going to lead us to Bellatrix."

Sorin once again was speechless. "Bella... she's here, where?"

Garrot was silent, he pointed to a distant star; barely a pinprick of light to it, which was giving off a purplish hue. Sorin stared, if he could form an expression like the digital version of Garrot, his expression of longing would have been painful to look at.

"Now, I need you to focus. Picture yourself and create an image like me, as best as you can, and then grab my arm." Garrot instructed carefully.

Sorin didn't need to be told twice. Whatever willpower he had, he used it to summon the best picture of himself that he could manage. Forcibly putting all his desperation and longing into his need to see her again. An arm, a hand, anything to grab hold of Garrot. And Songbird answered his call. From the spectral shape of his mind, a glimmer of light began to gather in front of him. It was data, pure raw data; a digital matrix of inverted characters, streaming forward in a green hue of digital light, not to dissimilar from the glow of a certain gem. Garrot's eyes became wide with astonishment, gazing in mute shock as the clawed glove of Songbird materialized from the millions of data fragments being gathered to form its shape. Soon, an arm, a shoulder, a neck, and finally the mask. Sorin's icon was a downpour of digital code, a transparent rainfall which continued to draw his avatar. Garret in a moment of silence could only stare as the gauntlet's fingers curled around his arm, barely able to encompass it in its entirety, the boys right hand was too small to fully grasp his forearm, but by god, Garrot was beyond impressed.

Was this the raw computing power of Songbird? Or was it the kids budding potential as a runner?

"Alright. Hold on, and pay attention."

Garrot put a digital finger to his temple. His image flickered, and too Sorin's amazement, the stars suddenly got closer. Too close. Each one surrounding them in a swirl of motion, and Garrot held out a hand; the stars froze in place, and something... was it a strand of data? Or a script of code? Multiple scrunched lines of code in front of Garrots face- typing themselves too fast for him to follow, an ever-growing script of directions, that looked more and more complicated as time went on. How was he doing this so fast!? Sorin could feel something stir from Songbird as he watched on, struggling to understand what was being done. There was a slow chill that traveled down his right arm; the gauntlet grasping his arm began to glow- the gem, its digital representation was active. Sorin felt his eyes behind the mask itch- was it a sensation from outside cyberspace, or was it something weirder? He couldn't be sure. But the effect was slowly revealing itself. The code in front of Garrot was slowing down...

Sorin felt his icon flicker and Songbirds digital copy chirped as more code typed itself before his eyes. The lines appearing near Garrot was strangely becoming clearer. More legible. Suddenly the script appeared in front of Sorin's face and his eyes widened at what he was able to decipher.

```
<Gateway_10595_B>..... Access_Granted.....

// GatewayBranch_Path_Selected\\

<<Gateway_10595_B >>>>>>> Gateway_36500_X>>

<<<WaypointsCharted_GatewayTravel_Execute>>>
```

"Sorin, where about to do a gateway jump! I need you to stay calm and hold on, this might be rough for your first time!" Garrot warned; Sorin, looking between the stars in front of them and Garrot, could only mutter an alarmed "What!?"

Whatever words that could have come next from Sorin quickly died in mid thought; there was a surge, a powerful force which zapped through his gauntlet, then arched directly towards his temple. His icon- now halfway completed- seized in mid materialization; Sorin could only watch as Garrot's icon was stretched- the data that comprised his digital avatar... seemingly ripped to shreds, as it was sucked up into the star itself, a blue thin filament of compressed data spaghettifying into the solar body with his arm quickly following in pursuit. "Just relax" Garrots voice ringed into his head as his form was sucked into the bright ball of light. Sorin besides himself with terror, could only get out a small yell of fright as his body was quickly broken down and sucked in. What happened next. Sorin would never forget. His out of body conscious was once again being slingshot into a narrow passage of light and sound. His brain lurched, his vision a frenzy of motion that made his earlier ventures on the hoverboard pale in comparison, his consciousness being stretched across a distance he couldn't even begin to fathom. But there was an eerie sense of familiarity to it... something he couldn't quite explain. Too quickly, the jaunt came to an abrupt end. And he was no longer in the building, no longer at the steel mill. Was this the middle of the desert!? Not a millisecond later he was compressed and shot out again. Like a bullet speeding out of its barrel, Sorin could only observe as the surrounding environment changed, his perspective a jumble, as his form was sent out in fixed points, as if he were traveling by way of a complex grid of coordinates.

And once again, as abruptly as possible, his velocity quickly and mercilessly halted. If it weren't for the fact that he wasn't in his physical body, he would probably be a shaking mess. Or vomiting out his lunch, in any case.

"Garrot... what the heck... was that?" his voice came out garbled, the syntax somewhat staticky in its output.

"Satellite arrays in hidden locations around the desert. Placed years ago; by either nomads, S.S officials, or the usual waster. They really come in handy when you need to make long reaching gateway jumps. Though... it's also really risky.

Can almost never tell when there spiked by hostile daemons or security I.C.E. Not something you should do often, unless you have no other way."

Looking up, his digital right hand was still latched on to Garrot's forearm. Letting go, he looked around- the surrounding environment had changed, the stars surrounding them were gone, replaced by something much, much, stranger. It was a room. A room that was seemingly built by thousands upon thousands of pixels. Shaded and given depth to make the surroundings almost photorealistic and translucent at the same time. A dark bluish tinge suffused the room, making Garrot and himself the most striking contrast against the rooms background. Their holographic icons where like floating neon ghosts standing at the very edge of the rooms interior. But what really had Sorin's attention, and likewise shock, was the rooms appearance.

It was the inside of the Seventh Nocturne. He could recognize the shapes of the tables, the booth chairs, and the bar stand from anywhere. But how...

"Garrot!" a familiar voice called "What's up! Do you have more intel on Sorin's..." Bellatrix's voice stopped.

Her red icon was now staring at them. Her avatar shimmered, the lone shape near the back of the bar... where Sorin's room would be located down the stairs to the basement.

"Bella..." Sorin said, his voice coming out almost in a whisper, not taking long in recognizing her face and... whatever it was that she was wearing. Not the same jumpsuit that she would normally be wearing. But some kind of suit. A plug suit similar to the runner from the bunker of Whitechapel.

The silence that dominated the scene was absolutely stifling. She stared past Garrot, her expression unreadable; her icon flickered again, eyes scanning Sorin's holographic avatar and the complete unraveling of her calm expression, second by second, the recognition painting her face in shock, before her eyes landed back to Garrot.

"What is this?" she breathed in total disbelief "How..."

Garrot glanced down to Sorin. "The artifact that Carver and his Shrikes stole from the black site... It bonded with his cyberdeck. The interface signal of his biomonitor... well... you see it for yourself."

Sorin felt nervous, Bella's silence and general uneasiness provoked a visceral instance of wrongness over what should have been a moment of relief. "He... that shouldn't... he's too young, and it's impossible for a model that old too..."

Garrot suddenly flickered, before reappearing in front of Bella's icon. He held out his open hand; Sorin felt time slow down, his perspective dilating along with the general view of the space around them. Songbird chirped, and text appeared, between the two icons as code script flew between them. The digital representation of Bellas consciousness widened her eyes; the data transfer ceased, and Bella was now looking horrified.

"The document I gave you was scanned from the file Sorin gave me earlier. It doesn't go into much detail about the artifacts origin, but, Carver didn't act alone. That much is obvious." Garrot said "Does your client know who could have hired him?"

Bella's icon stopped flickering, but, she shook her head "No... Raynor hasn't a clue, of who could have given him the means to pull off this gig. But… the damage is done and we're having a hell of a time cleaning it up."

She glanced back to Sorins' direction, she disappeared, reappearing right in front of him. Sorin froze, not at all use to the rapid movement of all present. She crouched down, looking at his avatar up and down; not really giving to much reaction to only half of his avatars body at present. But the mask on Sorin's face… that seemed to really get her attention; Sorin could almost feel the unease of its presence on his avatars face, but, she seemed to quickly shake herself from the brief moment of disturbance before focusing on him again. Her hand came to rest on his cheek, the data making up her hand mixing with clusters across Sorin's lower face. The sensation of her hand was faint, nowhere near as vivid in comparison to Garrot. But for Sorin it almost didn't matter in the slightest. Her expression was… he couldn't really read it… but, he did recognize the look of relief in there. As strained as it was.

"Hey, Scamp… you had us pretty worried there." She said, almost meekly, something he'd never would have thought, or, would have imagined hearing from her. "Sorry… I didn't mean.." Sorin began, his holographic image flickering. Bella shook her head

"No. This isn't on you, Sorin. Carver is… he's the only one to blame for this." Bellatrix said quietly, her tone becoming colder than jagged ice.

Sorin looked at Bellatrix, once again uneasy, he's seen her angry, but never like this… She seemed to notice the look he was giving her, her expression immediately softened, as her hand left his cheek, before gently gathering up his right hand. Songbird chirped on contact, making Bella flinch back in surprise. Sorin grabbed his wrist in reaction. "What in the world!" she breathed.

Sorin glanced down at Songbird. Grimacing at the likely need to explain Songbird's strange quirks; Garrot appeared next to Bellatrix, lightly touching her avatars shoulder. She stood up, giving him a brief glance before seizing up the gauntlet on his arm.

"Odd thing ain't it. I thought it would be better to show you what its capable of." he crouched down, held his hand up, and an image of one of the files materialized in his hand "And it's a direct match to the one in correspondence with Carver. When he and the other one got into a brief fight in the foundry."

Sorin suddenly felt himself grow cold, sounds of the gunfight immediately penetrating his skull. He grabbed Bella's wrist, getting her attention.

"Bella! Mr. Owens! Is he alright!?" Sorin blurted out, eyes behind the red lens of his mask searching, wild with pent up fear for his condition.

Bellatrix froze for a moment, before putting a comforting hand to his.

"It's okay. He's alive Sorin, we were able to get him help before the worst could happen." She said while averting her eyes, her expression once again becoming strangely unreadable.

Sorin paused, the good news of Mr. Owens' survival had a near instantaneous effect; like the terrible burden of the image in his head was given a powerful suppressant. Yet the way she averted her eyes. Something settled over Sorins heart, something heavy, maybe not as heavy as the earlier memory, but he was compelled to ask what was wrong. But before he could... she averted her gaze to Garrot, and the look made his question deflate, the thought disappearing in the throes of darkness.

"Garrot, the quasimorphs that are making a bee line for your Position, they're too fast for us to cut them off; the storm severely slowed us down, so there's no way were going to make it in time." Bella said, her expression becoming frustrated. "Tell me your back up will arrive to assist you..." her gaze sharpened "and are you sure they'll play ball? I've heard things about them... are they up to the task?"

Garrot nodded "There up to it. Right now, the Murdocks are there number one priority, and they're prepared to do whatever needs doing to extract them. I don't know how they'll will react to Sorin and Zoe when they get here."

Bellatrix scoffed "They'll help them of course! The quasis don't care a lick about who gets in their way! That, and Zoe is a deviant. As much as I hate to say that. She'll immediately be another target, just like the other two kids."

Sorin felt a wave of anger. The feeling causing him to clench his fist. A sudden reminder of what he felt in the aftermath of the supercell, reared its head and caused him to mumble "I doubt that."

Bellatrix turned to him, immediately confused about his comment. The edge in his voice catching her off guard. "Sorin, what's wrong?"

Sorin unclenched Songbird; the eyeless face of the quasi that continued to hunt him down, was now occupying a corner of his mind. The sheer certainty of its pursuit and eventual confrontation causing him to glance up at Bellatrix and Garrot. Sorin opened his mouth, but closed it; how could he explain this?

"Um... Bellatrix, I gotta ask you something," She focused on him, throwing him a questioning look "The quasimorph you're trying to find... did it have an eyeless look to it, and a blueish gem on its forehead."

Sorin continued to give details of the quasimorph to Garrot and Bellatrix, both of their digital holograms flickering inside of the digital space; both their faces looked stunned as he continued to accurately describe the beast in detail, none-more-so than Bellatrix, who looked very uncomfortable at the accurate summation of the monsters profile. After describing the hole that would have been left inside of its torso from the steel rebar which impaled it, did Bellatrix have a look of dawning horror on her face.

"Sorin... how do you know about all of this?" Bella questioned her eyes searching his own.

"Bella... that thing chased me across Whitechapel. It's not after Zoe or the others," he held up Songbird "It's after me."

CHAPTER

48

10/27/2061, Wednesday, 4: 58 pm

Sorin gasped out loud, as he exited cyberspace; his vision swimming as the domino-esc mask glanced around the room. A hand pushed him back against the chair.

"Hold up kid, don't lean to much or your liable to vomit... the first time is truly the roughest." Garrot said, taking off his visor headset and placing it near the laptop. "Just pace yourself, you'll come out of it quickly."

Sorin weakly nodded, before looking at the laptop, unsure if he was reading it right, he looked back at Garrot "It's only 4:58... weren't we in there for about an hour, tops." He questioned.

Garrot shook his head "Cyberspace runs much faster than the outside world. Technically, we've only been under for about five minutes."

Sorin blinked, surprised but quickly accepting the explanation. He looked out the wide windows; the sun was still high in the sky, but pretty soon the light of day would be extinguished, plunging them into further darkness. With the coming arrival of the three quasis.

"Bellatrix said there were three new ones. But, how? When I was being chased... the only one there was the big one." Sorin inquired, his vision finally clearing and his balance finally adjusting outside net space.

"I just wish I could have stayed longer..." Sorin sighed, grasping his temples.

Garrot shook his head "No. Five minutes in cyberspace is the limit. Especially if it's your first dive. But... I understand where you're coming from, you'll see her again in person soon. We just have to survive until help arrives."

Garrot eyed Songbird; the nomad had to admit it, the thing now attached to the boys arm was extraordinary. At his age and inexperience, being able to perceive cyberspace as clearly as he did was outside the norm. Most junior runners have to train extensively in order to get a bearing for net space. 15 to 19 years of age was the sweet spot so to speak for dipping one's toes into the digital waters.

Nevertheless, Garrot was still stunned by the gauntlets capabilities. How on earth was this thing able to neurally interface with his senses to such a degree? But, his digital avatar was proof. His consciousness was 100% being transmitted through the neural network. Watching the boy get up from his seat; Garrot was observing the armor around his upper torso, which, was now covering his other arm, lower back and chest. His eyes, and the bridge of his nose being covered by the life like mask. Strangely, the kids durag was left untouched by the pseudo-metal, the dark silver substance simultaneously moving around him as if it were alive.

The quasis from Whitechapel were abnormal. The other three, as Bellatrix informed them, seemed to be different variants of the larger one. One was faster and was extremely nimble. Another, which was seemingly able to interface with machinery. Something Bella found out the hard way when it almost breached past her I.C.E. And the last one was a walking tank; ripping through normal kinetic rounds and even shrugging off means of demolition; the main quasimorph or the leader, was unlike the other three, very intelligent and far more capable than the others- the ace of the lot, in other words. Something unheard of for the usual quasimorph, but, seeing how the gauntlet used Styx matter to power itself, it's likely the quasi evolved with its temporary possession of it. At least, that was his theory. He also noted Bella's description of how they fled through the desert. How eerily similar to that of a direwolf pack it was. The only notable difference being the lack of fear for a desert supercell.

Very dangerous indeed, he certainly had his work cut out for him. Garrot narrowed his eyes, he would have to address this soon.

Sorin meanwhile was thinking carefully about what Bellatrix told them. The description of the other quasis and of the main ones continued survival. It's determination to seek him out at this point was approaching bewildering levels of absurdity. The fear was still there of course, not as potent as it was in Whitechapel, but still ever present... He just couldn't help the dawning ridiculousness of his situation. Seriously... how couldn't he. When back at home he would go through the exact thing, only nowhere near as life threatening as it was now.

Sorin, to his horror, would have definitely preferred Chase's harassment over what he going through now. *Thing could give Chase a run for his money... it ran through a dang supercell just to reach me...* He thought in complete bafflement.

There was a sound of a door creaking open behind Sorin. He turned around, Mrs. and Mr. Murdock carefully came through the door, with the other three peaking from outside, out of curiosity. Both paused at the scene that greeted them; with Sorin giving them a confused gander, wondering what was up.

"Garrot, if your done with Sorin, could we have a word real quick." Mr. Murdock asked, his expression urgent.

Garrot after a moment nodded; he turned to Sorin, "Listen, will go over more of what happened later. Go on, you should have a talk with your friends, I'm pretty sure they've got a lot to tell you. Especially before things run their course." Garrot said, standing up.

Sorin at first wanted to argue; he really wanted to know when he could reenter cyberspace, but, the serious look that formed on Garrots face told him that something not for his ears was about to be discussed with Jack and Roxy's parents.

With a hesitant sigh, he got up and moved out, past the two parents and through the door leading out of the conference room.

10/27/2061, Wednesday, 5: 18 pm

"Come on Zoe! Its fine! See, perfectly safe." Jack called, as he sat down on the old office sofa near the window.

The sofa, unlike most of the other articles of furniture looked decently stable. Never mind its dirty, dust covered seats, its creaking armrests, and the headrests- which was also showing some spots of ripped upholstery. Its once brownish color now partly suffused in black particles of dust.

"Er... I'm good. You can have that all too yourself; I'll just stay over here." She deadpanned, near the other side of the window. "At least the view is good from up here... Goodness, this place is so old." She whispered.

She stood in front of the window, hands against the cool glass as she took it all in. The old steel mill stretched before them, and out there somewhere beyond the city limits of Hanover. Her dad was on his way, along with Sorins' family. She narrowed her eyes; the thing- or the quasimorph- was likewise on their heels as well. She felt a small shudder. Between her, Jack, Roxy, and Sorin. She still felt wholly unprepared for another confrontation with that thing. She could still remember the intense pain of getting smacked aside like an ant. As self-conscious of her strength (As well as the underestimation of her strength.) she was still struck by how powerful this monster was. It was humbling in the most horrific way possible.

Zoe sighed as she stepped away from the window. A chimera. That's the official name for deviants with her kind of power set. She wrinkled her nose at that, of all the names they could come up with, they chose that.

It could always be worse, I guess... But it sounds so... mean... She thought to herself.

A soft flicker of light grabbed her attention. She glanced askew to her left, and watched as electricity danced along Roxy's forearm, before surging to her hand and jumping from her pointed finger. The thin fork sailed towards a broken piece of wood standing near the opposite wall, which burst into a jumble of pieces; she took her finger and blew the smoke off it, like what those western gunslingers would do with their revolvers. The girl groaned in boredom, her cellphone on the table near her as she leaned against a wall (whose surface wasn't as drab and rotted as the others) her eyes gleaming with blue sparks, as she dismally looked at the burnt remains. Zoe regarded the two Murdock twins. Jack seating himself on the old sofa and seemingly in a world of his own, alongside his older sister. Both, more than likely thinking the same thing as her. Garrots contacts. The people that would be taking them from the wastelands, and simultaneously, from their parents. Zoe didn't really know what to say to that. Jack was still being his usual self, but there were tiny cracks in his carefree façade, after Sorin left he became a bit more quite, not unusually so, but it was noticeable; Roxy was somewhat more unusual, her phone lay on the table, and she wasn't getting on her brother nearly as much as she used too.

Zoe, too her frustration. Found herself likewise torn on the matter. Her father said that for her own safety, it might better for her to leave with the Murdocks. She had enough sense after her shock to ask him why. Instead, he assured her that he would answer her questions when he made it the mill. She grimaced, he also told her he would tell her more about her mom... She hugged herself. Her mom past away when she was just five years old. He- her dad, didn't talk much about her, but he told her enough to give her an idea of what she was like when she was still... here.

Zoe flinched, the door from across the room opened, and Sorin walked in. Jack sat up, a small grin on his face. "Yo! How'd it go?"

Sorin paused for the moment; the complex armor around his upper torso lightly reflecting the lights upon its dark material. She couldn't see his eyes under the red lens, but he seemed lost in thought, his mind in a daze similar to her own when she stepped out of the conference room. He seemed far more distracted- nothing unusual of course for Sorin... Somehow, compared to them he was seemingly in a greater spotlight for the weird.

Sorin was contemplating his experience with Cyberspace.

The endless data branches. The countless stars that were in actuality signals to other devices on the network. It was like a dream come true. Who would have ever guessed a sick kid like him would be able to witness something so cool, and all of it... because of his connection with Songbird. As much as he should have, and he did... He couldn't find it within himself to be nearly as creeped out of the gauntlet, as much as he used to be. At this point, he desperately wanted to keep it. Was it an experimental weapon- maybe. Was it something wholly incomprehensible, and somehow alive in its own right- also maybe. But the things he could do with it... the inner adventurer in him wanted to believe it was possible to keep it for himself. For the first time ever, he was able to explore something that, he'd only been able to imagine, from what Bella or Susan shared with him in their own experiences within the net. Only for their tales to be blown out of the water.

He was so happy. But he was also on edge. He forgot one important thing.

He didn't ask her what was inside of him. No, more like he couldn't. He was just so happy to see her again that he forgot about it completely. Honestly, nothing about that reunion went the way he thought it was going to go.

Yet... after everything he's gone through. He was glad of being able to see cyberspace with his own eyes. He could almost feel the armor around him tighten- nothing uncomfortable- but strangely it felt just as ecstatic.

"Yo! How'd it go?" Jack called on his seat, which Sorin paused, before grinning and taking a seat next to him.

Roxy and Zoe watched (with a small cringe as he sat on the old couch without so much as a moment of hesitation) curious to his sudden change of mood.

"Zoe- Roxy- come here- I gotta tell you guys something cool!" Sorin expressed, and even with the metallic mask covering half his face, you could tell he was highly thrilled; and Roxy noted the expression, it was the same one whenever he was in one of his nerdisms. She rolled her eyes before walking forward, grabbing her phone as she did so. Zoe sighed, already knowing she was going to struggle to understand him- as excited as he was.

Jack was simply wide-eyed at the energy rolling off the guy in his current exhilaration "Whoa, what happened in there to get you so excited? You look like your about to jump outta your armor." he observed, not able to help join in on the guys excitement.

"Guys... I was in cyberspace!" Sorin exclaimed, his grin stretching across his face.

Whatever worries of the future the four had, whether of possibly leaving there parents behind, the questions concerning their origins, or, the looming threat of the coming quasimorphs over the horizon.

For the moment, they were content.

CHAPTER

49

10/27/2061, Wednesday, 5: 50 pm

Garrot's avatar was a specter floating around the digital landscapes of his personal domain. The drones flew about the steel mill. Robotic centuries on high alert, as they hovered above buildings and streets. The cloaking devices were stable, yet, he still felt highly paranoid.

Bellatrix was one of the best ghost runners out there. But if someone of her caliber was nearly hacked into... then, he needed to adjust the security for his drones... just as added precaution. Quasimorphs having the ability to use the implants inside of them- after their transformation- wasn't unheard of per say, but the skill in which it possessed for nearly getting Bell was definitely not in the norm. His avatar floated in a void of darkness; the only source of light being the many screens in front of his lone silhouette, all four drone feeds, including some footage of cameras still able to function around the mill. He didn't have absolute control of the plants subsystem controls, but, he had enough to fortify some key features. The buildings old security features and the I.C.E of the surrounding plant. But the drones, unfortunately, would be his only defense for the other quasis in pursuit. He just hoped it would be enough to stall for time. Hosea's backup, and his partners from the republic. That's ultimately what this will come down too.

Would the quasimorphs be able to sense the three deviants in the building? Are they using Sorins connection with Songbird as a waypoint? Or was it a combination of both? Garret couldn't be sure. He just knew that it was only a matter of time.

10/27/2061, Wednesday, 5: 50 pm

Jack's eyes bulged from the descriptions of Sorins venture into cyberspace, with Zoe and Roxy having similar expressions of shock; it was something he found, personally, to be highly unfathomable. The way he went about explaining it was like he had slipped into another world... and all of it took place in less than five minutes.

Suddenly, his sonar powers didn't seem the coolest thing in the world. Although, he never really considered his powers something beyond ordinary. He was born with them after all. Along with his sister. Now here he was, in a building, in the middle of an abandoned steel mill, along with two other kids that he only just meet a few days ago. And somehow they had become his best buds in that short a time frame. He did have a few friends at school- but he couldn't share what he could do with them, on account of his parents wanting to keep their powers secret; now, in an even shorter spam of time, he's learned that normal people (barring his parents) probably consider deviants worser than outcasts, probably in the same league for their dislike of nomads (no offense to Sorin's lot). The whole thing honestly made his head spin. So, he didn't think about it much. Especially... the quasimorphs. Those he dared not put a needle in for the preservation of his head space.

But... all in all. For the moment, he was just psyched out by what Sorin was spouting. The whole explanation of radio waves, signals, avatar icons, and satellite uplinks... well, those just flew over his head. But, he could at least tell that he enjoyed himself.

"And then he pulls me out." Sorin finally finished.

Jack glanced at Zoe, and Roxy. And found himself unable to contain his laughter at their stupefied expressions. He just patted Sorin on the back (and was suddenly, thankfully, relieved the spiked armor going down his back didn't stab into his hand; which was strangely soft to the touch) "Yeah... that sounds... cool." Jack replied.

"Er... I didn't lose you guys did I?" Sorin asked, suddenly looking very sheepish. Once he realized the looks everyone was giving him.

"Well, I got the parts where you were floating in space. And the parts about the bar... but the satellite stuff, and the code stuff... well... yeah..." Zoe said weakly, scratching the back of her head.

Roxy snorted "Same."

"Oh." Sorin said "But you get the point. It was really, really, cool! And I gotta ask Garrot to let me go back in!"

Jack was shaking his head in fascination; to go from mostly quiet, to this excitable from his surprise expedition. Was so surreal that it was actually kind of funny. To think, he was so nervous about his super gauntlet, now he seems like an almost different person. Man... he'd kill to see what cyberspace loo-

Jack paused in his musing, he felt something, no, heard something strange. The ocean of sound surrounding him suddenly felt off. There was hardly any noise or feedback outside that drawed his attention. Simple stuff really: the groans of rotted wood, the subtle twisting of metal supports around the mill, which where rusting away from disrepair, the howls, chirps, squeals of critters around the very building they were in... He always had a general area around him that was his focal point, a limit so to speak for his hearing. Sometimes he had lapses of course, that's how he located Sorin and Zoe in the first place. But this wasn't like that at all... the sounds of the various critters, the desert wildlife that took shelter in the abandoned plant, they had suddenly and ominously went silent. He looked up and felt immediately on guard.

Everyone was silent. Sorin especially, clutching his head, eyes narrowed; Roxy and Zoe were no better. Roxy was tense, eyes looking towards the window as electricity slowly sparked around her arms, and Zoe looked murderous, her compound eyes scanning outside.

"I guess you guys can feel that too." Sorin said, "There close."

"Is that why the power out there feels so... on the fritz?" Roxy demanded, clicking her tongue in irritation. The surrounding presence of electricity in the air was a subtle comfort to her, yet in just an instant- it felt like something was robbing her of her piece of mind. Like she was feeling thirsty without its presence.

Sorin nodded grimly "Yeah, that's what the big one did when it was chasing me. Made everything freak out."

Jack winced "Never thought the animals would be scared too... heck, I didn't think cazadors or direwolves could get this quiet..." he said.

Legitimately, he was listening for the subtle buzz of Cazador wings, or the pensive growls or low howls of direwolves, but there was nothing, and he found himself genuinely unnerved by the lack of sound, not that he would ever admit it...

Zoe simply remained quiet; her instincts flaring in alarm, the danger, as Sorin said, was getting closer. She had to suppress the mad inclination to growl, to bare fangs at the general direction of the approaching danger to her being. A chimera's warning sense; as Garrot told her, he said he knew of it, but it really wasn't his expertise. That someone else, another deviant like her, would help to explain whatever questions she had concerning them. That is, if she was still breathing at the end of this. No pressure.

There was a sudden sharp sound which caused Jack's hands to slap over his ears. "Dang! Seriously!" Jack hissed. "Everyone, come into the conference room!" Garrot called from the hidden speakers on the ceiling.

Jack could only stare at the other four; all their faces in similar pale tension as his own; and as they hurried quickly towards the room where there parents were waiting. A moment of creeping dread spread over him. It has finally begun.

10/27/2061, Wednesday, 6:29 pm

Sorin was bathed by the red florescent lights of the buildings silent alarm system. The conference room, now periodically bleached in crimson did the opposite in calming him down; he watched as side windows of the room were slowly being draped over by sheets of metal barriers by the old buildings security measures. Long metal slabs covering the wooden panels blocking light into the room. The whole thing kinda reminded him of the looking glass armor which covered the windows of the Voyager.

Sadly they didn't seem to give an outside view. He felt an itch over his right temple, the lens of his hud suddenly popping a notification in front of his eyes.

A holocall!? The thought rocketed through his brain. *I have an actual holocall... but who...*

"Sorin... is that you sitting in the chair? What the heck is that thing on your arm and face!?" Sorin widened his eyes "Susan!" he said, holding his finger to his temple.

This small outburst had a few heads turn to Sorin. Who, in embarrassment said "Sorry... on call."

Garrot simply rolled his eyes "Okay, make it quick... and remember, your inside voice." He replied, much to everyone else's confusion.

"Wait, what?" Jack mouthed. Garrot simply sighed, "He's on a holocall."

Sorin got up and walked away, drowning out the conversation in the background as he stood alone in the far corner of the room away from the table.

"Susan, you still there?" Sorin said.

"Yes!" she answered quickly "And what happened? All we know, is what we learned from Raynor... Even he can't explain why it bounded to you. That thing on your arm hasn't made a peep since it was discovered years ago- other than a few incidents- where being close to it has caused headaches and hallucinations. Raynor said that a few days ago its readings went off the charts, and it was the same day you got kidnapped."

Sorin sighed in annoyance. Yeah, that sounded about right. Almost like all the planets had aliened the day he was forcibly taken from home. The only problem was that Sorin was past the point of believing it to be a coincidence.

"Raynor is Zoe's dad right? So does he know where Songbird came from?" Sorin asked.

"Songbird?" Susan said confused.

"The gauntlet- the armor all over me... I call it Songbird." Sorin explained, cringing at what he just said; not even having to imagine the look of bewilderment on her face.

Songbird, thankfully, piped in- releasing a subdued beat of twitters (Over the holocall no less) causing Susan to go silent over the line. "Yeah... I know, it's weird."

Sorin sighed heavily, as she seemed to sputter over the line. Crap... he'd likely have to go through this with Tom, Jade, Hosea and the rest when they inevitably asked about the gauntlet on his arm.

"Susan, if you're done... I need your help with this security node."
Another voice, Bellatrix's voice said briskly, with a tone of impatience
over the line.

"But... Okay, Sorin... will talk about this later." Susan said, before
cutting the line. Leaving him with the low alarm sounds of the now
bunkerfied conference room.

Sorin closed his eyes behind the lens of his mask. As scared as he
was getting, it was nice to hear her voice again. Whatever chance they
had of outlasting that thing before help arrived, well, Sorin could only
hope for a miracle. The dull needle of pain piercing his temple only
confirmed what he was dreading. Opening his eyes, he moved back to
the others. Garrot was busy talking to Mr. Murdock, with Zoe, Jack,
Roxy and Mrs. Murdock sitting around the table. Sorin took the seat
next to Zoe and Jack.

"It's incredible to me that only now were learning about these things.
If styx matter is really the thing that creates them- then why are they
so fixated on deviants?" Mr. Murdock asked, his brow furrowed in
thought, "All the years I've been a ichorsyte minor, and... it's disturbing
to know how much we don't know about styx matter." He got out with
a shiver.

Garrot sighed under his helmet "That's why it's so rare. Cognicrossis
is the main symptom of styx contamination; so the question that should
be asked, is how it triggers the change in the first place." he typed
commands into his laptop "It's a nasty situation. With there being no
cure for cognicrossis, it's almost a given when a deviant becomes aware
of their powers- or, if a deviant is powerful enough, then it's likely to
attract quasimorphs in the area. Whether their freshly turned or their
drawn from outside the settlement- it always results in a bloodbath." He
stopped typing "Especially if there's more than one deviant in the area."

Jack gulped before laughing nervously "Well, at least were in this
super secure, and airtight room. And the drones- don't forget the
drones-" He rambled, before a casual elbow shut him up, courtesy of
his sister.

"Don't forget us!" she hissed, eyes sparking with electricity "I'd dare
one of those freaks to come near us." She growled.

Mrs. Murdock looked uncomfortable, looking towards her children with complete worry. "Roxy, Jack... if anything happens you need to let Garrot handle it. Don't just throw yourselves into danger needlessly."

While Roxy seemed to get into a small argument with her mom, Sorin thought back on the news feed from Delta city. The ruined highway near the cliff... and all those deviants, along with the many wounded from the supposed scuffle.

Now, he wondered if any quasis, like the ones from Whitechapel had a hand in the carnage. Looking at Jack and Roxy he wondered, grimly, that if Jack hadn't heard his fight with the first quasimorph... then nether of them, including his parents, would be in this situation right now.

"Hey," Zoe said, touching his shoulder "You okay?"

Sorin nodded, quickly banishing the loose thought before it could get worse. "Just wondering how many of them there are out there- aside from the one's here."

Zoe shivered, the red alarm lights highlighting her red hood and jacket. He could just barely tell that she had closed her eyes. Her lips pursed from relative nerves, she could only nod in response. "You think the buildings defenses will hold? I mean, one was bad enough... now there's three more of em." She said, hugging herself.

Sorin gave a half smile "Yeah." maybe it was because of Susan and Bellatrix helping Garrot with his defenses, or maybe because he really wanted there to be a small spot of hope in this horrible situation. But... he couldn't help the answer that came automatically. For a second, Sorin with a small start, realized everyone had gone quite.

Garrots calm expression changed from his seated position, Sorin could see the harsh scowl settling on the veteran nomads lower face. Something was wrong. "Bella, Susan... your seeing this right?" he whispered.

Sorin looked to Zoe, who gave him similar looks of unease. The Murdocks watched, none of them really understanding what was happening on the other end of the coms. But from what Sorin could see, Garrot looked to be in deep concentration. Something must have been happening outside the building, somewhere inside the vicinity of the steel mill. Did they finally engage the four quasimorphs?

The lights of the alarm suddenly cut. Plunging them in the semidarkness of the room. The only lights coming from Garrots visor and his laptop.

"What was that!" Jack got out in a frantic whisper; looking towards Sorin, who couldn't have told him even if he wanted to.

"Don't know... Could be in cyberspace tracking them down." Sorin said unsure, as he gazed at the nomads still form. He didn't like this. He really hoped all three were all right.

I could connect with him... Maybe see what's going on...

He quickly thought against that. With a wince, he immediately knew, felt, he'd only get in the way; but, there had to be something he could do! He balled his fists, just what was going on out there?

10/27/2061, Wednesday, 6:49 pm

The drones screamed through the air. Racing past the ruined buildings on either side, as it tore through the streets. There was a sighting, a small glimpse of movement captured by one of the security cameras still operational. Near the old smelting facilities located at the west side of the mill.

The massive pipelines stretched from between building to building, linked together by miles and miles of industrial girders. An iron backbone which simultaneously acted as the beating heart of the mill. A towering factory that once held the facilities and equipment to smelt, process, and forge steel products of infrastructure and construction—now abandoned. The drones camera locked onto the building, its lenses scanning the environment for movement. The place was dark, with barely any sunlight able to reach past the dense tangle of pipes and steel girders present. Although, whatever light was shining down from the fading sun couldn't reach the drone as it was veiled under a cloaking device. Its form appearing barely visible under the naked eye.

The drone hovered, its medium sized frame floating idle above the canopy of buildings as it looked around from its vantage point. Bella and Susan's avatars where already in route of the security cameras feeds; with a little bit of luck, they could help him flush it out. Then again, they still needed to be on the lookout for the leader, and the quasi capable of accessing the net.

There are only four of them. Yet, from Bella's accounts... These things are highly dangerous, more so than any I've come across before... The gauntlet attached to Sorin– whatever it is... it somehow created this things... just what have we gotten ourselves into? Garrots watched from the drones feed, the expression from his avatars face hardening into a grim continence. *No. Actually. I'd be more inclined to say, what has Carver gotten us into? Him... and his clan...*

Garrot thought about the photos that Bellatrix captured from within the Whitechapel bunkers interior. The bodies, the signs of conflict, and the vault room housing the artifacts old containment unit. He had the means, and the contacts to steal, whatever it was now attached to Sorin's arm. But who in all of the wastelands, or, all of Pangaea for that matter, would go to such lengths to employ the likes of Carver?

Movement. There was a flicker of a shadow, quickly disappearing into the front entrance of the building. All thoughts of Carvers employer was dropped in an instant, a sudden stillness fell upon Garrot, his avatar within the digital domain of his hub focused on the screen. *Just what where this things playing at? It already knows where Sorin and the others are. If it was able to follow them from within a supercell, then by proxy, it wouldn't take them long to figure out their location.*

Garrot scowled, something was off; he lifted his digital arm and widened the video of the screen, Before stepping through the control module, allowing his avatar to interface fully with the drone- activating the hard points within; he switched on the scanner equipment.

If there was any old cameras, or electronics not too far in disrepair, then he should be able to map them out for Bella or Susan to scout ahead, and maybe, search for any possible daemons placed inside as a trap. He didn't know if it was possible for this things to execute tactics like that, but after everything he has heard, he'd rather stay on the side of caution.

"Garrot, you there? I just got done severing any way for this thing to interface with the buildings security systems." Susan said on his coms. "Sorin, Raynor's kid, and that family should be secure for the time being. Anything strange on your side?"

"So far, yes. There was four of them right? If this is one of them, where are the rest?" Garrot said, looking at the building with growing suspicion. "All the drones are still cloaked, but, I'm not sure it'll be enough to take them out."

"It won't." Bellatrix answered on coms. "We dumped all are ammo on the leader of the group; and we barely made it out with our lives." She sighed "and a few of Raynor's men paid the price for our mistake."

Garrot narrowed his eyes, and silently switched the hardpoints off standby. From under the cloaked drone, if it was visible under the naked eye, one would have noticed a small compartment open, followed by the extension of a miniature radar device. The SOCOM unit on the drone will help detect electronic signals; the next hardpoint to come online where the twin mounted guns hidden within the wings of the drone. The drone's ammo box was full of rivet rounds: A special type of caliber rounds made for recognizance units, powerful enough to puncture past kevlar and partway through concreate, but light enough as to not generate intense recoil on the drone itself. The only problem, sadly, would be the disruption of the drones cloak. The cloak wouldn't extend to the muzzle flash or mask the sound of the guns discharge, so... if he decided to confront this thing, he needed to make every shot count. He doubted it would have much trouble in taking this unit offline.

And he only had about three more drones.

"I'm scanning the inside of the building now. There doesn't look to be many access points inside... hold on, I think there's a few on the 2nd and ground floors. Bella, Susan, which of you are going in." Garrot said, watching the data scroll in front of him.

A lot of the access points were faded or non-operational. But there looked to be a few choices within. A few cameras, and some of the old lighting systems inside of the building looked to be somewhat operational. Whatever electrical switches and connectors that were linked across the building, should help the two find the target. Garrot aimed the scanner as it revealed the paths linking whatever junctions or components that lead inside of the old building. And he found himself unsurprised at the level of disrepair. Only a few good paths that could give satisfactory access inside, with each data branch connecting outside to the net being partially faded and or deteriorated.

Garrot sighed, these would have to do.

"Ok, sending you the coordinates. I would advise caution though, the gateways I gave you aren't too stable." Garrot said.

"Understood. The operating chairs that Raynor gave us have emergency desyncs, will be fine if the connection doesn't hold, but will be unable to direct your other drones if something goes wrong." Bella said.

"That's okay, just put the others on standby, I'll have them roam around the building on overwatch."

CHAPTER

50

10/27/2061, Wednesday, 7: 03 pm

Susan's grey icon traveled down the glitching mess that was their gateway, into the buildings subsystems. After a few years of ghost running, she's had leagues of experience going through raggedy pathways in worser conditions.

And as the gateway opened up, she found herself looking out of a... less than savory position. The camera was hanging by a thread. Upside down as the still image of the abandoned blast furnace greeted her. Now a bitter, and semi dark coffin. Its skeleton submerged in darkness; activating the cameras night vision, she saw the many old trollies of steel, the stoves, and cast houses, which revealed themselves to her with nary a spark of heat in their name. She sighed, this wouldn't do.

Taking a moment, she called up the grid paths connecting to this surveillance camera, and made her jump along the power junctions.

Her avatar, now nothing more than a grey comet striking through the electrical network. Struggled to find another outlet within the decrepit and faded gateways. Cyberspace was a plain of radio waves and electrical subsystems in constant communication with each other, didn't matter how faded or how old the data share was- so long as it was active, it would work. The glaring problem of course, were the moments where you encountered an unstable connection. And by god... was it bad here. The whole facility was shut down countless decades ago, and whatever connection it had with the old net was severely fractured. On more than one occasion she nearly found herself getting desynced by the bad path lines. Her body in the real world, cringing from pain of the surprise jolt from her cyberdeck, and the gosh darn feedback loop of encountering a bad gateway was head explodingly painful. The consequence of being so far from their organic bodies.

Her avatar bypassed another faulty gateway. The circuitry connecting this facility was like an endless labyrinth. Shooting forward in a digital surge to find the location of Garrots coordinates. If either of them. Bella or her, find this thing- then maybe they could get the drop in ambushing it from the net. And hopefully by time for Garrots' back-up to arrive.

One well-placed anti cyberdeck daemon to the noggin. Then boom. Or at least, she hoped it would work out like that.

Suddenly, a signal. She paused, her avatar stopping in a nanosecond of time as a message appeared in her line of vision. A network path, and coordinates, Bella... she found it... The basement level of the facility. That's where the network path led her. She transitioned into the power grid of the basement, taking care to scan ahead for any security measures along the way. Susan braced herself, the signal and coordinates pointing her to one final gateway. And with a flash, her vision was filled with a gruesome sight.

The quasimorph. The burnt remains of a ghost runner, the same one from the bunker of Whitechapel. Now a heavily mutated abomination. Its body was gaunt, nothing but burnt skin and bone, animated by the styx matter now flowing through its emulated remains. The plug suit which adorned its body was in tatters, with the operating chairs neural link cables trailing on the floor behind it. Its skull seeing sightlessly across the hall; Susan shuddered, how on earth could it even see without eyes?

There was sudden motion above. Cameras moving, but it wasn't her, or Bellatrix controlling them. So that's how... there was a surge of power around the thing. The fluorescent lights above flickering on and off.

It's using the net around it to see... Gotta be careful, last thing I need is to become a vegetable back at the Voyager. Susan thought grimly.

"You ready. Will only have one shot." Bellatrix said on coms, the transmission heavily encrypted.

Susan hardened herself. Bringing up every automated daemon online, every single program of defense to protect her avatar. The small icons in the corner of her vision switched on and she brought up her command prompt. Her cyber index was live, and she jumped position. Traveling ahead of where this thing was going.

The creatures unsteady steps took it into a large room. Circuitry lined the walls, electrical junctions on every corner, cameras and old sensors on the outside and inside corners of the space. In the center of the room, a chair and table with a large monitor on its cobwebbed and dust riddled surface. And behind it... cables, upon cables, and more junction boxes behind it. This had to be the main electrical room for the main facility. Susan paused in her pursuit, and unknowingly Bellatrix did too, this was a nexus of activity for the net in this area surrounding the steel mill. What on earth was it doing here!? They both moved quickly. Susan activating her defensive measures, and Bellatrix, activating her offensive measures. They both found sights on the creature, using the security cameras in the room.

Susan's avatar flinched, almost instantly, the exact moment she entered the camera, a massive discharge of energy crashed into the firewall surrounding her digital silhouette. A large sphere, a digital shape of hard light and code came charging from outside the gateway. Counter I.C.E program. But her firewall intercepted the hostile code script, and Bellatrix was quick on the counter hack. The shape exploded into a thousand pieces of code and light bricks.

Bellatrix's avatar appeared next to her, silently and briefly looking her up and down, making sure her digital avatar was secure; Susan nodded to her, and they both continued on.

The creature suddenly, and with a swiftness that made them both extremely unnerved- shot its fist forward- the computer crumpled under its strength- contrary to its thin and haggard appearance- its arm now elbow deep within its electrical components from inside the screen. They both watched as it ripped a bundle of cables attached to the ends of the console. And with a jerkish movement, the cables still attached to its suit ejected off. Quickly, it began inserting each cable from the monitor into the slots of its plug suit. What was it doing? Was it trying to access the mills mainframe? That many junction cables going through its interface nodes would make it easier to swarm it with daemons, but what was it really after? Susan and Bellatrix activated their command prompts holding their hand forward from the inside of the camera; as much as Bellatrix questioned its actions, this was the perfect time to obliterate its defenses, they sent out their daemons immediately, each program meant to destroy whatever I.C.E was between them and the abomination in the room.

There was a sudden red flash; Bellatrix and Susan paused in shock, the electrical arcs of red lighting streaking wildly around the room, casting the place in red hues and causing shadows to jump across the stretch of the hall behind it. The quasimorph was inexplicably generating an intense level of power, but how? And where was this coming from!? The daemons rushed from out of the camera, and traveled like a swarm through the cables and junction switches, before finally infiltrating the cables running into its plug suit. The interface nozzles around the suit began to radiate an orange glow; Susan couldn't be sure if it was the crimson energy pulsing from it, or, the power from the grid now running through its suit. But as the daemons scanned and drilled for whatever vulnerabilities through its I.C.E, she began to feel uneasy.

The pulsing red of the lighting looked disturbingly familiar... She froze, wait a minute... of course it looked familiar... this was...

She thought back a few days ago. When the quasis ran through their concentrated fire and broke out of Raynor's flank. The quasi in the room, it couldn't run, but the leader, its massive frame- carried it into the jaws of the rushing supercell. She still couldn't believe what she had seen, when the concentrated columns of red crashed into the group of quasis in pursuit of their goal. Bellatrix's digital hand landed on her shoulder, there was a look on her face that Susan only rarely has seen. The panic now coloring her face, froze her solid. "It's trying to overload the network!" She shouted in alarm "We gotta take it out now!" Bellatrix's avatar shot off into the power grid, and Susan immediately typed commands, understanding what the veteran runner was about to do. Bella recalled her daemons and immediately pulled up her I.C.E. She had to penetrate this things defenses. Susan transmitted the vulnerability in its security and Bella immediately took advantage of the intel. Her avatar crashed into the I.C.E wall, her subroutines keeping whatever hostile security measures from destroying her software integrity. Her connection with her real body. That's what the subroutines were for, not just protecting her physical body, but the cyberdeck within her head; if one goes, the other would soon follow suit.

She touched the I.C.E wall and called upon her command prompt, it was time to brute force an opening. Susan watched from inside the lens of the camera and was meet with a disturbing sight. The quasimorph was staring directly at her. Its burnt eyeless skull looking her square in the eyes from its position, the halo of energy arching from its body creating a horrible sight. Bellatrix sneered in frustration; the code script in front of her was probably the most complex thing she'd written yet; but this wouldn't be enough. Once she launched this, it would be a gamble if it could take this thing out. She shot her lethal counter hack into the hole of its security and dashed out of there. Just as her subroutines were nearly at their limit.

Like a shooting star, she traveled back through the network of cables and switches back to Susan's location. Susan turned her head, only to be greeted by Bellatrix's flickering icon, the visible band of protection of her programs creating a small light show around her.

There was a sudden sound which drew Susan's attention back outside the camera view. The right side quasimorphs head- to her disgust- was blown open. The black mist of inactive styx matter evaporated into the air as the red electricity raging from its body continued without measure. Bellatrix cursed, the program she sent fried its cyberdeck... but the thing was still standing. Susan recoiled back, and Bellatrix couldn't stop herself from flinching as an unearthly howl exploded from the things mouth. Electric volts ripped across the room, screams of electric discharges singed and caused sparks to rain everywhere. Susan suddenly felt faint, and Bellatrix's avatar began to glitch; she widened her eyes as her digital construct began to become unstable.

"WHAT IS THAT THING DOING!?" Susan yelled, her holographic avatar also glitching.

"I told you. It's trying to force the net into a blackout state, by overloading the network and electric grid." She growled out "It's trying to isolate Garrot's group to the building."

Susan widened her eyes, but before she could say anything, the net around them began to glitch and distort. There small domain from within the camera sputtered and seized, only for a red pillar of energy to strike the camera. Destroying it. and throwing them back into the main grid, which was as unstable as the camera.

The long network path before them began to fully distort and break apart. Susan could barely concentrate, let alone move as her avatar seemingly began to fall apart, the binary code linking her icon was slowly becoming undone. Bellatrix was no better, her avatar also becoming paralyzed by the swift dyssynchronization and just as abruptly, there was an error message, following the brightest light searing her cone of vision, before everything went dark. Susan seized and shook, opening her eyes, she was back inside the voyager. At the very back of the armored motorhome as Tom drove them towards the steel mill. Hosea at her side, as Jade and Raynor were already helping Bellatrix up.

"Damn thing!" Bellatrix cursed "It desynced us. Any news from Garrot?" she demanded.

"He already messaged us. He made it out of cyberspace safely, and has the drones still on standby. But what about the Quasimorph- is it dead?" Raynor asked back. His face hardened, and tired.

Susan stood up with the help of Tom "Don't know. It could be, I saw Bellatrix's hack blow the side of its head." Susan replied tiredly. "So maybe."

"Oh, it's dead. Just not by my own hands. You all should have seen it, I don't know how... but I think it absorbed the power from the supercell, and used it to overload both the net, and the electrical grid at the mill." Bellatrix said while leaning against Jade, who was looking pale at the state of Bellatrix.

"How long do we got until we reach the mill? Will it be in time to help Garrot?" Jade asked.

"Where fifty minutes off. Until then, it's up to Garrot to hold the line, and for his back up to arrive on time." Hosea said grimly.

10/27/2061, Wednesday, 7: 18 pm

The rooms emergency lights abruptly shut off, plunging them all in the semi- darkness of a barely lit conference room. Sorin could only watch as Garrot immediately took off the helmet, and set it down next to the still working laptop on the table. Its illumination the only thing keeping the darkness at bay.

You could practically hear a pin drop, the silence that fell after the lights and alarms went out was almost stifling. Zoe was frozen in her seat. Looking around the dark room, feeling uneasy as the veteran nomad slid out of his chair and moved to the other end of the room. He retrieved a large duffle bag from the ground, he quickly unzipped it, and brought something out; Sorin could barely make it out, but from what he could see, it looked like a gun of some sort. Suddenly there was a bright glare of light from the other end of the table. Sorin, cringing from the brightness, glanced over while holding a gauntlet clad hand to block some of the light.

Roxy held her hand up, an intense discharge of electricity traveling from up her arm to her hand. An impromptu light source. Mr. Murdock held Mrs. Murdock as her eyes widened at the gun in Garrots hands. Sorin's eyes bulged from under his mask, as Zoe and the Murdock twins stared at the device.

The rifle in his hands could best be described as experimental. The wires, tubes and apertures of the device seemed connected to its muzzle. The barrel looked like a hodgepodge of both high and low-tech instruments, attached and wielded onto a metal stock. Sorin paused, observing how the wires attached to the muzzle where connected to a... was that a beam emitter!? Sorin flabbergasted, remembered the time when Church showed him the small medical laser they had when traveling in the wasteland. A tool they used to originally operate on Susan's prosthetic arm.

"Garrot... What is that your carrying?" Mrs. Murdock asked dubiously. "Insurance." Garrot said simply.

He moved back over to the laptop and leaned the gun against the table as he typed away. Sorin eyed the thing; the many conversations he eavesdropped on between Jade and Tom, about some of the high-tech weaponry from the further corners of the conclaves and republic. Became very prominent at that exact moment.

"I-is that supposed to be a laser rifle?" Sorin asked unsurely.

Garrot locked a cursory glance at him, before focusing back on the screen "You could say that."

Sorin felt something poke his shoulder, sparing a look, it was Jack giving him a look of disbelief as he mouthed the word "Laser what!?" silently.

"What's going on out there? Is it those things?" Roxy questioned, looking tense. The electricity buzzing softly across her arms.

Zoe was silently standing up, her claws out, and a barely perceivable growl was coming from beneath her hoody; Sorin wasn't even sure when she had gotten out of her chair. The interface from his mask didn't reveal much information on what was going on, but, it did inform him on one tidbit of info. In a small data scroll, or notification- Two sentences...

>Cyberspace/Network signal missing: Gateway Proxy cutoff/severed<

But the last sentence of the notification is what really caught his attention.

>Quasimorph presence detected: Caution Advised<

Sorin felt the gooseflesh across his spine. The cold feeling of fear touched him in the form of a pinprick. He could sense its presence, the one true abomination of the litter was on the move. And was getting closer and closer.

Sorin stood up, there was an abrupt jolt of activity through the connection, causing him to stand; the chair falling backwards from how fast he stood up. Everyone's head turned to the sound of the chair falling, unlike Garrot, who noticed Sorin's sudden movement.

"Sorin! What the heck! Dude... you good!?" Jack exclaimed, startled by the sound.

"Hey... what's with that look?"

"Dear? What's the matter?"

"Sorin?"

His world began to lose detail, a fixation so absolute that everyone's attempt to get his attention failed miserably.

Time seemed to stand still, and all the while a feeling of intense dread began to shroud over him. Like something disastrous was about to happen. But what was it? What was this precognition warning him about? And why was it so strong...

He felt something, an almost magnetic pull forcibly turning his full attention to his immediate right. Towards the barrier shielding the window. Below the building, somehow, he could sense it... like his consciousness was being hurled into cyberspace again... but it wasn't that, no... it was the tether. It was showing him something. Pulling his mind's eye towards the danger, and like a light through the darkness he could see it...

The monster from Whitechapel. Its eyeless gaze glaring directly at him, the single glowing radiance of the indigo gem, protruding from its forehead; but what drew Sorin's attention and clear horror- was the swirling mass of dark energy gathering outside, over its wide-open mouth.

Zoe's hand reached for his shoulder, just as Garrot was seconds away from telling her to wait; Sorin suddenly snapped-

"EVERYONE GET DOW-"

Instantly, the whole party was overwhelmed by a massive explosion. Sorin's voice overshadowed by the sound of the windows outer barriers getting obliterated by the single volley of dark matter. Its spherical shape, crashing through the barriers like a giants fist. There was a small shockwave, followed by the bulge and separation of debris from the now ruined, right side portion of the building. The Murdocks, Zoe, Garrot, and Sorin were flown backwards by the impact. Away from the windows and towards the other side of the conference room, as the long table was flipped over by the velocity of the dark missile tearing through the air. The laptop and helmet belonging to Garrot getting flung across the room, with the laser rifle getting thrown into the air behind Garrot; Sorin landed in a heap, followed by Zoe, Jack, and Roxy. As his head spun, the tether connecting him to the beast was suddenly picking up a signal.

The all too familiar and loathed feeling of triumph.

CHAPTER

51

10/27/2061, Wednesday, 7: 39pm

Garrot coughed, spluttering in indignation as he pulled himself up. The smoke cloud surrounding them from whatever that was, was still in the air; but as he looked around, his immediate concern was completely shifted when he saw the damage of that one single attack.

The whole line of shutter barricades that once shielded the inside of the room where completely demolished. An ugly act of laceration that peeled the safety barricades, windows, and walls off the building as if it were an onion. The conference room was now open to the outside elements some six stories above the ground floor as pieces of debris still hung, attached by threads of scaffolding or rebar, while other fragments of the buildings simply fell down to the ground below. Fuses that once where inside of the walls sparked and popped, periodically lighting the horrible scene before him. Against the ebbing dusk over the horizon, this was quickly becoming a nightmarish scenario.

What on earth had it launched earlier to do such severe damage- to a *building* no less?

Sorin grabbed his head with one arm as he struggled to pull himself up. Zoe was already on her feet, but the fear on her face was mirroring partly how he felt at the moment. He gritted his teeth, the headache he was feeling, the soreness of his back from his resent landing, and the ringing of his ears from the sound of those barriers, no, the entire wall being erased by this things shot... he could actually understand how scared she was at the moment. But, strangely enough, he wasn't really feeling the worst of the demoralization of this gruesome discovery. No, instead, at this point, he just felt a complete exasperation of the fact instead.

Through the link he could comprehend how proud it was of this devastating power. And through it, he was becoming absolutely tired of this freaking thing.

Jack groaned, not at all prepared for the surprise cannonball which destroyed the entire right side of the room. The table was completely flipped over and the remains of Garrots laptop was lying pathetically across from him near the wall.

"Jack! Roxanne!" Mrs. Murdock cried out, her voice terrified.

Jack immediately felt someone pulling him to his feet. Sorin forced the pain of his headache down, as he helped Jack up, to his gratitude. As Zoe moved to check the closest person to her, which, ended up being Roxy. Mrs. Murdock wasn't far as she rushed to check both her children. Mr. Murdock seeing that his kids were mostly alright, dusted himself off and was about to move to see how Garrot was doing. Then halted on the spot. His eyes bulging, turning around, only to be greeted by the colossal gash that ran across what used to be the right side of the room.

"Christ... what on earth could have-" he started.

"Rob, we have to leave." Garrot's voice suddenly sounded next to him, quickly snapping him out of his shock.

"I... Okay, let's g-" Mr. Murdock wasn't able to finish his sentence.

A massive, horrible lurch from the floor he stood on caused him to widen his eyes in alarm, something was generating a rapid series of quakes. Like something was rattling the very ground they stood on. Sorin turned and his eyes- as well as the masks eyes- widened in panic. Across the link he could sense it, not just sense it, feel it. It was climbing up the building, and as Garrot rushed to gather his gun, the worst scenario happened. Sorin rushed forward past Zoe, the armor over him responding on instinct as tendrils of silver extended, three, four, Sorin wasn't counting. Just acting. Wither out of fear or panic he couldn't quite tell. All he knew was that a feeling of something through the link made him feel absolutely ill, a feeling of concentrated bloodlust, aimed for the two closest to the edge. A moment later, which felt like an eternity. The Beasts massive frame launched itself up and over the ledge;

Mr. Murdock and Garrot couldn't have done anything at all where they stood, as the beast crashed down in front of them. Its eyeless stare glaring past the both of them to its real target. Garrot fired the gun in his hand. The rifle let out a loud HISSS as the beam emitter pulsed with red light, shooting a condensed beam of energy from the guns muzzle.

Like a thick red javelin, the concentrated beam of light crashed into the side of the things head. Burning a brutal wound to its side as black mist shot out from the hole left behind. To everyone's horror, it didn't much react to it, nor did it give any hint that it was bothered by the wound, and quicker than they could react the beast was suddenly in motion.

Its massive hand winded up to pulverize them from overhead. Sorin's heart hammered into his chest, everything slowed down, as his perception seemed to heighten. He could feel the live styx matter coursing through his body, simultaneously, the armor lengthened, forcing Songbirds metallic chains to lash out by his mental command. Garrot and Mr. Murdock both cried out in alarm as two ropes of silver wrapped around them and pulled them both off their feet. The clawed, car door sized palm, swiped open air. Leaving a visceral backwind from its arc. He moved them, just in the nick of time, but there was yet another problem.

Sorin widened his eyes as they both sailed behind him, not expecting ether lines to pull that hard. But that wasn't exactly the crux of the issue. As the two roughly landed behind Sorin a few feet back. Suddenly, in an instant, Sorin found himself right in front of the monsters range- in arm's length of it.

The creature didn't hesitate in the slightest.

The hand shot out, its full length grabbing Sorin's entire torso. The pressure excruciating, head exploding in pain, as the air was squeezed from his lungs. From beyond the ringing of his ears and the throbbing headache of the connection going haywire. He could hear three- four- voices calling his name. Followed by panicked shouts. His field of vision was clouded, as something glaringly blue zapped the thing in its arm, followed by a funnel of compressed air to the face.

"LET GO OF HIM!" a loud roar behind him, as something sliced into the things other arm as it blocked two, three, slashes in succession.

Suddenly, there was a pained gasp; Sorin opened his eyes, and saw Zoe flying back into the wall next to Mrs. Murdock who scrambled to check if she was okay. Zoe was struggling to get back to her feet.

The monster crushing him roared in defiance. The bellow overshadowing everyone as they were forced to cover their ears. But, what it should have been doing was paying attention to the youth in his enclosed fist.

The rage boiled over inside of his heart. Barely able to concentrate, Sorin used every bit of his remaining nerve to give Songbird a command. A command of surreal retaliation. Which, Songbird replied by the sharpening of its armor. The once soft edges of the armor that were once safe to the touch by Jack's admission, grew dangerously serrated and jagged. Sorin's now sharpened talons for fingers dug into the hide of the fist holding him, as the tendrils adorning out of his back and sides turned hostile. They shot out, like brittle javelins, spearing into the sneering abominations face and lower neck. Catching it completely off guard for the first time. So swift was the blow that it tumbled over; Sorin still in hand, was forced to follow suit as the beast fell over the edge- bringing Sorin along with it. The trail of black vaper fumed from its various skewer marks, as the two fell down the buildings length.

Sorin could barely make out the shrill cries of his name, the high winds screaming, muffling the echo in the night air, as he struggled to figure a way out of this. As the winds howled in his ears, he spotted something rushing upward. A slim shape, almost as big as the creature holding him, but fast- it must have been the other quasi that's been traveling alongside the others. He could just make out the torn shreds of nomadic travel gear, but its mutation made it look snug on its muscular physique. Suddenly the beasts other arm lanced out, ripping into the brickwork of the building stopping its fall as it swung into the building, causing spider cracks to form on impact. Sorin could feel his lunch ripple in his stomach as he was still gripped by its fist. His gauntlet covered hands, now sharpened to talons gripped the metallic hide of its hand, bracing himself from the constant motion.

All this must have happened in two to three seconds- simultaneously, something was happening with the javelins penetrating through the creatures face. The interface seemed to glitch, sputter, as more text started to appear on screen.

>Missing Core found: Commencing Reclamation<

Tendrils exploded from behind his back, curving in air and skewering into his captors face. Sorin cried out, horrified, but strangely satisfied by whatever Songbird was doing. The monster roared, the bellow of rage causing him to let go of its wrist and slap over his ears. Suddenly, there was a pulse of energy. A feeling, no, a surge of power which caught Sorin off guard. The gauntlets gem blazed red, and light seemed to radiate from between the plates of his armor as the tendrils piercing the things face seemed to glow the same light. Sorin's eyes widened as the eyeless face of the thing began to ripple. The top layer of its smooth surface began to seemingly melt, the now liquid silver, poured off its head and dissipated in the air in a cloud of dark smog.

Sorin's was watching with batted breath; there was another face, someone that he immediately recognized. The guy that kidnapped him in the first place. Carver... his face and eyes were the same as the nomad from the bunker: horribly pale complexion, face riddled by spider webs of black lines, and his eyes- the blackest abyss in each one- starring hatefully into his own.

But the indigo gem, the last core Songbird apparently needed, was lodged into his forehead, which looked to be the source of the black veins. And the tendrils extending from his back was wrapped around said gem.

"The.... Gatekeeper... It.... Belongs to me..."

His voice, a gravely, harsh tone, was warped. A corruptive echo that seemed robbed of its usual presence. Sorin then, at that moment, became woefully disturbed. In the same breath another barrage of tendrils shot out from Sorin's shoulder stabbing into Carvers chest. Carvers face became enraged, a venomous expression settling over him as he cried out in pain.

Abruptly, his other arm blurred upward, clawed talons shredding through the tendrils in one swift motion. Sorin was suddenly screaming in alarm, as the hand holding him exploded forward in an arc.

Sorin found himself now flying through the air, turned into a literal projectile as the ex-nomad flung him away with all his strength. His vision blurred, arms reaching for something, anything, to grab onto in a blind panic. He was going to die! He was going to die if he didn't do something soon! His backpack! He still had his backpack, so that meant...

Sorin with barely any thought, sept survival, reached for his bag. The world was almost moving to a crawl, and his motion from the freefall was slowly ebbing, and as he caught sight of his falling reflection from the window. He finally caught the zipper of his backpack, he unzipped it in one swift motion.

"SONGBIRD! QUICK- THE HOVERBOARD!" Sorin screamed.

His vison slowing down as he found himself now approaching the hard ground at the bottom of the building. Only four stories to go. The board suddenly roared to life, extending and shooting out of his bag with a horrible SHRIPP! of fabric. The board was now free, and Sorin immediately grabbed it- moved it under him and with a blast of energy, the board was fighting his downward descent. His velocity altered, both hands gripping both sides of the platform as it shot forward, and incoherent curse flew from the boys lips as he swerved aside a massive steel girder in his way.

With a crash and a loud THOOM of energy dispersing from the impact, the board, and Sorin. Were finally, safely, on solid ground.

Sorin shivered, his belly still on top of the board as he couldn't believe, that once again, he had avoided oncoming death. Looking around, he realized he was now at the back of the building.

There was a crash behind him. Sorin jumped up to his feet on the platform and immediately kicked off, not even daring to look back.

Once again, riding for his very life.

10/27/2061, Wednesday, 7: 58pm

Garrot rolled as the quasimorph swiped for his face.

The veteran nomad could only grimace at the things appearance. The live styx matter animating his body and limbs have dramatically mutated him. Arms and legs longer than what could be deemed natural, an animalistic coat of fur and scales covering what use to be his skin from under the singed rags it was wearing. And its face... eyes of coal that where sunken into its sockets, mouth chockfull of razor-sharp teeth.

And it was incredibly strong and fast for its size. Nowhere near as big as the thing that took Sorin. But it was definitely quicker. The cuts and bruises he collected in the short time was testament to this. Zoe, and the Murdocks, where of course, the reason for why he wasn't worse off.

Zoe was like a mini hurricane of carnage. The first person the thing went after was Mrs. Murdock, who was closest to the edge after Sorin was pulled over. When out of nowhere the quasi appeared, pulling itself up from the far corner of the destroyed section of the room. If not for Zoe's intervention, Mrs. Murdock would have likely been dead. A massive, clawed hand gouging were she had been just a moment before. Zoe with incredible strength and agility, moved the woman back, as Jack and Roxanne in total fury over the attack to their mother went berserk with their powers.

Robert was quick to pull Meryle back to safety, while Zoe, in a ferocious trance, attacked the thing furiously with claws and pincers combined. Jumping past the two espers, and engaging directly with the freak. It was definitely a sight to see... but how long would it last?

Zoe dodged, leaped away, dived under, and vaulted over the monstrosities furious swings. All the while, she swiped, gouged and punched with her immense strength and speed. But from Garrots perspective, as he made pot shots with his laser rifle. Zoe's attacks, and by extension, his, and the other kids powers didn't seem to be doing all that much damage.

On the account that they couldn't hit it consistently.

Roxy with her powers would send massive surges of electricity at the things position- at first, she was doing an excellent job of punishing the things aggressiveness in pursuing Zoe, only for Roxy to come in and relieve said pressure. Jack sent massive shockwaves towards the creature whenever it tried to go directly for his sister, only for Zoe and Garrot to quickly come in and get its attention. All was going well at first. Now, it looked like the thing was adapting to their improvised strategy.

Zoe moved, barely able to jump out of the way in time. The mutant was in a frenzy, and no matter how many times Zoe slashed with her pincers, no matter how many times Roxy or Jack blasted it with electricity and soundwaves. Or the amount of shots Garrot fired, the thing continued forwards, relentless in its pursuit. The group was forced back into the building. Mr. and Mrs. Murdock, despite their protests, were led back inside by Garrot as Zoe- now sporting a multitude of cuts and bruises over her now torn clothes and jacket. Was slowly losing her zeal, along with Roxy and Jack who were also not doing any better.

Jack cried out in pain as the monsters closed fist nearly punched a hole through his chest. The sound wave barrier he hastily brought up saving his life- but sending him flying back from the force. He crashed back into the room, bruised and groaning in pain.

Roxy seeing the hit on her brother, lost her mind in a fury. The night outside of the office building exploded in pale blue light. The electric storm the teenager released floored the quasi as it was forced to shield itself from the maelstrom of plasma. Zoe could only shield her eyes from other corner of the room, safe from the deluge, but was able to feel the intense heat, the taste of copper invading her tongue.

The ex-nomad could only screech in agitation. Its torn clothing igniting from the volts of energy serenading its entire body, its skin, burning and dissipating in clouds of black smog, and its eyes, furious, enraged, seething, stared beadily at Roxanne's furious expression.

Roxy gritted her teeth, the electricity over her body slowly ebbing away. She was losing her charge! Her eyes scanned the room, looking for any devices still on, anything she could use to recharge her powers. But there was nothing. Nothing that could help her keep this up...

Zoe unshielded her face, eyes widening at Roxy's panicked look. Sure enough, her knees hit the floor and with an exhausted gasp. The surge was gone, the electricity was gone, and the now immolated abomination gave a horrible sneer- it lunged forwards, ready to rip the dark-haired teen into pieces. Suddenly with all the speed she could muster Zoe launched herself between the creature and Roxy; the quasi evaded the three sharpened pincers, and with inhuman precision swiped away at Zoe's face- causing her to go flying over Roxy's stunned form, past the doorway and inside the next room.

The girl crashed into the table next to Mrs. Murdock, to her absolute horror.

Zoe in absolute pain, groaned pitifully, her head spinning from the blow she received.

The quasi reeled back ready to smash the girl before it. Only for a massive shockwave to ram directly into it- sending the creature flying back. Roxy could only yelp as Mr. Murdock picked her up and, in one smooth motion, carried her through the doorway as Jack limped behind, followed by Garrot as he signaled for the panic shutters behind them. A large steel plate which fell from the slit above the doorway. Sealing the conference room.

BANG! Everyone flinched back, BANG! BANG! BANG!

Massive indents of the quasis fist hammered into the iron bullwork. Smashing a curve into the supposed impenetrable surface. Garrot narrowed his eye, looking back and scanning the room and its inhabitants. He came to a grim conclusion. The back up, his ace in the hole, would be there only salvation from this thing.

Looking back, everyone was a mess. Zoe, Roxy, and Jack were all being tended to by Mrs. Murdock, who was using the last of the supplies to patch them up. Garrot gave one look at each of their expression's, and he didn't like what he'd saw.

All of them looked to be demoralized. Roxy and Jack were both quiet, shellshock by the looks of it. Both of them had nearly died out there, and Zoe, she looked to be on the verge of tears. And it wasn't hard for Garrot to see why. At this point, he was struggling to find an actual light in the preverbal tunnel. Especially after what happened with Sorin. God, he couldn't believe what happened. In all his years as a nomad, he'd never come across something as dangerous as the quasimorph that had shot that energy blast at the building.

How was he going to break it to Bella and Hosea, if they did make it out of this?

Suddenly, his eyes shimmered. His interface notifying him of an incoming holocall- there was no number, no caller id; he narrowed his eyes, wondering what on earth could be happening now.

"Garrot! I need help! Carver is chasing me across the mill! Is there anything I can do to stop him!?" Garrot eyes widened, suddenly, the light was looking brighter than it did just mere moments ago.

Mr. Murdock steeped closer to Garrot, and stopped when he saw the look on his face. "Garrot, what's wrong, is it the backup- are they finally here!?"

Everyone's attention shifted to the old nomad, Mrs. Murdock paused on her bandage across Zoe's arm, Jack and Roxy both looked up with a morose expression. While Zoe didn't even seem to hear anything, her head bowed and lips trembling.

"It's Sorin, he's alive!" Garrot replied back, clear relief in his voice.

This seemed to wake up the two Murdock siblings, and for the first time, Zoe looked up, compound eyes wide and attentive.

CHAPTER

52

10/27/2061, Wednesday, 8: 12 pm

The last vestiges of sunlight was gone, plunging the steel mill into solid pitch blackness. The steel girders, industrial pipes, and blast mills now drab silhouettes across the abandoned expanse.

The darkness, only pushed back by the cerulean pulse of the hoverboards bottom vents; Sorin darted through the forsaken streets of the mill, not entirely sure where he was, or where he was going, all he knew was that he couldn't let Carver catch him.

He swerved left, avoiding the mass of dark energy which cleaved the old stop sign ahead of him. Its metallic makeup, seemingly erased by the black ball of death. The sign crashed down, right as Sorin sped past, his speed increasing by the second. Sorin could feel his heart hammering within his chest as he flew past the empty roads; one hit, one scratch, and he shuddered to think what that dark projectiles would do to him on contact.

It's the gem... It all comes down to Songbird... the red gem makes the armor appear... and the green signals cyberdeck use... but what the heck does the purple one even do?

Sorin focused his thoughts to Songbird, desperate for a plan and a way out of this. Garrot! He could call him, see if there was anything at all that he could do to get rid of Carver.

The interface shifted, and Songbird immediately began the dial up. There was a ringing in his ears as he swerved yet again to avoid another volley of dark energy from Carver, which tore a straight gash through the lower side of a building. Sorin focused, dodging more blasts and swerving from street to street, his path illuminated by the engine of his hoverboard. His heart beating a hole into his chest as the call finally went through.

"GARROT!" Sorin screamed through the wind and sounds of impact, as the road, streetlamps, sides of buildings got obliterated by the blasts from Carver. "I NEED HELP! CARVERS CHASING ME ACROSS THE MILL-" an explosion next to him, he was forced to cover his face as debris flew from the window and wall of a small building; he turned a hard right, barely evading another blast which sailed over his head; forcing himself to look forwards, instinctly pulling back left as he nearly hit another sign from lack of sight. "IS THERE ANYTHING I CAN DO TO STOP HIM!?" he screamed.

The road was a blur. Streetlamps, buildings, signs, and barricades flew by him in swift illumination, before once again being swallowed by darkness. All the while, Carver wasn't letting up.

"Sorin! Listen to me... the drones, the drones should still be operational! Lead Carver to the drones!" Garrots voice ordered over the line. "How do I find them!?" Sorin demanded.

"Here, this should lead you to them. I don't know if it'll work, but you have to keep him busy. Help will arrive soon, and you better keep yourself alive till then, you hear me."

Sorin numbly nodded "Y-yes."

He gunned the engines forward. Just as a marker appeared on his heads-up display, the arrow pointing him, where he needed to go. The red lens of the mask pressed against his face, the wind buffeting and screaming past him as he knifed through the roads towards his destination. 50mph, 70mph, his speed evening out to a solid 85mph. simultaneously, bobbing and weaving the volleys of shoots from Carver's maw. Quickly, he left the center of the steel mill behind. His waypoint taking him to the expansive industrial sector, ruled by massive steel warehouses and even bigger steel production plants. A large open space with plenty of loose machinery strewn about. Sorin couldn't have even guessed what all this equipment did. Blasting through the gravel paths at nearly 85mph would do that, especially out in the darkness of night, with barely a lick of illumination barring the bright glare from his hoverboard.

Sorin felt his nerves fraying from the constant pressure. His survival a constant tight rope of tension and danger, every shot from Carver tuning the string to its breaking point. At this moment he didn't have any buildings or large objects to veer between to throw off his aim, it was only a matter of time. Sorin looked back, Carvers distance was nearly that of two light poles, a far cry from how fast he was during Whitechapel. But the hair-raising danger of those energy shots! It more than made up for it!

Sorin veered, and ducked, throwing his weight onto the board to force it around one of the larger piles of steel rebar. Jumping over a few piles of discarded equipment, too old to really identify what they were. Forcing himself to remain focused, to remain concentrated on the goal at hand. Survive, survive, keep moving, keep living.

Suddenly, there was a crash in the darkness. It wasn't Carver, he was still in the far back... but why has he stopped firing?

There was abrupt tightening across the armor, a warning screech from Songbird, the gauntlet burning red. Sorin's eyes widened, there was a sound not coming from Carver's direction, which was behind him. But from the front...

A massive silhouette, an ear-splitting roar, human but not, the crashes of heavy foot falls so strong he could feel from on top his board. Sorin could only yelp as he was forced to slide, the massive bulk of something just as big or maybe bigger than Carver's armored hide. From the light, something mechanical, was it a man? No, a quasimorph.... but... Sorin felt a shiver, as time slowed down in recognition- the large nomad with the mechanical arms... he's been transformed!

The bulwark crashed into something off into the darkness, while Sorin continued forward, his path through the night becoming more desperate, more terrifying- there was another crash behind him and he could only curse as the quasimorphed cyborg began to quickly gain on him. Its body was heavily mutated, but the thing was partially covered by the same substance as Carver. Half its face and most of its torso was covered in it. And the mechanical arms, which seemed attached by the silver substance.

Sorin forced himself to look forwards- he needed to reach the drones, he needed to reach them now!

His path took him down the road, and slowly the distance between the marker began to dwindle and dwindle, he was close. Just a bit further...

Sorin felt something, a painful lurch in his chest which caused him to stumble on the board. He grasped over it, his hand going directly over his heart, the spot was absolutely burning! He could feel it through his shirt, what was going on? The interface seemed to glitch and spaz out. The marker going in and out of sync. Sorin growled, come on! This was the worst possible time for whatever this was!

Sorin was forced to close his eyes, as pain shot across his body, causing him to stumble on the board; this couldn't be a cogni attack, not now!

Opening his eyes again, he screamed in fright. A large truck or bulldozer was fast approaching. Steering the board to his right using the left fin propulsor, he was just barely able to avoid running headfirst into the massive vehicle. Now however, he's found himself zooming through an expansive line of the same large-scale vehicles. He looked behind him, the quasi was gone, and so was Carver... Sorin became suddenly panicked, looking around frantically as he continued forward; the pain was still festering in his chest, but he had other problems. There was a sound to his further right, and he barely had enough time to slow down and turn with a duck, as a massive mechanical hand almost slapped him where his head had been a mere second ago. The massive cyborg crashing into one of the trucks capsizing it with a horrible sound of warped metal, before bounding forwards after Sorin, ready to steamroll into him.

Sorin roared in a total fury, the pain, the chase, enough! He swiped to his side with Songbird, and the gauntlet more than obliged to his will. The metallic whip bursting into action, as its forward arc through the air slashed across the side of the mechanical monstrosity. The cyborg roared as its right arm was severed by the armpit. The silver whip, serpentine in its movement was hoisted in the air once again as Sorin slashed, simultaneously moving, pulling the hoverboard into a swift power slide around the beast as the metallic teeth of the whip split the other arm off the quasified cyborg. The quasi was airborne for a second, before crashing back onto the earth as it slid to a stop. Sorin blasted off once again, pulling his board into another steep turn to the left as he dashed past the line and back where he needed to go.

Not long after a familiar sound wheezed past him. The deadly projectile of energy screamed through the air as it vaporized another far-off target in the darkness. Carver was back, and he was much closer now.

Sorin sneered, taking the whip into his right fist like a trailing lasso. He will not go down like this. He will survive this, no matter what.

10/27/2061, Wednesday, 8: 21 pm

"Listen, stay back and keep down," Mrs. Murdock demanded "Your in no shape to do anything right now!" she almost cried out in frustration.

Roxanne was growling from where she stood, barely able to keep herself up from the barrage of power she threw earlier at the freak outside. The dents on the iron door barricading them inside where only getting worse, and it looked to be on its last legs.

"BUT MOM!!!" she shouted.

"NO BUTS! Keep down, and let Garrot do what he can. You did all you could do, and we both know what will happen if you keep using your powers without any electricity around!" She retorted with complete authority. Causing Roxy to hesitantly sit back flinching from the sounds of the door.

Jack held his hands to his ears, blocking out the thunderous impacts from barricade door. The ungodly racket was keeping him from focusing outside the building, and even though he could hear the tell-tale sounds of Sorin's hoverboard, he couldn't pinpoint it because of this thing outside.

"I can't get much of anything... if only it would stop it with that racket!" Jack growled out. Zoe gave a gentle touch to his shoulder "At least he's still alive. There's that at the very least." She replied back, her morale somewhat regained on the knowledge that Sorin was still with them. But for how long... she shuddered to think about.

Mr. Murdock held the small gun in his hand. The firearm felt heavy, a classic six-cylinder kinetic revolver, and this would probably be the first time he ever fired a gun in self-defense. But for his children, he was prepared to do anything at this very moment. But his mind wouldn't stop going back to the moment, the moment when Sorin quite literally saved both his, and Garrots skins. His hands steadied, if someone that young could make such a gut decision, then he had no right to be on the sidelines. The two were currently near the large window overlooking the steel mill. The old top floor office was still intact, but for how much longer Robert couldn't really tell. If that thing got in, he very much doubted the receptionist office would boast anymore surprises that could help them. Robert shook his head in disbelief, the kid that saved his and Garrots life was currently fighting out there alone. And there wasn't a damn thing he could do about it right now.

"That kid, he really is somethin... ain't he, Garrot." Mr. Murdock said.

"Yeah, that he is... You ready? I doubt the door is going to hold for much longer." Garrot replied, switching off the safety.

Mr. Murdock could only nod as the beating of the door continued. Zoe stood up from her spot on the dirty sofa, something that would have had her freaking out not to long ago, but, as of right now she didn't much care about it. Jack stood next to his mom, his eyes showing a subtle hue, and hands still clutching his ears. Watching Zoe and coming to a quick decision, he joined her side and using his powers whispered, *"Got your back when it gets inside."* Directly to her, loud and clear. Nobody else but her could hear him, and she nodded back in turn. Giving a nervous smile, gulping as her claws lengthened. Roxy stared beadily towards the entrance, eyes sparking subtly- preparing herself for the worst.

The door began to make a low groan. This was it, everyone could feel it, the door was at its breaking point.

Garrot crouched near the center of the room, behind an overturned desk with his laser rifle on top, pointing towards the door. He dialed up the switch on the side of the experimental weapon, ready to turn the beam emitter on high frequency. Hopefully the hodgepodge of parts wouldn't explode from the yield. But he was willing to do anything to slow it down.

Zoe carefully stood next to the window, ready to make a move the second that thing got near or past Garrot. Jack stood his ground, as Mr. Murdock got in front of all of them, gun in hand, ready to use it. Roxy watched on, her cellphone in hand as electricity crawled from it, to her arm.

BAM! BAM! BAM! The sound kept repeating over and over, the groans getting louder, and the sounds of metal bending and warping under the onslaught. Suddenly, the constant banging ceased.

Garrot tensed his muscles, the cessation of bangs across the barrier door coming across as unexpected. What was going on now? He kept the muzzle of the gun pointed at the door, and as he was about to speak. His eyes flickered green; the notification streaking across his eyes.

All was quiet. No sounds, no bangs, no talking. Everyone was silently tensed, wondering what was going on; was it toying with them? Or had it sensed something?

Zoe further back in the room, near the large window overlooking the now dark mill, was definitely sensing something. Every instinct in her body minutes ago was screaming at her, warning her of the danger approaching. But now something else was replacing it, a strange feeling which seemed not of her own making, a sense of calm in the middle of the storm, a sensation of phantom safety which felt alien to her, as it did to Jack, and Roxy. Both twins feeling the breech in their heads as if something was trying to comfort them, without physically touching them.

"What... what is that, what is going on?" Roxy stuttered, holding her head, trying to figure out where that feeling was coming from, as her parents gave questioning looks to her... and Jack.

"Something's coming, I can hear it." Jack said, feeling the same probe in his head. "But, why does it sound like its coming from above the-"

There was a massive BANG! Which shook the entire building and caused the large window behind Zoe to vibrate harshly. The group stumbled where they stood, with Zoe and Jack having to reach out and grab onto a chair or surface to keep from falling with Roxy grabbing onto a rail alongside her parents. Garrot, still crouched behind cover could only take his rifle off the door. Looking unaffected by the intense vibrations ruling over the room. A glaring light suddenly pierced through the window, nearly blinding everyone beside Garrot, as it brushed within the room for a few seconds before disappearing.

"W-what the heck was that!?" Jack stammered aloud.

Garrot sighed "Took them long enough..." he said calmly, as he stood up from cover. "Back up has finally arrived."

CHAPTER

53

The room rumbled. Zoe cried out, falling against the window as everyone struggled to hold on; Jack was frozen where he was crouched down, his eyes stared, amazed at the sound waves resonating past the iron door.

Something heavy just landed on the other side.

Everyone was slack jawed (minus Garrot) as the sounds of a titanic struggle rumbled through the room. Antagonistic shouts and screams, broken up by periods of objects getting tossed around or the sound of heavy impacts against other surfaces. It was fierce, it was brutal, and they could hardly tell who or what was getting the upper hand. For almost a minute they were silent, for almost a minute the fight raged on, and just as abrupt the noise ceased. Only for the barrier door sealing them inside too burst off its hinges. Zoe was just able to catch something pierce its way through the solid door like tinfoil, before it flew backward into the room. Garrot was forced to quickly move out of the way as it crashed into his cover. Which slide forward; for the second time in a row, minus Garrot, the group had their jaws on the floor. For on top of the massive door, was a man, a man who was the shade of black obsidian, his skin looked to be made of granite, and his eyes, as he looked up... glowed a piercing orange light. He wore a complex leather combat uniform, which seemed barely able to hide his muscles. He was clean- shaven and bald, and as he looked around, in the middle of the room, his expression transformed from bulwark series, to one of battle-weary relief.

Below him, laid the now dead quasimorph. Its body in the death throes of disintegrating into the usual black smog. Zoe and the rest were startled as the giant of a man, suddenly, ripped something from the chest of the abomination. His fist, which, seemed to have a jagged stone hook extended from his knuckles like stalactite. Zoe could only widen her eyes as the massive hook began to shrink down, disappearing back into his fist.

"That... was probably the strongest lesser quasi I've ever come across," The giant said, his deep voice with clear exhaustion. "If this is what the wastelands normally pump out, I'd hate to see the one from the expanse!" he said with a chuckle, moving off the door and straightening up.

"Holy.... crap...." Jack uttered, looking at the remains of the quasi and the giant of a man who towered over even his dad!

"Duncan," a woman called out from the entrance of the room. Wearing a similar combat uniform to the one named Duncan, she was of a darker shade similar to Jack and Mr. Murdock, and her dark hair was in a long-braided hairstyle. Her face was adorned with ink tattoos that were both beautiful and fairly complex. Zoe made a small intake of breath, for she was levitating off the floor a few feet from the ground. Her eyes glowing a piercing magenta. "Ah! I see you found them... Sorry for the delay Garrot. We were busy trying to get through Delta cities security blockade. They're really upping surveillance around the entire airspace, surrounding the outskirts." She landed next to Garrot, smiling apologetically, her eyes losing the glow revealing hazel irises. Duncan steeped up, his skin slowly but surely reversing the granite like hue to it, shifting back to regular skin as it were.

His clear complexion, followed by the orange glow of his eyes vanishing, leaving dark brown eyes in their wake. They both landed on Zoe with mild surprise.

"Oh, you didn't say there was a third." The woman said, suddenly noticing Zoe.

"That's not important Claire. There's another kid out there- his names Sorin- and was taken maybe thirteen minutes ago; he contacted me earlier through a holocall, but I don't know how much longer he can last on his own." Garrot quickly said.

Claire's expression became serious, her hands going to her temple as her eyes lit up with the same magenta flare. Her hair stood up, an aura of energy surrounded her, and she began to rise up. Zoe and the others could only look in amazement, wondering what was going on.

"I'm guessing y'all never seen a telepath in action before have you?" Duncan said, watching there expressions with a glint of amusement in his eyes. "Don't worry, she's the best deviant of her class when it comes to telepathy, she should get a reading on your friend soon."

Claire's eyes suddenly widened, magenta eyes becoming worried as her expression turned inward. Duncan suddenly narrowed his eyes "Claire? What's the matter?"

She landed back on the ground with a tired breath, eyes going back to normal, she gave him a series look. "We have to move, somethings really wrong with the boy."

10/27/2061, Wednesday, 8:24 pm

Sorin was not okay.

Something was really, really, wrong with his chest.

It wasn't painful anymore, but it certainly wasn't a comforting sensation either. By this point he was nearly at the last coordinates for the drones. So he bared with it like he would any other cogni attack.

Songbird's whip tendril was surprisingly effective, but he didn't dare try it on the freak chasing him across the mill. Especially, if he could fire such devastating shots from his mouth. All of that was somehow because of the gem lodged into his forehead. And Sorin had an idea. He couldn't risk getting any closer to Carver, but the drones could...

Maybe he could pry the gem from him and use the drones as cover. Even if he failed, he could give someone else the advantage of weakening him, and maybe, take him down. Or at least, that's what he hoped.

His path took him across the open yard, and into the heavy industrial side of the mill. Large, massive steel cranes, and iron girders which scaled across the sides of a few buildings, and there was probably more he was missing, but the illumination from his board just couldn't reach far away enough for him to see. This, of course, wasn't something he was really worried about at the moment.

The marker on his display pinged, and Songbird began to chirp rapidly. Sorin quickly glanced backwards; the shots from Carver had ceased, and the mutated nomad was nowhere to be found. He's disappeared without a trace. But Sorin wasn't complaining. He slowed down and made a sharp turn to the right, entering an alleyway and looked around. He couldn't see them, but they were somewhere around here.

Didn't he mention at one point that they were invisible? Crap! I really hope Songbird can interface with them... Or I'm done for...

He popped out of the alley and made another turn. Gliding through the street at a comfortable speed of 33mph, he looked upward trying and straining his eyes to find some outline or clue of the drones location.

There was another chirp from his right hand. And suddenly his reticle jumped; he turned his head following the marker and saw something which caused him to hit the brakes on his momentum. There was a strong draft of wind blowing near a large dumpster near the side of warehouse. Kicking the board back in gear, he quickly closed the distance. A moment later when he got close enough, the interface flickered, and a green outline formed just fifteen feet above the dumpster.

The drones camera was focused on him. Sorin didn't even have to will the gauntlet to act; automatically, the breach command took hold. The progress bar quickly filling up, as code script ran down the targeting reticule over the drones highlighted shape. Sorin grasped his chest in pain, an ugly sneer flickering over his features as the pain came and went. Whatever the heck this was, all he needed to do was get this drones on his side. Then maybe he could attempt his plan.

Please work... please, please, work....

Sorin could only sigh in relief when the bar finally finished. The drone suddenly reappeared, its body shimmering as electricity traveled around the device. The small turbines holding it in the air, was suddenly much louder. *Must be a silent running mode, or something close to it. Jack is so gonna freak when he sees I got a drone...* Sorin's interface lit up, the lenses of his mask showing the status of the drone, and the other one... which was currently idle near a warehouse, close to an even bigger building. He quickly commanded the other drone to come back to his location, and kicked off down the dark streets- the other drone following close behind. It was like he had almost forgotten the fact he was being hunted down.

Taking back glances at the drone and not able to help the big grin sliding across his lips. Maybe, just maybe, he would be able to stand a chance against Carver now.

I just gotta make sure he's focused on the drone... Then I can try and get em with Songbird... And, maybe I can finally get some answers from Hosea...

That last thought almost made him pause for a moment. Before he could properly shake it off, his head was suddenly hit with a horrible headache. The pain was definitely from the mental connection from Carver. The same, piercing sensation which burrowed into his brain.

He came to an abrupt stop in the middle of the road. Warehouses and sheds illuminated by the glow of his board and the beat of the drones turbines. But what he was feeling now, made it all fade into the background. He fell to his knees on the platform, his vision blurring from the intense migraine. But what was really odd about the scene was his chest. The same hot, cold sensation which was traveling throughout his body. His eyes widened behind the mask, as a horrible chill traveled down his back.

The sounds that now assaulted him were the very same from the containment chamber of the bunker. The old vault which originally held songbird, and worse yet, the stranger- torn, shabby, and gaunt. His dark silhouette standing within the mist as his pale white eyes stared beadily into his soul, from the shadowy concealment of his hood. The voices, countless monotone whispers muttering nonsense that he just couldn't understand. In a language that sounded like unintelligible gibberish.

The vision passed, and he was back on the board. The drone whirring behind him as the night wind sighed before him. Suddenly, from out of the blue; Songbird alerted him with a twitter as his interface lit up. From the darkness, a shape materialized in a flash of rippling light. It was the other drone. But this one was damaged; the second wing looked bent, and the front side of it, the camera, had what looked to be a scuff mark on it, like something had crashed against it.

From the data scroll of his interface, the systems were still green. But one of its main guns was broken... and one of the ammo stores was jammed...

Sorin at first blanched at this; guns, an ammo count, a targeting module, and full hacking suite (inoperable); he actually couldn't believe something of this size could be so... dangerous. And then he mentally face palmed. What was he thinking! This wasn't the time to have cold feet! Carver would be on him any moment, and he needed to be ready.

The indigo gem was the source of all this trouble. If he could pry it from Carvers head, then this would be all over. He would finally be free of this cross region chase. And he wouldn't be placing everyone near him in danger anymore... he stilled himself, the fear ever present, but... he felt... knew what had to be done... the gem was the answer.

He quickly grabbed his head, gritting his teeth from another pounding headache. His chest too, in the place where his heart was. The pressure building little by little. Why? Why was this reminding him of the garage?

He shuddered to himself. *I gotta end this now. I don't... I don't know what's going on anymore...*

Sorin abruptly began to brace himself. The needle-like incision from the teether began to seethe in agitation, as the mental link was already pulling him in the general direction of Carver... and Carver to him...

His time was almost up.

CHAPTER

54

10/27/2061, Wednesday, 8: 35 pm

Sorin's visor was full of status pages, each window detailing the general info of both drones. Too his mild discomfort, the third drone was already destroyed. By his best guest, he theorized the other quasimorphs must have found it. Or, maybe Garrot getting disconnected may have had something to do with it. The fourth was also gone... an EMP short circuited it...

Either way. He was trying to get some practice with them while he had the time. Although, his rushed testing of the two drones did lead to some... less than desired outcomes.

BANG! Sorin jumped in alarm. Creating the most embarrassing yelp he'd ever heard, originating from his own mouth. The drone's gun immediately extended from below its camera and fired a shot from behind Sorin to his left. His eyes the size of dinnerplates behind his mask as he saw the large chunk of damage it did to the side of a building. Pieces of brick and mortar crashing across the ground, near the edge of illumination from his board, the hole left behind was the size of a softball; he glanced behind himself, looking at the offending drone as it hovered innocently. The end of the barrel smoking lightly.

This incident caused him to forget manual control mode. And instead, use its auto lock on feature. He would simply try to keep himself far from the drones, and Carvers line of fire.

He raced across the paved paths between the large warehouses lined on either side; barely any light save the hoverboard and the lights produced by the two drones behind him. Sorin kept his speed at 30mph, his focus on memorizing the area. The block was chock full of warehouses, small buildings, and a lot of paved paths between each structure. There looked to be a system of train tracks going outside the warehouse section- a few open rail cars left on some of the tracks.

There wasn't many alleys, or short cuts between them. So, his path was actually a narrow grid. Add in the massive pipes suspended in the air, around the buildings. This was literally a steel jungle. Was there any other way he could navigate it? He had been thinking and riding around for the past three minutes, just trying to form a good game plan.

Sadly, he wasn't Hosea. Nor was he the same caliber of hacker like Bellatrix; crap, there wasn't anything he could hack... save the drones. He would just have to make it up as he went along.

Just like Whitechapel... but, at least I got the drones...

Sorin cringed, the moment of optimism suddenly fizzling out as his anxiety and unease got worse by the second. This... was increasingly looking like a horrible idea. He stopped again, feeling his head pounding; the teether was getting stronger, and he could sense it. Carver was now on his way. He quickly commanded the drones to fly upwards above the warehouses. And used the camera's to get a good view from above. Two windows of the drones feed popped onto his interface.

After the drone surpassed a height of 70ft in the air, that's when he got a lock on from each drones targeting module. The camera focused some two hundred meters further southeast of his location. And under the shadow of darkness, which was pierced by the drones night vision mode, did he appear, rapidly closing the distance from the open industrial sector, and into the steel jungle of the main industry sector.

"Here we go..." Sorin said, activating the drones autotargeting setting. Cutting off the feed, he watched as the drones rocketed off towards the marked target. And Sorin blasted off into the opposite direction.

"Heh, if this plan doesn't work... at least I can say I've controlled two combat drones." Sorin chuckled dryly to himself from under his breath.

At least there was something cool in this crappy situation.

Just as that private comment left his lips, did he hear the roaring sound of the machine guns from the distance. Carvers beastly roar, following closely behind as the sounds of bullet fire, and the hair-raising echoes of the energy shots rang out into the night air. The armor around his arms and shoulders constricted, the complex metal spawning the whip which twisted serpentine down his right arm and gathered in his closed hand. The twin tails of his durag flapping behind him, along with the coiled, sharpened whip trailing behind him. His muscles tensed, if and when Carver got close enough, he would strike and hope the drones could keep Carver preoccupied enough for him to get away.

Guerilla tactics. Or at least, that's what Jade called it.

Sorins momentum carried him from out of a narrow alley between to warehouses, followed closely by the fast-moving mutant that was Carver. His body getting pelted by machine gun fire on all sides. But he seemed to pay it all with no attention, with the occasional fire of energy towards the offending drones. Which, to Sorins relief were pretty good at evading them.

Sorin was forced to turn as Carvers shot nearly hit him directly in the side. Causing the youth to turn hard in order to avoid it, placing him out of the warehouse area and into the train car section. One of the drones began to strafe around Carver, its rounds tearing into his lower side. But with a frustrated cry, the beast shot two silver lines of metallic thread for the drone. Sorin cursed, watching in a quick glance as the tendrils nearly skewered into the drone, the device quickly course correcting and managed to just barely avoid the attack. The second drone took over shooting Carver in the back, much to the quasimorphs endless irritation. The area it was in getting pelted with stray rounds, as the ground, and sides of the warehouses where getting punctured full of holes. Carver slid to a stop, turning its open mouth to the metallic flies orbiting around and firing upon him. He too began to open fire with his own, the air ringing with the shots of monochrome energy from his sharpened maw.

Sorin seeing a possible opening, ordered the drones to evade. Which all but added to the quasis fury as the two drones circled around him. Giving Sorin the chance he needed to get behind the behemoth.

Sorin slid with the momentum he was gathering, breaking and forcing the boards side fin to help him maneuver into position. All the while, Carver fired on, oblivious to what Sorin was doing. And with a quick burst of acceleration, he was flying towards Carvers position.

He unfurled the whip in his hand, his trajectory putting him directly towards Carver and with as much precession as he could muster- swiped his arm in a vertical motion, the whip trailing a serpentine arc as he shot across Carver to the side, his whip striking the beast full on the face.

This... for the first time, caused the mutated nomad to cry out in alarm! Its eyeless visage, now adorned with an ugly vertical slash across its face, which oozed black fog. The creature reared its head and roared the loudest its ever roared, a bellow which had Sorins ears ringing, but confirmed he had scored a hit.

But something happened. Sorin could only gasp, as something began to change with the armor. He could feel it move, the complex metallic substance was growing, lengthening down his body. Before Sorin could question what was going on, did he hear something which caused him to turn back around. Carver was coming directly for him! The drones where firing on him, but now he was ignoring them completely, the slash mark on its face smoking out the dark mist.

Sorin moved, yelping in alarm as its hand nearly flattened him on the spot. He twisted his body, guiding the board into a swift curve around a rail car. Simultaneously, he lashed out again with the whip. The metallic thread slicing into Carver's upper arm, to the enraged howl of the quasimorph.

Along the way, Sorin was forced to recenter himself. His posture on the board nearly thrown off by the quick movement, and his earlier attack. He may have practiced riding around the hoverboard, but attacking with the whip was another matter entirely.

He glanced backwards and shivered. Carver was going ballistic, the wound along his arm was smoking the black smog. And... it seemed to be melting... looking at the quasi, its eyeless face was also rippling off, looking similar to wax melting under an especially warm candle. Sorin glanced down, the armor was continually spreading down, covering his chest and lower torso.

Yesss...

The one known as Carver is spent...

His fight against the dark oath is lost, hopeless...

But yours is still in progress... you still have the chance...

TAKE WHAT IS RIGHTFULLY YOURS!!!

Sorin roared in pain, the countless voices were like fingernails dragging across his brain!

NO! I'LL SHALL NOT BE DENIED!

Sorin glanced back in horror; the thought surged through the link connecting him to Carver. His voice, a dark and determined mental cry which put him immediately on guard, as the beast surged forward. His past savagery from Whitechapel returning full force as he barreled toward him like an unstoppable juggernaut.

The drones immediately opened fire. And Sorin was not prepared for what happened next. His eyes widened, a cold sensation of terror washing over him as Carver, now in a frenzy, proceeded to change direction and lift up a rail car next to him, in the most smoothest of motions which defied reality. What must have weighed thousands of tons was lifted upwards, with a horrible sound of metal groaning and asphalt crunching. The next few seconds were a blur; the train car rising into the air, one drone in the nick of time was able to dodge the column of metal thrown its way, but the other wasn't so lucky. As a small explosion was seen, at the exact moment the train connected with it. That was all Sorin could see, as he glanced back- kicking off into high gear as he went immediately from 40mph to 80mph in the blink of an eye. The sound of the train car crashing back down somewhere in the distance reached him from somewhere inside the darkness, maybe it landed directly onto the face of a building, or maybe into one of the massive industrial valves suspended over one of the buildings. Sorin didn't know, all he knew was that he needed to get some distance from Carver.

And pray, he could score a hit which would end this nightmare for good.

The two were once again locked into a deadly chase, Sorin's path across the railyard was repeatedly altered again and again; Carvers dark determination to end him was emboldened; no matter how much the drone fired upon him, his dogged determination to catch Sorin made him commit some of the most incredible, and the most horrifying feats imaginable. Sorin was forced to alter his path several times, because Carver was now implementing both tendril and energy beam in his pursuit.

This caused Sorin to think on the fly, improvising some of the most creative maneuvers he's done to date on the board.

The most memorable one, happened a measly two minutes of the dogged pursuit. Carver had trailed him back into the industrial jungle of the main industry section. Sorin in a desperate bid to get some distance, some meager shred of a break. Was not expecting Carver to aim his mouth upwards. Towards the massive tangle of pipelines; there was an explosion of light, the thick projectiles of dark energy cleaving through steel and iron, as the network came crashing down; Sorin in complete survival mode made a beeline forwards. The road between what was likely the main foundry, and another warehouse was probably the longest yet, as the steel beams collided around him- massive steel frames which could easily splatter him alongside the pavement- did something miraculous happen.

Sorin wasn't sure how he did it, or how Songbird had understood what he wanted to do at the time; after all, he wasn't really thinking, he was just instinctly doing what needed to be done to survive.

Tendrils of silver extended out from around his armor. Hooks, which hoisted him and the board up and over the few large pipes in his way. Shooting him upward, as more tendrils reached out pulling and yanking him aside from the other pipelines still tumbling down around him. His vision was a blur of motion, as he flipped midair- the board humming from the rapid motion of his descent back down, an instinctual trust in Songbird as he curved back downward- and with a mighty crash he landed back on the pavement- the board sending out a wave of energy as he shot off across the road- followed by Carver, who simply rammed through the debris in his way.

The chase went on for a few more seconds, too Sorin, it was almost an eternity; but eventually, Sorin came up with another plan. Using the whip, he sent it towards the nearest light pole, using his current speed, he held on as the whip yanked him backwards, which slingshotted him down the opposite street. Carver could barely turn in time as his gait had him crash into the opposite wall of the building.

Before he could even recover to give chase, the drone decloaked, diving at his position as the gun barrel sparked in rapid fire. Each bullet hitting him directly in the face, causing the beast to roar in fury, as bullet after bullet pierced through his armored helm. Sorin commanded the drone to pull out of its dive, directing it to go back into 'stealth' mode as he called it. Carver could only shoot empty air, as the drone once again vanished. Its twin turbines adjusting the beat of its blades to an almost silent hover. Sorin pulled around a corner, memorizing the path he was taking, he knew he would be pulling out of the main industry area soon. He just needed to get back to the warehouse area, there, he would have more cover from Caver direct line of sight, anything to keep him from getting a direct laser beam in the face.

Suddenly, a loud sound caught the youths attention. A rolling, thunderous boom which traveled through the night air, and... Sorin was almost gob smacked by what he saw in the distance... further away, back towards the main entrance of the steel mill. The boy could only widen his eyes at the main building where the others still were in the distance. The unmistakable shape of an explicably large aircraft, the spotlights hovering over the building was unmistakable.

"Holy" Sorin breathed, two pinpricks (aided by the interface zooming in) to Sorin's shock, were descending into the remains of the distant conference room. "What's going on over there?"

A roar caught his attention, turning around, Carver was once again back on his heels. "Crap!" Sorin ducked, a tendril slicing the air where his face was a moment earlier. He turned in the opposite direction, narrowly dodging another energy volley as Carver continued to gain on him. Sorin was forced to make evasive maneuvers, Carver was obviously done with his machinations because he was going rapid fire with the energy projectiles. Causing Sorin to use creative means to avoid each and every shot. The ground around him exploding from the impact of each volley.

Eventually, Sorin had enough. With a quick yank, his whip snagged a sign which he used to make another sharp maneuver. Throwing him into another line of abandoned heavy vehicles. Which Carver lit up. The assembly quickly erupting in fire and spare parts; Sorin on one or more occasions was forced to cover his face from the heat of the explosions and fire. Only getting a break when he commanded the drone to open fire. The shots coming from the other side of Carver, who was more than frustrated by the annoying bee stings coming his way.

Carver turned his head to fire. And Sorin took his chance, he curved, maneuvering the head of the board towards Carvers body, he zipped in front of him catching the beast unwary- as the unfurled whip sliced into him yet again. This time, too Sorin's confirmation as he looked back, the whip had sliced right into Carvers eyeless dome. The gems indigo radiance shining through.

Carver gave probably the ugliest roar Sorin had heard to date, the raw hatred he could feel from the connection was almost sickening to him. Suddenly, Sorin could feel a switch from within the link. A sensation so alien to him that he couldn't believe it originating from another human being.

An almost colorless, baseless sensation that made his skin shiver...

It's too late.

He's finally run out of time.

"What?" Sorin uttered "What do you mean by-"

Suddenly, the night air became heavy. Sorin chocked on his words, the tidal wave of panic which flooded his brain had him gagging. The beast convulsed, grabbing its head in anguish as the flood of panic gave way to something far worse, making the earlier pulse of hatred more preferable.

It was... entropy... a word that Sorin couldn't have possibly known of, until now. The personality, the emotions, the panic and desperation, draining away and leaving only the most hollow shell of a being, which stood robotically, its back against the flames of destroyed vehicles starring directly at Sorin as he continued to make distance.

And without a word, or a savage roar, or anything that could be considered a conscious action- it gave chase.

CHAPTER

55

10/27/2061, Wednesday, 8: 59pm

This thing wasn't Carver anymore.

Sorin found that out the hard way, as this thing, without nary a warning hit 65mph in a couple of seconds. The tendrils which lashed out ripped through his armor, causing Sorin to roar in pain, as the two slashes in his back bleed from under his shirt and armor.

He quickly blasted off, and with a panicked command, ordered the drone to open fire. The drone wasn't hitting a thing. Carver surged forward, faster than the drone could get a bead on, and it began to close in on Sorin; Sorin steered right, desperate to get some distance, as the eerie shine of the indigo gem radiated behind him like a flashlight. Sorin twisted and turned, diving and retreating, from between warehouse and building using his whip to complete extreme turns from path to path, street to street.

But it didn't matter, Carver wasn't falling for any of his maneuvers. Like a killing machine, there was no obstacle that could stand in its way. Even the drone, which had been essential for giving him breathing room, was quickly proving ineffective. The rounds puncturing his body, aimed specifically at his weak points, didn't faze the mindless automaton of death, nor did it give Sorin the room to strategize.

Sorin was losing hope. But, something else was rising within him. The voices, ever present, hounded him throughout the chase. Urging him more and more to strike back, to kill, to destroy. Sorin was in a nightmare, every action, every decision that led him here, was it all for nothing? Suddenly he became aware of the raging heartbeat within his chest.

By this point he accepted it for what it was, which was flowing throughout his body; how he was alive? He didn't now. But he couldn't take it anymore. He had to end this, he needed to end this. And every ounce of live styx matter flowing through him to Songbird was the key. His target hadn't changed, the last gem which was still nestled inside of the dead nomads head was the only way out of this. He made another turn, barely missing the corner of a warehouse and angled his body towards the sidewalk of the street.

His heartrate increased, the organ pounding from within his chest. As he willed whatever it was supplying him the cursed substance.

Songbird's main core burned red, the gauntlet taking whatever fuel it needed to power itself and directing it towards the armor- which hardened, the slash marks from behind Sorins back began to close shut, as the complex metal lengthened slowly down his body.

Sorin of course, was no longer paying attention to the armor, his focus hyper fixated on his task. He needed to confront Carver, the whip was one of the only things that could hurt him... but, what about the gauntlet itself? Hadn't it been absorbing whatever was covering Carver? Sorin narrowed his eyes, picturing every moment when Songbird pierced, cut, and slashed at the ex-nomad. Every moment, every recollection pointed to it. And even the recent status page from against the building pointed to this. If he was to stop Carver, what would happen if he grabbed the gem in his own hands? Sorin could almost feel his concentration waning; picturing himself getting so dangerously close to the things head where the gem lied.

Sorin closed his eyes, hearing the juggernaut closing in once again. He had no choice... this was the only option he had left... help, wasn't going to reach him in time... and he was on his last leg, barely any ideas left to stave off this desperate plan... He opened his eyes, his expression tired, but his eyes held a glint in them.

Determination for survival shoring up whatever nerve he had left. He had to make every move count, there would be no more attempts left after this... it was now or nothing.

And... he needed to put all his trust into Songbird if he wanted to get out of this alive.

Song, I don't really know what you are... I don't even know if you're actually alive or not, or I'm just being crazy... But... I need your help. Just, give me a sign that you've got my back on this...

Behind the mask, Sorin felt his eyes widen in alarm. Songbirds usual twitter was replaced by something far more predatory. The armor around him suddenly radiating a heat from between the inner layers of each plate, the soft glow from the more organic looking spaces becoming more pronounced, as the armor itself got sharper and harder. Sorin for once felt some measure of relief. Made intrepid by a roar cry, which seemed to resonate from out of the armors folds. A cry, strikingly similar to the territorial challenge of a duneraptor.

"I guess that's a yes." Sorin said.

Sorin began to fiddle with the masks interface, his thoughts pulling up the control settings for the one remaining drone.

Sorin navigated his way back into the central industry sector. He would need plenty of space to make this plan work. The only problem, he didn't know if this would be enough, or if it would have enough force to give him the time he needed for the task at hand. Strangely, Carver hasn't been using his energy beam for a few minutes now- opting to slash at him with his tendrils instead... Why was that? Taking a moment to brace himself, he made another turn for the street he was searching for, his memory of nearly an hour of being chased into the night paying off. The road here was lengthy, long enough to nearly kill him- Carver especially used the length to nearly land a couple of energy volleys his way, causing the path to have a war-torn look to it. Through the illumination of his board, he could tell from the signs that he was close, just a few more turns. The rolling carnage behind him was still at a cars length, and wasn't letting up. The blue violet of the core, looming over him with its ethereal glow. Oblivion was fast approaching.

Sorin made the final turn and blasted off. His speed jumping from a 80mph to 100mph. Simultaneously, he began to evoke the thing inside of his chest, forcing out an unquantifiable surge of styx matter to Songbird. He could feel his body burn from the exposure of the stuff.

A self-inflicted cogni attack by any other word.

But as the main core of the gauntlet was irradiated with vermillion red, so to was the organic like textures of his armor, which seemed to glare with the same reddish tinge. The interface glitched, and he was forced to grit his teeth from the pain. The board shot down the path like a rocket, its side and bottom vents pulsing with energy as both boy and platform were propelled forward at blistering speeds.

The quasimorph silently watched him inch away. And if Sorin had been paying attention, he would have noticed the beast once again, open its mouth- a single softball of swirling energy gathering just in the middle of its teeth.

The youth charged down the street his speed greatly outstripping the beast's pace with him. But the quasimorph wasn't bothering in trying to keep up, no, the swirling mass of energy was getting bigger- the larger sphere now shaking uncontrollably. Meanwhile Sorin was syphoning from the proverbial styx matter factory in his chest. Squeezing every bit of power he had, as he shot forward. The armor continuing to spread, as Sorin's concentration was truly tested, fighting against the hot agony spreading across his body.

He was about to enter the end of the street, where it led to a t-section, a hard left or right, with the side of a massive concreate wall greeting him as he got closer and closer. At the current speed he was going he would, most definitely, splatter against the wall if he didn't slow down and turn soon... But that wasn't really part of the plan.

No... what he had in mind was much, much crazier.

Sorin could feel Songbird assimilating the cursed substance with its armor, the sheer bulk of which was being focused across his back and torso. He really hoped this crazy plan would work, and also hoped the drone was ready to intercept if things got hairy.

There was a horrible CRUNCH! behind him, followed by the sound of something massive dragging across broken asphalt. He turned his head for a split second and stared. Carver had stopped, his sudden break tearing into the concreate as his claws broke into the ground to stop his forward momentum. Time stopped around him, as he saw the obvious sphere of doom being aimed at him. The ethereal glow of indigo, contrasted by the monochrome glint of the gathered mass of energy between its mouth, a lightshow which pierced through the darkness.

Sorin felt a cold shiver run through his body. It was now or never.

The hoverboard surged upward with a pulse jump. As songbird stretched out, a multitude of thick, silver strands lanced out in different directions. Some anchoring into walls, others wrapping around signs, light polls, anything nailed into place as Sorin braced himself, his momentum still pulling him forward as the various strands stretched- he gritted his teeth, holding the board upward as the propulsion continued to push him backwards. Facing the creature, he gave the command for the drone to approach. With one final moment of resolve. He cut the boards bottom vents and physics took over. He was almost unable to process what had happened, his body suddenly shot forward- like a silver bullet he was flying through the air faster than he could have thought possible. The quasimorph, no longer Carver- simply aimed the sphere, ready to shoot down the streak quickly approaching his position. Suddenly, sparks jumped from its head. The bullets ricocheting across his metallic helm, no longer melting, but still sporting the slash wound which revealed the blazing core in its depths- still attached to the forehead of Carver. The monster was still unflinching, ignoring the drones covering fire.

Sorin felt time halt to a crawl, whether it was the sheer amount of styx matter flowing through his body, or if it was somehow the adrenaline altering his perception. He gave the drone his final command.

The drone held its fire and drew in its gun barrel. With a quick turn of its propellers, the drone shot forwards. Sorin flipped over midair bringing his board up, and Carver widened his mouth, the unstable gathering of energy poised to greet Sorin in response. Only for Carvers aim to be irreversibly altered; the drone had completed its final task- crashing point blank into the quasimorphs cheek. With a large explosion of fire and metallic parts the ball of energy shot forwards- barely missing Sorin's face as he willed the bottom vents of the board to ignite. There was a roaring hum, which lit up the street as the vents payload of compressed energy crashed right into Carvers face.

The quasimorph was stunned. The sheer force of the forward ignition from the board punching the beast backwards; Sorin twisted around and with every shred of willpower he could manage sent every tendril of silver forwards, the metallic ropes wrapping around the quasimorphs body as Songbird pulled him towards the behemoths head. It was a slideshow of movement, tendrils fighting opposing sides, Sorin's right arm punching forwards to grab its target, and Carver slashing with his enormous claws. There was a horrible crunch, the feeling of something bellow him getting smashed aside, followed by the quick flash of something coming apart.

The hoverboard flew out from under him, suffering a direct hit from Carver as pieces of it disassembled from the savage strike. In the background it landed somewhere, but Sorin was too preoccupied to notice.

Because his right hand had landed exactly on top of the indigo core.

Sorin was blinded by the brilliant flash which pervaded his entire being. The street and warehouses were enveloped inside of an intense flare of light, and Carver was silently overwhelmed by the sheer force of this one act.

The complete sensory overload was beyond words. The pain from his earlier invocation of styx matter quadrupled, and the sudden congregation of voices which invaded his brain could barely be understood, much less comprehended. His body locked up, and his eyes behind the mask rolled into his eyes. But strangely, bizarrely, he could feel himself leaving. Much like the moment when he first entered cyberspace- his consciousness seemed to separate from his physical body, going somewhere he couldn't exactly fathom.

He felt out of place, like he was being dragged out of something constricting his movements. It was a tight space, where strange symbols where etched into every surface of the pod like assembly. An odd mix of strange, and bizarre technology. He couldn't describe it as futuristic, but he couldn't describe it in the analog sense either... alien, otherworldly, that was probably the best two descriptions that best fit the large capsule.

Looking down groggily, as if he'd been in a deep slumber, he noticed the familiar dark lines of cognicrossis spreading across his arms and legs. He was being carried, that much he was certain. His arm dangling freely as the robbed stranger rushed through the large concrete corridor. Signs of battle and bloodshed painted every corner and section of the long hallway. The hooded stranger rushed past a few bodies which laid on the stone floors, dawning strange armor, that looked vaguely familiar... The stranger was running down a series of winding corridors and circular expressways. But watching closely, the hallway wasn't exactly concrete. It was unsettling, especially to the young boy being carried through its dark, dimly lit space. For what kind of architect would build such an interior, where the hallways vagally resembled a skeletal like structure.

Ancient and abandoned, the structures even touched by signs of battle and death, seemed long suffused with an air of great melancholy. A deterioration so scarring it left a mark on the barely conscious youth. But this wasn't really the main issue for the boy, no, instead the only word that left his lips were...

"Mom?" he said weakly "Where's mom?"

The stranger looked down, his hood still concealing his or her face.

"I'm sorry child... but, we have to move. Your mother did everything she could. She loves you, and she'll always be close to you..." his voice, a soft but gravely one, spoke with clear sympathy. His hand moved, resting upon his chest. "No matter what, she'll always be there to protect you." His voice came off as resigned, his words of sympathy, coming off far more mysterious than the boy of merely six could begin to comprehend.

The stranger came to a stop, the large sealed opening couldn't be seen as a conventional door, but when the stranger pulled an odd-looking leaver, the opening expanded open with a whoosh of air, as a bright light flooded the corridor, the stranger and boy included. Sorin averted his eyes, and as he weekly covered them, something loose and rough brushed past his fingers. Averting his face, the boy opened his eyes, and he was somehow stranded in the middle of the desert. Standing in place, as the mid winds carried the sands, spreading them into a mid-air curtain which surrounded him.

It was night, and as he looked up at the star filled sky, he noticed an especially wonderous cluster of stars. A swirl of stars resembling a cosmic maelstrom.

Survive Sorin...

I'll always be with you...

But you have to survive... Promise me... you'll survive...

Sorin blinked, the six-year-old turning around to catch the source of the voice. A woman's voice, which seemed to be carried off by the severe draft of the turbulent winds.

Sorin looked around, not knowing what to do, where to go, but as he was frozen in indecision. A strong luminous light broke a path across the fanning winds. Sorin could only watch curiously as an armored car slowly stopped in front of him. The door opened, and a large man steeped out, his hand keeping his hat from flying across the desert landscape.

Sorin averted his eyes, the winds getting more severe as the light from the car got brighter and brighter. Sorin opened them again, and the blazing energy from the indigo core greeted him. His hand covering the brilliant glow, which escaped past his fingers, as the world spun. The quasimorph was lashing out desperately to get him off.

Sorin vaguely looked around, wondering why he hadn't swatted him like a fly yet. But the tendrils binding his arms quickly answered his question for him. The beast continued to buck around, and to Sorin mild unease (or perhaps shock that his plan worked) the quasi was starting to move forward, picking up speed as it began to charge for the warehouse on the side of the street. Now Sorin was slowly panicking, it was attempting to smash him against the wall!

Luckly, Songbird had him covered. The armor exploded into action, as more tendrils extended from his back, the four silver ropes moving to wrap up Carvers legs... only for Sorin to quickly curse, as the momentum Carver generated was not all together stopped.

Sorin could only yell in alarm as Carver flipped, his massive bulk crashing into the wall, and punching straight through- bringing Sorin with him.

CHAPTER

56

Sorin rolled over onto the ground, going into a fetal position as smoke and rubble fell around him. Carver's massive frame collapsing into a heap as he slide across the concreate ground next to him.

The overhead lights were dead, but the force of the impact through the wall caused them to swing audibly. A few falling to the ground, or smashing into the catwalks overhead. Causing fluorescent filaments, or shards of glass to rain around the beast and youth; the armor covering Sorin's face and upper body shielded him from some of the debris falling around him. Along with the wisps of tendrils connecting him and the beast together.

Sorin, through his disorientation, was struggling to get back to his feet. The quasimorph though was already in action, forcing its lumbering body back up. Not a sound, or growl to denote any emotion or feeling of the situation. It's massive bulk seemingly rooted to the spot, the indigo gem, now shining freely. Its core smoldering within the confines of Carvers forehead. Sorin was too tired to say anything, and too tired to feel any fear at being so close to this abomination. But as he stood up, something strange began to take place. The metallic threads of silver connecting him to the nomad was emitting a soft glow. And like a magnet, he felt himself drawn to the creature. He wasn't even aware of when he started to walk closer to him. He wasn't sure if it was himself, or Songbird reaching up with a free hand towards the husk of Carvers face. Now devoid of any life, save the hollow shell of his expressionless dark eyes. Now seemingly subsumed in a dark abyss.

What were those memories? A question which seemed to stain his soul, but, as his right hand finally grabbed onto the last core. The question became altogether meaningless, as the core began to radiate visible energy.

It was like molten lava was spreading across his skin, as raw electricity surged through his veins, forking down his arm, and into his chest. His heart exploded from the depths of his upper torso, as black veins traveled across his whole body. While outside, Sorin was silent in a trance state. The pain coming secondary to the intense connection going through his cranium, rendering the secondary mute in color and feel.

Songbird was evolving. The gauntlet which landed on the last core was rippling with monochrome energy. Every fold and muscle like texture between them irradiated in intense light; the armor was stretching, from front to back the armor was rapidly gaining ground, covering Sorins entire lower torso and spreading down his thighs and lower legs, and finally consuming his shoes and replacing them with a complex pseudo-metallic greaves. The organic texture between the sharpened plates giving the child an almost otherworldly appearance. While in his mind, images briskly played across his eyes in an uncontrollable torrent. There meaning coming across as unperceivable as the last, a macabre showcase of someone else's life put in a condensed spreadsheet of vibrant color and mundane tinctures. The gem was moving. The dark blue and violet stone was being swallowed by Songbird. Its oval shape levitating from Carvers forehead and into the palm of the gauntlet, sinking into it and disappearing altogether. Leaving a smoking hole in its place.

Sorin began to falter backwards. His trance state apparently broken as the armored youth began to grab his head; the sensation was uncomfortable, like something was moving from within the armor itself...

Sorin tried to breath, tried to keep himself steady, but something was traveling up his neck and throat, covering his Adams apple and finally stretching over his mouth and nose. He could still breath, but it didn't disguise the fact that another part of the mask had covered his mouth. Turning the half mask into a full functional mask. Funnily enough... the prized durag covering his head was still there, untouched.

But below the head bandanna something was emerging. A vibrant, indigo illumination was poking just below the dark fabric, right over Sorin's forehead. Sorin opened his eyes from within the mask and felt his equilibrium plummet drastically, falling to both knees in a stupor, his energy at an all-time low. The soft illumination which permeated across the armor was his only light within the now dark warehouse, the distant fires from outside, barely reaching within the egregious hole adorning the wall behind him.

Behind him, still extending from his back, the silver wisps of metallic tendrils hung in midair behind him, poised to strike in a moments notice. While Sorin grasped his head, currently undergoing a rough, splitting headache, because its not like the voices from earlier had decided to let up in their jeering. Now more than exuberant in his recent success.

Yes....

He's done it...

The bound is established....

The dark oath is yet to emerge...

A potential spawn, born of the dark...

She has succeeded...

"Shut up already!"

A voice, Sorin's voice... growled out in an altered tone...

His hand flashed to his throat, eyes widening in horror, the organic like mask detailing the alarm and dread of the situation. *No, no, this couldn't be happening, i can't be turning into him, i couldn't–*

Movement. Sorin looked up, and Carver was crawling towards him from the dark. His shell was disintegrating, turning into dust in front of his very eyes. But with silent determination, he was still coming, still stalking towards him. The paralysis from earlier broken.

Sorin shook his head, the rage boiling up, a steady rise too his feet; he snarled, the mask's expression altering on a dime with his fury. The lens of the mask glowing in response to his emotions, while the new location of the indigo core upon his forehead gave off the appearance of a third eye behind his durag. He held his right hand up, backing away as Carver got closer and closer.

"STAY BACK!" his voice echoed across the warehouse, an uncharacteristically, and intimidating tone, heightened by the altered echo from his voice, sounding neither natural nor electronic in origin.

Sorin narrowed his eyes in pain, the voices stopped, and suddenly the air became charged. His chest felt like it was constricting on itself, as the drumming within his ears became more pronounced. His right arm became rigged, as the indigo sphere began to radiate an intense glow. Sorin headless of the changes taking place, was still focused on Carvers approaching figure. The complex armor adorning his right chest and arm began to suddenly emit more light from within the organic textures of the suit. Each line between each plate, one by one, from chest all the way to his right hand, began to hum with a rising sound of energy. The folds between the plates began to glow with the same monochrome energy as something small started to gather in front of his right palm. A pinprick at first, but as the seconds counted down it grew and grew, the pinprick gathering untold mass, as a swirl of air started to gather around the now softball sized sphere. Sorin suddenly looked down, finally noticing the dark orb floating ominously over his palm. The sphere's humming grew more intense, more unsettling to Sorin, as an uncontrollable cackle of condensed energy began to emit a pale radiance. The interior of the warehouse was quickly flooded with light, the intense flare of pale shine causing shadows to jump from object to object, from the remains of the overhead cat walks, to the various forms of rubble on the ground, which, was slowly being sucked in by the ravenous maelstrom of energy gathering around the gauntlets palm.

Sorin began to panic, quickly putting to and to together as he held his arm, desperate to control it. But he fell to his knee. Somehow, his right arm stood firmly in place, still aimed directly at Carver, who, without any sense of self preservation, was still crawling forwards.

The sphere eclipsed the size of Sorin's hand... and he could only watch in mute horror as the condensed energy began to finally erupt...

The other side of warehouse was utterly demolished by the resulting explosion of energy. The scene was bleached white, as the sounds of cataclysm screeched into Sorin's ears. Carver wasn't simply destroyed, he was erased. His enormous, hulking frame, reduced to dust under an onslaught of condensed energy- a white pillar shooting continuously forwards. Sorin wasn't even able to keep remotely stable as the force of the beam caused him to slide backwards. The tendrils adorning his back were the only things keeping him from being blown back through the hole behind him. He was forced to close his eyes because of the brightness, as his arm shifted at an angle upwards, bisecting the wall and much of the ceiling in its wake. The rafters, catwalks, and any other object in the way was simply obliterated by the rogue emission.

Slowly the beam began to peter in power, and as the beam shortened and the glow of his armor diminished, Sorin found it harder and harder to keep his eyes open, his only thought on the matter was of clear omission. As his exhaustion finally ran its course. The warehouse around him steadily began to collapse, as metallic tendrils from the armor slowly began to fan out. Pulling his body to relative safety, as rubble crashed around him.

10/27/2061, Wednesday, 9: 37 pm

Roxy was perplexed where she was sitting at the moment.

The situation was urgent, and for the life of her she couldn't believe the crap that has been happening for the last few hours now. But even she... as loath as she was to admit it, couldn't disguise her amazement.

She, her parents, her knucklehead of a brother, Zoe, and Garrot. All of them currently flying inside of a jet airliner to Sorin's location. The Dark Star it was called. As Claire explained, it was one of their means of infiltrating, and exfiltrating, for a deviant pickup way out into the wastelands. Something about having to uphold there secrecy to the general public, or something along those lines.

Jack's face was pressed against the glass as Zoe was quietly sitting in the seat behind him, her eyes wide as she took in the speed they were going. The jet was fairly large. Big enough to hold all of them and seemingly have space for a few more people. Her parents where in front, along with Garrot. The two other deviants: Duncan and Claire were busy piloting... Well, Duncan was flying. Claire was apparently tracking his location by psychic signature.

"How close are we to Sorin?" Garrot demanded, his expression tense.

"Don't worry, were closing in on him..." Suddenly, Claire froze, her eyes widening. "Wait a minute... what in the wor-"

Roxy and the others jumped in their seats; from the cockpit, blazing through the windshield and glaring out the side windows of the jet. They were forced to shield their eyes, as Duncan had to frantically peel up in order to avoid getting blinded at the wheel. The jet curved upwards and, as he brought the aircraft back into position, Roxy, opened her eyes a smidge, the intense lights deeming, and couldn't believe what she was seeing. Roxy's parents and Garrot, all three watched in silent horror of what was going on below the jet. One of the warehouses, near the center industrial sector was currently getting cleaved in-two. The solid column of energy ripping the warehouse apart moved upwards in an angle, before colliding with the largest structure next to it. The main furnace, the three towering smoke stakes above the building was instantly obliterated. The narrow beam of condensed energy slicing through each in a rough angle, like a super-heated knife through butter.

Roxy and her brother could only gape at the level of destruction. Zoe had her hands clamped over her mouth as the rest looked on in frozen shock.

"Holy... shit..." Duncan whispered.

"Garot... I'm sensing more signatures approaching the warehouse." Claire said, breathless to what she had just seen. "And I'm not sensing the quasimorph anymore either."

"Y-yeah. Just set us down somewhere close... that might be Hosea your sensing. Let's meet them were Sorin is..."

10/27/2061, Wednesday, 9: 41 pm

Tom and Jade, along with Hosea and Raynor. Were caught well out of their guards when they witnessed the beams trajectory from the nearby warehouse.

None of them, where taking any chances.

Hosea, Jade, and him were wearing the standard combat armor. With Raynor wearing his own S.S issue gear, which, he was happy to supply them with standard grade laser rifles. Which of course Jade refused, wanting instead to carry her shotgun, a goliath arms fléchette round burst; supremely effective to cyberized opponents, and the usual quasimorph. Susan and Bellatrix were still out of it, from their venture into cyberspace. So they were linked to their visual feeds.

"The hell was that!" Came Susan's voice from his holo feed.

"Damn, and here I was thinking this couldn't get more complicated." Jade sighed.

"Everyone, I'd advise caution. The gatekeeper is more than likely going to enhance the quasi further. It'll probably be worse at this point in time, especially if Carver gets overwhelmed by the other half of the artifact." Raynor said on the radio, steeping behind Hosea's heels as they entered the ruined street.

"Hosea, I'm still reading Sorin's half of the artifact." Bellatrix responded. "Good, so long as he's in the area we still got a chance." Hosea said.

Jade and Tom entered the street on the other end. The long-paved road was completely totaled, fire and debris strew everywhere, what on earth could have gone down to cause this much carnage? Tom stopped immediately noticing the strewn web of mechanical parts on the curb and street. Taking a closer look near the source of the beam, did he finally recognize it.

One of Garrots drones... completely destroyed...

Scanning the environment slowly he happened on something that caused him to go into a cold sweat. The hoverboard laid on the street corner, the platforms various pieces was strewn around it, with some of the turning fins broken off and littering the pavement. It could be fixed with enough time, but its rider was nowhere to be seen...

"Guys," Jade called out "The side of the warehouse, look."

Tom, Hosea, and Raynor glanced at the massive hole in the side of the building. The interior of the warehouse was in ruins, with rubble and loose rebar littering the decrepit environment. There was no way Sorin could be in there. But... what if...

"Hey, Hosea... let me check inside real quick." Tom said. Hosea nodded, "Will circle around, see if he was able to get away from the blast." He said, as Raynor joined him.

"Alright, let's get looking... I swear, he better be okay." Jade growled. Tom could only nod as he followed her inside. Both their main arms at the ready.

The place was a broken maze; glass, debris, rebar, and even the melted remains of a few catwalks littered the grounds in a mix pile of destruction. At that moment, as the pair navigated the rough terrain, they came to a conclusion. They needed to split up. Tom going to the left section, and Jade the right. Tom, as he slung his rifles strap across his shoulder, let the gun dangle at his side, to better cross the rubble in his way. The ceiling of the warehouse was peeled off from the beam of energy, allowing some of the distant fires to light some of his surroundings. But, not enough to make it easy for him. Suddenly, his foot crunched on something, that didn't feel like debris or broken concrete. Looking down, and holding his right boot up. Did he notice the strange material on the floor. A silverish residue which was slowly disappearing into a dark mist.

He switched on his flashlight; unlike Hosea, or Susan, he didn't have any see in the dark implants. So, with general unease, he began to notice the web of silver littering the floor.

He once again held his rifle in hand, and followed the strange substance.

"Jade, found something. Need you to join up with me." Tom whispered into the holocall. "Copy." Her voice confirmed.

"Bellatrix, Susan, need your eyes on me." He whispered again, he didn't have to wait long to hear their confirmation.

Tom followed the trail slowly, keeping calm and listening closely for anything suspicious, other than the path he was following like a bizarre bread crumb trail. Tom paused, near the other end of the warehouse where the most debris was gathered he could hear something coming from directly ahead.

Footsteps. From either the left or right corner turning into the path he was currently on. He crouched to the side and aimed his weapon, not foolish enough to call for a name immediately when he couldn't be sure if Carver was really dead. But worry began to eat at his nerves. And with how dire the situation was...

He had to know...

"Sorin! is that you?" His voice echoed down the path. He waited, narrowing his eyes as the footsteps ceased.

"Tom?" a voice said, which caused him to shiver, that sounded like him, barely, sounded like him. Tom moved, rounding the corner and freezing dead in his tracks in alarm.

The thing that greeted him in the dark had him frozen in shock. His flashlight beam illuminated what could have been best described as a miniature version of Carver. But the otherworldly, and organic like carapace standing before him couldn't have been Sorin. The tendrils moving behind him lazily, was what made him almost fire his gun. Until, he noticed the familiar durag resting upon his head. As red predator-like eyes stared at him in bizarre recognition. He could barely tell that the youth before him was wearing a mask.

Or, he hoped it was a mask.

"T- tom? How did you.." the altered voice was unnerving, but it was definitely Sorin that was speaking to him. But that wasn't important, what was important was the way he was listing to the side, almost like he was...

Sorin fell over and Tom was barely able to respond due to his shock. He almost braced himself to be cut by the sharpened edges of the armor, only for it to soften to his touch. As Sorin laid in his arms, he couldn't even get a word out, before the armor suddenly and rapidly began to disintegrate. Causing him to go bug eyed as the suit completely disappeared. Leaving a disheveled and wounded Sorin in his grasp.

Jade, Hosea followed by Raynor joined him soon after. With Raynor noticing the gauntlet immediately covering his right hand, which unbeknownst to him gained another gem, on the bottom end near the elbow.

CHAPTER

57

Hours passed, and numerous things happened during that initial time frame. Hosea's group linked up with Garrot's entourage. Things were said, notes were shared, and Raynor was reunited with his daughter.

What shocked every member of the Voyager crew the most, was how worried everyone was for Sorin. Three kids that Tom had never meet before where immediately crowding around him, asking if he was okay. Much to his shocked confirmation to them. Even the two parents, the Murdocks, were worried sick.

The two deviants that came to rescue Garrot and the Murdocks, confronted Hosea asking if Sorin was a deviant too; Hosea of course, told them the truth, that he was just a victim of Carvers mania- which unfortunately or luckily- ended up involving the Murdock family in the chaos. For what it was worth, they were willing to keep the details of Sorin's part a secret.

For his sake. As Raynor put it; the artifact that was bonded to the boy couldn't become widespread knowledge. The group ended up relocating back to the main office building. For the time being they couldn't leave... on account of the recent sandstorm which was sweeping the steel mill. The Dark Star wasn't equipped to fly through such weather, and the voyager wasn't in top shape because of the past few days of trying to track Sorin's path through the wastes. They would have to ride the storm out, which would most likely take the full day. The building was still standing all things considered. Sorin would lay comatose for much of the night.

The gauntlet on his right arm, on occasion gleaming ever so brightly.

10/28/2061, Thursday, ??????????

The sounds gently rustled into his ears.

A gentle whisper created by the swishing of fabric. He opened his eyes, too tired to move, and too tired to say anything. His small body covered up by white comforter and soft linen sheets. Head sinking into the pillow behind him. He looked up, his vision for some reason was blurry, and his body... now that he was waking up, it felt sore...

The room was decent in size, that much he could at least tell; a small bedroom with blue colored wallpaper. A few loose furniture, and a small ceiling fan overhead which was lazily revolving around. His eyes searched the room, but he hadn't the slightest clue of where he was. Where was mom?

A hand rested on his head, gently rubbing across the hair of his scalp, he looked up- trying to find the hands source. But his blasted vision, he couldn't make anything out of the woman's face. Other than the dark hair which spilled across the bed.

"Mom?" a much younger voice inquired.

"Shhhhh." The woman responded calmly. Her voice was light, dulcet against his ears, and strangely calming... "It's not time yet... try to get some more sleep, okay." He tried to say something, but before he could even utter a single question her way...

"Midnight, calling, dusk unending, we're falling. Together, we spy, the chains are falling. By night, I see, the freedoms reign."

The lullaby touched him, a song which stilled his questions, and as the hand brushed his short hair, a feeling of tiredness started to take hold. His eyes blinked and the only thing that could be done was listen to its end.

"Be still, my sweet star, the light is calling. Praise to my purpose, blessed by the dawn, and bourne of devotion. The eternal dream."

The boy finally wasn't able to hold his eyes open any longer, as he sunk into the blissful state of sleep, a whisper touched his fading consciousness.

"Sleep well Sorin, I'll always be with you..."

10/28/2061, Thursday, 6 :49 am

Sorin opened his eyes hesitantly; wishing that the vision was real, hoping that he would see her again. But it wasn't meant to be. Tiredly, disappointedly, he looked around, the room was semi-dark- but with the occasional harsh draft of wind and sand from the window. Which was also barricaded.

Too his genuine shock, he was still alive... everything that happened, all of the pain, fear, and horror. He had actually come out alive at the other end. Of course it didn't excuse the current state of his body. The armor... Oh god, the armor! He looked over his body, and he was overcome with relief... and guilt. Hadn't he put all his trust in songbird to help him out of that mess? But looking down at his body, covered in blankets, he couldn't get the way he sounded out of his head.

His body was sore all over, and he was having a hard time of actually moving, looking over just a bit revealed the problem. A machine was hooked up to him. Laying on an old couch, the contraption was linked to his right arm, with a few wires sticking from under his shirt and over his chest... exactly over his heart... and a few other wires connected in other places, both legs and his other arm.

Glancing down at Songbird, which had the most wires... he gave it a reproachful look. *Sorry Song... Thanks for keeping me alive back there.* A glimmer of red from the main core, and a small chirp was the gauntlets answer.

That's when he noticed the occupants of the room. All around, either taking furniture of their own to sleep on, or laying on a matt on the floor. Susan, Jade, Tom, Zoe, Jack, and Roxy... all of them seemingly okay... his head laid back down on the pillow, a surge of relief hitting him without warning, as the memory of the other quasi racing up the building played in his head. Everyone was alive, and even better... Hosea and Bellatrix, they had to be here somewhere... He struggled to sit up. The soreness and exhaustion running through his limbs was honestly getting old; heck, the two past weeks have been nothing but a marathon of anxiety and dread, with the explosive occasions of life threating peril. But... not all of it was bad, per say. Sitting up on the couch finally. He glanced towards the other three... How on earth did he manage to find such good friends, during this unexpected adventure?

The small machines wires draped on the floor. Its lights casting a dim pinprick of lights in the dark room. Numbers and dials, with the occasional keyboard, and screened interface. Holding up Songbird, most of the other wires were connected to it. Which, were connected around the two gems on the back of his hand. While a single wire was connected near the bottom one, the concealed gem, which he still had no idea what its main function was.

Red signaled the armor spreading, green was the cyberdeck function, and indigo...

Sorin grimaced, the beam... he grabbed his head, a small headache tapping at the center of his cranium in an irritating gesture. Scenes of Carver blasting away at him played- in a not so amusing slideshow- of him barely getting disintegrated or worse.

"Aunt Dot and Church are never going to believe what happened..." he whispered to himself. "Definitely no way... how would I even..." he leaned on the couch, still in shock of his survival the more he looked back.

He studied the last gem on the bottom of the gauntlet. It looked like a filament of silver was covering it. His expression turned inquisitive, and a little worried... What if it goes off by mistake? Just like the green and red gems tended to do... He gulped, after remembering a full-sized industrial truck getting blown apart, he suddenly felt Roxy and Jack had the less insane powers. This was almost too much to think about.

"Sorin?" Sorin blinked, his reflection interrupted as Susan glanced at him in shock. Pulling herself up from her mat, and brushing her vivid red hair back, her face pale as if she were seeing a ghost. She was literally the closet one in his proximity to the couch he laid in.

"Hi." He responded back after a moment "What's with the-"

Susan had already jumped up, giving him a bear hug that would have probably rivaled Zoe.

"Oh my god are you okay!?" she jumbled out, much to Sorin's inability to talk because of how hard she was hugging him, her robotic right arm probably the main cause for this.

"Y-y-ye-yeah," he struggled to say. She released him, looking frantically at the machine.

"Wha... What's with this thing anyway? And... what are all these wires supposed to be doing?" Sorin questioned, raising an eyebrow at her.

She grabbed his right arm, much to his dismay, looking at it with obvious suspicion. "It's supposed to monitor the artifacts compatibility level. Raynor said he needed to be sure of its connection with you- which meant keeping it on you for the entire night- until you woke up," She summarized. "Just to see if there were any adverse effects."

Sorin blinked "Adverse effects? Songbird been keeping me alive for the past two weeks... well, mostly Songbird..." he said, scratching the back of his head.

"Really don't think I would have made it without Zoe, or the Murdocks." Susan looked at him, before chuckling.

Sorin looked her "What is it?"

"I think you got it other way around." She said "When Tom carried you out of the warehouse, every single one of them where saying how you saved *them*. Especially Zoe." She said, with a small raise of the eyebrow. "And Songbird... you named the super-secret weapon. Songbird, of all things." She was crossing her arms at this point.

Only for a small series of chirps to suddenly catch her off guard. The glint from the gauntlets main gem causing her to glance at the gauntlet in alarm.

"It certainly fits, am I right." Sorin replied casually.

Susan could only watch in disbelief as the gauntlet stretched across his arm, covering his shoulder and creating a type of red lens over his right eye. Sorin widened his eye at the text appearing on the quarter-masks interface.

<----------------{Results}---------------->

USER SYMBYOSIS GRADE... PERFECT
STYX MATTER SYNTHESIS... PERFECT
COMPONENT CORE... RETRIEVED
CORE ALIGNMENTS... SUCCESSFUL
GATEKEEPER PROTOCOL ON STANDBY

"Huh, that's new." Sorin said, trying to understand what the Gatekeeper protocol was supposed to mean.

"Hold up... that thing is creating an interface?" Susan said, giving the mask, and the gauntlet a mystified look. "How?"

Sorin shrugged "Beats me. But... I guess when Songbird jumped on my cyberdeck, it must have absorbed its functions... maybe."

"How did it even latch on to you in the first place?" she paused, then snarled. "Was it Carver? Did he force it on you?"

Sorin was silent. The stranger against the backdrop of flames from the gas station coming to mind. "Not exactly."

There was a strangled yawn from behind Susan, turning around she there was a sudden gasp, then Tom followed by Jade, quickly moved past the disheveled ginger; Sorin was not amused as the two immediately jumped on either side of the couch, with Jade putting him in a casual head lock.

"Gah! Jade! Get off!" Sorin roared out as he struggled to break out of the hold.

"Damn! Ya little Scamp! You had us worried there!" Jade growled out.

"Jade! For god's sakes, don't suffocate him! I have to know how he managed to survive against that thing- probably the strongest quasimorph I've ever seen!" Tom remarked.

Jade let him go, and as Sorin recovered from the short headlock he realized something. Something was missing. Only to freeze... his hoverboard... where was his hoverboard?

"Tom... do you know where my board is?" he asked him. Tom stiffened, and gave him a regretful look.

Tom sat up and walked off, only to come back a moment later... clutching the remains of the board. Sorin groaned at what he was seeing; the board was a wreak! Pieces of the metallic shell where missing, and a few fins on the side where also gone... there was cracked shaped forks running all along the top and bottom, with the vents underneath looking dented and bent out of place...

"It's fixable... but, it'll take a while to repair it back to working order." Tom said with a frown. Sorin's shoulder slumped "At least it is fixable.... What about Hosea and Bellatrix? There here too, right?"

Jade nodded "There in a meeting. I think. I haven't seen them since last night actually." Susan stood up and sat beside him, taking care to move some of the wires and cables from out of her way.

"There with the Murdocks and Raynor. I guess there still discussing what happens next. But forget that for now..." her expression became worried "Sor, tell us about the gauntlet. I mean, everything Raynor told us about it was bad news. But you stumble on to it, and suddenly, it's got a perfect score. Not that were complaining! But... has it done anything that should make us worried?"

Sorin grimaced "I mean, what else is there to say. Songbirds pretty much kept me alive for the past few days. I just wanna know about the thing inside my chest."

All three looked taken aback. Something telling Sorin that he had said the right words. Looking at all of them, neither of them looked comfortable to discuss it.

"Listen... we don't know everything about it. But, you should wait for Hosea and Bellatrix first. After everything that's happened, they'll probably tell you as much as they know." Jade said, her expression somber, but serious.

Sorin was silent for a moment, a bad feeling coming over him. If Jade was being this blunt about it, then how bad was this about to be?

"Sorin! He's up!" Came the excited voice of Zoe, who immediately came shooting from her covers. Along with the Murdock twins, both looking extremely relieved to see him up. Sorin could only force the worry back, as Zoe latched onto him, causing Susan to eke out an ignored 'Zoe, wait!' as the other two came on to him... Much to the quite amusement of Jade and Tom, who were just chuckling at the scene before them; of course, the seriousness of the conversation didn't completely dispel with the coming of the others.

Especially Susan, who dreaded Sorins reaction to the secret they've been keeping for so long.

CHAPTER

58

10/28/2061, Thursday, 7: 46 am

Sorin watched as the three deviants left the room. The earlier conversation of how Carver meet his end was interrupted. Mr. Raynor came to get the three for the inevitable talk.

Something about where there going after the storm ends. Thankfully, it looked like Mr. and Mrs. Murdock would indeed be traveling with their kids. Which left Sorin with Hosea and the rest. And a large puck shaped device on the floor. In front of the couch that Sorin sat on. The first thing to happen after the three deviants left, was a bear hug from Bellatrix, something that Sorin was strangely not apposed of... to his embarrassment. The next thing, was Hosea... he laid a hand on his shoulder, telling him how proud he was for staying as strong as he did. Something he wasn't expecting to hear at all from the old nomad. He couldn't help looking away, barely able to keep himself together, and after he calmed down, did he ask the question...

Which lead to the same large puck shaped device on the floor.

A portable holograph projector. Connected wirelessly to the holomap of the voyager, which held a heavily encrypted file about Sorin's deep scan the week after his discovery in the desert. Something, which caused everyone to swear secrecy when they laid eyes upon it.

Something they've kept secret from even the Circle itself.

The puck sparked to life; electronic machinery humming as the center exploded with light. Sorin watched, transfixed, as a cloud of holographic pixels launched into the air. They were moving like a swarm, coalescing into a detailed shape of a... heart. A human heart. Sorin's heart. Sorin's eyes widened, what in the world was going on?

In the center of the contracting muscle... there was a circular stone orb- seemingly merged within the organ. Sorin blanched, it was exactly like another core or gem, like the ones on Songbird...

The spherical core had branching vines intersecting inside and outside of his heart, like a growth from a bizarre looking tumor of obsidian, which seemed to pump alongside his very own heart. Monochromic discoloration seemed to travel inside of the wire like protrusions connecting the heart to the core. At least, that's what Sorin assumed from what he could see, from the blue shade of the hologram. Try as he might, he really couldn't tell the color of the gem... Which, wasn't really the least of his worries.

The list of notes to the side of the altered heart was what really got his attention. Ten notes in total, with the first five detailing the core's appearance... but the last five were what caught his rapt focus:

5.) <u>Unique mutation of a deviant</u> or <u>botched experimental aug?</u>

6.) The innervation of the <u>object</u> and <u>heart</u> are <u>mixed and fused together</u>, each <u>major nerve connecting to the peripheral nervous system</u>. It's too... smooth of an amalgamation to even count as a botched experiment. But... it's still a distinct possibility.

7.) In an unpredictable set amount of time, <u>the stone or spherical apparatus will suddenly start contracting and pumping lose styx matter</u> throughout the body causing patient <u>extreme pain</u>

8.) When sphere <u>ceases</u> function- the loose styx matter... seemingly dissolves, but leaves small traces around the bloodstream and <u>bleeds</u> into the: <u>Autonomic nervous system</u> and <u>Somatic nervous system</u>. Effectively... <u>the boy has LIVE styx matter throughout his system... and he is still alive and functioning with this... it's impossible.</u>

9.) When not active the sphere '<u>deflates</u>', collapsing into a... seemingly idle state or deep hibernation. Effectively hiding itself from <u>normal scanners</u> or <u>x-rays</u>. .. unless a <u>deep dive scanner</u>. Something of this caliber could hide itself from any known public use scanners, and even <u>corporate and S.S deep scans!</u> If not for the recent upgrades courtesy of the circle, and *by proxy- Ebondyne, then I'd doubt I would even be able to see this... Just, what on Pangaea could this thing be?*

10.) The cycles and periods of Cognicrossis go from severe to nearly nonexistent in mere moments... it is a complete impossibility; yet, the only signs of the sphere's activity is indeed when the patient has the tell-tale symptoms of Cognicrossis. And the patient has shown a complete... adaptability, towards this unfortunate circumstance. Yet, the pain and mental trauma of Cognicrossis is still deeply present.

Touching his chest with his gauntlet dominated hand he felt a cold shiver running across his body. What... how... could this have happened- where could this have happened?

"Silverwood." Hosea said, causing Sorin to look at him startled. As if the old nomad had read his mind.

"That's where I found you. The settlement that was wiped out by a reactor meltdown... and you were smack dap at the cities limit, well away from the blast."

Sorin paled, remembering the small convo on the way to the steel mill. Feeling that phantom moment of strange familiarity... but, he still didn't have any recollection of what happened before that moment, before Hosea found him... but the visions he gained from coming into contact with the last core...

"H-Hosea... there's something I gotta tell you guys." everyone looked at him "Ever since getting Songbird... I've been seeing things- I don't know if there memories or really weird dreams... But, I think might have seen my mom."

Everyone was rapt in attention. Bellatrix and the rest widening their eyes in genuine alarm. "But, that's good! Can't you tell us what she looks like?" Susan asked. Once the shock wore off, her expression immediately becoming a happy one.

Sorin frowned "I couldn't see her face." Susan immediately looked crestfallen "But... I did hear her voice... it's something at least- but, anyway, that's not important." Sorin found himself grimacing as he said this "It's everything else about it that feels wrong."

Hosea stepped closer and crouched to one knee. His expression searching, "What is it? What about it feels wrong per say? Tell us as much as you can, and try not to leave anything out."

10/28/2061, Thursday, 8: 25 am

Mr. Raynor scanned the readings from the machine with amazed interest. His eyes- cybernetically enhanced- could only widen as the machines report was filed into his interface.

The synchronization reading was through the roof! Surpassing previous users of the Gatekeeper by miles in comparison. Not even a hint of desynchronization to be seen... Of course, this begs the question. How on earth was the artifact within the boys chest, able to so thoroughly interface with the Gatekeepers neural and biological requisites in order to function? He frowned, grimly reminded of the artifacts track record in its dossier; a proverbial dragons tail, as dangerous as the old worlds handling of nuclear munitions. File after file, and incident after incident; the many test subjects who were negatively impacted by the dyssynchronization were far too many, with only a few on one hand escaping with their lives. Or what remained of their lives, at the very least...

Sorin was a miracle. There was no two ways about it. And he would forever be grateful in his part for saving his daughter. He closed the window to the reports and nodded to Hosea.

"As far as I can tell Hosea, he looks good. There's not even a trace of dyssynchronization in his biomonitor." He said.

Hosea, Bellatrix, Raynor and Garrot sat next to each other around a small table from inside the receptionist room of the top floor. Everyone else was on the bottom floor of the building as they had their meeting about the Gatekeeper and its current user.

"And there's no way of removing it?" Garrot asked "He's stuck with it."

"For the time being, yes." Raynor answered "Is that correct, Mr. Starke?"

The question, aimed at the laptop on the other unoccupied side of the table next to Garrot. Which, had a curious individual seated on the other end. The man was dressed in a crisp, well-tailored suit, a darkish texture with a seeming bundle of medals and red tie. Neatly combed black hair, with his square jaw and pleasant features insinuating his professional demeanor, but he seemed far more relaxed, belying his stoic appearance.

"Right you are Raynor. I hazard a guess, but I'm assuming Bella has already analyzed the specs I sent her for the artifact. And how stable was Sorin's icon... if you don't mind my asking?"

There was a subtle familiarity in the way he said her name. Something not so subtle was the casual eyeroll of the experienced runner. Brushing her wild hair aside, she gave him a small grin.

"Stable... unlike your track record. Now, how is it that you and Garrot managed to form such a good partnership with the deviants?"

Starke sighed, as Garrot smirked. "A lot of patience and compromise. I'll tell you two about it later, but what fascinates me is that your boy, Sorin, he's been put through the ringer for the last couple of days... kinda reminds me of those other three, when they were of his age."

Hosea shook his head. "That... that was different. What Sorin has, it has me worried. You got any way of finding out how deep this really goes? I can't rely on my contacts from the circle, and Raynor's contacts within S.S would definitely put too much of a spotlight on Sorin. Could there be a way to safely test his connection with the gatekeeper, and the artifact inside of him?"

Mr. Starke rested a hand to his chin. An expression of deep thought creasing his brow. "I might have something... but, one thing that needs to be agreed upon is his ties here in the conclaves. You know we might have to move him from the Conclaves reach, and the corporations reach too... right?"

Hosea and Bellatrix's expressions grew grim; Bella sighed, while Hosea with hesitation nodded.

"The contract Carver took, he knew exactly where to find Sorin. Even the information detailing the artifact's existence, was stolen by his crew." Hosea narrowed his eyes "Cameron Richards. A friend who did the deep scan.... he was found dead in his home, much to the shock of his family."

Starke narrowed his eyes "Any intel on who issued the contract?"

Hosea shook his head. "Carver's cyberdeck was obliterated in the blast. Whatever information that could have directed us to the ones responsible is completely lost; the quasimorphed runner was also a dead end, Bella wasn't given much choice to burn his cyberdeck."

"Damn... Well, will just have to keep our eyes open then. I'll make some calls and see if I can set up a new location for Sorin. In the meantime, I'll also see about booking a flight for our next meeting. I think it would be better call for me to meet him, Sorin I mean." Starke said.

Garrot turned to the screen "Meet him you say?"

Starke nodded "The location I have in mind for the deep scan, is the very same facility that once held the gatekeeper. And they need someone from S.S to gain clearance. I already have a few trustworthy contacts to help smooth it over."

Raynor raised an eyebrow "You know, I could go there instead Starke."

Starke smiled "It's alright, and I assumed you would have preferred to be with Zoe... She has been through a lot after all."

Raynor sighed "Yeah, that's... thanks Starke."

Bellatrix grinned "Yeah, go be with your kid. You've done more than enough for us Nathan. By the way Starke, it's going to be a while before we get there. You might wanna kick back if you get there before us. The voyager was pushed to its limits to reach this place."

He nodded "Alright, I'll see about getting everything set up. I'll call you later for a potential moving spot... it'll have to be somewhere past Delta, maybe towards sector 5 of the republic; I imagine you'll have to break it to him later I suppose."

Hosea nodded "Yes. But before that, he should at least be able to return to the nocturne before that happens." He turned to Garrot "Garrot? Since you're going with the Murdocks. What else will you be doing after your done assisting them with the move?"

Garrot glanced at the old nomad "I'm not going to be too busy, if that's what you're asking... I'm assuming you'll need help investigating what happened with Roberts, correct."

"Yes, I'll have my coms open for when your able to contact me back."

Garrot nodded in turn, as Starke stood up from his seat. Nodding to everyone in the room "Alright, if that's everything, I'll see about getting the wheels in motion. Garrot you take care. Raynor, I'll get in contact with you later on. And Bella, Hosea- I'll be awaiting you at the black site. Can't wait to meet him, he seems like an interesting kid."

With that everyone said their goodbyes. Starke switching off his feed, took a moment to process everything he's heard. The future meeting with the new wielder of the gatekeeper was now over the horizon. But as he made his way out of his private quarters, he couldn't shake the feeling that there truly was more at play.

Whether or not Sorin was a just a victim of callous machinations, or a wild card of something more ominous. He would have to wait and see.

CHAPTER

59

10/28/2061, Thursday, 10: 16 am

Sorin was completely amazed at the spectacle before him. Since Zoe's dad had cleared him of any negative effects from Songbird, he said he was free to go, and was even nice enough to tell him where Zoe was.

Currently he was in the 3rd floor of the building. As he stepped out, he witnessed another person- a woman named Claire- who was floating Jack mid-air with her mind! To the excited screams of the younger Murdock. With Roxy talking with the big guy... who was doing something with his arm. (it looked like he had black rocks growing out of his skin!) This caused Sorin too pause in silence, eyes shining at the feats in front of him. *That's so cool!* Was his only thought as two people approached his position unaware of his silent awe. Mr. and Mrs. Murdock upon seeing him stepping out of the elevator immediately came to see how he was doing. With Mr. Murdock thanking him for saving his life, which kinda flustered the boy, who completely forgot about what happened at the top floor... due to getting chased by a crazed nomad-turned quasimorph.

"So, your both going with Jack and Roxy, what about Zoe?" he asked.

"Yeah, I'm going with them too." She said, dropping from behind him, apparently hanging from the ceiling using her pincers. "And so is my dad." She said with a smile. "Are you coming with us?" she asked.

Sorin rubbed his head "Well, not really... Hosea said I'm going to the place where they originally had Songbird. Something about testing the synchronization of it."

"Oh." Zoe said, sounding somewhat crestfallen.

"Yeah," Sorin responded, in equal disappointment "But... at least were finally done with getting chased across the desert." Zoe laughed "Yeah, though you gotta admit the storm holding us here is kinda convenient."

"Definitely," replied Mr. Murdock "The way I see it, you four got another day to hang out before you go your separate ways... I'd take that chance if I were you."

Sorin and Zoe looked at each other. Their minds immediately made up. "Let's go get the others! The storms not too bad yet, I gotta show you what the voyager looks like!" Sorin exclaimed in excitement.

"Are you sure Hosea will let us do that?" Zoe immediately asked.

"Don't know. But, maybe Bella, Tom, or Jade will." Sorin said, a grin rivaling Roxy's splitting his lips. "Come on!" he grabbed her wrist and with a sigh, allowed him to pull her towards Jack and Roxy.

10/28/2061, Thursday, 10: 39 am

The hoverboard sat pathetically on the table.

Sorin, Tom, and Susan were looking at its broken state from within the Voyager, the front living quarters where the familiar couch chairs where set up next to the Holomap, where Zoe, Jack, and Roxy looked on in amazement. Especially Jack- all three sat around the projector like a campfire, as Bella and Jade taught them how it worked.

"Do you think we can fix it?" Sorin asked feebly, who was very much not happy with its current condition. All that work, now down the drain once more.

"Oh yeah, it's definitely fixable." Replied Susan, to the astonishment of Sorin. "Wait... how would you know that?" Susan shrugged "Who do you think helped Tom get the cyberdeck for you?"

Tom chuckled "I swear Sorin. You really shouldn't fall for the whole rule abiding sibling act... She can be really-"

Tom didn't get the chance to finish, as he was hit by Susan's mechanical elbow to the side of his arm. Causing him to chock on what he was about to say.

"Anyway, I'm pretty sure with enough spare parts... and a hammer. We can get it back good as new. And Tom can help with the tunning." She quipped, as if she didn't cause Tom to nearly bite his tongue in pain.

"Y-yeah sure." Tom groaned, wisely not saying another word.

"And Sorin, you can help me out with checking the operating system later. Since you can interface with it." Sorin nodded, trying really hard not to laugh at Tom's expense.

10/28/2061, Thursday, 11: 10 am

A strong breeze outside of the voyager carried with it a sand-turned gust, which blew against the looking glass shards, the reflective ripple humming from the strength of the winds.

And there was Sorin. Sitting with Zoe, Jack, and Roxy around the holomap projector. The holographic expanse of the conclavien regions displayed for all of them to see. The emerald hue of the map splashed across the semi-dark room. Roxy turned off the lights, saying the glow from the map was kinda cool. Like they were in some kind of sci-fi movie. Jack simply splayed himself out on the couch, watching the flickering lights of the map and the window. *Sure didn't take him long to get really comfortable with the couch...* Was Sorin's thought as he glanced over at Jack.

"So, is this really the last time were gonna see you?" Jack said from his position.

"Don't know," Sorin replied "I'm kinda shocked Bella let us stay here for the time being... you think she's spying on us right now?"

Jack suddenly froze "Oh crap, I forgot she could do that!" as he righted himself on the furniture, much to the snicker of his older sister.

"To be fair, Bella seems really chill. Well, she doesn't seem as scary as you made her out to be sometimes. Heck, even Jade didn't seem that bad." Roxy said. Moving next to her brother.

Sorin shuddered "You haven't seen them mad."

Zoe smiled. Brushing her blonde locks aside, she glanced at the holomap, her forest green eyes staring excitedly at the screen.

Sorin glanced at the map, then blinking at what was projected. On screen a massive swath of forest, and nearby, a large town. "Oh, so that's what Rosaria really looks like."

The small digital map that Mr. Murdock had given them couldn't possibly show such a detailed look of the town. It wasn't as massive as Gloomhaven's central district, but it was pretty large in its own right. Thinking back, when Jack was controlling the map, he showed his hometown of Ashton. Which still wasn't as big as Gloomhaven. But was mighty impressive for a settlement.

"But still. While were going with Duncan and Claire, you're going to be off somewhere else. Crap, you think will ever see each other again?" Jack groaned.

"Jack! Of course were gonna meet him again." Zoe stated, causing all three to look at her "If it comes down to it, maybe dad will let us come visit Gloomhaven one day. I kinda wanna see what the Nocturne looks like." Zoe admitted, scratching the back of her head in embarrassment.

Roxy shot up in her seat "Oh my god! How did I forget you live in a bar! Like, that's got to be the coolest place to live, ever." Jack also perked up, his brow furrowed in thought "Yo, Sor... wouldn't you by chance have a photo, or picture of the nocturne on this thing?"

Sorin gave shrug "Hold on, let me see-"

As his right hand went to touch the console, Songbird's green gem lit up. With a small chirp from the gauntlet, the holomap suddenly began to glitch out.

Sorin pulled his hand back with a quick "Oh crap!" and everyone watched open mouthed as Rosaria disappeared. Sorin widened his eyes, his reprimand to Songbird dying in his throat, as the holographic image of The Seventh Nocturne appeared over the projector in all its glory.

"Whoa!" Jack said. "It's certainly bigger than I imagined!"

Roxy laughed "Yeah, I have to see the inside of place. It looks really cool."

Zoe raised an eyebrow, as she glanced at Songbird "That's certainly a neat trick you got there."

Sorin nodded, as he patted Songbird on the wrist. "Yep, it certainly is."

She smiled "But seriously, I really hope will be able to see each other again. It's gonna be strange not having you around."

Sorin sighed "Yeah... It's only been what? Two weeks? And I now I can't imagine not having you guys around. Tomorrow sure is gonna suck."

The wind continued to beat at the windows, and all throughout, the pair of four continued to hang out with one another. An hour passed, and suddenly there time within the Voyager was cut short. The side entrance inside opened, letting out a lot of sand and dust within the large camper.

Hosea poked his head inside, grasping his hat as the wind danced around and within the Voyagers interior. "It's time to head inside!" he would shout at them "The storm is beginning to pick up speed!" The kids didn't need to be told twice.

One by one they filed out, following the old nomad back inside the building as the roar of the storm echoed over the horizon.

"One thing I'm not gonna miss is this weather!" Zoe would shout as she held onto her red hoodie, as Sorin followed behind.

"Don't worry about it! The wastelands got plenty of other things to look forward too!" he would shout "Maybe tonight will be able to catch the stars! I think Susan can show you where Nocturna major is!" He grinned "I bet you'll probably try to draw it once you see it!"

Zoe laughed "Okay, Sure, will see about that!" Sorin grinned "Don't worry, you'll definitely will!"

The two finally made it inside, and after a beat the door closed behind them.

The low roar of the wasteland being the only sounds which boomed outside the main building of the steel mill.

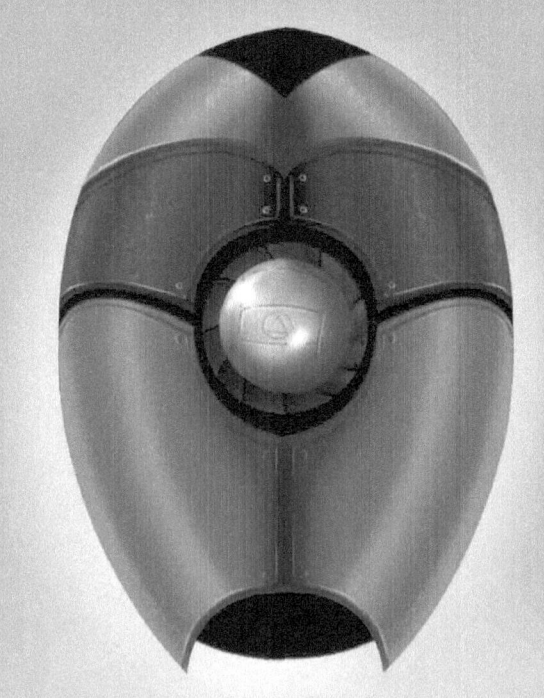
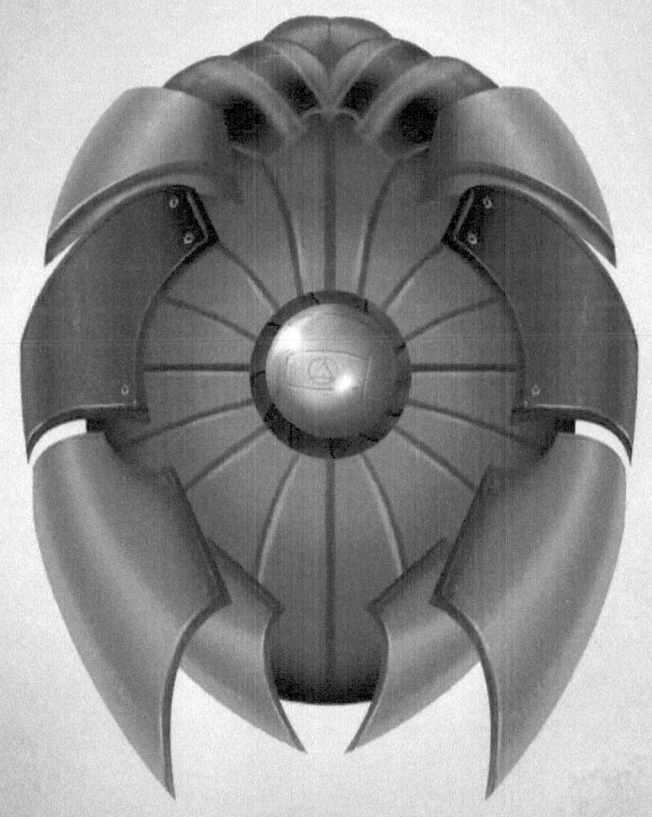